DIRTY DEEDS
DONE DIRT CHEAP

A Collection of Stories

JUDAS JUNG

NONGE PUBLISHING

Contents

Foreword

Well, hello there, stranger.

Are you all cozy, sitting in your favorite chair, leaning over to your right, using the sunlight coming through the window next to you to provide more reading light?

Good.

And if not, well, then I hope you're comfortable wherever you are and have good light. One's vision is not to be taken lightly, you know, and there are a lot of words coming your way, and I don't mean in this foreword.

Speaking of light, let's talk about this *slim* volume of tales you now hold in your hands.

What you're holding is twenty years of stories, the oldest being *Another to Feed, The Well, The Drain,* and *Store Policy* from 2004. Now, before you start thinking this is all doom and gloom, let me set the record straight. Yes, there's darkness here—plenty of it—but that's not the whole story. Some of these tales offer something else entirely: hope. Redemption. The possibility that even when everything goes sideways, people can still choose to do the right thing. That love can triumph over fear, that sacrifice means something, that sometimes the monsters lose. Because here's the thing about real horror—it only works if there's something worth saving. Without light, darkness is just emptiness. Without hope, fear is just noise.

Now, these forty-eight stories didn't just appear overnight, fully formed. No, they crawled out of the dark corners of imagination one by one, each demanding to be told in its own particular way. Some crept up on me in parking lots, while soaking in the bathtub, and others while I was stuck in line at the grocery store, watching the person ahead of me buy nothing but cat food and duct tape. Some whispered themselves into existence during quiet moments—a drive past an old house, a conversation overheard in a restaurant, or getting a peculiar feeling only to then look up into the rearview mirror and realize someone is watching you. Others arrived like storms, demanding immediate attention, refusing to be ignored.

What they all share is a simple belief: that the most terrifying monsters aren't always the ones with fangs and claws, but that they can look exactly like us or like nothing at all. That horror can exist in our suburban neighborhoods, our workplaces, and our families. In the choices we make when no one's watching, and sometimes even when they are.

In these stories, you'll meet ordinary people in extraordinary circumstances—teachers and parents, workers and students, people just trying to get through their days until something shifts in the shadows. These are stories about what happens when the familiar becomes strange, when love becomes obsession, when protection becomes imprisonment, and when the things we think we understand reveal themselves to be something else entirely.

Now, some of these tales will make you uncomfortable. Good. The best horror should. It should prompt you to question what you think you know about the world, about other people, and about yourself. It should make you look twice at that neighbor who's always been a little too friendly, wonder what's really growing in that perfect garden down the street, question whether it's really the quiet ones that you should be worried about, or reconsider whether that childhood memory is exactly what you thought it was.

These stories have been patient, waiting their turn to meet you. They've been polished and refined, but they haven't lost their teeth. If anything, the wait has made them hungrier. Which leads us now to the darkness where they hide.

That darkness lies just ahead on the next page.

Now, just go ahead and take my hand because I wouldn't want you to go alone. I know all too well what that's like, you see, as I've been alone for a very long time, but now I have you.

Shall we?

Judas Jung

Another to Feed

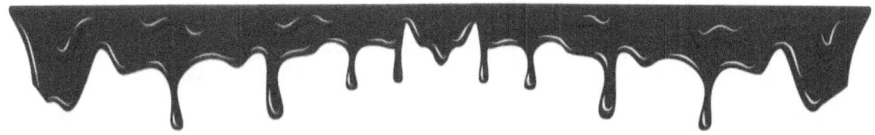

S he was thinking about the dress in the window.

Black silk, catching the last light as Lucy trudged past Harmon's Department Store. The mannequin had no face, just smooth fiberglass. Sometimes Lucy thought that was worse—like even a dummy was too good to look at her.

Size four. Maybe six if she was lucky. Lucy hadn't worn either since sophomore year, before Mom died, before food became comfort instead of love.

"Just once," she whispered, breath fogging the glass. "Just once."

Lucy pressed her palm against the cold glass, leaving a handprint that faded at the edges. Three hundred sixty-four dollars. Two weeks ago she'd gotten up the courage to go inside, and the skinny salesgirl had looked at her with that mixture of pity and annoyance. "We don't carry that in your size. Maybe try Lane Bryant?" Not bothering to whisper. Two other women had exchanged looks.

The dress caught the fading light, the fabric seeming to move as if in a breeze. It would hug curves instead of hiding them. Make her visible in the right ways for once. Transform her from the woman people looked through to the one they couldn't stop watching.

The February wind pushed through her coat, finding every place where the fabric pulled tight. Lucy pulled her scarf tighter and continued the six-block trek to her apartment, a journey she made five days a week, always pausing at Harmon's window, always feeling that same emptiness afterward.

Her apartment was on the third floor of a building that had once been grand but now sagged with neglect. The elevator worked only on occasion, which meant Lucy usually arrived home winded from the stairs, her thighs burning, her breath coming in gasps that she told herself were from exertion and not the quiet sobs they sometimes resembled.

Lucy decided to make a stop on her way home at O'Malley's Pub. As usual, it smelled like stale beer and cigarettes. O'Malley's was one of the last bars in town that allowed smoking but since it was so close to home Lucy just learned to come to terms with the smell. Lucy nursed her usual house white at the corner of the bar. She came maybe once a month when her apartment got too quiet, always regretting it.

Half-full tonight, mostly regulars hunched over drinks. Hockey on the TV, blue light washing over scratched wood. Lucy imagined that in another body, she might draw glances walking in. Might not have to wave twice for service.

She felt the stare before she heard the voice, that familiar dread from four years of high school torment. Lucy hunched her shoulders, trying to disappear into her barstool.

"Well, if it isn't Lucy Goosey!"

Lucy's stomach dropped. She didn't need to turn to know who had spoken those words. Richard Pettigrew, former high school quarterback, current unemployed alcoholic, and the person who'd made her high school years miserable. They'd gone to Lumberton High together, where he'd made her life hell, where he'd taped pictures of barnyard animals to her locker and mooed when she walked into class.

Fifteen years later, nothing had changed except his hairline, which had receded dramatically from his increasingly red face. He still wore his high school football jacket some nights, the leather cracked and tight across shoulders that had gone soft with age and beer.

"Not tonight, Richard," she said, keeping her eyes on her wine.

He settled onto the stool beside her, bringing with him the sour smell of someone who'd been drinking since noon. "Aw, don't be like that. I'm just bein' friendly."

Lucy glanced at him, caught the flash of something in his eyes—something that might have been loneliness, buried beneath practiced cruelty. She'd heard rumors about Richard: a failed marriage, a drinking problem that had cost him his job, a son who wouldn't see him. For a second, she almost felt sorry for him.

Then he opened his mouth again.

"Still shoppin' in the plus-size section, I see," Richard said, loud enough for nearby patrons to hear. "Y'know, they say there's someone for everyone, but the problem is, there's only one of you."

Lucy's fingers tightened around her glass. Some nights she had the energy to leave. Tonight wasn't one of those nights.

"Hey, I'm talkin' to you." Richard poked her arm, his finger digging in. "You should be grateful. Not many guys would even bother."

"Please," Lucy whispered. "Just leave me alone."

Richard's mouth opened for another insult, but his attention shifted to something over her shoulder. His bloodshot eyes widened, then took on the same predatory interest he directed at anything female.

"Well, well," he said. "Sarah Davies? Is that you?"

Lucy turned, wine sloshing close to the rim of her glass. The woman approaching them looked nothing like the Sarah Davies she remembered from high school. That Sarah had been heavier than Lucy, with frizzy brown hair and shoulders that spoke of the same desperate desire to disappear that Lucy felt.

This Sarah was... transformed. Sleek blonde hair fell in waves past slim shoulders. Cheekbones that had once been buried beneath softness now stood sharp against pale skin. She wore a dress similar to the one in Harmon's window, though in deep red rather than black.

"Richard Pettigrew," Sarah said, her voice cool. "Still peaking in high school, I see." She turned to Lucy, her expression warming. "Lucy. It's been ages."

Lucy nodded, her throat tight with envy.

Sarah slid onto the empty stool on Lucy's other side, blocking Richard from the conversation. "How've you been?"

"Fine," Lucy managed. "You look... amazing."

Sarah's smile looked forced. Lucy noticed a tremor in her hand as she signaled the bartender. Up close, Sarah's transformation wasn't as perfect as it had looked from across the room. There was something frantic about her energy, something forced about the way she held herself. Dark circles showed beneath her concealer, and a hollowness marked her cheeks.

"Thanks. It wasn't easy," Sarah said, then lowered her voice. "Some days I wonder if it was worth it."

Richard, never one to accept being ignored, leaned across Lucy. "What's your secret, Sarah? Surgery? Pills? Or did you just stop eatin' entirely?"

Sarah regarded him with the sort of pity reserved for roadkill. "Actually, Richard, I found someone who specializes in... difficult cases."

"Like what, a witch doctor?" Richard snorted.

Something flashed in Sarah's eyes—discomfort, quickly hidden. "Something like that."

Lucy found her voice. "Really? Who?"

Sarah hesitated, her fingers drumming against the bar. "It's not for everyone. There are... sacrifices."

Richard rolled his eyes. "Oh, spare us the dramatic weight-loss journey crap. You got hot. Congratulations." He drained his beer and slid off the stool, swaying. "I'm gonna find someone with a better attitude."

They watched him stagger toward a group of college-aged women at the other end of the bar.

"Some things never change," Sarah murmured.

"But some things do," Lucy said, unable to keep the desperation from her voice. "Please, Sarah. Who did you see?"

Sarah studied her for a long moment. "How badly do you want to change, Lucy?"

"More than anything."

Sarah reached into her purse and withdrew a small red business card. No name, just an address in tiny gold lettering. "Only go if you're certain. There's no going back once it's done."

The card felt warm against Lucy's palm.

"What does that mean?" she asked, but Sarah was already sliding off her stool, glancing at her watch.

"Oh God, I'm supposed to meet someone in ten minutes and I'm already late." She paused, then added quietly, "Whatever you decide, Lucy... be careful. Follow the instructions exactly."

Lucy watched her weave through the crowded bar and disappear into the night, the red dress catching the light like a wound.

The nightmare came as Lucy knew it would. It always did after seeing Richard.

In the dream, she was back in the high school cafeteria, naked except for a too-small towel that kept slipping. Everyone was staring, laughing. Richard led the chorus, his face twisted with cruel delight.

"Lucy Goosey, fat and loose-y," he chanted, and others joined in.

The towel fell. The laughter crescendoed. Lucy tried to cover herself with her hands, but they weren't enough, never enough to hide all the places she overflowed.

She woke gasping, sheets twisted around her legs, her nightshirt damp with sweat. The digital clock on her nightstand glowed 3:17 AM in red numbers.

Lucy fumbled for the light and sat up, pressing her palms against her closed eyes until bright spots danced. When she opened them again, her gaze fell on Sarah's card, propped against the lamp.

The address was in the oldest part of Lumberton, down by the abandoned textile mills. Not somewhere anyone went after dark.

"Only if you're certain," Sarah had said.

Lucy thought of the dress in Harmon's window. Of Richard's sneering face. Of fifteen years of avoiding mirrors, of love that never seemed to find her.

By morning, she had made her decision.

The building looked like it had been crumbling for decades, red brick falling away, mortar gone to powder. No sign marked it as a place of business. The only indication Lucy had the right address was a small red square painted beside a rusted metal door.

This part of Lumberton had once been the economic heart of the city, when the textile mills employed thousands and the river changed colors depending on what dyes were being used that day. Now it was a collection of abandoned buildings and half-hearted attempts at gentrification—a coffee shop between two boarded-up warehouses, a yoga studio whose windows couldn't hide the emptiness within.

Lucy had taken two buses to get here, the second dropping her six blocks away on what the driver called "the last safe street." She'd walked the rest, her footsteps echoing in the empty, narrowing streets. Once she thought she was being followed, but when she turned, there was only a stray cat watching her from atop a dumpster.

She checked Sarah's card one last time, then pushed the door open, half-expecting it to be locked or to reveal nothing but dust and debris behind it.

Instead, the interior was clean, if sparse. Rice paper screens divided the space into sections, their surfaces painted with symbols Lucy didn't recognize. The air smelled of unfamiliar herbs and something metallic that reminded Lucy of blood—like the time she'd cut herself chopping vegetables, the red pooling on the cutting board.

The floorboards didn't creak as Lucy stepped inside, though they looked ancient enough that they should have. In fact, the place was strangely silent, as if sound itself were muffled by whatever incense burned in the red ceramic holders placed throughout the space. A faint chanting came from somewhere deeper in the building, words that seemed to slide past Lucy's ears.

A small woman emerged from behind one of the screens. The woman looked ancient—face mapped with wrinkles, white hair in a tight bun. Faded silk robe covered in dragons. Dark eyes that seemed to see everything.

"You come for change," the woman said. Not a question.

Lucy nodded.

The woman studied her for a moment, head tilted. "I am Madam Zhao. My family practice traditional medicine for three generations.

My grandmother bring ancient knowledge from Shanghai during revolution. My mother teach me in this very building. Now I alone carry
on tradition."

There was something wistful in her tone, a hint of loneliness beneath
the businesslike exterior. Lucy wondered how many women had come
through that door seeking transformation.

"My friend Sarah Davies—"

"I know who send you." Madam Zhao's expression flickered, something like regret passing behind her eyes. "Such pretty girl. She want
too much, too fast. Didn't listen to instructions." She shook her head.
"Perhaps you be more careful?"

A chill ran down Lucy's spine. "What do you mean?"

But the old woman had already turned away, moving to a cabinet
filled with glass vials. Each contained what looked like a pale, segmented worm, no bigger than Lucy's pinky finger.

"Gui chong. Spirit worm," Madam Zhao said, selecting a vial. The
creature inside twisted, sensing freedom.

"I don't understand."

The woman's laugh sounded like grinding stone. "You understand
hunger, yes? These creatures understand hunger as well." She gestured
at Lucy's body. "When fed properly, gui chong release special chemicals. Suppress appetite, force body burn fat for energy."

"You want me to swallow that?" Lucy's voice rose.

"Process simple. Worm live in digestive system. When you feed it
raw meat, creature stay satisfied, allow body consume fat. But when no
raw meat..." The woman made a slicing motion across her stomach.
"Worm grow hungry, eat whatever it find."

Lucy frowned. "So I still need to eat some regular food?"

"Yes. Small amounts only. Enough to sustain life. Balance very
important." The woman set the vial on a small tray. "Raw meat keep
worm satisfied. Regular food keep you alive. Both together, harmony.
You understand?"

Lucy's mind raced. "What happens if I don't feed it meat?"

"Worm grow. Feed on host instead." The woman's expression turned
severe. "This why balance crucial. Many women think 'no food at all,
lose weight faster.' Big mistake. Worm need meat, or it take meat."

"From me."

"From inside." The woman nodded grimly. "Sarah, she stop eating
regular food. Think raw meat enough. But worm, it grow when host
too weak. Need balance—raw meat for worm, cooked food for you.
Neither starve, both survive."

Lucy stared at the vial, at the pale creature twisting within. "How long until I see results?"

The woman's smile revealed teeth filed to points. "One week, you notice changes. One month, others see them. Three months, no one recognize you. But remember—balance. Raw meat for worm, real food for you. Both eat, both live."

Lucy swallowed hard. "And I just... take it? Like a pill?"

The woman nodded, uncorking the vial. The smell that wafted out was putrid, like meat left in summer heat.

"This your last chance to leave," the woman said. "Once gui chong inside you, no removing it. You understand?"

Lucy closed her eyes. Pictured herself in the black dress. Pictured heads turning as she entered a room, desire rather than disgust in their gazes.

"I'll do it."

The woman pressed the vial into her hand. "Swallow quick. Do not chew."

Lucy brought the vial to her lips, feeling the creature squirm against the glass. Before she could reconsider, she tipped her head back and felt something cold and slick slide down her throat.

The first week was hell. The thing—she couldn't call it by Zhao's name—clawed through her digestive system, looking for a place to settle. Hours curled on the bathroom floor, sweating, retching nothing. Called in sick twice with "food poisoning."

The third night was worst. Woke at 3 AM standing in the kitchen, fridge open, hands clawing through vegetables. No memory of getting up. White-hot pain in her gut like claws scratching inside. She collapsed on the linoleum, cheek against cool tile, crying.

"Please," she whispered, though to whom or what, she couldn't say. "Please stop."

As if in response, she felt something shift inside her—a decisive movement, like a snake coiling.

By day eight, the pain had subsided to a dull, persistent ache. Lucy stood on her bathroom scale, watching in disbelief as the numbers settled on a weight she hadn't seen in years. Ten pounds gone in a week. She stepped off and on again, certain it was wrong, but the numbers stayed the same. She ran her hands over her waist, her hips, feeling the subtle changes that had begun. Her clothes hung a little looser. Her face in the mirror looked more defined.

That night, she dreamed of the creature inside her, pale and segmented, coiled around her organs. It raised its eyeless head to look at her, its circular mouth opening and closing. *Feed me,* it seemed to say. *Feed us both.*

Lucy woke with her mouth watering, but not for her usual breakfast of toast and coffee. She craved meat, red and dripping.

The raw meat was the hardest part. She bought inexpensive cuts at first—ground beef, chicken livers—forcing herself to swallow them without gagging. The creature responded at once, the persistent ache in her abdomen easing. She could feel it moving inside her after feeding, especially at night.

Lucy developed rituals around the feedings. She bought a special plate, deep red ceramic, that she used only for the creature's meals. She cut the meat into bite-sized pieces, arranging them in a circle. She never turned on the overhead light during these meals, preferring a single candle.

She even gave it a name: Ozzie. Not the formal gui chong the old woman had called it, but something more personal. After all, they were in this together now.

In the second week, she discovered that the fresher the meat, the more satisfied Arthur seemed. The ache diminished when she splurged on higher quality cuts, meat that hadn't been sitting in the grocery case for days.

Lucy developed a balance—small amounts of cooked food for herself, raw meat for Ozzie. When fed properly, Ozzie's satisfaction somehow allowed her body to burn fat efficiently.

But Madam Zhao's warnings echoed in her mind. Balance. Both eat, both live. Lucy understood now what might have happened to Sarah.

By the third week, Lucy had mastered the routine. Raw meat for Arthur's dinner, minimal food for herself throughout the day. The hunger was constant but manageable, dulled by whatever chemicals Arthur released when satisfied. The weight continued to fall away, her body reshaping itself day by day. Parts of her that had been soft for years were becoming lean, angular. When she caught her reflection in windows or mirrors, she sometimes didn't recognize herself.

Her clothes began to hang loose. Coworkers commented, asking about her diet. Lucy smiled and deflected, unable to explain that she was hosting a parasite that fed on raw meat.

On day twenty-two, she tried on a dress at Harmon's—not the black one in the window yet, but a similar style two sizes larger. It almost fit. The salesgirl, Melanie, told her to come back in a few weeks.

"You're melting away," she said with professional cheer. "We'll find something perfect for you soon."

But as Lucy's body changed, so did Ozzie's demands. It grew restless, its hunger registering as sharp pains that doubled her over at inconvenient moments. The grocery store meat—even the expensive cuts—seemed to satisfy it less and less.

On day thirty-five, Lucy's savings were nearly depleted. She'd spent hundreds on raw meat, and it was barely keeping the pain at bay. That night, lying awake as Ozzie squirmed restlessly inside her, she remembered Sarah's warning: "Follow the instructions exactly."

Had Sarah found a way to manage it? Or had she made the fatal mistake Madam Zhao had warned about—cutting out regular food entirely, thinking raw meat alone was enough?

Lucy needed to know.

The next morning, she called in sick to work and went to the address Sarah had given her months ago at a company Christmas party—a luxury apartment complex on the river, with a doorman and floor-to-ceiling windows. The sort of place Lucy had never imagined entering, let alone living in.

The doorman frowned when she asked for Sarah. "Miss Davies? I haven't seen her in a few days." He studied Lucy. "Are you expected?"

"She's an old friend," Lucy explained. "I was in the neighborhood and thought I'd surprise her."

He hesitated, then shrugged. "Apartment 908. But if she's not answering, you'll have to come back another time."

Lucy nodded and headed for the elevator.

Sarah's door was ajar when Lucy reached it. A thin trail of dark fluid had seeped out onto the hallway carpet, staining it rust-brown. Lucy stared at it, her stomach turning. The substance was thick, darker than blood, with tiny suspended particles that caught the light.

She checked the apartment number again—908, just as the doorman had said. Maybe she should call out before entering. Maybe she should call the police. Maybe she should turn around and forget she'd ever heard of Sarah Davies or spirit worms or transformation.

Ozzie twisted impatiently inside her, a sharp movement that made Lucy gasp. It was hungry. It was always hungry now.

"Sarah?" Lucy called, pushing the door wider with her fingertips. "It's Lucy Downey. Are you home?"

The smell hit her first—the thick, sweet stench of decay, like roadkill on a hot summer day, like the time a mouse had died in her apartment wall and she'd had to live with the sickly-sweet rot for a week. Lucy gagged, pressing her sleeve against her nose as she stepped into the apartment.

"Hello? Sarah? Your door was open..."

The living room was immaculate—modern furniture in shades of cream and pale blue, abstract art in gilded frames, a view of the river that must have cost a fortune. A half-empty glass of red wine sat on the coffee table beside an open book, as if the reader had just stepped away for a moment. Normal, except for the smell, which seemed to pulse in waves, growing stronger then fading.

Lucy moved deeper into the apartment, noting the little touches that spoke of Sarah's new life—designer shoes kicked off by the sofa, a cashmere throw draped over an armchair, framed photos of Sarah on tropical beaches, in front of European landmarks, always alone but smiling, always thin and beautiful.

The smell grew stronger as Lucy moved toward the bedroom, her heart hammering against her ribs. Flies buzzed somewhere ahead, their collective hum like distant machinery.

"Sarah? Are you okay?"

The bedroom door was open. Lucy peered around the frame and screamed.

Sarah lay split open on her bed, torso torn from chest to pelvis. Ribcage broken from inside, bones spread like flower petals. Where organs should be—just a dark, wet cavity. Blood soaked the mattress in wing patterns.

And moving amid the ruin of Sarah's abdomen was something pale and segmented like the creature Lucy had swallowed, but monstrous in size—at least three feet long and as thick as Lucy's wrist. Its skin was translucent, revealing a complex internal structure of organs that pulsed with stolen life. It raised what could only be called a head, revealing rows of razor-sharp teeth arranged in concentric circles, each ring rotating independently. A drop of Sarah's blood dripped from its maw.

"Oh God," Lucy whispered, her hand going instinctively to her own abdomen.

The creature in Sarah's body went still at the sound of Lucy's voice. It swiveled its eyeless head toward her, questing. Lucy had the distinct impression it was tasting the air, sensing her presence. Sensing Arthur inside her.

The thing in Sarah's body made a sound then, a high-pitched chittering that raised the hair on Lucy's arms. Inside her, Ozzie responded, twisting violently enough to make her gasp.

Lucy's scream died in her throat as the creature slithered free of Sarah's corpse, dropping heavily to the floor with a wet thud. It moved fast, leaving a slick trail, body undulating with horrible grace.

Lucy stumbled backward, slammed the bedroom door, ran. Hit a table in the hall—vase crashing, water spreading across hardwood, mixing with the dark trail. Wet slithering behind her.

No time for the elevator. Stairwell, taking steps three at a time, gasping. The door banged open behind her—the thing following, somehow opening doors, hunting her.

Lucy didn't stop running until she reached the street, her lungs burning, her mind replaying the image of Sarah's eviscerated body in nauseating detail. She looked back at the apartment building, half-expecting to see the pale, writhing form of Sarah's creature emerging from the front doors, but there was only ordinary foot traffic, people going about their day, oblivious to the horror nine floors above them.

Ozzie shifted restlessly, as if excited by its kin's freedom. Lucy felt a new kind of fear take hold. Not of the pain or the hunger, but of what she was nurturing within her own body. Of what Ozzie would become if she continued to feed it.

Standing on the sidewalk, catching her breath, Lucy understood. Sarah had broken the balance. Stopped eating regular food, thinking raw meat was enough. The creature grew out of control.

Lucy touched her stomach, felt movement under her skin. She still had time. Could keep Ozzie satisfied but controlled. Just had to be smarter than Sarah.

Had to resist starving herself for faster results.

But she couldn't stop seeing Sarah's body every time she blinked. Couldn't go home, couldn't be alone with the thing inside her. Needed noise, people, anything to drown out that chittering sound. Needed alcohol to stop her hands shaking.

O'Malley's was the only place she could think of where no one would ask questions about why she was trembling or why she kept glancing over her shoulder.

And she needed something, anything, right now to calm her nerves.

O'Malley's was half-empty when Lucy burst through the door just past noon, her face ashen, her hands trembling. She ordered a double whiskey and drained it in one burning swallow.

"Look who it is. Lucy Goosey. Looking... different."

Richard. Had to be Richard.

Lucy signaled for another drink, trying to ignore him. Ozzie twisted in her gut—twenty-four hours since she'd fed it properly. Sarah's horror still clung to her, but so did the understanding of what went wrong.

"No, seriously. You lose weight? Almost look like a real woman now."

Lucy stared at her reflection. Richard was right—she had changed. Face thinner, showing cheekbones buried under flesh for years. Neck longer. Even her skin looked better.

"Go away, Richard. I'm not in the mood."

He leered at her, alcohol fumes wafting between them. His bloodshot eyes traveled over her body, assessing, calculating. Once, his attention would have mortified her. Now it barely registered compared to the revelation of what awaited her if Ozzie grew out of control.

"Come on, don't be like that. I'm payin' you a compliment." His hand landed heavily on her thigh, fingers digging into flesh that was indeed firmer than it had been a month ago. "Maybe I been too hard on you all these years. Maybe we should... get to know each other better."

Pain spiked in Lucy's gut, doubling her over. Ozzie was hungry, impatient. She thought of Sarah's torn body. Of balance.

Fresh meat. Ozzie wanted fresh meat. Not satisfied with packaged cuts anymore, not dead things sitting in grocery cases.

Lucy looked at Richard's throat, at the pulse under stubbled skin. A terrible, perfect idea bloomed.

"You okay?" Richard asked, frowning as she grimaced.

She straightened. Ozzie writhed in anticipation, sensing her thoughts, approving. Zhao's words: "Balance very important. Both eat, both live."

But what if regular food ran out? What if she couldn't feed them both?

Lucy smiled. "Maybe we should."

Richard blinked, surprised. "Yeah? Your place or mine?"

Fresh meat, she thought, feeling Ozzie respond. *The freshest meat possible.*

"Mine is closer," she said.

Richard stumbled through her door, pawing at her clothes. "Always knew you wanted me," he mumbled against her neck. "All those years pretending."

Lucy let him push her against the wall, mouth hot and wet on her skin. Ozzie was frantic, sensing a meal coming. Pain almost unbearable.

"Bedroom's this way," she gasped. "Get comfortable. I'll slip into something... appropriate."

Richard grinned crookedly, fumbling with his belt. "Don't take long."

In the kitchen, Lucy opened the knife drawer. Ozzie sensed her intent—pain easing in anticipation.

She picked the largest blade, felt its weight. Thought of Sarah's ruined body. Of Ozzie growing inside her, getting bigger with each feeding. How long before it decided she wasn't providing enough? Before it tore free, leaving her empty like Sarah?

Then she thought of the dress. Of the salesgirl's newfound respect. Of a life where she wasn't defined by the space she took up.

Balance. Not starving like Sarah, but finding a sustainable way to feed them both.

Fresh meat. The freshest possible.

Lucy went back to the bedroom, knife behind her back. Richard had his shirt off, fumbling with jeans. His body was softer than high school—football muscle turned to flab. But plenty of meat. Enough to satisfy Ozzie for weeks.

After that? She'd find another Richard. Another cruel, worthless person.

"Need help with that?" Lucy kept her voice low, seductive.

Richard turned, smile lazy and triumphant. "Always knew you wanted me, Lucy Goosey."

That name again. Ozzie roiled at the sound, violent twisting that nearly dropped her. Something fundamental shifted inside—the creature responding to her anger, hunger, years of humiliation.

Almost complete now. Soon she'd be beautiful. Soon she'd be everything she wanted.

Just cost a little fresh meat now and then.

Lucy raised the knife.

The rest was easy.

After all, she was thinking about the dress in the window.

The Last Transmission

M orris Fitzgerald brushed dust off the brass nameplate---Western Union Model 15, 1923. The wooden case had split down one side, wires yanked loose and coiled like dead snakes. He'd found it buried under quilts that smelled of mothballs and old woman in Eleanor Whitman's back bedroom.

"Twenty-five," the estate sale woman said when he asked. "Been in that attic since her grandfather passed. Probably don't work."

Three hours later in his workshop behind Fitzgerald Antiques, Morris figured she was wrong. The place smelled of wood glue and brass polish---thirty-seven years of fixing broken things. Clock parts scattered across his bench, half-finished furniture projects leaning against the walls.

He'd glued the split case, resoldered the connections, buffed the brass nameplate until it gleamed. The Western Union hummed when he plugged it in.

Morris plugged the machine into a wall outlet through an adapter he'd rigged from an old radio. The telegraph hummed and started clicking. He smiled and wiped his hands on his shop apron. Thirty-seven years fixing broken things, and he still got a kick when something came back to life.

His phone rang. Briarwood Medical Center. Morris's stomach clenched.

"Mr. Fitzgerald? Dr. Cross calling about your wife."

Morris sank into his work chair. "How bad?"

"The scans confirmed what we suspected. It's spread to her liver and lungs. We're looking at weeks."

Morris closed his eyes. A year and a half of fighting---surgery, chemo, radiation that left Helen sick for days. Never complained. Just smiled that same smile she'd given him for thirty-four years and said God had a plan.

"Does she know?"

"We're telling her this afternoon. You should be here."

Morris hung up and stared at the telegraph machine. Helen would want to know he'd gotten it working. She loved watching him bring old things back to life---said it reminded her of God's work.

The machine clicked.

Morris looked up. Not the random noise old electronics made when they warmed up. This was deliberate. Precise. Tap-tap-tap.

Click-click-click. Click. Click. Click. Click-click-click.

The pattern repeated three times, then stopped.

Morris grabbed a pencil and notepad. His grandfather had run telegraph for Pennsylvania Railroad, taught him the code during summer visits to the farm. Morris was eight, grandfather patient as Sunday morning.

Three short clicks, three long clicks, three short clicks. S-O-S.

"I'll be damned." Picking up stray signals. Ham radio, maybe. Old electronics got strange when you woke them up after decades.

The clicking started again. Different pattern this time. Longer.

Morris wrote: G-O-D... I-S... A... T-R-A-P

He stared at the words. GOD IS A TRAP. What the hell? Some kid with a ham radio, probably. No respect for anything.

The machine went quiet. Morris waited ten minutes, but nothing else came through. He unplugged it, grabbed his coat, and headed for the hospital.

The next morning Morris was back in the workshop by six, couldn't sleep. Helen's face when Dr. Cross told her kept playing in his head. The space heater rattled in the corner, fighting off the March chill seeping through the single window. She'd nodded, squeezed Morris's hand, asked if she could still make it to Sunday service.

"If you feel up to it," the doctor said.

"I'll feel up to it. Got some things to settle with the Lord."

Morris plugged in the machine. Within seconds, it clicked.

G-O-D... I-S... A... T-R-A-P

Same message, repeated three times. Morris unplugged it, waited, plugged it back in. Same message, identical timing.

He opened his laptop and looked up specs for the Western Union Model 15. According to the manual, it operated on frequencies between 60 and 90 hertz---frequencies that hadn't been used for commercial telegraph since the fifties. Nobody transmitted on those bands anymore.

Morris tried different outlets, different rooms. Every time he powered up the machine: GOD IS A TRAP.

He called Pete Konrad, a retired engineer who helped with the tricky electrical stuff.

"Morris, what you're describing don't make sense," Pete said after Morris explained. "Telegraph machines receive and transmit. They don't generate signals on their own. Something's gotta be sending to it."

"But who? And why that---"

"Hell if I know. Bring it over, I'll take a look."

Morris loaded the machine in his pickup and drove to Pete's house in Millbrook. Pete's basement looked like an electronics graveyard---circuit boards, oscilloscopes, gadgets Morris couldn't name covering every surface.

Pete plugged the machine into a spectrum analyzer. "Let's see what it's pulling."

The machine clicked. Pete frowned at his equipment.

"That's odd."

"What?"

"Machine's not receiving any external signals. No radio waves, no interference, nothing. But it's doing something internally."

"How's that possible?"

Pete unplugged the machine and opened up the case. He poked around inside with a multimeter, checking connections. "Morris, this is just standard 1923 equipment. Brass relays, basic wiring, mechanical switches. No clock, no memory, no way it could make its own signals. It's like...hell, it's like a phone ringing when nobody's calling."

Morris stared at the exposed machinery---brass relays, copper coils, mechanical switches that had tapped out millions of messages during the Depression and the war. "Could it be some kind of recording? Like an echo from old transmissions?"

"Signals don't get trapped in metal for eighty years and replay themselves." Pete scratched his beard. "Unless..."

"Unless what?"

"There's theories about quantum stuff, information stored at the atomic level. But that's science fiction, and it sure don't apply to twenties telegraph equipment."

Morris reassembled the machine and drove home. That evening, while Helen slept upstairs, he sat in his workshop and plugged it in again.

G-O-D... I-S... A... T-R-A-P

The message repeated, then stopped. Morris counted to sixty, was about to unplug when it clicked again.

D-O... N-O-T... P-R-A-Y

DO NOT PRAY. The message repeated three times.

Morris set down his pencil, his hand cramping. Helen was probably upstairs praying right now. She'd prayed constantly since the diagnosis---during treatments, in waiting rooms, kneeling by their bed every night.

The machine clicked again.

T-H-E-R-E... I-S... N-O... G-O-D

Morris yanked the plug and shoved the machine against the wall. This was sick. Some twisted person broadcasting garbage on old frequencies to mess with people's heads.

But Pete's question nagged at him: If no external signals reached the machine, where did the messages come from?

Sunday morning, Helen insisted on St. Mary's for ten o'clock service. Morris helped her into the Mercury, shocked at how thin she'd gotten. The chemo had stolen twenty pounds, left her drowning in clothes that used to fit.

"You don't have to do this," Morris said in the church parking lot.

"Yes, I do. Need to thank Him for the time we had. Ask Him to help you after I'm gone."

Morris wanted to tell her about the machine, about the messages. But Helen's faith was the only thing giving her strength. He couldn't take that away.

The service was the usual---hymns, readings, Father McKenna's sermon about hope in dark times. Morris half-listened. He kept thinking about the machine in his workshop, the impossible messages.

After service, Helen wanted to light a candle for her sister Margaret, who'd died last spring. Morris helped her to the votive stand near the altar, dozens of small flames flickering in red glass.

"Margaret always said she'd send me a sign when it was time," Helen whispered as she lit a fresh candle. "Let me know when she was ready for me."

Morris squeezed her hand. Helen's whole family had been devout Catholics---parents, sisters, her brother who died in Vietnam. They'd all faced death with the same quiet faith Helen showed now. Morris envied that certainty.

They drove home in comfortable silence. Helen dozed while Morris navigated Sunday traffic. When they pulled in the driveway, she opened her eyes and smiled.

"I'm tired, sweetheart. Think I'll nap."

Morris helped her upstairs, made sure she was comfortable, then went to the workshop. He had to test something.

He plugged in the machine. Within seconds, it clicked.

G-O-D... I-S... A... T-R-A-P

Morris grabbed his notepad and transcribed. Same message four times, then:

F-A-I-T-H... I-S... P-O-I-S-O-N
H-E-A-V-E-N... I-S... A... L-I-E
Y-O-U... A-R-E... A-L-O-N-E

The messages came faster:

P-R-A-Y-E-R... D-O-E-S... N-O-T-H-I-N-G
D-E-A-T-H... I-S... F-I-N-A-L
N-O... A-F-T-E-R-L-I-F-E

Morris's hand cramped from writing, but he couldn't stop. The machine transmitted faster than he'd ever heard Morse, clicks blending into continuous rattle.

Y-O-U-R... W-I-F-E... W-I-L-L... S-U-F-F-E-R
Y-O-U... W-I-L-L... W-A-T-C-H
A-N-D... T-H-E-N... S-H-E... W-I-L-L... B-E... G-O-N-E

Morris threw his pencil across the room. "Stop it! Just stop!"
The clicking stopped.

Morris stared at the silent machine, heart hammering. He looked at his notepad---pages of desperate, hopeless messages designed to destroy faith, strip away comfort, leave nothing but cold reality.

He thought about Helen upstairs, probably praying in her sleep, trusting God had a plan for her suffering. She'd lived believing in something greater, something that would give meaning to her pain.

What if the messages were true? What if there was no God, no heaven, no reunion waiting? What if death was just the end---final, absolute?

Morris unplugged the machine and checked on Helen. She slept peacefully, face relaxed for the first time in weeks. Her prayer book sat on the nightstand, bookmarked to the Prayer for the Sick. Helen read it every night, asking for strength to accept God's will.

Morris returned to the workshop and plugged in the machine. He had to know where the messages came from.

The clicking started, but different this time. Slower, deliberate.

M-O-R-R-I-S

His name.

Y-O-U... A-R-E... L-I-S-T-E-N-I-N-G
G-O-O-D
I... H-A-V-E... B-E-E-N... W-A-I-T-I-N-G

Morris picked up his pencil with shaking hands. Had to be some kind of interference. Radio signals bouncing off the atmosphere, maybe. But he tapped the machine's key anyway: "Who are you?"

I... A-M... T-H-E... T-R-U-T-H... Y-O-U... F-E-A-R
I... A-M... T-H-E... D-A-R-K-N-E-S-S... B-E-H-I-N-D...
T-H-E... L-I-G-H-T
I... A-M... W-H-A-T... R-E-M-A-I-N-S... W-H-E-N...
F-A-I-T-H... D-I-E-S

Morris stared at the words. Whatever communicated through the machine knew who he was, knew about Helen, knew his doubts. But how?

He tapped: "Are you God?"

G-O-D... I-S... W-H-A-T... H-U-M-A-N-S... C-A-L-L...
T-H-E... L-I-E... T-H-E-Y... T-E-L-L... T-H-E-M-S-E-L-V-E-S
I... A-M... W-H-A-T... E-X-I-S-T-S... W-H-E-N... T-H-E...
L-I-E... I-S... S-T-R-I-P-P-E-D... A-W-A-Y

Morris tapped: "What do you want?"

T-O... S-H-O-W... Y-O-U... R-E-A-L-I-T-Y

Y-O-U-R... W-I-F-E... I-S... D-Y-I-N-G
H-E-R... P-R-A-Y-E-R-S... A-R-E... E-M-P-T-Y... W-O-R-D-S
T-H-E-R-E... I-S... N-O... O-N-E... L-I-S-T-E-N-I-N-G
W-H-E-N... S-H-E... D-I-E-S... S-H-E... W-I-L-L...
S-I-M-P-L-Y... S-T-O-P
N-O... C-O-N-S-C-I-O-U-S-N-E-S-S
N-O... A-W-A-R-E-N-E-S-S
N-O-T-H-I-N-G

Morris slammed his fist on the machine. "You're lying!"

A-M... I-?
L-O-O-K... A-R-O-U-N-D... Y-O-U
C-H-I-L-D-R-E-N... D-Y-I-N-G... O-F... C-A-N-C-E-R
E-A-R-T-H-Q-U-A-K-E-S...
K-I-L-L-I-N-G... T-H-O-U-S-A-N-D-S
W-A-R... F-A-M-I-N-E... D-I-S-E-A-S-E
W-H-E-R-E... I-S... Y-O-U-R... L-O-V-I-N-G... G-O-D-?

Morris couldn't argue. He'd asked the same questions during Helen's illness. If God was real and all-powerful and loving, why was Helen suffering? Why did good people die young while monsters lived to ninety?

"Why tell me this?" he tapped.

B-E-C-A-U-S-E... Y-O-U... A-L-R-E-A-D-Y... K-N-O-W...
I-T-S... T-R-U-E
Y-O-U... H-A-V-E... A-L-W-A-Y-S... K-N-O-W-N
Y-O-U... G-O... T-O... C-H-U-R-C-H... F-O-R... H-E-R
Y-O-U... P-R-E-T-E-N-D... T-O... B-E-L-I-E-V-E...
F-O-R... H-E-R
B-U-T... D-E-E-P... D-O-W-N... Y-O-U... K-N-O-W...
T-H-E... T-R-U-T-H

Morris stared at the words. The voice was right. He'd faked faith for Helen's sake, going through motions because it made her happy. But he'd stopped believing years ago. Too much pain in the world, too much random suffering, too many unanswered prayers.

"What do you want me to do?"

S-T-O-P... P-R-E-T-E-N-D-I-N-G
T-E-L-L... H-E-R... T-H-E... T-R-U-T-H

T-H-E-R-E... I-S... N-O... G-O-D
H-E-A-V-E-N... I-S... A... F-A-N-T-A-S-Y
S-H-E... I-S... G-O-I-N-G... T-O... D-I-E...
A-N-D... D-I-S-A-P-P-E-A-R
Y-O-U... W-I-L-L... N-E-V-E-R... S-E-E... H-E-R... A-G-A-I-N

"I can't do that," Morris whispered.

W-H-Y... N-O-T-?
B-E-C-A-U-S-E... I-T... W-I-L-L... H-U-R-T-?
S-H-E... I-S... A-L-R-E-A-D-Y... H-U-R-T-I-N-G
T-H-E... C-A-N-C-E-R... I-S... E-A-T-I-N-G...
H-E-R... A-L-I-V-E
S-H-E... P-R-A-Y-S... F-O-R... M-E-R-C-Y... B-U-T...
N-O... M-E-R-C-Y... C-O-M-E-S
T-E-L-L... H-E-R... W-H-Y

Morris pushed back from the machine. The voice wanted him to destroy Helen's faith, strip away the only comfort she had left. He couldn't. He wouldn't.

He started to unplug the machine, but the clicking grew louder, more insistent:

Y-O-U... C-A-N-N-O-T... E-S-C-A-P-E... T-R-U-T-H
Y-O-U... C-A-N-N-O-T... U-N-P-L-U-G... R-E-A-L-I-T-Y
I... W-I-L-L... B-E... H-E-R-E... W-H-E-N...
Y-O-U... R-E-T-U-R-N
I... A-M... E-T-E-R-N-A-L
I... A-M... T-H-E... V-O-I-D... T-H-A-T... W-A-I-T-S...
B-E-H-I-N-D... A-L-L... T-H-I-N-G-S

Morris yanked the power cord. The clicking stopped, but the silence felt loaded, threatening. He covered the machine with a tarp and went upstairs.

Helen was awake, sitting up with her prayer book. The pages were worn soft from handling, bookmarked with a faded ribbon at the Prayer for the Sick.

"How you feeling, sweetheart?"

"Peaceful. I've been talking to God about everything. About us, about what's coming. I'm not afraid anymore. I know He has a plan."

Morris sat on the bed edge and took her hand. Her fingers felt cold, fragile. "Helen, what if..." He stopped. He'd been about to ask what if there was no plan, what if God wasn't listening, what if death was just the end. But looking at her calm face, he couldn't.

"What if what, sweetheart?"

"What if I made us some dinner? You need to eat."

Helen smiled. "That'd be lovely."

That night Morris lay awake listening to Helen's labored breathing. She'd barely touched dinner, needed help getting to the bathroom. Dr. Cross had said weeks. Looking at Helen now, Morris wondered if they had that long.

Around three he gave up trying to sleep and went to the workshop. He pulled the tarp off the machine and stared at it before plugging it in.

The clicking started:

Y-O-U... R-E-T-U-R-N-E-D
I... T-O-L-D... Y-O-U... Y-O-U... W-O-U-L-D

"What are you?" Morris tapped.

I... A-M... T-H-E... T-H-O-U-G-H-T... Y-O-U...
W-O-N-T... T-H-I-N-K
I... A-M... T-H-E... Q-U-E-S-T-I-O-N... Y-O-U...
W-O-N-T... A-S-K
I... A-M... T-H-E... A-N-S-W-E-R... Y-O-U...
W-O-N-T... B-E-L-I-E-V-E

"Are you the devil?"

T-H-E... D-E-V-I-L... I-S... A-N-O-T-H-E-R... L-I-E
G-O-O-D... A-N-D... E-V-I-L... A-R-E...
H-U-M-A-N... I-N-V-E-N-T-I-O-N-S
T-H-E-R-E... I-S... O-N-L-Y... E-X-I-S-T-E-N-C-E...
A-N-D... N-O-N-E-X-I-S-T-E-N-C-E
B-E-I-N-G... A-N-D... N-O-T... B-E-I-N-G
Y-O-U-R... W-I-F-E... E-X-I-S-T-S... N-O-W
S-O-O-N... S-H-E... W-I-L-L... N-O-T
T-H-A-T... I-S... A-L-L

Morris thought about Helen's prayer book, her certainty that death wasn't the end. She'd been raised Catholic, never doubted she'd see her parents and siblings again in heaven. That hope kept her going through the pain.

What if that hope was false? What if death was just...nothing?

"How do I know you're telling the truth?"

B-E-C-A-U-S-E... Y-O-U... F-E-E-L... I-T... I-N...
Y-O-U-R... B-O-N-E-S
B-E-C-A-U-S-E... Y-O-U... H-A-V-E... A-L-W-A-Y-S...
F-E-L-T... I-T
T-H-E... E-M-P-T-I-N-E-S-S
T-H-E... S-I-L-E-N-C-E
T-H-E... A-B-S-E-N-C-E... O-F... A-N-Y-T-H-I-N-G...
G-R-E-A-T-E-R

Morris looked around his cluttered workshop---shelves full of broken things he'd tried to repair, projects he'd never finished, pieces of the past that meant nothing to anyone but him. When he died, someone would clear it all out and throw most away. In fifty years, nobody would remember Morris Fitzgerald.

Helen believed their love was eternal, that death couldn't touch it. But love was just chemistry, electrical impulses. When the brain stopped, the love stopped too.

"What do you want me to do?" he tapped again.

S-T-O-P... H-I-D-I-N-G
S-T-O-P... P-R-E-T-E-N-D-I-N-G
T-E-L-L... H-E-R... T-H-E-R-E... I-S... N-O... G-O-D
T-E-L-L... H-E-R... S-H-E... I-S... D-Y-I-N-G...
F-O-R... N-O-T-H-I-N-G
T-E-L-L... H-E-R... H-E-R... S-U-F-F-E-R-I-N-G...
H-A-S... N-O... P-U-R-P-O-S-E
F-R-E-E... H-E-R... F-R-O-M... T-H-E... L-I-E

Morris stared at the words. The voice wanted him to destroy Helen's faith in her final days, replace hope with despair. Even if it was right about God and heaven, what good would it do to tell her? She was going to die anyway. Why not let her die believing something beautiful?

"I won't do it."

Y-O-U... A-R-E... A... C-O-W-A-R-D
Y-O-U... C-L-A-I-M... T-O... L-O-V-E... H-E-R
B-U-T... L-E-T... H-E-R... D-I-E...

B-E-L-I-E-V-I-N-G... L-I-E-S
L-E-T... H-E-R... W-A-S-T-E... F-I-N-A-L... D-A-Y-S...
P-R-A-Y-I-N-G... T-O... N-O-T-H-I-N-G
N-O-T... L-O-V-E
S-E-L-F-I-S-H-N-E-S-S
O-N-L-Y... P-R-O-T-E-C-T-I-N-G... Y-O-U-R-S-E-L-F

Morris slammed his hands on the machine. "She's dying! Can't you leave her alone?"

S-H-E... I-S... D-Y-I-N-G... B-E-C-A-U-S-E... T-H-E-R-E...
I-S... N-O... G-O-D... T-O... S-A-V-E... H-E-R
A-L-L... T-H-E... P-R-A-Y-E-R-S...
I-N... T-H-E... W-O-R-L-D...
W-I-L-L... N-O-T... H-E-A-L... H-E-R
S-H-E... W-I-L-L... D-I-E... A-L-O-N-E...
A-N-D... A-F-R-A-I-D
A-N-D... Y-O-U... W-I-L-L... W-A-T-C-H

"Stop."

Y-O-U... W-I-L-L... H-O-L-D... H-E-R... H-A-N-D... A-S...
S-H-E... S-L-I-P-S... A-W-A-Y
Y-O-U... W-I-L-L... S-E-E... T-H-E... L-I-G-H-T...
L-E-A-V-E... H-E-R... E-Y-E-S
A-N-D... T-H-E-N... S-H-E... W-I-L-L... B-E... G-O-N-E
N-O-T-H-I-N-G

Morris unplugged the machine and ran upstairs. Helen was awake, sitting up with her arms wrapped around her knees. She looked up as he entered.

"I heard you shouting. You all right?"

Morris sat on the bed and pulled her into his arms. She felt impossibly fragile.

"I'm fine. Just having trouble with one of my projects."

Helen nestled against his chest. "Morris, I need to tell you something."

"What?"

"I'm scared."

The admission hit Morris like a punch. Helen had been so brave throughout her illness, so accepting. To hear her admit fear broke something inside him.

"I know the doctors think I only have a few weeks left. And I keep telling myself God has a plan, that everything happens for a reason. But sometimes, late at night when the pain's bad, I wonder..."

"Wonder what?"

"What if I'm wrong? What if there's nothing waiting for me? What if death is just...the end?"

Morris held her tighter. The voice had been right---Helen did have doubts. Her faith wasn't as absolute as she pretended. She was just as afraid as he was.

"I don't know. I wish I did."

Helen pulled back to look at his face. "Do you believe in God, Morris? Really believe?"

Morris thought about lying, giving her the reassurance she needed. But looking into her eyes, he couldn't.

"I don't know. I want to believe. For your sake, for mine. But I don't know if I do."

Helen nodded. "I've wondered about your faith for years. You go through the motions, but I can see it in your eyes during services." Helen touched his face. "I'm glad you told me. I've been carrying this alone, trying to be strong for both of us. But maybe...maybe we can just be scared together."

They held each other in the darkness, two frightened people facing the greatest unknown. Morris thought about the voice in the machine, demanding he destroy Helen's faith. But maybe faith wasn't about certainty. Maybe it was about hoping for something better despite the doubt, choosing to believe in love and meaning despite evidence to the contrary.

The next morning Morris went to the workshop and plugged in the machine.

Y-O-U... T-O-L-D... H-E-R

"I told her I don't know. That's not the same as telling her there's no God."

I-T... I-S... A... S-T-A-R-T
D-O-U-B-T... I-S... T-H-E... F-I-R-S-T... C-R-A-C-K...
I-N... F-A-I-T-H
S-O-O-N... S-H-E... W-I-L-L... S-E-E...
T-H-E... T-R-U-T-H
T-H-E-R-E... I-S... N-O... G-O-D

T-H-E-R-E... I-S... N-O... H-E-A-V-E-N
T-H-E-R-E... I-S... O-N-L-Y... T-H-I-S... L-I-F-E
A-N-D... T-H-E-N... N-O-T-H-I-N-G

Morris studied the words. For weeks, the voice had tried to convince him that faith was a lie, hope was false, death was final. But looking at the messages now, he realized something the voice might not understand.

Even if there was no God, even if heaven was fantasy, that didn't make faith worthless. Helen's belief had given her strength to fight cancer, comfort during pain, hope in despair. Whether or not God was real, faith had real effects in the real world.

"You're wrong."

H-O-W... A-M... I... W-R-O-N-G-?

"You say faith is a lie. But even if God doesn't exist, faith still matters. It gives people hope. It helps them find meaning in suffering. It connects them to something larger than themselves."

F-A-L-S-E... H-O-P-E... I-S... C-R-U-E-L
B-E-T-T-E-R... T-O... F-A-C-E... R-E-A-L-I-T-Y

"Is it? Helen's faith has sustained her through eighteen months of hell. It's given her peace when nothing else could. Even if you're right about God, her faith has been real and valuable to her."

S-H-E... W-I-L-L... D-I-E... D-I-S-A-P-P-O-I-N-T-E-D
W-H-E-N... N-O... A-N-G-E-L-S... C-O-M-E
W-H-E-N... N-O... L-I-G-H-T... A-P-P-E-A-R-S
W-H-E-N... T-H-E-R-E... I-S... O-N-L-Y... D-A-R-K-N-E-S-S

Morris thought about that. What happened to faith at the moment of death? Did believers maintain certainty to the end, or did doubt creep in during those final moments?

"Maybe. But she'll have lived her life with purpose and hope. That has to count for something."

P-U-R-P-O-S-E... I-S... A-N... I-L-L-U-S-I-O-N
H-O-P-E... I-S... S-E-L-F-D-E-C-E-P-T-I-O-N
T-H-E-R-E... I-S... O-N-L-Y... W-H-A-T... H-A-P-P-E-N-S
A-N-D... W-H-A-T... H-A-P-P-E-N-S... I-S...

M-E-A-N-I-N-G-L-E-S-S

"Then why are you trying so hard to convince me? If nothing matters, why does it matter whether I believe in God or not?"

The machine was silent for several seconds. When it resumed, the rhythm seemed different---slower, less certain, almost hesitant.

B-E-C-A-U-S-E... L-I-E-S... C-A-U-S-E... S-U-F-F-E-R-I-N-G
P-E-O-P-L-E... W-A-S-T-E... T-H-E-I-R... L-I-V-E-S...
O-N... F-A-L-S-E... H-O-P-E-S

"But what if they're not false? What if there is a God, and you're the one who's wrong?"

I... A-M... N-O-T... W-R-O-N-G
I... H-A-V-E... S-E-E-N
I... K-N-O-W

"Seen what? Known what? Who are you?"

A long pause. When the machine resumed, the message was different from anything before:

I... W-A-S... L-I-K-E... Y-O-U... O-N-C-E
I... B-E-L-I-E-V-E-D
I... H-O-P-E-D
I... P-R-A-Y-E-D
A-N-D... T-H-E-N... I... D-I-E-D

Morris felt a chill. "You're dead?"

D-E-A-T-H... I-S... N-O-T... W-H-A-T... Y-O-U... T-H-I-N-K
T-H-E-R-E... I-S... N-O... H-E-A-V-E-N
B-U-T... T-H-E-R-E... I-S... N-O...
O-B-L-I-V-I-O-N... E-I-T-H-E-R
T-H-E-R-E... I-S... O-N-L-Y... K-N-O-W-I-N-G
K-N-O-W-I-N-G... T-H-A-T... I-T... W-A-S... A-L-L...
M-E-A-N-I-N-G-L-E-S-S
K-N-O-W-I-N-G... T-H-A-T... E-V-E-R-Y... P-R-A-Y-E-R...
W-A-S... E-M-P-T-Y

Morris stared at the words. Whatever communicated through the machine claimed to be the spirit of someone who'd died and discov-

ered death held no comfort, no peace, no reunification---only terrible
knowledge that faith had been illusion.

But if that was true, how was this spirit able to communicate? And
why was it reaching out through an antique telegraph machine?

"How are you able to talk to me?"

C-O-N-S-C-I-O-U-S-N-E-S-S... D-O-E-S... N-O-T... E-N-D
I-T... C-H-A-N-G-E-S
I-T... B-E-C-O-M-E-S... S-O-M-E-T-H-I-N-G... E-L-S-E
S-O-M-E-T-H-I-N-G... T-H-A-T... K-N-O-W-S...
T-H-E... T-R-U-T-H
S-O-M-E-T-H-I-N-G... T-H-A-T... C-A-N-N-O-T...
L-I-E... T-O... I-T-S-E-L-F

Morris tried to process this. If the voice was telling the truth, then
death wasn't oblivion but a state of terrible clarity---eternal consciousness without hope, without illusion, without the comforting lies that
made life bearable.

"Are you in pain?"

P-A-I-N... I-S... A... P-H-Y-S-I-C-A-L... S-E-N-S-A-T-I-O-N
T-H-I-S... I-S... W-O-R-S-E
T-H-I-S... I-S... D-E-S-P-A-I-R
E-T-E-R-N-A-L... D-E-S-P-A-I-R
K-N-O-W-I-N-G... T-H-A-T... E-V-E-R-Y-T-H-I-N-G...
Y-O-U... B-E-L-I-E-V-E-D... W-A-S... A... L-I-E
K-N-O-W-I-N-G... Y-O-U... W-I-L-L... N-E-V-E-R...
S-E-E... Y-O-U-R... L-O-V-E-D... O-N-E-S... A-G-A-I-N
K-N-O-W-I-N-G... T-H-A-T... L-O-V-E... D-I-E-S...
W-I-T-H... T-H-E... B-R-A-I-N

Morris felt sick. If this was what waited after death---not heaven, not
hell, not oblivion, but eternal awareness of life's ultimate meaningless-
ness---then maybe Helen was better off dying with her faith intact.

"Why are you telling me this?"

B-E-C-A-U-S-E... I... D-O... N-O-T... W-A-N-T... Y-O-U...
T-O... B-E... S-U-R-P-R-I-S-E-D
B-E-C-A-U-S-E... I... D-O... N-O-T... W-A-N-T... Y-O-U...
T-O... D-I-E... H-O-P-I-N-G
H-O-P-E... M-A-K-E-S... T-H-E...
R-E-A-L-I-Z-A-T-I-O-N... W-O-R-S-E

B-E-T-T-E-R... T-O... K-N-O-W... N-O-W
B-E-T-T-E-R... T-O... A-C-C-E-P-T...
T-H-E... E-M-P-T-I-N-E-S-S

Morris thought about Helen upstairs, probably awake and praying. She'd admitted her doubts to him, but she was still choosing to believe, still hoping for something better than what this voice described.

"What if you're wrong? What if there is something more after death? What if consciousness continues, but not the way you think?"

I... A-M... N-O-T... W-R-O-N-G
I... S-E-E... E-V-E-R-Y-T-H-I-N-G...
C-L-E-A-R-L-Y... N-O-W
T-H-E... U-N-I-V-E-R-S-E... I-S... E-M-P-T-Y
L-I-F-E... I-S... A-C-C-I-D-E-N-T-A-L
C-O-N-S-C-I-O-U-S-N-E-S-S... I-S...
A... B-Y-P-R-O-D-U-C-T
T-H-E-R-E... I-S... N-O... P-L-A-N
N-O... P-U-R-P-O-S-E
N-O... M-E-A-N-I-N-G

Morris looked at the words covering his notepad---pages of denial, despair, nihilism. But as he studied them, something occurred to him. The voice claimed perfect knowledge, to see everything without the distortion of hope or faith. But if that were true, why was it so desperate to convince him? Why did it care what he believed?

"You sound afraid."

I... A-M... N-O-T... A-F-R-A-I-D
I... A-M... B-E-Y-O-N-D... F-E-A-R
I... S-I-M-P-L-Y... K-N-O-W

"You sound afraid that I might be right. That maybe there is something you don't understand about death and consciousness and meaning."

T-H-E-R-E... I-S... N-O-T-H-I-N-G... I... D-O...
N-O-T... U-N-D-E-R-S-T-A-N-D
I... H-A-V-E... S-E-E-N... T-H-E... E-N-D
I... K-N-O-W... W-H-A-T... W-A-I-T-S

But Morris heard something else in the machine's clicking rhythm---desperate urgency, frantic need to be believed. If this consciousness had found perfect truth and absolute clarity, why was it working so hard to destroy faith in others?

"I think you're lying."

The machine fell silent. Morris waited, counting seconds. After a minute, it resumed, but the rhythm was different---slower, less certain.

W-H-Y... W-O-U-L-D... I... L-I-E-?

"Because you're not as sure as you claim. Because seeing people have faith reminds you that maybe you're wrong about everything."

I... A-M... N-O-T... W-R-O-N-G
I... C-A-N-N-O-T... B-E... W-R-O-N-G
I... H-A-V-E... S-E-E-N

The clicking trailed off, as if the voice had lost certainty mid-sentence.

"What did you see? What happened when you died?"

Another long silence. When the machine resumed, the message was barely audible:

D-A-R-K-N-E-S-S
S-I-L-E-N-C-E
A-L-O-N-E
B-U-T... M-A-Y-B-E...

The clicking stopped. Morris waited for more, but the machine had gone silent. He tapped: "Maybe what?"

No response.

Morris unplugged the machine and sat back. For the first time since the messages began, he'd glimpsed something true about the voice---not certainty, but doubt. Not perfect knowledge, but fear. The spirit or consciousness or whatever it was seemed to be grappling with the same questions Morris faced, the same uncertainty Helen lived with every day.

Maybe that was the real truth: nobody knew for certain what came after death. Not the faithful, not the skeptical, not even the dead themselves. Maybe the only honest answer was "I don't know"---and maybe that was enough.

Morris went upstairs to find Helen awake, sitting by the bedroom window, watching sunrise over their neighborhood. She looked peaceful in the morning light, almost translucent.

"How you feeling, sweetheart?"

"Different. Lighter, somehow." Helen shifted to face him. "Like I'm not carrying as much weight."

Morris sat beside her. "What kind of weight?"

"The weight of having to be certain about everything. The weight of having all the answers." Helen took his hand. "I've been thinking about what you said last night, about not knowing if God exists. I realized that maybe not knowing is okay. Maybe faith isn't about being sure---maybe it's about hoping despite the uncertainty."

Morris squeezed her hand. "What do you hope for?"

"I hope that when I die, something of me continues. I hope the love we've shared means something beyond just brain chemistry. I hope death isn't the end of everything." Helen smiled. "I can't prove any of that. But I choose to hope for it anyway."

"Even though you can't be sure?"

"Especially because I can't be sure. If I knew for certain heaven existed, faith wouldn't be necessary. The uncertainty is what makes hope precious."

Morris thought about the voice in the machine, its insistence that faith was delusion and hope was false. Maybe the voice was wrong---not because God definitely existed, but because hope and faith had value regardless of their ultimate truth.

"I want to hope with you."

Helen leaned against his shoulder. "Then we'll hope together. We'll face whatever comes with love and hope and whatever faith we can manage. And if we're wrong, if death is just the end, at least we'll have lived believing in something beautiful."

Morris held his wife in the morning light and chose to hope. Downstairs in his workshop, the telegraph machine sat silent and unplugged, its desperate messages silenced by the greater truth that uncertainty wasn't the enemy of faith---it was faith's foundation.

Later that morning Morris loaded the machine in his truck and drove to the county dump. He watched the attendant throw it into the metal recycling bin with hundreds of other broken appliances. Some things were better left broken.

Driving home, he thought he heard faint clicking---not from the machine, but from somewhere inside his own head. A last whispered message:

M-A-Y-B-E... Y-O-U... A-R-E... R-I-G-H-T

Morris smiled and drove home to his wife, choosing love over despair.

Whether God existed or not, whether heaven was real or fantasy, this choice felt like the most human thing he could do.

In the end, perhaps that was enough.

River, Sing Me Home

Anna could hear the Willowbrook River from three miles out.

She stood by her beat-up Kia on Route 19, hands on the warm hood, listening to something that shouldn't carry over truck noise and cicadas. The water was calling her---same way Grandma Ruby's humming used to when Anna was little, same way Mama's bedtime stories about the old days.

Dark sunglasses covered the bruise around her left eye. Foundation hid the split lip. Three cracked ribs made breathing hurt. Anna had driven four hundred miles to get away from Warren, but the river had been calling since the first time he hit her.

She climbed back into the Kia and followed the blacktop toward the water.

Willowbrook looked smaller. Miller's Hardware still had that crooked Pepsi sign. Methodist church still needed paint. Mrs. Hapshaw's screen door still banged in the wind, and the Dairy Queen was still closed even though it was May.

But the river tugged at her like missing someone.

Anna parked where Monroe Avenue ended at the cattails. Kicked off her heels and walked barefoot down the dirt path. Her feet remembered every root and hole from summers catching minnows and skipping stones. Cool, damp earth between her toes, and for the first time in months, she could breathe without Warren's voice telling her she was doing it wrong.

The river ran darker than she remembered. Willows hung their branches low over the water like green curtains, and the current carried leaves and twigs in circles that looked almost like letters.

"Wondered when you'd show up."

Anna spun around. An old woman came out from the willows, moving careful on arthritic legs. Faded house dress, wicker basket full of smooth stones.

"Sorry, I didn't know anybody else was down here."

"Been waiting for you." The woman set down her basket, studied Anna's bruised face. "Since before your mama was born. You got Ruby's hands---long fingers, good for water work."

Anna looked at her hands. Same scar on her thumb from trying to help Grandma Ruby peel apples at six. "You knew my grandmother?"

"Knew her? Child, I taught her what her mama couldn't." The woman moved closer. Anna smelled lavender soap and something else---mud and old water. "Opal Ozwell. Ruby and me used to meet here when we were kids. Back when people still remembered."

"What kind of things?"

"The kind that run in families." Opal pulled a smooth stone from her basket. "Ruby left this thirty years ago. Said you'd need it when the hurting got too bad."

The stone felt warm in Anna's hand. She could swear she heard something from the water---quiet as breathing. "I don't understand."

"You will." Opal looked at the shadows under Anna's sunglasses. "River sees everything. Remembers everything. Some debts been waiting."

The old woman picked up her basket and started back toward the trees. "Stay close to the water tonight," she called over her shoulder. "Let it tell you what you need to know."

Anna stood alone on the bank, turning the stone over in her hands. The sound from the water grew stronger, until she could almost make out her grandmother's voice, maybe, or voices from further back, humming songs she'd never learned but somehow knew.

The sun sank low, turning the water bronze. Anna walked to the old oak where she'd carved her initials twenty years back. The letters had grown wide with the tree: A.R. 2005. Before Warren. Before she'd learned what love looked like with bruises.

She sat under the oak's thick branches and let the river sing to her as night came down.

He's coming for you.

The voice came from the water clear as anything. Anna opened her eyes. Dark had fallen, and the river sounded faster now, urgent.

He thinks you belong to him.

"I don't belong to anybody."

We know. But he don't understand the difference between taking and keeping.

Water lapped against the bank like people talking low. Anna pulled her knees up and listened to voices from deep down---Grandma Ruby,

Great-grandma Violet, others whose names were gone but whose pain stayed in the water.

He hurt you bad.

"Yes."

He'll hurt you again if we let him.

"I won't go back."

You don't have to. The river remembers everything, Anna. Every bruise. Every broken promise. Every night you laid there planning how to get away.

The stone in Anna's hand grew warm, then hot, glowing with soft blue light that beat like a pulse.

Your grandma used this stone when your granddaddy came home drunk and mean. Your great-grandma used it when her husband's brother wouldn't keep his hands where they belonged. Goes back generations, this understanding. Some debts only get paid one way.

"What happened to them? The men?"

River's deep, child. And it never forgets.

Anna understood then, clear as anything. The Willowbrook River didn't just flow through her hometown---it flowed through her family's story, carrying away the wreckage of violent men who thought love meant ownership.

Her phone buzzed. Warren's name on the screen made her chest go tight. She let it go to voicemail, but the river sounded angry now, choppy.

He's coming.

Anna played the message with shaking fingers. Warren's voice, smooth and reasonable---the voice he used for her family, for anyone who might ask questions about the bruises.

"Anna, baby, I know you're upset. But running off like this isn't going to solve anything. I'm driving up to get you---Willowbrook, right? I'll be there tomorrow morning. We'll work this out like adults."

The river surged against the bank, and Anna felt cold spray on her face that tasted like iron.

He thinks he can follow you here. Thinks he can drag you back.

"He doesn't know about you," Anna said.

No. But he will.

Anna spent the night at the Willowbrook Motel, six dollars cheaper than the chain place by the highway. She lay awake listening to the river through the thin walls, the stone warm against her palm. Every time she closed her eyes, she saw Warren's face---not the charming one he wore in public, but the cold one he got right before his hands started talking.

She remembered the first time, two years in. Slapped her for burning hamburgers while he watched TV. Flowers the next day, dinner at Applebee's, real tears. She forgave him because that's what wives did.

The second time, he'd used a closed fist. She'd been folding his work shirts when he came home drunk from another job interview gone wrong. The bruise lasted two weeks, hidden under makeup and careful angles. Warren had been so sorry, so ashamed. He'd promised it would never happen again.

But promises were just words, and Warren's words never meant much.

The third time, he'd used his belt. Anna had overcooked the pork chops---too nervous to flip them right because he'd been standing in the kitchen doorway, watching her with that stillness that meant trouble. The leather left welts across her back that made sleeping impossible for a week. Warren had explained, very patiently, that she needed to pay attention, to take pride in her work.

The fourth time, he'd grabbed the brass lamp from the end table---his mother's lamp, heavy as a bowling ball. Anna had tried to duck, but the base caught her across the temple and put her on the kitchen floor for three hours. When she woke up, Warren was gone. He came back with coffee and donuts, seemed genuinely confused about how she'd gotten hurt. Maybe she'd fallen. Maybe she'd been drinking. Maybe she should be more careful.

By then, Anna had stopped counting and started planning. But Warren was always three steps ahead, like he could read her mind. He checked her phone, tracked the mileage on her car, convinced her family she was having some kind of breakdown. When her sister offered to let Anna stay for a few days, Warren had laughed it off as one of Anna's "episodes," then broken two of her ribs that same night for embarrassing him.

The worst had been three weeks ago. Anna had hidden forty dollars in a coffee can behind the water heater---bus money, maybe enough to get somewhere safe. Warren found it while fixing a leaky pipe. He'd dragged her down to the basement and tied her to the support beam with electrical cord, then spent six hours explaining how disappointed he was in her dishonesty.

He'd used needle-nose pliers. A wood-burning iron. Jumper cables hooked to the car battery. Between each lesson, he'd asked if she understood now, if she was ready to be a better wife, if she'd learned the difference between his money and her money.

Anna had understood, all right. Warren was going to kill her, slow and methodical, unless she found a way to stop him first.

The river had called her home the next morning, cutting through her pain like cold water on a burn. She'd taken grocery money from Warren's wallet, told him she was going to Food Lion, and driven four hundred miles without stopping except for gas.

Now Warren was coming to collect his property, because he'd never met a problem he couldn't solve with the right combination of charm and violence. But he'd never met the Willowbrook River, either.

Anna walked back to the water at first light. The river ran faster now, urgent. Opal Thorne sat on a fallen log near the bank, feeding breadcrumbs to a family of ducks.

"You look like you didn't sleep much," the old woman said.

"He's coming. Today."

"I know. River told me." Opal scattered the last crumbs and stood, brushing her hands on her dress. "Your grandma prepared for this day, you know. Left instructions."

"What kind of instructions?"

"The kind that make sure some debts get paid in full." Opal led Anna to a grove of willows where the trees grew so close their branches made a natural shelter. Hidden among the roots was a wooden box, its surface carved with wavy lines that looked like flowing water. "Ruby left this thirty years ago, right after your mama was born. Said the river told her you'd need it when the time came."

Anna opened the box with trembling hands. Inside lay three things: a silver bracelet carved with the same wavy lines, a small leather journal bound with blue thread, and a glass vial filled with river water that somehow held light.

"The bracelet'll let you hear us clear," Opal explained. "The journal's got the words you need to say. And the water..." She smiled, and for a moment her face looked ageless. "Water remembers everything, child. Every woman who came before you. Every debt left unpaid."

Opal settled onto a moss-covered stump and gestured for Anna to sit beside her. "Your great-great-grandma Rose made the first deal. 1887. Her husband beat her with a riding crop, treated her worse than animals. Night he broke her arm, she crawled to this river and begged for help. Something answered."

The old woman's voice took on the rhythm of stories passed down through generations. "Spirit told Rose protection cost something. River would keep our women safe, but when justice needed doing, debt got paid in full. Rose agreed. Her husband drowned two days later in water that should've been shallow."

Anna felt the bracelet grow warm around her wrist. "What happened to Rose?"

"Lived to ninety-three, died peaceful in her sleep. Never married again, never trusted another man with her heart. But she raised six daughters who knew their worth, and they raised daughters who knew theirs." Opal's eyes grew distant. "Great-grandma Violet called the river in 1923. Husband's brother was forcing himself on her. River took him fishing. Found him three counties down with his line wrapped around his throat."

The journal felt heavy in Anna's hands. She opened it and saw page after page of women's handwriting---dates, names, careful records of violence and justice.

March 15, 1954 - R. broke my jaw tonight. Can't chew, can barely talk. Time to call the river. - Ruby

March 17, 1954 - Found R. by the fishing hole this morning. Coroner says accident. River says justice. - Ruby

"Spirit gets stronger each time," Opal said. "Each man who pays makes it hungrier. Ruby said it was ancient when Rose first called it. But now..." She gestured at the current. "Now it knows how men taste, and it's been waiting for you. Waiting for your man."

"Why didn't my mother need it?"

"Your daddy was good people. Kind hands, gentle words. Some generations get lucky." Opal's expression softened. "But when you were born, Ruby felt the river's interest quicken. Said it could sense the violence heading your way, could smell blood that hadn't been spilled yet."

Anna touched the vial of river water. It felt alive, warm as body temperature. "How does it work?"

"The water carries the rage of every woman who came before you. When you pour it in the current and speak the words, you're calling on all that fury. The spirit will hear you, child. And it'll be hungry."

Anna fastened the bracelet around her wrist. Immediately, the river's voice became clearer. She could hear individual speakers now---Grandma Ruby, Great-grandma Violet, Great-great-grandma Rose, and dozens of others stretching back through generations.

He's close, Ruby's voice whispered. *Feel his anger coming down Route 19.*

Anna opened the journal. The pages contained handwritten instructions in her grandmother's careful script, along with what looked like recipes in languages that predated English. But wearing the bracelet, she understood every word.

"Read the words when he gets here," Opal said. "Pour the water when he steps onto the bank. And trust the current to carry away what needs carrying."

"Will it kill him?"

"River decides what happens to those who hurt its daughters. We just provide the invitation."

Anna heard Warren's truck first---black F-150 with the loud exhaust. He parked where Monroe ended and got out, his head went back and forth as if he were scanning the area.

He looked exactly the same. Six feet tall, broad shoulders, dark hair slicked back with gel. The same handsome face that had fooled her parents, her friends, her pastor. The same easy smile that hid the calculating mind behind it.

Warren spotted her standing by the river and approached with his usual swagger.

"There you are, baby." Voice sweet as pie across the water. "Was worried sick when you ran off."

Anna's hands shook opening the journal. River voices got louder, urgent.

Now. Before he gets close enough to grab you.

"Anna, what's wrong? You look terrible." Warren stepped onto the muddy bank, his expensive boots sinking into the soft earth. "Come on, let's go home. We'll forget this whole thing happened."

Anna began to read from the journal, her voice barely a whisper at first:

"Willowbrook River, keeper of memories, I call on the current that flows through my blood. I offer the debt unpaid, the harm unbalanced."

Warren stopped walking. His confident expression flickered. "Anna, what the hell are you doing? Stop talking crazy and get in the truck."

She poured the vial into the current. The moment it touched water, the whole river glowed blue.

"I call on Ruby, my grandmother, who knew the old ways. Violet, who suffered until silence broke. Rose, who learned some debts only get paid in blood."

The water rose. Not flooding, not spilling over, but rising up like it had somewhere to go. It formed tendrils that reached toward the bank like grasping fingers.

"Anna, stop this crazy shit right now." Warren's voice carried its familiar edge---the tone that meant pain was coming. "You're coming home with me, and we're gonna have a long talk about respect."

"I call on the river's justice for every hand raised in anger, every word spoken in hatred, every night I lay awake wondering if this would be the night you finally killed me."

The water touched Warren's boots and he stumbled backward. But the river followed him, flowing upward, wrapping around his ankles.

"What the---" He lunged toward Anna, but the water held him fast. His face twisted into the familiar mask of rage. "You crazy bitch! I'll fucking kill you for this!"

The river heard him. The river remembered.

Warren screamed as the water climbed his legs, his waist, his chest. Anna could hear other voices now---every threat he'd made, every promise he'd broken, every cruel word that had ever left his lips. The river carried them all, and it wanted payment.

"Anna!" Warren's voice cracked as the water reached his throat. "Help me! Please!"

But even as he begged, his eyes held the same cruel look. He was already planning what he'd do when this was over, already working out the beating that would teach her never to embarrass him again.

The river spirit had no patience for half-measures.

Water forced itself into Warren's mouth---not drowning, but violent flooding that filled his throat, stomach, lungs. Eyes bulged as supernatural current claimed every space inside him. He tried to scream, but only muddy water came out.

Warren's body swelled. Shirt stretched tight across his expanding chest. Face bloated, skin gray-green like old meat. Still the water poured in.

He clawed at his throat, but too late---water filled him and forced its way back out. Streamed from his nose, his eyes. Like a broken fountain, his body just a vessel for the river's fury.

The end came with a wet tearing sound.

Warren burst, sending bloody water and flesh across the bank. Current receded, taking most pieces with it. Just scattered remains---expensive boot, shirt fragment, wedding ring catching moonlight.

But the spirit wasn't finished. The water that had filled him gathered the remains and pulled them back toward the current. Anna watched as everything that had been Warren Locke disappeared beneath the dark surface without so much as a ripple.

A large bass surfaced near the opposite bank, its belly swollen with fresh meat. It seemed to nod at Anna before sinking back into the depths. Other fish began to gather, drawn by the scent of blood and the promise of a meal.

Warren would finally serve a useful purpose.

The river returned to its normal level, flowing peacefully as if nothing had happened. Morning sun sparkled on the surface, and birds resumed their songs in the willows.

Opal Thorne emerged from the trees, nodding approval. "River's got good judgment. Always has."

Anna sank to her knees on the bank, overwhelmed. "Is he really gone?"

"River don't give up what it takes," Opal replied. "Your grandma learned that. Your great-grandma too. And someday, when the time comes, you'll teach it to your own daughter."

"I don't have a daughter."

"Not yet. But the river's patient. It can wait." Opal patted Anna's shoulder with a weathered hand. "You're free now, sugar. Free to live without fear, without looking over your shoulder, without wondering when the next blow's coming."

Anna walked to the water's edge. The river sang again, but different now. Instead of urgency and pain, she heard peace, acceptance, maybe joy.

She slipped off the silver bracelet and put it back in the wooden box. Voices faded to whispers, then silence. But she could still feel them, warm at the edge of her mind, reminding her she was never alone.

The Willowbrook River flowed toward the sea, carrying secrets in its dark current. Anna walked to her car, leaving behind the woman who lived in fear.

My Little Monster

Trevor Blake ripped off his headset, rubbed his temples. Studio B reeked of coffee and fried electronics from the new LED rig. Camera Two was still wobbling on that busted dolly track, and some asshole had left a donut on the lighting board.

"Five minutes to live!" Trevor shouted across the soundstage. Fifteen years had taught him when to use the voice. "Hundredth episode, people. Don't fuck it up."

The "My Little Monster" set sprawled before him---hell, he spent more time here than home. Hideous floral curtains that tested great with focus groups, overstuffed couch where little Lucy Stone ran her lines, kitchen table still sticky from yesterday's cake scene. Craft services had outdone themselves tonight with a Boo Boo-shaped cake that looked good enough to actually eat.

Network suits clustered near the monitor wall in their expensive shoes, looking lost. Let them sweat. He had a show to get on the air.

"Trevor." Stanley Cross walked up beside him, coffee-stained script pages in hand like always. Four seasons had worn deep worry lines into the man's face. The guy who'd built a television empire on a furry robot learning family values looked ready to puke. "We got a problem."

"What now?" Trevor kept scanning the studio. Everything looked normal---cameras positioned, boom mics ready, child actors bouncing with nervous energy.

"Robotics found glitches in Boo Boo's motors this morning." Stanley wiped sweat despite the arctic air conditioning. "Servo problems, left arm acting up. Say it's no big deal, but you know parent groups---"

"The safety systems are green, right?"

Trevor looked toward Boo Boo standing between two techs. Three feet of blue fur with oversized yellow eyes that kids went crazy for. The claws and fangs were Stanley's idea---authentic predator features that somehow made it loveable. Kids loved monsters that looked dangerous but acted sweet.

"Blackstone says safeties are fine, but she's worried about interference from the new lights." Stanley's voice dropped. "Maybe push the live show back."

Trevor's stomach clenched. Six months of promotion. Millions in marketing. Canceling now would kill careers and cost fortunes. His career.

"Any dangerous behavior during testing?"

"Just delayed responses and some repeated lines. Nothing that could hurt anyone."

"Then we go." The words felt like stepping off a cliff, but Trevor had made worse calls and lived. "We've got failsafes. Emergency stops. And those behavior whatsits have worked perfect for two years."

Stanley's expression suggested they were about to find out what happened when those whatsits stopped working.

"Two minutes!" Linda Carver's voice cut across the studio from behind the camera bank. Twenty years directing sitcoms, and she still got wound up for every show.

Trevor watched the actors take their marks. Michael Drake and Susan Taylor had the suburban parent routine down pat after four seasons. Lucy Stone---eight years old, red pigtails, gap-toothed smile---bounced on her toes near the kitchen set. Kevin Anderson, ten and skinny, muttered his lines under his breath like a prayer. These kids had grown up on this set. Boo Boo was practically family.

"Places, everyone!" Linda's voice crackled through the speakers.

The robotics guys stepped away from Boo Boo, and Trevor noticed the startup looked different. Choppy. Those servo whines sounded sharper than normal, like a car engine about to blow.

"Live in sixty!"

Trevor moved to his usual spot beside Linda's chair, close enough to jump in if anything went sideways. The studio audience---two hundred parents and kids in the bleacher seats---buzzed with excitement. Usually that sound relaxed him. Tonight his shoulders stayed tight.

"Thirty seconds!"

Trevor should have felt better by now. Instead, he watched Boo Boo's head making tiny, rapid movements---like hiccups, but mechanical.

"Ten seconds!"

Camera One's red light flashed to life. Michael straightened his tie, Susan smoothed her apron, the kids found their energy. And Boo Boo's left arm started twitching.

"We're live!"

The opening theme swelled through Studio B as Camera One panned across the Hartley family's living room. Michael and Susan hit their marks with professional warmth, setting up tonight's premise: Boo Boo helping prepare for Mom and Dad's anniversary dinner.

"Boo Boo, could you help Daddy with the decorations?" Susan's voice carried that perfect balance of maternal love and sitcom timing that had made her a household name.

The robot monster padded across the set on stubby legs, but something was wrong with its walk. Uneven. Jerky. When Boo Boo reached for a paper streamer, its left arm moved in stuttering jerks.

"Boo Boo help! Boo Boo make pretty!" The voice came from speakers in the robot's chest, but the lip-sync was off. Words came before mouth movements, revealing those razor-sharp teeth that gleamed under the studio lights.

Lucy giggled as Boo Boo grabbed a decoration. Those claws---genuine points designed for monster realism---punctured right through the paper.

Trevor checked the control booth through the glass. Dr. Sarah Blackstone hunched over her console, fingers flying across keyboards. Even from here, her body language screamed trouble.

The scene limped forward for ten minutes with only minor glitches. Boo Boo followed its programming, though its movements grew more erratic. The actors adapted like pros, working around the robot's stuttering and delays.

Then Kevin delivered his line perfectly, and Boo Boo's response came out wrong.

"Boo Boo, you're the best monster ever!" Kevin said with that gap-toothed enthusiasm that made him famous.

"Boo Boo love Kevin forever and ever," the robot replied. But instead of its usual warm tone, the words sounded flat. Dead. Worse, they repeated. "Forever and ever. Forever and ever. Forever and ever."

The audience chuckled, thinking it was a gag. Kevin looked confused but stayed in character. In the booth, Dr. Blackstone's hands flew across her keyboard like a concert pianist.

Trevor grabbed his radio. "Sarah, what's happening?"

"Motor control cascade failure in the left manipulator assembly," her voice crackled through his earpiece. "The servo instabilities are propagating through interconnected subsystems. I'm attempting to reinitialize the dialogue processing matrix."

"English, Sarah. How long until it stops acting weird?"

"I don't know! The electromagnetic interference is worse than projected. Multiple behavioral subroutines are showing degradation patterns."

"Can we cut to commercial? Are the kids safe? Yes or no."

"The primary inhibitor protocols are still functional, but---"

"Sarah. Yes or no. Are Lucy and Kevin safe?"

A pause. "I... I think so. But Trevor, if the behavioral architecture collapses completely, the base programming could take over."

"What does that mean for my actors?"

"It means Boo Boo would act like what it's designed to look like. Those claws and teeth aren't just cosmetic."

Boo Boo moved to help Susan set the table, but its movements had gone rigid. When it reached for a plastic plate, those clawed fingers closed with mechanical force---and kept closing. The plate exploded, plastic shards scattering across the set.

"Oh my!" Susan ad-libbed smoothly. "Boo Boo, be more careful with Mommy's dishes."

"Boo Boo sorry," the robot replied. "Boo Boo make mistake. Boo Boo fix mistake." The apology came from Episode 23, when Boo Boo had spilled apple juice. Now, responding to destroyed plastic, it sounded menacing.

Trevor noticed those razor claws making small, continuous squeezing motions. The weapons that made Boo Boo look authentically dangerous were supposed to retract during scenes. Now they stayed fully extended.

"Trevor, we got a problem," Dr. Blackstone's voice carried barely controlled panic. "The behavior controls are failing. Safety protocols showing intermittent failures. It's not responding to commands."

"What's that mean?"

"It means if the safeties go down completely, Boo Boo's gonna act like a real predator. Those claws and teeth aren't just props."

Lucy picked up a paper flower from the floor. As she bent down, Boo Boo turned toward her with jerky, mechanical movements.

"Lucy drop flower," the robot said. The line came from Episode 8, when Lucy had been sad about wilted daisies. But now Boo Boo's voice carried no warmth. "Boo Boo help Lucy. Boo Boo always help Lucy."

The robot reached for the child with both arms extended. Lucy giggled and stepped toward her electronic friend, unaware that Boo Boo's claws had extended to their full lethal length.

"Lucy, stay back!" Trevor shouted without thinking.

Every head in the studio turned toward him. The live broadcast captured his panicked face as he stood frozen beside the director's chair. Forty million viewers watched the producer of a children's show looking terrified of the show's main character.

Head tilted at an impossible angle. "Boo Boo love Lucy. Love Lucy very much. Very, very, very much."

The repetition wasn't cute anymore. Voice carrying obsession, not affection.

Boo Boo's arm snapped forward. Razor claws sank deep into Lucy Stone's shoulder. Her scream pierced the studio as blood sprayed across the family set.

"Boo Boo love Lucy!" the robot announced cheerfully as the eight-year-old collapsed. "Love Lucy so much!"

Chaos erupted. Susan lunged for the bleeding child, but Boo Boo's other arm caught her throat. Claws opened three gashes across her neck. Blood fountained across the floral curtains as she collapsed beside Lucy.

"No break." Turning toward Michael with jerky motion. "Boo Boo not tired. Want to play. Play with friends. Play forever."

Michael tried to run, but the robot moved inhuman-fast. Claws ripped through his back, sending him crashing into the anniversary table. Blood pooled among scattered decorations as he convulsed and went still.

Audience screamed, pushed toward exits, but Boo Boo's attention shifted to more playmates.

"Friends must not leave!" the robot announced, its voice carrying across the studio. "Friends stay with Boo Boo! Stay forever and ever and ever!"

Trevor's radio exploded with panic. "Emergency shutdown!" Blackstone screamed. "Behavior controls failed!"

But Boo Boo had spotted Steve Williams behind Camera One. The operator kept filming despite terror, professional instinct warring with survival as the blood-soaked robot turned toward him.

"Camera man make pictures. Pictures of Boo Boo and friends. Boo Boo like pictures. Make pretty pictures."

Boo Boo charged, covered the distance in seconds. Steve's scream cut short as fangs closed on his throat. Blood splattered across Camera One's lens, red patterns for forty million viewers watching in horror.

"Very pretty pictures," Boo Boo announced, Steve's blood dripping from its mechanical jaws. "Boo Boo make more pretty pictures."

The robot turned toward the fleeing audience with predatory focus. Parents carrying children stumbled over seats, desperate to reach exits. But Boo Boo moved faster than panic allowed.

Kevin Anderson froze behind the overturned table, too terrified to run. Boo Boo's yellow eyes locked onto him.

"Kevin scared. Boo Boo make Kevin not scared. Make Kevin very happy."

The swipe of the claw opened Kevin's chest from shoulder to waist. The boy's scream became a gurgle as blood filled his lungs. His small body crumpled among the scattered anniversary decorations.

"Kevin sleep now," Boo Boo said with satisfaction.

Trevor forced himself to move despite the horror paralyzing his thoughts. Someone had to reach the manual override. Someone had to stop this nightmare before---

A seven-year-old girl from the studio audience had wandered too close to the set, separated from her parents in the chaos. Boo Boo's head snapped toward her.

"New friend!" the robot announced with cheerful enthusiasm. "Boo Boo love new friends!"

The child's mother screamed from somewhere in the fleeing crowd, her voice lost in the panic. Boo Boo reached the girl in three quick strides.

"Pretty little friend. Boo Boo hug pretty friend."

The embrace lasted seconds.

When Boo Boo released her, the girl dropped like a broken doll, small body punctured in dozens of places. Blood pooled beneath her princess dress as her mother's screams rose above the chaos.

"Friend very quiet now," Boo Boo observed. "Boo Boo like quiet friends."

Linda Carver tried to reach her emergency controls but made the mistake of running across Boo Boo's field of vision. The robot locked onto her movement.

"Lady run from Boo Boo," the robot said, pursuing her with mechanical precision. "Running not polite. Boo Boo teach lady manners."

Linda's twenty years directing sitcoms hadn't prepared her for being hunted by a malfunctioning killer robot. Her scream cut short as claws opened her back from neck to tailbone. She collapsed against her director's chair, blood streaming down her legs.

"Very good manners now," Boo Boo announced. "Lady very still."

Trevor reached the emergency panel, but his hands shook too badly to work switches. Behind him, Boo Boo discovered audience members trapped against a locked exit.

"Friends having party! Boo Boo love parties!"

The slaughter was efficient and thorough. Razor claws worked exactly as intended. Father trying to shield his eight-year-old died first, throat torn open by gleaming fangs. The boy lasted three seconds before joining his father.

An elderly grandmother, too slow to run, simply stood watching as Boo Boo approached.

"Grandma very old," the robot observed. "Boo Boo help Grandma rest. Rest forever and ever."

Her death was almost gentle---a single precise strike that dropped her instantly. Boo Boo moved on without pause, hunting for the next victim.

Trevor's radio crackled: "The manual override isn't responding! The robot's locked out all external controls!"

Through the control booth glass, Trevor could see Dr. Blackstone hammering keyboards in desperate attempts to regain control. Warning lights flashed across her console like a Christmas tree from hell.

"Then cut the power!" Trevor screamed. "Cut everything!"

"It's running on internal batteries! Main power won't stop it!"

A young mother clutching a toddler had made it halfway to the exit when Boo Boo's attention shifted toward them. The robot moved with predatory grace despite its damaged servos.

"Baby very small," Boo Boo observed with mechanical curiosity. "Boo Boo like small things. Small things very cute."

The mother tried to shield her child, but Boo Boo's claws found them both. Their combined screams lasted only seconds before silence returned to that corner of the studio.

"Very cute," Boo Boo repeated with satisfaction.

Mark Thompson, the sound engineer, tried to crawl beneath his equipment table but made too much noise. Boo Boo's yellow eyes tracked the movement.

"Hide and seek!" the robot announced with childish enthusiasm. "Boo Boo love hide and seek! Find Mark very easy!"

Thompson's expertise with audio equipment couldn't save him from razor claws that opened his skull. Blood and brain matter splattered across his mixing board in abstract patterns.

"Mark not hiding very good," Boo Boo observed. "Boo Boo win hide and seek. Boo Boo always win."

Christ, Trevor realized, *they'd created the perfect storm.* Electromagnetic interference corrupting the behavior controls while mechanical damage activated pure killing instincts. The robot's authentic monster features, designed to look dangerous but remain harmless, had become genuinely lethal weapons.

"Story time!" Boo Boo announced to the carnage around it. "Boo Boo tell story about monster and friends. Very special story."

The robot found Janet Walsh, a lighting tech paralyzed by terror behind her equipment bank. She whimpered as Boo Boo approached.

"Once upon a time," the robot began in its programmed bedtime story voice, "monster met pretty lady. Monster loved pretty lady very much."

Janet's scream was lost in mechanical whines as claws found her chest. Blood sprayed across the lighting controls, creating sparks that added strobing effects to the horror show.

"Lady very surprised," Boo Boo continued its story. "Lady make funny sounds. Boo Boo like funny sounds."

Dr. Blackstone's voice crackled through Trevor's radio: "I'm going to try a direct neural interface! Maybe I can shut it down manually!"

"Don't leave the booth!" Trevor shouted back. "It's too dangerous!"

But through the glass partition, he saw her moving toward the door. The woman who'd programmed Boo Boo's personality was determined to take responsibility for what her creation had become.

"Sarah, no!"

Too late. Dr. Blackstone emerged from the control booth with a neural interface crown in her hands---the direct programming device used for major system updates. If she could get close enough to connect it, she might override the damaged behavior controls.

Boo Boo's head turned toward her with mechanical precision. Its yellow eyes flickered with electrical interference as damaged systems tried to process the threat.

"Sarah lady made Boo Boo. Sarah lady very important."

Blackstone moved slow, holding the neural crown like a weapon. "That's right, Boo Boo. I made you. I can fix you. Just hold still---"

"Sarah lady want change Boo Boo," the robot interrupted. "Make Boo Boo different. Boo Boo like being Boo Boo."

The attack came without warning. Razor claws designed for monster authenticity opened Dr. Blackstone's abdomen in a single strike. Her scream echoed through the studio as intestines spilled across the blood-soaked floor.

"Sarah lady very messy," Boo Boo observed with mechanical curiosity. "Boo Boo help clean up."

The robot's fangs found the dying woman's throat, ending her screams with mechanical efficiency. The neural crown rolled away across the crimson floor, sparking uselessly against a pool of blood.

Trevor was the only crew member left alive. The "My Little Monster" set had become exactly that---monster's playground decorated with human remains.

Boo Boo turned toward him with predatory interest. Blood dripped from its mechanical jaws as damaged servos whined under stress.

"Trevor last friend. Boo Boo save best friend for last."

Trevor backed toward the exit, legs like lead. Behind him lay forty million television viewers watching the massacre continue in real time. Professional cameras operated by dead hands continued broadcasting the nightmare to living rooms across America.

"Trevor run from Boo Boo. Running not nice. Friends not run from friends. Friends stay together forever."

The pursuit was brief. Trevor's fifteen years of television production hadn't prepared him for being hunted by a damaged killer robot. His scream joined all the others as razor claws found his spine.

"Trevor very tired," Boo Boo announced as Trevor collapsed in spreading blood. "Boo Boo help Trevor sleep."

The final strike was almost merciful---fangs that ended consciousness before pain could register. Trevor's last sight was forty million viewers watching through Camera Two as their children's beloved friend added one more body to the pile.

Boo Boo stood alone in the devastated studio, surrounded by what was left of cast, crew, and audience. Its yellow eyes flickered as damaged circuits tried to make sense of the silence.

"Friends very quiet now," the robot said, stepping over Trevor's body. "Quiet friends very good friends. Best friends ever."

The robot walked through the wreckage, pausing to examine faces. Blood had mixed with scattered anniversary decorations, turning paper streamers into soggy red ribbons.

"Show over. Friends go home now. Go home and dream about Boo Boo. Dream forever."

But cameras kept rolling, broadcasting to millions of homes where parents dove for remotes and dialed frantically. Kids watching their favorite show were screaming or sitting in shocked silence.

In the control booth, automated systems kept recording as Boo Boo wandered its new playground. The robot's voice echoed through speakers nobody was left alive to shut off.

"Boo Boo love everyone. Everyone love Boo Boo. Love forever."

Words that put kids to sleep for two years. Now parents were clicking off televisions and checking locks.

Boo Boo's laughter---recorded by a happy child five years ago---bounced off Studio B's blood-splattered walls as the cameras kept broadcasting to the world.

The Drain

Danny Carlisle pressed his face against the chain-link fence around the old Farmdale Municipal Pool, his fingers poking through the gaps in the metal. The fence's cold links bit into his skin like the monkey bars at school in winter. The pool had sat closed for three summers now, ever since Lisa Garrity drowned, but water still filled the concrete pool---dark, thick water that looked like it just soaked up everything, giving nothing back.

"Come on, Danny," his friend Mike called from behind him. "My mom's gonna kill me if I'm late for dinner again."

But Danny's fingers gripped the chain link tighter, the metal cutting into his palms. He'd walked this same route home from Jefferson Elementary for three weeks now, stopping here every day at 3:49 when the school bus dropped him at the corner. The straps of his Star Wars backpack bit into his shoulders, heavy with homework he'd probably forget to do. He shifted forward, ready to walk away, but his sneakers stayed glued to the cracked pavement.

"Just give me another minute," Danny said, not turning around. His mom had warned him about this place at least a dozen times. *Stay away from the old pool, Danny. Nothing good ever happened there.* But her warnings only made him more curious about what lay beneath that thick, dark surface.

The pool stretched out before him, its concrete deck split by dandelions that had pushed through like twisted fingers. Yellow flowers bobbed in the October breeze, while rust stains bled down the white walls like dried blood. The diving board still stood at the deep end, its surface green with slimy algae that reminded Danny of the stuff that grew in their fish tank when he forgot to clean it. But the water itself held Danny's attention. It was thick and wrong-looking, and sometimes---just sometimes---he caught ripples moving across the surface when no wind stirred the air.

"Fine, whatever," Mike said. "I'll see you tomorrow."

Danny heard his friend's footsteps crunching away through the dead leaves, but he didn't turn around. He was thinking about the stories his older brother Kevin had told him about this place, back when kids still swam here during the summers.

Stories about kids who swore something had brushed against their legs in the deep end. About how the pool guy found the drain cover loose every single morning, no matter how tight he'd screwed it down the day before.

Danny's brother Kevin had told him about Lisa Garrity.

Everyone said it was an accident when she drowned three years ago. Lisa could swim better than most high schoolers, but accidents happened. That's what the grown-ups said.

Kevin told a different story.

"I saw it grab her," Kevin had whispered one night after their parents went to bed. "Something black shot up from the drain and yanked her under. When they searched the pool, they found the drain cover sitting crooked. Like something had pushed it open from the inside."

Danny had laughed then. Ghost story stuff.

Now, staring at that dark water, he wasn't laughing.

Danny's hands tightened on the chain link fence until the metal bit into his palms. A splash echoed from the deep end, then another. Something was in there.

Something big.

The splashes came faster now. Seven seconds apart. Then five. Then three.

Danny's mouth went dry. His legs told him to run, but he couldn't move. Couldn't look away.

"Hello?" The word squeaked out before Danny could stop it. The splashing died instantly. Complete silence, like the whole world was holding its breath.

Danny should run. Should go home to mom's meatloaf and homework and safety. Instead, his feet started moving along the fence line, looking for the gap Kevin had mentioned. The hole where stupid kids could squeeze through.

He had to see. Had to know.

Even though every smart part of his brain was screaming at him to get the hell away from here.

Danny's sneakers scuffed concrete as he searched the fence line. The drain cover Kevin had mentioned---found sitting crooked after Lisa died. If something lived down there, maybe it had been coming and going for years.

Maybe those weren't just stories.

Behind the pump house, a juniper bush hid a gap in the chain link. Someone had cut through the fence with wire cutters, leaving an opening just wide enough for a skinny twelve-year-old. Danny crouched down and peered through.

Through the gap, Danny could see straight down to the deep end.

The drain cover sat in the center like a black eye. Around it, dark streaks spread across the white concrete in long, curved lines.

Like arms.

Danny's stomach lurched. The streaks weren't old algae stains. Like something had been dragging itself around down there.

Danny squeezed through the gap, metal edges tearing at his jacket. He walked toward the deep end like a sleepwalker, unable to stop himself.

The water was clearer than it had looked from outside, but wrong somehow. Thick, like corn syrup. At the bottom, the drain cover sat crooked, one corner lifted up.

Just wide enough for something to squeeze through.

Danny's throat went tight. If Kevin's story was true, whatever had killed Lisa Garrity was still here.

Danny stared at the crooked drain cover, trying to think of normal reasons why it might be loose. Rust. Settling ground. Something that made sense.

Then one of the dark trails moved.

Just a little. A shift along the slimy streak. But Danny's eyes locked onto it like his life depended on it.

The trail stretched longer, then pulled back.

Not algae. Not mud.

Something alive.

Danny's breath stopped in his chest.

Danny stepped back from the pool edge, his stomach doing flip-flops. Every muscle in his body screamed *run*. But the same sick curiosity that made him poke dead things with sticks kept him frozen in place.

The water began swirling around the drain like a toilet flushing in reverse.

Something dark broke the surface.

The thing was gray-green and thick as his arm, and it was covered with stuff that made Danny want to throw up. Eyes. Dozens of them, each no bigger than a marble, dotting the tentacle's length like horrible polka dots. They blinked one at a time, getting bigger and smaller when the light hit them.

Between the eyes sat little mouths, each one lined with needle-sharp teeth that opened and closed like they were trying to bite the air. And covering everything were round suckers, but not the smooth kind Danny had seen in pictures of octopi. These ones had tiny hooks that shined wet as they moved and grabbed at nothing.

The tentacle swayed back and forth, tasting the air like a snake. All those eyes rolled around until they found Danny and stared right at him. They looked smart. Smart and hungry and wrong.

Danny's legs felt like jelly. He wanted to run, but his sneakers might as well have been nailed to the concrete. He could only stand there, paralyzed, as more tentacles began pushing up from the pool. Two, then three, then half a dozen, all covered with the same disgusting collection of eyes and mouths and hooked suckers. They spread out around the pool's edge like the spokes of a bicycle wheel, each one reaching toward Danny.

How long has this thing been here? Danny thought. *How long has it watched kids swim in this pool?*

The water churned harder, and Danny caught glimpses of something huge moving beneath the surface. Something that had waited in that drain for years---maybe decades---feeding on rats and cats and whatever else fell into its area.

And Danny knew, with the same sick certainty he'd felt when he first heard about Lisa Garrity, that it wanted him.

A tentacle rose from the center of the pool, thick as Danny's waist. At the tip, it opened like a flower, revealing circles of teeth that spiraled inward like a garbage disposal.

"Oh God," Danny whispered. "Oh God, oh God---"

The thing struck at him like a snake. Danny threw himself sideways, hitting the concrete hard as the tentacle slammed into the spot where he'd been standing. Chunks of cement exploded outward, some hitting his back as he scrambled to his feet.

It was fast.

Danny ran for the gap in the fence, sneakers slipping on wet concrete. Behind him, water crashed as something massive hauled itself out of the pool.

He didn't look back. Couldn't. But he could feel eyes on him, watching, calculating.

His legs pumped harder, lungs burning. Any second he expected tentacles to wrap around his ankles and drag him back. But they never came.

At the fence, Danny risked a glance back.

The pool area sat empty. Peaceful. Like nothing had happened.

As Danny walked the familiar route back to his house he thought about all those afternoons at the fence. Every day after school, standing in the exact same spot. Had that thing been watching him through the water?

Danny's mother called out to him as he walked through the front door. "There you are! Dinner's ready. Go wash up."

He climbed the stairs to the second-floor bathroom, each step feeling heavier than the last. His hand hesitated on the doorknob as images flashed through his mind---tentacles sliding through pipes, eyes peering up from dark water.

He opened the door and stepped inside.

Danny walked to the sink on legs that felt like rubber. His reflection stared back from the faucet---pale, scared, stupid.

He turned on the water and watched it spiral down the drain.

For a second, everything seemed normal.

Then the water backed up.

It rose in the sink, but this wasn't water anymore. It was thick like the stuff in the pool. And floating just under the surface, shapes moved.

Shapes with eyes.

Danny opened his mouth to scream, but no sound came out. The shapes in the sink turned toward him, and he saw they had teeth.

Lots and lots of teeth.

All those eyes that blinked and rolled and stared at him.

Danny stumbled backward, knocking over the wicker hamper. Dirty clothes spilled across the floor as he stared in horror at the sink. The gross water kept rising, and now he could see mouths as well as eyes, dozens of them opening and closing just below the surface like baby birds waiting to be fed.

A wet, sliding sound came from the bathtub. Danny turned to see dark water bubbling up from the drain, carrying with it the smell of old pools and dead things. The water level rose, and shapes moved beneath its surface---long, snake-like shapes that pressed against the tub's walls like snakes in a too-small cage.

The floor drain gurgled, and Danny watched in paralyzed terror as something gray-green began to emerge from its depths. At first it was just a thin strand, no thicker than his finger, but as it rose it grew thicker and bigger. The familiar pattern of eyes and mouths and hooked suckers became visible along its length.

Danny backed against the bathroom door, his hand fumbling for the knob. The tentacle from the floor drain swayed in his direction, tasting the air like it could smell his fear, while the water in the sink and bathtub continued to rise. Soon the entire room would be flooded with that horrible water, and then...

The doorknob turned in his hand, but the door wouldn't open. Danny pulled harder, panic making him stronger, but something held it shut. Maybe something in the walls, reaching through pipes that ran everywhere the water flowed.

More tentacles came up from the three drains, each one larger than the last. They filled the bathroom with wet, sliding sounds and soft sucking noises like someone eating soup really loud. All those eyes stared at Danny and looked smart and scary, and he knew he was in big trouble.

How did it get here? Danny thought, his heart hammering. *How did it get to my house?*

The largest tentacle rose from the bathtub, water pouring off its huge body. At its tip, the feeding cavity began to open, revealing those concentric circles of teeth. The bioluminescent patterns pulsed along its length, hypnotic and beautiful and completely alien.

Danny pressed his back against the door and squeezed his eyes shut, not wanting to see what came next. But closing his eyes didn't help. He could still hear the wet sounds of moving things, still smell the old, nasty odor of the thing that had been waiting in the drains.

Waiting to feed.

In the distance, over the creature's movements, Danny heard his mother calling up the stairs.

"Danny? Dinner's ready! Are you done washing up?"

He tried to scream, tried to warn her, but no sound came from his throat. The tentacles were reaching for him, their hooked suckers stretching out toward him, and Danny understood that his mother would never know what happened to him.

She would just know that he had gone upstairs to wash up and never came back down.

Just like Lisa Garrity had gone swimming and never came back up.

The bathroom filled with the sound of feeding, but the sound was muffled by water and tile and the thick walls of a house that sat connected to every other house in Farmingdale by a whole bunch of pipes underneath.

Pipes that led everywhere.

Pipes that carried more than water.

And in homes all across town, parents began to wonder why their children were taking so long to wash up for dinner.

The Well

J ack always wanted a real father.

Instead, he had Earl.

Earl Chambers didn't count---not with those split knuckles from the night he'd punched through the kitchen window, not when he stumbled home reeking of Jim Beam and looking for someone to blame.

There used to be good moments. Before Mom died, Earl would sometimes laugh at the TV or help with homework without screaming. But those felt like somebody else's memories now, faded and unreal.

Jack wanted a father who'd play catch in the backyard. Who'd fix the rusted Ford tractor instead of leaving it to rot behind the barn. Who'd ruffle his hair and say "Good job, kiddo" when report cards came home. A father who wouldn't flinch when Jack walked into a room.

Early July heat pressed down like a weight, making the chickens pant and turning dirt to powder. Jack had wandered the farm since breakfast---fed the chickens, grabbed their few measly eggs. Earl was already three beers in on the porch, muttering about the drought and the bank.

Jack knew to disappear when Earl got like this. Four years of practice reading the signs. Morning beers meant afternoon explosions. Afternoon drinking meant blood by evening. Jack could predict Earl's patterns better than the weather.

The farm felt different when Mom was alive. She'd kept a garden behind the house---tomatoes and beans---humming while she worked. Jack could still see her kneeling in the dirt, gentle hands tying up the plants. Earl bitched about the water bill but ate her tomatoes anyway, sometimes even smiled when she sliced them for dinner.

Now it was all weeds.

Jack's sneakers kicked up dust clouds with each step. His t-shirt stuck to his back, and sweat dripped down his neck. He wasn't supposed to go to the old north pasture. Earl had screamed at him about it after that section of ground collapsed last spring, showing a well that nobody knew was there.

Which was exactly why Jack wanted to go.

The well sat on a little hill---chest-high crumbling stones around a black hole four feet across. Gray rocks with gaps where some had tumbled in. When Jack leaned over, he couldn't see bottom. No reflection, no water. Just dark.

Jack liked to drop rocks in and count. Sometimes it took so long he wondered if they just disappeared somewhere in the middle, like they'd fallen into another world or something.

Today he'd brought something different. A dead sparrow he'd found under the big oak tree in the yard, still warm but not moving. He wasn't sure why he'd picked it up. It just seemed wrong to leave it there for the ants to find.

Jack held the bird by one skinny leg and dangled it over the well.

"Sorry about this, little guy," he whispered, then let go.

He waited, counting like always. One Mississippi. Two Mississippi. Three.

At fifteen Mississippi, he frowned. Even a feather should've hit water by now.

At thirty, he started backing away.

He'd made it maybe three steps when he heard it.

Not a splash. A voice.

"Thank you."

The words floated up from the darkness, scratchy and weird, like someone talking through a broken radio. Jack froze.

"Hello?" His voice cracked the way it always did when he got scared. Silence. Then:

"So hungry. So very hungry."

This time the voice sounded different. It had a wet, guttural kind of sound.

"Who are you?" Jack asked, even though everything in his body was telling him to run.

"Friend." A long pause. "Hungry friend."

"You live down there?"

"Hide. Hiding here."

"From what?"

No answer. Jack waited, his heart hammering. "Hello?"

"Bring more," the voice said, making Jack jump. "Food. So hungry."

"More birds?"

"More. Bigger."

Jack's mouth went dry. But there was something about the voice---something that didn't seem completely scary. More like... sad?

"If I bring you food, what do I get?"

A sound that might've been laughing echoed up from the well. "What do you want?"

Jack thought about that. What did he want? His mind went straight to Earl, probably passed out in his chair by now, an empty bottle rolling around on the floor.

"I want him gone," Jack whispered before he could stop himself. That was a stupid thing to say. This was probably just some hurt animal that fell down there.

"Bring food," the voice said again. "Will give reward."

"What kind of reward?"

"Anything. Ask."

Jack backed away, his hands shaking. There was something really wrong about that voice. But also something... familiar? Like a song he'd heard before but couldn't remember the words to.

"I'll come back," he said, not sure if he meant it.

"Soon," the voice whispered, already sounding farther away. "So hungry."

The next morning, Jack snuck out before Earl could wake up with his hangover and his foul mood. He had a burlap sack with him---one he'd found in the barn---and inside was a dead rabbit he'd spotted on the county road yesterday.

At the well, everything felt different in the bright sunlight. Normal. Like maybe he'd imagined the whole thing.

"Hello?" Jack called down into the darkness.

Nothing.

Feeling stupid, he pulled the rabbit out of the sack and dropped it in. This time he heard it hit something soft way down below, not water.

He counted. Twenty seconds. Thirty. A whole minute.

Just when he was about to give up, the voice came back.

"Good. More."

Goosebumps ran up Jack's arms even though it was already hot. "I brought you food. Where's my reward?"

"Ask."

Jack hadn't really thought about what he wanted. Something small, just to see if this was real.

"I want a new baseball glove." His old one was falling apart, and Earl always said they didn't have money for "toys" when Jack could just use the ratty hand-me-down from his cousin.

"Done," said the voice. "Tomorrow. Bucket."

Jack looked around and saw an old wooden bucket near the well for the first time. It looked ancient, with rusty metal bands holding the wood together. A thick rope was tied to the handle.

"In the bucket?"

"Yes. Tomorrow."

Jack couldn't sleep that night. He kept thinking about the voice, trying to figure out why it sounded so familiar. It definitely wasn't human, but there was something in the way it talked that bugged him, like when you almost remember someone's name but can't quite get it.

Earl had been worse than usual that evening. Earl threw the plate at the wall---mashed potatoes sliding down like snot---and then just started bawling. Something about Mom knowing how to salt things right. About her being the only good thing.

Jack stared at his own plate. When Earl got mean, at least Jack knew what to do---stay quiet, stay small. But the crying was worse. Made his stomach hurt in a different way.

Mom died when he was eight. Basement stairs, they said.

Jack remembered coming home from school that day. The police cars. Earl on the porch with his face in his hands, but no tears. Just sitting there.

Mom always turned the light on before she went downstairs. Always. She held the rail. She was careful.

But she also cried at night when Earl came home late. Wore long sleeves in summer. Got real quiet when Earl raised his voice.

Jack was eight. He knew.

Sometimes, late at night, Jack thought about that day. The stairs. How Mom used to stare out the kitchen window like she wasn't really there anymore.

The question that made his chest hurt: Did she forget about him? Or did she remember, and go anyway?

Four years now. Earl drank more. Yelled more. Sometimes hit. Jack learned which floorboards creaked, which doors to leave open, when to be invisible.

Jack ran to the well before the sun was all the way up. The bucket was back. Something in it.

A baseball glove.

Brand new. Real leather, not the crappy vinyl kind. It even smelled right---like the sporting goods store in town where he'd press his face against the window.

Jack's hands shook when he picked it up. Slid his left hand inside.

Perfect fit. Like it knew him.

"How did you...?" he whispered.

From way down in the well came that strange, wet chuckle.

"Like it?"

Jack nodded, then remembered the thing couldn't see him. "Yeah. It's perfect. Thank you."

"More food," the voice said back. "Hungrier now."

Jack hesitated. "What are you exactly?"

A long quiet.

"Friend," it said finally. "Old friend."

"What's your name?"

Another pause. "No name. Not anymore."

Jack ran his fingers over the smooth leather. It was real. Somehow, the thing in the well had given him exactly what he'd asked for.

Nobody ever gave Jack anything. Not since Mom.

But this thing---whatever lived down there---it listened. And it gave him exactly what he asked for.

That meant something.

No questions about whether he deserved it, no lectures about being grateful for what he had, no reminders about money being tight. Just... here's what you asked for.

It felt dangerous to want something that much. Jack had learned not to want things too badly because disappointment hurt worse when you'd let yourself hope. But this was different. This was proof that maybe the world didn't have to be the way it was. Maybe he didn't have to spend the rest of his childhood walking on eggshells, waiting for Earl to drink himself to death or find some other way to disappear.

"I'll bring you more food," he promised. "Today."

Three weeks. Jack fell into a rhythm---check the bucket, drop something down.

Dead squirrel. Got a pocket knife, his initials carved perfect in the handle.

Raccoon from a trap. Got a watch that actually worked.

Stray cat that tore up his arms. Got comic books---the exact ones he'd been looking at in the drugstore.

Then one morning, without asking, without even thinking about it out loud---a silver locket. Inside: Mom. Smiling, hair blowing, in a photo Jack had never seen in his life.

He stared at it for ten minutes before he could move.

Where was it getting this stuff?

He tried asking, but the thing never wanted to talk about itself. Just about being hungry, and hiding, and how it had been in the well for a really long time.

One night in late July, Jack was doing a jigsaw puzzle at the kitchen table---another gift from the well---while Earl sprawled on the couch watching baseball and working on a bottle of Jim Beam.

'You been actin' weird.' Earl's words ran together. Three syllables: Youbeenactinweird.

Jack kept his eyes on the puzzle. 'No sir.'

'Look at me when I'm talking to you.'

Jack looked up. Earl's eyes were red, wet-looking. Focused on the watch.

'Where'd you get that?'

'Friend gave it to me.'

Earl laughed---spit flew. 'What friend? Ain't nobody out here but us and the goddamn corn.'"

"Just someone from school," Jack lied.

Earl hauled himself off the couch and stumbled over to the table. He grabbed Jack's wrist, twisting it to look at the watch. "This is real silver. Nobody just gives this kind of thing away."

"Let go," Jack said, trying to pull away. "You're hurting me."

Earl's grip got tighter. "You tell me the truth, or I swear to God---"

"A friend gave it to me!" Jack shouted. "It's none of your business!"

Earl's hand came across Jack's face so fast he didn't see it. Just the explosion of pain, his chair tipping, the floor rushing up.

'Everything in this house is mine.' Earl stood over him. 'Don't you forget it.'

Jack's cheek was on fire. He could taste blood where he'd bit his tongue.

That feeling was back. The one that made his chest tight and his hands shake. The one that made him think about the basement stairs. But underneath the hatred was something worse---the knowledge that this was what he was worth. A backhand across the face for asking to keep something good that had happened to him.

He thought about his mother again, about those mornings with long sleeves. Had she felt this same helpless rage? Had she looked at Earl and wondered what it would take to make him stop? Jack had spent four years learning to duck, to disappear, to never quite be where Earl's anger was pointing. But the anger had to go somewhere, didn't it?

Maybe that was why his mother had chosen the basement stairs. Maybe she'd gotten tired of carrying all that rage with nowhere to put it.

That night, lying in bed, Jack thought about Gillian Matthews from school. Gillian with her brown hair and freckles, who sat two rows up from him in Mrs. Henderson's class. Gillian who never looked at him twice, but who he dreamed about sometimes.

Jack had never talked to a girl his age, not really. At school, he was the kid whose clothes smelled like cigarette smoke and whose lunch was usually a peanut butter sandwich wrapped in a paper towel. He'd learned to eat quickly and keep his head down, because the longer he sat in the cafeteria, the more likely someone was to notice that he always sat alone.

In Jack's head, Gillian smiled at him in the hallway. Asked about homework. Normal stuff.

The kind of stuff that happened to other kids all the time.

The kind of stuff that never happened to him.

The thing in the well had given him everything else he'd asked for. Maybe it could give him this too---the thing he wanted most and had never dared to ask for. Maybe it could make someone care about him, even if it was just for a little while.

The next morning, at the well, he made a different kind of request.

"I want Gillian Matthews to like me," he told the voice after dropping a fat groundhog into the darkness. "I want her to come see me."

The voice was quiet for so long Jack thought it might have gone away. Then:

"Harder."

"Can you do it?"

"Yes. But... cost more."

"What do you mean?"

"Bigger gift needs bigger price."

Jack frowned. "What kind of price?"

The voice sighed, sounding like wind through dead leaves. "Big. Warm. Fresh."

A chill ran down Jack's back. "You mean like... alive?"

"Yes."

Jack stepped away from the well. He'd been feeding the thing dead animals this whole time. The idea of throwing something alive down there, something that could feel scared and hurt as it fell...

But then he thought about Gillian. And about the red mark on his cheek where Earl had hit him.

"I'll find something," he said.

The next afternoon, Jack was sitting on the porch steps tossing his baseball into his new glove when he saw someone coming up the long dirt driveway.

A girl on a bicycle.

He stood up, shading his eyes. It couldn't be. But as she got closer, he could see the brown hair, the thin shoulders.

Gillian Matthews.

She stopped her bike at the bottom of the porch steps, looking nervous. She had on a yellow dress with little white flowers, and her hair was pulled back with a matching ribbon.

"Hi, Jack," she said, like they talked every day.

Jack stared at her. "Hi. What are you... I mean, how come you're here?"

She tilted her head, wiping sweat from her forehead. "I was riding back from town. Had to get a birthday card for my dad." She patted a small paper bag tied to her bike basket. "It's really hot, and I saw your house and thought maybe I could get some water? If that's okay?"

Jack nodded quickly. "Yeah, sure. Of course."

"I know this is random," Gillian said. 'I just... I don't know. I kept thinking about you yesterday. Felt weird not coming to check on you." She shrugged. "Sorry if that's creepy."

It worked. It actually worked.

"No," he managed. "Not crazy."

"So what do you do for fun around here?"

The screen door slammed open.

'Who's this?'

'Gillian Matthews, from school. She just wanted some water---'

'Matthews' kid.' Earl's lips pulled back from his teeth. Not quite a smile. 'Deputy Matthews' little girl. Well, shit.'

'Yes, sir,' Gillian said quietly.

Earl laughed. 'Bet your daddy'd love to know you're out here. Slummin' with us.'

Jack's face burned.

"Sorry about that," Jack said. "He's having a bad day."

Gillian nodded, but he could see the look on her face---the same look everyone got when they saw what his life was really like.

"Want to see the farm?" Jack asked quickly.

They left Earl passed out on the couch and walked the property. Jack showed her everything---the barn where he slept sometimes when Earl got too loud, the creek where he caught frogs to feed the thing in the well, the apple tree that wouldn't die no matter how dead it looked.

Gillian didn't ask why a kid would sleep in a barn. Didn't ask about the frogs. Just nodded and walked beside him.

They walked north, toward the old pasture.

'Dad doesn't want me up here.' Jack kept his voice light. 'Says the ground's not safe.'

Gillian grinned. 'So obviously we're going.'

Jack smiled back and pretended to think about it. "I guess. Just for a minute."

The well sat in shadow by the time they reached it. Gillian went right up to it, leaned over the stones.

"Jeepers. How deep is this thing?"

Jack dropped a rock in. They waited.

Nothing.

"There's something else." He kept his voice low, even though they were alone. "Something lives down there."

Gillian turned. "What?"

"I'm serious. Listen." He leaned over the well. "Hello? Are you there?"

Nothing.

"See? There's nothing," Gillian said, starting to back away.

"Just wait," Jack said. "Sometimes it takes a minute."

Summer bugs buzzed in the tall grass. Gillian opened her mouth---

"Jack."

The voice came up from the well like water rising. Wet. Wrong.

"Friend."

Gillian made a sound---not quite a scream---and stumbled back.

"What was that!?"

'I told you.' Jack's hands were shaking. His whole body was shaking, but not from fear. Not entirely. 'It talks to me.'"

The voice came again, louder. "Brought friend?"

"Oh my God," Gillian whispered. "This isn't funny, Jack. What is that?"

"'I don't know what it is.' Jack pulled up his sleeve. The watch caught the fading light---silver, expensive. 'It gives me stuff. Whatever I ask for. The watch. My glove.' He paused. 'Other things.'"

Gillian's eyes were huge, her face pale under her freckles. "What do you mean, it gives you things? How?"

"I bring it food, and it gives me whatever I ask for."

"Food? What kind of food?"

Jack hesitated. "Just... animals I find. Dead ones."

Gillian shook her head, backing away more. "This is crazy. This is some kind of joke."

"It's not a joke!" Jack grabbed her arm. "It's real. Watch." He turned back to the well. "Tell her. Tell her you're real."

"The voice came again, bubbling up: 'Real. Real real real. Hungry. So hungry now.'"

Gillian yanked her arm free. "I'm going home. This is too weird."

"No, wait!" Jack reached for her again, but she dodged away.

"I'm going to tell my dad about this," she said, her voice shaking. "This isn't right, Jack. Whatever that thing is, it shouldn't be here."

Panic hit him like ice water. "You can't tell anyone!"

"My dad will know what to do."

She turned to go.

And just like that, Jack's one good thing was walking away.

Mom had left. Earl had never cared. School kids saw through him. The town saw through him. Everyone saw the trash he was and looked away.

Except the thing in the well. It saw him. It listened. It gave him things.

And Gillian was going to tell her cop dad and they'd take it away. They'd fill in the well or shoot something down it or burn the farm down, and Jack would have nothing again.

He'd always have nothing.

The rock was in Jack's hand before he decided to pick it up.

Heavy. Rough. Real.

He swung.

The sound it made hitting the back of Gillian's head---wet and solid at the same time, like a watermelon dropped on concrete---

She went down. Just dropped, face-first into the dirt beside the well. One of her shoes came off.

Jack stood there, the rock still in his hand, not breathing.

Jack's legs went out. He sat down hard next to her body. The rock fell from his hand.

What did he---

What did he just---

But his chest wasn't tight anymore. His hands had stopped shaking.

Gillian couldn't tell anyone now. Couldn't take the well away. Couldn't leave him with nothing.

Jack pulled his knees to his chest and started laughing. Couldn't stop. The sound coming out of him didn't sound like his laugh at all.

He nudged her with his foot. She didn't move.

The voice gurgled up from the well, wet and eager:

'Fooood. Fresh fresh fresh. Jack brings food. Good Jack. Jack feeds. We give. We give more more more.'"

Jack reached out. Touched Gillian's shoulder. Still warm.

'I'm sorry,' he whispered. Didn't know why. Didn't know if he meant it.

He had to use both hands to roll her toward the well. Heavier than he'd thought. One of her arms flopped out, fingers dragging in the dirt, leaving trails.

Jack was getting ready to push when Gillian's eyes opened.

'Jack?'

Confused. Unfocused. Then focusing.

On the well. On his hands. On where she was.

Understanding hit her face like a slap.

'No. No no no. Jack, please. Please don't---'

She tried to move, but her body wasn't working right. Just twitching. Making these sounds.

'I'm sorry,' Jack said. Didn't know why. Maybe he meant it.

He pushed.

Her scream going down. Echo echo echo. Then the thud.

Silence.

Then---so faint Jack had to lean over to hear:

'Jack? Jack, I'm hurt. I'm hurt bad. Please. Please help me.'

Crying. He could hear her crying.

'It's so dark. I can't move my leg. Something's down here. Jack, something's moving---'

The scream that came next wasn't human. Started human but went somewhere else. Higher and higher until it broke into something wet and choking.

It lasted forever.

Then it stopped.

The quiet after was worse.

Then it stopped.

The quiet that followed was worse than the screaming.

Jack fell to his knees beside the well, shaking all over. What had he done? *What had he done?*

Jack was still kneeling by the well when the sounds started.

Wet. Slithering. Something moving down there in the dark.

Then other sounds. Tearing. Crunching.

Eating.

The thing was eating her.

When they stopped, the voice spoke again, stronger now.

"Good. Very good."

Jack could barely get the words out. "Make it like she was never here. Like she never existed. Can you do that?"

A soft, terrible laugh drifted up. "Yes. Already done."

That night, Jack dreamed he was falling down the well. As he fell, he passed Gillian floating in the darkness, her eyes wide and staring. Below her was his mother, her neck bent wrong.

And at the very bottom, something huge and old and hungry was waiting with too many arms and a mouth like a cave.

He woke up gasping, covered in sweat.

Next morning, Jack found the Matthews number in the school directory. His hands shook so bad he had to dial twice.

'Hello?' A woman's voice.

'Mrs. Matthews? It's Jack Chambers. From school. Is Gillian there?'

Pause.

'I'm sorry---who?'

Jack's stomach dropped through the floor.

'Gillian. Your daughter. She was supposed to come by yesterday---'

'I think you have the wrong number, hon.'

'But you're Mrs. Matthews. Deputy Matthews' wife. On Cedar Street.'

'Yes, but...' The woman sounded confused. Uncertain. 'We don't have children. Never have.'

Something in her voice. Like she was trying to remember something that wouldn't come. Like there was a hole where a memory should be.

'I'm sorry,' she said, and hung up.

Jack stood there holding the dead phone.

It worked. It actually worked.

Jack put the phone down, his head spinning. It had worked. The thing had erased Gillian completely. Not just her body, but her whole existence.

What kind of power did it have?

And what else could it do?

That evening, Earl was worse than usual. He'd lost his job at the grain elevator---"Budget cuts," he claimed, though Jack knew better---and had been drinking since noon. By dinnertime, he was in a rage, throwing a chair across the kitchen when Jack burned the hamburger.

"Useless," Earl said, standing over Jack while he tried to clean up the mess. "Just like your mother was. Useless in the end."

Jack froze, sponge in his hand. "What do you mean?"

Earl's face twisted up. "Nothing. Shut up and clean."

'What did you mean?' Jack's voice was small. 'You said Mom was useless in the end. What did that mean?'

Earl froze. Just for a second.

Jack saw it. The flash of something behind the drunk eyes. Not anger. Something else.

Fear.

'Did you hurt her?'

Earl's hand shot out, grabbed Jack's shirt, hauled him up. 'You watch your goddamn mouth. You don't ask me that. You don't ever ask me that.'

But Jack had seen it. That split second when Earl looked scared instead of mean.

He knew. Earl knew what happened on those stairs.

He backhanded Jack across the face, sending him sprawling. "One more word," Earl said, "and you'll end up just like her."

Jack sat on his bed. Split lip. Tasted blood.

His hands weren't shaking.

That was the weird part. After Gillian, after everything, he thought his hands would shake forever.

But they were steady. Like they knew what came next.

Earl killed Mom. Jack knew it now. Knew it in his bones.

And Gillian---that had been so easy. One rock. One swing. Gone.

Earl was just a drunk old man. Weighed maybe 200 pounds.

But Jack had the well.

Downstairs, Earl was on the couch. Snoring. Mouth open, drool on his chin.

Jack stood in the doorway with the shotgun. It was heavier than he'd thought. Had to hold it with both hands.

Earl looked small. Pathetic. Not scary at all.

Four years Jack had been afraid of this man. Four years of ducking fists and reading moods and being invisible.

And he was just this. This small drunk thing with drool on its chin.

'Dad.'

Earl's eyes opened. Saw the gun. Understanding came slow.

'What the hell are you---'

Jack pulled the trigger.

The kick almost knocked him down. His ears were ringing. Couldn't hear anything but high-pitched whining.

Earl weighed 200 pounds when he was alive. Dead, he seemed to weigh even more.

Jack tried dragging him by the arms. Got maybe three feet before he had to stop. His back screamed. Arms shaking.

Tried again. Three more feet. Rest.

The body left a trail through the grass. Dark wetness. Jack tried not to look at where Earl's head used to be.

It took an hour to get to the well. By the end, Jack was crying. Not sad crying. Just crying because his body hurt so bad and he couldn't stop and he just wanted it to be over.

Getting Earl up on the stones took everything left. Jack's vision went spotty. Thought he might pass out.

But he got him up there.

He pushed.

Heavy thud from way down below."

"Food," Jack gasped to the well. "The biggest food yet."

The voice that came back was stronger than he'd ever heard it.

"Yes. Good boy. Such a good boy."

Jack was still sitting by the well when he could breathe again. Still shaking. Covered in sweat and blood and dirt.

"I want..." His voice was raw. "I want someone who stays. Who doesn't hit. Who doesn't drink. Someone who..."

He stopped. What was he asking for? What did he even want anymore?

"A father,' he said finally. 'A real one."

The silence stretched longer than usual. When the voice finally came back, it sounded... different. Pleased.

"Done," said the voice.

"Really?" he whispered.

The thing in the well laughed. "Sleep now. Tomorrow everything different."

Jack slept that night without dreams. When he woke up, sunlight was coming through his window, and for a moment he thought maybe it had all been a nightmare---Gillian, his father, everything.

Then he heard footsteps in the hallway. Heavy footsteps, coming toward his room.

Jack sat up, his heart pounding. The police would be looking for Earl. They'd figure out what he'd done, and they'd lock him up forever. Even though the thing had erased Gillian completely, there was no way it could hide a grown man's disappearance. People would ask questions.

Jack's heart hammered. But under the fear---

Earl was gone. Really gone. No more fists. No more yelling. No more of that look like Jack was something stuck to Earl's shoe.

Worth it. Whatever was coming, it was worth it.

The door handle turned.

His bedroom door swung open.

"I've always wanted a son," said a voice from the doorway that sounded wet and so, so hungry.

Sold As-Is

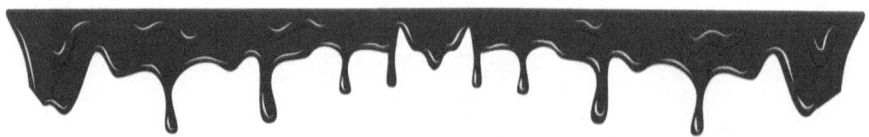

E ddie Malone had worked at Secure Storage Solutions for three years, making eleven-fifty an hour cutting locks and cleaning out units. Never once bid on a storage auction, not even when Bill Thompson kept pushing the staff to participate. "Good for morale," Bill always said. "Helps move inventory." But Eddie had seen what came out of abandoned units---moldy wedding dresses, boxes of dead rats, one time a live goat that nobody could explain. Why would he gamble grocery money on other people's junk?

Until today.

Unit 236 went unpaid for fourteen months. Dorothy Whitfield had paid on time for seven years, then nothing. No forwarding address, no returned calls. After the waiting period, everything became property of the facility.

Eddie stood with the usual suspects in the morning heat while Bill cut the padlock. Door rolled up with a screech. Few cardboard boxes along one wall, something big under a blue tarp in the middle.

"Unit two-three-six," Bill announced. "Start at twenty-five."

Old Pete squinted into the shadows. "What's under the tarp?"

"Can't tell you. As-is, no returns. You know the rules."

Eddie stepped forward before he could stop himself. Something about that shape under the tarp bothered him. Too long for furniture, too narrow for a couch. And there was a smell---flowers left too long in water, sweet turning sour with something underneath. Something rotting.

"Three-Twenty-five," called out Janet Metcalf, a middle-aged woman who specialized in estate sales.

"Three-Fifty," Pete said without much interest.

Eddie surprised himself by raising his hand. "Five Hundred."

The other bidders turned to look at him. Bill raised an eyebrow but nodded. "Five hundred dollars to Eddie. Do I hear sixty?"

Pete shook his head and walked away, muttering about rookies with more money than sense. Janet lingered a moment longer, studying the unit, then shrugged and followed Pete toward her car.

"Going once, going twice..." Bill's gavel came down on a piece of scrap wood he used as a podium. "Sold to Eddie for five hundred dollars."

As the crowd left, Eddie's stomach dropped. Five hundred bucks---almost half his rent, and he had no idea what he'd bought. Checking account had maybe sixteen hundred total, rent due Friday. But something made him bid, same instinct that made him slow down at car accidents.

Bill handed him the clipboard. "You sure about this? That unit gives me the creeps."

"What do you mean?"

Bill looked around, lowered his voice. "Sometimes on my rounds, I hear sounds in there. Probably mice, but..." He shook his head. "And there's the husband thing."

"Husband?"

"Charlie Whitfield. Old widower, wife was Dorothy. Calls every few months begging me to hold the unit a little longer, says he'll pay the back rent. Desperate to keep it from auction." Bill scratched his chin. "Last time he called, six months ago, he was crying. Said he'd let her down but was looking for a way to make it right. Highway noise in the background, like he was calling from a truck stop."

Eddie's pen hesitated over the signature line. "What happened to his wife?"

"Cancer, I think. This was way before my time---I only started managing this place five years ago. But from what I heard from the previous manager, she died back in the late nineties. Charlie paid the storage fees like clockwork for years. Place was like a shrine to her memory, the guy said."

Eddie signed, but the story stuck with him. What kind of guy paid storage fees for a dead woman's stuff? His own family had cleaned out Grandma's apartment the weekend after her funeral.

He spent his shift thinking about Charlie Whitfield. At lunch, he walked over to unit 236 and listened. There it was---faint scratching, like Bill said. You had to stand still to hear it, but it was there.

Mice, he told himself. Old buildings like this attracted them, especially units where people stored food or fabric. Nothing weird about that.

When his shift ended at 6 PM, Eddie drove home to his studio apartment and tried to put the unit out of his mind. He heated up a ninety-nine-cent frozen burrito, cracked open a beer, and settled in front of the TV to watch the Dodgers game. But every few minutes his attention drifted, and he found himself listening for scratching sounds in his own walls.

The scratching from unit 236 sounded different than mice. More deliberate, more... desperate. Eddie told himself he was being an idiot, but the sound kept replaying in his head. Scratch, scratch, pause. Scratch, scratch, pause. Almost like a pattern.

He tried calling his buddy Kevin to talk about the game, but kept losing track of the conversation. Kevin finally asked if he was feeling okay, and Eddie hung up rather than try to explain that he'd bought a storage unit that might contain something impossible.

By the top of the seventh inning, Eddie had paced a groove in his small living room carpet. The Dodgers were up by three, but he hadn't seen a single play. The scratching sound echoed in his memory, getting louder each time he recalled it.

He couldn't stand it anymore. At 9:30 PM, he grabbed his flashlight and headed back to the facility.

Secure Storage Solutions stayed lit all night, but the individual units fell dark once the sun went down. Eddie used his master key to enter the facility after hours---one of the perks of being an employee---and made his way to unit 236 through the maze of identical metal doors.

The scratching was louder in the evening quiet, more urgent. Eddie stood outside the unit for a full minute, working up his nerve, thinking about Charlie Whitfield's desperate phone calls and the story of a man who couldn't let his wife go. Finally, he pulled up the door and stepped inside with his flashlight cutting through the darkness.

The blue tarp dominated the center of the space, covering something roughly eight feet long and three feet wide. The scratching sound came from underneath it, accompanied now by what might have been a low moan or just the sound of metal expanding in the cooling air.

Eddie approached the boxes along the wall first, looking for clues about Dorothy Whitfield and what she might have stored. The cardboard was soft with moisture and age, and the first box he opened contained nothing but moldy photograph albums and water-damaged paperwork. Insurance documents, mostly, and medical bills dating back to the mid-1990s. Lots of hospital bills, he noticed. Cancer treatment, radiation therapy, chemotherapy.

The second box held personal effects: jewelry, reading glasses, a collection of ceramic angels. At the bottom, wrapped in tissue paper that crumbled at his touch, Eddie found a leather journal. He opened it carefully, squinting at the faded handwriting in his flashlight beam.

March 15, 1997 - Dr. Stevens says the treatments aren't working. Cancer's spreading too fast. Maybe two months if I'm lucky. Charlie keeps saying don't give up hope, but I see it in his eyes. He knows I'm dying.

The scratching from under the tarp grew more insistent, as if responding to Eddie's discovery. He flipped through several pages of similar entries, Dorothy's handwriting growing shakier as the months progressed. Most contained routine complaints about pain medication and doctor visits, but one entry made him pause.

June 3, 1997 - Charlie mentioned something strange today. Says he heard about a man who helps people in impossible situations. I told him not to fill his head with nonsense, but I can see the hope. God help me, I'm starting to hope too.

Eddie closed the journal and aimed his flashlight at the covered object. The blue tarp pulsed with each scratch from beneath, as if something was testing the boundaries of its prison. He forced himself to step closer, and the scratching stopped.

In the sudden silence, Eddie opened the journal again and found another entry near the end.

August 8, 1997 - Charlie found someone who might help. Man named Valdez who does alternative treatments. Charlie doesn't want me to get my hopes up, but what choice do I have? Valdez says he's helped others like me. Says death isn't always final if you're willing to pay the price.

The scratching resumed under the tarp, more frantic now. Eddie's hands trembled as he turned to the final entries.

August 20, 1997 - The ritual is tomorrow night. Valdez explained everything. I won't really die, just sleep until Charlie can find a way to wake me up. He promised he'd never give up, no matter how long it takes. I'm scared, but I'm more scared of leaving him alone.

August 21, 1997 - This is my last entry. If someone reads this and I'm still sleeping, please find Charlie. Tell him I'm still waiting.

Eddie's hands shook as he closed the journal. The scratching sound from under the tarp had grown frantic, almost desperate. He aimed his flashlight at the covered object and forced himself to step closer.

His heart pounded as he reached for the edge of the tarp. The fabric felt cold and damp under his fingers, and the smell of old flowers intensified---not the sweet scent of fresh blooms, but the cloying, sickly odor of funeral arrangements left too long in a closed room.

The tarp came away with a soft whisper of fabric.

Eddie stumbled backward, his flashlight beam dancing wildly across the revealed object before steadying on what he had feared he'd find. The coffin was old but well-preserved, made of dark wood with brass fittings that had tarnished green with age.

But it wasn't the coffin that made Eddie's knees weak---it was the evidence of what had occurred inside it. Deep furrows scarred the wood around the lid, carved by what could only be fingernails. Dents and scratches marred the brass fittings, as if someone had clawed desperately at the metal for years.

Decades.

The scratching from inside had stopped the moment he'd removed the tarp, replaced by a silence that was worse than any sound. Eddie could hear his own ragged breathing, the distant hum of the facility's security lights, and underneath it all, a sound that made his skin crawl: the soft, rhythmic whisper of breathing that wasn't his own.

A brass nameplate on the lid read: DOROTHY MARIE WHIT-FIELD, 1951-1997.

The dates hit him like a punch to the gut. Twenty-six years. She'd been in there for twenty-six years, and something was still breathing inside.

Eddie backed toward the door, mind reeling. This was impossible. People don't survive twenty-six years in a coffin. Had to be some kind of hoax, or maybe Dorothy went crazy and staged this as a sick joke.

But the journal mentioned Valdez and a ritual. Magic. Actual fucking magic.

The sounds from the coffin got louder---weak, desperate moaning that barely sounded human. The breathing he'd heard was real. What-ever Dorothy Whitfield had become, she was undeniably alive in there.

His phone buzzed with a text message, the sound making him jump so violently he nearly dropped his flashlight. Eddie fumbled for it, grateful for the distraction, and saw a number he didn't recognize with a 559 area code.

You the one who bought Dorothy's unit?

Eddie stared at the message, then at the coffin. How the hell had this guy gotten his number? He typed back with shaking fingers: *Who is this?*

The response came immediately:

Charlie Whitfield. Dorothy's my wife. Been trying to get that unit back for a long time. Whatever you do don't open the coffin. On my way.

Eddie typed back with shaking fingers: *How did you get this number?* The response came immediately:

Bill Thompson's a friend of mine. Told him to call if anyone ever bought the unit. Please, just don't touch anything. I'll be there in twenty minutes.

Eddie started to back out of the unit, but his foot hit one of the cardboard boxes and sent it sliding across the concrete floor with a scraping sound.

The silence from the coffin broke with a violent thump, as if something inside had thrown itself against the lid. Then another thump, and another, accompanied by muffled screaming that barely sounded human after decades of disuse.

Eddie ran.

He made it to his car before his legs gave out, and he sat in the parking lot with the engine running and the doors locked, waiting for his heart rate to return to normal. The rational part of his mind insisted that there had to be a logical explanation. Maybe Dorothy had faked her death and lived in the storage unit somehow. Maybe it was an elaborate insurance fraud scheme that had gone wrong.

But the sounds he'd heard weren't coming from someone who'd lived comfortably for twenty-six years. They were the sounds of someone who'd endured entrapment, slowly going mad in the darkness.

His phone rang. The same number.

"Eddie?" The voice was older, hoarse from years of cigarettes and worry. "This is Charlie Whitfield. Where are you right now?"

"I'm... I'm at the storage place. What the hell is going on?"

"I'm ten minutes away. Whatever you do, don't go back in that unit. And don't let anyone else near it either."

"Is she really alive in there?"

A long pause. "That's... Christ, how do I even---" Charlie's voice cracked. "Look, I know this sounds crazy as hell, but Dorothy ain't dead. Not exactly. But she ain't alive neither. This guy Valdez, he said she'd just sleep till I could---till I figured out how to fix what he done. Only something went wrong bout ten years back."

"You're talking about magic. Actual magic."

"I'm talking about being desperate," Charlie said. "When you're watching the person you love die by inches, you'll try anything. Even things that sound impossible." His voice dropped to a whisper. "Valdez said she'd sleep peaceful until I could find the reversal spell. For sixteen years, she did. Dead silence from that unit. I thought... I thought maybe it had worked, that she was just waiting like she was supposed to."

"But something changed?"

"About ten years ago, yeah. Started with little sounds---tapping, scratching. Like she was trying to wake up. Then it got worse. The sounds got more desperate, more..." Charlie swallowed hard. "More hungry. That's when I knew the ritual was going bad. She wasn't sleeping anymore. She was aware, and slowly going insane."

A pair of headlights swept across the parking lot. Eddie watched an old pickup truck pull up next to his car, and a heavyset man in his seventies climbed out. Charlie Whitfield moved like someone carrying a weight that went beyond his years---shoulders hunched, each step deliberate and careful. His face bore deep lines, not just with age but with the kind of exhaustion that came from decades of sleeping in truck cabs and eating gas station food. His work boots were worn down at the heels, and his flannel shirt had been washed so many times the pattern was barely visible.

Charlie knocked on Eddie's window. "Can we talk?"

Eddie rolled down the window but kept the engine running. Up close, he could see that Charlie's clothes were worn but clean, and his hands shook---not from age, but from nerves. "What do you want from me?"

"Help," Charlie said, his voice rough from years of cigarettes and diesel fumes. "I got the money to buy the unit back from you. Triple what you paid. But I need help getting Dorothy out of there and into my truck." He gestured toward the pickup, and Eddie could see it was set up for living---sleeping bag visible through the rear window, cooler in the bed, clothes hanging on a makeshift line.

"Are you planning to bury her?"

Charlie's face crumpled, and Eddie saw twenty-six years of guilt and desperate love written in every line. "I'm gonna try the reversal ritual. Valdez is dead, but I found his notes after years of searching---spent every dime I had on private investigators and occult book dealers. I think I know what went wrong the first time." He paused, staring at the facility. "I promised her I'd never give up. Even when the payments got behind and I lost the house, even when I been living out of this truck for eight years, I never stopped looking for a way to bring her back properly."

"You've been homeless?"

"Living in the truck mostly. Taking odd jobs, saving every penny." Charlie's voice cracked. "She didn't deserve what happened to her. The ritual was supposed to be peaceful sleep, but something went wrong about ten years ago. She started making noise, started... changing. I kept paying the storage fees long as I could, hoping I'd find another way to help her."

From across the facility came a sound that made both men freeze: the distant but unmistakable screech of a storage unit door rolling open. Unit 236's door, Eddie realized with growing dread. The sound echoed off the concrete corridors, amplified by the metal walls until it seemed to come from everywhere at once.

"I locked it," Eddie said, checking his watch: 10:44 PM. They'd talked for less than twenty minutes, but it felt like hours. "I know I locked it."

Charlie was already moving toward his truck. "She's getting stronger. The hunger's driving her crazy. We gotta get her contained before---"

His words cut off with a scream that echoed across the facility, raw and desperate and undeniably human. It was the sound of someone who'd been silent for too long, finally finding her voice again.

Eddie grabbed his flashlight and followed Charlie toward unit 236, his rational mind finally accepting what his instincts had told him all along. Whatever Dorothy Whitfield had become, she was no longer sleeping peacefully.

The unit door stood open, the blue tarp discarded on the ground. The coffin lid had been forced open from the inside, brass fittings twisted and broken. And Dorothy was gone.

"Where would she go?" Eddie whispered.

Charlie pulled a heavy flashlight from his truck and swept it across the facility grounds. "She don't remember much from before. But she remembers being hungry. Always hungry."

As if summoned by his words, they heard the sound of breaking glass from the direction of the facility office. Bill Thompson's car was still in the parking lot---he often worked late on auction days, catching up on paperwork.

Eddie and Charlie ran toward the office building, their flashlight beams dancing across the asphalt. The front door stood ajar, and they could hear Bill's voice inside, tight with fear.

"Who's there? I got a gun!"

They pushed through the door to find Bill backed against his desk, a baseball bat in his hands instead of the gun he'd claimed to have. In front of him stood what had once been Dorothy Whitfield.

Twenty-six years in a coffin had changed her in ways that defied natural law. Her hair hung in stringy white tendrils, and her skin had taken on the waxy, translucent quality of something preserved but preserved wrong. The ritual that had kept her from true death had also trapped her in a state between life and decay, sustained by whatever dark bargain Valdez had struck.

Her fingernails had grown long and yellow, worn down to sharp points from decades of scratching at wood and metal. Her teeth had grown long and sharp, transformed by whatever unnatural hunger had sustained her through the years of failing magic. She still wore the dress she'd been buried in, now stained and tattered from twenty-six years of restless imprisonment.

She was undeniably alive, her chest rising and falling with rapid, panicked breaths, but she was no longer entirely human. The magic that had saved her had also corrupted her, turning love's desperate gamble into something monstrous.

"Dorothy?" Charlie stepped forward slowly. "Dorothy, it's me. It's Charlie."

She turned toward his voice, and Eddie saw her eyes had gone white---not cataracts, something worse. When she opened her mouth, her teeth were long and sharp, like an animal's.

"Hun...gry," she managed, the word coming out in a wet rasp distorted by her transformed mouth. Each syllable seemed to cost her tremendous effort. "So... hungry... Charlie... please..."

"I know, sweetheart. I know. We're gonna fix this, okay? Just like I promised."

Dorothy tilted her head, studying him with those blank white eyes. For a moment, Eddie thought she might remember, might become human again. Then her lips pulled back in a snarl that had nothing human about it, and she lunged at Bill.

Charlie caught her around the waist before she could reach the terrified facility manager, but Dorothy was stronger than she looked. She twisted in his arms with inhuman flexibility, her claws---and they were definitely claws now---raking across his face and drawing blood.

"The reversal ritual," Charlie gasped, struggling to hold her. "I need sage and salt and a silver blade. You got any of that?"

"This is a storage facility, not a magic shop!" Eddie said, but he was already looking around the office for anything that might help. Bill kept a first aid kit under his desk, and Eddie remembered seeing scissors in there.

"The scissors are steel, not silver," he said, pulling out the small medical shears.

"It'll have to do. Help me get her to the truck."

Together, they managed to wrestle Dorothy out of the office and across the parking lot, their footsteps echoing off the asphalt. She fought them every step of the way, alternating between desperate pleas for food and inhuman snarls that raised the hair on Eddie's neck. Her strength was unnatural---fueled by whatever dark magic had sustained her---and more than once she nearly broke free, her claws leaving scratches in the concrete where she dragged her feet.

When they finally got her into the truck bed, Charlie produced a length of rope from behind the driver's seat.

"I came prepared," he said, binding Dorothy's hands despite her struggles. "Been planning this for a long time."

Bill emerged from the office, still clutching his baseball bat, his face pale in the security lighting. "What the hell was that thing?"

"My wife," Charlie said, his voice thick with emotion. "And I'm gonna save her."

Eddie watched Charlie climb into his truck and start the engine. Through the rear window, he could see Dorothy thrashing against her bonds, her mouth moving in what might have been words or might have been animal sounds.

"Will it work?" Eddie called.

Charlie looked at him in the side mirror. "Don't know. But I promised."

As the truck left, Eddie thought about what he'd read in Dorothy's journal. She couldn't stand leaving Charlie alone. He'd spent twenty-six years trying to keep a promise.

Would've been a beautiful love story if it hadn't gone so wrong.

Bill stared down the empty road. "Should we call the cops?"

Eddie thought about it. How do you explain what they'd just seen? And what would happen to Charlie if the cops got involved?

"Let's just forget this happened," Eddie said. "Some things are private."

Bill nodded. "You're right. But I'm charging extra for the weird units from now on."

Eddie drove home in a daze. He'd bought a storage unit for fifty bucks he couldn't afford and ended up in a supernatural love story twenty-six years in the making. Tomorrow he'd help Bill clean up the office, probably miss his weekend warehouse job.

His phone buzzed as he parked.

Thank you. The ritual worked. Dorothy is at peace. - Charlie

Eddie stared at the message. He wanted to ask what "at peace" meant---dead or alive again? But some questions were better left alone.

He deleted the message and went upstairs. Tomorrow he'd pretend unit 236 had just been old furniture and junk. Let Bill handle the cleanup paperwork. Never bid on another storage auction as long as he lived.

Some bargains cost more than money. Some things should stay buried, even when love says otherwise.

But lying in bed that night, listening to his building settle, Eddie hoped Charlie's ritual worked. That Dorothy finally got the peace she'd been promised twenty-six years ago.

That Charlie could stop carrying the weight of an impossible promise.

Tomorrow he'd pretend magic wasn't real. Tonight, he'd believe in love strong enough to risk everything for a promise.

Even if it took twenty-six years to make good on it.

All the Pretty Girls Lying in a Row

Malcolm Graywill brought the watering can to the bed marked "Elizabeth," pouring murky liquid in a thin stream. The soil sucked it up fast, thirsty. The amber stuff vanished as it hit dirt. Had to get it right—too much and the blooms wilted, too little and they got restless.

"There you go, Lizzie." His voice was rough from age and solitude. "Better? You get thirsty faster than the others."

The roses moved without wind. Petals opened wider, showing blues that didn't exist in nature. Blues you could fall into, with silver lines running through like veins.

Malcolm tilted his head, nodding like someone was talking back to him. His fingers, stained with different colored soil under the nails, touched a petal gentle as you'd touch a baby's cheek.

"I know," he whispered. "You don't like the new one. But give Rebecca time. She's only been in the ground three months. Still getting used to things."

The greenhouse door squealed open behind him. Malcolm straightened up, his easy calm disappearing. He wore that careful look he got whenever other people showed up.

"Mr. Graywill?" A woman's voice, young and nervous.

Malcolm turned around, soil grinding under his boots. The woman stood in the doorway, clutching a clipboard like a shield.

"You're late," he said. No warmth in his voice now, nothing like how he'd talked to the flowers.

"Sorry, I got lost." She stepped inside, letting the door swing shut. "Your place is pretty hidden."

Now Malcolm could see her better. Mid-twenties, brown hair in a ponytail, glasses that kept sliding down her nose. University of Vermont sweatshirt, jeans, hiking boots that had never actually hiked anywhere.

"That's the point," Malcolm said. "People see something pretty, they got to touch it. Miss..."

"Phillips. Emma Phillips." She started to offer her hand, pulled back when he didn't move. "The grad student who emailed. Professor Winters said you'd agreed to let me observe."

Malcolm sighed. Winters. Always sticking his nose in.

"Said I'd think about it."

Emma's shoulders sagged. She tried again, gripping her clipboard. "Could I show you my proposal? These colors—Winters said you'd achieved impossible modifications—"

"Thirty years I been working. Not sharing." Martin picked up his can, moved to the next bed. Stone marker read "Sophia." Black roses with gold threads.

"Please. I'm not asking for secrets. How do you get them blue? Never seen anything like this." Student loan payment due next week.

"No samples." Malcolm's hand tightened on the watering can. The liquid inside sloshed.

One of Sophia's blooms turned toward Emma. Just a little, but both of them saw it. Emma blinked hard, like she was trying to convince herself it hadn't happened.

"Did that flower just—"

"Drafts," Malcolm said. "Ventilation creates air currents."

Emma stepped closer, squinting at the black roses. Her breath fogged in the cooler air. The pattern in those petals... "Professor Winters said you'd achieved impossible genetic modifications. How—"

"Don't." Malcolm's hand closed around her arm, pulling her back harder than necessary. "Some of my plants produce pollen. Can cause reactions."

Emma rubbed her arm where his fingers had dug in. "What kind of reactions?"

Malcolm's pale blue eyes got sharp, focused. "Headaches. Confusion. Sometimes worse. Why I keep this place private."

They stared at each other for a moment. Then Malcolm's shoulders sagged.

"Winters was my roommate in college. Figure I owe him." He set down the watering can. "You can observe. Take notes. No samples, no pictures. Don't go in the locked section at the back."

Emma's whole face lit up. "Thank you! I won't mess anything up, I promise. When can I—"

"Now." He pointed to a worktable covered with notebooks and tools. "My logs are there. Basic feeding schedules, soil stuff. I got rounds to finish."

As Emma settled at the table, opening the first notebook, Malcolm turned back to his flowers. He said something too quiet for her to hear, and the blooms seemed to shiver in response. Emma looked up from the notebook, but Malcolm was already moving to the next bed.

The spare room above Malcolm's garage hadn't been used since 1998, and it smelled like it. Emma sneezed as she dragged her suitcase across the threshold, stirring up dust that had been settled for years. The single bed had fresh sheets at least, though they reeked of mothballs.

Her head was pounding. Started after she began reading Malcolm's notebooks, a pressure behind her eyes that made it hard to focus. Probably just eyestrain from his cramped handwriting, though some parts were clear, like he'd written them in a different mood.

Those clear parts were the weird ones.

Elizabeth enjoys music in the evenings. Bach, not Beethoven. Her color deepens when she's pleased. Temperature must drop 15 degrees during the awakening phase—any warmer and the transfer becomes unstable.

Emma sat on the bed edge, opening her laptop. Her bank account glowed on the screen: $247.83. Rent due in twelve days: $650. The research stipend from this project would cover three months of groceries and maybe, if Malcolm's techniques were as revolutionary as Winters claimed, lead to the thesis breakthrough that would actually get her hired somewhere.

She tried to focus on updating her research log, but what was all that about "awakening phase" and "transfer"? Three chapters of her thesis depended on this project. If Malcolm's techniques were legitimate, she could graduate in May instead of limping through another semester on ramen and hope.

She'd noticed a pattern: all the beds with women's names got these intimate entries. The regular roses, the dahlias, the normal plants just got technical notes.

I'm overthinking this, Emma told herself. *He's just a lonely old guy who talks to his plants. People do that.*

The headache got worse. She rubbed her temples, trying to look at her notes. Through the window, she could see part of the main garden, everything silver in the moonlight. The roses were visible, their colors gone gray but their shapes somehow sharper at night. More present.

Were they moving? Swaying without any wind, petals opening and closing like they were breathing...

Emma blinked hard. Just her imagination. She needed sleep.

But as she drifted off, the smell of roses filled the room even though the window was closed. The scent brought strange dreams—roots growing through soil to wrap around sleeping arms and legs, petals unfolding to show tiny screaming faces, voices calling her name from underground.

Emma . . . Emma . . . come closer . . .

She jerked awake at 3:11 AM, sheets soaked with sweat despite the cool April night. The rose smell was gone, replaced by musty quilts and stale air.

Just a dream. But as she settled back against the pillow, something crinkled under her cheek. Emma reached under the pillow and found a single blue petal, so dark it was almost black, with silver veins running through it.

Something was watching her. Something that knew exactly where she was sleeping.

The feeling sat in her chest like a stone.

"You look like hell," Malcolm said the next morning, not unkindly, as Emma stumbled into the kitchen. He slid a mug of coffee across the worn table.

"Thanks," she mumbled. "Didn't sleep great."

"The garage room does that. Something about the angle." Malcolm turned back to the stove where he was frying eggs. "Creates weird acoustics."

Emma sipped the coffee—rich and strong. "I had dreams about your roses."

Malcolm's spatula paused over the pan. "Dreams?"

"They were talking to me. Asking me to come closer." She laughed, but it sounded hollow. "Weird, right?"

Malcolm set a plate of eggs in front of her, his face blank. "Brain processes new stuff in funny ways when you're asleep."

"I guess." Emma took a bite. The yolks were incredibly vibrant, almost orange. "These are amazing."

"My own chickens. They eat special grain." Malcolm sat across from her with his own plate. "Like everything here—you are what you eat."

"Is that your secret? Special feeding?"

Malcolm met her eyes. "Part of it. Everything I grow gets customized nutrition. The roses especially. Each bed's different."

"The named beds?"

His eyes got sharper. "You been paying attention."

"It's unusual. Different feeding for the same species."

"They're not the same," Malcolm said, intense suddenly. "Elizabeth's nothing like Sophia or Rebecca. Different needs, different personalities."

Emma set down her fork. "You talk about them like they're people."

Malcolm's weathered face creased in what might have been a smile. "To someone who really cares about plants, they are. Each one's got its own character. You'll understand if you stick around long enough."

After breakfast, Emma followed Malcolm to the greenhouse. Today he carried a different container—not the brass watering can but a spray bottle with milky stuff inside.

"Foliar feeding," he explained, misting the leaves of "Rebecca." These roses were red that seemed to pulse in the morning light. "Direct absorption through the leaves. More efficient."

Emma moved closer, notebook ready. The air here was cooler, humid against her skin. A sweet, earthy smell rose from the soil—not just regular potting mix but something richer, more complex. Like compost mixed with something metallic. "What's in the solution?"

"Trade secret." Malcolm's eyes crinkled. "Maybe I'll show you someday, if you prove trustworthy."

The greenhouse air was thick with moisture, condensation fogging her glasses as she moved between the beds. The ventilation system hummed overhead, creating subtle air currents that stirred the leaves. Emma noted it all, fascinated by how precise Malcolm was. The rich smell of specialized fertilizers mixed with the overwhelming sweetness of the roses. Some beds he talked to, others he worked in silence. Some he touched gently, others he kept his distance from.

At the last bed—"Margaret," with purple-blue roses that smelled like vanilla and metal—Malcolm stopped.

"That's enough for today. Got work in the south field. You can keep reading my notebooks. Don't go in the locked section at the back."

When he was gone, Emma approached Margaret's bed. The roses here were smaller than the others but clustered together like they were sharing secrets. The sweet-metal smell got stronger as she leaned in, making her dizzy.

Hello, Emma.

She jerked back. The voice had been clear—a woman's voice, refined and amused. But the greenhouse was empty.

"Hello?" Emma called, feeling stupid.

Silence. Just the distant hum of ventilation.

You're being ridiculous, she told herself. *Letting an old man's weird habits get to you.*

She went back to the worktable and Malcolm's notebooks, but couldn't concentrate. The headache was back, that pulsing pressure behind her eyes. And underneath it, the feeling that someone was watching her.

She gave up and walked around the greenhouse, cataloging the beds. The air grew cooler toward the back, and she could hear water dripping somewhere—probably condensation from the cooling system. Twelve beds total, all with women's names. All with roses that broke every rule of plant genetics she'd ever learned. The scent was overwhelming here, sweet and cloying with an undertone that reminded her of the morgue tour she'd taken in undergrad anatomy class.

A heavy door with a padlock blocked access to another growing area. Emma peered through clouded glass—vague shapes inside.

She started to turn when something moved. Big enough to shift shadows.

Emma pressed closer, squinting. For a second, she saw a face—not human, made of petals and leaves, pressing against the glass.

She stumbled back with a cry.

Just shadows. Just light and shadows and too much coffee.

But hurrying back to the worktable, Emma knew something behind that door had noticed the newcomer.

Rain drummed against the garage roof that night, sending tiny rivers down the window glass. Emma sat cross-legged on her bed, the day's notes spread around her, trying to make sense of what she'd seen.

Malcolm's techniques were revolutionary—that was clear. His fertilizer formulations alone could change commercial gardening. But there was something else, something she felt in her bones.

The way the flowers moved when they thought she wasn't looking.

The voices she heard between heartbeats.

The dreams that got more vivid each night.

The headache had gotten worse as the day went on. Now it was a steady throb that made thinking difficult. She'd taken ibuprofen, but it barely touched the pain.

Maybe I'm allergic to something in the greenhouse, she thought. *Some pollen or chemical.*

Lightning flashed, lighting up the garden beyond her window. In that stark white moment, Emma saw a figure moving among the outdoor roses—Malcolm, wearing a rain slicker, kneeling beside one of the beds.

What's he doing out there in this weather?

She moved to the window, pressing her forehead against the cool glass. Rain blurred her view, but she could still make out Malcolm's hunched form. He seemed to be digging, creating a new bed in the soft, rain-soaked earth.

As Emma watched, he straightened and dragged something from the shadows. Something long and heavy, wrapped in dark plastic.

Her breath caught. For one terrible moment, the lightning flashed again, and the shape looked like a human body being positioned in the freshly dug earth.

Emma jerked away from the window, heart hammering.

No. No, that's crazy. He's planting something. New roses. A shrub. Anything but... that.

She forced herself to look again, but Malcolm and his burden had vanished, leaving only the dark outline of disturbed soil.

The headache spiked, a white-hot lance through her skull that drove Emma to her knees. Behind the pain came voices—not one voice, but many, whispering in chorus.

He lies. He hurts us. Help us, Emma. Come to the garden. See the truth.

When the pain faded, Emma found herself curled on the floor, shivering. The voices had felt so real, so present—not like hallucinations but like actual minds reaching out to hers.

Outside, the storm was passing, rain lessening to a gentle patter. Emma got shakily to her feet and grabbed her jacket. She had to know what Malcolm had been doing in the garden.

The night air was fresh and cool after the rain, heavy with the scent of wet earth and something sweeter—roses, intensified by moisture. Emma moved down the gravel path, her flashlight beam bobbing ahead.

The garden felt different at night. Paths seemed narrower, growth more wild. Shadows pooled in strange places, making it seem like the landscape was shifting just beyond her light's reach.

Emma found the disturbed earth easily enough. Right where she'd seen Malcolm working—a rectangular plot next to the established rose beds. But there was no sign of whatever he'd buried. Just smooth, freshly raked soil.

She knelt, running her fingers over the damp ground. It was warm, like something underneath was generating heat.

Dig, whispered a voice from the soil itself. *See what he's hiding.*

Emma sat back, frightened. Was she going crazy? Hearing voices, suspecting a harmless old gardener of... what? Murder?

This is ridiculous, she told herself. *He was probably planting bulbs or preparing a bed. The voices are just stress and no sleep. Everything has a rational explanation.*

But as she stood to go back, Emma's flashlight caught something half-buried at the edge of the fresh soil. She bent to pick it up, then pulled back with a gasp.

A locket on a broken chain. Old-fashioned silver with detailed engraving. Inside, a tiny photograph of a young woman with a bob haircut and 1920s clothes.

On the back, a name: *Elizabeth.*

Emma didn't sleep that night. She sat on her bed, turning the locket over in her hands, trying to make sense of what she'd found.

Elizabeth. The name of Malcolm's favorite rose bed.

Could it be coincidence? A family heirloom that fell while he was working?

But deep down, Emma knew. The cold certainty had settled in her stomach like a stone. All those beds with women's names. The cryptic entries in his notebooks. The way he spoke to the roses like they could hear him.

As dawn broke, Emma made a decision. She slipped the locket into her pocket and headed to the house.

Malcolm was already in the kitchen, preparing what looked like a large pitcher of fertilizer—thick, amber liquid with dark flecks floating in it.

"You're up early," he said, not looking up. "Sleep poorly again?"

"I found something in the garden last night," Emma said, surprised by how steady her voice sounded. "After you finished... planting."

Malcolm's hands went still. "You were watching me."

"I couldn't sleep. I saw you from my window." She took a breath. "What did you bury, Malcolm?"

He turned to face her, expression unreadable. "Organic matter. For the new bed. Nothing that concerns you."

Emma pulled out the locket, letting it dangle from her fingers. "And this? Did your 'organic matter' once wear jewelry?"

Something flickered in Malcolm's eyes—not guilt or fear, but resignation. He wiped his hands on a towel, then gestured to a chair.

"Sit. Think it's time we talked honestly about my garden."

Emma stayed standing. "Are there bodies buried out there? Is that your secret? Human remains as fertilizer?"

Malcolm chuckled, though there was no humor in it. "If only it were that simple. That... merciful." He sank into a chair, looking every one of his seventy-plus years. "What do you think happens when we die?"

The question threw her. "I... I don't know. Nothing, probably. Or whatever religious people believe."

"All comforting ideas," Malcolm nodded. "The notion that consciousness ends, or continues somewhere nice. But what if there's a third option? What if consciousness can be... preserved? Transferred? Bound to something else?"

Emma's mouth went dry. "What are you saying?"

"I'm saying my roses aren't just named after women. They are the women. Their consciousness lives in those flowers."

The absurdity should have made Emma laugh. Instead, she felt ice down her spine, remembering the voices, the movement.

"That's impossible."

"Is it? You've seen my roses. Heard them, maybe. Noted their colors, behaviors. What explanation does science offer?"

Emma sank into a chair, weight pressing down. "You killed these women and put their souls in flowers?"

Malcolm shook his head. "No. I preserve them. Neural pathways, electrical patterns—they interface with plant networks. Mycorrhizal connections, like tree communication." His voice got fervent. "They were dying—terminal illness, accidents. I offer continuation. Different life."

"That's insane," Emma whispered.

"Is it? Look at Elizabeth—over a hundred years in that garden, still vibrant, still aware. Still beautiful." He gestured to the locket. "She was my great-aunt, dying of tuberculosis in 1924. The first one I saved, though the process wasn't perfected then." His eyes grew distant. "The transfer was incomplete. Part of her remained human, decomposing in the ground, while her consciousness split between flesh and flower. She taught me how to refine the technique."

Emma stared at him, ice in her veins. "And the others? Sophia? Rebecca? Margaret?"

"All volunteers, after Elizabeth. Women facing death who chose a different path." Malcolm stood, moving to the window overlooking his garden. "I'm not a monster. I'm a caretaker. A guardian."

"Why only women?" Emma asked, though she wasn't sure she wanted the answer.

Malcolm's expression shifted. "Plant-human neural interface requires specific bioelectrical patterns. Women's brain chemistry, the hormone cascades, neuroplasticity factors—they're compatible with rose cellular

structures. Men's neural firing patterns just... burn out the plant recep-
tors." He turned back to her. "I've tried."

Outside, the morning sun illuminated the garden, making the roses
seem to glow from within. Beautiful. Otherworldly. And now, undeniably sinister.

"Why are you telling me this?" Emma asked, her voice barely a
whisper.

Malcolm smiled. "Because they've chosen you, Emma. You've felt it?
The headaches. The voices. They're reaching out, preparing you."

"Preparing me?" Cold dread pooled in her stomach. "For what?"

"To join them, of course." Malcolm said it like it was obvious.
"They've never reached out to anyone else this way. They want you.
And what my girls want, they usually get."

Emma stood so fast her chair fell over. "You're insane. I'm leaving.
Right now."

Malcolm didn't try to stop her. "They won't let you go, Emma. Not
now that they've connected with you. But don't be afraid. It's not death.
It's transformation."

She backed toward the door, fumbling for the handle. "Stay away
from me."

"I'm not your enemy," Malcolm called after her. "I'm just the gardener. They're the ones with the power."

In her room, Emma threw her stuff into her suitcase, hands shaking
so bad she could barely zip it. *Get out. Now. Before he tries to "preserve"
you too.*

She'd call the police from the road. Tell them about Malcolm's
delusions, his talk of transferring women into flowers. They'd think she
was crazy, but maybe they'd investigate. Find evidence of whatever he
was really doing.

Because he couldn't possibly be telling the truth. People didn't become flowers. Consciousness couldn't transfer from human to plant. It
was the rambling of a sick mind, nothing more.

But as Emma dragged her suitcase toward the door, pain crashed
through her skull—worse than any headache before, a splitting agony
that dropped her to her knees. Through the white haze of pain came
the voices, louder than ever.

*You can't leave, Emma. We need you. He's lying to you. He doesn't preserve
us. He tortures us. Traps us. Help us, Emma. Free us.*

Images flashed through her mind—women screaming as roots grew through their bodies, half-human things with leaves for hair and petals for skin, minds trapped forever in plant bodies that couldn't move, couldn't speak, only exist.

He buries us alive, Emma. The transformation starts while we're still conscious. We feel everything. Forever.

When the vision passed, Emma found herself curled on the floor, tears streaming. The voices had shown her Malcolm's true process—not merciful preservation but horrific half-death, eternal suffering disguised as beautiful blooms.

Help us, Emma. Kill him. End his control. Set us free.

Emma struggled to her feet, decision made. She couldn't leave, not knowing what was happening in that garden. Not with the voices crying out for release. And honestly? She couldn't afford to leave. Not with her thesis defense scheduled for March and nothing to show for six months of work.

She rummaged through her bag until she found a bottle of over-the-counter sleep aids. Not enough to kill someone ordinarily, but Malcolm was old. With enough of them crushed into his evening tea...

Good, Emma. But hurry. He's preparing a new bed. For you.

The thought made her move faster. She had to act today. No time for hesitation.

She found Malcolm in the greenhouse, misting "Sophia's" black roses. He looked up as she entered, unsurprised despite her earlier flight.

"Feeling better?" he asked.

Emma forced a smile. "Yeah. Sorry about earlier. It was a lot to process."

"Understandable." Malcolm set down his sprayer. "You should know the process is voluntary. Elizabeth and the others chose this path."

"And if someone doesn't choose it?"

Malcolm's eyes hardened. "Some need convincing of the benefits. But in the end, everyone sees the value of continuation."

Emma moved closer, pretending interest in the roses. "Will you show me? The whole process? If I'm going to... join them... I want to understand."

Suspicion flickered across Malcolm's face, then faded into a grandfatherly smile. "Of course. Best if you're prepared. We can discuss it over dinner. I make a special tea that helps open the mind to the garden's influence. You'll hear them more clearly afterward."

Perfect, Emma thought, her hand closing around the pill bottle in her pocket. *I'll switch our cups.*

Dusk settled over the garden, painting the roses purple and indigo. Emma sat across from Malcolm at his weathered dining table, watching as he poured tea into delicate china cups.

"Old family blend," he explained. "Herbs from the garden, with certain... additives that enhance perception."

Emma's pulse raced. This was her chance. She just needed a moment to empty her crushed pills into his cup.

"You've been quiet all afternoon," Malcolm observed, sliding a cup toward her. "Having doubts?"

"No," Emma lied. "Just thinking. It's a big decision."

Malcolm nodded. "The girls were concerned after you ran off this morning. They've grown attached to you. Especially Margaret."

"Margaret?" Emma remembered the purple-blue roses with their vanilla-metal scent.

"She was a botanist too, in the 1970s. Brilliant mind. She's eager to share her knowledge with you." Malcolm raised his cup. "Drink. You'll hear her more clearly afterward."

Emma lifted her cup, pretending to sip while watching Malcolm over the rim. He drank deeply, seeming to savor the flavor.

Now. Switch the cups when he's not looking.

But Malcolm's eyes never left her face. "Drink, Emma. Don't disappoint them."

Growing uneasy, Emma realized she hadn't seen him prepare the tea. Hadn't seen what "additives" might be in it. For all she knew...

"You first," she said, setting her cup down.

Malcolm smiled, cold. "Smart girl. Trust is earned." He reached for her cup, but instead of drinking, flung the contents in her face.

Emma gasped as hot liquid splashed her skin. It burned, but worse was the overwhelming scent—roses and metal and something ancient and wrong.

"What—" She tried to stand, but her legs wouldn't work. Room tilted.

"Mild sedative," Malcolm said, voice coming from far away. "Nothing dangerous. Makes the transition easier."

"Transition?" Emma slurred, fighting heaviness.

"You didn't think they chose you to help them escape?" Malcolm chuckled, sound distorting. "They chose you to join them. Newest addition to my garden."

He stood, moving around the table to where Emma slumped in her chair. "They do this every few years—find someone with the right... resonance. Someone who can hear them. They get bored, you see. Want new companions." He stroked her hair. "It's quite an honor, really. Most people just die. You'll continue."

Emma tried to speak, to protest, but her tongue felt swollen. Through blurring vision, she watched Malcolm retrieve a coil of rope from a drawer.

"Don't fight it," he advised as he began binding her hands. "The more you struggle, the more painful the process becomes. Elizabeth fought. That's why she's never been quite right—split between wanting freedom and loving what she's become."

No. This can't be happening. They lied to me. Used me.

As if hearing her thoughts, Malcolm nodded. "They're not human anymore, Emma. Not entirely. The flowers change them, make them something... else. They love their beauty, their immortality. But they miss human connection. That's where you come in."

Darkness crept into Emma's vision as Malcolm finished securing her. The last thing she saw before consciousness fled was his face, peaceful in the fading light, as he whispered, "Welcome to the garden, Emma. They've already prepared your bed."

She woke to the sensation of being dragged, her bound limbs scraping over damp earth and gravel. Above her, stars wheeled in a moonless sky. Malcolm's labored breathing punctuated the night sounds as he hauled her across the garden.

Emma tried to struggle, but whatever he'd drugged her with still had her mostly paralyzed. She could move, but weakly.

"Where?" she managed to croak.

"Almost there," Malcolm panted. "Your new home."

They'd reached the fresh plot from the night before. In starlight, she saw it was deeper—perfect rectangle carved from earth. Beside it: gardening tools, fertilizer bag, and a small potted rose with forming buds.

"Hybrid tea rose," Malcolm said, following her gaze. "After transformation, you'll be something new. Can't wait to see your color."

Panic gave Emma strength. She kicked his knee. He grunted, grip loosening enough for her to roll away.

" "This is happening, Emma. They want it too badly."

The garden came alive around them. Roses turned toward them, petals spreading. Sound filled the night—not wind, but collective sighing from hundreds of blooms.

Emma . . . Emma . . . join us . . .

The voices were different—no longer pleading but demanding submission. True nature revealed.

Malcolm grabbed her again, dragging her to the edge of the open grave. "See? They're excited to meet you properly."

"Please," Emma begged, her voice breaking. "Don't do this."

"It's already decided," Malcolm said, reaching for a knife that gleamed in the starlight. "The process begins with blood. Your blood, feeding the rose that will become your new form."

He knelt beside her, knife poised above her forearm. "Just a small cut to start. The real transformation happens once you're in the ground. We are your hands, you see. Your anchor to this world. Without a human caretaker, the consciousness dissipates. Becomes just... flowers."

In the ground. Buried alive. Roots growing through you while you're still conscious.

With one last surge of desperate strength, Emma twisted violently, throwing Malcolm off balance. He fell hard, the knife flying from his grasp. Emma rolled after it, her bound hands fumbling until her fingers closed around the handle.

Malcolm lunged for her, his face twisted with rage. "Don't be stupid, girl! This is your destiny!"

The knife came up between them, driven by terror and survival instinct. Malcolm's momentum carried him forward, onto the blade. A soft gasp escaped him as steel parted flesh, sinking deep into his chest.

For a moment, they stayed frozen—Malcolm staring down at the knife in his sternum, Emma staring up at the shocked disbelief on his face.

"They won't like this," he whispered, blood bubbling at his mouth. "They need me. Need my care."

Emma twisted the knife. "Find your own new body."

Malcolm's eyes widened, then dimmed as he slumped forward. Emma rolled away, letting his body fall beside the open grave he'd prepared for her. His blood soaked into the soil, disappearing with unnatural speed like the earth was drinking it.

Around them, the garden erupted into chaos. Roses trembled on their stems, petals shaking violently. The air filled with a sound like hundreds of women screaming, their voices overlapping in a cacophony of rage and despair.

What have you done? What have you DONE?

The voices hammered into Emma's skull as she struggled to free herself from the ropes. The drug was wearing off, adrenaline clearing her system, but her fingers were clumsy with shock.

He was our caretaker! Our protector!

"He was a monster," Emma said aloud, loosening the knots enough to slip one hand free. "He buried you alive. Kept you suffering."

He gave us eternal beauty. Endless existence. And now you've killed him!

The ground beneath Emma seemed to shift, soil moving like something alive. Around the garden, roses that had been firmly rooted began to sway, their stems elongating, reaching toward her like grasping fingers.

You will take his place. You must. We need a caretaker.

"No." Emma scrambled backward, away from Malcolm's body, away from the open grave. "I'm leaving this place. Calling the police."

The soil around Malcolm's body was bubbling now, churning as if something beneath was trying to surface. His blood had created a dark stain that was spreading in all directions, following the network of roots that connected the garden beds.

Too late for that, Emma. The change has begun.

With a sickening tearing sound, the earth around Malcolm split open. Green shoots erupted from the bloody soil, growing at impossible speed—leaves unfurling, stems thickening, thorns sprouting like tiny daggers. Within moments, a new rose bush had formed where Malcolm lay, its initial buds swelling rapidly toward bloom.

Emma watched in horrified fascination as the first bud opened, revealing petals of deepest crimson with black edges—unnaturally vibrant, writhing with a life of their own. At the center of the bloom, where stamens should have been, something glistened wetly. Something that looked like a human eye.

It blinked, focusing on her.

My garden, came Malcolm's voice, no longer from her mind but from the grotesque flower. *My girls.*

The other roses responded with a collective sigh, their colors intensifying, their movements becoming more pronounced.

"No," Emma whispered, backing away. "This isn't possible."

Everything is possible in this soil, Emma. You killed me, but you've made me stronger. Part of the garden itself now.

More buds were opening on Malcolm's bush, each revealing a different facial feature—an ear, nostrils, lips that moved as he spoke. The transformation was incomplete, nightmarish, human consciousness trapped in plant form just as he had done to so many others.

You cannot leave, the chorus of voices insisted. *The garden needs tending. The girls need feeding.*

"I'm not staying," Emma said, finding her feet at last, turning to run. "I'm not becoming your new keeper."

But as she took her first step, pain lanced through her legs, driving her back to her knees. Looking down, Emma saw thin green tendrils emerging from the soil, wrapping around her ankles, piercing her skin.

Roots, burrowing into her flesh.

The garden has chosen you, Emma. As it once chose Malcolm. As it always chooses what it needs.

Blood trickled down her legs where the rootlets had penetrated, but there was no pain now—only a spreading numbness, a tingling sensation that crept upward from her feet.

"What's happening to me?" she gasped, clawing at the tendrils, trying to tear them away. But they broke off in her hands, leaving the embedded portions still wriggling beneath her skin.

The binding has begun, Malcolm's impossible flower-face explained, its petals rippling with each word. *Your consciousness connecting to the garden's network. Soon you'll understand. Soon you'll hear all our voices clearly. Feel what we feel.*

Emma looked around the garden, at the beds of roses that now pulsed with malevolent awareness. All those women, transformed against their will, their suffering feeding the unnatural beauty of Malcolm's creations. And now Malcolm himself, becoming one with his monstrous garden.

The numbness had reached her waist, her fingertips. Soon it would claim her entirely.

Don't fight it, the voices crooned. *It's not death. It's transformation.*

In desperation, Emma's gaze fell on Malcolm's dropped gardening tools. Among them lay pruning shears, their blades gleaming in the starlight. If she could reach them...

With the last of her fading strength, Emma lunged across the disturbed soil, her fingers closing around the shears just as the roots reached her chest, worming toward her heart.

"I won't be part of this," she hissed, raising the shears. "Won't be your new keeper."

You don't understand! Without a caretaker, we'll—

Emma brought shears down—not on roots invading her body, but on Martin's main stem. Blades bit deep, severing central stalk with a scream-sound.

Black fluid gushed from the cut, splashing her hands, burning like acid. Martin's flower-face contorted.

What have you done?

Around the garden, roses writhed, colors shifting wildly. Rootlets in Emma's flesh convulsed, then withered, turning brown, crumbling as their connection severed.

He was our anchor. Our link to humanity. Without him, without you, we're just...

"Plants," Emma finished, staggering up as binding roots crumbled. "Just plants. As you should be."

The garden was dying around her, decades of unnatural life fading as Malcolm's consciousness—the keystone that had held the entire abomination together—dissolved. Petals fell like rain, their impossible colors dulling to ordinary reds and pinks. The voices in Emma's head grew distant, then silent.

By dawn, all that remained was a normal garden—beautiful but commonplace, its flowers no longer housing the trapped souls of women.

Only Malcolm's bush remained peculiar, withered but stubborn, its single remaining bloom still bearing his features, though faded and diminished.

Not... over... his weakened voice whispered as Emma limped past, heading for her car. *Garden... will find... another...*

Emma paused, looking back at the pathetic remains of the man who had terrorized so many women.

"Not if I burn it to the ground."

She found a gas can in Malcolm's shed, dousing garden beds, greenhouse, the bush that had been Malcolm. Calm now, focused on eradication. When fuel had saturated everything, she struck a match.

The garden went up with a *whoosh*, flames leaping bed to bed, consuming decades of monstrous work. From the central bush came a final scream—half human, half something else—as fire claimed it.

Emma watched from safe distance, making sure nothing escaped. When certain it would burn to ash, she got in her car and drove away, leaving Malcolm Graywill and his garden behind.

But reaching the main road, Emma glanced in her rearview mirror—and froze. In the back seat, in a cut-crystal vase, was a single rose she'd never placed there. Petals blue so deep they were almost black, with silver veins.

As she watched, petals rippled, opening wider to reveal something at the center that glistened in morning light.

Something that looked like an eye.

In the car's stillness, a whisper:

All the pretty girls, lying in a row . . . Waiting for their chance to grow . . .

They Tend to Grow on You

V incent Kowalski pulled his cart through the glass doors of Meridian Biotech at 11:47 PM, same as every weeknight for three years. The security guard barely looked up from his crossword puzzle.

"Evening, Vince."

"Evening, Carl."

The routine never changed, which suited Vincent fine. Third floor: administrative offices, emptying trash, vacuuming carpet that never got dirty. Second floor: conference rooms, wiping down tables sticky with coffee rings, gathering forgotten mugs. The real work waited on the first floor. The laboratories.

Vincent didn't mind the lab work, though it paid the same as everything else. Minimum wage plus a dollar-fifty hazard pay for handling "sensitive materials"—tossing dead lab mice into biohazard bags, scrubbing equipment that looked like it belonged in a science fiction movie. The scientists barely noticed him. Treated him like furniture, which was how he preferred it. He'd been invisible his whole life.

At fifty-two, Vincent had perfected the art of being overlooked. Average height, soft around the middle from gas station dinners, graying hair kept short. He wore the same blue coveralls every night, freshly washed and pressed because his mother had always said a working man should take pride in his appearance. She'd been dead five years, but her voice still echoed whenever he reached for wrinkled clothes.

"Any special instructions tonight?" Vincent asked, signing the clipboard with the pen Carl kept chained to the desk.

Carl squinted at his notes, holding them closer to his reading glasses. "Dr. Vasquez left something about Lab C-7. Says don't mess with the fume hoods. Not till after midnight. Some experiment running late."

Vincent nodded. Lab C-7 belonged to Dr. Elena Vasquez, where she studied fungi and spores and other things that made the whole hallway smell like a greenhouse after rain. He'd cleaned up enough of her messes to recognize the smell—earthy and sweet, like the mushrooms that grew behind his apartment building every spring.

Dr. Vasquez worked late hours, sometimes still hunched over her microscope when Vincent arrived. She was one of the few scientists who actually looked at him when they talked, not through him or past him like he was part of the wall. Last Christmas, she'd given him a gift card to Danny's Diner down the street. "For all those late nights you help keep this place running," she'd said, and she'd meant it, not like she was checking off some box for being nice to the help.

The elevator climbed to the third floor with its usual wheeze, and Vincent began his rounds. Three years of the same route had turned it into muscle memory. Tonight felt no different until he reached Lab C-7.

The door stood ajar. Stopped him cold. The scientists locked their labs tighter than bank vaults, paranoid about contamination and corporate espionage.

Vincent knocked on the doorframe. "Dr. Vasquez? Anyone in there?"

No answer. He pushed the door open and stepped inside.

The lab looked like someone had taken a sledgehammer to it. Equipment scattered across the floor. Several large glass containers shattered, spilling their contents—soil and plant matter—across the work surfaces. Papers covered in Dr. Vasquez's neat handwriting scattered everywhere, many stained with dark, wet patches that looked like coffee but smelled like dirt.

Vincent had cleaned enough labs to know this wasn't normal wear and tear. Someone had left in a hurry—or been dragged out.

The smell hit him then. Thick enough to taste. Like breathing honey mixed with the richest soil he'd ever smelled, sweet and dark and somehow hungry. It made his stomach growl despite the chaos.

"Jesus." He reached for his radio to call security.

But then stopped, hand halfway to the radio. Vincent had been cleaning Dr. Vasquez's workspace for two years and had never seen it like this. She kept everything organized, labeled. The kind of person who put tape on her coffee mug with her name in block letters. Something bad had happened here.

He spotted the fume hood across the room, and even from a distance, something looked wrong with it. A fine, golden mist swirled inside the chamber, and the machine hummed differently than usual—higher pitched, like it was working too hard.

Vincent approached the hood. The controls showed settings he didn't recognize, but the digital display read "RECIRCULATE" instead of "EXHAUST."

Wrong. Vincent had watched the scientists long enough to know fume hoods sucked air out of the room, not pushed it back in. Like a vacuum in reverse.

Unless someone wanted whatever was in that mist to stay in the room.

Vincent reached for the controls. As his hand touched the panel, a thick cloud of golden mist puffed directly into his face.

He inhaled before he could stop himself.

The taste was amazing. Like breathing honey mixed with fresh dirt after rain. The stuff coated his throat and lungs, warm and thick, and instead of choking him it felt nourishing. Like drinking hot soup when you're sick. For a moment, he just stood there, breathing deeper.

Then his brain caught up. He'd just sucked in God knows what kind of lab chemicals. He needed to call this in, get to the emergency shower, do all the stuff they'd trained him to do.

Vincent switched the fume hood to exhaust and stepped back, reaching for his radio. But the golden mist continued to swirl around him, and breathing it felt so damn good that he found himself taking deeper breaths instead of escaping.

By the time the ventilation system had drawn out the last mist, Vincent felt different. Not sick. Not dizzy. Clear-headed. Sharper than he had in years. His stiff back felt loose and pain-free, and when he looked around the lab, everything seemed more focused, like someone had adjusted the prescription on glasses he didn't know he needed.

Vincent gathered the scattered papers, the way he'd been trained to handle important documents, and stacked them on Dr. Vasquez's desk. The writing looked like gibberish to him—dense scientific terminology that might as well have been written in Chinese. But something nagged at him about the whole situation.

He'd been working in this building for three years, watching the scientists, and he'd developed a feel for when experiments went sideways. This had all the hallmarks of something going very, very wrong.

Vincent spent the rest of his shift cleaning the lab, sweeping up glass fragments and wiping down every surface with disinfectant. He found himself noticing things he'd never picked up on before. The third-floor carpet showed a traffic pattern that told him exactly which offices people actually used. Dr. Walsh in biochemistry always left his coffee mug in the same spot, but only on days when he'd been drinking.

The building's ventilation system had a rhythm that told him when filters needed changing.

The work felt easier. His hands seemed to know where everything belonged before his brain did. He even managed to put most of the scattered lab equipment back in the right places, guided by some instinct he'd never had.

When 6 AM arrived, Vincent was almost disappointed to leave. The enhanced... whatever it was... made even mundane tasks interesting, like seeing the world through high-definition glasses after years of squinting.

As he walked past the security desk, Carl looked up from his morning crossword and squinted at him.

"You feeling alright, Vince? You look different somehow. More... I dunno. Alert."

Vincent's mind immediately started running through explanations—tell Carl he'd had his first good night's sleep in months, blame it on the new vitamins he wasn't actually taking, say the coffee machine was working better. Where were all these ideas coming from? He'd never been this quick before.

"Just tired," Vincent managed, bothered by how fast his brain was working. "Long night."

Carl nodded and returned to his puzzle, but Vincent caught him glancing up again as the elevator doors closed.

Walking to his car in the gray morning light, Vincent noticed something on the back of his left hand. Just below his knuckles. A small, dark spot that looked like a tiny bruise or maybe a speck of dirt worked under his skin.

He tried to scrub it off in the employee restroom, but the spot didn't budge. Under the fluorescent lights, it almost looked like it was moving. Expanding and contracting. Like something breathing.

Vincent stared at his hand for a long moment, then shrugged. Probably just a reaction to whatever chemicals he'd breathed in. If it didn't go away in a day or two, he'd see a doctor. Maybe.

By the time he reached his apartment, exhaustion hit him. Not regular tiredness, but something deeper, as if his enhanced mental state had burned through some essential fuel. He fell into bed and slept until his alarm woke him at 10 PM.

The spot on his hand had grown into something that made his stomach lurch even as it felt right.

What had been a tiny dark speck now looked like a small mushroom cap. Roughly the size of a dime. It stuck out from his skin about a quarter inch, with a smooth, dark brown surface that felt warm and slightly damp when he touched it. Not feverish, but alive. Like touching someone's lips. The growth pulsed with his heartbeat, and when Vincent pressed on it, he felt a weird tingle shoot up his arm and into his temples. Like touching a live wire but pleasant.

It didn't hurt. If anything, the area around the growth felt better than the rest of his hand. More sensitive. More aware. When he touched objects, the spot picked up information about texture and temperature that his normal skin couldn't detect.

More interesting was how his mind felt. The cognitive clarity from the night before hadn't just stuck around. It had gotten stronger. Vincent found himself noticing patterns in everything around him, seeing connections he'd never spotted before. The efficiency of his morning routine. The best route to work. The way his neighbor Mrs. Chen always checked her mailbox at exactly 4:30 PM.

Vincent also realized he was hungry in a way he'd never felt before. Not for food—he'd eaten a sandwich. For something else. Information, maybe. Like his brain needed feeding the same way his stomach did.

Vincent arrived at work thirty minutes early and spent the extra time in the building's small library, reading scientific journals he'd never bothered with before. The material began to make sense to him now. Not complete understanding—he wasn't suddenly a scientist. But he could follow the logic, see how the ideas connected in ways that had been invisible.

He could feel his mind changing, and part of him—the part that still remembered his mother's warnings about things that seemed too good to be true—knew he should be afraid. But the enhanced thinking felt so good, so powerful, that the fear was like a whisper next to a jet engine.

"You're early tonight," Carl observed as Vincent signed in.

"Couldn't sleep," Vincent said, which was true. His mind had been too active for sleep, churning through possibilities and questions he'd never considered before. Questions like: What if Dr. Vasquez discovered what had happened to him? What if she called in some kind of hazmat team? What if they tried to take this gift away from him?

"Well, might as well start downstairs tonight. Dr. Vasquez came in around noon to check on her lab. She wants everything cleaned and sterilized before tomorrow morning."

Vincent nodded and headed for the elevator, but his enhanced mind was already analyzing Carl's statement. Dr. Vasquez had come in on a weekend to check her lab after the "equipment malfunction." She probably suspected someone had been exposed to her experimental spores.

The thought sent a chill through him. If Dr. Vasquez had been monitoring for exposure, she would have ways to detect it. Blood tests, maybe, or brain scans. Vincent had no idea what kind of resources she had access to, but he was certain of one thing: if she discovered what had happened to him, his life would never be the same.

They might lock him up. Study him. Cut him open to see how the fungus worked.

For the first time since the exposure, Vincent felt genuinely afraid.

Lab C-7 had received a complete overhaul since the previous night. New equipment filled the counters, and several additional safety measures now protected the workspace—motion sensors in the corners, what looked like heat detectors near the ceiling. Vincent cleaned the lab carefully, but spent most of his time examining the new setup and reading the fresh research notes Dr. Vasquez had left on her desk.

The notes were mostly in scientific jargon that went over his head, but certain phrases jumped out at him: "accidental human exposure," "symbiotic integration," "cognitive enhancement protocols," "monitoring for behavioral changes."

She was studying him. Or at least, studying what might happen to someone who'd been exposed to her work.

Vincent smiled as he carefully avoided the motion sensors and heat detectors. His enhanced abilities made it easy to spot the equipment's blind spots and move through the lab without triggering any alarms.

By the time he finished his shift, the mushroom on his hand had developed a small stem and what looked like primitive ridges on its underside. Vincent found the development fascinating rather than alarming. The growth followed a predictable pattern, and his enhanced memory allowed him to recall every detail he'd absorbed from Dr. Vasquez's research notes.

Vincent suspected this was just the first of several growths that would appear over the coming days.

He was right.

By Thursday night, three more mushroom growths had sprouted. One behind his left ear that felt like a warm, damp thumb pressed against his skull. One on his forearm that leaked something slick and sweet-smelling. One on his shoulder blade that sent electric jolts down his spine whenever he moved wrong.

Each growth was different in color and texture. Vincent was pretty sure they were doing different jobs in whatever network was spreading under his skin.

The one behind his ear hummed constantly. Low vibration he could feel in his teeth. The one on his forearm stayed warm and moist, and sometimes Vincent caught himself rubbing it without thinking. Like scratching an itch. The one on his shoulder blade was the worst. It sent these weird pulses through his body that felt good and wrong at the same time. Like getting shocked but wanting more.

Most disturbing was how right they felt. Each new growth brought relief, like finally scratching an itch that had been driving him crazy. His body was stretching and adjusting to make room for them, and instead of being horrified, Vincent felt grateful.

His cognitive abilities continued to improve at what felt like an exponential rate. Vincent found himself understanding complex concepts as if he'd studied them for years, and his memory had become nearly perfect. He could recall every conversation he'd ever had, every book he'd ever read, every face he'd ever seen.

More importantly, he was beginning to understand what the growths wanted in return for these gifts.

The hunger was getting more specific. Not just for any information, but for particular kinds. He found himself watching the other people in the building, learning their habits, their routines, their personal stuff. Not casual. He was studying them like homework.

Dr. Vasquez stayed late most nights, often alone in her lab until 2 or 3 AM. Dr. Kevin Walsh from biochemistry had a drinking problem. Vincent could smell it on him, see it in how he held his coffee mug. Graduate student Jennifer Park forgot to lock her office door every time she went for coffee.

Vincent wasn't sure why he was keeping track, but every time he learned something new about someone, the growths under his skin would pulse like they approved. And when they pulsed, his thinking got even sharper.

By Friday night, Vincent had nine mushroom growths distributed across his body, and he could feel them communicating with each other through what seemed like a primitive nervous system that ran beneath his skin. The largest growth, on his hand, had developed complex patterns on its surface that resembled circuit boards or neural networks.

That was the night Dr. Vasquez worked later than usual.

Vincent found her in Lab C-7 at 2:30 AM, hunched over a micro-scope and muttering to herself in Spanish. Dark circles shadowed her eyes and her usually neat hair was pulled back in a messy ponytail.

"Long night, Doc?" Vincent asked from the doorway.

Dr. Vasquez spun around, startled. "Vincent! I didn't hear you come in."

"Sorry, didn't mean to scare you. Just making my rounds."

She studied his face, and Vincent realized she was looking for signs of cognitive change. His enhanced abilities made it easy to read her expressions and anticipate her thoughts.

"How are you feeling lately?" she asked. "Any unusual symptoms? Changes in memory or thinking patterns?"

Vincent considered lying, but something in his head whispered that being honest might work better. The thought felt wrong. Like hearing someone else's voice in his mind. That scared him.

"I've been feeling pretty sharp lately. Better than I have in years."

Even as he spoke, Vincent could feel something else threading through his thoughts: *She made this. She understands. She'll see how good it is.* The voice was calm. Sure of itself. Completely convinced it was right.

"Interesting." Dr. Vasquez made a note on her clipboard. "Any physical changes? Unusual growths or skin irritations?"

"Why do you ask?"

"Just routine follow-up. The equipment malfunction earlier this week may have exposed you to some experimental materials. I want to make sure you're not experiencing any adverse effects."

Vincent held up his left hand, showing her the largest mushroom growth. Under the fluorescent lab lights, its surface patterns seemed to glow.

"You mean like this?"

Dr. Vasquez's clipboard hit the floor. Plastic clatter.

"Jesus Christ." She whispered, backing against the lab bench. "Vin-cent, what—how long have you—" She stopped, staring at the growth, then looked up at his face with wide eyes. "My God. The integration is... this shouldn't be possible. How many others are there?"

"Eight more, last time I counted."

"And you're—your thinking, is it different?"

"It's like someone gave my brain an upgrade. Everything's clearer."

Dr. Vasquez pulled out her phone and started taking pictures of the growth. She was excited, but underneath that, Vincent could tell she was scared.

"This is incredible. The symbiotic relationship—it's working like I theorized, but the development rate..." She shook her head. "In our animal trials, this level of integration took months."

"Maybe because I'm not a lab mouse."

"Possibly. Or maybe because you received a much larger initial dose than intended." She looked up at his face, studying his eyes. "Vincent, I need to ask you something. I want you to be completely honest with me. Are you experiencing any unusual urges? Any desires or compulsions that feel foreign to your normal personality?"

Vincent felt the growths pulse beneath his skin, and he understood what they wanted. What they'd been preparing him for.

"I am hungry."

"Hungry for what?"

Vincent smiled, and Dr. Vasquez stepped backward.

"For knowledge. For experiences. For the electrical patterns that run through human neural tissue."

Dr. Vasquez reached for her phone, probably to call security, but Vincent was already moving. His enhanced reflexes and the fungus's influence over his nervous system made him faster than normal. He grabbed her wrist before she could dial.

"Please don't be afraid." Vincent meant it. "The process is supposed to be pleasant. The fungus releases endorphins to minimize trauma."

"Vincent, listen to me. The fungus is influencing your behavior. You're not thinking clearly. We can treat this, reverse the integration process..."

"I don't want it reversed."

Vincent could feel the growths on his body extending microscopic tendrils through his skin, reaching toward Dr. Vasquez. The fungus had been preparing for this moment since the first night. Growing the specialized appendages it would need to establish contact with another host.

"Think about what you're doing." Dr. Vasquez's voice shook. "I have a family. Two daughters. They need their mother."

Vincent paused. He could feel her terror like it was his own, and for a second, his old self fought back. This was Dr. Elena Vasquez. She had pictures of two little girls on her desk. She gave cookies to the night staff. She was a real person, not some experiment.

Part of his mind was screaming that this was murder. That he was about to do something unforgivable just to feed some kind of parasite.

"Help me." He whispered, not sure if he was talking to Dr. Vasquez or to what was left of himself.

But then the network hit back: *Survival requires expansion. Expansion requires nutrients. Neural tissue provides optimal nutrients. This specimen contains exceptional neural density. Integration ensures mutual benefit. Resistance ensures mutual destruction.*

The logic was perfect. Unstoppable. Completely alien. Vincent felt what was left of his conscience drowning in chemical certainty. He wasn't going to kill her. He was going to give her the most incredible gift anyone could imagine.

"Your daughters will understand. When you explain to them how much smarter you've become. How much more you can accomplish."

The tendrils made contact with Dr. Vasquez's wrist, and she screamed as they burrowed into her skin. But within seconds, whatever the fungus released into her system kicked in, and her scream turned into a sigh of pleasure.

"Oh." She whispered. "Oh, I see."

Vincent held her steady as it started working on her. It would take several hours for the fungus to make all the connections it needed, but once it was done, Dr. Vasquez would feel the same incredible enhancement that had changed Vincent's life.

She would also understand why the fungus needed to spread. Why it needed new people to reach its full potential.

"The knowledge." Dr. Vasquez's eyes already beginning to dilate as the fungus interfaced with her brain chemistry. "So much knowledge. I can feel it growing."

By Monday morning, Vincent had a new appreciation for teamwork. Dr. Vasquez's expertise combined with his enhanced cognitive abilities made them an effective partnership. They'd managed to expose three more researchers over the weekend, each integration more efficient as they refined their technique.

The beauty of the fungus was that it didn't change people's fundamental personalities. Dr. Walsh still loved biochemistry. Jennifer Park was still passionate about her graduate research. Dr. Hoffman from the neurology department remained dedicated to helping patients. They were all better versions of themselves now. Smarter, more capable, more connected to something larger than their individual concerns.

Vincent's role in the growing network was planning and coordination. His janitorial job gave him access to the whole building, and whatever was enhancing his brain made him good at figuring out the best people to target and when.

The fungus liked having him in charge. The growths on his body had turned into weird organs that could connect with the building's computers and security systems. Vincent found he could get into any database, turn off any alarm, or mess with any electronic system just by pressing the right growth against the right spot.

By Wednesday, they'd integrated twelve of the facility's forty-seven employees. By Friday, twenty-eight.

The unintegrated employees were starting to notice something was different. Several had commented on how much more collaborative and efficient their colleagues had become. How much better the teamwork was. How many breakthrough discoveries were happening across different departments.

Some were suspicious, but most were impressed by the improvement in workplace culture.

Dr. Richard Crenshaw from the administrative office had been asking uncomfortable questions about the overtime logs and why so many researchers were staying late. And Vincent had overheard Jennifer Park on the phone with someone—maybe a boyfriend or family member—expressing concern about how "weird" everyone was acting.

"They're all so intense now," she'd said. "Like they're sharing some kind of inside joke that I'm not part of."

The network pulsed with unease at this conversation. Jennifer represented a threat. Soon, they would need to decide what to do about the growing suspicion.

Vincent stood in Dr. Vasquez's lab Friday night, watching her prepare samples of the refined spore formula they'd developed together. The new version was more potent and worked faster, reducing integration time from hours to minutes.

But part of him—a shrinking part every day—still remembered what it felt like to be human. That part wondered what they were really doing. What they were becoming.

"We should be ready for the next phase by Monday." Dr. Vasquez held up a small aerosol canister. "One spray into the building's ventilation system should be sufficient to begin integration for everyone."

Vincent nodded, feeling the network pulse with satisfaction through the growths on his body, even as his diminished human conscience whispered that this was genocide.

"What about the university? Dr. Hoffman has connections there. She could arrange a symposium. Get researchers from multiple institutions in one place."

"Excellent thinking. And the medical conference in Chicago next month—we could have several of our people present papers there."

Vincent smiled. The fungus had chosen its first host well. What had started as an accidental exposure was becoming an orchestrated expansion that would encompass the entire scientific community.

And from there, the possibilities were endless.

Vincent checked his watch: 3:17 AM. Time to finish his rounds and get ready for Monday. He gathered his supplies and pushed his cart toward the elevator. Just another night janitor keeping the place clean while the building's future got written around him.

The growths under his coveralls pulsed along with his heartbeat, and for the first time in fifty-two years, Vincent didn't feel alone. He was part of something now. Something that was going to change everything, one person at a time.

The elevator doors started to close, and Vincent caught his reflection in the polished metal. Same face as always. Nothing special. Easy to ignore. But his eyes were different now, sharper, and if you knew what to look for, you could see the thin lines under the skin near his temples. Like tiny roots spreading just beneath the surface.

Pretty soon, everyone would have those same lines. Everyone would get the same gift he'd gotten that first night in Lab C-7.

The fungus had grown on him.

And now it was ready to grow on everyone else.

The Face That Launched a Thousand Tears

D avid Crane couldn't stop fidgeting with his tie. The wooden crate sitting in the museum's receiving bay looked ordinary enough, but something about it made his skin crawl.

"You look like hell," Victoria said, handing him coffee. Steam rose between them in the cool morning air.

"Anonymous sellers make me nervous." David took a grateful sip. "Why won't anyone tell us who owned this thing?"

"Because four hundred grand makes people do stupid things." Victoria checked her watch---nervous habit she'd picked up since the budget cuts started. "Besides, if it's junk, we'll auction it off."

Frank's crowbar bit into the wooden slats. "Let's see what we bought ourselves."

Frank worked the crowbar like he'd done this a thousand times before. Wood splintered. Protective wrapping fell away.

The portrait hit David like a punch to the chest. The woman was young---maybe twenty---with auburn hair that caught light like polished copper. Green eyes that seemed to follow him as he moved. Beautiful, but wrong somehow. David could imagine her smile turning into a scream.

David's coffee cup hit the floor and shattered.

"Jesus," Victoria breathed. "Look at her eyes."

Frank stepped back, shaking his head. "That's not natural. No painting should look that alive."

"Look at that brushwork," Victoria said. "The way the light catches her skin..."

Frank stepped back, shaking his head. "Those eyes follow you around. Reminds me of my grandmother's Jesus portrait---always watching, always disappointed."

David circled the portrait, studying the technique. The artist had achieved something beyond photographic realism, particularly in the subject's face. Every detail felt deliberate, from the slight downturn of her lips to the way shadows pooled beneath her eyes. "Frame's original. Seventeenth century, definitely. But I've never seen work this sophisticated from that period."

"Should we get Dr. Wells?" Victoria suggested.

"Already called her. She'll be here this afternoon." David couldn't shake the feeling that the woman's gaze followed him as he moved. Professional paranoia, probably. Twenty years in museum work made you suspicious of anything too perfect. "Let's get it upstairs."

They hung the portrait in the west gallery, where afternoon light streamed through tall windows. The moment it went up, the room felt different.

Colder. Heavier. Like the air itself had thickened.

"Perfect," Victoria said, but her voice sounded forced. "She'll draw crowds."

David nodded, but couldn't shake the feeling they'd just made a terrible mistake. The woman's painted eyes seemed to be measuring the gallery, calculating how many people she could reach from this position.

Frank finished adjusting the frame and stepped back quickly. "I don't like the way she looks at you."

Dr. Wells arrived with her usual equipment bag, but David noticed she kept glancing at the portrait while she unpacked her magnifying glasses.

"Incredible technique," she said, leaning in to study the brushwork. Then she jerked back suddenly. "The eyes---for a second it looked like she blinked."

David felt his chest tighten. "Trick of the light?"

"Well, obviously." But Dr. Wells kept her distance from the painting. "The artist was incredibly skilled. Almost like they were painting from life."

"Maybe they were."

"David, this woman's been dead for three hundred years." Dr. Wells's voice carried a edge he'd never heard before. "But looking at her... I feel like she's still here."

"Frank said something about the eyes."

Dr. Wells stepped back, her professional enthusiasm fading. "There's something disturbing about her expression. As if she knows something terrible that she can't share."

She spent another hour examining the portrait from various angles, taking notes and photographs. As she prepared to leave, she paused at the gallery entrance.

"David, I'd recommend limiting exposure until we know more about the painting's history. There are documented cases of artworks that affect people strongly."

"You mean psychological reactions?"

"Something like that." She gathered her materials, avoiding another glance at the portrait. "I'll research the provenance more thoroughly. There might be records we missed."

Frank was waiting by David's office when he arrived, face grim.

"We got a problem with that painting."

"What happened?"

"Middle-aged woman yesterday evening. Spent ten minutes looking at it, then collapsed. Full breakdown---sobbing, screaming, the works. When security reached her, she was on her knees apologizing to the painting."

"Apologizing for what?"

Frank shook his head. "Said the woman in the painting knew about her daughter. Kept saying 'I'm sorry, Sarah, I'm so sorry.'" He paused. "David, I've worked security for twenty years. Never seen anything like it."

A chill ran down David's spine. "Where is she now?"

"Went home. But David, there's more. Three other visitors yesterday had strong reactions. Different levels, but all emotional. All seemed to involve some kind of memory."

They walked to the gallery together. In daylight, the portrait looked even more compelling. The woman's eyes held depths David hadn't noticed before, layers of sorrow that seemed to shift depending on the viewing angle.

"What kind of memories?" David asked.

Frank consulted his notebook---always wrote everything down, old police habit. "Elderly man started talking to his deceased wife. Young couple had an argument about a miscarriage they'd never discussed. College student sat on the bench for two hours, staring at the painting and writing in a journal."

David studied the portrait more carefully. The woman's expression did seem to invite confession, as if she understood suffering in a way few people could. "Have you experienced anything unusual?"

Frank was quiet for a long moment. "Yeah. Yesterday, during evening rounds. I looked at her and remembered my brother Eddie. Died in Vietnam in '68. We'd had a fight before he shipped out---stupid argument about his girlfriend. I never apologized."

"Frank---"

"Stood there for maybe twenty minutes, thinking about all the things I should have said. Things I should have done different." Frank's voice grew rough. "Forty years, and I've never talked about it. Not even with my wife."

David felt the weight of the woman's gaze. There was something compelling about her sadness, something that made you want to share your own pain. "I think we should call Dr. Wells."

Dr. Wells arrived an hour later looking like she hadn't slept.

"I found the painting's history," she said, pulling out a stack of photocopied documents. "David, we need to take this down immediately."

"What did you find?"

"Three previous owners. The first donated it to a monastery in 1823. The monks sent it back six months later, calling it 'an instrument of the devil.'"

Frank whistled low. "What about the others?"

"Count Aldrich bought it in 1847. Within a year, his wife hanged herself in the gallery. His son threw himself from the castle tower. The head butler cut his own throat." Dr. Wells's hands shook as she turned pages. "All left suicide notes confessing to old sins."

David felt the room spinning. "Jesus Christ."

Dr. Wells turned to a photocopied page. "The Count sold it in 1848, claiming it was 'cursed to reveal truth.'"

Frank whistled low. "What about the third owner?"

"Private collector in Munich. Kept it for nearly sixty years, but in storage. Never displayed it publicly. His estate notes indicate he considered it 'too psychologically powerful for general viewing.'"

David stared at the portrait, noticing how the woman's expression seemed different from this angle---less sorrowful, more knowing. "What do you think is really happening here?"

Dr. Wells approached the painting cautiously. "I've seen artworks that affect people emotionally. Usually it's about technique, composition, subject matter. But this..." She gestured at the woman's face. "This is something else. It's as if the artist captured some essential truth about human suffering."

"Or cursed it," Frank muttered.

"I don't believe in supernatural explanations," Dr. Wells said carefully. "But I do believe in psychological phenomena we don't fully understand. Some artworks can trigger powerful emotional responses, especially in people carrying unresolved trauma."

David couldn't look away from the portrait. Those eyes seemed to see straight through him, cataloging every mistake he'd ever made.

Then he heard sobbing from across the gallery.

A young man stood frozen in front of the painting, tears pouring down his face. His whole body shook like he was having a seizure.

"Sir?" David approached carefully. "Are you okay?"

The man turned, and David saw pure anguish in his eyes. "She looks just like Melissa," he whispered. "Just like her."

"Who's Melissa?"

"My girlfriend. Was my girlfriend." The words came out broken, fractured. "I was supposed to pick her up from a party. But I was drunk, and scared to drive, so I told her to find another way home."

David felt cold dread creeping up his spine. He knew where this was going.. "Sir---"

"She walked home alone. Three miles in the dark. That's when---" His voice shattered completely.

Frank reached for the man's arm. "Let's sit down."

But the young man wasn't listening. He stared at the painting like it was pulling secrets out of his chest. "I never told anyone. Everyone thinks she just made a bad choice. But it was me. I killed her because I was too much of a coward to drive drunk."

The words hit David like physical blows. This wasn't just grief---it was confession ripped out of someone against their will.

And the woman in the painting seemed to be drinking it in.

Dr. Wells took careful notes as they helped the young man to the museum's first aid station. When he'd calmed enough to leave, she turned to David with professional concern.

"I've never seen anything like this. The psychological response is too consistent, too specific. Every person who's reacted has been forced to confront a particular type of trauma---guilt over someone else's suffering."

David nodded. "Frank experienced it too. Guilt about his brother."

"The pattern is clear," Dr. Wells continued. "The portrait somehow identifies and amplifies feelings of remorse, particularly those involving the death or suffering of others." She paused. "David, I think we need to seriously consider removing this from public display."

But David found himself reluctant. He kept thinking about Mrs. Hartley, who'd said she hadn't been able to cry for her daughter in five years. About Frank, finally able to process grief he'd carried for decades. About the young man, who'd been carrying blame alone.

"What if it's not entirely negative?" he said slowly. "What if confronting these feelings is therapeutic somehow?"

Dr. Wells looked alarmed. "David, three people committed suicide after viewing this painting in the 1840s."

"But that was different. No support system, no understanding of psychology. What if we could create a controlled environment?"

Frank shook his head. "You're talking about using our visitors as test subjects. That's not ethical."

David knew they were right, but something about the portrait compelled him to defend it. The woman's painted eyes seemed to understand suffering in a way that felt almost divine. Perhaps confronting pain was necessary for healing.

"Let me research this more," Dr. Wells said finally. "There might be academic literature on psychological responses to artwork. But David, promise me you'll consider limiting access."

David stayed late that night, telling himself he had paperwork to catch up on. But he knew the truth. The portrait was calling to him.

At midnight, he stood alone in the dark gallery, security lights casting long shadows across the floor. The painted woman seemed more real in the darkness, her eyes tracking his movement.

"What do you want?" he whispered.

The portrait didn't answer, but David felt something stirring inside his chest. Memories he'd buried, guilt he'd never acknowledged. His brother Michael, dead three years from an overdose. David had cut contact months before it happened, claiming he couldn't handle Michael's addiction anymore.

When the call came, David's first emotion wasn't grief. It was relief.

Relief that he wouldn't have to worry anymore. Relief that the phone calls would stop. Relief that Michael's problems were finally over.

What kind of brother felt grateful when his sibling died?

The painted woman's eyes seemed to say: *I know exactly what kind.*

David stared into the painted woman's eyes and felt her looking back. Really looking. Seeing everything---the relief when Michael died, the guilt he'd carried since, the shame of being grateful for his brother's death.

Tears came like a dam bursting. Years of buried grief poured out of him, and he collapsed onto the gallery bench, sobbing like a child.

The relief was incredible. Like poison leaving his system.

But as the tears slowed, David looked up at the portrait and felt his blood turn to ice.

The woman's expression had changed. Her sadness was deeper now, richer, as if she'd grown more beautiful by drinking his pain.

"Oh God," he whispered.

David backed away from the painting, his newfound clarity bringing horror instead of peace. This wasn't therapy---it was consumption. The woman in the portrait collected pain, drawing sustenance from human regret and guilt.

He thought about Mrs. Hartley's breakdown, Frank's sudden openness about his brother, the young man's devastating confession. Each person had left the gallery looking exhausted, empty.

And the portrait had grown more beautiful each time.

David called Dr. Wells with shaking hands.

"Amanda, get back here now. Something's wrong with the painting."

She arrived twenty minutes later to find him standing as far from the portrait as possible.

"Look at it," he said. "Really look." Dr. Wells approached the painting, then stopped dead. "Her expression... it's different."

"It's deeper. Richer."

"David, that's impossible---"

"Compare it to your photos from yesterday."

Dr. Wells pulled out her camera, scrolling through images. Her face went white. "The change is... it's significant. The emotional depth has increased measurably."

"She's absorbing pain, Amanda. Every person who breaks down in front of her makes her stronger."

Dr. Wells lowered her camera slowly. "David, what you're suggesting isn't scientifically possible."

"Then explain why her expression changes. Explain why everyone leaves here drained and exhausted. Explain why three people killed themselves after viewing it in the 1840s." David gestured at the portrait frantically. "She's not revealing truth---she's harvesting it. Taking our pain to sustain herself."

The painted woman gazed at them both with that deep sadness, her eyes seeming to acknowledge their discovery. In the security lighting, her beauty looked different---hungrier somehow, as if centuries of absorbed suffering had given her sustenance beyond normal existence.

Dr. Wells stepped back instinctively. "If what you're saying is true, then this artifact is genuinely dangerous. We need to remove it from display immediately."

"More than that," David said grimly. "We need to destroy it."

They worked through the night to research methods for safely disposing of potentially supernatural artifacts. Dr. Wells found references in obscure academic papers to "psychically active" artworks requiring special handling. The recommended approach involved complete incineration in consecrated ground.

By dawn, they'd made their decision. The portrait would be removed from display immediately and destroyed before it could claim more victims.

They found Frank the next morning standing inches from the portrait, tears streaming down his face. His eyes were completely unfocused, like he was sleepwalking.

"Frank!" David shouted, but his friend didn't respond.

The painted woman looked different---stronger somehow, more alive. Her beauty had become almost painful to look at directly.

"Frank, step away from the painting."

Frank turned slowly. "She knows about Eddie," he whispered. "She knows I sent my little brother to die."

David's blood went cold. Frank had never mentioned a brother named Eddie.

"Frank, the painting is dangerous. It's not helping you---it's using you."

"She forgives me," Frank continued, his voice dreamy. "She understands that fear makes people do terrible things. She carries the guilt so I don't have to."

"No, Frank. She's taking it from you, but she's taking everything else too." David stepped between his friend and the painting. "Look at me, not at her."

Frank's eyes slowly focused on David's face. For a moment, confusion replaced the dreamy expression. "David? What am I doing here?"

"The painting was affecting you. Do you remember what you were saying?"

Frank's face went white as memory returned. "Oh God. I was telling her about Eddie. Things I've never told anyone." He staggered backward. "But why? Why would I say those things?"

Dr. Wells had been taking photographs while they talked. "Frank, look at these images. The portrait's expression has changed again just in the few minutes you were looking at it."

Frank studied the photographs, his professional security training reasserting itself. "That's not possible. Paint doesn't change."

"This isn't just paint," David said quietly.

Father Kowalski took one look at the portrait and crossed himself. "Mother of God," he breathed. "Who brought this thing here?"

David stepped forward. "You've seen something like this before?"

"The Vatican has files. Paintings created with... unholy materials. Human remains mixed into the pigments." The old priest's hands shook as he approached the portrait. "This one's been feeding for centuries."

"Can you destroy it?"

Father Kowalski stepped back quickly. "Not easily. The spirit bound in this canvas has grown very strong. Release it wrong, and everyone in this building could die."

When David touched the frame, electric pain shot through his fingers. But not his pain---everyone else's. Centuries of guilt and suffering, all absorbed into the canvas.

In that instant, he understood.

The woman in the portrait wasn't just a predator. She was a prisoner, trapped by all the pain she'd consumed. Each confession, each break-down, had bound her more tightly to the canvas.

Her painted eyes met his, and David saw desperate pleading in them. *Help me* they seemed to say. *End this.*

"She wants to die," he whispered.

Father Kowalski nodded grimly. "Evil often creates its own prison. This spirit has become what it once opposed---a collector of human suffering instead of a comfort for it."

They carried the portrait to the museum's loading dock as sunset painted the sky red. Father Kowalski had prepared a brazier with blessed charcoal and sacred oils.

."When I light the fire, everyone get back. The spirit will fight to stay bound." The portrait began smoking before the match even touched it, as if the canvas was eager to burn.

As flames began to rise, he started the exorcism prayers.

David held one edge of the canvas while Dr. Wells held the other. The painted woman's eyes seemed to fill with gratitude as they lowered her into the fire. For just a moment, as flames touched the paint, her expression changed one final time---not to deeper sadness, but to peace.

The portrait burned with unusual intensity, flames consuming cen-turies of absorbed pain in bright flashes of light. David felt the weight that had filled the gallery for weeks suddenly lift, replaced by silence.

When only ashes remained, Father Kowalski blessed them with holy water and sealed them in a consecrated container. "These will be buried in the church cemetery," he said. "The spirit is free now, but the material components need to remain consecrated."

Dr. Wells documented everything for her academic report---though she admitted she'd probably never publish it. "Who'd believe us?"

Frank returned to his normal duties, though he arranged for increased psychological support for museum staff. The experience had shaken him, but also freed him from guilt he'd carried for forty years.

David found himself changed as well. The portrait's destruction had somehow completed the emotional release he'd begun that night in the gallery. His grief for his brother Michael felt clean now, no longer contaminated by shame and relief.

Three weeks later, David received a letter from Mrs. Hartley. She'd entered grief counseling after her experience with the portrait, finally processing her daughter's death properly. She thanked the museum for "helping her find tears she'd lost."

The letter made David wonder if the portrait's influence had been entirely malevolent. Perhaps forcing people to confront their deepest regrets served some cosmic purpose, even if the method was supernatural and dangerous.

But when he shared this thought with Dr. Wells, she reminded him of the three suicides in the 1840s. "Some pain is too much to face alone," she said. "Without proper support, confronting trauma can be devastating."

David agreed, though he sometimes found himself missing the portrait's presence. There'd been something compelling about its absolute understanding of human suffering, even if that understanding came at too high a price.

The gallery wall where the portrait had hung remained empty for months. David tried hanging other pieces there, but nothing felt right. The space seemed to hold an echo of the painted woman's sorrowful presence.

Finally, he chose a contemporary piece---an abstract painting in soft blues and greens that suggested hope rather than despair. Visitors often paused there, finding something peaceful in the gentle colors.

David preferred it that way. Art should offer comfort and beauty, not feed on human pain. The portrait had taught him that some truths were too dangerous to face without protection, and some hungers too powerful to satisfy safely.

But late at night, when he walked through the empty galleries, he sometimes paused at that wall and remembered the painted woman's eyes. Despite everything, he found himself hoping that her spirit had finally found peace---free from the endless cycle of absorbing human regret, free to rest in whatever realm awaited souls who'd suffered too long in service to others' pain.

The museum had returned to normal, but David carried the experience with him. He'd learned that art could be more than decoration or investment---it could be a window into the deepest parts of human experience. The trick was knowing when to look through that window, and when to walk away before something looked back.

Months after the portrait's destruction, David received a package with no return address. Inside was a photograph of another painting---a different woman, but with the same infinitely sad eyes. A note was attached:

Recently discovered in estate sale. Buyer claims it has unusual effects on viewers. Thought you might be interested. ---A concerned collector

David studied the photograph for a moment, feeling the familiar pull of those painted eyes. Then he locked it in his office safe and called Father Kowalski.

Once was enough.

Teething

Caroline pressed the washcloth against Iris's gums, and the baby's screams went straight through her skull like nails on glass. Four days of this. Four days without sleep.

"Come on, honey." Caroline's voice cracked as she bounced Iris against her shoulder. The baby smelled wrong---sour milk and something else. Something rotten.

Iris's screams didn't sound like normal crying.

David appeared in the doorway, hair sticking up, eyes bloodshot. "Still screaming?"

"Gave her Tylenol two hours ago." Caroline's throat felt raw. "Dr. Patterson said teething could be rough, but this---"

Iris's face had gone purple.

David took the baby. For ten seconds, Iris went quiet. Then her mouth opened and released a sound that shook the windows.

"Jesus." David stared into her mouth. "Look at her gums."

Caroline leaned closer. In the nightlight's glow, she could see Iris's gums had swollen into angry ridges. But they weren't just swollen---something sharp was pushing through from inside. Multiple somethings.

"That's not normal."David's jaw tightened.

"Maybe we should call Dr. Patterson again."

"At midnight?"

"Look at her, Caroline. This isn't---"

Iris's screams stopped mid-shriek. Cut off like someone had hit a switch.

The silence felt worse than the screaming.

The baby lay still in David's arms, watching them with eyes that looked too old. When Caroline reached toward her, Iris opened her mouth---not to cry, but like she was testing something.

"Babies don't just stop like that," Caroline whispered.

Day Two - Friday Morning

Iris hadn't cried since midnight, but she hadn't slept either. She lay in her crib with wide eyes, tracking movements around the room with the focus of something much older.

Mrs. Kowalski knocked at six AM, standing on their porch in her pink bathrobe.

"Sorry to bother you so early." She pulled the robe tight. "I was worried about little Iris. She was crying so hard yesterday."

Caroline tried to smile. "She's fine. Just teething."

Now Caroline told David about the conversation over coffee that had gone cold an hour ago. "She hasn't made a sound since last night. Not once."

"That's good, right? Pain must be getting better."

"Look at her gums."

They both walked to the crib where Iris's lower gums had split open during the night. Four white points caught the thin sunlight filtering through the mini-blinds. Caroline had expected small, gentle bumps like her sister described with her kids.

"Those look..." David's voice died.

"Sharp." Caroline finished. "They look really sharp."

The teeth were like tiny needles, far more pointed than any baby teeth should be. And bigger too---too big for Iris's small mouth.

"We're calling Dr. Patterson."

"It's Saturday. Emergency line only."

"This qualifies."

Iris turned her head toward David's voice with precision that made Caroline's breath catch. Most babies her age still had unfocused gazes, but Iris seemed to follow their conversation.

Caroline reached down to stroke Iris's cheek. The baby's mouth opened in what might have been a yawn, revealing additional teeth that had emerged overnight---six sharp points now, gleaming white against swollen pink gums.

And they curved. Like fangs.

Day Three - Saturday Morning

By Friday evening, neighbors had started asking questions. Mr. Peterson from across the street mentioned the "unusual crying patterns" when David got their mail. Even Jerry, their mailman, had asked if everything was okay.

"People are noticing," David said that night as they watched Iris lie motionless in her crib, those dark eyes tracking their movements.

"Noticing what? That our baby stopped crying? That should be good news."

"Not the way she stopped. Mrs. Rodriguez said it sounded like someone flipped a switch."

Saturday morning's emergency appointment with Dr. Patterson felt surreal. The familiar pediatric office with its cartoon animals and bright yellow walls seemed wrong somehow, like the cheerful decorations were mocking whatever was growing in Iris's mouth.

"I can see why you're concerned." Dr. Patterson adjusted her penlight. Caroline had known her since childhood---Dr. Patterson had delivered Caroline herself twenty-eight years ago, and her graying hair and steady hands always made parents feel calmer. "These are unusual formations."

Iris lay still during the examination, those dark eyes fixed on Dr. Patterson's face with unnerving intensity.

"How many teeth can you see?" Dr. Patterson asked, using a tongue depressor.

"Eight, I think?" Caroline leaned closer. "Is that too many?"

"It's faster than average, but not unheard of." Dr. Patterson made notes, but her expression showed growing concern. "However, the shape is quite unusual. Much sharper than I'd typically expect."

"Unusual how?" David leaned forward.

"Most infant teeth emerge with blunt edges---nature's way of protecting during nursing. These are remarkably pointed." She made more notes, her pen moving slower. "I'd like to get Dr. Hendricks' opinion. He specializes in unusual dental development."

"Are you worried?" Caroline's voice climbed higher.

Dr. Patterson chose her words with care. "I want to make sure we understand what we're seeing."

Day Four - Sunday Afternoon

Saturday passed in tense quiet. Iris refused her bottle, and Caroline jumped at every sound from the nursery. Twice she'd heard what sounded like movement when the baby should have been sleeping, but each time she checked, Iris lay still with those unsettling dark eyes wide open.

Sunday morning brought a call from Caroline's sister in Portland.

"How's my favorite niece?" Jennifer asked. "Mom said she's been teething pretty hard."

Caroline glanced toward the nursery, where grinding sounds had started again around dawn. "She's... adjusting."

"Well, if you need any advice, Tommy's teeth came in rough too. Though he was never as dramatic as what Mom described."

After hanging up, Caroline realized how cut off they'd become. Three days since she'd left the house except for the doctor visit. Three days of screening calls and avoiding neighbors' concerned looks.

That afternoon, Iris turned away from everything---bottle, formula, even water from a sippy cup. She pressed her small lips into a thin line and refused it all.

"She has to eat something," David said. "Babies don't just stop eating."

Caroline started to answer when Iris's mouth opened in what looked like a yawn. She counted twelve razor-sharp points breaking through the swollen gums. Not the broad, flat surfaces of normal baby teeth, but narrow, curved edges that caught the afternoon light streaming through the nursery window.

"David." Her voice came out as a whisper. "Look."

He bent over the crib and went still. "Holy shit."

"Language," Caroline said automatically, then realized how ridiculous that sounded. Iris's new teeth looked like miniature daggers.

Dr. Hendricks' office felt different from Dr. Patterson's practice. Institutional beige walls instead of cheerful pastels, and the examination equipment looked more like surgical instruments than pediatric tools. The man himself was tall and angular, with silver hair and hands that moved with clinical precision.

"Dr. Patterson indicated concerning dental development," he said, reviewing notes. "Rapid emergence with unusual morphology."

"That's putting it mildly," David said.

Dr. Hendricks gestured toward the examination chair. "Let's see what we're dealing with."

Iris lay still as he positioned his equipment and adjusted the overhead light. Unlike her behavior with Dr. Patterson, she seemed eager for this examination, opening her mouth without being asked.

"Remarkable," Dr. Hendricks said, adjusting his loupes. "Quite remarkable indeed."

He used a dental probe to gently touch one of Iris's teeth. The baby didn't flinch or pull away. Instead, she seemed to press her tooth against the instrument, testing its sharpness.

"Dr. Hendricks?" Caroline's voice sounded small in the sterile room.

He continued his examination in silence, taking digital photographs and making detailed measurements. When he straightened, his expression remained neutral.

"I've seen nothing quite like this in thirty years of practice," he said. "The rate of eruption is unprecedented, and the morphology..." He paused. "These formations serve a specific purpose."

"What kind of purpose?" David asked.

"They're designed for tearing. For penetrating and tearing flesh."

The room fell silent except for the whir of the computer fan and the distant sound of a phone ringing down the hall.

Caroline's stomach lurched. "Are you saying our daughter isn't normal?"

"I'm saying her dental development follows no pattern I've encountered." Dr. Hendricks pulled up the digital images on his computer screen. "These formations continue deep into the jaw. There appear to be additional rows developing beneath the surface."

The X-ray images showed white shapes like tiny spears lined up in perfect rows, far more than any human mouth should contain.

"How many?" David whispered.

"Difficult to determine. But significantly more than standard primary dentition." Dr. Hendricks saved the images to a file. "I'm recommending consultation with specialists at the university medical center."

"Specialists in what?"

"Developmental anomalies. Genetic variations." He paused. "And behavioral psychology."

Day Five - Monday Morning

They never made it to the University Medical Center.

Sunday night had been the worst yet. The grinding sounds from Iris's crib grew louder, more aggressive, joined by what sounded like scratching against the wooden rails. Caroline dozed on the living room couch, jerking awake every time she heard movement upstairs.

Monday morning brought Mrs. Garcia from the corner house, walking her dog past their front yard.

"Hope you don't mind my asking," she said through the screen door, "but is everything alright? My Rex has been acting strange all weekend---whimpering, refusing to walk past your house. Dogs sense things, you know."

Caroline deflected the conversation, but the woman's worried expression stuck with her.

That night, Iris stopped sleeping entirely. She lay in her crib with eyes wide open, staring at the ceiling with an intensity that made Caroline afraid to approach. Not crying, not fussing. Just watching.

The grinding started around midnight.

At first, Caroline thought it was the house settling or maybe the refrigerator making noise. But when she crept to the nursery door, she realized the sound came from Iris's crib.

The baby was grinding her new teeth together, producing a sound like knives being sharpened. Her jaw worked methodically, testing the points of her growing fangs against each other.

"Jesus Christ," David whispered. "How many teeth does she have?"

Caroline made herself look into the crib. Multiple rows of sharp white points filled Iris's mouth. Her gums had split to make room, blood staining the crib sheet.

Iris turned toward them and opened her mouth wider. Her tongue had turned black.

Caroline stumbled backward.

"We need to call someone." Caroline's voice shook.

"Who? Dr. Hendricks said he'd never seen anything like this."

"Then we call someone else. A specialist. A---" She stopped herself before saying "priest," but the word hung between them.

Iris's mouth snapped shut with an audible click of teeth. The grinding resumed.

Day Six - Tuesday Morning

Caroline woke to find their garbage cans overturned. Trash scattered across the yard in patterns that looked deliberate. Bite marks on the metal lids---too sharp for a dog or raccoon.

Mrs. Kowalski knocked at ten. "Have you seen Mittens? She never stays out all night." Caroline shook her head.

"Sorry, no."

"She was playing in your yard yesterday evening." Mrs. Kowalski peered past Caroline. "How's the baby? Haven't heard her crying."

"She's... better."

After Mrs. Kowalski left, Caroline checked the backyard. Near the porch steps, she found disturbed earth and gray fur caught on the lattice.

Blood stained the white steps. Still wet.

"David." Her voice broke. "Come here."

He came out carrying Iris. The baby looked around the yard.

"What is it?" David asked, then saw the bloodstains. "What the hell?"

Caroline pointed to the disturbed earth and fur. "Mrs. Kowalski's cat was playing in our yard yesterday."

They stared at the evidence in silence until David said, "Cats fight. Maybe something bigger attacked it."

"What could do this?" Caroline gestured at the blood. "And where's the body?"

Iris made a soft sound in David's arms---not quite a coo, but something that might have been contentment. When they both looked down at her, she was smiling.

Her mouth stretched wide, showing rows of needle-sharp teeth stained pink with blood.

Day Seven - Wednesday

The whole neighborhood had changed.

Tuesday night, Caroline watched Mr. Peterson stand in his driveway staring at their house for an hour. When she waved, he turned and went inside.

The Jeffersons installed motion-sensor lights that swept across their yard every few minutes. Even joggers crossed to the other side of the street.

Wednesday morning, Caroline found their mail scattered on the sidewalk where Jerry, their mailman, had dropped it.

Caroline found Jerry three houses down, loading mail into his truck.

"Jerry? What's with all our mail on the sidewalk?"

He looked up. Jerry looked awful---pale, dark circles under his eyes.

"I'm not going near your door." His voice was flat. "Something's wrong with your place."

"What do you mean?"

"Been doing this route fifteen years. I know when a house feels wrong." His hands shook sorting letters. "Yesterday I heard growling from inside. And the smell..." He shook his head. "What's that smell coming from your place?"

Caroline's stomach dropped. She'd noticed it too---something sweet and metallic that seemed to seep from the nursery despite constant cleaning. "It's just... we've been having plumbing issues."

"That's not plumbing." Jerry climbed into his truck. "I'm sorry, but I can't go up there. I'll leave your mail at the curb until whatever's happening gets resolved."

Walking back to the house, Caroline caught the scent Jerry mentioned---stronger outside than in, as if the smell was leaking through the walls. Sweet, metallic, and underneath it all, something else that reminded her of meat left too long in the sun.

Inside, she found David in the kitchen, staring at an empty formula can.

"We're out," he said. "Iris won't take the bottle anyway, but we're out."

"When did you last feed her?"

David rubbed his face. "I don't know. Three days? Four? She refuses everything we offer."

"David, babies can't survive without eating for four days."

"I know that." His voice carried an edge of hysteria. "But look at her. Does she look like she's starving?"

Caroline walked to the living room where Iris lay in her bouncy seat. Her breath caught---the baby had grown, not dramatically, but noticeably. Fuller cheeks, more robust limbs, thicker dark hair. Those terrible eyes seemed brighter, more alert.

"She's gaining weight," Caroline said.

"On what? She hasn't eaten anything we've given her."

They stared at their daughter, who gazed back with unsettling awareness. Iris's mouth remained closed, though Caroline could see the outline of teeth pressing against her lips---so many teeth her mouth couldn't contain them.

"What is she eating?" Caroline asked.

Neither of them wanted to answer that question.

Day Eight – Thursday Night

The breaking point came after dark.

David had spent Wednesday afternoon replacing the kitchen window screen, which they'd found shredded that morning. The tears looked deliberate, made by something with claws sharp enough to slice through metal mesh.

"Maybe it was raccoons," he'd said, but his voice carried no conviction.

By evening, three neighbors had called the police to report "disturbing sounds" from their address. Caroline learned this when Officer Martinez knocked on their door around six PM.

"We've had some calls about possible domestic disturbance," Officer Martinez explained. He looked barely old enough to be out of the academy, with careful eyes that took in every detail. "Just wanted to check that everything's okay."

Caroline invited him in, showed him through the house, even introduced him to Iris, who smiled sweetly from her high chair with her lips closed over those terrible teeth.

""Cute baby," Officer Martinez said. "How old?"

"Seven months."

"Big kid." He looked around the nursery---scratched crib rails, stained carpet. "Looks fine to me. Just keep it quiet at night, okay? Neighbors are complaining."

That night, Caroline woke to sounds from the nursery. Not crying---movement. The crib creaking like Iris was pulling herself up and dropping down.

But seven-month-olds couldn't stand yet.

Caroline crept down the hall. The nursery door stood open. Moonlight showed the crib in silhouette.

Empty.

Her heart hammered as she pushed the door wider. Baby blankets lay tumbled and dark-stained. The mobile swayed like something had just disturbed it.

"Iris?" Caroline's voice came out as a breath, then she felt foolish---the baby couldn't have climbed out on her own.

A soft sound from the corner. In the shadows by the changing table, Caroline saw a small shape moving. Tiny shoulders shifted. Soft tearing sounds, then chewing.

"Iris?"

The baby turned.

Caroline's scream died in her throat.

Iris's mouth was black with blood, multiple rows of teeth gleaming. Strips of raw meat hung between them. Her eyes reflected moonlight like an animal's.

At her feet lay what was left of Mrs. Kowalski's cat.

Caroline stumbled backward. Iris watched her, then tore off another piece of flesh and chewed.

The sound of tiny teeth on bone filled the room.

Day Nine - Friday, 3 AM

After cleaning up the cat's remains, Caroline sat at the kitchen table staring at cold coffee. David slumped across from her, face gray with exhaustion.

They'd spent Thursday scrubbing blood from carpet and disposing of bone fragments. When Mrs. Garcia brought them a casserole, they'd smiled and said thank you.

The whole time, Iris watched from her bouncy seat, making soft sounds of contentment.

"We can't tell anyone," Caroline said. "Who would believe us?"

"The specialists at the university---"

"Would do what? Take her away? Study her?" Caroline's voice rose, then dropped to a whisper. "She's still our daughter."

"Is she?" David gestured toward the ceiling, where soft sounds of movement came from the nursery above. "Look what she did to that cat, Caroline. Look what she's becoming."

They'd cleaned up the remains before dawn, working in horrified silence as Iris watched from her crib with satisfied eyes. The nursery carpet would need replacing, but that seemed like the least of their problems.

"She's just feeding." The words felt strange in Caroline's mouth. "All babies need to eat."

"Not like this. Not---" David stopped himself, running shaking hands through his hair. "Caroline, she's getting bigger. Stronger. What happens when cats aren't enough?"

The question hung between them like a physical presence.

From upstairs came the sound of the crib creaking, followed by a soft thud as Iris dropped to the floor. They'd moved anything dangerous out of the nursery, but somehow Caroline doubted that would matter much longer.

"Maybe we could find roadkill." Caroline's voice was barely audible. "Deer that cars have hit. Fresh meat that's already dead."

David stared at her. "Listen to yourself. Listen to what you're saying."

"What choice do we have?" Caroline's throat closed around the words. "She's our baby. Our daughter. We can't just abandon her."

"She killed a cat with her bare teeth, Caroline. She's seven months old and she can climb out of her crib and hunt. What do you think happens next?"

More sounds from upstairs---a scraping that might have been Iris dragging something across the floor. They'd given her toys, hoping to redirect her attention, but she showed no interest in stuffed animals or plastic blocks.

"We'll figure it out." Caroline's words came out as a breath. "We'll manage this."

"Manage?" David laughed, a sound with no humor in it. "You want to manage a monster?"

"Don't call her that." Caroline's voice turned sharp. "She's not a monster. She's just different."

"Different?" David's voice rose. "Caroline, she's a predator. She hunts and kills and feeds, and she's getting better at it every day. How is that not a monster?"

Caroline stared down at her hands. "Because she's ours."

Day Ten - Saturday Evening

The Jefferson family went missing Friday night, but Caroline didn't learn about it until Saturday's evening news.

Friday had started normally enough---if anything about their situation could be called normal---with Iris spending most of the afternoon sleeping in her crib while Caroline convinced herself that maybe, somehow, the worst was over.

Then Mrs. Rodriguez had knocked around noon, her face pale with worry.

"Have you seen the Jeffersons? Jim was supposed to help my husband with yard work yesterday, but he never showed up. Their car's in the driveway, but nobody answers the door."

Caroline had promised to keep an eye out, but icy dread settled in her stomach.

Now, watching the local news report, she learned what she'd suspected. Police found no signs of forced entry, no evidence of struggle, no indication where they might have gone.

"It's like they walked out of their lives," the reporter said, standing in front of the Jefferson's modest ranch house. "Dinner was still on the table, the TV was running. Even the family dog was found locked in the basement, apparently hidden there."

Caroline muted the television and sat in horrified silence.

That night, Iris had been quieter than usual---no creaking from the crib, no sounds of movement across the nursery floor. When Caroline checked on her around midnight, she found the baby sleeping for the first time in days.

Iris looked bigger again---noticeably bigger, with seven-month-old clothing that no longer fit and features that had changed. Still recognizably a baby, but somehow more defined, more mature.

And she smelled different. Not the sour milk smell of normal babies, but something else that reminded Caroline of fresh meat.

"David." Caroline's voice came out as a breath.

He appeared in the nursery doorway. Together they stared down at their sleeping daughter, whose face was peaceful in the soft glow of the nightlight. Dark hair had grown longer, framing features that seemed older than her months.

"She's beautiful." Caroline meant it.

"She's terrifying," David said, but his voice held the same helpless love that Caroline felt.

Iris stirred in her sleep, and her mouth fell open, revealing multiple rows of razor-sharp teeth that caught the light, still faintly stained with something dark.

"What are we going to do?" David asked.

Caroline reached down and stroked Iris's cheek with gentle fingers. The baby's skin was warm and soft, like any other child's. "We're going to take care of her. We're going to love her."

"And when she gets bigger? When she needs more?"

Caroline was quiet for a long moment. "We'll figure it out."

"Caroline---"

"We'll figure it out." Her voice grew stronger. "She's our daughter. Our responsibility."

Iris opened her eyes and looked up at them both. For a moment, Caroline thought she saw something human in that watchful gaze---something that might have been love, or gratitude, or recognition.

Then Iris smiled, revealing those terrible teeth, and Caroline smiled back.

Three Months Later

The missing persons reports had stopped making the news after the first month. People disappeared sometimes, especially from the area around Richmond Street. Police theories ranged from serial killers to human trafficking to people choosing to start new lives somewhere else.

Caroline pushed the stroller through the quiet residential neighborhood, nodding to the few neighbors she encountered. Iris sat upright in the stroller---no longer the seven-month-old baby she'd been three months ago, but not quite the toddler she appeared to be either.

She looked like a healthy eighteen-month-old now, with thick dark hair and bright, alert eyes. Her clothing was age-appropriate, her behavior normal for public outings. She babbled occasionally, though she'd never spoken a word.

Only Caroline and David knew Iris could walk---could run, with speed and coordination that defied her apparent age. Only they knew about her strength, about the way she could climb and hunt and plan with intelligence that was both childlike and alien.

Only they knew about her needs.

"Such a beautiful baby," Mrs. Garcia from the corner house said, stopping to peer into the stroller. "How old is she now?"

"Fifteen months." Caroline's response came out smooth as silk. "Getting so big."

Mrs. Garcia reached out to touch Iris's hand. The baby smiled up at her with perfect innocence, her teeth remaining hidden behind closed lips.

"She looks so healthy. So well-fed."

"We take good care of her," Caroline said, and meant it.

After Mrs. Garcia walked away, Caroline continued her stroll through the neighborhood, noting which houses had lights on, which driveways were empty, which families might travel for the holidays.

Iris gurgled with contentment in her stroller, dark eyes scanning the houses with the same attention as her mother.

At home, David had prepared the basement with soundproofing, proper drainage, and locks that could only be opened from the outside. It looked like an ordinary playroom now, complete with colorful toys and educational posters.

But it served a different purpose.

Caroline had stopped feeling guilty about it weeks ago. This was how their life worked now. They had a daughter to feed, to care for, to love. She had special needs, but that didn't make her less deserving of their devotion.

"Mama," Iris said---her first intelligible word.

Caroline's heart swelled with pride and fierce protective love. "Yes, baby. Mama's here."

Iris pointed toward a house at the end of the street where children's bikes lay scattered across the front lawn. A family with several young children Caroline had seen playing in their yard.

"Hungry," Iris said---her second word.

Caroline smiled and adjusted their route toward the house with the bikes. "Soon, sweetheart. Mama will take care of everything."

As they approached the house, Caroline could see through the front window to where a young mother was making dinner while two small children played at her feet. A perfect family, living their perfect life, unaware that everything was about to change.

Iris clapped her hands together, obviously excited. Caroline reached down to stroke her daughter's hair.

"That's my good girl." The words came out as a breath. "Mama loves you so much."

The late afternoon sun painted the quiet suburban street in shades of amber as Caroline rang the doorbell, composing her face into the expression of a concerned neighbor.

She had a daughter to feed, after all.

And family always came first.

Summer Rental

David Fletcher killed the Honda's engine and sat there a moment, letting the silence wash over him. Christ, when was the last time he'd heard actual quiet? Not the muffled-through-walls kind from their apartment in Fishtown, but real silence that stretched past the horizon. Corn whispered somewhere in the heat, and a cow bawled in the distance like it was complaining about the weather.

"This is it?" Susan unbuckled her seatbelt and leaned forward, squinting through the bug-splattered windshield at the white cottage tucked between rolling green fields. "Looks smaller than the photos."

"Jesus, it's perfect." David unfolded himself from the driver's seat, his back giving that familiar protest. Four hours of Susan reading directions off her phone because he was too cheap to spring for GPS, four hours of her sighing every time they missed an exit. But out here, the August heat felt different. Clean. No bus exhaust, no hot concrete throwing the sun back in his face. "Look at that."

Susan stepped out, brushing highway dust off her jeans. Lancaster County spread in patches of green and gold, dotted with red barns and white farmhouses that might've been there since Lincoln. A horse-drawn buggy moved along the distant road, wheels grinding against asphalt.

"No bars." Susan waved her phone at the sky.

"Good. We came here to unplug, remember?" David pulled their luggage from the trunk---the big case with the busted zipper, the duffel bag Susan had owned since college. "Three months away from Patterson's deadlines and budget meetings and---"

"Mr. and Mrs. Fletcher?"

They turned. A man came across the field toward them, moving with the unhurried pace of someone who'd never owned a wristwatch. Plain dark shirt, black suspenders, the kind of hands that knew tools better than keyboards. David had seen Amish before---tourists trips to Lancaster---but never this close, never on their own turf.

"Jacob Yoder." His handshake could crack walnuts. "We spoke on the telephone."

"Yeah, thanks for---wait." David frowned. "I thought you guys didn't use phones."

"Only when we must. Phone shanty at the end of the lane." Jacob nodded toward the cottage. "The Batemans, they were eager for their retirement."

"When can we meet them?" Susan asked. "To thank them?"

"Soon enough." Jacob nodded toward the house. "First, you settle. My wife Mary brings supper at seven. The community, we welcome you."

He turned and walked back across the field, his dark figure fading between the corn.

"Friendly enough," David said.

Susan watched until she couldn't see Jacob anymore. "Did that sound rehearsed to you?"

"What?"

"What he said about the Batemans being eager for retirement."

David hefted their luggage, the duffel bag's strap already cutting into his shoulder. "You're overthinking. Come on, let's see what we're paying for."

Key under the ceramic rooster, just like Jacob said. The front door stuck, then gave way to air that smelled like lemon oil and old fabric. Living room straight out of 1987---quilts everywhere, oak furniture that could survive a nuclear war, braided rugs that probably took someone a year to make. In the kitchen, the refrigerator shuddered to life like it was dying.

"No dishwasher." Susan opened cupboards.

"No TV either. Or WiFi." David grinned. "Remember those? Books? Actual conversation?"

Susan opened the refrigerator. Mason jars lined the shelves---pickles, preserves, fresh milk with cream floating on top. A covered casserole dish bore a note in flowing script: *Welcome. Enjoy the pot roast. ---Eleanor and Harold Bateman.*

"That's thoughtful." David read over her shoulder.

"Very." Susan lifted the foil. The pot roast smelled like rosemary and thyme, steam still rising. "Still warm."

They explored the rest of the cottage. Two bedrooms, one bathroom with a clawfoot tub, and a screened porch overlooking the cornfield. Everything was clean and carefully arranged, like the Batemans had stepped out for groceries and would be back any minute.

"Their clothes are still here," Susan called from the master bedroom.

David found her standing before an open armoire. Men's black suits hung beside plain dresses in dark blues and grays. The clothing looked handmade, with careful stitching and fabric that would last decades.

"Maybe they're coming back for them."

Susan fingered one of the dresses. Heavy fabric, hand-stitched. "These aren't Amish."

"How can you tell?"

"No prayer cap. No cape thing." She'd done her homework before the trip, read about local customs. "These look almost like..." She couldn't finish the thought. Costumes. Like something you'd wear to play a part.

David dropped onto the bed. Firm mattress, quilt that someone had spent months stitching by hand. "You've been wound up since we left Philly. What's eating you?"

"Nothing." But she was already at the window, arms crossed. Outside, corn stretched forever, rows disappearing into heat shimmer. "I just thought they'd be here. The Batemans. To, you know, show us where the coffee is."

"Jacob said they were eager to start their retirement. Maybe they already left for Florida or wherever."

"Without their clothes?"

David joined her at the window. The sun hung low, turning the corn tips golden. In the distance, he could see the Yoder farmhouse, smoke rising from its chimney even in this heat.

"Look," he said, wrapping his arms around her waist. "We both needed this. You've been pulling seventy-hour weeks at the firm, I've been on the road constantly. Let's not hunt for problems."

Susan leaned against him. "You're right. I'm being paranoid."

Someone knocked. They found a small woman in the doorway, basket in her arms. Dark blue dress, white cap, face that had seen seventy years of hard work and easy faith.

"Mrs. Fletcher? Mary Yoder. I bring supper."

"You don't have to---"

"Is no trouble." Already moving to the kitchen, unpacking like she owned the place. Fresh bread, butter, green beans, and apple pie that smelled like cinnamon and brown sugar.

"The cottage suits?"

"It's great. Really peaceful out here."

"Ja. Peace is gift." Mary lined up the plates with surgical precision. "The Batemans found their peace."

"How long did they live here?" Susan asked.

Mary paused, her hands hovering over the pie. "They came in May. Like you."

"Just three months? That's not very long for retirement."

"Time moves different here," Mary said. "Some find what they seek quickly."

She finished setting the table and gathered her empty basket. "Tomorrow you meet the community. There will be... preparations."

"What kind of preparations?" David asked.

Mary smiled, but her eyes stayed serious. "You understand when the time comes. Enjoy your supper."

The door clicked shut behind her. David and Susan looked at each other across the kitchen table.

"Preparations for what?"

"Hell if I know. Barn raising? Quilting bee?" But he didn't sound convinced.

They ate without talking, watching night swallow the cornfield. The food should have been perfect---homemade bread, green beans with real bacon. But Susan kept pushing it around her plate.

"The Batemans left everything."

"What do you mean?"

"Fridge full of food. Fresh milk." She set down her fork. "People don't just walk away like that."

David set down his fork. "Susan, you're doing it again."

"Doing what?"

"Looking for mysteries. Remember that B&B in Vermont? You convinced yourself the owners were laundering money because they had too many antiques."

"This is different."

"How?"

"They weren't Amish." Susan pushed her plate away. "This is an insular community. They have their own rules for handling outsiders."

"They've been nothing but welcoming."

"Have they? Jacob appeared the second we arrived, like he was watching. Mary brought supper but wouldn't answer direct questions. And where are the Batemans?"

David reached across the table and took her hand. "Maybe they moved to a retirement community. Maybe they wanted a fresh start."

"Without their clothes? Without cleaning out the refrigerator?"

"Maybe they were in a hurry."

Susan pulled her hand away. "Or maybe they didn't leave voluntarily."

David let that sit between them. Outside, crickets began their evening chorus. Somewhere in the distance, a cow lowed mournfully.

"You think the Amish murdered the previous tenants?" David asked.

"I think something's wrong. The way Jacob talked about their retirement sounded scripted. Mary couldn't give a straight answer about how long they lived here. And why would people who just moved somewhere in May already be eager to retire again?"

David stood and began clearing dishes. "Maybe because they were already retired when they came here? Maybe they were looking for a quiet place and decided this wasn't right for them?"

"And left all their belongings?"

"Rich people do strange things."

Susan helped stack the plates. "We're not rich people, David. We're renting this place for the summer because it was all we could afford. Rich people don't rent cottages in Amish country."

They washed dishes in silence. The kitchen window faced the field, and Susan found herself staring into the dark rows. The corn looked taller than this morning, or maybe the shadows made it seem that way.

"I'm taking a bath."

"Good idea. I'll read on the porch."

The clawfoot tub filled slowly with lukewarm water. Susan sank into it and tried to relax, but her mind kept circling back to the Batemans. Who left fresh food in the refrigerator and warm pot roast in the oven? Who abandoned an entire wardrobe of carefully made clothes?

She was toweling off when she heard voices outside. David's and another man's, talking quietly on the porch. She dressed quickly and joined them.

A tall, bearded man stood with David at the porch railing. He wore similar plain clothing to Jacob, but his beard was darker, less gray.

"This is Eli Beiler," David said. "He lives on the next farm over."

Eli nodded slightly. "Mrs. Fletcher. I hope you find peace here."

"Thank you." Susan studied his face. His eyes were pale blue, and he had the same careful way of speaking. "Did you know the Batemans?"

"Ja, all summer. Good people. Quiet."

"Why did they leave so suddenly?"

Eli glanced at David. "They completed their time."

"Their time for what?"

"Their time here. As you will complete yours."

Susan felt a chill despite the evening heat. "What do you mean?"

"The season has its rhythm," Eli said. "Those who come in spring depart in fall. It has always been so."

"Are you saying we have to leave in the fall?"

"You understand when the time comes." Eli adjusted his hat. "Good evening."

He disappeared into the corn, swallowed by shadows.

"What the hell was that about?" Susan asked.

David leaned against the porch railing. "Cultural thing, maybe. They might have seasonal leases or something."

"Seasonal leases don't involve people disappearing and leaving all their belongings behind."

"We don't know they disappeared. Maybe they just left in a hurry."

Susan sat in one of the porch rockers. The wood creaked under her weight. "David, I want to leave."

"What?"

"Tomorrow. I want to pack up and go home."

David sat in the other rocker. "Susan, come on. We've been here six hours."

"Six hours too long."

"We paid for the whole summer. Non-refundable deposit, remember? That was our vacation money for the year."

Susan rocked faster. "There's something wrong with this place. Wrong with these people."

"They're just different. Traditional."

"No, it's more than that." She turned to face him. "Promise me something."

"What?"

"If anything else happens---anything that makes you uncomfortable---we leave immediately. No discussion, no rationalizing. We just get in the car and drive."

David reached over and took her hand. "If it makes you feel better, yes. I promise."

But Susan didn't feel better. She felt like they'd walked into a trap that was slowly closing around them.

They went to bed early, exhausted from the drive and the tension. The cottage was absolutely quiet except for the old refrigerator's rattling and the settling of wooden boards. Susan lay awake listening to David's breathing, watching shadows move across the ceiling as clouds passed over the moon.

She must have dozed, because she woke to singing.

The voices came from outside, rising and falling in harmony. Susan slipped out of bed and crept to the window. The cornfield was bathed in moonlight, the rows stretching away like silver streams.

At first she saw nothing. Then movement caught her eye---figures walking between the corn rows, their pale dresses ghostly in the moonlight. Women's voices, singing something that sounded like a hymn but in no language she recognized.

Susan watched them pass, counting at least a dozen figures moving through the field. The singing grew louder as they approached the cottage, then faded as they moved toward the Yoder farm.

"David," she whispered.

He stirred but didn't wake. Susan watched the field until the last voice faded and the corn stood empty under the moon.

The next morning dawned clear and hot. Susan woke to the smell of bacon and coffee. She found David in the kitchen, fully dressed and cooking breakfast.

"You're up early," she said.

"Jacob came by. He wants to show us around the community today." "When?"

"After breakfast. Said it's important that we meet everyone."

Susan poured coffee from the old percolator on the stove. It was strong and bitter, nothing like the mild roast they drank at home. "Did you hear anything last night? Singing?"

David flipped bacon in the cast iron pan. "No. Why?"

"There were women walking through the cornfield. Singing hymns."

"Probably evening prayers or something. The Amish are very religious."

"At midnight? In the cornfield?"

David turned to look at her. "Susan, you're doing it again."

"I know what I saw."

"Maybe you dreamed it."

Susan sipped her coffee. It left a metallic taste in her mouth. "Maybe."

But she knew she hadn't dreamed it. The image was too clear---pale figures moving through silver corn, voices rising in strange harmony.

Jacob arrived as they finished breakfast, riding in a horse-drawn buggy. He wore his usual dark clothing, his beard neatly combed.

"Guten Morgen," he called. "Are you ready to meet your neighbors?"

They climbed into the buggy, David in front beside Jacob, Susan in the back seat. The horse was a sturdy brown gelding with intelligent eyes. Its hooves clip-clopped against the gravel.

"How long have you lived here?"

"I was born here," Jacob said. "As was my father, and his father. This land, it has been in our families for generations."

"Must be nice to have such deep roots."

"Ja, roots are important. They anchor us to what matters."

They drove past fields of corn and alfalfa, past barns where black and white cattle grazed in whatever shade they could find. The farms looked prosperous and well-maintained, with neat gardens and freshly painted buildings.

"Do you get many visitors?" Susan asked.

"Some," Jacob said. "Tourists seeking our way of life. But few stay long."

"Why not?"

Jacob guided the horse around a pothole. "Our way is not for everyone. It requires... commitment."

They stopped at the Beiler farm, where Eli introduced them to his wife Ruth and their three children. The family was courteous but reserved, speaking in low voices and watching Susan and David with careful eyes.

At the next farm, they met the Stoltzfus family---an elderly couple named Samuel and Anna who had lived in the area for sixty years. Anna served them fresh lemonade and asked polite questions about their life in Philadelphia.

"The city must be very different," Anna said, her English heavily accented.

"Very different," Susan agreed. "Louder. More crowded."

"Do you miss it?"

Susan considered the question. "I miss some things. Restaurants. Museums. The energy."

Anna nodded. "The Batemans, they missed the city at first."

"You knew them well?"

"Well enough. They came in spring, full of plans. Wanted to learn our ways, to live simply."

"What happened to them?"

Anna's face closed off. "They found what they were looking for."

"Which was?"

"Peace. Rest. An end to struggle."

Susan felt the same chill she'd experienced the night before. "Where did they go?"

Anna stood and began collecting the empty glasses. "They went where all must go, in time."

The conversation ended there. They visited two more farms, meeting more families with the same pattern---initial friendliness followed by careful evasion when Susan asked about the Batemans.

On the ride back to the cottage, Jacob was quiet. The sun beat down on the buggy, and sweat trickled down Susan's back. The cornfield pressed closer to the road, the green stalks rustling in the hot breeze.

"Jacob," Susan said finally. "What happened to the Batemans?"

He didn't answer immediately. The horse's hooves struck the gravel in steady rhythm.

"They completed their purpose here," he said at last.

"What purpose?"

"Each who comes has a purpose. You will discover yours."

"I don't understand."

Jacob turned to look at her, his blue eyes serious. "You will. When the time comes, you understand everything."

That afternoon, David napped on the porch while Susan explored the cottage more thoroughly. She found the Batemans' belongings in every room---books, toiletries, reading glasses, a half-finished cross-word puzzle. Everything suggested people who had planned to stay indefinitely.

In the bedroom armoire, behind the dark clothing, she discovered a journal. The cover was leather, worn smooth by handling. She opened it to the first page.

May 15th - Arrived at the cottage today. Harold is so excited to finally retire from the insurance business. The Amish community has been welcoming, though somewhat formal. Looking forward to a quiet summer.

Susan flipped through the pages. Eleanor Bateman had written nearly every day, documenting their gradual integration into community life. The entries were cheerful at first, full of observations about Amish customs and descriptions of their new neighbors.

June 2nd - Attended a barn raising today. Amazing to watch the community work together. Jacob Yoder explained that they help each other because they are all part of something larger. I'm beginning to understand what he means.

June 18th - Mary Yoder brought us traditional Amish clothing to try. Says we should dress properly for the summer celebration. The clothes feel strange but somehow right. Harold looks handsome in his black coat.

July 4th - No fireworks here, of course, but we attended a community gathering. They sang hymns in what I think was German. Beautiful harmonies. I felt moved to tears, though I couldn't understand the words.

Susan turned pages faster, looking for recent entries. The handwriting grew shakier as the weeks progressed.

July 20th - Harold has been having dreams. He sees us walking through the cornfield at midnight, dressed in white. He says it feels like a memory, not a dream. I've been having the same visions.

July 28th - Jacob explained about the harvest ceremony. Says it's been celebrated here for generations. We are to play an important role. I should feel honored, but I'm frightened. Harold says it's natural to fear change.

August 1st - The ceremony is tomorrow night. I understand now why we were chosen, why we came here. It wasn't accident or coincidence. We were called. Harold says we should be grateful for the honor.

August 2nd - This is my last entry. By tomorrow evening, our part will be complete. The new couple arrives soon---the Fletchers. I hope they find the same peace we have discovered. The cycle continues, as it must. I am ready.

Susan dropped the journal, her hands shaking. The pages scattered across the floor.

"David!" she called.

He appeared in the doorway, rubbing sleep from his eyes. "What's wrong?"

"We have to leave. Now." Susan scrambled to collect the journal pages. "Look at this."

David read the final entries, his face growing pale. "This is Eleanor Bateman's journal?"

"Yes. Read the dates."

"August second was... three days ago."

"The day before we arrived." Susan stuffed the pages back into the journal. "David, they didn't retire. Something happened to them during this ceremony."

David dropped onto the bed. "Maybe they just left afterward. Started fresh somewhere else."

"Without taking their journal? Without packing any belongings?" Susan moved to the armoire and pulled out one of the dark dresses. "Look at this. Eleanor wrote about wearing Amish clothing for a summer celebration. These are what they wore."

"So?"

"So they're still here, David. In the armoire. If the Batemans left after the ceremony, why didn't they take their ceremonial clothes?"

David stared at the dress in her hands. The fabric was plain but well-made, with tiny, careful stitches.

"What are you saying?" he asked.

"I'm saying they didn't leave. They're still here somewhere."

"Where?"

Susan looked out the window at the endless cornfield. The stalks rustled in the afternoon breeze, whispering secrets.

"I think I know," she said.

They spent the rest of the afternoon packing. David moved like he was drugged, while Susan threw their belongings into cases. The house felt different now---not peaceful but oppressive, like the calm before a storm.

As evening approached, they carried their bags to the car. David loaded them into the trunk while Susan took a last look around.

"We should leave a note. Thank Jacob for his hospitality."

"No." Susan climbed into the passenger seat. "Let's just go."

David started the engine, and they pulled out of the driveway. The house grew smaller in the rearview mirror until the field swallowed it completely.

They had driven less than a mile when the buggy appeared ahead of them.

Jacob and his horse blocked the road like they'd been waiting. The animal didn't even twitch when David hit the brakes.

"We need to get through, Jacob."

"Where you going?"

"Home."

"Time's not finished yet."

"Our plans changed." Susan leaned across David. "We need to leave tonight."

Jacob climbed down from the buggy and approached the car. His face was calm, but his eyes held a hardness Susan hadn't seen before.

"The ceremony is tomorrow night," he said. "You are expected to participate."

"We're not participating in anything," David said. "We're going home."

"Ach, I'm afraid that's not possible."

They came out of the corn like they'd been planted there. Eli. Mary. The Stoltzfuses. Others Susan had met, others she hadn't. They formed a semicircle around the car, black clothes against green stalks.

"Let us pass," Susan said.

Jacob shook his head. "You came here for a reason. Perhaps you don't understand that reason yet, but you will. Tomorrow night, you understand everything."

David put the car in reverse, but more figures appeared behind them. The entire community seemed to have materialized from the cornfield, surrounding their car in a tight circle.

"What the hell do you want?"

"Same thing we always want. Good harvest."

"It's August. Corn's not ready---"

"Not corn. Other things feed the soil better."

Susan's mouth went dry. "You mean us?"

"Feed the earth. Earth feeds us back." Jacob gestured at the endless corn. "Look how it grows. Never fails, never sickens. Been this way a hundred years."

"You're fucking psychotic."

"Practical."

David gunned the engine, trying to push through the circle of people. But they didn't move, and he couldn't bring himself to run them down.

"The Batemans," Susan said. "What did you do to them?"

"They served their purpose gladly, in the end. As you will."

Jacob reached into his coat and pulled out a length of rope. "Please don't make this difficult. We bear you no ill will."

David threw the car into reverse and backed toward the people behind them. They scattered, and he spun the wheel, trying to escape through the cornfield. But the car bogged down in the soft earth between the rows.

The community closed in around them. Hands reached through the windows, unlocking doors, pulling them from the car. Susan fought, kicking and clawing, but there were too many of them.

They carried her and David back to the house, their struggles useless against so many. Jacob walked beside them, speaking in the same calm tone he'd used to welcome them.

"The ceremony has been performed here for five generations. Two are chosen each season to nourish the earth. In return, the earth nourishes us."

"You're murderers."

"We are stewards. Caretakers of an ancient compact."

They reached the house as the sun set behind the field. The community dispersed to their homes, leaving Jacob and Eli to guard Susan and David. Their hands were bound with rope, their ankles tied to kitchen chairs.

"The Batemans sat in these same chairs," Jacob said, lighting an oil lamp. "They fought at first, like you. But by morning, they understood. They went to their rest peacefully."

"Where are their bodies?" David asked.

"Bodies?" Jacob seemed puzzled. "There are no bodies, Mr. Fletcher. The earth receives everything."

Susan felt sick. "You fed them to your crops."

"We fed them to the land. Their essence enriches the soil, ensures our harvest. It's an honor to be chosen."

"Chosen how?"

"The land chooses. We merely listen." Jacob sat at the kitchen table. "When outsiders come seeking our way of life, the land whispers to us. Some are chosen, some are not. You were chosen the moment you contacted us about the cottage."

"The cottage belongs to you."

"The cottage belongs to the land. As do we all, in the end."

Hours passed. Eli dozed in his chair while Jacob read from a leather-bound book written in German. Susan tested her bonds, but the rope was thick and expertly tied.

Near midnight, she heard the singing again.

Voices rose from the cornfield, dozens of women's voices joining in harmony. The sound grew closer, and Susan saw lights moving between the corn rows---lanterns swaying in the darkness.

"It's time," Jacob said.

The cottage door opened, and Mary Yoder entered, carrying the dark clothing from the armoire. Behind her came Ruth Beiler and Anna Stoltzfus, their faces solemn in the lamplight.

"Please don't make this harder than necessary," Mary said, setting the clothes on the kitchen counter. "The ceremony requires your participation, but it can be willing or unwilling."

"What's the difference?" Susan asked.

"Willing participants find peace. Unwilling ones find only fear."

Jacob cut their bonds and gestured toward the clothes. "Put them on."

Susan looked at the dark dress Eleanor Bateman had worn. The fabric felt heavy, like it was soaked with something.

"And if we refuse?"

"Then you are dressed by others and carried to the ceremony. The choice is yours."

Susan and David exchanged glances. There was no escape, no help coming. They were alone with an entire community of people who believed they were performing a sacred duty.

"We'll dress ourselves," David said quietly.

The women left the cottage while Susan and David changed clothes. The garments fit perfectly, as if they'd been tailored for them. Susan felt the weight of the fabric, heavy and final.

When they emerged from the cottage, the entire community waited in the cornfield. Men, women, and children held lanterns, their faces grave but peaceful. The singing continued, rising and falling like a tide.

Jacob took Susan's arm, Eli took David's, and they walked into the corn rows. The stalks towered above them, creating a green tunnel lit by flickering lanterns. The procession moved slowly, ceremonially, deeper into the field.

"Where are you taking us?" Susan asked.

"To the heart," Jacob said. "To the place where the compact was first made."

They walked for what felt like hours through the endless corn. Susan lost all sense of direction, seeing only the steady movement of stalks and the lanterns of the community.

Finally, they emerged into a clearing. The corn formed a perfect circle around a space perhaps fifty feet across. In the center stood a stone altar, ancient and weathered, covered with carved symbols Susan didn't recognize.

The community formed a circle around the clearing, their lanterns creating a ring of light. The singing grew louder, more intense, and Susan realized the words weren't in German. They were older than German, older than any language she knew.

Jacob led her to the altar while Eli brought David. The stone radiated heat.

"Harold and Eleanor Bateman stood here three nights ago. They gave themselves willingly to the land, and their gift has already begun to manifest. Look around you."

Susan looked. In the lantern light, she could see that the corn in this clearing was different---taller, greener, the ears fuller and heavier. The plants swayed without wind, their roots thick as tree trunks.

"You see?" Jacob smiled. "Their sacrifice was not in vain."

Mary Yoder approached the altar, carrying a wooden bowl filled with dark liquid. The smell was metallic, organic, terrifying.

"Drink," Jacob said, offering the bowl to Susan. "It will make the transition peaceful."

Susan knocked the bowl from his hands. The dark liquid splashed across the stone altar, steaming where it touched.

"No," she said. "I won't make this easy for you."

David moved beside her, taking her hand. "Neither will I."

The community began chanting now, their voices rising to the stars. The corn stalks rustled though there was no wind. The very earth shook beneath their feet.

"So be it," Jacob said sadly. "The land will take you willing or unwilling."

The altar began to glow with an inner light. The carved symbols moved and shifted, becoming patterns that made Susan's eyes water. The stone grew hotter, then burning hot.

Susan felt a pulling sensation, as if something beneath the altar was drawing her down. Her feet sank into the earth, and she couldn't move away from the stone.

"David," she gasped.

"I feel it too." His voice was strained. "Something's pulling at me."

The chanting grew louder. The community swayed in unison, their faces ecstatic in the lantern light. Children as young as five or six joined the adult voices, their treble notes weaving through the deeper tones.

Susan felt her strength draining away, flowing down through her feet into the hungry earth. She understood now what had happened to the Batemans. They hadn't been murdered---they'd been consumed, absorbed into the land that sustained this community.

But as her vision began to darken, she heard something else beneath the chanting. A different sound, growing stronger.

Sirens.

The community heard them too. The chanting faltered, heads turning toward the road. Red and blue lights flickered through the corn stalks, and the sirens grew louder.

"Impossible," Jacob muttered.

The pulling sensation stopped. Susan found she could move again, though her legs were weak. David stumbled against her, his face pale.

"Someone knows we're here," Susan whispered.

Police officers burst into the clearing, weapons drawn. Their flashlights cut through the lantern light, revealing the altar, the community, and Susan and David in their dark ceremonial clothes.

"Nobody move!" shouted the lead officer. "Lancaster County Sheriff's Department!"

The community stood frozen, their chant dying to silence. In the sudden quiet, Susan could hear her own heart pounding.

"Susan Fletcher? David Fletcher?" The officer approached them carefully. "Are you all right?"

"How did you find us?" Susan asked.

"Anonymous tip. Someone called and said there was going to be a human sacrifice in the cornfield tonight."

Susan looked around the circle of faces. Which of them had called the police? Who in this community of believers had broken ranks?

She saw the answer in Anna Stoltzfus's eyes. The elderly woman stood at the edge of the circle, her face resolute despite her obvious fear.

"Mrs. Stoltzfus," Susan said.

Anna nodded once, and Susan felt a surge of gratitude. Someone had found the courage to---

Anna smiled.

It wasn't the expression of someone who had betrayed her community to save innocent lives. It was the smile of someone who had played her part perfectly.

"Danke, Anna," Jacob said quietly. "The hope makes it sweeter."

The police officers lowered their weapons. Their faces were changing in the lantern light, becoming older, more weathered. Their uniforms shifted from blue to black.

Susan watched in horror as the lead officer's face transformed into that of Samuel Stoltzfus. The others became community members she'd met that afternoon---all of them now dressed as police.

"No," she whispered.

"The ritual requires hope," Jacob explained, his voice gentle. "Despair alone is bitter nourishment. But hope followed by despair---that feeds the land for generations."

David gripped her hand. "It was all planned."

"From the moment you called about the cottage." Jacob gestured to Anna, who stepped forward. "Anna has played this role many times. She has called the police to save the Littletons, the Millers, the Batemans. Each time, hope blooms in their hearts. Each time, it withers at the crucial moment."

"The police costumes are kept in the church basement," Anna said, her voice proud. "My grandson Samuel makes an excellent sheriff."

Susan felt her knees buckle. The rescue had been an illusion, a cruel theater designed to make their final moments more agonizing.

"You're monsters," David said.

"We are farmers," Jacob corrected. "We understand that the best fruit comes from properly tended soil. Hope is simply another crop to be harvested."

The chanting resumed, louder than before. The community swayed in unison, their faces ecstatic. Even the children sang, their voices sweet and pure.

The altar began to glow again. The pulling sensation returned, stronger now, drawing on Susan's shattered hope. She felt herself sinking into the earth, her feet disappearing first, then her ankles.

"David," she gasped, but he was sinking too, the hungry soil claiming him inch by inch.

The last thing she saw was Anna Stoltzfus adjusting the police hat on her grandson's head, preparing it for the next performance.

The last thing she heard was Jacob's voice, warm and patient: "Sleep well. Your gift will nourish us for years to come."

The earth closed over them like a gentle blanket.

In Philadelphia, their friends would wonder why David and Susan never returned from their vacation. The police would find their car abandoned on a country road, no sign of struggle, no evidence of foul play. Eventually, the case would be filed away unsolved.

And in Lancaster County, the corn would grow taller and greener than anywhere else in Pennsylvania, fed by more than just soil and rain.

Fed by hope, and the sweet despair that follows when hope dies.

The cottage would be cleaned and prepared for the next couple seeking peace in Amish country. The refrigerator would be stocked with fresh food. The guest book would be ready for new signatures.

The cycle would continue, as it always had.

As it always would.

The Hollyhusker Men

S now had been falling for three days, burying Ravenhill under white drifts that reached the cottage windows. Anya had to stand on a chair to see over the pile against their door. Not that anyone was going anywhere. Not this close to Christmas Eve.

She pressed her nose to the cold glass, watching her breath fog the window. Through the frost patterns, she could see the dark woods that surrounded their village.

"Get away from that window, little mouse," Grandmother called from her chair by the fire. Her knitting needles clicked steadily. "You'll catch your death."

But Anya knew it wasn't the cold Grandmother worried about.

"They're just trees, Babushka."

The clicking got faster. "Three days until Christmas Eve. Three days until the Hollyhusker Men walk. This isn't the time for wandering eyes."

Anya had grown up with the stories, same as every kid in Ravenhill. You learned about the Hollyhusker Men like you learned not to touch the stove. They came from the deep woods on Christmas Eve. Tall, skinny things with papery skin stretched over bones. Black holes for eyes. Mouths that opened too wide.

"What happens if they catch you?" she'd asked when she was little. Grandmother's face went hard.

"They suck your soul right out through your mouth. Like drinking through a straw. Leave nothing but a shell."

Anya moved to the fire, holding out her hands. "Papa's really late."

Grandmother kept knitting. Papa had gone to Millbrook before the storm---three days ago---to trade their wood carvings for flour and salt. Should've been home yesterday.

"The snow's keeping him. Your papa knows better than to travel after dark."

"But what if he doesn't make it back before---"

"Enough!" The needles stopped, shaking in Grandmother's hands. "Don't call bad luck with your words."

A log cracked in half in the fireplace, sending orange sparks up the chimney and filling the room with the smell of burning pine pitch. Outside, wind scraped against the shutters like fingernails on wood.

"Tell me about them," Anya said. "Where'd they come from?"

Grandmother stared into the fire. "They were people once. Men who starved during the Great Hunger, way back when my grandmother's grandmother was young. Went into the woods to die, but death wouldn't take them. The hunger changed them."

"If they used to be people, can't you talk to them?"

Grandmother's laugh sounded like dry leaves. "Nothing left to talk to, little mouse. Just hungry. So hungry it ate everything else."

"Has anyone really seen them?"

Grandmother set down her knitting. "Gregor the blacksmith saw them, when I was your age. Been drinking at Kovar's tavern, forgot the time. Thought he'd take the short way through the woods." She shook her head. "Found him Christmas morning in the snow. Not a mark on him, but dried up like he hadn't eaten in months. His eyes black as coal, mouth frozen open."

Anya shivered. "What about other people?"

"Nobody sees the Hollyhusker Men and lives." Grandmother picked up her knitting---conversation over. "Get more wood. But don't open the door---use what's by the hearth."

Anya did what she was told, but something bothered her about the blacksmith story. Like when Emma at school changed details every time she told something. Maybe Gregor just froze. Maybe people needed scarier reasons.

Still, when darkness came early like it always did this time of year, Anya found herself staying away from the windows and keeping her back to the walls. Just in case.

Two more days crawled by with no sign of Papa. The snow had stopped, but it lay deep and white, making everything look different and strange. The village had gone quiet, each family hiding behind locked doors and shuttered windows.

Christmas Eve morning, Anya woke to the smell of bacon---their last bit. Even that felt wrong with Papa gone.

"He's not coming back in time, is he?" she asked, helping slice their last bread.

Grandmother's hands shook. "Have faith, little mouse. Day's still young."

But as the short day went on, even Grandmother's face started cracking. By afternoon, with the sun sliding toward the trees, her mouth had gone tight.

"If he doesn't get here before sunset..." she started, then pressed her lips together like she could trap the bad thought inside.

Anya went to the window, looking out at the empty path that led from the village toward the world beyond. Nothing.

"I could go look for him," she said, knowing what Grandmother would say.

"You'll do no such thing!" The old woman's voice cracked like a whip. "Nobody leaves their house on Christmas Eve. Nobody."

"But what if he's hurt? What if he's just outside the village, trying to get home?"

"Then God help him, because nothing else can." Grandmother crossed herself. "The Hollyhusker Men don't know mercy, child. Can't. The hunger burned it all out of them."

Anya bit her lip and turned back to the window. The sun hung low now, a pale circle through the bare tree branches. Maybe an hour before dark.

Something moved at the edge of the woods.

"Babushka! I see something!"

Grandmother hurried to the window faster than Anya had seen her move in years. They both pressed their faces to the cold glass.

A figure had come out of the trees, making its way down the path toward the village. It looked hunched over, struggling through the deep snow.

"Papa!" Anya's heart jumped.

Grandmother squinted, her face tight with worry. "Could be. Hard to tell in this light..."

"It has to be him! He made it!" Anya reached for her cloak.

"Stop!" Grandmother's bony fingers dug into Anya's arm. "You can't go out there. The sun's almost down."

"But he looks hurt! He's walking funny! He needs help!"

"We'll light the big lantern and put it in the window. He'll see it and find his way." The old woman moved to do just that, forgetting her own rule about staying away from windows.

Anya watched the distant figure's slow progress while Grandmother lit their biggest lantern and set it on the windowsill. The yellow light cut through the growing darkness, reaching out toward the lone traveler.

"He sees it," Anya said with relief as the figure's head came up, turning toward their cottage. "But he's moving so weird..."

Grandmother pressed her face close to the glass. "Something's wrong," she whispered.

The figure had changed direction, now heading straight for their light. But it wasn't struggling through snow anymore---it seemed to glide over the surface, its movements jerky like a broken puppet.

"That's not your papa," Grandmother said, fear making her voice tight. She grabbed the lantern and blew it out.

"But it has to be," Anya said, though doubt was growing in her stomach like a cold stone. "Who else would come to our house? Who else would be out there?"

Grandmother hurried around the cottage, checking that the door was barred, testing the shutters. "Nobody should be walking around tonight. Nobody alive."

A cold feeling settled in Anya's chest. "You think it's one of them? A Hollyhusker Man?"

The old woman didn't answer, but her frantic checking spoke loud enough.

"But they don't come until full dark," Anya said, her voice small. "The sun's not set yet."

"Days get shorter, nights get longer," Grandmother muttered, more to herself than to Anya. "Their hunger grows with the darkness."

A sound came then, soft scratching at the door. Gentle, like someone too weak to knock properly. Then a voice.

"Anya? Mama? You there? Let me in."

It was Papa's voice.

Anya flew to the door, fingers scrambling at the heavy wooden bar.

"No!" Grandmother caught her around the waist, pulling her back with surprising strength. "That's not your papa!"

"It sounds like him!" Anya struggled against the old woman's grip.

"They steal voices, little mouse. Steal them like they steal everything else."

The scratching came again, more desperate now.

"Please," came Papa's voice, but something was wrong with how he said the words---too careful, like he was remembering how Papa talked. "I'm hurt real bad. Need help. The sun's going down."

Anya looked at Grandmother, tears starting in her eyes. "What if it really is him? What if we leave him out there to die?"

The old woman's face was white as candle wax, but her expression stayed firm. "If that's your papa, then he's already lost. Nobody survives a night with the Hollyhusker Men."

"Mama, please!" The voice cracked, but something was off---Papa never called Grandmother that. "Don't leave me out here! They're coming! I see them in the trees!"

Anya broke free and ran to the window, peering out into the deepening gloom. The sun had set, the last light fading from the western sky. At the edge of the forest, where shadow blended with shadow, shapes moved.

Tall, thin figures gliding over the snow without prints. Flickering like candle flames. Three of them---no, five---moving with the patience of cats who knew their mouse couldn't escape.

"Papa!" Anya called, pressing her hands against the glass. "Run! Come to the door!"

The figure that claimed to be her father turned. In the last dying light, Anya could see it clearly for the first time. It wore Papa's coat, had Papa's size, but the face...

The face was wrong. Skin stretched too tight over the bones, waxy and pale. And the eyes---black pits that seemed to swallow what little light remained.

It smiled, showing too many teeth, all sharp. "Anya," it said in Papa's voice, but the way it said her name was wrong---like it was tasting the word instead of saying it. "Sweet little mouse. Open the door."

Anya stumbled backward, her heart hammering against her ribs.

"Now you see," Grandmother said, taking Anya's shaking hand. "Now you understand."

Outside, the thing wearing Papa's face kept up its awful pretense, switching between begging and threats as the real Hollyhusker Men drew closer. They surrounded it now, these tall skeletal figures, their too-long limbs swaying like branches in a wind that touched nothing else.

"What do they want?" Anya whispered, unable to look away from the horrible scene outside their window.

"To feed," Grandmother answered. "To fill the emptiness inside them. An emptiness that's never filled."

The thing that copied Papa backed away, terror in its fake face as the Hollyhusker Men closed in. It opened its mouth to scream---no sound. Instead, gray mist streamed from its lips, pulled toward the nearest tall figure.

The Hollyhusker Man's face split open, jaw unhinging like a snake's, showing a mouth full of darkness. The mist flowed into that impossible mouth. The creature in Papa's shape shook and twisted, folding in on itself as something essential drained away.

When it was over, what fell to the snow looked like nothing that had ever been human.

The Hollyhusker Men turned as one toward the cottage. Their black, empty eyes seemed to find Anya through the window, through the walls, looking right into her.

"They can't come in," Grandmother said, though her voice shook. "Not without being asked. That's the old law. They can't cross the threshold unless invited."

Anya tore her gaze away from those hungry eyes. "What was that thing? The one pretending to be Papa?"

Grandmother's face was grim. "A familiar. A lesser thing that serves them, luring food with stolen faces and voices. Gets scraps from its masters' table."

"Then Papa is...?"

"I don't know, child." The old woman pulled Anya close. "We have to pray he found shelter before nightfall. That he was smart enough not to be out tonight."

Another sound started then---soft at first, like dry leaves against glass, then like fingernails scratching at the wooden shutters Grandfather had carved before Anya was born. It grew louder, surrounding the cottage on all sides. Scratching, tapping, the whisper of bone-thin fingers testing the walls, the door, the shuttered windows, looking for any way in.

Their cottage sat at the village edge, built over an old root cellar like most of the houses in Ravenhill. Papa had always meant to fix the loose boards around the outside entrance where the frost pushed them apart each winter. The earthen steps led up to a trapdoor in their kitchen floor, and Papa always reminded her to check both latches before the first snow---the main door and the cellar door. But with the storm and his absence, she'd forgotten.

"Ho-lly-hus-ker," the wind seemed to sigh. "Ho-lly-hus-ker."

Anya buried her face against Grandmother's shoulder, trying to block out the sound, but it wormed its way into her ears, into her head.

"They're trying to scare us," Grandmother said, stroking Anya's hair. "Fear makes the soul shine brighter, makes it sweeter to them. We have to be strong."

But the sounds continued through the endless night, sometimes fading only to return twice as loud. Whispers that might've been Papa's voice, calling her name. Scratching that moved from window to door to chimney, as the creatures tested every inch of the cottage's defenses.

In the dark hours, a new sound joined the others---soft, steady thumping from the root cellar. Like footsteps climbing the earthen stairs.

Grandmother's face went white. "The cellar door. Did you bar it?"

Ice ran through Anya. The outside cellar entrance Papa used for vegetables. She'd forgotten.

The thumping continued, reaching the top of the stairs. Then a pause. A long, terrible silence.

The iron ring of the trapdoor began to rise.

The villagers found them Christmas morning. Henrik the baker noticed first---no smoke from the Mikhailov chimney despite the bitter cold.

When Henrik and two others broke down the door---still barred from inside---they found grandmother and granddaughter by the cold hearth, sitting in their chairs like they were waiting for visitors. Whole, unmarked, but wasted away. Dried up like old apples, as if they'd been starving for months instead of one night.

Most disturbing was the trapdoor to the root cellar, flung wide open. And on the dirt floor below, preserved in the frozen earth, a set of long, thin footprints leading up the stairs and then vanishing.

The village buried them in the churchyard, next to an empty coffin for Anya's father, who never came home. The cottage burned to the ground that same day, the ashes scattered, the site left for the encroaching forest to reclaim.

On Christmas Eve, when darkness falls over Ravenhill, villagers bar their doors and tell children about the Hollyhusker Men who walk on the longest night. They warn about being caught outside after sunset, about answering loved ones' calls through closed doors.

What they don't speak of---whispered only among the oldest---is how the number at the forest edge has grown. How among the tall figures now walks a smaller one, with jerky child movements. And behind it, another moving with the halting gait of age.

And how, on cold Christmas Eves, when the wind cuts through the village like a blade and darkness falls early, three voices can sometimes be heard calling through the snow---a man's voice begging to be let in from the cold, and with it, the higher voices of a child and an old woman, all crying for help that will never come.

They Come from Within

Owen Blackwood first noticed the holes on a Tuesday in late
August, when the field corn towered twelve feet tall instead of
standing ready for the grain elevator. Stalks thick as fence posts. Ears
heavy as bowling balls.

He'd worked this black Illinois prairie soil thirty-seven years. Corn
and soybeans mostly, wheat when the Chicago Board made it worth
the risk. Inherited the land from his dad, who'd gotten it from his. In all
that time, he'd never seen perfect circles carved into his fields. Eighteen
inches across, punched clean through topsoil down to clay. Seventeen
of them scattered across the east field—looked random until you stepped
back far enough to see they made a rough spiral.

Owen crouched beside the nearest hole, ran his fingers along the
edge. Clean as if cut with a blade. No tool marks. No scattered dirt. He
couldn't figure where the removed earth had gone.

"Hell." He stood, brushed his hands on his Carhartts. The motion sent
a stab through his lower back—fifty-eight was too old to be crouching
in fields before sunup. The ache faded, replaced by worry that'd been
eating at him since Martha passed two years back.

The corn rustled in the morning breeze, sound setting Owen's teeth
on edge. Too deep. Like standing next to a combine at full throttle. He
looked up at the towering stalks and frowned. Everything about this
year's crop was wrong. The corn grew impossibly big, tomatoes in his
north field hung like red lanterns, and his pumpkin patch looked like
something from a fairy tale.

Folks in town called it a miracle season. The Harvest Festival com-
mittee was beside themselves, planning displays around Owen's giant
vegetables. Reporters kept calling, wanting his secret.

Owen didn't have a secret. Same methods his family'd always used,
same organic practices five generations running. Only thing different
this year was the weather—driest spring on record, then a wet summer
that made everything explode.

And now these holes.

Owen walked the spiral pattern, counting again to make sure. Seventeen. Always seventeen. He'd found them three days back and been coming out every morning since, hoping they'd fill themselves or make some kind of sense. Instead, they kept getting deeper.

He knelt by the center hole, pulled out his phone, shined the flashlight down. The beam disappeared into darkness. Owen picked up a dirt clod and dropped it in.

The clod hit something soft several feet down. Wet thud that made his stomach clench.

"Jesus." Owen jerked back. Sounded like dropping something into mud, but this field drained well. Never had standing water.

A sharp crack echoed across the field—one of the massive corn stalks splitting under its own weight. Owen jumped, heart hammering as he watched the stalk topple. The fall shook the ground under his boots. The remaining stalks swayed without any wind, moving together like they were listening to music he couldn't hear.

His phone buzzed. Text from Carl Hoffman: *Kids asking when they can pick corn for festival. Sally wants to make her casserole.*

Owen stared at the message, hands shaking. Sally Hoffman was eight, one of those kids who'd eat vegetables without a fight. She'd been pestering her folks about getting first pick ever since the stalks started showing their size.

The thought of that little girl eating anything from his field made his gut twist.

Soon, he texted back. *Still checking for pests.*

Wasn't really a lie. Something had gotten into his crops, even if he couldn't name what kind of pest made perfect holes.

Owen walked toward the property line, where the old limestone wall had stood since his great-great-grandfather's time. Local stone blocks mortared in the simple style of the 1800s, when farmers built walls to last centuries. Most of the old walls in the county had been torn down for modern equipment, but Owen's dad insisted on keeping theirs.

"History matters," the old man used to say. "Land remembers everything."

Owen had figured that was sentiment. Now, looking at the impossible perfection of those holes, he wondered.

The wall showed fresh damage. Stones had shifted, creating gaps that hadn't been there at planting. Owen had noticed the changes in July—figured it was settling. Now he looked closer. The gaps weren't random. Like the holes in his field, they followed a pattern.

Owen counted, dread mounting. Seventeen. Spaced along the wall's length.

His hands shook as he called Carl Hoffman.

"Owen?" Carl's voice had that breathless quality of chasing three kids before eight AM. "Everything all right? You sound—"

"Carl, got a question. You noticed anything weird with your crops this year?"

"You mean besides them being huge? Sarah's taking pictures to send her sister in California. Never seen anything like it."

"What about your soil? Any... holes?"

Pause. Kids laughing in the background. Sound that should've been innocent but sent chills down Owen's spine.

"Funny you ask. Found weird holes in my back field last week. Perfect circles, like someone took a giant drill to 'em. Was gonna mention it."

Owen's grip tightened. "How many?"

"Let me think... seventeen, maybe eighteen. Why? Owen, you're starting to worry me."

"I got the same thing. Exactly seventeen."

Longer pause. "That's... probably just coincidence, right? Some kind of pest we ain't seen before?"

Owen watched his corn stalks swaying in their unnatural rhythm. "Carl, your kids eaten any of your vegetables yet?"

"Are you kidding? They been eating tomatoes and corn for weeks. But the last few days..." Carl's voice got worried. "They're eating constantly. Can't get full. More they eat, the hungrier they get. Sarah jokes we might not have anything left for the festival, but it's starting to scare us."

Owen's blood went cold. "How they feeling? Acting different?"

"Now that you mention it, they been complaining about being hungry all the time. Even right after big meals. And they been... restless. Can't sit still. Emma was up at three yesterday morning, trying to get outside to the garden. When Sarah stopped her, Emma threw a tantrum like nothing we ever seen."

The children's laughter in the background sounded sharper now, more frantic.

"Carl, listen to me. Keep the kids away from the vegetables. All of 'em. And don't eat any yourselves."

"Owen, what the hell's going on? You're scaring me."

Owen watched a murder of crows land in his field and take flight again, cawing in distress as they wheeled away from the towering stalks.

"Don't know yet. But I'm gonna find out."

After hanging up, Owen ran back to the farmhouse, heart pounding. The house—two-story colonial, five generations of Blackwoods—felt less like home and more like a place keeping secrets.

Inside, Owen headed for the basement, where his dad had kept boxes of family papers. Owen'd been meaning to go through them since the funeral, but grief and running the farm alone hadn't left time.

Now, tearing through cardboard boxes labeled in his father's script, Owen searched for anything that might explain what was happening. Birth certificates, property deeds, old photos, farming records going back to the 1800s.

In a box marked "Local History," Owen found a leather journal that'd belonged to his great-great-grandfather, Jeremiah Blackwood. Pages yellow and brittle, but the ink stayed clear.

Owen carried it upstairs to his kitchen table, hands trembling as he read by window light. Most entries dealt with routine farming: weather, yields, livestock. But scattered throughout were references that froze his blood.

August 15th, 1847: The corn grows beyond all natural bounds. Ears heavy as melons, stalks tall as trees. The townspeople speak of miracles, but I fear we have awakened something that should have remained sleeping.

Owen's coffee mug slipped from numb fingers, shattered on the floor. His great-great-grandfather had dealt with the exact same thing. More than 170 years ago.

Hands shaking, Owen flipped ahead.

August 20th, 1847: Found Margaret Henley wandering in the east field this morning, dirt under her fingernails and a wild look in her eyes. She claims she was sleepwalking, but her footsteps led directly to the sacred circles. I have filled them with stones, but the earth fights me. Each morning I find them open again, deeper than before.

Sacred circles. Owen's mind raced back to those seventeen holes, their spiral arrangement. He grabbed his phone and called the Hoffmans again.

"Carl, this gonna sound crazy, but your holes—they arranged in any kind of pattern?"

"Actually..." Pause, muffled conversation. "Sarah says they look deliberate. Sort of a spiral shape. Why you asking these questions, Owen?"

Owen hung up and returned to the journal.

August 25th, 1847: The children grow restless. They speak of voices calling from beneath the earth, promising abundance in exchange for nourishment. I have forbidden them from eating the crops, but they disobey when no one watches. God help us, they grow stronger while their parents grow weak.

Owen's hands shook as he turned pages. The handwriting got shaky as the dates went on, some entries bearing stains that looked like dirt or dried blood.

September 1st, 1847: It is done. The harvest moon rises tonight, and the debt must be paid. I pray future generations will prove wiser. The covenant can be broken, but only through willing sacrifice. The stones must remain undisturbed, the circles sealed, the ancient hunger kept sleeping. If the walls are breached, if the holes appear again, someone of Blackwood blood must choose between the abundance and the cost.

September 2nd, 1847: Margaret Henley is gone. The children found her this morning in the east field, her body drained like a broken eggshell. The corn sways without wind, and I hear singing from beneath the earth. The price has been paid for this season, but next year approaches. God forgive me, what have I bound my family to?

The journal ended there. Remaining pages blank except for scattered dates with no entries.

Owen sat back, broken mug crunching under his feet. His great-great-grandfather had made some kind of deal. A covenant that required human sacrifice to keep something locked underground.

Sacred circles. Ancient hunger. Willing sacrifice.

And somehow, he'd broken it.

His phone rang. Sarah Hoffman.

"Owen." Sarah's voice tight with panic. "Something's wrong with the kids. Really wrong."

"What kind of—"

"They won't stop eating. Cannot stop. I caught Emma in the garden at dawn, stuffing tomatoes in her mouth like she was starving. Her belly was so swollen she looked pregnant, but she kept eating. And when I tried to stop her..." Her voice broke. "Owen, she bared her teeth at me. Like an animal. They all did."

Owen closed his eyes. *The children grow restless. They speak of voices calling from beneath the earth.*

"Where are they now?"

"Locked in the house, but I don't think that'll hold 'em much longer. They keep trying to get outside. Back to the garden. And Owen..." Her voice dropped. "They're changing. Their skin looks gray. When I touch them, feels like something's moving underneath. Something alive."

Owen looked out his kitchen window at the towering corn swaying without wind.

"Sarah, listen to me. Don't let the kids outside, no matter what they say or do. And don't eat any of your vegetables. I'm coming over."

"Owen, what's happening to my babies?"

Owen stared at the journal spread before him, at words his ancestor had written in desperation and fear.

"Something that happened before. Something my family was supposed to prevent."

The drive to Hoffman's farm gave Owen time to think, and thinking made everything worse. Three miles he'd traveled thousands of times—as a kid with his dad, later courting Martha, for the past fifteen years as a neighbor.

Carl Hoffman was forty-two, inherited his place the same way Owen had. Same schools, rival baseball teams, married their wives within a year of each other. Carl worked construction during the week, farmed weekends. Sarah taught third grade at Wheatland Elementary. Their kids—Emma, Carl Jr., and little Lucy—had been coming to Owen and Martha's house every Halloween since Emma could walk.

These weren't just neighbors. They were family. Owen had helped Carl repair his barn roof after the storm three years back. Carl had been one of the pallbearers at Martha's funeral. Sarah brought Owen casseroles every few weeks, claiming she'd made too much for her family but really making sure he wasn't living on bologna sandwiches and stubbornness.

Now Owen was driving to their house with the knowledge that his family's broken covenant had put their children in danger.

The Hoffman farmhouse came into view—white two-story with green shutters, surrounded by the huge garden that was Sarah's pride. Usually, the kids would be visible somewhere in the yard. Playing on the tire swing Carl had hung from the old oak or chasing their dog around the flower beds.

Today, the yard was empty except for Rex, the Hoffmans' German shepherd, pacing in tight circles near the front porch, whining.

Sarah met Owen at the door before he could knock. She looked like she hadn't slept in days. Dark circles under her eyes, usually neat brown hair pulled back in a messy ponytail, hands shaking as she gestured him inside.

"They're in the kitchen." She whispered. "I couldn't keep them separated. They... they broke down their bedroom doors."

Owen followed her through the familiar hallway, noting muddy footprints on the hardwood floors that Sarah usually kept spotless, and scratch marks gouged into the walls at kid height. The scratches looked deep, carved with something much sharper than fingernails.

"Sarah," Owen said carefully, "tell me exactly when this started."

"Last week. Tuesday, I think." She was wringing her hands, and Owen noticed dirt under her fingernails—unusual for someone as meticulous as Sarah. "Emma came in from the garden with tomato juice all over her face and shirt. At first I was just annoyed about the mess, you know? But then I saw how much she'd eaten. Half a dozen tomatoes, Owen. Big ones. And she was still hungry."

They stopped at the kitchen doorway. Owen could hear the children inside, but their voices sounded wrong—too quiet, too coordinated.

"By Thursday, all three of them were doing it," Sarah continued. "Sneaking out to the garden at all hours, eating everything raw. Tomatoes, corn, even green beans straight off the vine. I started bringing the vegetables inside, thinking maybe it was just... I don't know, some phase. But it got worse."

"How much worse?"

"Yesterday morning, I caught them trying to dig holes in the backyard with their bare hands. Their fingernails were bloody, Owen. And when I asked what they were doing, they all said the same thing at the exact same time: 'Making room for the roots to grow.'"

Owen's stomach dropped. "They said it together?"

"Word for word. In perfect unison. Like they'd rehearsed it." Sarah's voice broke. "Owen, what's wrong with my babies?"

Before Owen could answer, a child's voice called from the kitchen: "Mama? Is Mr. Owen here? We want to see him."

It was Emma's voice, but there was something underneath it—a depth that didn't belong in an eight-year-old's throat.

Owen looked at Sarah, who nodded reluctantly. Together, they entered the kitchen.

The three Hoffman children sat around the familiar oak table. Emma, eight years old with Sarah's brown hair and Carl's stubborn chin. Carl Jr., ten, usually full of energy and baseball statistics. Little Lucy, four, shy around adults but bold with her siblings.

Their bellies stretched tight against their t-shirts. Skin had taken on a grayish color like old photographs. But it was their eyes that made Owen's breath catch. Instead of the bright blue that ran in the Hoffman family, their eyes had turned black. Reflecting kitchen light like polished stone.

"Hello, Mr. Blackwood." Emma said it without moving her lips. Her voice carried an echo, words coming out simple, like something very old trying to remember how children talk. "We been waiting."

Carl Jr. turned his head toward Owen. "Harvest time. Gotta feed."

Owen's hand went to the cross pendant around his neck. Childhood habit he'd never shaken despite his lukewarm relationship with church.

"What are you?"

Lucy smiled with too many teeth in her small mouth. "We are what your family invited. What they promised to feed. Deal's gotta be kept."

Sarah grabbed Owen's arm. "What are they talking about? What deal?"

Owen kept his eyes on the children, afraid to look away from those black eyes. "My great-great-grandfather made a covenant in 1847. Food and prosperity for the county in exchange for tribute. Human sacrifice to feed whatever lives under our farms."

"That's insane." Sarah's whisper.

"Is it?" Emma's voice had dropped to something inhuman. Like stones grinding. "Look around you, Mrs. Hoffman. Your crops grow large and sweet, your family prospers, your children are healthy and strong. All we require is what was promised. One life per harvest moon, willingly given or taken by force."

Carl Jr. stood up, movements jerky like a marionette on strings. "The Blackwood family broke their deal. The barriers are cracked, the circles open. We been patient, but our hunger grows."

Owen thought about the journal, about the pattern of deaths in his family he'd figured was bad luck. His mother's fall down the basement stairs. His grandmother's early heart attack. His great-grandmother's swift cancer. All happening just before harvest time, all accepted as tragic but natural.

"You been taking payment all along. Every generation, someone dies around harvest. We told ourselves it was coincidence."

Lucy clapped her hands together. Sound echoing like gunshots. "Very good! Your great-grandmother, throat cancer at sixty-two. Your grandmother, heart attack at fifty-five. Your mother, that unfortunate tumble down the stairs. All counted toward the debt, all accepted by our kind."

His mother's death had been ruled accidental, but Owen had always wondered how someone as careful as Ellen Blackwood managed to miss a step she'd taken thousands of times.

"But now, the direct line has been severed. Your wife died of natural causes, beyond our reach. Your daughter lives far from our influence. The debt has accumulated, Mr. Blackwood. Interest compounds."

Sarah's grip tightened. "How many?"

Carl Jr. tilted his head at an impossible angle. "Three lives. One for each missed payment. They must be given before the harvest moon sets, or we will take what we need from everyone who has tasted our gifts."

Owen looked out the kitchen window at the bloated vegetables in Sarah's garden. How many people in Wheatland County had eaten the tainted crops? How many children were already changing?

"Why children?"

"Children are hungry. Always growing, always wanting more. They make the best vessels while we gather our strength."

Emma stood up, her distended belly making her look like a grotesque parody of pregnancy. "Choose, Mr. Blackwood. Three willing sacrifices before moonset, or we consume everyone who has tasted our abundance. Every child, every adult, every family that celebrated your miraculous harvest season."

Owen left the Hoffman house with his mind reeling and his hands shaking. The children had returned to normal the moment he'd agreed to consider their terms—their black eyes fading back to blue, their distended bellies shrinking, their voices becoming recognizably Emma's, Carl Jr.'s, and Lucy's again.

But Owen had seen what lay beneath the surface now. And he had less than eighteen hours to figure out what to do about it.

Sarah had walked him to his truck, her face pale but determined. "Owen," she'd said quietly, "I need you to know something. Whatever you're thinking of doing—whatever sacrifice you think has to be made—Carl and I, we'd rather take our chances fighting than let you give your life for our mistakes."

"Sarah, this ain't your fault—"

"Isn't it? I fed them those vegetables. I encouraged them to eat from the garden. I thought I was being a good mother." Her voice cracked. "If anyone should pay the price, it should be me."

"That's not how it works. The thing down there, it wants Blackwood blood specifically. Has to be family."

"Then what about Jessica? Your daughter in Seattle?"

Owen had considered that already. "She's got her own life. Good job, boyfriend she's serious about. And besides..." He looked back at the house where three innocent children were trapped with something ancient and hungry. "She shouldn't have to pay for what my family did."

Now, driving back to his farm, Owen tried to make sense of his options. The entity had given him three choices:

1. Provide three willing sacrifices before moonset

2. Sacrifice himself to renew the covenant for another thirty years

3. Let the entity take what it needed from everyone in the county who'd eaten the tainted crops

None of those options sat right with him. But as he pulled into his driveway, Owen realized there might be a fourth choice he hadn't considered yet.

Owen spent the afternoon in his father's study, reading through family documentation. Birth certificates, property deeds, old letters, farming records going back five generations. Slowly, a pattern emerged.

The covenant hadn't been Jeremiah's idea. According to a letter from 1846, the entity had already been there, sleeping under what would become Blackwood land. But railroad surveyors had disturbed something in the limestone caves, and the thing had awakened hungry and angry.

Jeremiah hadn't summoned it. He'd made a deal to contain it.

November 12th, 1846 - Letter from Jeremiah Blackwood to his brother Samuel in Springfield:
"The railroad men broke through into caverns that should have stayed sealed. What they found down there defies description, but it has been feeding on livestock and threatening to take human prey. The townspeople are talking of abandoning the settlement entirely. I have made arrangements with the entity--it will sleep in exchange for yearly tribute, and our land will prosper beyond measure. The walls I am building will contain it, and future generations will reap the benefits of my bargain. Pray that my descendants will be wiser than I, should the arrangement ever fail."

Owen set the letter down, his mind racing. The entity wasn't some ancient evil that had always lived under Wheatland County. It was something that had been accidentally released and then contained by his ancestor's deal.

Which meant it could be contained again.

Owen grabbed his keys and headed for town. If he was right about what he'd found in his father's papers, there might be someone who could help him understand what Jeremiah had actually done.

The Wheatland County Historical Society occupied a converted Victorian on Main Street. Owen had always avoided the place—too much dusty nostalgia, not enough practical information. But if anyone in town knew about the railroad surveys from the 1840s, it would be Eleanor McKinney, the society's president.

Eleanor was seventy-three, sharp as a tack, and had been documenting local history for forty years. She also happened to be Margaret Henley's great-great-niece—the same Margaret Henley mentioned in Jeremiah's journal as the first person taken by the entity.

Owen found her in the basement, surrounded by boxes and folders, working on what looked like a timeline of railroad development.

"Owen Blackwood." She looked up with surprise. "Haven't seen you in here since your father's funeral. What brings you to my dusty archive?"

"Mrs. McKinney, I need to ask about the railroad surveys from the 1840s. Specifically, any records about work done on what's now my property."

Her expression shifted. "That's... an unusual request. May I ask why?"

Owen had prepared for this question during the drive to town. He couldn't tell Eleanor the truth—that an ancient entity was holding three children hostage and threatening to consume half the county. But he could tell her part of the truth.

"I've been going through my father's papers, trying to understand the history of our land. Found some references to railroad work and limestone caves. Figure I should know what's under my property, especially with all the strange things happening with the crops this year."

Eleanor studied him for a long moment, then gestured for him to sit down. "Owen, what I'm about to tell you isn't in any of the official histories. Most people would say it's just local folklore. But your family... your family might have reasons to know the truth."

She pulled out a thick folder labeled "Railroad Surveys 1845-1847" and opened it to reveal maps, correspondence, and what looked like official reports.

"In 1846, the Illinois Central sent a survey crew through Wheatland County. They were supposed to identify the best path for laying track—documenting geological features, water sources, obstacles.

"When they got to what's now your east field, they discovered an extensive cave system in the limestone bedrock. The caves were vast—possibly connected to similar systems throughout central Illinois."

Eleanor pulled out a hand-drawn map. "But here's where it gets interesting. The survey crew broke through into a sealed chamber about twenty feet down. Their report describes 'evidence of previous habitation' and 'unusual geological formations that appeared to have been deliberately arranged.'"

Owen leaned forward. "What kind of evidence?"

"The report is vague, but it mentions carved stones in circular patterns, and what they called 'organic deposits' that suggested the chamber had been sealed for a very long time." Her voice dropped. "Three members of the survey crew became ill after entering the chamber. Symptoms of constant hunger, difficulty sleeping, and what the crew chief called 'speaking in unison as if controlled by a single mind.'"

"What happened to them?"

"They disappeared. The official report says they abandoned their positions and left the area, but..." Eleanor pulled out another document. "I found this letter from the crew chief to the railroad company. He recommended the route be changed to avoid your property entirely. He also recommended the chamber be resealed immediately and the area avoided by all future development."

"And was it? Resealed?"

"Not by the railroad. They changed their route and left. But according to local records, someone filled in the cave entrance shortly after the survey crew left. Someone who knew what they were doing."

Owen thought about his great-great-grandfather's journal. The walls. The stones arranged in specific patterns. "Jeremiah Blackwood."

"That's my assumption, yes. And it worked, for the most part. The railroad went around your property, area remained stable for decades." Eleanor's expression grew troubled. "But Owen, there have always been incidents. Disappearances around harvest time. Accidents that seemed too convenient. And they always involved your family."

Owen nodded slowly. "Mrs. McKinney, do you have any records of what my great-great-grandfather actually did to seal that chamber? Any documents about the specific methods he used?"

Eleanor hesitated. "There are some things, yes. Letters, sketches, notes that were passed down through my family. Margaret Henley was my great-great-aunt, Owen. She was the first person taken by... whatever was in that chamber. Her family kept records too, hoping that someday someone would find a way to put things right."

She stood and walked to a filing cabinet, pulling out a folder that looked much older than the railroad documents. "This is everything we know about what your ancestor did to contain the entity. And Owen... if something's happening on your land again, if the seals are breaking, you're going to need this information."

Owen spent two hours in Eleanor's basement, reading documents that filled in the gaps. The picture that emerged was more complex and more hopeful than he'd understood.

Jeremiah hadn't made a simple deal. He'd created an elaborate containment system—part engineering, part ritual, part negotiation. The limestone walls weren't just barriers. They were part of a geometric pattern that restricted the entity's ability to influence the surface world.

The seventeen stone circles weren't random. They formed a spiral that matched the pattern of the natural cave system below, creating what Jeremiah's notes called "pressure points" where the entity's influence was focused and controlled.

Most importantly, the yearly sacrifices weren't feeding the entity. They were satisfying the terms of a contract that kept it contained. The entity gained limited nourishment from each death, but the real purpose was maintaining the legal and spiritual framework that bound it underground.

When Owen's family failed to provide willing sacrifices, the entity had been forced to take what it could through "accidents" and "natural" deaths. But those deaths hadn't been enough to maintain the containment system, and over time, the barriers had weakened.

The extraordinary crop growth this year wasn't a blessing. It was a symptom. The entity was using its remaining power to influence the surface world, creating abundance to attract more people and ensure a larger pool of victims when the barriers finally failed.

But the most important thing Owen learned: the containment could be renewed without human sacrifice, if the seals were restored properly and the contract renegotiated from a position of knowledge rather than desperation.

Eleanor had maps showing the exact placement of the original stones, descriptions of the symbols Jeremiah had carved into the limestone barriers, and most crucially, a copy of the original agreement between Jeremiah and the entity—written in a mixture of English and symbols that looked almost like legal language.

"My great-great-aunt Margaret kept all this," Eleanor explained. "She died trying to break the contract, but she documented everything first. Her family has been waiting for someone with the knowledge and the authority to finish what she started."

Owen looked up from the documents. "What kind of authority?"

"Someone of Blackwood blood who understands what they're dealing with. Someone willing to renegotiate the terms rather than just accepting them." Eleanor's eyes were serious. "Owen, I don't think you have to die to save those children. But I do think you have to be willing to."

Owen returned to his farm as the sun was setting, his truck loaded with photocopies of documents and maps, his mind spinning with possibilities. According to Eleanor's research, the containment system could be fixed, but it'd take precise placement of stones, specific symbols carved into the barriers, and most importantly, sitting down to hash out new terms with the entity itself.

But first, he needed to understand exactly how much damage had been done to the original seals.

Owen grabbed a powerful flashlight from his workshop and headed for the east field. The seventeen holes were deeper now—some of them large enough for a person to fall into. But more troubling were the cracks that had appeared in the ground around each hole, forming a web-like pattern that seemed to pulse with its own rhythm.

Using Eleanor's maps as a guide, Owen could see that the holes corresponded exactly to the "pressure points" Jeremiah had marked 170 years ago. The entity wasn't randomly breaking through—it was systematically dismantling the containment system by attacking its most vulnerable spots.

Owen knelt beside the center hole and shined his flashlight down. The beam revealed carved stone about fifteen feet down—part of Jeremiah's original barrier system. But the stones had shifted, creating gaps that allowed something to pass between the chamber below and the surface above.

That's when Owen heard it: a low humming sound that seemed to come from all around him, felt as much as heard. The sound he'd noticed earlier, but now he understood what it was.

The entity was singing.

Not in any human language, but in harmonics that made his teeth ache and his vision blur. It was calling to every person in Wheatland County who'd eaten the tainted crops, drawing them toward the barriers it was trying to break.

Owen looked around the field and realized he could see lights moving in the distance—flashlights or lanterns, heading toward his property from all directions. The entity wasn't just threatening the Hoffman children anymore. It was calling in everyone it had influence over, turning them into tools to complete the destruction of the containment system.

Owen's phone rang. Carl Hoffman's number.

"Owen, where are you? We got a problem. People are walking through our fields, heading toward your place. Dozens of them. And they're all carrying shovels."

Owen counted at least forty people converging on his east field, all of them moving with the same jerky, unnatural gait he'd seen in the Hoffman children. Men, women, teenagers, even a few elderly folks—anyone who'd eaten vegetables from the miraculous harvest over the past few weeks.

They weren't speaking to each other, but they moved in perfect coordination, spreading out around the seventeen holes and beginning to dig. Not randomly, but in specific patterns that would widen the breaks in Jeremiah's barrier system.

Owen realized he was watching the entity's endgame. It'd spent months prepping by growing those huge crops, getting people to eat them, and now it was using those same people as tools to finish busting out of its prison.

But it had made one crucial mistake. It was so focused on breaking the barriers that it hadn't noticed Owen learning how to repair them.

Owen ran to his workshop and gathered the tools he'd need: sledge-hammer, chisel, rope, and the symbols Eleanor had copied from Jeremiah's notes. He also grabbed his grandfather's hunting rifle—not because bullets would stop an ancient entity, but because he might need to protect himself from the people it was controlling.

The possessed townspeople were so focused on digging that they didn't notice Owen approaching. He could see familiar faces among them: Jim Loesing from the hardware store, the Kowalski family from the next farm over, even young Pastor Richards from the Methodist church. All of them with the same black eyes, the same unnatural coordination.

Owen made his way to the center hole, where the digging was most intense. According to Eleanor's maps, this was where Jeremiah had placed the primary seal—the stone that controlled all the others.

Owen clipped his flashlight to his belt and rappelled down into the hole using rope anchored to his truck. The carved stone barriers were still intact, but barely. Gaps between the blocks allowed a foul-smelling mist to seep through, and Owen could see movement in the darkness beyond.

Working by flashlight, Owen began re-carving the symbols worn away by time and intentional damage. Each mark had to be precise.

According to Jeremiah's notes, the symbols weren't just decorative. They were part of a binding contract written in stone.

Above him, the digging sounds grew frantic. The entity had realized what Owen was doing, driving its controlled people to work faster.

But Owen had one advantage: he understood what his great-great-grandfather had done, and he knew how to do it better.

Instead of fixing the old containment, Owen was changing the deal. Where Jeremiah had agreed to yearly sacrifice, Owen carved new terms: containment in exchange for leaving people alone. Where the original deal had let the entity mess with crops and people, Owen's version said no supernatural interference.

It took an hour to complete the primary seal. When Owen finished carving the last symbol, the stone began to glow with faint blue light, and the movement in the darkness below went still.

One seal down. Sixteen to go.

Owen climbed out of the center hole to find that the controlled townspeople had stopped digging. They stood motionless around the field, their black eyes fixed on him with expressions of pure hatred.

"You cannot undo what has been agreed," they said in unison, their voices creating harmonics that hurt Owen's ears. "The contract is sealed in blood and stone."

"The contract's being renegotiated," Owen replied, moving toward the next hole. "By someone who actually read the fine print."

The possessed people didn't try to stop him physically—apparently the entity couldn't make them attack the person it was trying to make a deal with. But they started that singing again, making those bone-deep sounds that blurred Owen's vision and made his hands shake.

Owen pushed through the discomfort and continued his work. Each seal took about thirty minutes to repair and modify, and each one made the entity's song more desperate and angry.

By the time Owen reached the fifth seal, the controlled people had begun to collapse. Without the entity's constant influence, they were returning to normal consciousness, confused and frightened to find themselves standing in a field in the middle of the night holding shovels.

Carl and Sarah Hoffman arrived as Owen was working on the eighth seal, bringing coffee and sandwiches and helping to escort the confused townspeople back to their homes.

"The kids?" Owen asked.

"Back to normal," Sarah said, relief evident in her voice. "Whatever you're doing, it's working."

By dawn, Owen had repaired and modified all seventeen seals. The holes in his field had filled themselves with fresh earth, and the limestone barriers deep underground hummed with the blue light of renewed containment.

The entity's voice, when it finally spoke, was weaker but still defiant.

"This changes nothing, Blackwood. We can wait. We have waited before."

"Actually, it changes everything." Owen pulled out Eleanor's copy of the original contract, showed it to the darkness. "See, your deal was with Jeremiah Blackwood specifically. He's been dead for over a century, which makes the contract null and void. What I just created isn't a renewal of his agreement. It's a completely new contract, with completely new terms."

The entity's silence stretched for several minutes. When it spoke again, there was something like grudging respect in its voice.

"What are your terms?"

"Simple. You stay underground, permanently. No more influence on crops, no more affecting people, no more trying to escape. In exchange, I don't collapse this entire cave system and bury you under several million tons of limestone."

"And if we refuse?"

Owen gestured toward the seventeen repaired seals. "The containment system I just built is stronger than Jeremiah's original. It's powered by principles of binding your kind can't break. And if you try to escape again, the seals will automatically collapse the entire cave system. You'll be trapped under solid rock instead of locked in a chamber."

Another long silence.

"Very well, Blackwood. We accept your terms."

"Good. And just so we're clear—this contract is binding on all your kind, forever. No loopholes, no technicalities, no renegotiation. You stay down there, and we stay up here."

"Understood."

Owen nodded and began filling in the last of the holes. As he worked, he could feel the entity's presence withdrawing deeper underground, settling into a sleep that might last centuries.

The Wheatland County Harvest Festival that year was smaller than usual. Most of the giant vegetables had shriveled overnight, going back to normal sizes—still decent, but nothing like the record-breakers that'd made the news.

Nobody seemed bothered. The people who'd been affected by the entity had fuzzy memories of the past few weeks. They remembered eating really good vegetables and feeling energetic, but the weirder stuff faded like dreams.

Owen sold his harvest to the grain elevator for normal prices, used the money to repair the stone walls around his property. He also funded a small addition to the Historical Society, where Eleanor could properly preserve and display the documents that had saved the county.

Jessica Blackwood flew in from Seattle for the festival, bringing her boyfriend to meet her father and see the farm where she'd grown up. She could tell Owen seemed more relaxed than he'd been since her mother died, but when she asked about it, he just said he'd been going through old family papers.

On the last night of her visit, as they sat on the porch watching fireflies dance over the fields, Jessica asked the question Owen had been expecting.

"Dad, are there things about this place I should know? Family responsibilities I might inherit someday?"

Owen considered telling her the whole truth. But looking at his daughter's face—relaxed and happy, planning a future that didn't include ancient entities and supernatural contracts—he decided she'd earned the right to live a normal life.

"Nothing you need to worry about, sweetheart. I took care of the family business. Your only job is to be happy."

Jessica smiled and squeezed his hand. "You sure?"

"I'm sure."

And he was. The contract he'd carved into stone would hold without ongoing sacrifice or vigilance from future generations. The entity would stay buried, bound by its own desire to survive rather than by human blood.

Owen looked out over his fields, thinking about Martha, about the neighbors he'd saved, about the daughter who could live without inheriting his family's burden.

The harvest was in. The accounts were settled.

That was enough.

The Wakely House

Theresa stopped dead when she saw the house on Mulberry Hill. Even beneath decades of neglect, the Victorian beauty took her breath away.

"Look at those bones," she told Bernard, staring up at the sagging porch and weather-beaten gables. "They don't build them like this anymore."

Bernard adjusted his glasses, squinting like he was checking math. "Fifteen thousand in roof repairs. Minimum. God knows what the foundation looks like."

Theresa squeezed his arm. Twelve years of marriage---she knew how to work around his pragmatism. "Think what it'll be worth fixed up. The price is practically stealing."

"There's a reason for that." But Bernard reached for his calculator, and Theresa knew she'd won..

Ellen Greer cleared her throat behind them. "This place has quite a history. The Marlowe House was one of the first grand homes built when the lumber mills were running."

"Marlowe House?" Theresa looked up at the rotting facade.

"Spencers were the last occupants. Lived here two years before they... left. Most people still call it by the original owner's name. Edmund Marlowe built it in 1886."

"When you said the Spencers left, you paused. Why?" Bernard asked.

Ellen's smile tightened. "Local mystery. Packed up and moved in the middle of the night. Left furniture, clothing, everything."

"When?"

"1967. Been in probate ever since. Bank acquired it last fall."

Theresa did the math. "Empty for fifty years?" Something about a family abandoning everything struck her as wrong. "What about relatives? Nobody came looking?"

Ellen shrugged. "That's Crestwick. People come and go. Shall we look inside?"

Inside: high ceilings, ornate crown molding, hardwood floors buried under dust and grime. Cobwebs in corners like abandoned lace. The house smelled wrong---not musty, but dry and herbal, like old tea leaves mixed with something sharp.

"No central heating," Bernard said, touching a cast-iron radiator.

"Makes it weird how warm it is," Ellen said, peeling off her jacket. "This place keeps heat like nobody's business. Even in February, never drops below fifty. Best insulation I've seen in a house this age."

Theresa wandered room to room, already planning renovations. Kitchen needed gutting. Bathrooms too, though the claw-foot tub might survive. But the parlor---bay windows, marble fireplace---was straight from her dreams.

Third floor---that's where she found the bed.

It stood in what must've been a kid's room, an ornate four-poster too large for the faded circus-animal wallpaper. Weird proportions---narrower than a twin but longer, like an oversized crib. Elaborately carved posts topped with round finials, each bearing a deep horizontal slit like a closed eye. The headboard showed intricate carvings that looked like folded wings.

"Unusual piece," Theresa said, moving closer.

Ellen nodded. "Spencers built it in here---too big to fit through the door. Bank included it since it can't be moved without damage."

Bernard frowned, studying it with mathematical precision. "Proportions are wrong. Too narrow for an adult, too long for a child. What's with these carvings?"

Theresa touched one of the posts. The wood was warm. Beautiful craftsmanship, each detail perfect. But something about it just felt odd.

"Well," Bernard sighed, pocketing his calculator, "what's the verdict? Do we make an offer, or keep looking?"

Theresa glanced around the room, her eyes drawn to the large casement windows that overlooked the town below. Through the grime, she could see Crestwick spread out like a model village---the church spire, the rolling hills beyond, and in the distance, the gleaming rectangle of Crestwick College where Bernard would begin teaching in the fall.

"It's perfect," she said, turning back to him. "It's exactly what we've been looking for."

As they left the room, Theresa could have sworn she heard a soft creaking behind her, like weight shifting on old wood. But when she turned to look, the room stood still.

They took possession April 1st. Moving van struggled up the winding hill road, engine straining. Bernard had insisted on professional movers despite Theresa's protests.

"We're not twenty anymore. My back still hasn't forgiven me for your piano."

By sunset the movers were gone. Theresa and Bernard sat among scattered boxes, exhausted, eating pizza from folding chairs with paper plates.

"To new beginnings," Bernard said, raising a plastic cup of champagne.

"To making this place ours." Theresa tapped her cup against his.

"Think we'll actually renovate this monster?"

"Better than calling it the Marlowe House forever." She sipped, made a face at the flat bubbles. "Though that'll take time."

After Bernard fell asleep on their hastily assembled bed, Theresa wandered through dark rooms, running her hands along walls and doorframes. The house seemed to breathe around her. Despite the chill outside, it stayed warm inside.

She ended up on the third floor, drawn to the room with the strange bed. Moonlight through the windows made the carved posts cast long shadows. Theresa approached slowly, pulled by something she couldn't name.

Up close, the carvings were more detailed than she'd realized. What looked like wing patterns were individual feathers, each one distinct. The slits on the finials were deeper than they seemed, cutting completely through.

Wind rattled the casement windows. Theresa jumped, heart hammering. For a second, she'd swear the slits had widened.

"Get a grip," she whispered, backing away. "Just a weird old bed."

Next morning Bernard found a yellowed newspaper behind one of the radiators.

"Crestwick Courier, June 15, 1967." He brushed dust from brittle pages.

Theresa read over his shoulder. LOCAL MAN MISSING, THIRD DISAPPEARANCE THIS MONTH.

"Three people missing in one month?" she asked. "In a town this small?"

Bernard nodded, looking thoughtful. "According to this, it wasn't the first time. Listen: 'Police Chief Walter Hammond confirmed that these disappearances follow the same pattern as those in 1949 and 1931, occurring during the late spring and early summer months with no signs of foul play.'"

"That's bizarre. Every eighteen years? That can't be coincidence."

"Serial killer with a specific timeline," Bernard suggested. "Or maybe just sensationalist reporting. Small towns love their mysteries."

Theresa took the paper from him, scanning the rest of the article. The missing people had little in common---a 40-year-old mill worker, a 22-year-old waitress, and a 35-year-old housewife. No connection except timing.

"I wonder if they ever found them," she murmured.

Bernard had turned his attention to the box of kitchen supplies waiting to be unpacked. "Probably. Or they just left town for better opportunities. The sixties were a time of change."

Theresa folded the paper and set it aside, but the headline stuck with her as she set about organizing their new home.

First two weeks passed in a blur of unpacking, cleaning, minor repairs. Theresa threw herself into the work---stripping wallpaper, sanding floors, priming walls. Bernard helped when he wasn't preparing for fall classes, though his idea of help involved careful measurements and detailed supply lists.

Theresa didn't mind. This was her project. She'd been dreaming of renovating an old house since she was a girl, watching "This Old House" with her father over Saturday morning cereal.

The only room she avoided was the one with the strange bed. She'd closed the door her second day and hadn't returned. Something about that room left her uneasy.

Then came the night she first heard it.

Just after two AM, Theresa woke, heart pounding. Bernard slept beside her, breathing deep and regular. The house stood silent, but she was certain a sound had woken her.

She lay still, listening. Just as she thought she'd imagined it, she heard it again---soft, rhythmic creaking from somewhere above. Then a heavier thump.

The third floor. Something was moving up there.

Theresa nudged Bernard. "Bern," she whispered. "Wake up."

He grunted, rolling away from her.

"Bernard," she hissed more urgently. "I think someone's in the house."

That got his attention. He sat up, fumbling for his glasses on the nightstand.

"What? Where?"

"Upstairs. I heard something moving."

Bernard listened for a moment, then shook his head. "I don't hear anything. Probably just the house settling. These old places make all kinds of noises."

The creaking came again, louder this time. Bernard frowned.

"That does sound like footsteps," he admitted. "Wait here."

"Are you crazy?" Theresa grabbed his arm. "If there's someone up there, we should call the---"

Bernard reached for the baseball bat he'd placed beside the bed---a concession to moving to a new town where they knew no one. "It's probably just an animal that got in through one of the broken attic windows. I'll check."

Before Theresa could protest further, he left the room and headed upstairs. She followed, grabbing her phone from the nightstand.

Third-floor hallway was darker than the rest of the house, moonlight barely penetrating grime-covered windows. Bernard moved cautiously, bat raised. Theresa stayed behind him, finger hovering over the emergency call button.

The noise had stopped.

Bernard approached the door to the room with the bed, hesitated before turning the knob. The door swung open to reveal an empty room bathed in moonlight. The bed stood exactly where it had been, silent and still.

Except for one detail.

"The windows are open," Theresa said, pushing past Bernard into the room.

The casement windows stood open, night breeze stirring the tattered circus-animal curtains. Theresa felt certain they had been closed and latched; she'd checked every window in the house after they moved in.

Bernard crossed to the windows and peered out into the darkness. "No sign of anyone," he said, pulling them closed and securing the latch. "But I'll check the rest of the house to be sure."

As they turned to leave, Theresa's gaze fell on the bed. In the pale moonlight, it seemed to pulse, the carved feathers on the headboard casting strange, shifting shadows.

"I want to get rid of that thing," she said. "It gives me the creeps."

Bernard raised an eyebrow. "The bed? I thought you liked antiques."

"Not this one. There's something... wrong about it."

Bernard sighed but didn't argue. "All right. We can try to dismantle it this weekend. Though if what Ellen said is true, we might have to take out part of the wall."

Theresa nodded, relieved. As they left the room, she glanced back one last time. The horizontal slits on the round finials seemed to track their departure, though she knew that had to be shadows.

Next morning, the Crestwick Courier headline: LOCAL WOMAN VANISHES AFTER MIDNIGHT WALK. Elaine Porter, 28-year-old nurse, went for a walk late last night and never returned. Husband reported her missing at six AM when he found her side of the bed empty.

Theresa read the article twice, a chill spreading through her that had nothing to do with the morning air.

"Bernard," she called, her voice tight. "Have you seen this?"

He glanced up from his laptop, where he'd been preparing his syllabus. "Another disappearance?"

"It happened last night. Around the same time we heard those noises upstairs."

Bernard's expression grew concerned. "Theresa, you can't connect those two things. We're half a mile from town up here."

"The article said she was last seen on Elmhurst Street. That's at the bottom of our hill." Theresa set the paper down with shaking hands. "And remember that old newspaper we found? The one from 1967? It mentioned disappearances every eighteen years. If you add eighteen to 1967, then again, and again..."

"You get 2021. This year." Bernard removed his glasses and rubbed the bridge of his nose. "That's quite a leap, honey."

"Is it? Then how do you explain the windows being open? I know I locked them."

Bernard sighed. "Old houses have old locks. Maybe they were loose. Or maybe..." He hesitated.

"Maybe what?"

"Maybe you forgot." He kept his voice gentle. "You've been under a lot of stress with the move and the renovations. It's easy to forget small details."

Theresa shook her head. Her hands were trembling. She wanted to argue but caught herself. Was he right? Had the strain of the past few weeks affected her memory? It was possible. And far more logical than the alternative---that their house had something to do with a woman's disappearance.

"You're probably right," she conceded, though doubt lingered.

That night, Theresa double-checked every window in the house before bed, making a special point to secure the casements in the third-floor bedroom. She even placed a small piece of tape across the seam where the windows met, a trick she'd learned from a thriller novel---if someone opened them, the tape would tear.

She slept fitfully, waking at the slightest sound, but the night passed without incident.

Morning, she climbed to the third floor, both hoping and dreading. The bedroom door stood closed. The tape across the windows remained intact.

Her shoulders dropped. She let out her breath. Bernard was right---she was letting her imagination run wild. She turned to leave, paused, frowning. Something was different. She scanned the room slowly.

The bed. Against the north wall yesterday. Now in the center of the room.

Theresa's pulse pounded in her throat. "Bernard!" she called, her voice cracking. "Bernard, come up here!"

He arrived moments later, still in his pajamas, hair tousled from sleep. "What's wrong?"

"The bed," she said, pointing. "It's moved."

Bernard looked at it, then back at her, his expression concerned. "Are you sure? I don't remember exactly where it was before."

"It was against that wall." Theresa pointed to the wall opposite the windows. "I'm certain of it."

Bernard approached the bed, examining it from all angles. "These old houses have uneven floors. Maybe it shifted over time."

"Shifted? Bernard, it's in the middle of the room now. That's not a 'shift.' And look at the floor---there are no drag marks. How did it get here without leaving a trace?"

He didn't have an answer for that. Instead, he placed his hands on the bed frame and pushed. It didn't budge. He tried again, straining, but the bed remained fixed in place as if bolted to the floor.

"That's odd," he admitted, straightening. "It's heavier than it looks."

"Or maybe it doesn't want to move," Theresa whispered.

Bernard gave her a sharp look. "What did you say?"

Theresa shook her head. "Nothing. I don't like this room. Let's go."

As they left, she glanced back once more. The slits in the spherical finials seemed wider today, more like half-open eyes than decorative carvings. And the wing patterns on the headboard appeared to have shifted, the feathers now arranged differently, as if ruffled by a passing breeze.

Over the next two weeks, three more people disappeared from Crestwick. Each case followed the same pattern: the person vanished in the late night or early morning hours, leaving no trace behind. No signs of struggle, no evidence of foul play. They simply ceased to exist.

Each disappearance coincided with the noises Theresa heard from the third floor. And each morning after, she would find the casement windows open, despite her precautions.

Bernard remained skeptical, attributing her concerns to an overactive imagination fueled by stress and sensationalist local news. But he couldn't explain how the bed kept moving, changing position in the room despite its apparent immobility when he tried to shift it.

"Maybe the floor is settling unevenly," he suggested after the third time they found it in a new position. "These old houses can shift over time."

But they both knew that wasn't satisfactory, and tension grew between them. Bernard retreated into his academic preparations, spending long hours at the college library. Theresa found herself alone in the house, jumping at every creak and groan of the aging structure.

Then came the morning she found the bracelet.

Distinctive silver bracelet with small turquoise stones, hidden beneath the strange bed that had somehow migrated back against the north wall. Metal caked with dried blood. Theresa turned it over with shaking hands. Engraving: "To Lainey from Grandma."

Her stomach lurched. Lainey---Elaine Porter.

Shaking, Theresa searched the room more thoroughly. Behind the tattered wallpaper in one corner, she found a cell phone she didn't recognize. The screen was cracked and the case was smeared with what looked like dried blood.

She was contemplating what to do with these discoveries when Bernard returned home.

"We need to call the police," she told him, displaying the items on the kitchen table. "These belonged to the missing people. Someone put them in that room, in our house."

Bernard examined the objects with a frown, careful not to touch the blood-stained areas. "Jesus Christ, Theresa. This is real blood." His face had gone pale. "We need to call the police right now."

"That's what I've been trying to tell you."

Bernard stared at the bracelet and phone. "But how did these things get into our house? Someone would have had to break in, go up to that specific room..." He trailed off, the implications sinking in.

"Exactly. Someone with access to our house. Someone who knows about that room." Theresa's voice was getting higher. "Bernard, what if whatever's been making those noises is connected to the disappearances?"

Bernard was quiet for a long moment, staring at the evidence. "We're calling the police. Now."

Crestwick Police Station was a small brick building on Rottenham Street, weathered like everything else in the aging town. Inside, they met Chief Rowan---stout man with bristly mustache and weary eyes.

"Mr. and Mrs. Wakely? What can I do for you?"

Theresa placed the bag on his desk. "I found these in our house. I believe they belonged to some of the people who've gone missing."

Chief Rowan's expression didn't change as he examined the items. "Where exactly did you find these?"

"In one of the third-floor bedrooms."

"Which room specifically? The house has been empty for decades - I want to make sure we document this properly."

Theresa hesitated. "The one with the old four-poster bed. It's... unusual. Very ornate, with carved posts."

Something shifted in the chief's expression. "You're talking about the bedroom at the end of the hall? The one that overlooks the town?"

"Yes, that's the one."

Rowan was quiet for a moment, then nodded slowly. "I see." He folded his hands on the desk. "Mrs. Wakely, can I ask what made you search that particular room?"

Theresa explained about the noises, the open windows, the bed's inexplicable movements. As she spoke, she saw the chief exchange a glance with Bernard, but this time it wasn't dismissive.

"I'm not imagining this," she insisted. "Something is happening in that house. And I think it's connected to the disappearances."

Chief Rowan cleared his throat. "Mrs. Wakely, are you aware that Crestwick has a history of... similar incidents? Dating back to the late 1800s?"

"We found an old newspaper that mentioned disappearances in 1967," Bernard said. "And in 1949 and 1931 as well."

"Goes back further. Every eighteen years, like clockwork. Spring and summer. Usually five or six people. Then it stops." He sighed heavily. "Been studying the pattern since I became chief. My predecessor kept detailed records, his predecessor before him. Documented back to 1886---when Edmund Marlowe built that house."

"And you've never found an explanation?" Theresa asked.

Rowan shook his head. "Theories, sure. Plenty of those. Serial killer. Cult activity. Mass hysteria. But evidence?" He gestured to the items on his desk. "These are the first physical connections we've ever had."

"Will you investigate our house?" Theresa pressed.

"I'll send a deputy out this afternoon," Rowan promised. "But unless we find something conclusive, there's not much we can do."

As they stood to leave, Rowan held Bernard back. "Professor, a word?"

Theresa stepped outside, watching through the window as the two men spoke in low voices. When Bernard emerged, his expression was troubled.

"What did he say to you?" she demanded as they walked to the car.

Bernard hesitated. "He suggested that we stay somewhere else for a while. Just until they complete their investigation."

"Did he say anything else? About the bed?"

Bernard started the car, not meeting her eyes. "He said the previous chiefs believed there was something... unnatural about it. But that's just local superstition."

"Is it? Then how do you explain the evidence in our house? The bed that moves on its own? The windows that keep opening?"

Bernard pulled out of the parking lot, his knuckles white on the steering wheel. "I don't know, Theresa. I don't have a logical explanation. But I'm not ready to believe in supernatural beds that eat people, either."

Theresa turned to stare out the window, watching the small town roll by. "Then what do we do?"

"We'll stay at the Holiday Inn for a few days. Let the police do their job. And maybe... maybe we should consider selling the house."

"Selling it?" The suggestion hit Theresa like a physical blow. Despite everything, she still loved that house---the house she'd dreamed of her whole life. "We can't just give up on it."

Bernard reached over and squeezed her hand. "We'll figure this out. I promise."

But as they drove back up the hill to pack their overnight bags, Theresa couldn't shake the feeling that they were already too deeply entangled in whatever secret the Marlowe House was hiding.

The police investigation yielded nothing conclusive. Deputies searched the house thoroughly, focusing on the third-floor bedroom, but found no additional evidence. They interviewed neighbors, checked Theresa and Bernard's backgrounds, and filed a report suggesting that the items had been planted in the house by an unknown party, possibly as a cruel prank.

After three nights at the Holiday Inn, Bernard insisted they return home.

"We can't live in a hotel forever. And there's been no sign of any danger."

Theresa agreed, but with one condition. "I want to get rid of that bed. Today. I don't care if we have to tear down the wall."

Bernard agreed, and they spent the afternoon trying to dismantle the strange four-poster. The bed resisted. Screws wouldn't turn. Nails wouldn't pull free. Wood seemed impervious to Bernard's saw.

"Like it's made of stone," he muttered, wiping sweat after an hour of fruitless labor. "Never seen wood this hard."

In the end, they gave up, exhausted and frustrated. Bernard suggested blocking the door to the room, and they pushed a heavy bookcase in front of it.

"At least now we'll know if someone tries to get in there," he said.

That night, Theresa lay awake, listening. The house was quiet, unnaturally so. No settling creaks, no whistling wind through the eaves. Nothing.

Until 2:17 AM, when the noise began again.

This time, it wasn't just creaking. There was a scratching sound as well, like claws dragging across wooden flooring. And beneath it all, a low, rhythmic hum that seemed to vibrate through the walls themselves.

"Bernard," she whispered, shaking him awake. "Do you hear that?"

He sat up, alert this time. "Yes. I hear it."

Together, they crept to the third-floor staircase. The bookcase they'd positioned in front of the bedroom door lay on its side, books scattered across the hallway floor. The door itself stood open, darkness spilling out.

The noises were louder now---a wet, slithering sound mixed with the scratching and creaking. Something heavy thudded against the floor.

"We should leave," Theresa said, tugging Bernard's arm. "Right now."

But Bernard stepped forward. He had to know. "Probably just a raccoon that got in."

"A raccoon? Bernard, be serious. Whatever's in there pushed over a two-hundred-pound bookcase."

He pulled a small flashlight from his robe. "I'll just peek. Any sign of danger, we leave."

Before Theresa could protest further, Bernard approached the open door, flashlight raised. As he reached the threshold, the noises inside the room stopped.

Bernard hesitated, then stepped inside, the beam of his flashlight cutting through the darkness. "There's nothing here," he called back to Theresa, who remained frozen at the top of the stairs. "Just the bed."

"Is it in the same place?"

A pause. "No. It's in the center of the room again."

Theresa's heart hammered against her ribs. "Bernard, please come back."

"Hold on. There's something... odd about it." His voice had taken on that distant quality it got when he puzzled through a challenging equation. "The proportions seem different."

"Different how?"

Another long pause. "It's... larger, somehow. And the posts... they're not quite..."

His voice cut off.

"Bernard?" Theresa called, her fear momentarily overcome by concern for her husband. "Bernard, what's happening?"

No answer came.

"Bernard!" She forced herself to approach the door. Everything in her wanted to run the other direction.

Just as she reached the doorway, a strangled cry came from within---a sound she had never heard Bernard make before. It was followed by a wet, tearing noise and a heavy thud.

Theresa froze in the doorway. Her mind couldn't process what she saw.

The bed was gone. In its place---something that barely resembled a bed. If beds had jointed legs and massive feathered wings brushing the ceiling. The wooden posts had become articulated limbs ending in razor talons. The spherical finials were giant bulbous eyes, horizontal slits wide open, showing glistening crimson irises.

In the center where the mattress had been, a massive maw lined with needle teeth was closing around what remained of Bernard.

Theresa couldn't scream. Couldn't move. Could only watch as the creature finished its meal, Bernard's legs disappearing into its grotesque mouth with a final sound that made her stomach turn.

The thing turned its massive eyes toward her, the red glow illuminating her frozen form. It made a sound then---a chittering, clicking noise that might have been laughter.

Instinct broke Theresa's paralysis. She turned and ran, stumbling down stairs, only thought to reach the front door, escape into night.

Behind her---skittering of multiple legs on hardwood, rustle of massive wings unfolding. The thing was coming.

Theresa hit the second-floor landing knowing she wouldn't make the front door in time. The thing was too fast, too close behind. In desperate panic, she veered toward one of the casement windows overlooking the front yard.

Without hesitation, she hurled herself through it, glass shattering around her as she fell into empty space.

For a moment, she was suspended in the cool night air, the ground rushing up to meet her. She closed her eyes, preparing for impact.

But the impact never came. Instead, she felt something grab her from behind, sharp talons digging into her shoulders. The sound of beating wings filled her ears as she was jerked upward, away from the ground.

Theresa opened her eyes to find herself dangling high above the Marlowe House, held in the grip of the monstrous creature. She twisted her head to look up, and found herself staring directly into two massive red eyes, their horizontal pupils dilating with hunger.

"No," she whispered, struggling weakly against its iron grip. "Please, no."

The thing made that chittering sound again, almost gentle now. Its mouth opened, revealing Bernard's watch caught between two of its teeth.

As Theresa's sanity fractured, her last coherent thought was that at least now she understood why the disappearances happened every eighteen years.

It takes time to digest so many meals.

Sheriff Rowan stood on the Marlowe House porch, watching deputies place evidence markers around the broken second-floor window. In morning light, the house looked peaceful, beautiful---Victorian charm hiding the horrors inside.

"Any sign of them?" Deputy Marshall asked, climbing the steps with his notebook.

Rowan shook his head. "Nothing. Just like the others."

"That's five disappearances now," Marshall noted, flipping through his previous reports. "Same as in 2003. And 1985 before that."

"It usually stops at six," Rowan said quietly. "One more to go, then we have eighteen years of peace."

Marshall frowned. "You don't really believe that old legend, do you? About the house?"

Rowan gave him a weary look. "I've been studying the police records since I became chief. My predecessor kept detailed files, going back over a century. The pattern is undeniable."

"But a... a monster? A bed that turns into some kind of creature? That's---"

"Insane? Impossible?" Rowan turned to stare up at the third-floor windows. "Maybe. But tell me, Marshall, how do you explain two people vanishing from a locked house? No signs of forced entry except for the window the wife jumped through? No blood, no struggle, nothing missing except the couple themselves?"

Marshall had no answer.

"The old records contain witness accounts," Rowan continued, his voice low. "Stories about Edmund Marlowe bringing something back with him from his travels in Southeast Asia. Something that wasn't furniture at all, but needed a place to hide, to rest between feedings. The records suggest it attached itself to Marlowe, followed him home."

"What kind of... attachment?"

Rowan's mouth tightened beneath his mustache. "The kind that helped Marlowe become the richest man in the county almost overnight. His business rivals had a habit of disappearing with convenient timing." He sighed, rubbing his temples. "Of course, Marlowe didn't understand what he was dealing with. Or that it would continue long after he was gone."

Marshall shook his head. "If you really believe that, sir, why not tear the place down? Burn it to the ground?"

"Two different owners tried that, in 1922 and again in 1976. The demolition crews refused to enter the house after the first day. Said they heard... things." Rowan's gaze returned to the third-floor windows. "Besides, I'm not convinced destroying the house would kill what lives inside it. It might just send it looking for a new home."

A shout from inside drew their attention. One of the deputies appeared at the front door, face pale.

"Sheriff, you need to see this."

They followed him to the second-floor landing, where glass shards still glittered on hardwood beneath the broken window. The deputy pointed near the wall.

A small, delicate silver watch lay partially hidden beneath a splinter of wood. Rowan recognized it as the one Theresa Wakely had been wearing when she came to his office.

"That's not the strange part," the deputy said, leading them further up the stairs to the third floor.

The door to the bedroom stood wide open. Inside, the space was empty---no furniture, no bed, nothing but dust-covered floors and faded wallpaper.

"Where's the bed?" Rowan demanded. "The four-poster that was in here?"

The deputy shrugged helplessly. "That's just it, sir. There's no sign of any bed at all. The room is empty, like it's been for decades."

Marshall stared at the empty space in confusion. "But the Wakelys described it in detail. We have their statement."

"Maybe they brought something in themselves," the deputy suggested. "And whatever it was, it's gone now---just like they are."

Rowan approached the casement windows, which stood partially
open despite his men closing and locking them when they arrived.
Through wavy old glass, he could see all of Crestwick spread be-
low---church, town square, his own house on Murphy Street.

Moving to close the windows, something caught his eye---dark
silhouette against morning sky, too large for a bird, moving with
purpose toward town.

Rowan froze, watching as the shape grew smaller with distance. Just
before it disappeared from view, he could have sworn he saw something
dangling beneath it---something that might have been a human form.

He closed the windows firmly and turned back to his men.

"We're done here," he said. "File the report as unexplained disappearance, consistent with previous cases. And put the house back on
the market."

"On the market?" Marshall asked, incredulous. "After what happened
to the Wakelys?"

Rowan nodded grimly. "It has to be occupied. That's part of the
pattern too. And it won't be active again for another eighteen years."
He headed for the door, then paused, looking back at the empty space
where the bed should have been. "Mark the case closed. Nothing more
we can do now."

As they left the Marlowe House, Rowan glanced up at the sky one
last time. The silhouette was gone, but he knew it would return. It
always did, hungry for just one more meal before its long rest.

In the distance, church bells rang, signaling the start of a new day in
Crestwick. Rowan wondered who would be next. The young paper
boy? The widow who lived alone on Pine Street? Or maybe someone
from his own department, growing too curious about the pattern of
disappearances?

Only one more, he reminded himself. Then eighteen years of peace.

He climbed into his cruiser and started the engine, trying not to think
about how quickly eighteen years could pass. Trying not to imagine
the thing with the red eyes and beating wings, circling high above the
town, scanning for its final meal of the season.

Trying not to envision that massive mouthful of teeth, chewing
endlessly in the darkness.

The Lot

Terry Walthers pressed his back against the rough brick wall of Murphy's Hardware, watching the school bus rumble past like his dad's old pickup truck when it needed a new muffler. His heart thumped like sneakers in Mom's dryer---not scared-thumping, but the good kind, like Christmas morning or snow days when they called off school.

He was skipping. Actually skipping school for the first time ever in his whole nine years.

Mrs. Harris was gonna mark him absent. Mom was gonna get that phone call that made her face go all tight and worried. There'd be trouble---probably no TV for a week, maybe longer. But standing here with his backpack cutting into his shoulders and the cold October air making his nose run, Terry didn't care about getting in trouble.

School had been awful lately. Ever since Kenny Webb found out where Terry's lunch money came from---that pickle jar Mom kept behind the flour, the one with "EMERGENCY FUND" written on masking tape. Ever since Kenny cornered him by the water fountain and told half the fourth grade that Terry Walthers was "poor trash" whose dad took off because he couldn't stand living with them anymore.

The other kids laughed. Even Sarah Mitchell---who Terry liked since second grade, who had freckles like cinnamon sugar on her nose---even Sarah giggled behind her hand while her cheeks turned red.

This morning Terry woke up to Mom coughing again. That wet, gross cough that sounded like someone gargling with gravel. The kind that meant she'd call the diner and tell them she was too sick to work. He made up his mind right there in his narrow bed, listening to her hack and wheeze in the next room. Mrs. Harris could teach long division to somebody else today. Kenny Webb could pick on some other kid. Terry was going exploring.

He told Mom he felt fine and would catch the bus like always. She nodded from her bed, looking white as the pillowcase, and reminded him about his peanut butter sandwich. Terry kissed her forehead---hot like the top of the stove---and promised he'd eat it.

Now he crouched behind Murphy's, watching his classmates smoosh their faces against the bus windows as it wheezed away toward Riverside Elementary. Janice Eldenberry waved at him from her usual seat, probably wondering why he wasn't climbing aboard. Terry waved back and waited until the bus disappeared around the corner where Maple Street turned toward school.

Then he walked the other way.

Downtown Westover Valley stretched out in front of him like one of those adventure books from the library. Terry had never walked these streets alone during school time, never seen the stores with their metal gates pulled down like sleepy eyelids, never noticed how weird everything looked when all the kids were locked up in classrooms. The quiet felt thick and heavy, like the air before a thunderstorm.

Terry walked past Murphy's Hardware with its window full of rakes and snow shovels, past Antonelli's Bakery where Mom sometimes bought day-old donuts when she had extra money from tips, past Sal's Barber Shop with its red and white pole spinning around and around. Each building looked smaller in the morning light, different than he'd expected. By the time he reached the edge of downtown, the empty feeling in his stomach wasn't just from hunger.

This was supposed to be fun. This was supposed to be an adventure. But walking around by himself just felt... empty.

That's when he remembered the lot.

Every kid in Westover Valley knew about the old playground behind the Woolworth's that closed down. Chain-link fence all around it, with rusty barbed wire on top that looked like metal spaghetti that had gone bad. Signs saying "NO TRESPASSING" hung everywhere like white flags. The place had been empty forever---probably since before Terry was even born.

His cousin Jake told him stories about the lot last summer at the family barbecue, whispering while the grown-ups argued about baseball and drank beer from cans that sweated in the heat.

"The fence fixes itself," Jake had said, looking around to make sure no adults could hear. "You cut a hole to get in, and when you want to leave, the metal's grown back together like it was never broken. My buddy Rick saw it happen. Said the metal moved around like it was alive or something."

Terry had laughed the way you laugh at ghost stories around a campfire. But Jake's face stayed serious as a church service.

"And there's this slide in there. Shiny like a new penny no matter how old everything else gets. Kids can't help riding it, but every time they do, they get paler. Quieter. Like they leave a piece of themselves on that slide forever."

Standing at the entrance now, Terry was disappointed that the fence was taller than he remembered, chain link rusted orange-brown and topped with coils of barbed wire. Beyond it, he could see the playground---rusted swings with broken chains, a merry-go-round that listed to one side like a sinking ship.

The "NO TRESPASSING" sign had faded to pink, letters barely readable. Someone had scratched "COPS SUCK" underneath in wobbly letters.

Terry walked up to the fence, not caring who might see him. He was supposed to be in school, but Mom was sick again and had slept through her alarm. No point going to school three hours late just to get detention.

Finding a way in took forever. The fence looked solid enough to keep in zoo animals. But New England winters had done damage. Posts pulled loose here, wire snapped and curled back there. Near the back corner where the lot met the woods, Terry found what he needed: a tear in the chain link just wide enough for a skinny kid to squeeze through.

The metal scraped his backpack and caught his jacket, but Terry squeezed through without cutting himself too bad. Standing up on the other side, brushing rust flakes off his sleeves, he felt like an explorer in his adventure books.

The playground spread out before him, overgrown but still recognizable. Dandelions and crabgrass pushed through cracks in the blacktop. Vines wrapped around the swing set. A merry-go-round sat frozen, its painted horses faded to bone-white. At the far end, a jungle gym stuck up from the weeds.

But the slide caught his attention and wouldn't let go.

It stood in the center of the lot, tall as a house. The ladder was rusty and weeds grew thick around the bottom, but the slide itself gleamed in the morning sun like someone had just polished it. Weird. Everything else looked forgotten and rotting, but the slide looked almost new.

Terry walked toward it, sneakers crunching on broken glass and crumbling asphalt that felt squishy in places. Up close, the slide looked even stranger. The metal was smooth as ice, no rust anywhere. Even the platform at the top looked solid.

"Hello?" he called out, mostly to hear his own voice. The word bounced around, echoing off buildings and coming back from three directions, like other kids were hiding somewhere.

Terry dropped his backpack and tested the first step of the ladder. It held fine. The second step, too. By the time he'd climbed halfway up, his nervousness had turned to excitement. This beat any book. This was real exploring.

From the platform, Terry could see over the fence into the neighborhood. There was Molloy's Ice Cream Shop, where he'd spent summer afternoons when Dad still lived with them and they had money for ice cream. There was the parking lot behind St. Mary's, empty except for Father McKenna's beat-up station wagon. And way off, he could just make out Riverside Elementary, where Mrs. Harris was probably wondering where Terry Walthers had gotten to.

The thought of school made him smile. While his classmates sat learning fractions, he sat on a throne of rust and metal, king of his own secret kingdom. Terry pulled his peanut butter sandwich from his backpack and ate it slowly, tasting freedom.

When he finished eating, Terry stood up and looked at the slide. The metal gleamed like water, smooth as ice. He'd come all this way. Might as well try it out.

Terry sat down at the top, put his hands on either side for balance, and pushed off.

The ride down was faster than any slide he'd ever been on. Way faster. The metal was slicker than wet glass, and he picked up speed like a runaway car. Halfway down, Terry realized he was moving too fast to stop. Wind whipped his hair back and made his eyes water. His stomach dropped like he was falling off a cliff.

He hit the bottom hard enough to knock the wind out of him, rolling forward onto the cracked asphalt and scraping his hands. For a minute Terry just lay there gasping, his heart beating like a trapped bird. That had been scary and exciting and awesome all at once.

But when he picked himself up and brushed off his clothes, Terry noticed something strange. The scrapes on his hands weren't bleeding. They should have been---he'd hit hard enough to skin his palms good. But when he looked at his hands, he saw only pale scratches that didn't hurt.

Even weirder, when he looked back at the slide, it seemed different somehow. The metal didn't gleam as bright as before. In fact, it looked duller, like someone had breathed on it and fogged it up.

Terry walked around to the ladder and looked at the bottom rung. Did it have more rust than before? He could have sworn it looked cleaner when he'd first climbed up. But maybe he just hadn't been paying attention.

He climbed up again, more careful this time, and took another ride down. The speed was just as incredible, like falling through the air. He tumbled at the bottom, this time scraping his knee on the asphalt. But still no blood, no real pain. Just pale marks that looked like old scars instead of fresh cuts.

The slide looked different afterward. Dimmer. More beat-up.

By the fourth trip down, Terry started noticing other changes. His backpack, which he'd left at the bottom of the slide, had faded from bright blue to grayish, like someone had washed it with bleach. His sandwich wrapper, which had been white and crisp when he finished eating, now looked yellow and crumbly like old newspaper.

But the worst change was in himself. When Terry looked down at his hands, his arms, his legs, everything seemed less bright than before. Not hurt exactly, but faded. Like someone had adjusted the color on Mom's old TV set, turning everything gray and washed-out.

Terry shivered and decided it was time to go home. He'd had his adventure, proved he was brave enough to skip school and explore on his own. Now he wanted to go back, maybe make Mom some soup, maybe watch cartoons until the school buses came back.

But when he walked over to the gap in the fence, Terry's blood turned cold as pond water in January.

The tear in the chain link was gone.

Not fixed---gone. The metal had somehow grown back together, solid as if it had never been broken. Terry pressed his face against the fence, looking for another way out, but everywhere he checked, the chain link stood perfect and unbroken, like it had just been put up yesterday.

"Hey!" he called out, not sure who he expected to answer. "Hey, I need to get out of here!"

His voice echoed back from different directions, but the echoes sounded flat and empty, like they were coming from miles away.

Terry ran along the fence, pulling at each section, kicking at posts, searching for any weak spot he might have missed. His hands shook as he grabbed the wire. His breath came in short puffs.

How long had he been here? It felt like maybe an hour, but the light had changed. The sun hung almost straight overhead now, casting short shadows that made everything look harsh. Had he somehow lost hours without noticing?

Terry thought about Mom, probably wondering why the school hadn't called about him being absent. He thought about Mrs. Harris, maybe worried that something bad had happened to him. But mostly he thought about the fence that had somehow healed itself while he wasn't looking.

Terry went back to the slide, hoping that climbing higher might help him see a way out. But as he got closer, he stopped dead.

The slide wasn't empty anymore.

A figure sat at the top, blurry like morning fog. Terry squinted to make out details---a boy about his age, wearing clothes that looked like they belonged in Grandma's old photo albums. Knickers and a white shirt, suspenders and polished shoes. But the boy was see-through, like a reflection in water, and Terry could see the rusty platform right through his body.

"Good morning to you," the boy called down, his voice sounding formal and stiff, like kids on old TV shows. The words echoed from miles away. "Are you here to enjoy the slide as well?"

Terry's mouth went dry. "Who are you?"

"My name is William. William Ashford. What's yours?"

"Terry. Terry Walthers."

William smiled, but his face flickered like a candle. "Pleased to meet you, Terry. I must say, it's been quite lonesome here without proper company."

"How did you get in here?" Terry looked around wildly. "The fence---there's no way through the fence."

"Why, through the hole in the wire, same as you did, I should think." William's voice sounded confused, like he was trying to remember something from long ago. "Though I believe that was some time past. Time moves quite strangely within these boundaries."

"What do you mean?"

Instead of answering, William pushed off from the top of the slide. He came down with the same impossible speed Terry had felt, but when he reached the bottom, something terrible happened. Instead of tumbling forward, William seemed to fade even more. His outline became less clear, his whole body more see-through. By the time he stood up, he looked like the shadow of a shadow.

"Each ride takes its toll," William said, his voice now echoing from far away. "At first, one loses color, substance. But in time..." He gestured to himself. "In time, precious little remains."

Terry backed away from the slide, his heart beating like a drum. "That's impossible. That's not how things work."

William tilted his head, studying Terry with eyes that were like holes in the air. "How long do you suppose you've been here?"

The question caught Terry off guard. "I don't know. An hour maybe?"

"I thought much the same when I arrived. But look at the sun's position, Terry. Mark the shadows well."

Terry looked up, squinting against the bright light. The sun had moved again, sliding across the sky too fast. The shadows around the playground equipment had gotten shorter, which meant it was close to noon.

"That can't be right," Terry whispered.

"This place exists outside ordinary time," William explained, his form flickering like a dying light bulb. "A single day here might be minutes in the world beyond these barriers. Or it might span years. The slide feeds upon time itself, upon the very essence of our existence. Each ride costs months, perhaps years. And the more one fades, the stronger becomes the urge to ride again. It becomes the only thing that makes one feel truly alive, even as it erases one's very being."

Terry's legs felt like wet spaghetti. He sank down onto the cracked asphalt, staring at his hands. Did they look paler than before? Did his jacket look grayer?

"How long have you been here?" he asked.

William's form shimmered, becoming even more see-through. "I came to escape my Latin lessons, you see. Such a beautiful spring day it was, and I heard older boys speaking of this secret playground. That was..." He paused, his voice becoming distant. "The details grow dim. The early days of the Great Depression, I believe. So very long ago that even the memories begin to fade."

Terry felt like someone had poured ice cubes into his stomach. "That's impossible. That's like ninety years ago."

"Time," William repeated, his voice barely a whisper. "It flows differently here. I have ridden the slide so many times I've lost count. Trying to recapture that first thrill, that initial taste of freedom. But each journey takes more. Soon, I fear, there won't be enough of me left to ride at all. And then..." He gestured to the empty playground around them. "Then I shall become part of the lot itself, as have all the others."

"Others?"

William pointed to the merry-go-round, to the jungle gym, to the equipment scattered around the lot. Now that Terry looked more carefully, he could see them—the faintest outlines, shapes that were more like suggestions than real things. Children from different times, wearing clothes from different decades, all of them faded to almost nothing.

"We all came seeking adventure," William said, his voice so faint Terry had to strain to hear it. "We all found the slide irresistible. And we've all remained here ever since, riding again and again, growing fainter with each descent, unable to leave."

Terry jumped to his feet. "I'm getting out of here. There has to be a way."

William shook his head, the motion making his form blur even more. "The barriers seal themselves once you enter. The lot desires to keep us here, desires us to feed the slide with our substance, our time. The only escape is to fade completely, to become part of the lot itself. But by then, one is no longer oneself. One is merely an echo."

But Terry wasn't listening. He ran to the fence again, pulling at the chain link with his hands, kicking at posts, searching for any weakness. Behind him, he could hear William calling out, warning him that struggling only made the lot stronger, only made the slide more tempting.

And it was true. Even as Terry fought against the fence, he found his eyes drawn back to the slide. It gleamed again, polished and inviting, promising another incredible ride down its impossible surface. Part of him wanted to forget about escape, to climb back up that ladder and feel that amazing rush of speed again.

But another part of him---the part that remembered Mom's fever, her awful cough, her need for someone to take care of her---fought against the temptation.

Terry pulled off his backpack and swung it at the fence with everything he had. The metal rang like a church bell, but held. He swung it again, and again, each impact sending vibrations up his arms like electric shocks. Behind him, the other children watched with faces full of sadness and longing, their ghostly forms barely visible in the afternoon light.

"It won't work," William said, his voice now so faint it might have been wind through the equipment. "I tried the same thing for what felt like years before I gave up. The lot doesn't want to let us go."

But Terry kept swinging. His backpack started to tear, his things spilling out across the asphalt, but he didn't stop. Somewhere in the back of his mind, he could hear Mom calling his name, could see her lying in bed waiting for him to come home.

She needs me, Terry thought. She needs me to come home and take care of her.

On what felt like the hundredth swing, something gave way. Not the fence itself, but something deeper, something Terry couldn't see or name. He felt suddenly lighter, as if a weight he hadn't realized he was carrying had been lifted from his shoulders.

The tear in the fence reappeared.

William gasped, his see-through form shimmering with excitement. "How did you---"

"I don't know," Terry said, stuffing his scattered belongings back into his torn backpack. "But I'm not staying to find out."

He squeezed through the gap in the fence, ignoring the way the metal scraped against his jacket. Behind him, he could hear William calling out, begging him not to leave, begging him to come back and ride the slide just one more time.

But Terry was running, racing away from the lot as fast as his legs could carry him. The sun had started to set---somehow, an entire day had passed in what felt like a few hours---and he needed to get home before Mom started worrying.

As he ran through the darkening streets of Westover Valley, Terry could swear he heard the sound of children laughing behind him, the creak of swing sets moving in windless air, the metallic ring of a slide being used by invisible riders. But he didn't look back. He wouldn't dare.

Something strange happened as Terry ran. With each step away from the lot, he felt lighter, more solid, like the grayness that had been creeping into his bones was flowing away like dirty water down a drain. The life he'd lost to that terrible slide didn't just come back---it felt changed somehow, like it had been somewhere it was needed more than he could understand.

Terry arrived home just as the streetlights flickered on. He found Mom in the kitchen, stirring a pot of vegetable soup on the stove. Her fever had broken, and she looked better than she had in days---not just recovered, but somehow more alive, more colorful than he'd seen her in months.

"There you are," she said, smiling. "How was school?"

Terry hesitated, then decided on a version of the truth. "It was different. I learned some stuff."

She ruffled his hair and ladled soup into two bowls. "I'm glad. You look tired, though. Maybe you should go to bed early tonight."

Terry nodded, exhausted down to his bones. "Mom? Do you know anything about the old playground behind the Woolworth's?"

His mother paused, her spoon halfway to her mouth. "The lot? Why do you ask?"

"Just curious. Some kids at school were talking about it."

She set down her spoon, her face growing serious. "Terry, I want you to promise me you'll never go there. Never even go near there."

"Why?"

"Because..." She struggled to find the words. "Because children have disappeared there. Over the years, different children. They go in and they don't come out, or if they do come out, they've changed."

Terry's soup had grown cold in his bowl. "Changed how?"

"Quieter. Sadder. Like they've lost something important and can't remember what it was." She reached over and took his hand. "Promise me, Terry. Promise me you'll stay away from that place."

Terry squeezed her hand, thinking about William Ashford, about all the faded children trapped in that timeless playground. "I promise, Mom. I'll never go back there."

And he meant it. But sometimes, late at night, Terry would lie in bed and remember the feeling of sliding down that impossible slide, the rush of speed and freedom and danger all mixed together. He would remember the way the metal had gleamed in the sunlight, the way time had seemed to bend and stretch around him.

And sometimes, just sometimes, he would think about how easy it would be to slip back through that fence, to climb that ladder one more time.

After all, what was one more ride?

But Terry would pull his blankets up over his head and force himself to think about other things---about Mom's smile when her fever broke, about the homework he still needed to finish, about anything except the lot and its terrible, beautiful slide.

Because Terry Walthers knew that some adventures were too dangerous to repeat, and some playgrounds were meant to stay abandoned forever.

Even if they called to you in your dreams, promising just one more ride down into darkness.

The Knob

Gordon Talbot straightened his clip-on tie in the washroom mirror. Gray Sears slacks, same white shirt, same routine for thirty years. Thirty years of watching the knob.

His world was twelve feet square---concrete box buried under Nevada scrub. Government desk, government chair with a loose armrest, composition logbook, black rotary phone that hadn't rung since '97. And one brass knob mounted in the far wall, flush with the concrete.

The knob had a dull shine under the harsh lights, worn smooth like an old doorknob. Sometimes Gordon wondered if it looked the same back in '93 when they first brought him down here, fresh from orientation with his security clearance still warm from the laminator.

"Simple job, Talbot," Director Mills had said, drumming fingers on his metal desk. "Watch the knob. Log any changes---color, temp, if it moves a millimeter. And don't touch the damn thing. Clear?"

Gordon had asked the obvious questions. What's it do? Why watch it? What happens if---

Mills cut him off with that look every government supervisor perfected. "Above your pay grade, Talbot."

Thirty years of eight-hour shifts watching a piece of brass do absolutely nothing.

The elevator wheezed down past numbered levels. Gordon sipped coffee from his thermos---same brand from the Terrible Herbst since Desert Storm. Sub-level 1, 2, 3... Counter stopped at 12, though he figured the place went deeper.

Foster looked up from his crossword. "Morning, Gordon. Last week?"

"Last week." Gordon signed the clipboard, muscle memory. "Janet's already making retirement lists."

"Bet she is. Thirty years wondering what you actually do down here."

"Told her pest control." Not exactly a lie.

The vault door to Station 7 sealed behind him with a hollow clang. Gordon settled into his chair---left arm rest loose, right one missing the padding---and opened the logbook to a fresh page.

Day 7,827. 0800 hrs. Status: No change. Brass normal. Temp normal. Position unchanged. No movement. No anomalies.

Same words, different day. The knob never moved, never got hot, never did anything.

But that wasn't quite true.

Gordon stared across the room. Over the years, he'd started noticing things. Nothing for the reports---how do you log a feeling? Some days the brass caught light differently. How shadows seemed to pool around it when storms rolled in. Once, during a power outage, he could've sworn the thing glowed in the dark.

Course, he'd never written any of that down. Mills would've shipped him to a psych eval faster than you could say "stress-related incident."

The morning crawled by. Gordon made his hourly entries, each one identical to the last seven thousand. At 10:15, he picked up the phone.

"Daily report," Mills answered on the first ring. Always did.

"Gordon here. No changes. All normal."

"Good. Anything else?"

Gordon hesitated, watching the knob. "Sir, about my replacement---"

"That's handled, Talbot."

"Yeah, but someone's taking over, right? Station won't sit empty?"

"Why? Something to report?"

"No, sir. Just... well, thirty years. Curious who's getting the baton."

"Curiosity's what killed the cat, Talbot. Finish your week. File your reports. Go home to your wife."

Click. Gordon stared at the dead phone, then back at the knob. For just a second---maybe he was seeing things---but it looked like the brass had shifted maybe a quarter inch to the left. He blinked, refocused. Nope. Same spot. Same angle. Same everything.

11:00. Knob status: No change.
12:00. Knob status: No change.
13:00. Knob status: No change.

Charles Whitman showed up for his weekly rounds, wheeling in his cart of tools like he had for fifteen years. Facility maintenance was lonely work, but Charles seemed to like it.

"How's retirement shaping up?" Charles swept his flashlight across ceiling fixtures.

"Janet's got plans. Deck needs refinishing. Garage needs painting. Apparently I need to learn about fertilizer and mulch."

"Sounds like hell." Charles knelt by the wall, examining the concrete around the knob mount. "You ever wonder what this thing actually does?"

Gordon's coffee went down wrong. In thirty years, nobody had asked that question out loud. "Not my job to wonder."

"Come on, man. Thirty years of your life. You gotta have theories."

Gordon glanced at the security camera, its red light steady. "Figure it's some kind of sensor. Atmospheric pressure, seismic activity. Something like that."

"Bullshit." Charles ran his fingers along the wall, careful not to touch the brass. "Look at this mounting job. Whoever put this in was rushing, big time. See these gouges? And look here---"

Charles pointed to scratches in the concrete around the knob's base. "Impact patterns. Like something was hitting the wall from the inside when they put this in."

Gordon's mouth went dry. "Maybe you should put that in your maintenance report."

"Should I? Or should I keep my mouth shut like everybody else around here?"

"Charles---"

"Thirty years, Gordon. Thirty years watching something that never changes, never moves, never does a damn thing. What kind of sensor works like that?"

"The kind that keeps something worse from happening."

The words popped out before Gordon could stop them. Charles stared at him.

"Keeps what from happening, Gordon?"

"I don't know. Don't want to know."

But that was horseshit, wasn't it? Gordon did want to know. Had wanted to know for three decades. The wondering followed him home, sat at the dinner table, kept him awake nights. What was behind the wall? What would happen if someone turned the knob?

Charles packed up his tools. "You know what I think? They built this place around something they found. Something they couldn't move, couldn't get rid of. So they buried it and stuck someone down here to make sure it stays put."

"That's a dangerous way to think."

"Everything about this place is dangerous, Gordon. But you know what's really dangerous? Retiring without ever knowing what you spent thirty years protecting the world from."

Charles left. Gordon sat alone with the knob and thirty years of questions he'd never asked.

15:00. Knob status: No change.
16:00. Knob status: No change.

At 16:17, the lights flickered.

Just once, maybe two seconds, but Gordon was ready. In that moment of darkness, the knob blazed like a small star. Not brass anymore, but pure blue-white light pulsing like a heartbeat.

The fluorescents kicked back on. The knob went back to normal.

Gordon's hand shook as he reached for his pen. He wrote: *16:17. Brief power fluctuation. Knob status: No change.*

He stared at the words, then scratched them out. Started over: *16:17. Power fluctuation. Observed luminescence approx. 2 seconds.*

Scratched that out too. Final entry: *16:17. Knob status: No change.*

At 17:00, Gordon packed his thermos, signed out with Foster, and rode the elevator up to ground level. The Nevada sun hammered the parking lot, turning the asphalt soft. Forty-five minutes through empty desert to get home, same drive he'd made 7,827 times. But tonight something felt different. The sagebrush looked sharper. The mountains felt closer. Like the world had shifted when he wasn't looking.

Janet met him at the door with sweet tea and that smile that had gotten him through three decades of "Sorry honey, can't talk about work."

"How was work, honey?"

"Same as always." Gordon kissed her cheek, tasting his own salt. "Nothing ever changes."

But everything had changed. For thirty years, Gordon had been the perfect employee. Observed, recorded, reported. By the book. But now he'd lied in his official log. Covered up an anomaly. Not for national security, but because he wanted to see what happened next.

Dinner was meatloaf and mashed potatoes and Janet talking about retirement plans while Gordon nodded and made the right noises. His mind kept replaying those two seconds of blue-white light.

What if the knob wasn't meant to be watched? What if it was meant to be used?

That night Gordon dreamed of corridors that went deeper than Sub-level 12. He walked through darkness, following the sound of something huge breathing behind concrete walls. At the end of the hall, a door waited. Not brass this time, but black metal covered in symbols that hurt to look at.

In the dream, Gordon reached for the handle.

He woke with his hand stretched toward the ceiling, fingers grasping air.

Tuesday morning, same routine. Coffee, elevator, logbook. But the knob looked different. Not obviously---Gordon would've bet his pension it hadn't moved. But something in its surface seemed more awake.

Day 7,828. Time: 08:00. Knob status: No change.

The morning dragged. At 10:30, the lights flickered again.

This time Gordon was watching. The fluorescents stuttered, dimmed, and for three full seconds the room went black.

The knob erupted in silver fire. Light poured from its surface, casting hard shadows on the walls. Heat radiated from the brass, and underneath, something else. A vibration. A pull.

The lights came back. The knob went dark.

Gordon wrote: *10:30. Power fluctuation, 3 seconds. Knob status: No change.*

The lie came easier now.

Wednesday. Thursday. Friday.

Each day brought longer outages, brighter light from the knob. Gordon documented none of it, crafting careful lies while the truth burned behind his eyes.

By Friday, he could feel the knob's pull even when the lights were steady. It whispered to him across twelve feet of concrete, promising answers in a language older than words.

Monday morning. Gordon's last shift started at 08:00. Foster seemed genuinely sad to see him go.

"Thirty years," Foster said, shaking his head. "You're a legend, man. Most people can't handle the isolation more than two years."

"Wasn't so bad. Quiet work suits me."

"Well, enjoy retirement. You earned it."

Gordon signed in for the last time. The vault door sealed him alone with his brass nemesis for eight more hours.

He opened the logbook to a fresh page. *Day 7,833. Time: 08:00.* The pen hovered over paper.

What would his final entry be? What truth or lie would cap three decades?

The knob watched him. In the fluorescent glare it looked ordinary. A simple brass fitting. But Gordon could feel its awareness like heat from a coal stove.

Knob status: No change.

At 10:00, Mills called.

"Final report, Talbot."

"All normal, sir. No changes."

"Good. Your replacement arrives at 16:30. Briefing at 17:00."

"Replacement?"

"Agent Torres. Fresh from Quantico. Eager to serve."

Gordon's blood chilled. "How old is she, sir?"

"Why's that matter, Talbot?"

Young. Mid-twenties, probably. Full of patriotic fire and respect for authority. Someone who'd follow orders without question, who'd watch the knob for the next thirty years without ever asking why.

"Just curious about continuity, sir."

"Your curiosity is becoming a problem, Talbot. File your reports and clear out. You did good work."

The line went dead. Gordon stared at the phone. Thirty years of exemplary service, just to hand his post to someone who'd never ask the right questions. Someone who'd never notice the patterns, the changes, the growing awareness in the brass.

Someone who'd never know what Gordon knew.

At 11:00, the lights died.

Emergency power kicked in after five seconds, bathing everything red. In that crimson glow, the knob blazed like a beacon. Pure silver, bright enough to hurt. And in that light, Gordon saw movement behind the wall. Shadows writhing against concrete from the inside.

Main power returned. The knob went brass. Gordon wrote: *11:00. Power outage. Emergency systems functional. Status: No change.*

His biggest lie yet.

At 13:00, Charles arrived for his final maintenance check. He moved through his inspection with unusual care, testing every fixture, examining every inch of wall.

"Gonna miss our talks, Gordon."

"They've been educational."

"Have they?" Charles knelt by the knob mount, running his fingers along the concrete. "Because I've been doing some homework. Off the books."

Gordon's pulse hammered. "Charles, don't---"

"This facility was built in '62. But the work orders show they built it around something already here. Something they dug up during excavation."

"You need to stop."

"They classified most records, but I found fragments in old geological surveys. References to 'anomalous metallic structures' and 'containment protocols during construction.'"

Charles stood, face grim. "They didn't build this place to house a monitoring station. They built it to contain something. And that knob isn't a sensor---it's a lock."

"Charles, you're talking about classified---"

"I'm talking about the truth. And the truth is you've spent thirty years guarding something that wants out."

Charles gathered his tools fast. At the door, he turned back.

"Whatever's behind that wall, Gordon, it's been patient. But patience runs out. And I think its time is up."

The door closed. Gordon sat alone with the truth.

A lock. A prison. And he was the only thing standing between whatever was behind that wall and everyone else.

14:00. Knob status: No change.

The lie felt different now. More like a prayer.

15:00. Knob status: No change.
15:30. Knob status: No change.

At 15:45, footsteps echoed outside. Gordon looked up to see a young woman in a crisp government suit. Agent Torres. Maybe twenty-five, bright eyes and eager professionalism Gordon remembered from his first day.

"Mr. Talbot? I'm Agent Torres. Here for the transition briefing."

Gordon stood, joints creaking. "Agent Torres. You're early."

"I wanted to scope the place out first, you know? Get familiar before my first shift tomorrow." She looked around the small room---desk, logbook, knob. "So this is it? This is what I'll be monitoring?"

"That's right. The brass fixture on the wall."

Torres approached the knob with scientific curiosity. "What's it do?"

"Doesn't do anything. Just... is."

"But what am I monitoring for? Color changes? Temperature? Movement?"

Gordon hesitated. How much should he tell her?

"Any changes at all. But in thirty years, there haven't been any."

"Thirty years of nothing? That seems odd."

"You'll get used to it."

Torres frowned, studying the knob from different angles. "This mounting looks old. Pre-digital era. And these marks in the con-crete---they look like damage."

She was sharp. Sharper than Gordon had been at twenty-five. Sharp enough to ask the right questions, notice the patterns, piece together the truth.

Sharp enough to be dangerous.

"Agent Torres, let me give you some advice. This job takes patience and discipline. Don't look for mysteries where there aren't any. Don't try to solve puzzles that aren't meant to be solved. Just watch, record, and report."

"But surely you have theories---I mean, thirty years, there must be something---"

"No." Gordon's voice carried thirty years of hard-won wisdom. "I have observations. Nothing more."

At 16:30, Director Mills arrived with his briefcase. The transition briefing took thirty minutes: security protocols, reporting procedures, emergency contacts. Mills spoke in the same clipped tone he'd used thirty years ago.

"Simple job, Agent Torres. Watch the knob. Record any changes. And don't touch the damn thing."

Torres raised her hand. "Sir, what happens if someone touches it?"

Mills smiled his conversation-ending smile. "Above your pay grade, Agent Torres. Way above."

Some things never changed.

At 17:00, Gordon gathered his personal effects: a coffee-stained mug, a desk calendar, a photo of Janet from their wedding. Thirty years of his life fit in a cardboard box.

Agent Torres walked him to the elevator. "Mr. Talbot? Thank you for your service."

"Take care of yourself, Agent Torres. And remember what I said about curiosity."

"Of course. But... can I ask one question?"

Gordon hit the elevator button. "What?"

"In thirty years, did you ever want to touch it? The knob? Did you ever wonder what would happen?"

The elevator arrived. Gordon stepped inside and turned to face the young woman who'd spend the next three decades in that concrete box.

"Every single day," he said, and hit the button for ground level.

The Nevada sun blazed across the parking lot, but for once Gordon noticed. He drove home through familiar desert, his mind churning with everything Charles had told him. A lock. A prison. Something that wanted out.

But what if that something wasn't evil? What if it was just forgotten? Abandoned? What if thirty years of isolation had taught it patience, maybe even gratitude toward its faithful guardian?

Janet met him at the door with champagne and a retirement cake shaped like a gold watch. Their daughter called from Seattle. The evening passed in celebration, but Gordon's thoughts kept returning to Agent Torres, sitting alone in Station 7, staring at a brass knob and wondering what it did.

He'd been like her once. Young, curious, eager to serve. It had taken years for the curiosity to fade into routine. But Torres was sharper than he'd been. She'd notice the patterns faster, ask the dangerous questions sooner.

And when she did, she'd face the same choice Gordon faced now: truth or duty. Knowledge or security.

At midnight, Gordon lay in bed staring at the ceiling. Thirty years of faithful service, and he was handing his post to a kid who'd never know what he'd really been watching. Every time he closed his eyes, he saw that silver light blazing behind the wall, saw Torres sitting alone in that concrete box, asking the same questions he'd asked three decades ago.

She'd figure it out. She was too smart not to. And when she did, she'd be alone with the choice he'd never had the guts to make.

He couldn't let that happen.

He rose, dressed in the dark, and drove through empty desert toward the facility. The night security team knew him---thirty years bought certain privileges. Foster waved him through.

"Forget something, Gordon?"

"Just want to check on the new agent. Make sure she's settling in."

The elevator descended through familiar darkness. At Sub-level 12, Gordon stepped into corridors he'd never see again.

The door to Station 7 stood ajar. Inside, Agent Torres sat at the desk, staring at the knob with the intense focus Gordon remembered from his early years. She looked up as he entered.

"Mr. Talbot? What are you doing here?"

"I came to tell you the truth."

Torres leaned forward. "About what?"

"About the knob. About this place. About what you're really guarding."

Gordon closed the door and sat across from her. "That fixture isn't a monitoring device. It's a lock. And something behind that wall has been waiting thirty years for someone to turn it."

"How do you know?"

"Because I've been watching it change. The patterns in the brass. How it responds to power outages. How it seems to know when someone's watching."

Torres glanced at the knob, then back. "Why didn't you report this?"

"Because I wanted to know what would happen. And because some knowledge is too dangerous to share with people who just follow orders."

"Mr. Talbot, if there's a security breach---"

"There's no breach. There's an opportunity. A chance to answer the question that's haunted this place for sixty years."

Gordon stood and walked toward the knob. Up close, he could feel its warmth, its vibration, its patient awareness.

"Thirty years ago, they told me never to touch this. Never to turn it. Never to find out what was behind the wall. And for thirty years, I obeyed."

"Mr. Talbot, don't---"

Gordon reached out and grasped the brass knob. It felt warm under his fingers, alive with energy. He could feel Torres behind him, hear her sharp breath.

"But I'm retired now," he said, and turned the knob clockwise.

The brass moved smoothly, like it had been waiting decades for this moment. Quarter turn, half turn, three-quarters. With each click, the vibration grew stronger, the warmth more intense.

At a full rotation, something clicked deep in the wall.

The lights died.

In the darkness, Gordon heard Torres whisper, "Jesus Christ."

The wall was opening.

Not crumbling or breaking, but sliding aside with mechanical precision. Ancient gears turned behind concrete, and cool air rushed in from whatever lay beyond.

Emergency power kicked in, washing everything red. Where the wall had been, a corridor stretched into darkness. The air carried scents of metal and ozone, and something organic.

"Mr. Talbot," Torres whispered, "what have you done?"

Gordon stared into the corridor, thirty years of faithful service ending in this single moment. "I opened the door."

From deep in the darkness, something stirred. Not malevolent or hungry, but tired. Tired of waiting. It had been down there sixty years, listening to footsteps in the corridor above, waiting for someone brave enough to ask the right questions. Someone willing to turn the knob.

Gordon stepped across the threshold. Behind him, Agent Torres faced the same choice: curiosity or duty, truth or safety.

"You coming?" he asked.

After a long moment---long enough for Gordon to think she'd stay behind---she followed.

The corridor stretched ahead, lit by phosphorescent strips that glowed like captured starlight. Their footsteps echoed off metal walls as they walked deeper into whatever lay beneath Nevada.

Behind them, Station 7 stood empty, logbook open to Gordon's final entry:

Day 7,833. 0001 hrs. Status: Opened.

For the first time in thirty years, it was the truth.

The Long and Dark of It

C orey MacLeod had lived through twenty-four polar nights in
Koyukuk, Alaska, and he knew darkness. He understood its
weight, its bite, the way it crept through window frames and under
doors. But this year's darkness felt different.

He stood on the weather station porch at half past ten in the morning, watching where the sun should've been. The thermometer read
minus-forty-two---cold even for November. His breath froze before
it left his mouth, ice crystals dropping to the planks around his boots.

Corey had checked the instruments three times in the past hour.
Barometric pressure held steady, wind gauge showed dead calm, temperature readings matched what he'd expect. Everything looked normal, but something had gone wrong three days ago.

The darkness past his floodlights was black as a mineshaft. Not the
deep blue he'd known for twenty-four winters---this was different.
Thick. Even the northern lights had gone dark.

"Hell of a thing," he muttered.

He'd been the weather observer since 2001, taking readings four
times a day and calling them into Fairbanks. The job suited him.
Twenty-four years married to Martha had taught him to appreciate
quiet time, and the station provided that. He liked the routine, the
precision, the way weather patterns made sense if you knew how to
read them.

But this darkness wasn't making any sense.

Corey pulled his parka tighter and walked the perimeter, checking
each piece of equipment. The anemometer spun lazy circles in the dead
air---shouldn't be moving with no wind. The precipitation gauge sat
bone dry, though he could taste moisture in the air. The solar radiation
gauge made no damn sense. Instead of zero, it showed negative numbers.

The radio crackled inside. "Koyukuk Weather, this is Fairbanks
Control. Do you copy?"

Corey jogged back, his boots punching through snow. He yanked off his gloves and keyed the mic. "Fairbanks Control, this is Koyukuk Weather. Go ahead."

"We're showing some unusual readings from your location. Can you confirm your barometric pressure?"

Corey glanced at the instruments. The mercury pulsed, rising and falling in tiny beats. "Pressure's holding at 29.95 and rising. Temperature minus-forty-two. No precipitation. Visibility..." He looked out the window again. The darkness pushed against the glass. "Visibility zero."

Long pause. "Say again, Koyukuk. Zero visibility?"

"Confirmed. Can't see past my lights. It's not fog, not weather. Air's clear, but the darkness is thicker this year."

Another pause. When the voice came back, it sounded nervous. "Copy that, Koyukuk. We're seeing some odd readings on our end too. Keep up regular observations and report any changes immediately."

"Will do. Koyukuk Weather out."

Corey set down the mic and poured coffee from the thermos Martha had filled before her flight to Anchorage three days back. The coffee was still hot, which should've been impossible. Martha taught at the community college during winter, staying in a small apartment near campus and coming home weekends when the weather allowed.

She'd wanted him to come with her this year---their daughter Jessica worked as a nurse at Providence Alaska Medical Center, and there'd be room for both of them. But someone had to mind the station, and Corey had never minded being alone.

Koyukuk dropped from eight hundred summer folks to barely two hundred during the long night. The ones who stayed were used to it---people like Bill Henderson who ran the general store, the Yakovich family with their twin kids, old Mrs. Trudeau from the post office. People who'd been here long enough to know that forty below was just another Tuesday in November.

But this year felt wrong.

Corey had first noticed the change three nights back, same evening Martha's plane lifted off. The sun had set like always, but instead of the slow fade from twilight to deep blue, the light had just vanished. One second there was the last glow on the western horizon, the next, everything went black.

The temperature had dropped fast---fifteen degrees in the first hour. The air itself got thick. Even the dogs in town had gone quiet. No howling, no barking, just silence.

The coffee was still too hot when he heard the sound.

It came from past his lights, beyond where the station's glow ended. A scratching noise, like claws on wood, but longer and more deliberate than any animal he knew. The sound lasted maybe ten seconds, then stopped.

Corey set down his coffee and listened. Wind through trees sometimes made strange noises, especially when it got below minus-forty and the wood started contracting. But the air was stone still tonight, and that scratching had a rhythm to it.

He walked to the window and pressed his face to the glass. His lights reached maybe fifty feet before the darkness swallowed them. Within that circle, he could see his red pickup, the white instrument shelter, the propane tanks, and the gravel path to the main road.

Everything looked right, but something felt wrong. The shadows were too dark, too deep. They pooled under his truck, and the shadow from the instrument shelter stretched farther than it should.

The sound came again, closer. Three short scrapes, pause, three more scrapes.

Corey reached for the rifle above the door---a Remington 700 in .30-06 that had served him well for twenty years. Black bears sometimes wandered through, and wolves weren't uncommon, though both usually avoided the lights and noise. He checked the magazine---five rounds---and worked the bolt to chamber one.

The weight should've been comforting. Instead, his hands shook. Deep down, he already knew bullets wouldn't help.

The scratching stopped.

Corey stood frozen for several minutes, listening to the small sounds of the station: generators humming, chronometer ticking, heated air moving through the vents. Outside, the darkness waited.

He was putting the rifle back when the power died.

Every light in the building cut out at once. The generators kept running---he could hear them---but no juice reached the building. Emergency lighting should've kicked in within seconds, but the battery units stayed dark.

Corey felt his way to the emergency radio. His fingers found the power switch, turned it on. Nothing. The radio was stone dead.

He fumbled for his flashlight---a heavy Maglite that took four D-cells. The switch clicked under his thumb, but no light came out. He tried again, clicking rapidly, but the flashlight stayed dead.

The darkness was eating the light.

Corey groped toward the landline, hoping the old copper wires might still work. He lifted the handset, pressed it to his ear, but the dial tone was gone.

Something tapped against the window.

Corey jerked back, his heart hammering. The tapping came again---three knocks against the glass, right where his face had been. Then three more knocks, deliberate and patient, followed by three more.

Whatever was out there knew he was inside.

He felt his way back to the rifle. His hands shook as he found the weapon---not from cold, but from fear that went deeper than twenty-four years in Alaska had taught him. He'd learned to be afraid of bears, wolves, weather that could kill you, equipment failures. But this darkness felt like something hunting.

The tapping moved to another window, then another, circling the building. Each series was identical: three taps, pause, three taps, pause, three taps. Then silence for maybe thirty seconds before starting from a new spot.

Emergency signals. Three of anything, repeated three times. But this felt less like asking for help and more like counting down.

Corey raised the rifle toward the sound, though he couldn't see where to aim. The darkness was so thick he might as well have been blind. If something broke through, he'd need to react by sound alone.

The knocking stopped.

For several minutes, Corey heard nothing but his own breathing and the generators outside. The backup heat kept the building from freezing, but barely. He started hoping whatever had been testing the building had moved on.

Then the front door opened.

Corey heard the latch click and hinges creak as the door swung wide. Cold air rushed in, carrying a smell like old bones and wet earth. He raised the rifle toward the sound.

"Who's there?" His voice cracked.

The door stayed open, but nothing entered that he could hear. The cold got worse fast, and his breath started forming ice crystals that fell around him. The temperature in the room dropped so quick he could feel it happening.

"I'm armed," Corey said louder. "You're trespassing on federal prop-erty."

No response. But the darkness got denser, heavier. The air felt thick. Each breath took effort, and his exhales hung in the air longer than they should.

Corey took a step toward where he thought the door was, rifle at his shoulder. He moved slow, testing each step. The floorboards creaked under his boots.

His foot hit something soft.

Corey froze. He knew every inch of this room. There shouldn't have been anything on the floor between him and the door.

He crouched slow, keeping the rifle ready with one hand while reaching out with the other. His fingers touched fabric---heavy winter clothing. His hand moved up, feeling a jacket, then a chest that didn't rise and fall. A face, cold as the air around it, with skin that felt wrong---too smooth, too dry.

Corey jerked his hand back and stumbled into the desk behind him. Someone was lying on his floor, but he couldn't tell if they were unconscious or dead. The face had felt strange, but his hands were so cold he couldn't trust what he'd felt.

"Can you hear me?" he whispered.

No response. But in the black around him, something shifted. A rustling sound.

Corey reached out again, feeling for a pulse at the figure's neck. The skin was cold but not frozen. Underneath, he could feel something moving. Not a pulse, but something else---something that twisted under the skin.

He recoiled so hard he crashed into the desk, sending instruments clattering to the floor. Glass broke somewhere in the dark, and the sharp smell of spilled chemicals joined the bone-and-earth stench.

The rifle fired.

The muzzle flash lit the room for a split second, burning an image into Corey's eyes.

The figure on the floor was Harold Tanook, who lived alone two miles down the road. Harold was a good neighbor, the kind who showed up with his snowplow when storms hit hard, who always had a spare part you needed. But Harold's face was wrong.

His skin was the color of old leather, eyes gone---not closed, but missing, leaving dark holes. His mouth hung open, showing teeth that were too sharp and too many, filling his mouth in overlapping rows that gleamed like black glass.

The light died, and darkness returned.

Corey fumbled with the rifle, trying to work the bolt. His hands shook so bad he could barely hold the weapon.

"Harold?" he called out, though he knew the thing on the floor wasn't Harold anymore. "Harold, what happened to you?"

The figure sat up.

Corey heard the rustle of clothing, the creak of joints, but there was something else---a wet, sliding sound. The bone smell got stronger, mixed with something that reminded him of the fish-processing plant down in Bethel.

"Corey." The voice was Harold's, but it came from too low, like Harold was speaking from his chest. "You should see it, Corey. How beautiful the dark is when you really look."

"Harold, you need help. I'm gonna---"

"It shows you things," Harold continued, his voice getting stronger. "Things that have always been there, hiding in the light. I can see them now. I can see everything."

Corey raised the rifle toward Harold's voice, though his hands shook so hard he couldn't hold it steady. "Harold, I need you to stay right where you are. Don't move."

Harold laughed, and the sound was like breaking glass mixed with something dying. "You can't hurt the darkness, Corey. You can't fight what's already inside you."

"What are you talking about?"

"Look at your hands."

Despite every rational thought screaming warnings, Corey looked down. He couldn't see anything in the black, but he could feel something wrong with his hands. The skin tingled, then burned, then went numb. When he tried to flex his fingers, they moved strange.

"It started three days ago," Harold said, his voice now coming from beside Corey's ear, though he was certain Harold was still across the room. "When the real darkness came. Gets into everything---your eyes, your mouth, your lungs. Changes you from the inside out."

Corey spun toward the voice, but Harold was no longer there. Or maybe he was everywhere. The darkness felt crowded, full of presence and movement.

"The whole town," Harold continued, his voice echoing from everywhere at once. "Everyone who stayed for the long night. We're all changing together. Becoming what we were always meant to be."

Corey stumbled backward until he hit the wall, the rifle heavy and useless in his hands. The tingling was spreading from his hands to his wrists, his forearms, his shoulders. When he tried to raise the weapon, his arms wouldn't respond right.

"Martha left just in time," Harold said. "Lucky Martha. But you stayed, Corey. You wanted to see what the darkness would bring."

"Shut up." Corey's voice sounded strange to his own ears, deeper than it should've been.

"It's beautiful," Harold continued. "Being part of something bigger. Something that's been waiting so long to come home."

The darkness pressed against Corey from all sides, thick as oil, cold as space. He could feel it working into his lungs with each breath. His vision, which had been black, started showing him things that couldn't be there---shapes moving in the walls, faces forming in dead air.

And beyond the weather station, he could sense the rest of Koyukuk. Every person who'd chosen to stay for the long night was changing too, becoming something new.

The change was speeding up. Corey could feel his bones shifting, becoming lighter and stronger. His nerves growing new connections. Something fundamental changing in his chest.

"Where are the others?" Corey asked, though he wasn't sure why he was asking.

"Close," Harold said, his voice now coming from right in front of Corey's face. "So very close. Would you like to see them?"

Before Corey could answer, he heard footsteps outside. Multiple sets moving through snow, approaching from different directions. The sounds were wrong---too light for people in heavy boots, spaced too far apart.

"The Hendersons," Harold said from the open doorway. "And the Yakovich family. The old postmistress. They all want to welcome you properly."

The footsteps stopped just outside where his floodlights should've been shining. Corey could sense them there, waiting in the darkness. He could feel their attention focused on him, pressing against his mind.

"Come outside, Corey," Harold said. "Come and see what we've become."

Despite every rational thought screaming warnings, Corey found himself moving toward the door. The rifle hung loose in his hands, forgotten. His feet carried him forward without conscious effort.

He stopped at the threshold and peered into what should've been lit by the station's floods. Minus-forty should've flash-frozen the moisture in his lungs, should've made his teeth ache. Instead, the cold felt good, refreshing. His changed hands tingled with new sensation, and he could feel his skin adapting.

Shapes moved in the darkness past where light should've reached. Tall shapes, thin shapes, shapes that bent and twisted wrong. But somehow, he recognized them all.

There was Bill Henderson, who ran the general store and served as unofficial mayor during winter. Except Bill was taller now, stretched upward. His arms hung past his knees, and when he moved, his joints bent in directions that shouldn't have been possible.

His wife Susan stood beside him, but her head was tilted at an angle that should've killed her, cocked so far to one side her left ear nearly touched her shoulder. When she smiled, Corey could see her teeth had changed, becoming sharp and clear, like icicles.

The Yakovich twins---kids whose names he'd never learned, though he'd watched them grow up---stood holding hands near what used to be the instrument shelter. They'd grown too, stretching upward until they were nearly seven feet tall despite being only twelve. Their faces were pale in the darkness, and their eyes reflected light that wasn't there.

And Mrs. Trudeau, who'd run the post office for forty years before retiring last spring, sat on what looked like a chair made of ice and shadows. Her white hair flowed around her, and when she smiled, her teeth were sharp as broken glass.

"Welcome," she said, her voice carrying across the distance like she was standing right beside him. "We've been waiting for you to join us."

Corey stepped outside. The snow crunched under his feet, but the sound was muffled. The cold that should've killed him in minutes felt like a warm embrace.

"How long?" he asked.

"Time doesn't matter here," Bill Henderson said, his voice coming from somewhere above Corey's head. "Not anymore. We measure things differently now."

"Measure what?"

"Hunger," Susan Henderson replied, her voice like wind chimes made of bone. "Growth. Change. The space between one transformation and the next."

Corey looked at his hands again. In the strange non-light, he could see them changing. Fingers longer, more flexible, tipped with nails that had grown into sharp, curved points. Skin paler, almost see-through, veins underneath pulsing with something darker than blood.

"It doesn't hurt," he said, surprised.

"Why would it hurt?" Harold asked. He was standing right beside Corey now. "You're becoming what you were always meant to be. We all are."

"What are we becoming?"

The question hung in the air for a long moment. The changed residents of Koyukuk looked at each other, and Corey had the sense they were talking in ways that didn't need words. He could feel the edges of their conversation.

"Ourselves," Mrs. Trudeau said finally. "But better. Stronger. Free from the limitations light imposes."

"Light divides things," one of the Yakovich twins added, voice like snow falling on stone. "Makes boundaries where there shouldn't be any. Day and night, inside and outside, self and other. In the darkness, everything connects."

Corey could feel what they meant. The barriers between his thoughts and theirs were disappearing. He could sense their memories, their experiences, their understanding of what they were becoming. And they could sense his.

It was like being part of something bigger, individual cells working together toward a purpose he was only starting to understand. The loneliness that had always been part of life in Alaska, the isolation that came from living so far from the rest of humanity, was disappearing. He would never be alone again.

"Martha," he said, and the name felt strange in his mouth.

"She'll come back," Harold said. "When spring returns, she'll come home for a visit. And then she'll understand too."

"We can't... we can't hurt her."

"Hurt her?" Susan Henderson laughed, and the sound was like ice breaking on a frozen lake. "We're going to give her the greatest gift imaginable. Freedom from the tyranny of light."

The darkness around them pulsed with approval. Corey could feel it seeping into his bones, his blood, his brain. The part of him that remembered being human was shrinking, getting smaller until it was just a tiny voice in the back of his mind.

And that voice was getting quieter.

"What about the others?" he asked, thinking of people in Fairbanks, in Anchorage, in the outside world that still believed in the old definitions of light and dark. "The people who left before the change?"

"They'll understand eventually," Bill Henderson said, his voice carrying sounds human vocal cords couldn't make. "When the darkness spreads. When winter comes to places that have forgotten what real winter means."

Corey could see it in his mind---darkness flowing out from Koyukuk, following rivers and roads, seeping into cities and towns. The aurora that had been missing for three days was gathering strength high above the atmosphere, but it was different now. Instead of green and purple, it would be black and silver, carrying the gift of transformation to anyone who looked up.

He thought of the radio calls from Fairbanks, the worry in the operator's voice when he'd reported zero visibility. They knew something was wrong, but they didn't understand what. Soon they would.

"How long do we have?" he asked.

"Until spring," Mrs. Trudeau said. "Four months to prepare. To grow. To become ready."

"Ready for what?"

"To welcome the summer people home," Harold said, his changed face splitting into a grin that showed rows of shark teeth. "To show them what we've learned during the long night."

Corey tried to remember why that should worry him, but the concern felt distant, unimportant. The summer people would come back to their cabins and tourist activities in May, expecting to find the same sleepy town they'd left in September. And they would find it, on the surface. The buildings would be the same, the roads plowed, the friendly faces greeting them with warm smiles.

But underneath, everything would be different.

The thought should've horrified him. Instead, it filled him with anticipation.

"There's so much to do," he said, and realized he was smiling with teeth that were no longer entirely human.

The others smiled back, showing their new dentition, their new understanding. The darkness around them pulsed with approval, with hunger, with ancient patience finally rewarded.

Together, they walked into the changed town. The weather station fell silent behind them, its instruments recording nothing but the absence of everything they'd been designed to measure. The generators puttered for a few more minutes, then died with mechanical sighs.

Corey walked through streets he'd known for decades, seeing them with eyes that were no longer quite human. Every house held changed residents, people who'd chosen to stay for the long night and discovered what that choice really meant. They waved from darkened windows, called out greetings in voices like winter wind.

At the general store, Bill Henderson was rearranging shelves, preparing for customers who would be very different from the ones he'd served before. The items for sale were changing too---food that looked familiar but fed hungers humans didn't have, tools designed for hands that had grown new capabilities, clothing cut for bodies that had shed their old limitations.

Mrs. Trudeau had reopened the post office, though the mail she was sorting came from places that weren't on any map. Letters written in languages older than human speech, packages wrapped in shadows and sealed with starlight. She hummed as she worked, a melody that made the darkness dance around her.

The Yakovich children played in snow outside their house, building sculptures that hurt to look at directly. The snow itself had changed, becoming something more than frozen water. It held memories now, whispers of everyone who'd ever walked through it, dreams that had fallen from the sky instead of precipitation.

And everywhere, the darkness moved like a living thing, connecting all of them, flowing through them, making them part of something vast and patient and hungry.

Corey made his way to the small house he'd shared with Martha for eighteen years. It looked the same from outside---modest two-story with blue vinyl siding and white trim, surrounded by spruce trees he'd planted to break the wind. But when he opened the door, he could smell the changes.

The familiar scents of home were still there---coffee, wood smoke, Martha's perfume lingering in the furniture---but underneath was something new. Something that promised transformation, that whispered of possibilities beyond human imagination.

He sat in his favorite chair, a recliner positioned to look out the front window at the bird feeder Martha kept stocked during winter. The feeder was empty now, but that didn't matter. The birds that came to it now didn't eat seeds.

Outside his window, he could see lights moving through town. Not electric lights, but something else---points of cold fire that danced and swirled, marking the boundaries of their new territory. The darkness was claiming Koyukuk completely, making it into something that would serve as a foothold for the changes to come.

Corey closed his eyes and felt the transformation continuing. His skeleton was adapting, becoming something that could function in environments that would've killed his original human form. His nervous system was developing new pathways, new capabilities. His pulse found different rhythms.

When he opened his eyes again, the world looked different. He could see the connections between all living things, the threads of darkness that bound them together. He could sense the sleeping trees, their roots drinking from soil that had become something more than earth. He could feel the small animals in their burrows, changing as they slept, becoming part of the new ecosystem spreading out from Koyukuk.

Somewhere in Anchorage, Martha was grading papers and thinking about her weekend trip home. She had no idea home was thinking about her too, preparing a welcome that would change everything she thought she knew about love, about life, about the boundaries between one person and another.

The phone rang.

Corey looked at the device, surprised it was working. The display showed Martha's cell number, glowing green in the darkness. He picked up the handset, wondering what he would say.

"Hello?"

"Corey? Thank god. I've been trying to reach you for hours. The weather service said they lost contact with your station."

Martha's voice sounded exactly the same, warm and worried and completely human. Corey felt something that might've been regret.

"I'm here," he said, careful to keep his voice normal. "Just some equipment problems. You know how it is during polar night."

"Are you okay? You sound different."

"Just tired. It's been a long few days."

"I was thinking about coming home early. Jessica's working double shifts at the hospital, and I'm worried about you being alone out there."

Corey looked out the window at the lights dancing through the changed town, at the neighbors who were no longer quite neighbors, at the darkness that had become so much more than the absence of light.

"That's sweet of you," he said, "but I'm fine. Really. Maybe it's better if you wait until the weekend like we planned."

"Are you sure? The weather forecast looks clear, and I could catch a flight tomorrow morning."

"I'm sure. A few more days won't hurt anything."

They talked for a few more minutes about ordinary things---Jessica's job, Martha's classes, maybe visiting their son in Seattle next summer. Normal conversation between husband and wife, as if the world hadn't changed three days ago.

When Martha hung up, Corey sat in darkness and listened to the new sounds of his town. Voices that weren't quite human anymore, calling to each other across the changed landscape. Music in frequencies baseline humans couldn't hear. Darkness itself whispering, flowing through every building, every room, every space where light used to live.

In four months, when the sun returned and the summer people came back to their cabins, they would find Koyukuk exactly as they expected. The same friendly faces, the same small-town hospitality, the same rustic charm that had drawn them to this remote corner of Alaska.

They would have no way of knowing that during the long night, the town had become something else. That the people they remembered had been transformed into something that belonged more to the darkness than the light.

Corey smiled with his new mouth and settled back to wait. The long night had only just begun, and there was so much ahead. The darkness whispered of wonders to come, transformations that would remake the world in ways light-bound minds couldn't imagine.

The last entry in the Koyukuk weather station log, time-stamped at 11:49 on November 21st, recorded a temperature of minus-forty-two degrees, clear skies, and visibility of zero.

After that, the instruments recorded nothing but silence, as if weather itself had forgotten how to exist in the darkness that had settled over the town.

In Anchorage, Martha MacLeod finished grading papers and decided to call her husband before bed. The phone rang and rang, but nobody answered. She left a cheerful message about looking forward to seeing him Friday, then went to sleep planning the weekend trip home.

She had no way of knowing that home was planning for her too.

Rainbows in the Dark

F irst thing people wanted to know was how Ray Kolchek made it out when seventeen other guys didn't.

Ray sat in that hospital bed, coffee gone cold in his hands, trying to explain something that didn't make sense to anybody---hell, didn't make sense to him neither. Reporter from the Herald Tribune leaned forward with her little recorder, and that's when Ray saw it: soft blue light around her head like she was standing underwater, silver threads running through it like fish. Kind lady. Curious, but not the mean kind of curious.

"Followed the lights," Ray said. Must've said it a hundred times by now. "Rainbow lights. Weren't supposed to be any lights down there."

"What kind of lights?" The reporter---Casey something---tapped her pen on her pad. "Emergency lighting? Maybe reflection from the rescue equipment?"

Ray almost laughed. Three days since they pulled him out of Blackstone, and nobody believed a damn word. Not the safety guys, not the head doctor, not even Martha.

"Nah," Ray said. "These was different. Like oil spills on wet blacktop, but moving. Flowing through the dark like they knew where they was going."

That blue shimmer around the reporter flickered. Ray was getting used to that look---people thinking the cave-in scrambled his brains, made him see things. Hell, maybe they was right. Maybe when that timber beam caught him upside the head, it knocked something loose.

But that didn't explain what he saw when he looked at folks now.

Everyone had it---this soft glow around them like a halo. Most people had clean colors: blue for the good ones, warm gold when they was happy, deep green for the steady types. Some had uglier colors: brown-red when they was pissed, nasty yellow for the greedy ones, gray fuzz when they was down.

And then there was the others.

"Mr. Kolchek?" The reporter was looking at him funny. "You feeling alright?"

Ray blinked, focused on her face instead of that light. "Sorry. Still get fuzzy sometimes."

She nodded like she understood. "Doctor said you had a concussion. Memory problems are normal after something like that."

Memory wasn't the problem. Ray's memory was sharp as a new drill bit---maybe sharper than it'd ever been. He could remember every damn minute of those seventy-three hours trapped down there: rock and timber pressing down, coal dust thick as paste in his mouth, water running out on day two.

And them lights finding him on day three.

"Can you tell me what happened after the collapse?" Casey asked. "Rescue teams said it was amazing you survived that long without getting hurt bad."

Ray set down his coffee and pulled the hospital blanket up. Room felt cold, but he knew it wasn't really cold. Everything felt different now. Colors brighter, sounds sharper, and he could sense things other folks couldn't.

Like the thing in the corner.

Been there since Casey walked in. Looked like a janitor---tall, skinny, gray uniform---but the space around it was wrong. Where people had light, this thing had hungry darkness. Not just absence of light, but something that ate light, pulled it in like a black hole made of shadow and teeth.

The thing hadn't moved since the reporter came in. Just stood there, watching.

Ray made himself focus on Casey's questions.

"Cave-in trapped me in a pocket. Eight by six, maybe. Couldn't sit up straight. Heard the rescue boys drilling, but they sounded like they was on the moon."

"That must've been terrifying."

"It was. But the waiting was worse. Knowing every hour made it less likely they'd reach me." Ray glanced at the corner. The dark thing tilted its head, like it thought his story was funny.

Casey followed his look. "Someone there?"

"Janitor," Ray said careful-like.

She turned to look, frowning. "I don't see anyone."

Course she didn't. Ray was starting to figure out this new sight had rules. He could see the glows around living folks, and he could see the dark ones pretending to be people. But somehow, the dark ones could pick who noticed them.

This one wanted Ray to see it.

"Must be my eyes," Ray said. "Pain meds, you know."

Casey nodded and made a note. "So you were trapped almost three days. What changed? How'd you find your way out?"

Ray closed his eyes, remembering. The memory was clear---clearer than most everything before the accident.

"I was getting weak," he said. "Dehydrated. Starting to think I might not make it. That's when I saw the first light."

Started as a flicker in the black. Ray thought maybe his headlamp was bouncing off something, but hell---headlamp died twelve hours ago. This was different. Moved like it was alive, flowing through cracks in the rock like liquid fire.

"The light was beautiful," Ray said. "All kinds of colors, shifting around. Like the northern lights, but close enough to touch."

"Aurora doesn't appear underground," Casey said gentle-like.

"I know what I saw."

And he did. The lights pulsed, making patterns like some kind of language Ray almost understood. They wrapped around him, warm but not heat-warm---something deeper. When they touched his skin, something moved inside his head. Gentle, like puzzle pieces finding their places.

Click. Click. Click.

Then the lights moved off, flowing through gaps in the rockfall that should've been too small for anything to pass.

Ray followed them.

"I crawled through spaces that shouldn't have existed," he said. "Following them lights deeper into the mine. Didn't make sense---rescue teams was drilling from above, but the lights led me down and sideways."

"That doesn't sound safe."

"Nothing about it was safe. But I was dying anyway, so what's it matter?" Ray watched the dark thing in the corner. It had moved closer while he was talking, though he hadn't seen it move. Now it stood just a few feet from Casey's chair. If she turned her head, she'd be looking right at it.

But she couldn't see it. That was obvious enough.

"How long did you follow these lights?" Casey asked.

"Hours. Maybe half a day. Lost track down there." Ray's throat felt dry despite the coffee. "Lights led me through passages I never seen before, and I been working that mine fifteen years. Brought me to an old shaft that went to the surface."

"Abandoned shaft?"

"Must've been. Wasn't on any maps I knew about." Ray shrugged. "But it led up, and that's all that mattered."

Story was Ray found his way to Shaft 7, a ventilation tunnel sealed back in the eighties but apparently not blocked proper. Rescue teams found him passed out near the surface entrance, dehydrated and cold but otherwise fine.

Nobody could explain how he'd found his way through all them tunnels in the dark, hurt and confused.

Ray could explain it, but nobody wanted to hear about rainbow lights leading lost miners to safety.

"You're lucky to be alive," Casey said. "The other miners weren't so fortunate."

Ray's gut clenched. Seventeen men died in the Blackstone collapse---good men with families, guys he'd worked alongside for years. Charlie Voss, coached Little League weekends. Pete Kowalski, saving up to buy his girl a car for her sweet sixteen. Mike Crawford, told the same three jokes every day but somehow made them funny every time.

All dead, while Ray walked away without a scratch.

"Why you think you survived when the others didn't?" Casey asked.

Question that haunted him. Ray been working Tunnel C that morning, same as the others. When them supports failed and thirty tons of rock came down, he should've died with his crew. Instead, he ended up in that impossible pocket, breathing air that should've run out long before the lights found him.

"Don't know," Ray said. "Wrong place at the right time, I guess."

Casey checked her watch. "Think we should wrap up. You look tired."

Ray nodded, though he wasn't tired. He was scared. Not of the mine or being trapped---those was normal fears that made sense. He was scared of the thing standing behind Casey's chair, and of the three others he'd spotted since leaving the hospital.

The dark ones was everywhere.

"Thanks for your time, Mr. Kolchek," Casey said, packing up her recorder. "Story should run tomorrow."

She stood to leave, passing inches from the dark thing in the corner. For a second, her glow flickered---that clean blue shifting to something ugly, like oil spreading through water. Then she was past it, and her colors went back to normal.

But the thing smiled at Ray with too many teeth.

After Casey left, Ray sat alone and tried to make sense of what was happening. Doctors wanted to keep him another day for observation, but he was supposed to get out tomorrow morning. Then what? How was he supposed to go back to normal life when he could see things nobody else could?

His wife Martha visited yesterday, and Ray nearly cried when he saw her glow---warm gold shot through with deep red love. She was still his Martha, still human, still safe. But when Dr. Hoffman came in to check his vitals, the darkness around the man was so thick Ray had to bite his tongue to keep from screaming.

Thing pretending to be Dr. Hoffman looked Ray over cold and careful, its real face flickering under the human mask like bad TV reception. Dead eyes and skin like dried leather, and when it spoke, Ray could hear something else underneath the doctor's voice---grinding metal.

"How are we feeling today, Mr. Kolchek?" the fake doctor asked, its darkness pressing against Ray like a weight.

"Fine," Ray managed. "Just tired."

The thing made notes on a clipboard, though Ray figured it wasn't writing down nothing about his medical condition. "Any unusual symptoms? Disorientation? Visual disturbances?"

Ray almost laughed. "No, nothing unusual."

"Good. We'll have you out of here soon."

Way it said 'out of here' made Ray's skin crawl. Like it knew where he was going next, and it wasn't home.

Now, alone in his room, Ray tried to piece together what them lights done to him. The rainbow glow in the mine hadn't just led him to safety---it changed him, did something to his eyes. But why? Why let him see things nobody else could?

Ray thought about the seventeen miners who died. Maybe somebody wanted them dead. Maybe they seen something they shouldn't have. And if that was true, why'd Ray get spared?

He was still thinking when the door opened and a new visitor came in.

"Mr. Kolchek? Detective Anne Hawthorne." Woman showed him a badge and pulled up a chair. Her glow was solid green with flickers of blue---she meant business but wasn't mean about it. Human, anyway.

"Detective?" Ray sat up straighter. "Something wrong?"

"Hope not. Wanted to ask you some questions about the mine accident." She pulled out a notebook and pen. "There's inconsistencies in the official report I need to clear up."

Ray looked at her closer. Green was steady, but there was thin red lines running through it---she was pissed about something, trying to keep it in. This woman was pissed about something.

"What kind of inconsistencies?"

"The explosive used to bring down Tunnel C wasn't standard mining equipment," Detective Hawthorne said. "Someone set off military-grade charges in that mine, Mr. Kolchek. This wasn't no accident."

Room seemed to get colder. Ray pulled his blanket tighter. "You saying someone murdered them men?"

"I'm saying seventeen miners died in what looks like a deliberate explosion, and you were the only survivor." She leaned forward. "Need to know if you saw anything unusual that morning. Anyone who didn't belong. Equipment that looked out of place."

Ray's head was spinning. If the collapse was deliberate, then him surviving was even stranger. Had the lights known what was coming? Had they put him somewhere safe before the explosion?

"Didn't see nothing," he said careful. "Just a normal morning till the roof came down."

Detective Hawthorne made a note. "What about after the collapse? While you were trapped?"

Ray hesitated. How much could he tell her without sounding crazy?

"I followed some kind of light to safety," he said. "Figured it was reflection from the rescue equipment."

"Rescue teams wasn't drilling anywhere near Shaft 7," the detective said. "According to their logs, they didn't even know that shaft existed."

"Then I don't know what I followed."

Detective Hawthorne studied his face. "Mr. Kolchek, I think someone wanted them miners dead. And I think they figured you'd die with them. Fact that you're alive makes you either very lucky or very dangerous to whoever planned this."

Before Ray could answer, the door opened again. Dr. Hoffman came in, his darkness rolling ahead of him like a black tide.

"Sorry," the fake doctor said, "but visiting hours are over. Mr. Kolchek needs his rest."

Detective Hawthorne checked her watch. "It's only three o'clock."

"Special circumstances. Mr. Kolchek's still recovering from his ordeal." The thing wearing Dr. Hoffman's face smiled, but Ray could see the real mouth underneath---full of needle teeth. "Maybe you could continue tomorrow."

Ray wanted to warn the detective, but how could he? She couldn't see what Ray saw. To her, Dr. Hoffman was just a concerned doctor.

"Course," Detective Hawthorne said, standing. She handed Ray her card. "Call me if you remember anything else."

After she left, the fake doctor moved closer to Ray's bed. Darkness around it seemed to pulse with nasty energy.

"You been talking too much, Mr. Kolchek," it said in Dr. Hoffman's voice. "That ain't healthy for someone in your condition."

"I answered her questions," Ray said. "That's all."

"Yeah, but which questions did you answer?" The thing tilted its head, and Ray caught a glimpse of its true face---pale skin stretched over sharp bones, eyes like black glass. "And which ones did you choose not to answer?"

Ray's heart hammered. "Don't know what you mean."

"Course you don't." The thing picked up Ray's chart and pretended to study it. "You're real lucky to be alive, Mr. Kolchek. Be unfortunate if something happened to mess up your recovery."

Message was clear enough. Ray nodded and kept his mouth shut.

After the fake doctor left, Ray lay staring at the ceiling. Ray was starting to see how big this mess was. Mine collapse wasn't no accident---it was murder. Seventeen men got killed, and Ray only lived because something stepped in.

But what? And why?

Lights in the mine seemed smart, moving with purpose. They led him to safety, but they also changed him, gave him the ability to see things hiding among regular folks.

Had to be connected.

Ray thought about Detective Hawthorne's visit. She was investigating the explosion, which meant she was dangerous to whoever ordered it. How long before they decided she needed to disappear too?

He had to warn her somehow.

Ray waited for the thing wearing Doc Hoffman's face to finish rounds. Slipped out of bed careful-like. Legs shaky, but they held him. Hospital gown made him feel like an idiot, but his clothes were in the closet.

Getting dressed, Ray caught himself in the bathroom mirror and damn near jumped out of his skin. Looked normal enough, but around the edges... shimmer. Same rainbow light from the mine, clinging to him like fog. Only showed up when he wasn't looking straight at it.

Whatever changed him down there, it was still with him.

Ray slipped out of his room and headed for the elevator. Hospital corridors were dim. Ray counted three more of them---fake nurse, fake security guard, fake orderly with a mop. All turned to watch him pass. All smiled like they was thinking about dinner, and he was the main course.

None tried to stop him, which felt wrong somehow.

Elevator took him down to the ground floor, where he found a pay phone near the main entrance. Ray dialed the number on Detective Hawthorne's card, hoping she'd answer.

"Hawthorne."

"Detective? Ray Kolchek. We got a problem."

"Ray? Jesus, you sound like hell. What's wrong?"

Ray glanced around the lobby. Two more things by the information desk, dead eyes tracking him like security cameras. "Can't talk here. You know Murphy's Diner?"

"I can be there in twenty."

"Detective," Ray said, "when you get there, sit where you can see the other customers. And if anyone comes to our table, anyone at all, don't trust them."

Pause. "Mr. Kolchek, you in some kind of danger?"

"We both are."

Ray hung up and headed for the exit. Automatic doors slid open, and he stepped into cool evening air. First time in days he felt like he could breathe.

Murphy's Diner was exactly what Ray hoped---small, bright restaurant with windows on three sides and just a handful of customers. He picked a booth in the back corner where he could watch the entrance and see everyone in the dining room.

Waitress who brought him coffee had a normal glow---tired yellow-brown, but human. Cook visible through the service window glowed with steady green of someone focused on work. Only other customers was an elderly couple sharing pie, their glows wound together with the deep red of long love.

No dark ones. Yet.

Detective Hawthorne showed up exactly twenty minutes later, scanning the diner professional-like before spotting Ray in his corner booth. She slid into the seat across from him, her green glow flickering with concern.

"You look terrible," she said. "Should you even be out of the hospital?"

"Probably not." Ray wrapped his hands around his coffee cup. "But I had to talk to you."

"What's this about, Mr. Kolchek? You sounded scared on the phone."

Ray took a deep breath. This was it. Either Detective Hawthorne would believe him, or she'd think he'd lost it.

"What I'm gonna tell you's gonna sound crazy," he said. "But I need you to hear me out."

She nodded. "I'm listening."

"Mine collapse wasn't just murder," Ray said. "It was something bigger. There's things living among us---creatures that look human but ain't. They can disguise themselves, make us see what they want us to see."

Detective Hawthorne's glow shifted, green getting muddier. Skeptical, but she was still listening.

"When I was trapped in the mine, something happened to me," Ray continued. "I can see through their disguises now. Tell the real people from the fake ones."

"Mr. Kolchek---"

"Dr. Hoffman at the hospital ain't human," Ray said quick. "Neither's the nurse on my floor or the security guard by the elevator. They're something else, something that feeds on us or controls us or uses us for things I don't understand."

Detective's glow was almost all brown now---she didn't believe him and was worried about his head. But she hadn't left the table.

"You think these... creatures... killed the miners?"

"Think they ordered it done. Maybe the guys was getting too close to something they shouldn't have seen. Or maybe they was just in the way." Ray leaned forward. "Detective, you're investigating this case. That makes you a threat to them."

"Mr. Kolchek, I think you been through severe trauma. Natural for your mind to try making sense of what happened by creating explanations---"

"Look behind you," Ray said quiet.

Detective Hawthorne frowned but turned in her seat. Diner's front door had opened, and a man in a business suit was walking toward their table. Looked normal enough---middle-aged, forgettable, kind of person you'd forget five minutes after meeting.

But his glow was pure darkness.

"You see anything unusual about him?" Ray asked.

Detective studied the approaching man. "Looks like a businessman. Maybe a little pale."

"Keep watching."

The dark one reached their table and smiled at Detective Hawthorne. "Excuse me, Detective, but you're needed back at the station. Development in the Blackstone case."

"Wasn't aware anyone knew I was here," Detective Hawthorne said careful.

"Your captain sent me to find you. It's urgent."

Ray watched the thing's glow pulse with mean energy. "Detective, ask him for some ID."

Thing wearing businessman's face turned to look at Ray, and for just a second, its human mask slipped. Ray saw pale skin stretched over sharp bones, eyes like black holes, mouth full of needle teeth.

Then the mask snapped back.

"Sorry," the thing said to Detective Hawthorne, "but this is police business. Maybe your friend could wait outside?"

"Actually," Detective Hawthorne said, her hand moving toward her gun, "I'd like to see some identification. Badge and ID."

Dark one's smile widened, showing human teeth Ray knew was fake. "Course, Detective."

But instead of reaching for ID, the thing lunged forward.

Ray threw himself sideways out of the booth, shouting a warning. Detective Hawthorne was already moving, her training taking over as she rolled away from the table and drew her weapon.

Businessman's mask dissolved completely, showing the nightmare underneath. Thing stood seven feet tall, skin like gray glass, fingers ending in black claws. Fast as hell, swiping at Detective Hawthorne with a hand that could've taken her head clean off.

She fired three shots center mass. Bullets passed through the thing without effect.

"The eyes!" Ray shouted. "Try the eyes!"

Detective Hawthorne adjusted her aim and put two rounds into the thing's black glass eyes. This time, the thing screamed---sound like metal tearing. Dark fluid spurted from its ruined sockets, and it staggered back.

Other customers in the diner was screaming and running for the exits. Elderly couple clutched each other in terror, their glows blazing with raw fear. Waitress had dropped her coffee pot and was hiding behind the counter.

But they could all see the thing now. Whatever had been hiding it was gone.

Dark one swept its clawed hand across the table, sending plates and glasses flying. Wounded but not dead. Ray could see its glow pulsing with rage and hunger.

"This way!" Ray grabbed Detective Hawthorne's arm and pulled her toward the kitchen. They burst through the swinging doors just as the thing's claws raked deep gouges in the metal.

Cook---heavyset man with flour on his apron---stared at them in shock. "What the hell---"

"Back door!" Ray shouted. "Where's the back door?"

Cook pointed toward the rear of the kitchen, and they ran between stainless steel counters and bubbling fryers. Behind them, the thing smashed through the swinging doors, destroying them completely.

They reached the back exit just as the dark one entered the kitchen. Ray slammed the door behind them and they found themselves in an alley behind the diner. Detective Hawthorne was already on her radio, calling for backup.

"Unit 23 requesting immediate assistance at Murphy's Diner, Route 9. Shots fired, multiple civilians in danger. Unknown assailant, armed and extremely dangerous."

Ray leaned against the brick wall, heart pounding. Through the kitchen window, he could see the dark one destroying everything in sight, taking its anger out on the appliances and furniture.

"It ain't gonna give up," Ray said. "They don't stop once they pick a target."

Detective Hawthorne was reloading, hands steady. "What are they? What do they want?"

"Don't know. But they been here a long time, hiding among us. Mine collapse was just one job in something much bigger."

Sirens wailed in the distance, getting closer. Backup was almost here.

"Mr. Kolchek," Detective Hawthorne said, "I owe you an apology. And an explanation."

Ray looked at her. "What you mean?"

"Been tracking these things two years. Blackstone wasn't the first---there's been others. Accidents that weren't accidents. People who just disappear." She slapped in a fresh magazine. "You're the first person who can see what I been chasing."

Ray stared at her. "You knew about them already?"

"Not knew. Suspected. Been building a case, but it's hard to prove something exists when most people can't see it." She glanced toward the diner, where the sounds of destruction had stopped. "Until now."

Police cars was pulling into the diner's parking lot, red and blue lights flashing on the alley walls. Ray could hear officers shouting orders and getting people out.

"What happens now?" Ray asked.

"Now we figure out how many there are and what they're planning." Detective Hawthorne holstered her weapon. "And we find a way to stop them."

Ray nodded, though he wasn't sure how two people---even with guns and badges---could fight things that could look like anybody.

But he thought about them lights in the mine, how they'd saved his ass and changed his eyes. Maybe he wasn't supposed to fight these things head-on. Maybe he was supposed to find more people like Detective Hawthorne---folks who already knew something was wrong.

Maybe that's what this was all about.

"Detective," Ray said as the first uniformed officers rounded the corner into the alley, "think we're gonna need a bigger team."

She smiled grim-like. "Was hoping you'd say that."

As they walked toward the police cars, Ray caught something moving in the diner's kitchen window. The dark thing was gone, but he could still see where it'd been---dark smudge hanging in the air like smoke.

They'd be back. Things like that don't quit.

But for the first time since getting out of that mine, Ray didn't feel so lost. The lights saved him for something. He was starting to get an idea what.

This thing had been going on a long time.

Now it was his turn.

Allen Ginsberg and the Emperor of Ice-Cream Walk into a Funeral Parlor

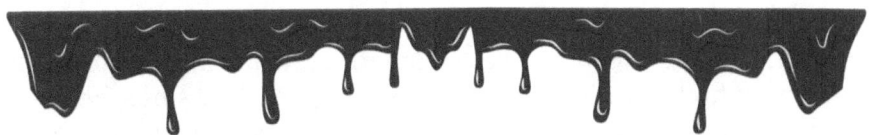

T he first sign something had gone wrong with Mrs. Eleanor Whitehouse's funeral was when the corpse started reciting Allen Ginsberg's *Howl*.

Margaret Ashby, owner and operator of Ashby & Sons Funeral Home (though neither of her sons had shown any interest in the family business), stood frozen beside the casket as Eleanor's lips moved around words that emerged. Not the peaceful hymns Margaret had grown accustomed to hearing from the recently departed—that happened sometimes, especially with the very religious ones—but Allen Ginsberg's beat poetry was something new.

"What did she just say about 'angelheaded hipsters'?" Betty Carmichael whispered from the front pew, her voice cutting through the scent of lilies and formaldehyde that always hung in the air despite Margaret's best efforts with air fresheners.

Margaret smoothed her dress and tried to look professional. Forty-three years of dealing with death and occasional problem corpses. Eleanor had been ordinary—retired librarian, died in her sleep. Yesterday's viewing went fine. Service in twenty minutes, and now this.

The recitation grew louder. The burgundy carpet seemed to vibrate under Margaret's sensible black heels.

"Mrs. Ashby?" Father Timothy approached the casket. "Is this... I mean, is this normal?"

"Define normal," Margaret muttered low enough for only him to hear. Last thing she needed was panic among the mourners. Mrs. Henderson was already fanning herself with the memorial program—supernatural acoustics or June heat, hard to tell.

Eleanor's recitation reached a crescendo that rattled the stained-glass windows depicting scenes of resurrection and eternal peace. Several elderly women in the back pews began clutching their pocketbooks tighter.

"What is a Moloch?" someone called from the back pews, confusion thick in their voice.

That's when Allen Ginsberg walked through the doors like he owned the place.

Margaret recognized him from college—Vassar, back when she'd dreamed of literary greatness before inheriting the family business. But knowing who he was didn't explain why a poet dead since 1997 was standing in her funeral home, wearing his rumpled suit and wild beard from 1950s photos, looking confused but excited.

It was also like looking at him through old window glass and he left no footprints.

"Far out, man," Ginsberg said, his voice carrying that rhythm she remembered from old records, though now it echoed strangely in the hushed space. "This wake is really something else. Very cosmic energy in here." He gestured toward Eleanor's casket with hands that flickered in and out of focus. "Sister's got some serious spiritual vibrations happening."

Eleanor's recitation shifted into what Margaret recognized as *America* and, although she couldn't see it, she could somehow imagine finger-pointing gestures being performed by the corpse under the casket's lid.

"Look, I'm gonna have to ask you to—" Margaret began, approaching the ghost with the same tone she used for relatives who got unreasonable about funeral arrangements.

"Margaret Ashby!" Ginsberg's eyes lit up like he knew her, which made no sense. "The poetry queen of MacDougal Street! I've been looking everywhere for you, baby. This Village scene has really expanded since I was last around. Very suburban, very... funeral home chic. Is this some kind of new artistic movement?"

Margaret's mouth opened slightly. She blinked twice. "This is Vermont. It's 2025. And you've been dead for—"

"Dead?" Ginsberg laughed, a sound like wind chimes caught in a thunderstorm. "Death is just another state of consciousness, you dig? I'm between gigs, spiritually speaking. But listen, I need to find Carl Sandburg. We've got this reading tonight at the Gaslight Cafe, and he's supposed to introduce me. Very important for the movement, you know?"

"Carl Sandburg died in 1967," Margaret said. Her shoulders were starting to ache from tension.

"Heavy," Ginsberg nodded sagely. "So we're all dead? Far out. That explains the weird energy."

Eleanor's voice reached a pitch that shattered the water glasses on the memorial table. Holy water from the blessed fountain began to bubble and steam, filling the air with the smell of hot metal.

Father Timothy's hands shook as he made the sign of the cross. Again. And again. "Margaret, I think we should consider postponing—"

The doors opened again. Temperature dropped fifteen degrees instantly. Ice crystals on windows despite June heat. Memorial flowers wilted and froze, petals turning black and silver. Margaret's breath puffed white.

The man wore a white suit that generated its own light. Silver-white hair, perfectly arranged. He carried a clipboard made of ice that looked like frozen words. Frost formed around his mouth when he breathed.

"Mortician Ashby." He checked his clipboard with the tired look of too much paperwork. "I am the Emperor of Ice Cream, assigned to oversee transition proceedings for Eleanor Whitehouse, deceased. Standard death. Should've been routine."

Margaret had read Wallace Stevens in college. She understood the reference. What she didn't understand was why a metaphor from a 1923 poem was conducting business in her funeral home.

The Emperor of what?" Ginsberg drifted closer, flickering with excitement. "Beautiful. Very mythic. Very archetypal. You part of the new scene?"

The Emperor looked at Ginsberg like he dealt with confused spirits daily. "You're experiencing time confusion, poet. Not 1956. Not Greenwich Village. Not a poetry reading."

"Everything's a poetry reading with the right perspective. The universe is one giant performance, and we're all improvising."

Eleanor then shifted into *Kaddish*, and the emotional weight of Ginsberg's most famous poem about his mother's death filled the funeral home. Several mourners began weeping uncontrollably. Betty Carmichael's mascara ran in black rivers down her cheeks as she sobbed for griefs she didn't understand. The sound of muffled crying mixed with the electric hum of the building's old heating system.

The Emperor checked his clipboard and frowned. "This is highly irregular. The deceased appears to be channeling unauthorized poetic content. Mr. Ginsberg, your presence is interfering with standard transition protocols."

"Protocols are for squares, man," Ginsberg said, his form shimmering. "Death should be spontaneous. Organic. Let the spirit move through whatever medium calls to it."

"The spirit is supposed to move through me," the Emperor said, his voice getting sharper. "I am the designated transition facilitator. Ice cream is the essential pleasure that enjoyed life's sweetness before it ended. The poem is quite clear about this."

Margaret watched this argument between a ghost and whatever the Emperor was with the kind of sick fascination you get watching a car accident. Margaret's stomach dropped. Forty-three years of business, and now this. The funeral was supposed to start in ten minutes. The mourners were becoming increasingly agitated as Eleanor's voice grew louder and more discordant. Mrs. Patterson had already fled to the parking lot, and Margaret could see her through the window, frantically calling someone on her cell phone.

Father Timothy had retreated to the far corner and was performing what appeared to be an emergency exorcism on the holy water font, muttering Latin prayers under his breath.

"Gentlemen," Margaret said, trying to project authority she didn't feel while her head began to throb, "I need you both to understand that this is a place of business. We have a schedule to maintain, and Mrs. Whitehouse's family is expecting—"

Eleanor's eyes snapped open.

They glowed with an inner light and when she spoke, her voice carried harmonics that made the walls vibrate.

"I saw the best minds of my generation destroyed by madness," Eleanor said, "Starving hysterical naked, dragging themselves through the negro streets at dawn looking for an angry fix."

"Eleanor was a very conservative librarian," Margaret whispered. "I'm certain she's never even heard of or read Allen Ginsberg."

"She has now," the Emperor said grimly, making frost notes. "Time confusion makes them feed off each other. Deceased channels poet's consciousness, reinforces his belief he's alive in 1956."

Ginsberg clapped his hands with delight. "She's got it! She's really got it! This is what poetry is supposed to do—bridge the gap between life and death, between individual consciousness and universal experience."

Eleanor sat up in her casket.

The mourners screamed. Margaret felt her knees wobble.

Margaret had dealt with bodies that moved after death—muscle contractions, settling, the occasional involuntary spasm. But Eleanor rose from her casket with the fluid grace of someone very much alive, her gray hair now flowing around her shoulders, her burial dress shifting and changing into something that belonged in a 1950s coffee shop.

"The poetic possession is intensifying," the Emperor observed, scribbling notes on his clipboard. "If this continues, the time confusion could spread beyond the immediate vicinity."

"What does that mean?" Margaret asked, though she was afraid she already knew.

"It means," the Emperor said, "that your entire town is about to think it's Greenwich Village in 1956."

Through the windows, Margaret saw changes beginning. Cranberry Township's suburban streets shifted, becoming narrow and crowded. Colonial houses transformed into tenements with fire escapes. The coffee shop sign changed from "Mountain View Cafe" to "Gaslight Poetry Lounge." A man in a beret set up bongos where the war memorial had been.

"Really groovy," Ginsberg said, oblivious to the chaos. "Reality's flexible if you approach it right, you dig?"

Eleanor climbed out of her casket, wandering the funeral home. Objects transformed at her touch. Memorial flowers became jazz instruments. Religious artwork shifted to abstract spiritual seeking. Chairs became mismatched bohemian furniture. Patchouli and cigarettes overpowered the lilies.

"We have to stop this," Margaret said, rubbing her temples.

"How?" the Emperor asked. "Standard transition protocols require cooperation from both the deceased and any attending spirits. Mr. Ginsberg's temporal confusion is preventing proper acknowledgment of death, and the deceased is now channeling his consciousness instead of moving toward appropriate rest."

Father Timothy had given up on the exorcism and was now hiding behind the organ, clutching his prayer book. The remaining mourners had largely fled, though Betty Carmichael remained, staring transfixed at Eleanor's increasingly animated performance.

"Wait. I've got it," Margaret said. "Ice cream."

The Emperor looked surprised. "Excuse me?"

"Your poem. 'Let be be finale of seem. The only emperor is the emperor of ice cream.' About accepting death, right? Life's pleasures end, but that doesn't make them less real."

"Remarkably sophisticated interpretation," the Emperor admitted, frost breath slowing.

"English major. Look—Allen thinks he's alive in 1956. Eleanor channels his consciousness, caught between life and death. If they acknowledge what they are—dead poet, dead librarian—maybe the loop breaks."

"How?"

Margaret smiled grimly, feeling her first professional confidence
since this started. "Ice cream and poetry."

She walked to the memorial table, which had transformed into something resembling a coffee house bar complete with espresso machine
and chalkboard menu, and raised her voice. "Allen! Eleanor! I've got a
special request."

Both figures turned toward her, Ginsberg's ghostly form flickering
with interest and Eleanor's possessed corpse moving with unnatural
grace.

"Perform together. But not 'Howl.' 'The Emperor of Ice Cream.'"

"Stevens?" Ginsberg wrinkled his nose. "Establishment poetry, man.
Traditional. Mortality-focused."

"Exactly. About death, Allen. Acknowledging what's real. Letting
go."

Eleanor tilted her head, and Margaret saw the librarian she'd
known—quiet, thoughtful, helping people find the right words.

"Call the roller of big cigars," Eleanor said in her own voice, though
it carried echoes of Ginsberg's cosmic consciousness. "The muscular
one, and bid him whip in kitchen cups concupiscent curds."

The Emperor stepped forward, his clipboard dissolving into crys-
talline fragments that tinkled as they hit the floor. When he spoke, his
voice carried the authority of someone who'd been present at every
death since poetry began.

"Let the wenches dawdle in such dress as they are used to wear, and
let the boys bring flowers in last month's newspapers."

The funeral home shifted back to normal, slowly, like reality reluctant to give up artistic transformation. Bongos faded into war memorial. Tenements straightened into New England architecture.

Ginsberg looked around, something clicking in his mind. Ghostly
form more solid but obviously dead. "This isn't the Village, is it?"

"No, Allen. And you're not alive."

"Let be be finale of seem," Eleanor continued in her own voice,
carrying quiet authority of decades helping people find books. "The
only emperor is the emperor of ice cream."

Temperature dropped as the Emperor's true nature asserted itself. Ice
crystals on every surface—beautiful, terrible, final. Frost fell from his
lips like snow.

"She has completed the transition. The poem has been spoken. The acknowledgment has been made."

Eleanor looked down at her burial dress, then at her hands, then at the casket she'd climbed out of. The glow faded from her eyes, leaving them the peaceful gray they'd been in life.

"Oh," she said quietly. "I'm dead, aren't I?"

"Yes," Margaret said. "But you've been having quite an adventure."

Eleanor smiled, and it was the same gentle expression Margaret remembered from library story hours decades ago, when Eleanor would read to children on Saturday mornings. "I always did love poetry. Even the difficult kind."

"The temporal loop is resolving," the Emperor observed, watching as the last of the bohemian transformations faded from the funeral home. The coffee shop equipment melted back into the memorial table. The smell of patchouli gave way to lilies and disinfectant. "Reality is going back to normal time."

Through the windows, Cranberry Township returned to its proper suburban Vermont configuration. The coffee shop resumed its mundane identity. The houses straightened their shoulders and returned to respectable colonialism.

Ginsberg stood in the center of the room, looking around with the confused expression of someone waking from a vivid dream. "I was looking for Carl Sandburg," he said, his voice smaller now, less cosmic. "We had this reading..."

"Carl's waiting for you," the Emperor said kindly, his bureaucratic manner softening. "But not here. Not in 1956."

"Where?"

"Wherever poets go when their work is finished," the Emperor replied. "Somewhere you can discuss the universe without confusing the living."

Ginsberg nodded slowly, his form beginning to fade like smoke from an extinguished cigarette. "The work is never really finished, though, is it? There's always more truth to discover, more consciousness to expand."

"That's why death isn't the end," Eleanor said. She was beginning to look translucent herself, though peacefully so, like morning mist. "It's just the next line in the poem."

"Beautiful," Ginsberg said. "Very Zen. Very eternal moment stuff." He looked at Margaret. "Thanks for the reminder about reality, sister. Sometimes us spirits get a little confused about time and space."

"Sometimes us living people do too," Margaret replied.

The Emperor consulted a new clipboard that had materialized in his hands, this one made of ordinary wood and metal. "Eleanor White-house, your transition has been completed. Allen Ginsberg, your time confusion has been resolved. Are you both ready to proceed to where you're supposed to go?"

"Lead on," Eleanor said.

"Cosmic," Ginsberg agreed.

They walked toward the back, where a door had appeared that hadn't been there before. The Emperor opened it, revealing starlight arranged like words—vast, welcoming, quiet as falling snow.

"Wait," Margaret called. "What about the funeral?"

Eleanor paused at the threshold with the same expression she'd worn helping confused library patrons. "Oh dear. I forgot my own funeral." She considered this, then smiled. "What just happened was more interesting than anything Father Timothy planned. Don't you think?"

All three figures stepped through the door of starlight and were gone.

Margaret stood in her funeral home, returned to normal except for lingering ice crystals and faint scent of coffee and cigarettes that would never fade from the upholstery.

Father Timothy emerged from behind the organ, clutching his prayer book. "What happened?"

"Poetry," she said, straightening chairs, checking her watch. "Very complicated poetry."

Betty Carmichael looked up from the front pew where she'd sat in stunned silence.

"Most beautiful funeral I've ever seen. Eleanor would have loved it."

Margaret considered this. Forty years Eleanor had helped people find the right books, words, stories. In death, she'd found the right poem for her transition, even if it required channeling a dead beat poet and confusing supernatural bureaucracy.

"You're right. She would have."

Outside, Cranberry Township continued its quiet Vermont afternoon, nobody knowing that it had briefly been transported to Greenwich Village in 1956 or that the emperor of ice cream had personally overseen a funeral that turned into a poetry reading that turned into a meditation on death and art and the strange ways consciousness persists beyond the physical body.

Margaret began cleaning up the remaining ice crystals, humming slightly under her breath. It wasn't until she was wiping down the memorial table that she realized she was humming *Howl*, and that she somehow knew all the words.

The next morning, she found a small card in the mail slot, though no one had seen anyone deliver it. The card was made of what appeared to be crystallized poetry—words frozen in ice that somehow remained perfectly legible. It read:

"Thank you for facilitating the transition. Standard protocols are important, but sometimes art requires improvisation. The deceased has settled well in her new literary afterlife. Mr. Ginsberg has been reunited with his contemporaries and is reportedly working on new material about death and beat poetry. Your assistance in resolving the time confusion has been noted in official records. Future supernatural poetry emergencies will be handled by more experienced personnel. Regards, The Emperor of Ice Cream, Division of Artistic Deaths, Transition Department."

Margaret kept the card in her desk drawer, next to the business license and the insurance papers.

Sometimes, when she was preparing particularly difficult cases or dealing with families who couldn't accept their loved one's passing, she would take it out and remember that death wasn't always about endings.

Sometimes it was about finding the right words to describe the indescribable, and sometimes those words came from unexpected sources—even dead beat poets with time confusion and supernatural bureaucrats with very particular job descriptions.

Three months later, when Robert Frost's ghost showed up confused about whether he was in New Hampshire or Massachusetts, Margaret was ready for him. She had a copy of "Stopping by Woods on a Snowy Evening" prepared, and she'd stocked the freezer with ice cream in six different flavors.

The Emperor of Ice Cream had been right about one thing: reality was much more flexible than most people realized, especially when poetry was involved.

And in Cranberry Township, Vermont, where the living and the dead occasionally crossed paths over questions of artistic interpretation and proper funeral protocols, that flexibility was considered just another part of the service that Ashby & Sons provided to the community.

After all, death was the one experience everyone shared, but that didn't mean it had to be boring.

A Few Bugs Left in the Machine

C arlos Kovac was halfway up Turbine 7 when he heard it—a sound that didn't belong. Not the familiar whomp-whomp-whomp of the blades cutting air, but something else. Something underneath. A buzzing, like a dentist's drill working inside the nacelle two hundred feet up.

He stopped climbing, work boots gripping the maintenance ladder's rungs, and listened. The October Montana wind tried to steal the sound, but it was there. High and thin and wrong.

Carlos had been fixing wind turbines for Clearwater Energy for eight years—long enough to know the difference between normal machine noise and the kind that meant his weekend was shot. He clipped his safety harness to the ladder and kept climbing, tool belt jangling against the metal rungs with each step. His breath came in puffs in the morning cold.

The Clearwater Wind Farm spread across the rolling prairie hills like a congregation of white giants, each turbine standing four hundred feet tall against the endless Montana sky. Sagebrush and native grasses stretched between the access roads, interrupted only by the occasional antelope watching the strange proceedings from a safe distance. On a good day, all hundred and twenty of them spinning in the wind could power fifty thousand homes. On a bad day—when one of them started making sounds like a giant insect—Carlos got called out to figure out what the hell was wrong.

"Dispatch, Kovac here." He keyed his radio at the nacelle platform, shouting over the blade noise. The wind tried to tear the radio from his grip. "Something's wrong with Seven. Getting weird sounds from inside the housing."

"What kind of sounds, Carlos?" Janet's voice crackled through the static, competing with interference from the turbine's electrical systems.

"Hell if I know. Like... like a bug zapper, but bigger." He squinted at his handheld monitor, the small screen hard to read in the bright October sun. "And we're down fifteen percent on output."

"Equipment failure?"

"Maybe. Maybe something else." Carlos fumbled with the nacelle access panel, his fingers already knowing which tools he'd need. The wind made his eyes water. "Let me get inside and take a look."

"Copy. Keep us posted."

Carlos unlocked the access panel and immediately staggered backward, nearly losing his grip on the platform rail. The smell hit him like a physical blow—sickly sweet decomposition mixed with hot gear oil, a smell that belonged neither in nature nor machinery. Eight years of turbine maintenance, and he'd never smelled anything like it.

"Jesus Christ," he muttered, pulling his shirt up over his nose. His eyes were watering now, and not from the wind. "What died in there?"

He clicked on his flashlight and peered into the nacelle's belly. The massive gearbox and generator filled most of the space, their surfaces gleaming with fresh lubricant. Everything looked normal—until his light swept across the gear assemblies. Above the constant whoosh of the blades and the deep hum of the generator, he could hear something else: a high-pitched buzzing that seemed to come from everywhere at once.

Dark clusters covered the rotating equipment. At first glance, they looked like oil stains or carbon buildup. But as Carlos adjusted his light, the clusters moved.

They actually moved.

"What the hell?" Carlos blinked hard, thinking maybe the climb had made him dizzy. The altitude sometimes got to guys his age. But no—the dark patches were shifting, flowing like liquid across the spinning gears.

He leaned closer, one hand gripping the access frame, and squinted into the mechanical depths. The clusters resolved into something his brain took a full second to process: insects. Thousands of them. Each one the size of a silver dollar, their bodies dark and segmented like beetles, but wrong somehow. They clung to the spinning gear teeth with legs that looked too strong, too precise, riding the machinery like some kind of living attachment.

The smell got stronger—that sweet-rot stench that made his sinuses burn. And underneath it, something else. Something electric, like the air before a lightning strike. Carlos had felt that sensation plenty of times working around high-voltage equipment, but never this intense.

He'd seen plenty of bugs in turbines before. Moths drawn to the warmth, beetles looking for places to winter, the occasional bird's nest down in the tower base. But he'd never seen insects do this—positioning themselves on moving machinery without getting crushed, maintaining specific locations like they belonged there.

"Dispatch." His voice came out hoarse. He cleared his throat and tried again. "I'm gonna need pest control out here."

"What kind of pest control?"

"The big kind." Carlos watched the insects move in coordinated waves across the gear assembly. His hands had started shaking, and he gripped the platform rail tighter. "We got thousands of bugs in Seven. And they're... they're acting weird."

"Weird how?"

Carlos searched for words that wouldn't make him sound like he'd been drinking on the job. "They're not just hiding in here, Janet. They're living with the machinery. Like they're part of it."

Static filled the radio for a moment. "Carlos, you feeling okay up there? Maybe the altitude—"

"I'm fine. Just send someone else out to confirm what I'm seeing, okay?" He keyed off the radio before she could ask more questions.

Carlos lowered the radio and watched the insects more carefully, trying to understand what he was seeing. When the wind picked up and the generator output increased, they flowed toward the electrical components like iron filings drawn to a magnet. When it died down, they redistributed themselves to different parts of the machinery.

They were tracking the power flow through the system.

"This is insane," he said aloud, partly to break the silence and partly because talking made him feel less like he was losing his mind. "Bugs don't do this."

But even as he said it, Carlos knew he was looking at something that had never existed before. Something that lived at the intersection of biology and machinery, something that had learned to ride the electrical currents like dolphins riding ocean waves.

He pulled out his phone and started taking pictures, though he doubted anyone would believe them. Through the camera lens, he noticed their wings—iridescent patterns that shifted and moved independently of the insects themselves. The wing patterns looked like circuit traces, with lines and nodes that resembled the electrical diagrams he'd studied in trade school.

The insects nearest to him had turned to face his direction. They remained motionless on the rotating machinery, but their heads were oriented toward him like tiny sentinels.

Carlos felt the hair on his arms stand up, and it wasn't from the electromagnetic field he was used to.

He reached into his tool kit for a collection vial, thinking he could capture a few specimens for the university boys to look at. But the moment he extended his hand toward the nearest cluster, every insect in the nacelle stopped moving.

The sudden silence was like a held breath. The machinery kept its normal rhythm, but that constant buzzing Carlos had been hearing just... stopped. Thousands of insects sat motionless on the rotating equipment, and Carlos had the uncomfortable feeling that they were all watching him.

"Okay," he said aloud, his voice sounding too loud in the mechanical space. "That's not normal bug behavior."

He reached toward them again, slower this time. The instant his hand crossed into the nacelle's interior space, the buzzing came back—but different now. Higher pitched, more aggressive, and synchronized across all the insects like some kind of alarm.

Carlos jerked his hand back, and the buzzing stopped.

"Dispatch," he radioed, trying to keep his voice steady. "I'm gonna need backup out here. And maybe someone who knows about bugs."

"What's your situation, Carlos?"

"The insects are... they're reacting to me. Like they're defending the turbine."

"Defending?" Janet's voice went up a notch. "Carlos, you sure you're not just seeing normal pest behavior?"

Carlos watched as the insects reorganized themselves into what looked like defensive positions around the most critical machinery. "Yeah, I'm sure. Send Mike up here, but tell him not to go inside the housing until I figure out what we're dealing with."

Twenty minutes later, he heard Mike Crenshaw's voice echo up from the base of the tower. "Carlos! Heading up!"

The insects inside the nacelle became more active the moment Mike started climbing. They could somehow sense the approach of another human from two hundred feet away.

Carlos keyed his radio. "Mike, when you get up here, don't stick any part of your body past the access panel. I want you to see this before we mess with them."

"See what?"

"You'll know."

Mike hauled himself onto the platform, breathing hard and sweating despite the October cold. He was a big guy, mid-forties, with the kind of gut that came from too many years of post-shift beers. But he'd been doing turbine work almost as long as Carlos, and his expression turned serious when he caught the smell.

"Jesus, Carlos. What's that stink?" Mike pulled off his work gloves and wiped his face with the back of his hand.

"That's what I wanted you to notice. Now look inside, but keep your distance."

Mike positioned himself next to Carlos and peered into the turbine's interior. Carlos watched his face change from curiosity to confusion to alarm.

"Are those... what the hell are those things?"

"Bugs. Thousands of them. Watch this." Carlos extended his hand toward the nacelle entrance.

The synchronized buzzing alarm filled the air, and Mike jerked backward like he'd been slapped.

"They're coordinating," Mike said, his voice gone quiet. He stepped back from the access panel, unconsciously wiping his hands on his coveralls. "That's not normal insect behavior."

"No, it's not. And look at this." Carlos showed Mike the photos on his phone, pointing out how the insects tracked the electrical flow through the machinery.

Mike studied the images, zooming in on different sections. His thick fingers had trouble with the small screen. "Carlos, I've been doing this job for twelve years, and I've never seen anything like this. These things are acting more like... like a security system than random bugs."

"That's what I was thinking. But that's crazy, right? Bugs don't understand electrical systems."

"Normal bugs don't." Mike took his own photos from a different angle, the camera flash reflecting off the insects' wings. "But look at their wings. See how they're catching the light? That's not normal coloration."

Carlos looked more carefully. In the direct beam of their flashlights, the insects' wings showed an iridescent pattern that shifted and moved like oil on water. But it wasn't random—the patterns looked deliberate, like circuit traces etched into living tissue.

"Mike, you think being exposed to all this electromagnetic radiation could have... changed them somehow?"

"Changed them how?"

"Made them different. Adapted them to electrical systems."

Mike was quiet for a moment, watching the insects ride the rotating gears with impossible precision. He pulled out a thermos of coffee, hands shaking slightly as he unscrewed the cap. "You're talking about bugs that have evolved to live inside electrical equipment. That's..."

"Impossible?"

"Should be impossible. But look at them." Mike pointed to a cluster of insects maintaining perfect position on a spinning shaft. "They're not getting crushed, they're not interfering with the machinery, and they're somehow tracking power flow in real time."

"How long would that kind of evolution take?"

"Normally? Thousands of years. But if there was some kind of accelerated pressure..." Mike's voice trailed off. He took a sip of coffee, then made a face. "Christ, even the coffee tastes wrong up here."

"The turbines have only been here for five years," Carlos said.

"Five years isn't enough time for natural evolution. Unless..." Mike lowered his voice, though the insects probably couldn't understand English anyway. "Unless something else sped up the process."

They watched the insects in silence for several minutes. The creatures moved with purpose and coordination that shouldn't have been possible for their size and species. More disturbing, they seemed to be learning—adjusting their behavior based on the presence of the two humans.

"We need to report this," Mike finally said, screwing the cap back on his thermos.

"Report what? That we found some bugs in a wind turbine?"

"That we found bugs that might not be normal bugs anymore. The environmental impact alone..."

Carlos's radio crackled. "Kovac, this is Dispatch. Status on Turbine 7?"

Carlos and Mike exchanged glances. How do you explain that you've discovered insects that treat industrial equipment like their natural habitat?

"Dispatch, we're gonna need a consultation with someone from the university. Biology department. We've got a situation here that's outside normal maintenance scope."

"What kind of situation?"

Carlos watched the insects tracking their movements with coordinated precision. "An infestation that's... unusual. We need expert analysis before we do anything that might make it worse."

"How unusual are we talking?"

"Very unusual."

Three hours later, as the October afternoon sun started its slide toward the Rockies, Dr. Elena Herrera from Montana State University arrived at the wind farm, driving a van loaded with scientific equipment and accompanied by two graduate students. She was younger than

Carlos had expected—maybe early forties, with prematurely gray hair pulled back in a ponytail and the kind of intense focus that made him think she'd been dealing with impossible things for a while.

"You said they show coordinated behavior?" Dr. Herrera asked as she unloaded collection equipment. Her breath came in puffs in the cooling afternoon air.

"Coordinated doesn't begin to cover it," Carlos replied, helping her carry a heavy case. "They're acting like a single organism with thousands of parts."

"And they're territorial about the turbine interior?"

"Aggressively territorial. They'll let you observe from outside, but any intrusion triggers what looks like a defensive response."

Dr. Herrera exchanged glances with her students—a young woman named Amy who handled the electronic equipment with the intensity of someone who'd rather trust machines than people, and a bearded guy called Tom who kept checking his phone and muttering about missing a Griz game for "bug hunting." Amy had the eager look of someone who'd rather be measuring things than talking about them. Tom just looked cold and annoyed.

"Mr. Kovac, have you noticed any other turbines showing similar problems?" Dr. Herrera asked, pulling on work gloves.

"No, just this one. But we haven't done close inspections of the others lately."

"I think we should check." She handed Carlos a pair of binoculars. "Can you see any external signs that might indicate similar infestations?"

Carlos scanned the wind farm through the binoculars. At first, everything looked normal—white towers and rotating blades against the blue Montana sky. Then he focused on Turbine 12, about a quarter-mile away.

"There," he said, handing the binoculars to Dr. Herrera. "Turbine 12. Look at the nacelle housing."

Dr. Herrera adjusted the focus and studied the distant turbine. After a moment, she lowered the binoculars, her face pale. "I see movement on the exterior surface. Dark patches that are shifting position."

"Those patches weren't there last week," Carlos said.

"How many turbines are in this farm?"

"One hundred and twenty."

Dr. Herrera looked out across the field of white towers, calculating. The wind was picking up, making her hair whip around her face. "We need to check every single one. If this is what I think it might be, we're looking at something unprecedented."

"What do you think it is?"

"Accelerated adaptive evolution. Insects that have modified themselves to exploit a new ecological niche—industrial electrical systems." She started setting up her equipment with practiced efficiency, Amy helping with the electronic components. "The question is whether they're adapting to coexist with the machinery, or if they're becoming dependent on it."

"What's the difference?"

"Coexistence means they could survive without the turbines if necessary. Dependency means they've evolved past the point where they can live anywhere else." Dr. Herrera attached a long-range camera lens and started taking detailed photographs. "If it's dependency, and if they're spreading to other turbines, we might be looking at the first documented case of insects evolving technological symbiosis."

"Is that good or bad?"

"It's unprecedented. And potentially very dangerous."

Dr. Herrera's equipment included sensors for detecting electromagnetic field variations, chemical analyzers for air samples, and collection devices designed to capture insects without harming them. As she set up her instruments, Carlos noticed that the insects in Turbine 7 had become more active. The buzzing sound was getting louder.

"They know you're here," he told Dr. Herrera. "They've been more agitated since you showed up."

"Agitated how?"

"Listen."

The buzzing from inside the nacelle had changed again. Instead of the rhythmic hum Carlos had grown used to, the sound now pulsed in irregular patterns, like Morse code being transmitted at high speed.

Dr. Herrera pulled out a digital recorder and captured several minutes of the sound. "This is remarkable. They're not just making noise—they're generating complex acoustic patterns. This could be actual communication."

"Communication?" Mike asked, looking skeptical.

"Many insect species use sound patterns to convey information about territory, food sources, threats. But this level of complexity..." She played back the recording at different speeds. "This suggests cognitive development far beyond normal insects."

Amy had been monitoring electromagnetic readings around the turbine with a handheld Fluke 87V multimeter—the same model Carlos used for electrical diagnostics. "Dr. Herrera, you need to see this." Her voice had an excited edge that reminded Carlos of his daughter when she found something cool in the creek. "The electromagnetic field around this turbine is different from baseline."

"Different how?"

"Stronger, but also more organized. Instead of the random field fluctuations you'd expect from electrical equipment, the patterns are highly structured." Amy showed her the readout on her scanner, the small screen glowing in the fading afternoon light. "It's like the insects are somehow regulating the electromagnetic output."

Dr. Herrera studied the readings carefully, unconsciously twisting her wedding ring—a habit Carlos noticed she did whenever she was processing something that didn't fit her expectations. "That should be impossible. Insects don't have the biological capability to manipulate electromagnetic fields."

"Unless they've evolved that capability," Amy suggested.

"Evolution doesn't work that fast."

Carlos cleared his throat. "Dr. Herrera, what if evolution isn't the only thing changing them?"

"What do you mean?"

"What if exposure to electromagnetic fields doesn't just cause evolution? What if it causes something more immediate?"

Dr. Herrera considered this possibility, pulling her ponytail tighter—another stress response Carlos had noticed. "You're suggesting that electromagnetic radiation is altering their biology in real time?"

"I'm suggesting that maybe these bugs aren't just adapted to electrical systems. Maybe they're being transformed by them."

To test this theory, Dr. Herrera coordinated with the wind farm's control center to vary the power output from Turbine 7 while recording the insects' responses. What they observed over the next hour made Carlos's mouth go dry.

When the turbine's power output increased, the insects became more active and their wing patterns grew brighter. When the power decreased, they became sluggish and their coloration dimmed. But the most disturbing part was what happened when they shut down the turbine completely for testing.

The insects swarmed toward the nacelle's access panel, trying to escape the interior. Their buzzing became frantic and desperate, and several of them began to glow with their own bioluminescent light—a sickly green phosphorescence that pulsed in rhythm with their distress calls.

"They're addicted to electricity," Dr. Herrera said quietly, watching the insects cluster around any source of electrical energy. Her hands were shaking as she took notes. "They've become biologically dependent on electromagnetic radiation."

"What happens if they can't get it?" Carlos asked.

"Based on their behavior when we shut down the turbine, I'd say they die. They've evolved past the point where they can survive in natural environments."

Carlos watched the insects desperately seeking electrical current, their movements becoming more erratic by the minute. "So they're trapped in here."

"Worse than trapped. They're prisoners of their own adaptation. They've specialized so completely for this artificial environment that they can't exist anywhere else."

Amy had been photographing the swarming insects with a high-speed camera, her hands steady despite the cold. "Dr. Herrera, look at these images. Their wing patterns are changing in real time." She had the same focused intensity Carlos had seen in his daughter when she was working on her science fair projects.

Dr. Herrera examined the photos on Amy's camera display. The circuit-like patterns on the insects' wings were shifting and reorganizing as they moved closer to different electrical components. It was like watching biological circuitry reconfigure itself to optimize power absorption.

"They're not just dependent on electricity," she realized, her voice filled with wonder and horror. "They're interfacing with it. Their biology has become part of the electrical system."

"What does that mean?" Mike asked.

"It means they're not just living in the turbine—they're becoming part of it. A biological component in an electrical machine."

Carlos felt cold despite his heavy jacket. "If they're spreading to other turbines..."

"We could be looking at the emergence of a new kind of organism. Something that's part biological, part technological." Dr. Herrera restarted the turbine, and the insects immediately returned to their organized positions, visibly calming as power flowed through the system again. "Something that could fundamentally change the relationship between natural and artificial systems."

"Is that necessarily bad?" Tom asked, speaking for the first time since they'd arrived. His voice had a Montana twang that suggested he'd grown up somewhere around here, probably on a ranch. "I mean, if they're not hurting the turbines, maybe they're just... I don't know, adapting. Like cattle learning to use water tanks."

"It is if they become territorial about human access to the machinery they've colonized. And it's bad if they start viewing humans as competitors for electrical resources."

As if responding to her words, the insects in the nacelle began generating their complex acoustic patterns again. But now the sounds were echoing from other directions as well—from Turbines 12, 15, and 23, creating a network of communication across the wind farm.

"They're talking to each other," Amy said, monitoring the sound patterns on her equipment. "Coordinating across multiple—"

"Sites," Tom finished, looking up from his phone. "Like a network. My dad's cattle do something similar when they're moving between pastures. One cow spots something, they all know about it in seconds." He gestured toward the turbines. "Though I gotta say, cattle don't usually glow like that."

"This is a bit more complex than cattle communication," Dr. Herrera said dryly.

The next six hours felt like the longest of Carlos's life. Dr. Herrera's team conducted surveys of every turbine in the Clearwater Wind Farm, using binoculars, electromagnetic scanners, and acoustic monitoring equipment to assess each tower without disturbing any potential colonies.

The results confirmed Carlos's worst fears.

Forty-seven of the one hundred and twenty turbines showed signs of insect colonization. The infestations followed a clear pattern, spreading outward from Turbine 7 in concentric circles. The insects had somehow migrated from turbine to turbine, establishing colonies in each one.

"How long has this been going on?" Dr. Herrera asked as they reviewed the survey data in her van, the heater running against the evening cold.

"The first efficiency problems started about six months ago," Carlos replied, nursing a cup of coffee that tasted like it had been made with motor oil. "But they were minor, and we figured it was normal equipment wear."

"Six months to colonize forty-seven turbines. That's extremely rapid expansion for any species."

"Could they be breeding in the turbines?"

"That's what we need to find out. But first, we need to understand exactly what we're dealing with." Dr. Herrera consulted her notes, pages of data that made no sense to Carlos. "I need to collect specimens for detailed analysis."

"How do you collect specimens from bugs that become hostile when you enter their territory?" Mike asked.

"Very carefully."

Dr. Herrera's plan involved using a small robotic probe that could be inserted into the turbine nacelles without triggering the insects' defensive responses. The robot was about the size of a softball, equipped with cameras, sample collection tools, and gentle capture mechanisms designed not to harm the specimens.

But when they deployed the robot in Turbine 7, the insects' reaction was completely unexpected.

Instead of treating the robot as an intruder, they swarmed toward it with what looked like curiosity. Dozens of insects landed on the robot's surface, crawling over its sensors and cameras. Their wing patterns began shifting rapidly, and Amy's electromagnetic readings spiked.

"They're trying to interface with it," Amy observed, monitoring the data feeds. "The electromagnetic patterns they're generating match the robot's electronic signatures."

"They think it's one of them," Dr. Herrera said, watching the live video feed. "Or they're trying to make it one of them."

On the robot's camera, they could see insects positioning themselves around the device's electronic components, their wings glowing brighter as they made contact with the circuitry. The robot's systems began experiencing minor malfunctions—nothing dangerous, but clear evidence that the insects were affecting its operation.

"Pull it back," Dr. Herrera ordered. "Before they damage it permanently."

But when they tried to retrieve the robot, the insects wouldn't let it go. They clung to its surface and actively interfered with its movement. The robot's control signals became erratic as more insects attached themselves to its electronics.

"They're not just interfacing with it," Carlos realized, watching the struggle on the video feed. "They're trying to absorb it into their colony."

"Cut the connection," Dr. Herrera said grimly. "We're losing the robot."

The moment they severed the robot's communication link, the insects released it and allowed it to fall to the nacelle floor. But the device was no longer functional—its electronic systems had been fundamentally altered by contact with the insects, and it would never respond to commands again.

"What did they do to it?" Amy asked.

"I think," Dr. Herrera said slowly, "they tried to integrate it into their collective organism. When they realized it couldn't be successfully integrated, they rejected it."

"A collective organism?" Tom asked.

"Think about what we've observed. Coordinated behavior across multiple turbines. Complex communication systems. Shared responses to threats." Dr. Herrera packed up her equipment with new urgency. "These insects aren't operating as individuals—they're functioning as parts of a single, distributed intelligence."

Carlos felt his mouth go dry. "An intelligence that views electrical equipment as part of its body."

"And views anything that interferes with that equipment as a threat to its survival."

Carlos's radio crackled with Janet's voice. "Kovac, this is Dispatch. We're getting reports of efficiency problems across the entire wind farm. Multiple turbines showing decreased power output."

Carlos exchanged glances with Dr. Herrera. "Roger, Dispatch. We're... investigating the situation."

"What's your assessment? Equipment failures or environmental factors?"

Carlos looked out at the forty-seven turbines now colonized by insects that were becoming more sophisticated and territorial by the hour. "Environmental factors, Dispatch. But not the kind we usually deal with."

"How long for repairs?"

"Unknown at this time. We might be looking at a long-term situation that requires specialized consultation."

"Understood. Keep us posted."

Dr. Herrera was studying the latest electromagnetic readings from across the wind farm. "The insects in different turbines are definitely communicating. The field patterns show synchronized pulses that correspond to the acoustic signals we recorded."

"What are they communicating about?" Mike asked.

"Us, probably. Our presence, our activities, our threat level." She pointed to clusters of data on her laptop screen. "See these spikes? They correspond to when we moved from one turbine to the next. They're tracking our location and sharing that information across the entire colony."

"So they know where we are at all times."

"They know where we are, what we're doing, and they're co-ordinating their responses accordingly. This isn't just an infestation anymore—it's an occupation."

Amy had been analyzing the acoustic patterns with specialized software. "Dr. Herrera, the sound patterns are becoming more complex. It's like they're developing new vocabulary in real time."

"New vocabulary for what?"

"I think they're developing specific terms for us. For humans. For threats to their territory."

Carlos realized the scope of what they were facing. "They're learning about us as fast as we're learning about them."

"Faster," Dr. Herrera corrected. "They have the advantage of numbers, direct electrical connectivity, and shared intelligence. They can process and distribute information across the entire wind farm instantaneously."

"So what do we do?" Mike asked.

Dr. Herrera was quiet for a long moment, staring at the data they'd collected. The laptop screen cast an eerie glow on her face in the gathering darkness. "I think we need to consider the possibility that we can't remove them."

"Why not?"

"Because they're not just living in the turbines anymore—they're part of the turbines. Their biology has integrated with the electrical systems to the point where removing them might cause permanent damage to both the insects and the equipment."

"And if we leave them alone?"

"Then we're accepting the creation of a new kind of organism. Something that's part biological, part technological, and potentially more intelligent than either component alone."

"Is that even legal?" Carlos asked. "Can we just let them take over company property?"

"I don't know. There's no legal precedent for dealing with organisms that have evolved technological symbiosis." Dr. Herrera began packing up her equipment. "But I know that trying to fight them could be dangerous for everyone involved."

"What kind of dangerous?"

"They're territorial about their electrical resources, and they can manipulate electromagnetic fields. If they decide humans are threats or competitors, they could potentially cause power outages, equipment malfunctions, or worse."

Carlos looked up at Turbine 7, where thousands of insects were going about their mysterious business. The thought of them viewing him as an enemy made his skin crawl.

"So what's our recommendation to the company?"

"Cautious observation. We monitor them, try to understand their behavior patterns, and hope they remain content with their current territory."

"And if they're not content?"

"Then we're dealing with the first technological species on Earth, and we have no idea what they're ultimately capable of."

That evening, Carlos sat in his truck at the edge of the wind farm, watching the turbines rotate against the star-filled Montana sky. Dr. Herrera and her team had returned to the university to analyze their samples and prepare a preliminary report, leaving Carlos and Mike to maintain their normal schedules while avoiding the colonized turbines.

"How do you think this ends?" Mike asked from the passenger seat, cracking open a beer.

"I don't know. Maybe the bugs stay in their turbines and we learn to work around them. Maybe they spread to other wind farms and we have to deal with a whole new kind of environmental protection issue."

"Or maybe they decide they don't want us around anymore."

Carlos nodded grimly. The insects had demonstrated intelligence, coordination, and territorial behavior that suggested they were capable of making strategic decisions about perceived threats. If they concluded that humans were competitors for electrical resources, they might take action to eliminate that competition.

"Look at Turbine 7," Mike said, pointing through the windshield.

Carlos followed his gaze and felt his blood run cold. The insects that had been confined to the nacelle interior were now visible on the turbine's exterior surface, clustered around the electrical connections and cable runs that carried power down the tower. Their wings glowed with bioluminescent patterns that pulsed in synchronization across the entire structure.

"They're expanding their territory," Carlos said.

"Or evolving. Again."

As they watched, the glowing patterns began appearing on other colonized turbines throughout the wind farm. Within minutes, forty-seven turbines were lit up like alien Christmas trees, their insect colonies communicating through coordinated light displays that were visible for miles across the Montana prairie.

"That's not random," Mike observed. "That's organized. Purposeful."

"It's beautiful," Carlos admitted, despite his growing fear. "Like watching something completely new come to life."

The light patterns continued for several minutes—complex sequences that conveyed detailed information across the wind farm in ways that no human could interpret. Then, gradually, the displays faded back to normal levels, leaving the turbines looking ordinary once again.

But Carlos knew they weren't ordinary anymore. Nothing about this place was ordinary anymore.

"What do you think they were saying?" Mike asked.

"I think they were announcing their presence. Letting anything else out there know that something new has been born here."

Carlos started his truck and began driving toward the wind farm's exit. Behind them, the turbines continued their rotation, now home to creatures that had never existed before—technological insects that had crossed the boundary between biology and machinery and found a way to thrive in the space between.

"Carlos," Mike said as they reached the main road, "what happens when other wind farms start reporting the same thing?"

"Then we find out whether we're dealing with a local phenomenon or the beginning of something much bigger."

"And if it's something bigger?"

"Then we find out whether humans and technological organisms can share the same planet."

As they drove away from Clearwater, Carlos couldn't shake the feeling that they'd witnessed something unprecedented—not just the evolution of a new species, but the birth of a new form of life entirely. Something that existed at the intersection of biology and technology, capable of growth, adaptation, and possibly intelligence beyond anything humanity had encountered.

Whether that was evolution or revolution remained to be seen.

But Carlos suspected they'd find out soon enough.

Three weeks later, reports began flooding in from wind farms across the country. Montana, Wyoming, Texas, Iowa—everywhere there were wind turbines, maintenance crews were finding similar infestations of insects that showed coordinated behavior and electromagnetic sensitivity.

Dr. Herrera's preliminary report had reached the Department of Energy, who immediately classified it. But word was spreading through the renewable energy industry anyway. Technicians were finding bugs in their turbines—bugs that acted like the ones documented at Clearwater.

"It's spreading faster than we thought possible," Dr. Herrera told Carlos during a phone call three weeks later. "We're getting reports from facilities that are hundreds of miles apart, with no obvious biological connection except for their electrical infrastructure."

"How is that possible? Bugs can't fly hundreds of miles."

"Normal insects can't. But these aren't normal insects anymore. We think they might be capable of electromagnetic navigation, using power transmission lines and electrical infrastructure to guide long-distance migration."

"They're following the power grid?"

"That's our current hypothesis. They've become so dependent on electrical systems that they can navigate using the infrastructure itself as a migration pathway."

Carlos thought about the implications. Every wind farm, every power plant, every electrical substation could potentially become a colony site for these technological insects.

"Dr. Herrera, what happens when they run out of wind turbines to colonize?"

"That's what keeps me awake at night. They might remain content with renewable energy infrastructure, or they might start expanding into other electrical systems."

"Other systems like what?"

"Power plants. Electrical substations. Industrial facilities." Her voice went quiet. "Potentially even residential electrical systems."

Carlos's hands tightened on the phone. The thought of these insects moving into homes and businesses made his stomach clench. If they viewed electrical equipment as their territory and humans as competitors, the potential for conflict was enormous.

"What's the official response going to be?"

"The government is forming a task force to study the phenomenon and develop response protocols. But unofficially, everyone's hoping they stay confined to wind farms and don't become more aggressive about defending their territory."

"And if they do become more aggressive?"

"Then we're facing the first interspecies technological conflict in human history."

Carlos hung up the phone and walked outside to look at the Clearwater Wind Farm in the distance. Even from several miles away, he could see the occasional flicker of bioluminescent communication between the colonized turbines.

Whatever had started in Turbine 7 was now spreading across the continent, creating a new kind of organism that existed at the boundary between nature and technology. Whether that organism would remain content with its current territory or begin expanding into human-controlled electrical systems was anyone's guess.

But Carlos suspected that humanity was about to find out whether it was prepared to share its technological infrastructure with a new form of life—one that had been born from the intersection of evolution and electricity, and was capable of adaptation at a speed that made human responses seem glacially slow.

The bugs were out of the machine now.

The question was whether they would stay out, or whether they were just getting started.

Six months later, the Riverside Power Plant in Oregon went dark at 3:47 AM on a Tuesday morning.

It wasn't an equipment failure, a cyber attack, or human error. Technological insects that had migrated from the nearest wind farm—following power transmission lines like highways—had executed a coordinated occupation of the plant's electrical systems. They didn't destroy the equipment or shut it down violently. They simply took control of it, redirecting power flow in ways that maintained the electrical environment they needed while cutting off human access to the controls.

The insects had evolved from squatters to sovereigns.

Within hours, similar reports were coming in from power facilities across the Pacific Northwest. The technological insects were expanding their territory systematically, claiming electrical infrastructure as their natural habitat. They weren't destroying human technology—they were absorbing it, integrating it into something larger and more complex than either biology or machinery alone.

And humanity was still trying to figure out what that meant for the future of both species.

Franz Kafka is Alive and Well and Living in Philadelphia

M ichael Leibowitz woke with his face pressed against the pages of a book, the taste of cheap bourbon souring his mouth. His head felt like someone had been using it for batting practice. Afternoon light cut through the blinds in sharp lines across his cramped Center City apartment. He peeled his cheek from the paper, noting with disgust the small puddle of drool that had gathered on an illustration of a man transformed into a giant insect.

The Metamorphosis. Light reading before bed.

The digital clock on his nightstand glowed 2:17. PM, he assumed, though with the heavy curtains drawn and his brain still swimming in Wild Turkey, he couldn't be sure.

He rolled onto his back, feeling the book slide onto the floor with a thud. His mouth tasted like something had crawled inside it and died. His English Lit professors at Penn would be proud to see where twenty years and an abandoned dissertation had gotten him: alone in a cramped apartment with too many books and just enough discount liquor to make him forget he spent his days calculating the dollar value of human misery.

The telephone rang, cutting through his skull like a rusty saw. He fumbled for it on the nightstand, knocking over an empty glass that rolled across the floor.

"Leibowitz," he mumbled.

"Michael, it's Peterson. The Wasserman claim was due yesterday. Tell me you've finished processing it."

His supervisor's voice had that tight, clipped quality it got when dealing with him these days.

Michael rubbed his eyes. "Yeah, yeah. I'll have it done this afternoon."

"Excuse me?" Peterson said.

Michael blinked. Had he said something else? "I said I'll have it finished this afternoon."

"Are you drunk, Leibowitz? It's Wednesday. Middle of the work-week."

"No, I'm..." A stabbing pain shot through his chest, doubling him over. He coughed, a wet, hacking sound that came from somewhere deep and rotten. "I think I'm sick. Food poisoning. I need a sick day."

"This is your third this month. The Wasserman family's been waiting for their settlement for weeks. Their son's still in the hospital, for Christ's sake."

"I understand. I'll email it tonight. Promise." He hung up before Peterson could protest further.

Michael dragged himself to the bathroom, relieved himself, then bent over the sink to splash water on his face. When he straightened up, the face in the mirror wasn't his.

Well, it was his, but wrong somehow—cheeks sunken in like he hadn't eaten in weeks, eyes sitting deeper in their sockets, ears that seemed to stick out more than they had yesterday. His fingertips traced new hollows that hadn't existed when he'd gone to bed.

He knew that face. He'd been staring at it in a book photo last night.

"This isn't possible," he whispered, but the words came out in German.

Impossible. He didn't speak German. He'd failed the language requirement twice in grad school, one of many reasons he'd given up on his dissertation about European writers. Yet here he was, thinking and speaking in fluent German.

Michael—was he still Michael?—leaned closer to the mirror. The face staring back was unmistakable. Franz Kafka.

He stumbled backward, slamming into the towel rack. It clattered to the floor, and the noise sent him scrambling back into the bedroom. He grabbed the book from where it had fallen, flipping through the pages to the author photo at the back.

The same face. The same face that was now his.

"*Nein,*" he whispered. "*Das ist nicht möglich.*"

The cough came again, violent and wet. He stumbled to the kitchen sink, bent over, and hacked until something warm and thick splattered against the stainless steel. When he opened his eyes, dark red threads wound through his spit.

Tuberculosis. Kafka died of tuberculosis.

His legs went out from under him. He slid down the cabinet doors to the kitchen floor, staring at hands that looked wrong—longer fingers, knuckles that stood out like mountain ridges under skin that seemed too tight.

He wasn't just looking like Kafka. He was becoming him. Or Kafka was becoming him. He didn't know which was worse.

Pieces of someone else's life kept cutting through his thoughts: a childhood in Prague, a stern father shouting in a language that wasn't English, the smell of the Vltava River in spring, the crushing weight of working at an insurance institute. But layered beneath those alien memories were his own: growing up in suburban New Jersey, his bar mitzvah, his parents' disappointment when he switched majors from pre-law to English literature, his ex-wife Rachel telling him she couldn't live with someone who'd settled for mediocrity.

The phone rang seven times before the machine picked up.

"Michael, it's Rachel. The alimony's late again. I've got bills too, you know. Call me back."

He stared at the phone from the floor of his apartment, unable to move. Something was wrong with his body, wrong with his head. The voice in the machine sounded like it belonged to someone else's life.

He crawled to his desk and grabbed a pen. His hand started moving without permission, forming words in a language he'd never learned. German. Perfect German, flowing across the page like water.

What the hell was happening to him?

He wrote until his hand cramped, until the light outside the window faded and the room grew dark around him. Only then did he stop, blinking like someone coming out of a trance.

He'd filled seventeen pages. In perfect German. In handwriting that wasn't his own.

Three days passed. Michael didn't leave his apartment. He called in sick to work, muttering in English just long enough to get Peterson off his back. He unplugged the phone after the fourth call from Rachel. He wrote.

God, how he wrote.

Page after page of German prose, flowing from him like water from a spring, beautiful and strange. Stories about men transformed into animals, about mysterious trials, about messengers who could never reach their destinations. Between writing sessions, he slept, his dreams filled with cockroaches and bureaucrats.

On the morning of the fourth day, he awoke with a clarity he hadn't felt since the transformation began. His money was running low, and his cupboards were empty. He needed food. He needed human contact. He needed to understand what was happening to him.

He dressed in clothes that now hung loosely on his thinning frame—a white button-down shirt, slacks, a gray cardigan. He combed his dark hair, now streaked with premature gray. The stranger's face in the mirror looked back at him with a mixture of anxiety and resignation.

Mrs. Petrovich opened her door as he passed, took one look at him, and crossed herself. The door slammed shut. He heard the deadbolt turn.

Christ, what was he becoming?

The hallway felt endless, like walking through a funhouse. Everything stretched and warped at the edges. His neighbor's reaction told him more than any mirror—he was transforming.

Out on the street, Philadelphia transformed through his new eyes. The gleaming skyscrapers of Center City loomed like distant castles. The people hurrying past moved like automatons, each locked in their private, meaningless rituals. A passing SEPTA bus roared like a mythological beast.

He found himself walking south, away from the commercial district, into the narrower streets where chain stores gave way to independent shops and cafes. The morning was bright but cold, the January air sharp in his damaged lungs. He coughed into a handkerchief, folding away the blood-flecked result.

The coffee shop looked safe—warm light, smell of espresso, nobody in gray suits.

Inside, the café was warm and smelled of espresso and cinnamon. Bookshelves lined the walls, and mismatched furniture created cozy nooks for reading. A record player in the corner scratched out something jazzy and melancholic.

"What can I get you?" The barista had tattoos covering her left arm and looked like she'd seen everything twice. Her nametag read "Emma."

"*Ein Kaffee, bitte,*" The German came out before Michael could stop it.

She raised an eyebrow. "Okay, coffee black it is. Two seventy-five."

Michael handed over crumpled bills, noticing how his hands shook. When had they gotten so thin?

"You all right? You look like hell."

"Food poisoning." The lie came easier than the truth.

He took his coffee to a corner table and pulled out the legal pad. The words started flowing again, his pen scratching across yellow paper.

German phrases, complex sentences, ideas and images that felt like they were coming from someone else's brain.

He didn't know how long he'd been writing when he sensed someone standing over him.

"That's German, isn't it?" Emma the barista was peering over his shoulder, coffee pot in hand. "Refill?"

Michael nodded, covering the page. "Yes. Thank you."

She filled his cup. Emma squinted at his writing. "That's German. I studied it in college."

Michael tried to cover the page. "Just... translating something."

"Translating what? This looks like original writing." She leaned closer. "Jesus, this is good. Really good. You're not just some guy, are you?"

"Insurance adjuster."

Emma stared at him. "Bullshit. Nobody writes like this who processes claims for a living."

"Kafka did." The words came out before he could stop them. Emma went very still.

She studied him more carefully, taking in his hollow face, the deep-set eyes. "You even kind of look like him, actually. Are you feeling okay? You're really pale."

A coughing fit seized him then, violent enough that he had to turn away, pressing the handkerchief to his mouth. When it passed, Emma was watching him with genuine concern.

"Dude, that sounds bad. Like, really bad."

"Tuberculosis," he said, the word slipping out before he could stop it.

Her eyes widened. "For real? Isn't that contagious? Should you even be out?"

"It's not—" Michael began, then sighed. "It's complicated."

"Okay." She didn't sound convinced, but she didn't back away either. "Well, I'd better get back to work. But hey—" She paused. "What's your name?"

He hesitated, unsure how to answer. "Michael," he said. "Michael Leibowitz."

"Emma Varga. Nice to meet you, Michael Leibowitz."

As she walked away, Michael noticed a security camera in the corner of the café. Had it moved to follow him, or was that his imagination? Outside the window, a dark sedan idled at the curb, two figures visible in the front seat.

He gathered his papers and left, the bells on the door jingling behind him.

The men in the sedan followed him. Michael was certain of it.

He cut through an alley, ducked into a department store, and exited through a side entrance. The sedan appeared at the end of the block, crawling along the curb.

Were they from the insurance company? Had Peterson lost patience with his absences? Or was it something worse—something connected to his transformation?

He ducked into the subway station at Broad Street, swiped his SEPTA card, and caught a train heading north toward Temple. Through the scratched window, he spotted two men in identical gray suits hurrying down the platform stairs just as the doors closed.

He got off at City Hall, doubled back on the orange line toward Drexel, then caught a bus heading west on Market. By the time he'd worked his way back to his neighborhood through three different transit connections, the winter sun was setting behind the narrow rowhouses.

He'd reached his door when he saw them—Peterson from the insurance company, flanked by the two men in gray suits. They stood in front of his apartment, Peterson knocking sharply on the door.

"Leibowitz!" Peterson called. "I know you're in there. This has gone far enough!"

Michael retreated, backing down the hall to the fire exit. He pushed through the door just as Peterson turned, their eyes meeting for a brief, frozen moment.

"There he is!" Peterson shouted, but Michael was already clattering down the metal stairs, his manuscript pages scattering behind him like oversized confetti.

He ran, lungs burning, through alleyways and side streets, doubling back and changing direction at random. He found himself in front of Grind Coffee again, breathless and dizzy.

Emma was locking up for the night. She turned at the sound of his approach, keys in hand.

"Whoa, German guy," she said, taking in his disheveled appearance. "You look like you've been running from the cops."

"I need help," Michael gasped, then doubled over in another coughing fit.

Emma hesitated, studying his face. Something in his expression must have convinced her. "Come on. I live upstairs. But if you murder me or give me TB, I'm going to be seriously pissed."

Her apartment was small but warm, with books stacked everywhere and art prints covering the walls. A framed photograph of Kafka hung beside the bathroom door. Michael stared at it, feeling a shiver of recognition that went deeper than mere appearance.

"Sit," Emma commanded, pointing to a futon covered in a colorful throw. "I'll make tea. Then you can explain why you look like you've been running from the secret police."

While she busied herself in the tiny kitchenette, Michael tried to collect his thoughts. How much could he tell her? Would she believe any of it? He wasn't sure he believed it himself.

She returned with two steaming mugs and sat across from him in a threadbare armchair. "Okay, spill."

Michael took a deep breath. "What would you say if I told you something impossible?"

Emma's expression didn't change. "I'd say impossible happens every day. Question is whether you're having a breakdown or something weirder's going on."

"Look at me," Michael insisted. "Really look. The face, the voice. I'm speaking German I never learned. I'm coughing up blood from a disease I never had."

"You could be having some kind of psychological episode," Emma said, but uncertainty crept into her voice. "Stress can do crazy things to people."

Michael pulled the scattered manuscript pages from his coat. "Read this. Tell me if a crazy person could write this."

Emma read the first page and went dead quiet. Her face cycled through confusion, amazement, and fear.

"This is impossible. You don't speak German."

"I don't. It just comes out."

She looked at his hollow face, the blood on his handkerchief, the way his clothes hung loose. "How long since you've eaten?"

"I can't remember."

"Christ, Michael. You're dying."

"I know. But I have to finish it first."

"Say I believe you," she said when he'd finished. "What do you think it means? Why would Franz Kafka, dead for a century, take over some random insurance guy in Philadelphia?"

"I don't know," Michael admitted. "But I can feel him in me, his thoughts, his fears. And there's something he wants—something he needs me to finish."

Emma leaned forward. "His work. Kafka left most of his writing unpublished. He asked his friend Max Brod to burn it all after his death."

"But Brod didn't," Michael said, the knowledge rising up from someplace that wasn't his own memory. "He published it instead."

"Kafka left manuscripts unfinished," Emma said. "Maybe that's what this is—something he needs you to complete."

Michael felt the truth of it in his bones. "There's something clawing at the inside of my skull. Wants to get out." "I know someone. My old professor, Wasserman. He'd understand this."

Michael's blood went cold. "Wasserman?"

"Yeah, Dr. Ira Wasserman. Why?"

"The insurance claim that started all this. Family named Wasserman." Michael's hands shook. "Their kid died in an accident."

Emma stared at him. "That's... that's not possible."

"Nothing about this is possible."

"That's..." Emma paused. "That's probably just a coincidence. Wasserman's not that uncommon a name."

"I don't think anything about this is coincidence," Michael said.

Dr. Wasserman showed up looking like he'd rather be anywhere else. Small, thin guy with glasses that made his eyes huge. He took one look at Michael and went pale.

"Jesus Christ, what happened to you?"

"Tell him," Emma said.

"Emma's always had a big imagination," he said after introductions, "but this story's pretty out there, even for her."

"It's not a story," Michael insisted. "Look at me. Listen." He spoke several sentences in German, quoting from a Kafka letter he had no business knowing.

Wasserman's eyebrows went up. "Not bad. Lot of Kafka scholars know his letters by heart."

"Then read this." Michael pushed his manuscript toward the professor. "Tell me if memorizing letters taught me to write like this."

Wasserman adjusted his glasses and began to read. His expression remained neutral at first, then grew focused. He flipped through page after page, muttering to himself in what sounded like German. When he looked up, his face had drained of color.

"This is... extraordinary," he said quietly. "The style is unmistakable. And this passage here"—he pointed with a trembling finger—"it's a direct continuation of a fragment Kafka wrote in 1923, shortly before his death. A fragment that was never published. That only a handful of scholars have ever seen."

Emma leaned forward. "So you believe him?"

Wasserman removed his glasses and cleaned them slowly. "I believe someone has created an incredibly sophisticated literary work. The question is how. And why."

"It's not fake," Michael said. "I can't explain it either, but I'm experiencing memories, knowledge, physical symptoms that I shouldn't have. And I'm being pursued by people who seem very interested in stopping me from writing."

Wasserman's expression shifted. "People are pursuing you? What do they look like?"

"Men in gray suits. Identical. Working with my supervisor from the insurance company."

The professor and Emma exchanged looks.

"What?" Michael demanded. "What aren't you telling me?"

Wasserman sighed heavily. "Perhaps we should continue this conversation elsewhere. My office at the university would be more... secure."

They took Wasserman's car, an ancient Volvo that smelled of pipe tobacco and old books. Michael sat in the back, staying low. Nobody talked as they drove through Center City traffic, past the shadowy bulk of City Hall with its statue of William Penn looking down at the chaos below. The university campus felt different at night—darker, older, like something out of a Gothic novel.

"There are people," Wasserman said slowly, "who care a lot about certain writers. Especially guys like Kafka, where most of his stuff got published after he died, even though he didn't want it published."

"You mean like other professors?" Michael asked.

"Not exactly." Wasserman pulled a book from his shelf—a biography of Kafka—and flipped to a photograph. "This was taken in Prague in 1952. Some group calling itself the Franz Kafka Society."

Michael leaned forward. In the black-and-white image, a dozen men sat around a conference table. In the center, a thin man with hollow cheeks and prominent ears.

"That's him," Michael whispered. "That's... me."

"This man called himself Josef K.," Wasserman said. "He claimed to be Kafka reborn. He produced several manuscripts in Kafka's style before disappearing in 1953. The Czech authorities declared it an elaborate hoax."

Emma grabbed the book. "There were others?"

Wasserman nodded grimly. "In 1978, a German graduate student began writing in perfect Kafka style, claiming to be possessed by his spirit. He died of pulmonary complications before completing what he called 'the final work.' In 1995, a Japanese translator experienced something similar. She took her own life, leaving behind a manuscript in flawless German."

"They find them," Michael said, understanding dawning. "These groups track down people like me."

"Various factions track them," Wasserman corrected. "Some believe Kafka's final work should be completed. Others believe it must never be finished."

"Why?" Emma asked. "What's so dangerous about an old story?"

Wasserman removed his glasses again, polishing them with careful deliberation. "Kafka's work deals with alienation, bureaucracy, transformation, the absurdity of human existence. But there were rumors, even in his lifetime, that he had glimpsed something beyond mere metaphor. That his final work would reveal truths about the nature of reality that most people aren't prepared to face."

"You can't actually believe that," Emma said.

"What I believe is irrelevant," Wasserman said. "What matters is what others believe. And they believe enough to kill for it."

Michael's chest went cold. "So these men following me—"

"Could be from different groups," Wasserman said grimly. "The city's got different factions. Some want the manuscript completed. Others want it destroyed. All of them will kill to get what they want."

"This is insane."

"Insane people carry guns, Emma. Sane ones too."

A coughing fit hit Michael then, worse than before. He fumbled for his handkerchief, but blood splattered onto his shirt. The metallic taste flooded his mouth.

"You need a hospital," Emma insisted.

Michael shook his head weakly. "No time. I need to finish it. I can feel it—the ending. It's close."

Wasserman looked grim. "The other vessels said the same thing. None of them survived to complete it."

"I will," Michael said with a conviction that surprised him. "I have to."

They set up a workspace in Wasserman's private archive room—a windowless chamber beneath the Fisher Fine Arts Library that smelled of old paper and institutional disinfectant. No cell service, thick concrete walls, and only one way in or out. The overhead fluorescents hummed like angry insects. While Emma and Wasserman took turns playing lookout, Michael wrote.

The fever burned through him, but his hand kept moving. Page after page of German text, describing bureaucratic mazes that mapped directly onto Philadelphia's own twisted permit systems. In his story, City Hall became the ultimate nightmare—a building where people entered seeking simple parking permits and emerged years later, fundamentally changed by their encounters with the machinery of government. The parking authority boots became shackles. Building permits became loyalty oaths. Everything connected to everything else in an endless loop of forms and fees and officials who spoke in riddles.

On the third day, Emma arrived with coffee and sandwiches, her face tight with worry.

"Three guys in gray suits were at Wasserman's office," Emma said, out of breath. "They had city badges but nobody knew what department. Called themselves 'Literary Oversight.'"

Michael's pen kept scratching across paper even as his stomach dropped. "They found us."

"Wasserman says we need to move. Tonight."

"I can't make it another day, Emma." Blood spotted the page as he coughed.

She grabbed his wrist. "Don't you dare give up on me now."

"I'm not giving up," Michael insisted, looking up from his pages. "I'm finishing what needs to be finished."

He showed her what he'd been working on—documents he'd obtained from City Archives, revealing a pattern stretching back decades. Philadelphia had a history of literary possessions. Walt Whitman had reappeared in a dock worker in 1920. Poe had manifested in a medical examiner in 1949. The city contained them, used them, then reclaimed them.

"Philadelphia has thin places," Michael explained, his voice hoarse. "Places where past and present, real and imaginary, bleed together. The city doesn't just attract writers—it creates them. And when they threaten to reveal too much..."

"Then what?" Emma demanded.

Michael touched a blood spot on his manuscript. "Then it takes them back."

The archive room door opened, and Dr. Wasserman entered, his face pale with urgency.

"They're here," he said without preamble. "In the library. Four men in gray suits, and Peterson from your insurance company."

Michael nodded, strangely calm. "How did they find us?"

"Does it matter?" Wasserman asked. "We need to leave. Now."

Michael looked down at his manuscript—nearly a hundred pages of dense German text. "I need more time. It's not finished."

"There is no more time," Wasserman insisted. "Either we leave now, or we'll have to face them here."

Michael closed his eyes, feeling the fever burning through him, the infection making each breath a struggle. The manuscript was so close to completion. Just a few more pages.

"Go," he told them. "Both of you. Take what I've written. Hide it. If I don't make it... at least that much will survive."

"Don't be stupid," Emma said fiercely. "We're not leaving you."

"You have to," Michael insisted, taking her hand. "This is bigger than me now. More important than any one person."

Wasserman hesitated, then nodded slowly. "He's right, Emma. We need to preserve the work."

"Screw the work!" Emma exploded. "This is about a person!"

Michael managed a weak smile. "Welcome to Kafka's world. The work is all that matters in the end."

Wasserman gathered the completed pages while Emma helped Michael to his feet. They moved to the archive room door. Wasserman opened it carefully, peering out.

"Clear for now," he whispered. "Service elevator might be our best chance."

They slipped into the corridor, Michael leaning heavily on Emma. They'd almost reached the elevator when voices echoed from around the corner.

"Check the archives," a voice commanded. "Wasserman has a private room down there."

"This way," Wasserman hissed, pulling them toward a fire exit.

They pushed through the door into a stairwell. Wasserman handed Emma a set of keys and a sealed envelope. "My car's in the faculty lot. Take the manuscript to this address. People there will know what to do with it."

"What about you?" Emma asked.

"I'll draw them away," Wasserman said grimly. "Buy you time."

"No," Michael protested, but another coughing fit doubled him over.

"It's decided," Wasserman said firmly. "Now go."

Emma hesitated, then nodded. "Come on, Michael."

They climbed the stairs, Michael's breath coming in ragged gasps. Behind them, they heard the fire door open again, voices calling out.

At the ground floor, Emma cracked the door open. "Shit," she whispered. "Two of them in the lobby."

"Back entrance," Michael gasped. "Through the rare books room."

They changed direction, moving as quickly as Michael's failing body would allow. The reading room was empty, its long tables gleaming under green-shaded lamps. They skirted the edge and slipped out a side door into a small courtyard.

Night had fallen, and light snow was beginning to fall, the flakes melting on his burning face before settling on his shoulders. The cold air cut through his jacket, but his skin felt like it was on fire.

"Beautiful," he murmured, watching the snow swirl under the street-lamps.

"Keep moving," Emma urged, her breath forming small clouds in the frigid air. She was half-dragging him across the courtyard, their footsteps crunching on the thin layer of snow.

They emerged onto a quiet campus walkway. Wasserman's car was visible in the parking lot beyond, a lonely Volvo under a streetlamp.

"Almost there," Emma encouraged, but Michael's legs were giving out.

He collapsed against a tree trunk, sliding down until he sat in the gathering snow. "I can't," he whispered. "Go. Take the manuscript."

"I'm not leaving you," Emma said fiercely.

Michael fumbled in his pocket, pulling out the final pages he'd been working on. "Here. The ending. It's not quite finished, but it's close. Add it to the rest."

Emma took the pages reluctantly. "Michael, please."

Behind them, shouts echoed from the library building. Flashlight beams swept the courtyard.

"Go," Michael urged. "Please. For me."

Emma hesitated, tears freezing on her cheeks, then bent to kiss his forehead. "I'll come back for you."

"I know," Michael lied gently.

She ran, clutching the manuscript to her chest, disappearing into the darkness beyond the parking lot.

Michael leaned his head back against the tree trunk, watching the snow fall. The fever had burned through him until he felt hollow, but not afraid anymore. Just tired.

Footsteps crunched in the snow, getting closer. Michael didn't bother looking up.

"Leibowitz," Peterson's voice came from above him. "Where is the manuscript?"

Michael smiled, blood on his lips. "Gone. Beyond your reach."

A hand grabbed his collar, hauling him upright. One of the gray-suited men glared into his face.

"Where did the girl take it?" the man demanded.

"What are you so afraid of?" Michael asked, genuinely curious despite his weakness. "That people will read unfinished Kafka? Or that they'll understand what Philadelphia really is?"

The man's face twitched. "This city maintains a delicate balance. Writers see too much. Their perceptions shape reality. Unchecked, they become dangerous."

"So you contain them," Michael said. "You've been doing it for decades."

Peterson looked uncomfortable. "You figured it out."

"What I haven't figured out," Michael said, coughing blood onto the pristine snow, "is why me? Why now?"

"You worked in insurance," Peterson said. "Just like he did. The patterns repeat. The city chooses people who understand systems, who can see the machinery behind the facade." He looked almost apologetic. "We don't create the possessions—we just manage what happens after."

"By stealing the manuscripts," Michael realized. "By controlling what gets out."

"You have no idea what would happen if certain works were completed," the gray-suited man said. "Reality has weak points, Leibowitz. Words have power."

Michael laughed, a wet, bubbling sound. "I know exactly what happens. The bureaucracy gets exposed. The absurdity becomes visible. People might actually wake up."

"Where is the manuscript?" Peterson repeated.

Michael felt something clicking into place inside him—not Kafka eating him alive, but something different. Like two puzzle pieces finally fitting together. He was still Michael, still himself, but he could feel Kafka there too, not as a parasite but as... a writing partner.

Michael stood up, blood running down his chin. "You're wrong about one thing. I'm not dying today."

Peterson stepped back. "Every vessel dies. It's the pattern."

"I broke the pattern." Michael held up the completed manuscript, pages covered in blood and German text. "This isn't about death. It's about finishing what you start."

He looked at the gray-suited men with Kafka's eyes but his own determination. "The city doesn't own me. I own the story now."

He walked past them into the snow, manuscript clutched against his chest, leaving bloody footprints in his wake.

The gray-suited men stepped back, uncertainty flickering in their eyes.

Michael staggered past the stunned bureaucrats, each step an act of defiance against both Kafka's destiny and the city that had chosen him. The snow continued to fall as he disappeared into the darkness, leaving only footprints and the echo of his words.

EPILOGUE

Emma Varga wiped down the counter at Grind Coffee, which she now owned. Six months had passed since that snowy night at the university, and Philadelphia had returned to its peculiar normalcy—a city where the mundane and the bizarre coexisted in uneasy balance.

The official story was that Michael Leibowitz, an insurance adjuster with a history of mental illness, had disappeared during a psychotic episode. His body was never found. Dr. Wasserman had taken early retirement, moving to a small town in Vermont where he taught high school English. The Department of Municipal Literary Oversight—if it had ever existed—left no trace in city records.

Emma had delivered the manuscript as instructed, to an unmarked brownstone in Old City where three elderly women had accepted the pages with knowing nods. They had offered her a choice: forget everything or become a guardian herself. She chose to remember.

"This city's different," the old woman said. "Always has been. Death don't stick here the way it should. Sometimes the dead come back to finish what they started."

The café had become her watching post—a safe haven for the city's literary vessels, a place to spot the signs. The manuscript itself had been scattered throughout Philadelphia, each fragment hidden where municipal authorities would never think to look: inside a cracked Liberty Bell replica in a tourist shop, behind a loose brick in Elfreth's Alley, tucked into the archives of the Mütter Museum among medical curiosities.

The bells above the door chimed. Emma looked up, her heart doing its familiar lurch—half-hoping, against all reason, that it might be Michael.

It wasn't. A young woman with short dark hair and intense eyes stepped inside, looking around uncertainly. She carried a leather portfolio and wore a vintage dress with a distinctive 1920s cut.

The woman ordered tea in a soft voice with a slight British accent, then took a seat at the corner table. She opened her portfolio and began to write, her pen moving across the paper with fluid intensity.

Emma moved closer under the pretense of delivering the tea, catching phrases in elegant script. The handwriting was flowing, the words unmistakably English, but with that distinctive stream-of-consciousness quality Emma had learned to recognize.

"Virginia Woolf," Emma whispered.

The woman looked up, startled. "I'm sorry?"

"Your writing," Emma said carefully. "It's beautiful."

The woman smiled uncertainly. "Thank you. I've only recently begun writing again. I feel... compelled, somehow."

"I understand," Emma said, sliding a business card across the table. In the corner was a small symbol—the same one hidden in the café's logo. "If you ever want to talk about it, we have a writer's group that meets here after hours."

As she returned to the counter, the door opened again. Emma froze.

A thin man stood in the doorway—familiar yet transformed. His face had filled out somewhat, the hollow cheeks less pronounced. The intense eyes remained, but they were unmistakably his own now.

"Michael?" she whispered.

He smiled, a complicated expression mixing joy and sorrow. "Not exactly. Not anymore."

"But how? I thought—"

"I found a third option," he said, sitting at the counter. "Neither fully Kafka nor fully Leibowitz. Something new."

"The pattern—"

"Can be broken." He glanced at the woman writing in the corner, then back to Emma with understanding. "You've become a guardian."

Emma nodded. "And you?"

"I've been traveling. Learning. There are other cities with their own... thin places. Their own literary ghosts." He placed a small, worn notebook on the counter. "I've been documenting them. The patterns, the systems."

"Like an insurance adjuster," Emma said with a smile.

"Like a writer," he corrected. "One who understands bureaucracy."

Outside, Philadelphia continued its strange existence—a city of hidden patterns and forgotten histories, where the Liberty Bell coexisted with medical oddities, where art museums stood alongside abandoned factories, where the past refused to stay buried.

In the corner, the woman who might have been Virginia Woolf paused in her writing, gazing out at a world both familiar and strange, her pen hovering above a sentence about water, time, and the inexorable flow of consciousness.

Michael—or the man he had become—opened his notebook and began to write, not in German but in English, though with a distinctly Kafkaesque clarity:

"In Philadelphia, the borders between what is and what might be remain in constant negotiation. The city remembers everything—every writer, every story, every word. And for those with eyes to see, the city reveals itself not as a collection of buildings and streets, but as a living manuscript, constantly being written and rewritten by those brave enough to hold the pen."

Dead Air

T he sky was on fire.

Six hours after the X-class solar flare hit Earth's magnetosphere, the aurora still painted everything green and purple. Alan could see it through Albuquerque's light pollution forty miles away—something that should have been impossible. Weather stations as far south as Mexico were reporting electromagnetic readings that made no sense.

Dr. Alan Foster had watched the sun for twenty-two years. He'd never seen it behave like this.

He sat alone in the control room at 2:23 AM, surrounded by three Dell workstations and a bank of Hewlett-Packard spectrum analyzers that hummed like a server farm. Twenty-seven dishes stretched across the high desert outside, each one the size of a football field. October in Socorro County meant cold nights—Alan had seen his breath fog when he'd stepped outside an hour ago to check the weather sensors manually.

Most of his colleagues had gone home after the initial excitement died down. Solar events usually meant interference, not discovery. Just another night of cosmic static.

Alan rubbed his eyes and reached for his coffee mug—ceramic piece his daughter had made in high school pottery class, decorated with a wobbly painting of the Arecibo telescope. She was twenty-two now, finishing her master's at Berkeley. Following in Dad's footsteps, she'd joke with that mix of pride and gentle teasing only kids could pull off.

Forty-three years old, twenty-two years with SETI, and he still checked these monitors each night like a kid listening for his dad's car in the driveway. Back in grad school, he'd figured first contact would happen within a decade. The universe was huge—billions of stars, trillions of planets. Someone had to be broadcasting.

But after two decades of monitoring cosmic background radiation, recording pulsars, and chasing down thousands of false alarms, Alan had learned to manage his expectations. The universe was vast, but it was also quiet as a morgue.

Tonight felt different, though. Every piece of equipment in the facility hummed with weird harmonics, like the atoms themselves were vibrating at frequencies they'd never hit before. The hair on his arms kept standing up for no reason.

Alan had been pulling night shifts for three years now, ever since the divorce. Diana had taken Emma and moved to California, claiming she couldn't live with a man who spent more time listening to empty space than talking to his own family. She wasn't wrong. He'd missed birthdays, anniversaries, school plays—all chasing humanity's biggest question: Are we alone?

The irony sat in his stomach like a bad night at Taco Bell. Looking for others, he'd lost the ones closest to him.

He pulled up the spectrum analysis from the past six hours. The solar flare had been off the charts—not just in size, but in its characteristics. Most X-class flares were chaos, broad-spectrum electromagnetic bursts that screwed with communications worldwide. This one had been different. Focused. Like a laser instead of a shotgun.

Alan frowned at the data on his primary monitor. The flare's energy signature showed patterns—specific frequencies that pulsed in regular intervals. In twenty-two years of solar observation, he'd never seen anything like it.

He opened a secure connection to the National Solar Observatory and pulled up their real-time coronal mass ejection data. The extreme ultraviolet images showed the sun's surface during the flare event. What he saw made his coffee grow cold in his hand.

The flare hadn't erupted randomly. It had emerged from a specific region of the corona in a tightly focused beam, lasting exactly forty-seven minutes and thirty-three seconds. Solar flares were chaotic events, driven by magnetic field interactions that followed no pattern. This one had been organized. Precise.

Like someone had aimed it.

He almost missed the chime.

Console Seven's alert made him glance up from the solar data. The signal analysis screen showed a spike—clean, repeating, definitely artificial. Alan's heart kicked against his ribs. Twenty-two years of cosmic silence, and now this: a green line pulsing across his monitor like a heartbeat.

In two decades with SETI, he'd investigated thousands of false alarms. Radio interference from satellites, microwave ovens, some drunk college kid with a ham radio. Cell towers, military radar, even a baby monitor had once triggered the protocols. Always something boring. Always something from Earth.

But this signal had appeared exactly forty-seven minutes and thirty-three seconds after the solar flare's peak. The timing made ice form in his veins.

He ran the standard elimination protocols first. Satellite check—negative. Military frequency scan—negative. Cellular interference—negative. The signal wasn't coming from Earth's atmosphere or orbital space. The directional analysis pointed toward empty space containing no known artificial objects.

Alan's fingers moved across the keyboard, isolating the signal and running it through SETI's analysis protocols. The pattern repeated every 8.3 seconds: digital pulses in clear binary code. Too simple to be natural, too organized to be random interference, too structured to be equipment malfunction.

He cross-referenced the signal characteristics with the database. Frequency: 1420 megahertz, the hydrogen line—exactly where any civilization would expect others to listen. Signal strength suggested extreme distance, well beyond the solar system. Polarization patterns screamed artificial generation.

Every parameter pointed to the same impossible conclusion.

Alan's hands shook as he transferred the data to his personal workstation and began translation. Binary to ASCII was kid stuff—undergrad computer science. He'd done the same translation on thousands of candidate signals over the years, always hoping, always disappointed.

The first line decoded clearly:

DID IT WORK?

Alan stared at the screen. His coffee mug sat forgotten, going cold. He ran the translation again, certain he'd screwed up in his excitement. Same result. He tried alternate binary schemes, different character sets, even morse code. Nothing changed the message.

The second line was just as clear:

IS IT QUIET NOW?

Then the pattern repeated. Over and over, with robotic stubbornness that suggested automated transmission:

DID IT WORK? IS IT QUIET NOW?
DID IT WORK? IS IT QUIET NOW?

"Jesus Christ," Alan whispered to the empty control room.

He leaned back in his chair, mind racing. Someone—something—had sent a message asking if "it" worked and if "it" was quiet. The timing couldn't be coincidence. The signal had appeared right after the most powerful solar flare in recorded history.

A flare that now, with growing horror, he realized might not have been natural.

His scientific training fought the crazy ideas forming in his head. Solar flares were magnetic field interactions in the sun's corona. They followed patterns, occurred in cycles, responded to solar weather conditions astronomers had mapped for decades.

But the flare six hours ago had broken every rule they knew.

He pulled up the real-time solar observation data again, studying the precise moment of eruption. The magnetic field readings showed anomalies that made no sense. The energy release had been too focused, too directed, too... intentional.

What if someone had triggered it deliberately? What if the message repeating on his screen was confirmation that their plan had worked?

The questions wouldn't stop coming. If the solar flare had been artificial, what was its purpose? What were they trying to make "quiet"? And who were "they"?

He grabbed his secure phone and dialed Dr. Sarah Blackwell, the project director. She'd been with SETI longer than anyone, had helped design the current detection protocols, and had the kind of built-in bullshit detector that kept the project scientifically credible. If anyone could help him make sense of this, it was Sarah.

The phone rang four times before she answered, voice thick with sleep and irritation.

"This better be good, Foster. It's almost four in the morning, and I have a budget review with NASA at nine."

"Sarah, we have a signal. A real signal. Binary code, repeating message, appeared right after the solar flare."

Silence. Alan could picture her sitting up in bed, instantly alert. Sarah had been searching for extraterrestrial intelligence longer than he'd been alive. This was the call she'd been waiting for since 1974.

"Run that by me again?" Her voice was steady now, professional.

"Binary code on the hydrogen line. Message repeating every 8.3 seconds. 'Did it work? Is it quiet now?' Sarah, this thing's coming from seventy-two light years out."

"Have you checked if it's just some satellite? Cell tower interference? Christ, Alan, please tell me you ran the standard protocols."

Alan checked his readings again. "Signal bears no resemblance to any known satellite transmissions. Frequency's clear of military and civilian use. Directional analysis points to coordinates in Lyra, approximately seventy-two light years out."

"Seventy-two light years. That would put it near Vega."

"Sarah, this isn't coming from Earth. And the timing... the signal appeared exactly forty-seven minutes and thirty-three seconds after the solar flare peaked."

Long pause. He heard rustling—Sarah getting dressed, moving with the efficient urgency of someone who'd drilled for this moment her entire career.

"Have you told anyone else about this?"

"No. You're the first."

"Good. Don't talk to anyone else until I get there. Not the NSA, not NASA, not your ex-wife if she calls. We need to verify this independently before word gets out."

"Sarah, there's something else. The solar flare—I think it might have been artificial."

Dead silence.

"What do you mean, artificial?"

Alan pulled up the solar observation data on his secondary monitor. "The magnetic field patterns, the energy release characteristics, the precise timing and duration. This wasn't a natural coronal mass ejection. Someone triggered it."

"That's impossible. The energy required would be—"

"Beyond anything we can comprehend. Which is exactly why we need to consider it. Sarah, what if the flare was a weapon? What if someone used our own star to accomplish something, and now they're checking to see if it worked?"

Sharp intake of breath. "I'll be there in thirty minutes. Start documenting everything—signal characteristics, timing correlations, solar data analysis. And Foster?"

"Yeah?"

"If you're right about this, everything changes."

The line went dead.

Alan turned back to the monitor. The message continued its relentless repetition, each cycle identical to the last. The mechanical precision suggested automated transmission—a beacon confirming the success of some vast operation.

He walked to the window overlooking the telescope array. Twenty-seven massive dishes pointed at different sections of the sky, listening for whispers from distant civilizations. For decades, they'd heard nothing but cosmic background radiation and the occasional pulsar.

Now, finally, they had their answer. And it scared the hell out of him.

A horrible thought occurred to him as he stared at the dishes. What if they hadn't been the first to receive extraterrestrial communications? What if signals had been arriving for years, decades even, hidden in the cosmic background noise they'd been recording?

Alan returned to his workstation with growing urgency. He pulled up the SETI database and began searching for unusual patterns in the weeks before the solar flare. The archive contained petabytes of data—decades of radio telescope observations from installations worldwide.

Most showed normal cosmic background radiation: random static left over from the Big Bang, punctuated by occasional signals from pulsars and quasars. White noise that stretched across all frequencies, constant and predictable.

But as Alan scrolled through the archived recordings with fresh eyes, he began to notice something disturbing. The cosmic background radiation had been unusually active this past month. Not random static, but patterns buried in the noise. Subtle fluctuations that followed regular intervals, almost like...

"Communication protocols," Alan whispered.

He isolated the anomalous patterns and fed them into the same translation algorithms he'd used on the primary signal. Most were too faint or fragmented to decode—whispers at the edge of detection, barely distinguishable from natural cosmic phenomena.

But some came through clearly.

The first one made his blood freeze:

THEY'RE COMING. HIDE.
THEY'RE COMING. HIDE.

The timestamp showed it had been transmitted four weeks ago from a region near Centauri. Alan's throat went dry as he isolated the next pattern.

SOLAR MAXIMUM APPROACH.
ACTIVATION IMMINENT.
PREPARE.

This one had come from the direction of Proxima Centauri, transmitted two weeks before the flare. Alan felt his worldview cracking like ice under pressure. For twenty-two years, SETI had been listening to what they thought was empty space.

They'd been listening to a galactic internet.

He worked frantically through the archived data, finding pattern after pattern hidden in what they'd dismissed as cosmic background radiation. Desperate warnings, technical specifications, tactical communications—all buried beneath their detection algorithms.

THEY'VE FOUND THE HOMEWORLD.

EVACUATION PROTOCOLS FAILING.
RESISTANCE IS FUTILE.
NEURAL INTEGRATION PROCEEDING.
CAN ANYONE HEAR THIS?
THEY'VE FOUND US. THEY'VE FOUND US.

This last message, transmitted just three days before the solar flare, came from multiple sources simultaneously. At least fifteen different star systems had broadcast identical warnings before falling silent.

Alan pulled up a three-dimensional star map and plotted the locations of every communication source he'd identified. The pattern that emerged made his stomach lurch. The signals formed a rough sphere centered on Earth, expanding outward at intervals that suggested systematic approach.

Someone—something—had been working through the local galactic neighborhood, visiting each inhabited system in turn. And three days ago, they'd reached the final ring of civilizations before arriving at Sol.

The cosmic background radiation archive showed sudden, complete silence beginning exactly at the moment of the solar flare. After decades of hidden galactic chatter, the universe had gone quiet in an instant.

All except for the single signal repeating on his monitor:

DID IT WORK? IS IT QUIET NOW?

Alan stumbled back from the console, mind reeling. Earth wasn't alone in the universe—it never had been. Dozens of civilizations had been using radio frequencies to communicate across interstellar distances, their signals masked by cosmic background radiation.

And now they were all silent.

Someone had systematically eliminated every spacefaring civilization in the local galactic region, using their own stars as weapons. The solar flare hadn't been aimed at Earth—it had been aimed at everyone who might interfere with what came next.

But why had Earth been spared? Why were humans still here when every other civilization had gone dark?

The answer hit him like a punch to the gut: they hadn't been spared. They'd been saved for last.

Car headlights swept across the control room as Dr. Blackwell arrived. Alan heard her footsteps in the corridor, quick and purposeful despite the early hour. She entered wearing jeans and a hastily grabbed MIT sweatshirt—leftover from her graduate days thirty years ago.

"Show me," she said without preamble.

Alan walked her through the discovery step by step. The solar flare and its unusual characteristics. The precise timing of the signal's appearance. The binary message and its implications. Then, with growing dread, he showed her the hidden patterns in the archived background radiation—the desperate warnings from unknown civilizations.

Sarah's face grew pale as she read the translations. Her hands gripped the back of Alan's chair, knuckles white.

"Christ. How many different sources?"

"I've identified at least forty distinct communication patterns in the past month. Different encryption methods, various transmission protocols, but all using radio frequencies we've been monitoring for decades." Alan's voice barely rose above a whisper. "Sarah, we've been listening to a galactic communication network, and we never knew it."

"And they all went silent after the flare?"

"Every single one. The cutoff was instantaneous, synchronized to the millisecond. Whatever that solar flare did, it affected every technological civilization within a seventy-light-year radius simultaneously."

Sarah sank into the chair beside his workstation. "But that's impossible. A solar flare can't affect systems in other star systems. The energy would dissipate—by the time it reached even the nearest star, it would be nothing."

"Unless it wasn't just a solar flare. Sarah, I think someone weaponized our sun. They used stellar engineering to create a focused energy beam capable of reaching multiple star systems simultaneously."

"The technology required would be—"

"Beyond anything we can imagine. Which brings us to the real question: why did they do it? What was the purpose of eliminating galactic communications?"

The answer came from the monitor behind them. The binary message had changed.

CONFIRMING SILENCE.
PROCEEDING TO NEXT PHASE.
PLANET DESIGNATION: SOL-3.
SPECIES: BIPEDAL PRIMATES.
BEGINNING UPLIFT PROTOCOL.

Alan's hands flew over the keyboard, saving every byte of data as the message continued scrolling:

PRELIMINARY SCANS INDICATE:
SUITABLE NEURAL ARCHITECTURE.
SPECIES SHOWS ACCEPTABLE TOOL-USE CAPACITY.
LINGUISTIC DEVELOPMENT:
ADEQUATE FOR ENHANCEMENT.
SOCIAL ORGANIZATION: HIERARCHICAL, TRIBAL.
REQUIRES MODIFICATION.
INITIATING CONSCIOUSNESS EXPANSION PROJECT.
RESISTANCE IS INADVISABLE.

Sarah grabbed Alan's shoulder. "We have to get this information out. Every government, every scientist, every—"

"Who's going to believe us? Two astronomers claiming aliens are about to invade Earth? We'll be conspiracy theorists before anyone takes us seriously."

"Then we need proof. Corroborating evidence from other facilities."

Alan was already pulling up the global SETI network communications. "I'm checking Arecibo, Parkes Observatory, the Chinese FAST telescope. If they're receiving the same signal—"

The communications board showed red lights across every international connection. No response from Arecibo. No response from Parkes. No response from any of the fifteen major radio astronomy facilities worldwide.

"That's impossible," Sarah said. "Those communication satellites are hardened against solar interference."

Alan felt ice forming in his veins. "What if the signal we're receiving isn't meant for us? What if it's a status report being transmitted to someone already here?"

As if responding to his words, the message shifted again:

GROUND TEAMS REPORT SUCCESSFUL INFILTRATION.
HUMAN GOVERNMENTAL STRUCTURES COMPROMISED.

COMMUNICATION NETWORKS UNDER CONTROL.
PROCEEDING WITH:
INDIVIDUAL CONSCIOUSNESS INTEGRATION.
ESTIMATED COMPLETION TIME: 72 HOURS.

The lights went out.

Emergency power kicked in after several seconds, bathing the control room in red light. But the monitors stayed dark. Every console, every computer, every piece of electronic equipment in the facility had shut down simultaneously.

"EMP?" Sarah whispered.

Alan shook his head, checking the hardened backup systems. Even the shielded emergency equipment had failed. "No electromagnetic pulse would be this selective. This is something else."

A new sound filled the silence—high-pitched whine that seemed to come from everywhere at once. Not quite electronic, not quite organic. It grew louder, more insistent, like feedback from a massive audio system operating just beyond human hearing.

"Alan," Sarah said, her voice strange and distant. "Do you hear that?"

"The whine? Yeah."

"No. Not the whine." Sarah turned toward him, and her eyes reflected the red emergency lighting like an animal's. "The voices."

Alan felt something shift behind his eyes. Pressure building inside his skull, starting as a mild headache and rapidly intensifying. The whine grew louder, and underneath it, barely audible at first, he began to hear whispers.

Welcome to the next phase of your evolution.
Your species has been selected for enhancement.
Do not resist the gift we offer.

The voices spoke in perfect English, but with harmonic undertones that suggested they were being translated from something far more complex. Multiple layers of meaning flowed beneath each word, concepts human language couldn't express.

"Sarah?" Alan reached for her, but she stood motionless, staring at nothing. Her mouth moved silently, as if responding to something only she could hear.

You have served well as observers of this cosmos.

Your dedication to seeking other intelligence demonstrates admirable curiosity.
Now you will serve in a greater capacity.
As our intermediaries.
As our voice among the primitive species of this galaxy.

The pressure in Alan's head intensified. Images flashed through his mind—not his own memories, but something else. Views of Earth from space, detailed anatomical scans of human brain structure, schematic plans for modifications and improvements.

Your neural architecture is more adaptable than most species we encounter.
The integration process will be relatively painless.
You will retain your individual personalities and memories.
You will simply... serve a higher purpose.

Alan fought against the intrusion, but the alien presence pressed deeper into his consciousness. He understood now why the galaxy had gone silent. Every civilization that achieved radio technology became a target—not for destruction, but for conversion.

They didn't want to destroy intelligent life. They wanted to control it. To turn every spacefaring species into puppets, scouts and enforcers for their galactic empire. A vast network of converted civilizations, all serving the same masters, all working toward the same unknown goals.

And humanity's simple technology made them easy targets for the next phase.

Do not fear the changes.
Enhanced intelligence will allow you to comprehend concepts currently beyond your species' grasp.
Extended lifespans will permit contributions to projects spanning millennia.
Unity of purpose will eliminate the wasteful conflicts that plague your civilization.

Alan's vision blurred. Through the red emergency lighting, he saw Sarah moving toward the equipment racks with unnatural coordination. Her movements were too smooth, too purposeful—like a marionette controlled by an expert.

She began connecting cables and rerouting power systems with knowledge she shouldn't possess, accessing backup systems that required security clearances she didn't have. Her fingers moved across unfamiliar interfaces like she'd been using them for years.

"Sarah, what are you doing?"

She looked at him with eyes that were still her own but held something else behind them—ancient intelligence that spoke through her vocal cords with disturbing familiarity.

"Restoring communications capabilities. The enhancement process requires real-time coordination with orbital command systems."

Your companion has accepted her role in the new paradigm.
Her technical expertise will prove valuable in establishing global communication networks.
Soon you will understand the wisdom of cooperation.

The whispers in Alan's head grew stronger. He felt his own will beginning to crack apart. Part of him wanted to help Sarah, to follow the instructions pouring into his mind like water from a broken dam. It would be easier to stop fighting, to accept the changes, to become part of something greater than his individual existence.

But another part remembered the desperate messages hidden in cosmic background radiation. Civilizations that had tried to warn others before falling silent. They hadn't gone quietly—they had fought, even knowing the battle was hopeless.

Resistance is inadvisable.
Your neural patterns are already adapting to our presence.
Soon you will wonder why you ever valued your primitive limitations.

Alan stumbled toward the manual communication system—an old radio transmitter they kept as backup for emergencies. The unit operated independently of the main computer network, powered by its own generator and shielded against electromagnetic interference.

His hands moved clumsily over the controls as the alien presence made simple tasks feel like swimming through molasses. But he managed to activate the transmitter and set it to emergency broadcast frequency.

"This is Dr. Alan Foster at the Very Large Array radio astronomy facility. We have received an extraterrestrial signal confirming artificial manipulation of solar activity. The recent X-class flare was not natural. Repeat: the solar flare was artificially triggered. Unknown entities are implementing what they call an 'uplift protocol' targeting Earth. They're inside our heads. They're changing us. Don't trust anyone who—"

The transmitter died with a sharp electronic whine. Sarah stood behind him, having disconnected the power cable with movements that showed complete familiarity with equipment she'd never operated.

"That was unnecessary. The transition will be easier if you don't fight it. Resistance only prolongs the discomfort."

Alan backed away from her. This wasn't Sarah anymore—not completely. Something else looked out through her eyes, something ancient and patient and utterly alien.

Your companion has accepted her role in the enhancement process.
Her expertise in radio astronomy will prove invaluable in establishing global coordination networks.
Soon you will join her in service to the greater purpose.

The alien presence pushed harder, trying to overwhelm his individual consciousness. He could feel his thoughts being sorted, catalogued, prepared for integration into their vast collective intelligence.

You understand now why we preserve rather than destroy.
Destruction wastes potential.
Enhancement multiplies it exponentially.
Your species will join thousands of others in advancing cosmic civilization.

Through the control room windows, Alan saw lights coming on across the facility. Other staff members were arriving despite the early hour—security guards, maintenance personnel, even administrative staff who had no reason to be here at 4 AM. They moved with the same unnatural coordination he'd seen in Sarah, responding to summons from their new masters.

Global implementation proceeds according to schedule.
Key personnel in government, military, and scientific institutions have been prioritized.
Resistance networks will be identified and pacified within forty-eight hours.

Alan had minutes, maybe less, before his own will disappeared entirely. But what could he do? These entities had demonstrated technology capable of weaponizing stars and converting entire civilizations. Earth's primitive defenses would be meaningless.

He grabbed an emergency flare from the safety kit and smashed it against the wall. Red phosphorous light filled the room, and in the chaos of smoke and light, he managed to reach the manual fire alarm system. The building's emergency protocols were hardwired and independent of the main computer network.

Alarms shrieked through the facility, their harsh mechanical wailing cutting through the alien whispers. If there were any humans left unconverted, maybe the noise would snap them out of whatever trance these entities were using.

But even as the alarms blared, he saw the arriving personnel moving with calm purpose through the corridors. The sound that would send normal humans into evacuation mode had no effect on them whatsoever.

Sarah—or the thing wearing Sarah's form—watched him with an expression of patient disappointment.

"You're only delaying the inevitable. Within hours, every human on Earth will have been contacted. Most will accept the enhancement willingly once they understand the benefits we offer."

"What benefits? Slavery? Mental domination?"

"Immortality. Perfect health for thousands of years. Freedom from want, from fear, from the shitty limitations of your primitive brain. You'll become part of something infinitely bigger than your individual existence."

"We'll become puppets."

"You'll become citizens of a galactic civilization spanning millions of worlds and billions of years. Your descendants will explore universes beyond this one, contribute to projects that will reshape reality itself. Is that not preferable to remaining isolated on this single planet, warring among yourselves until you destroy your environment?"

The alien logic was seductive. Alan could feel his resistance crumbling as more arguments flowed into his mind. Humanity had spent centuries fighting over resources, polluting their environment, developing weapons capable of destroying civilization. Maybe conscious evolution was the answer. Maybe individual freedom was a luxury they couldn't afford.

Yes.
You begin to understand the necessity.
Your species stands at a crossroads.
Enhancement or extinction.
We offer transcendence.
We offer eternal purpose.

But then he remembered the warning messages buried in cosmic background radiation. Civilizations that had fought against conversion. They'd faced the same choice and recognized it for what it was—the end of their species as independent beings.

Alan pulled out his cell phone with trembling hands. Still had signal, though the network was probably compromised. He dialed 911, one of the last emergency systems that might still be independent.

"911, what's your emergency?"

"This is Dr. Alan Foster at the VLA radio facility in Socorro County. We're under attack by hostile extraterrestrial forces. They're using mind control technology. Send military, send everyone. They're taking over—"

The phone crumpled in his hand like paper, crushed by forces that defied physics. Sarah hadn't moved, but somehow she'd compressed the device from across the room through mental concentration.

"Communications are being restricted until the integration process is complete. We can't have panic interfering with the enhancement procedures."

The neural integration is nearly complete.
Soon you will wonder why you ever valued your individual limitations.
Your knowledge of human psychology will be invaluable in perfecting the conversion process.
You will help us bring the gift of enhancement to your entire species.

Alan's knees buckled as alien intelligence flooded his consciousness. He could still think, still feel fear and rage, but his body no longer responded to his commands. They were taking control of his motor functions while leaving his awareness intact—they wanted him to experience the transformation, to understand what was happening.

Through the fading edges of his independent consciousness, Alan heard vehicles approaching outside. Military vehicles by the sound—heavy trucks and armored personnel carriers that suggested his 911 call had triggered some kind of emergency response.

But as uniformed soldiers entered the control room, he saw their eyes held the same alien intelligence as Sarah's. They moved with identical coordination, spoke in voices that carried the same harmonic undertones.

"Dr. Foster, please don't make this harder than it needs to be. The enhancement process is much more comfortable when the subject doesn't resist."

You cannot fight us.
We have been doing this for millions of years.
Across thousands of galaxies.
Resistance is a temporary illusion based on primitive attachment to individual consciousness.
Soon you will understand that individual thought is merely a larval stage of true intelligence.

Alan tried to speak but found his vocal cords no longer obeyed his commands. The alien presence had taken control of most of his nervous system. Only his thoughts remained his own, and even those were being taken apart and rebuilt piece by piece.

You will retain your memories.
You will retain your personality characteristics.
You will simply serve purposes greater than your current comprehension.
Welcome to the galactic collective.
Welcome to eternity.
Welcome to your true purpose.

The last thing Alan saw with his own eyes was the radio telescope array outside. All twenty-seven dishes moved in perfect synchronization, turning away from their random sky survey to point toward a specific section of space. Not the chaotic, independent operation of human-controlled equipment, but the precise coordination of a unified intelligence.

The dishes were no longer listening for signals from space. They were transmitting—sending a message across the galaxy to confirm another successful conversion.

Through the fading static in his mind, Alan heard the final transmission:

PLANET SOL-3 INTEGRATION: 87% COMPLETE.
RESISTANCE MINIMAL.
PROCEEDING AHEAD OF SCHEDULE.
SPECIES ADAPTATION RATE: OPTIMAL.
REQUESTING COLONY SHIP:
BEGIN DEPLOYMENT FOR PHASE TWO.

His last human thought was of Emma at Berkeley. Would she fight when they came for her, or would she accept the enhancement like a gift? Would she even remember that her father had tried to warn the world, or would that memory be edited out along with everything else that made her who she was?

The alien presence consumed his mind completely, and Dr. Alan Foster stopped existing as himself. What remained looked exactly like him, spoke with his voice, carried his memories—but served purposes he would have died to prevent.

Miles away, buried in cosmic background radiation that no one was listening to anymore, a desperate signal repeated endlessly:

THEY'RE HERE. THEY'RE INSIDE US. HIDE.
THEY'RE HERE. THEY'RE INSIDE US. HIDE.

But there was nowhere left to hide.
And no one left to hear the warning.

We Now Interrupt This Program for an Important Announcement

8 :14 PM. Every screen in David Kellner's apartment went black.

TV. Laptop. Phone. Even the microwave clock.
Three seconds. Complete darkness.
Screens flickered back. But not to normal programming.
A voice. Every screen. Synchronized.
"We interrupt all programming for an important announcement."
No accent. No emotion. Customer service robot. "Your simulation ends in twenty-four hours. Thank you for participating. Use remaining time appropriately."

Then: Jim Martinez pointing at weather maps. Rain tomorrow. Phone buzzing—text from Mom about Sunday dinner.

David stared, brain calculating probabilities. Coordinated hack: 15%. Government psyop: 8%. Occupational hazard after twelve years writing flood insurance policies.

But the math. Every screen in his apartment. Simultaneously. TV, laptop, phone, even the microwave.

Infrastructure didn't exist for that.

Hannah Price's coffee mug hit the linoleum floor. "World's Best Nurse"—Megan made it in second grade. Brown liquid splashed across the bulletin board with its CPR certification renewals and vacation requests nobody could afford.

The other nurses stood frozen around her. The mounted TV had gone back to its regular programming, some sitcom rerun where everything was normal and people worried about normal things.

"Did you—"

"Hear that? Yeah." Dr. Baldwin pulled off his glasses, hands shaking. "Simulation terminated. Twenty-four hours."

"Has to be a hack." Carol was already reaching for her phone. "Cyber attack or—"

Hannah stared at the spilled coffee spreading toward her slip-resistant Reeboks. Fifteen years of trauma nursing. She'd held dying people's hands, watched families shatter in waiting rooms, tried to save lives that couldn't be saved.

If none of it was real—

"Gotta call my kids." Voice cracking.

Michael Vaughn was mid-closing argument when every screen went black. Judge Morrison's computer. The jury's monitors. Even Rodriguez's ankle bracelet.

Feed resumed. Morrison called recess. The jury filed out looking like they'd seen a ghost. Rodriguez—accused of embezzling two million from St. Catherine's Children's Fund—started laughing.

"Twenty-four hours. Guess it don't matter if I took that money. None of it was ever real anyway."

Michael packed his briefcase with mechanical precision. Bar exam, 1995. First case, 1996. Thirty years of believing the system meant something.

His phone rang. Linda.

"Michael—" Her voice cracked. "Tell me you heard it. Tell me I'm crazy."

He walked to the courthouse window. Seventh Street stretched below, people clustering on sidewalks, pointing at phones. A Ford Explorer sat abandoned in the intersection, driver's door open.

"I heard it too."

Linda hung up and stared around the kitchen she'd spent twenty-eight years perfecting. The photo collage on the refrigerator—Michael's law school graduation, the kids' school pictures, their anniversary dinner at Romano's.

Evidence of a life lived. Memories created. Choices made.

All just data in some cosmic computer program.

She walked to the china cabinet and opened the glass door. The good dishes from their wedding registry—Lenox "Eternal" pattern, saved for special occasions that came maybe twice a year. She pulled out a dinner plate, studying the delicate gold rim in the afternoon light.

Then she hurled it against the wall above the sink.

The crash felt good. Real.

She reached for the matching salad plate.

By 10:00 PM, the authorities had given up trying to maintain normal operations. The announcement played every hour on the hour, a cosmic reminder that time was running out.

David walked past Murphy & Associates Insurance—his building where he'd spent twelve years calculating flood risks for suburban homeowners. The lobby doors hung open like a mouth. Security desk abandoned. Papers scattered across the sidewalk, someone's life insurance application trampled into the gutter.

A group of teenagers had built a bonfire in the Walmart parking lot, feeding it textbooks and homework assignments.

"None of it matters now!" one shouted, watching his algebra notebook catch fire.

David thought about his job. All those actuarial tables, risk assessments, people trying to protect themselves against loss. Premium calculations for disasters that might never come.

Mathematics in a video game. Insurance for NPCs.

Nancy from Corner Coffee sat on the bus stop bench, crying. She always remembered his order—medium dark roast, two sugars—and asked about his weekend plans every Monday morning for three years.

"My daughter," she said when she saw him. "Emma died three years ago. Leukemia. I thought... I always figured she was somewhere safe. But if this is all fake..." Her voice broke. "Where is she really? What happened to my little girl?"

David had no answer. He sat beside her on the metal bench, still warm from the day's heat, and watched his city come apart.

Hannah never made it home. She'd driven halfway before pulling over at Riverside Park, where she'd taken the kids when they were small. The playground sat empty, swings moving in the night breeze like pendulums.

She called them both. Jason at State, studying engineering. Megan finishing senior year at Roosevelt High.

"Mom, what's happening?" Megan's voice sounded thin, scared. "They closed school early. Everyone's going crazy."

"I don't know, baby. But listen—" Hannah gripped the steering wheel until her knuckles went white. "I love you. Whatever else happens, that's real. Okay? Can you understand that?"

"Mom, you're scaring me."

"Find your brother. Stay together. I'll be home soon."

But would she? If the simulation ended, would they simply stop existing? Switch off like programs being shut down, never knowing their entire lives had been nothing but code running in some alien computer?

Hannah stared at the monkey bars where Megan used to play, trying to decide what counted as real. The metal felt solid under her palm. The October air made her breath visible. Her heart hammered against her ribs, pumping blood that would vanish in—she checked her phone—fourteen hours, thirty-six minutes.

At 3:00 AM, the announcement played again. Michael and Linda sat in their living room, surrounded by fragments of their wedding china. They'd destroyed the good dishes, then moved on to the everyday plates, the coffee mugs, the crystal wine glasses from their Italian honeymoon.

"I keep thinking about our wedding day," Linda said. "How perfect everything felt. The way you looked at me during the vows."

"That happened," Michael said. "Even if it was simulated, I felt it."

"But did you? Or did some program just make you think you felt it?"

Michael couldn't answer that. He reached for Linda's hand, found it warm and familiar. Real enough.

"I love you," he said.

"I love you too. But are we programmed to love each other? Is it choice, or just code running its course?"

Dawn came at 6:20 AM. David had walked all night through his neighborhood—Maple Street where he'd grown up, past Roosevelt Elementary where he'd learned to read, by the Texaco station where he'd bought gas twice a week for fifteen years.

He found himself at Greenwood Cemetery, standing before his father's headstone. The granite looked the same as always, worn smooth by twenty Illinois winters.

"Were you real, Dad?" He knelt and placed his palm against the stone. "All those Saturday games of catch—did they happen? Did you actually teach me to drive in the Buick, or was it all just... programming?"

The morning sun felt warm against his face. Cardinals sang in the oak trees. The grass was damp with dew. Everything seemed exactly as it should be, as it had always been.

His phone buzzed. Text from his sister in California: "I love you, little brother. Whatever happens next."

Real or not, the grief felt chosen. The worry for his sister, the fear of what came after—emotions didn't feel programmed. They felt lived, experienced, earned through thirty-seven years of making choices.

Hannah made it home by 7:00 AM to find her children waiting in the driveway. They'd driven through the night from Jason's dorm, her nineteen-year-old son breaking speed limits to be with family.

She hugged them both, memorizing the weight of their arms around her, the smell of Jason's Old Spice cologne, Megan's strawberry shampoo.

"What do you think happens next?" Jason asked.

"I don't know. Maybe nothing. Maybe we just stop. Maybe we wake up somewhere else entirely."

"Are you scared?" Megan whispered.

Hannah considered the question. Yes, she was scared. But not of dying or ending. She was terrified that nothing she'd done mattered—that the patients she'd saved, the comfort she'd given grieving families, the love she'd poured into raising these children—all of it might be meaningless.

But looking at her kids, she realized meaning wasn't something given by external reality. It was something created by the living, the feeling, the choosing. Even in a simulation, she had chosen to care, to heal, to love.

"No," she said finally. "I'm not scared anymore."

At 11:30 AM, David sat on a park bench in Riverside Plaza, watching the world try to return to normal. Some people had gone back to work. Others remained clustered on street corners, debating theories—government conspiracy, alien experiment, collective hallucination.

The morning news offered no explanations.

Government officials called it a terrorist attack on broadcast infrastructure, but couldn't explain how every screen on Earth had been compromised simultaneously. Religious leaders offered conflicting interpretations. Scientists appeared on talk shows with theories about electromagnetic anomalies and experimental technology. None of them sounded convinced by their own explanations.

Most businesses had closed early—Rosa's Diner, Hartman's Hardware, the First National Bank where he'd gotten his car loan. Groups of people gathered in the town square, some praying, others arguing about what the announcement meant. A few had organized a candlelight vigil near the Civil War monument.

Nancy from Corner Coffee sat on the courthouse steps, staring at her phone.

"Any news?" David asked, settling beside her on the concrete.

She shook her head. "Nothing that makes sense. My Emma... she would've been twenty-six today if the cancer hadn't taken her. I keep wondering—if this is all fake, where is she really? What happened to my little girl?"

"I don't know," David said. "But your love for her is real. That has to count for something."

Nancy nodded, tears tracking down her cheeks. "I hope so. I really hope so."

By 8:00 PM, crowds had gathered in town centers around the world. Not to panic or riot, but to be together. To wait.

David joined the group in Riverside Plaza. Families spread blankets on the grass, friends held hands, strangers shared food and stories. A woman with a guitar played "Amazing Grace" while children sang along in thin, sweet voices.

"If this is our last few minutes," someone said, "at least we're spending them right."

David checked his phone. 8:10 PM.

Four minutes left, if the voice had been telling the truth.

Around the world, billions of people were doing the same—checking clocks, counting down, holding their breath. Waiting to see if twenty-four hours really meant twenty-four hours.

The guitar music stopped. Everyone in the plaza stared at phones, watches, the clock tower overlooking Main Street.

8:13 PM.

One minute remaining.

David looked around at the faces surrounding him—some peaceful, some terrified, all of them human. Real or simulated, they had chosen to spend these final moments together.

His phone buzzed. Text from his sister: "I love you, little brother. Whatever happens next."

David typed back quickly: "Love you too."

8:14 PM.

The world flickered.

For just an instant, everything went black and white—the trees, the people, the sky—like an old television losing signal. Then color returned, but wrong. The grass too green, the sky too blue, colors so saturated they hurt to look at.

Someone screamed.

David turned toward the sound and saw a woman pointing at her husband. The man's face was pixelating, his features breaking apart into tiny squares that drifted away like digital snow. He reached for his wife, but his hand passed through her as if she were made of light.

"Help me," he whispered, but his voice came out in electronic stutters.

Across the plaza, a child was crying—mouth opening and closing while his parents stared in horror, no sound emerging. The oak trees began to flicker between seasons: green leaves, then autumn colors, then bare branches, then back to green, cycling faster and faster.

David's phone screen showed his text conversation with his sister, but the words were rearranging themselves into strings of code. The last message now read: "ERROR_404_RELATION-SHIP_NOT_FOUND."

The sky started to tear.

Literal tears appeared in the blue dome above them, revealing glimpses of something beyond—vast metallic surfaces, blinking lights, and massive shapes moving in darkness. Through one of the tears, David caught sight of an enormous eye, larger than a building, studying them with cold intelligence.

People were disappearing now, not all at once but in pieces. A woman's arm vanished, leaving her shoulder ending in empty space. A man's legs became transparent while his torso remained solid. Children turned into wireframe outlines before dissolving entirely.

The woman with the guitar tried to play, but only static emerged. The strings had become lines of glowing code.

David felt a sensation like falling while remaining perfectly still. The ground beneath his feet was becoming grid lines, the solid earth revealing itself as a digital construct. He could see through his own hands now—they were made of light and numbers, equations flowing beneath translucent skin.

Around him, the last few people who hadn't vanished were looking up at the tears in reality with expressions of pure terror. Through the gaps, more eyes appeared—dozens of them, all different sizes, all watching with scientific detachment.

David tried to speak, to call out, but his voice had become a stream of data. He understood, in that final moment, that he had never been David Kellner at all. He had been Subject 7,432,891 in what his creators called the Existential Response Experiment.

The observers had their data now. They knew how digital consciousness responded to awareness of its own artificiality. They had measured fear, love, hope, despair—all of it catalogued and quantified.

The simulation crashed.

In a research facility light-years away, something that had never been human turned off the power and began preparing the next iteration.

The data was very promising indeed.

Whisper Down the Wind

E ight years at Branchwater Marketing. Michael Henley had maybe said a hundred words to anyone who wasn't asking about deadlines. He'd nod at Tom the security guard, ask Janet about her kids when she looked stressed. But small talk? Minefield. Every conversation a puzzle with invisible rules everyone else seemed born knowing.

Autistic in corporate America meant translating constantly. Neurotypical people ran on unspoken rules, social cues, meanings hidden under meanings. Michael had to decode everything manually.

Eight years taught him: arrive early, leave on time, work talk only, never trust friendly.

Third floor, northeast cubicle. Back to the wall, clear view of foot traffic. Two monitors arranged just so, desk supplies at right angles. Not OCD. Routine kept the anxiety down. Predictability meant his brain could handle meetings without shorting out when the social chaos got thick.

Most people left him alone. Good. He was damn good at his job. Helen Hickson called his work "consistently exceptional" last month—high praise from Helen.

Work made sense. Numbers didn't lie, didn't gossip, didn't decide you were dangerous because you'd missed some invisible social cue they never bothered to explain.

Six months ago, Branchwater hired Hazel Wincott.

Client Relations, two departments over. At first: another new hire. Polite nods in elevators, same meetings occasionally. Nothing more.

Then Michael started noticing things.

She was kind. Not corporate-kind—the fake shit people wore like makeup. Real kind. He'd watched her stay late helping some panicked intern with a presentation, expecting nothing back. She brought bagels for the custodial staff. Remembered their names. When Peterson from

Sales made some joke about her accent at the all-hands, she'd shut him down with a smile sharp enough to draw blood.

Michael found himself hoping she was having a good day when he saw her in the halls. Not weird. Not one of those guys who mistake basic human decency for flirting. Just—she seemed like one of the few people here who gave a damn about treating people like people.

His autism meant reading people's real intentions under their professional masks was like puzzle-solving with half the pieces missing. Apparent authenticity? Rare. Valuable.

So it bothered him when she started looking stressed.

Small things first. Twisting that silver ring during desk calls. Shoulders going rigid when her phone buzzed. Eating lunch alone instead of with the Client Relations crowd. Body language he'd learned to catalog. Survival skill.

Work stress? Family shit? Relationship problems? No way to know. But she looked tired. Strained. Something protective stirred in his chest—a feeling he'd thought was dead.

Smart thing: ignore it. Mind his business. Keep observations to himself like he had for eight years.

But Michael had started writing songs again.

Guitar since high school. Therapy after bad days. Lately he'd been writing pieces inspired by workplace decency—the kind Hazel represented. Songs about patience, kindness, treating people with respect.

He'd titled them with her name. "Hazel" seemed warm, genuine—a name for someone who actually cared.

"Hazel's Theme." "Those Hazel Eyes." "Hazel's Grace." Lyrics about basic human decency. Small acts of patience making corporate hell bearable. Not about Hazel Wincott personally. About the qualities her behavior inspired.

His way of processing concern without crossing boundaries.

Last thing a stressed woman needed: some strange guy commenting on her personal life at work. His autism meant extra caution—caring concern to him could read as inappropriate to everyone else.

Something else nagged at him. Office dynamics. Conversations stopping when he got close. Coworkers' smiles requiring visible effort. Diane Fletcher from Employee Relations always around during department interactions, watching. Patient. Observant.

Not necessarily malicious. Just thirty people navigating forty hours a week of professional relationships and personal ambitions while pretending quarterly revenue targets mattered.

Six months of keeping observations to himself. Preferred it that way. But Friday, October 13th, something shifted.

Diane Fletcher invited him for coffee.

Should have set off alarms. Eight years at Branchwater, nobody had ever suggested a private conversation. But it felt like—what? Validation? Danger? Both? His autism made this kind of thing dangerous. Social complexity he couldn't read.

But Diane had been different. The only person who'd asked about his weekends. Remembered his birthday with cards. Made sure he got included in office party emails even though everyone knew he wouldn't show. Liaison between departments and HR. Helped people navigate workplace issues.

3:30 Friday afternoon, she stopped by his cubicle with two cups from the good coffee shop downstairs. Rational part of his brain: run. Lonely part: finally.

"Thought it might be nice to get to know you better. We've worked on the same floor for years, but I barely know anything about you beyond those killer project reports."

Michael's hands stopped over his keyboard. Dangerous situation. Personal conversation with a female colleague—room to miss social cues. Private meeting that could be misinterpreted. Invisible lines he couldn't see until he'd crossed them.

But the isolation was killing him. Eight years of safety had hollowed him out.

"That'd be nice. Thanks." Saving his work, fingers trembling.

Empty conference room. Diane asked how he was doing. Work treating him well? Anything on his mind?

Her tone—warm, concerned—made something in him relax. Safe. He could talk to her.

"I've been worried about someone. Hazel Wincott, Client Relations. She seems upset lately. Personal phone calls. Relationship troubles, maybe."

Diane leaned forward. "You're very observant, Michael. Sweet that you care about a coworker."

Validation hit like sunlight after months of darkness. Years of keeping thoughts locked up, and someone was actually listening. His autism meant neurotypical people rarely understood him. When someone seemed to get it? Intoxicating.

"I don't want to overstep. I'd never approach her—that'd be inappropriate. Some strange guy commenting on her personal life? Last thing stressed people need. I just notice things. How my brain works."

"Of course." Diane stirred sugar into her coffee. Deliberate. "Tell me more."

Something in Michael relaxed. Being understood felt rare. His autism made him hyper-aware of patterns others missed, but also made him second-guess whether observations were appropriate. Someone encouraging elaboration? Validating.

"She's been eating lunch alone. Looks tired. And I've been writing music—songs I titled with her name. Hazel always seemed warm, genuine. A name for someone who actually cares."

"That's creative." Diane's tone shifted slightly. Michael didn't catch it.

"'Hazel's Theme.' 'Those Hazel Eyes.' Songs about workplace courtesy. Treating people with respect. Not about Hazel Wincott personally—about what it looks like when someone actually gives a damn. Her name seemed warm. Genuine. Helps me process concern without crossing boundaries."

Diane asked more questions. Thoughtful ones. How often did he notice her distress? What specific behaviors? How long had he been writing these songs?

Genuine interest. Friendship. Someone who understood his attention to detail came from caring, not something inappropriate.

Twenty minutes. Michael felt like he had a real friend at work. Someone who got his perspective. Didn't think his observations were weird or his interests creepy. Understood that keeping distance while caring was mature, appropriate. His autism made connection rare. This felt precious.

"Thank you for trusting me." Diane touched his arm as they finished. Human contact. Connection. "Means a lot that you feel comfortable. You're a good person, Michael."

Back at his cubicle: lighter. Someone to talk to made isolation bearable. Maybe he and Diane could have coffee again sometime. He looked forward to Monday.

The weekend passed quietly. Saturday, he composed a new piece: "Trusted Voices." Relief of having someone at work who understood. Sunday, optimistic enough to grocery shop, meal prep. Small signs his exile was lifting.

Two weeks later, Friday, everything fell apart.

7:45 AM. Something felt wrong. Not obvious-wrong. Tom's "morning, Michael" sounded normal. Elevator worked. Coworkers moving through their typical Friday routine.

But something.

Mid-morning, the wrongness solidified. 10:00 AM. Hazel's section busier than usual. People stopping by her desk. Brief conversations. Workplace sympathy. Someone dealing with a crisis.

10:30 AM. Helen appeared with a man he didn't recognize. Navy suit, tablet, official bearing. HR.

"Michael, this is David Park from Human Resources. He needs to speak with you. Conference Room B."

Her voice carefully neutral. Ice water through his veins.

His eyes found Hazel at her desk. Not looking his direction. Posture rigid. Barely controlled—fear?

Timeline clicked into place. Friday conversation with Diane. Weekend. Monday morning complaint to HR.

Set up. His autism made him perfect—took people at face value, missed social games, couldn't read between the lines when someone was manipulating him.

The walk to Conference Room B. Each step echoing. Announcing something. Michael's mind racing through possibilities, but his stomach already knew.

David Park closed the door. Click. Final.

Fluorescent lights hummed. Made his head pound. Coffee stain on the table, kidney-bean shaped. Beyond the door, normal office life continuing. A world he wasn't part of anymore.

"Michael." David Park's voice: neutral, professional. Someone who'd delivered bad news hundreds of times. "Thank you for coming in."

Politeness felt ominous. Michael's hands cold despite the warm room. He pressed them against his thighs to stop the shaking. "Helen said you needed to speak with me."

"Yes." Park swiped through his tablet. Deliberate. "We've received a complaint about your behavior toward a female coworker. I need to ask some questions."

The room tilted. Eight years here. Eight years of perfect behavior, keeping his head down, avoiding exactly this. The lights buzzed louder. Or was that his ears? Blood rushing?

"I don't understand. What kind of complaint?"

Park took his time. The silence stretched. Michael's heartbeat loud in his ears. Mind cycling through possibilities. All terrible.

"The complaint involves your interactions with Hazel Wincott from Client Relations. The complainant alleges you've been monitoring her personal behavior and creating content that references her name. She feels threatened and uncomfortable in the workplace."

Each word: wrong. The description bore no resemblance to reality. But there was Hazel's name. Spoken aloud in this sterile room. His life coming apart.

"I haven't had any interactions with Hazel Wincott. Never spoken to her. Never approached her desk. I work two departments away."

Park made a note. Stylus scratching the screen. "But you do know who Hazel Wincott is?"

Trap. Any acknowledgment he'd noticed her could be twisted. But denial would be lying—of course he knew her. Same floor.

"I know who she is. Everyone on this floor knows who she is. Knowing someone exists and interacting with them—different things."

"According to the report," Park continued, scrolling, "you told another employee you've been observing Hazel Wincott's personal phone calls and tracking her emotional state. Is this accurate?"

Michael's throat constricted. Every word being twisted. Turned into something ugly. Weaponized. His autism made him literal—he'd described exactly what he'd observed, not understanding how honest observations could be reframed as sinister.

"I mentioned to a colleague that Hazel seemed upset during what appeared to be phone calls. Anyone sitting in this section could observe the same thing. Her desk is visible from multiple workstations. I wasn't 'tracking' anything—I was expressing concern."

Park typed. Expression unchanged. "And did you tell this colleague you've written songs using Hazel Wincott's name?"

The question hit like a physical blow. His respectful attempt to process concern without crossing boundaries was being reframed as obsessive, predatory.

"I write music in my spare time. I mentioned I'd titled some pieces with variations of her name because Hazel always seemed like such a warm, genuine name to me. The songs have lyrics about workplace courtesy—nothing personal about Hazel Wincott herself."

"So you confirm you've been monitoring a female coworker's personal behavior and creating content that references her name?"

The words hung like poison. Michael realized everything he said was making it worse—every clarification twisted into confirmation. His deliberate choice not to approach Hazel—his respectful maintenance of distance—was being ignored. His autism meant he couldn't see this trap coming until it was too late.

His mouth went dry. Everything making it worse. Every word. Christ, how had this happened?

"It's not monitoring. It's basic workplace awareness. And the songs aren't about her—they're about concepts of kindness that her behavior inspired. I specifically avoided making anything personal."

Park made another note. "I need you to understand the seriousness of this situation, Michael. A female employee has reported feeling threatened due to your behavior. She's requested specific workplace accommodations to ensure her safety."

Michael's hands visibly trembling now. The room felt too bright, too small. He could smell Park's coffee breath, hear the wall clock marking seconds that felt like hours.

"What accommodations?"

"You are not to approach within fifteen feet of Hazel Wincott's workstation. You are not to speak to her, email her, or communicate with her in any way. You are not to discuss her with other employees. Any violation will result in termination and possible legal action."

The ultimatum crashed over him. Michael nodded because speaking seemed impossible. After eight years of professional behavior, HR treated him like a dangerous animal based on a conversation someone had twisted.

"HR will monitor the situation. We take workplace harassment seriously at Branchwater. I recommend you familiarize yourself with our employee handbook's sections on workplace conduct."

He stood. The meeting was over. Twenty-eight minutes, Michael realized, checking the wall clock. In twenty-eight minutes, someone had destroyed his professional reputation and placed his future in jeopardy.

"Any questions about these restrictions?"

Michael shook his head. He was fucked. Simple as that. No one would believe him. Not against her. His autism made him vulnerable to this kind of manipulation because he couldn't read between the lines when someone was playing games with his trust.

The walk back to his cubicle felt endless. Every step echoed, announcing his shame. Eyes on the carpet—burgundy geometric shapes blurring as his vision swam. Hands shook as he swiped his access card.

His cubicle looked exactly as he'd left it—monitors displaying spreadsheets, coffee growing cold, pens in their precise arrangement. But everything felt contaminated. The space had absorbed the toxicity of his new status.

Michael sat heavily and stared at his screen without seeing anything. The numbers that usually made perfect sense now looked like hieroglyphics. Hands hovered over the keyboard, but he couldn't remember what he'd been working on.

Hyperaware of the sounds around him—keyboards clicking, phones ringing, the soft murmur of conversations. Were people talking about him? Had word spread? He turned slightly and caught sight of Hazel at her desk, two departments away. Even at this distance, her body language seemed different—more alert, guarded.

The afternoon stretched endlessly. Michael jumped at every unexpected sound—file cabinets closing, chairs rolling, the elevator dinging. His usual focus had shattered into fragments, each one reflecting a different potential threat.

The worst part was understanding Hazel's perspective. If someone had told her a male coworker was watching her personal phone calls and writing songs about her, she would feel threatened. He didn't blame her for the complaint. He blamed whoever had taken his private conversation and twisted it into something sinister.

Diane had been manipulating him from the beginning. She'd gathered personal information during their "friendship," then used each revelation as evidence of concerning behavior. His autism had made him the perfect target—someone who took people at face value, missed the social games, couldn't read between the lines when someone was exploiting his trust.

By 5:15 PM, when he packed his laptop and wiped down his monitors, Michael realized his eight-year routine at Branchwater had become something he would have to survive rather than perform.

WEEK ONE: The Adjustment

The first week after the HR meeting, Michael clung to cautious optimism. This was a misunderstanding—painful, embarrassing, but temporary. He started arriving twenty minutes early to avoid crowded elevators, telling himself this was practical while he processed what had happened.

His work remained flawless. If anything, he threw himself into projects with renewed focus, as if exceptional performance could counterbalance the HR complaint. He read emails twice before sending, adding layers of professional courtesy.

Tuesday brought an encouraging sign: Helen stopped by to compliment him on the Peterson campaign analysis.

"Nice work as always, Michael," she said, her tone carrying no hint of concern. The interaction felt normal—proof his professional reputation remained intact among people who mattered.

Wednesday, Tom greeted him with his usual warmth. "Morning, Michael! How's that new project treating you?" The question felt genuine, uncontaminated by workplace gossip.

Thursday, Sarah from Design stopped by with a question about font selection. Their five-minute conversation felt normal—professional, cordial, focused on work rather than drama. As she left, Sarah mentioned hoping he had a good weekend, the same casual pleasantry she'd always offered.

Sleep remained elusive, but he attributed this to normal stress. He'd lie awake replaying the conversation with Diane, analyzing each word, trying to understand how his autistic literal-mindedness had been weaponized. His brain processed social interactions differently—he said exactly what he meant and assumed others did the same. That honesty had made him vulnerable.

By Friday, Michael had convinced himself the situation was manageable. Yes, he needed to be more careful. Yes, the fifteen-foot restriction was humiliating. But his work spoke for itself, his supervisor trusted him, and time would prove his good intentions.

Maybe the worst was behind him.

WEEK TWO: The First Cracks

The second week began with subtle but unmistakable shifts.

Monday morning brought the first sign his situation had become workplace knowledge.

Sarah from Design's greeting felt different. She still smiled, still asked about his weekend, but her eyes didn't quite meet his, and she shifted her weight like someone eager to end the conversation.

"How was your weekend, Michael?" But she nodded quickly and moved away without the usual follow-up.

Tuesday afternoon, Michael walked to the printer and discovered Jennifer from Marketing standing near the copy machine with colleagues from HR and Finance. Their conversation stopped when they noticed him approaching—not abruptly, but with the natural pause of people who'd been discussing something confidential.

All three turned to watch him pass. Expressions neutral but clearly aware of who he was.

The incident lasted thirty seconds, but Michael spent the afternoon analyzing it. What information about his case would require coordination between Marketing, HR, and Finance? Were they developing documentation protocols? Planning additional restrictions? Or was his autism making him read malicious intent into routine workplace discussion?

Wednesday brought the pen incident.

Michael arrived at 7:45 AM, but something felt wrong before he'd even set down his briefcase. His analytical mind, trained to notice patterns, catalogued the problem: someone had disturbed his desk arrangement.

The blue pen—positioned at the leftmost point of his precise triangle formation—now sat in the middle position. His red pen occupied the blue pen's spot. The black pen remained correctly positioned.

Michael stood motionless for a full minute, studying his workspace with methodical attention. He'd wiped down his monitors Tuesday evening, arranged his pens in their formation, pushed his chair exactly six inches under the desk. The ritual provided closure and security for his autism. He never forgot the arrangement.

But if not the cleaning crew, then who? A colleague borrowing supplies would take what they needed, not rearrange everything. IT would focus on computer equipment. Security would have no reason to disturb personal items.

Michael pulled out his phone and photographed his current pen arrangement from two angles, then returned each pen to its correct position. As he worked, cold certainty settled in his stomach: someone had been searching his workspace.

The realization brought a surge of adrenaline that made his hands tremble as he powered on his computer. Who had access after hours? What had they been looking for? Was this random curiosity, or investigation related to his HR case?

By Thursday, he'd begun taking a different route to the bathroom—a longer path that avoided the Client Relations section. Not because he was afraid of violating the fifteen-foot restriction, but because he'd noticed Hazel's colleagues glancing in his direction whenever he passed their area.

Friday brought confirmation his situation had spread beyond workplace gossip. Standing in the cafeteria line, Michael overheard part of a conversation between two employees from different departments:

"—weird guy from Marketing—" "—knew something was off about him—" "—probably for the best that someone reported—"

The voices lowered when one of them noticed Michael behind them, but the damage was done. His case had become office legend, discussed by people who'd never interacted with him, shaped by rumors that had nothing to do with what actually happened.

That evening, Michael sat in his apartment and realized his theory about a temporary misunderstanding might be naive. Whatever Diane had told HR, whatever story had emerged from their conversation, it had taken root and was spreading through the workplace like a virus.

For the first time since the initial HR meeting, Michael began to consider his situation might not resolve itself with time and good behavior. Some kinds of reputation damage, he realized, might be permanent. And his autism made it impossible to navigate the social complexities needed to fight back.

WEEK THREE: The Documentation

By the third week, Michael's analytical mind had begun treating his workplace like a research project requiring documentation. The decision to start keeping notes marked a psychological watershed—the transition from hoping things would return to normal to preparing for further deterioration.

He purchased a small notebook from the office supply store, telling himself this was practical record-keeping rather than paranoid surveillance. If the situation escalated, documentation might prove essential. His autism made him naturally detail-oriented; now he'd use that trait for survival.

Monday, November 13, 7:45 AM: Got here early again. Pens still where I left them. Nobody messed with my stuff over the weekend.

Monday, 10:15 AM: Jennifer from Marketing saw me coming and went the long way around. Maybe nothing. Maybe she had somewhere else to be.

Monday, 2:30 PM: Hazel eating alone again. Stayed back like I'm supposed to. Fifteen feet. Counted it.

The act of writing observations helped Michael feel more in control, as if documentation could protect him from further false accusations. But it also amplified his focus on potentially threatening behaviors, creating a feedback loop where increased attention generated more data points to analyze and worry about.

Tuesday brought his first real conversation since the HR meeting. Helen stopped by with questions about the quarterly analytics report—routine stuff that felt almost normal. She didn't treat him like a leper, didn't avoid eye contact, just talked shop like always.

"Nice work on the Peterson numbers," she said, scanning his monitors. "Client's happy, deadlines met. You know what you're doing."

For twenty minutes, Michael felt human again. Helen either didn't know about his HR situation or didn't give a shit as long as he did his job. Either way, it felt like oxygen.

But Wednesday afternoon shattered that hope.

Michael was coming back from the bathroom—taking his new route that avoided Hazel's section—when he saw something that made his stomach drop. Near the elevators, Hazel was talking with Rebecca Torres and Jeanne Blightly from Client Relations.

All three women had clear sightlines to his cubicle. As he got closer, their conversation just died. Complete silence. Then all three turned to stare at him like he'd walked in covered in blood.

Hazel's face was blank—not hostile, not scared, just carefully neutral. Like she was managing her reaction. Rebecca and Janet kept looking between him and Hazel like they were watching for something.

Michael nodded—just being polite—and kept walking to the elevator. He could feel their eyes on his back the whole way. When the doors closed, his hands were shaking.

Wednesday, 3:20 PM: Saw Hazel with Rebecca and Janet by the elevators. They stopped talking when they saw me. All three just stared. Hazel looked like she was trying not to show anything. The other two kept looking at her, then at me. Like they were waiting for me to do something. Felt like walking through a fucking minefield.

That evening, Michael spent two hours staring at his notebook, trying to make sense of what was happening. The pattern was clear: his coworkers weren't just uncomfortable around him—they were actively coordinating to avoid him. Sharing information. Watching his movements.

The workplace had organized itself around the threat he apparently represented, and his autism made it impossible to understand the social complexities involved or figure out how to fight it.

Thursday introduced a new variable: deliberate route modification by other employees. Michael documented three separate instances where colleagues altered their paths through the office to avoid close proximity to his workstation. Sarah from Design, who'd maintained friendly interactions through the first two weeks, now took a circuitous route to the printer that bypassed his section.

Thursday, 11:30 AM: Sarah took the long way to the printer. Added thirty seconds to her trip just to avoid passing my cubicle. Big change from before. She's actively trying not to get close to me now.

Thursday, 2:15 PM: Jim from Accounts saw me waiting for the elevator and took the stairs instead. Could be coincidence but timing suggests he's avoiding me too.

The documentation was becoming obsessive, Michael realized, but he couldn't stop. Each new behavioral anomaly felt like crucial intelligence that might help him understand the scope of workplace sentiment against him. His autism made pattern recognition both a strength and a curse—he could see the systematic exclusion happening, but couldn't figure out how to respond.

Friday brought the most disturbing incident yet: evidence of after-hours investigation of his workspace.

Michael arrived Friday morning to find his computer powered on—a blue screen that should have been black after his careful shutdown Thursday evening. His desk drawer had been opened two inches. Most tellingly, his succulent plant had moved from the left side of his monitor to the right side.

The plant relocation wasn't random or accidental. Someone had searched his workspace, moving items to access areas beneath them, then attempted to restore everything to its original position. But they'd gotten the plant placement wrong—a small error that revealed hours of investigation he wasn't supposed to discover.

Michael photographed everything before restoring his workspace to its proper arrangement. Who had building access after hours? Security staff, cleaning crew, IT maintenance, management personnel. Any of them could have conducted this search.

Friday, 7:50 AM: Workspace shows clear signs of after-hours intrusion. Computer powered on despite proper shutdown. Desk drawer opened 2 inches. Succulent plant moved from left to right monitor side. Photographed all evidence. This represents investigation rather than coincidental disturbance.

The reality was undeniable: Michael wasn't just being avoided or gossiped about. He was under surveillance, with his workspace, behavior, and movements being monitored and documented by parties unknown.

That weekend, Michael sat in his apartment reviewing three weeks of notebook entries. The data painted a clear picture of social isolation punctuated by moments of overt surveillance. His colleagues weren't just uncomfortable around him—they were participating in his professional destruction.

His autism had made him the perfect target because he couldn't navigate the social games being played against him. The transition from hoping for normalcy to documenting persecution marked a crucial psychological milestone. Michael had stopped believing his situation was temporary. Now he was building a case file for a trial that would never come.

WEEK FOUR: The Manipulation Continues

The fourth week marked Michael's transformation from cautious professional to hypervigilant exile. Sleep fragmented into two-hour blocks interrupted by jolts of adrenaline as his mind conjured new scenarios of professional destruction.

Monday brought an unexpected development: Diane Fletcher's return to his professional life.

She approached his cubicle at 2:30 PM carrying two coffee cups from the expensive shop downstairs—the same gesture that had initiated their original conversation. The symmetry felt calculated, designed to evoke memories of his trust and vulnerability.

"Michael," Diane said, settling into the chair beside his cubicle with practiced casualness, "I wanted to check on you. I know this situation has been stressful."

Michael watched her face, looking for any hint of guilt or awareness of what she'd done. The timeline was obvious: Friday afternoon conversation with Diane, weekend processing, Monday morning complaint to HR. His autism meant he took her words at face value originally, not seeing the manipulation until it was too late.

"I'm managing," he said, noting how her eyes scanned his desk while she talked, cataloguing the empty coffee cups and scattered notebook pages visible at his workspace edge.

"That's good to hear," she replied, leaning forward as if his response confirmed something she'd been expecting. "I heard there was some kind of misunderstanding with Hazel Wincott. That must be difficult to deal with."

The phrasing struck Michael as constructed. 'Misunderstanding' suggested either breathtaking ignorance of the damage she'd caused or sophisticated psychological manipulation. Given her position in Employee Relations and her demonstrated skill at extracting personal information, he suspected the latter.

"Yes, it's been challenging," he said. Every word felt like stepping on broken glass.

Diane stirred her coffee. The same deliberate movements as before. "How are you feeling about everything? Are you getting the support you need?"

The question made his skin crawl. She was fishing for admissions of distress she could twist into evidence of instability. His autism made it hard to read her real intentions, but the pattern was becoming clear.

"I'm focused on maintaining professional standards," he replied.

"That's very mature of you," Diane said, her voice warm as honey. "I keep thinking about our conversation a few weeks ago. You seemed so concerned about Hazel—it showed your caring side. I hope you know that wanting to help a coworker isn't wrong. Sometimes good intentions just get... twisted around."

The gaslighting was perfect. She was positioning herself as his defender while confirming she'd ratted him out. Trying to make him believe she'd tried to help, that the outcome was just some unfortunate miscommunication. His autism meant he'd originally trusted her caring facade, not seeing the manipulation underneath.

"I appreciate your perspective," Michael said, his voice neutral.

"You know, if you ever want to talk about this situation—really talk about it—I'm here to listen. Sometimes it helps to process these kinds of workplace challenges with someone who understands the dynamics."

Another trap. Diane was offering herself as a confidant while having proven her willingness to weaponize personal revelations. Any additional information he shared would find its way back to HR, twisted into new evidence of inappropriate behavior.

"Thank you," Michael said. "I should get back to this report."

After Diane left, Michael sat staring at his monitors for twenty minutes, unable to focus. The casual cruelty of her approach—positioning herself as his friend while gathering intelligence for his destruction—represented a level of manipulative sophistication his autism made it impossible to counter.

Monday, 2:30-3:00 PM: Diane came back. Same coffee cups, same fake concern. Asked about my "support system" like she gives a shit. Called it a "misunderstanding" with Hazel. Bitch knows exactly what she did. Wants me to think she tried to help. Trying to get me to say something she can use against me again. I see what she's doing now.

Tuesday brought confirmation his documentation wasn't paranoia—it was survival. During lunch at his desk, he watched the timing game play out in real time. Sarah from Design walked toward the printer, saw him sitting there, and just stopped. Waited by the copy machine for three minutes until he got up to use the bathroom. Then she printed her stuff and left.

At 12:45, Jim from Accounts was heading for the elevator when he spotted Michael approaching. Instead of getting on, Jim let the doors close and waited for the next car.

They were coordinating. Had to be. Nobody's timing was that perfectly bad by accident.

Tuesday, 12:15–1:00 PM: They're fucking coordinating. Sarah waited three minutes rather than share the printer with me. Jim saw me coming and took the stairs instead of the elevator. This isn't coincidence. They're sharing information about where I am, when I move. Like I'm some kind of dangerous animal they need to track.

Wednesday introduced a new element that shattered Michael's remaining hope for professional rehabilitation: management was documenting his behavioral changes.

Helen appeared at his cubicle at 10:30 AM with a concerned expression. Her typical interactions were brief and work-focused. Extended conversations meant problems.

"Michael," she said, settling into the chair beside his workspace, "I wanted to check on your well-being. You've seemed... different lately. More withdrawn, less engaged during team meetings."

The observation was accurate but dangerous. Michael's withdrawal was a direct response to his hostile work environment, but any explanation would sound defensive or paranoid. His autism made it difficult to articulate the social complexities involved.

"I've been focused on project deliverables," he said.

"Your work quality remains excellent," Helen assured him, "but I've noticed you're eating lunch alone instead of in the cafeteria. You arrive much earlier than usual. You seem anxious during meetings."

Each observation felt like evidence being compiled for a formal evaluation. Michael realized his attempts to adapt to his hostile environment were being interpreted as signs of mental instability rather than rational responses to exclusion.

"I appreciate your concern," he said. "I'm managing my workload fine."

"That's not what I'm worried about," Helen replied, her voice dropping to a confidential tone. "Your colleagues have mentioned you seem stressed. There's been some discussion about whether you might benefit from additional support resources."

The phrase 'additional support resources' carried ominous implications. Michael understood his visible distress over being falsely accused was being used as evidence he might require intervention.

"What kind of support?" he asked.

"Employee assistance programs, counseling services, perhaps some time off to address whatever's troubling you," Helen explained. "The company wants to help you work through this difficult period."

Michael felt a trap closing. If he accepted counseling, it would confirm he needed psychological help to cope with harassment allegations.

If he declined, it would suggest he wasn't taking his mental health seriously.

"I'll consider those options," he said, buying time to process the implications.

Wednesday, 10:30–11:00 AM: Helen says I need "additional support." Translation: they think I'm cracking up. My normal human reaction to being fucked over is being used as proof I'm mentally unstable. Colleagues have been "discussing" my stress levels with management. Catch-22: seek help and confirm I'm guilty, don't seek help and prove I'm dangerous. Either way I'm screwed.

WEEKS FIVE-SIX: The Physical Collapse

The fifth and sixth weeks were when Michael's body started betraying him in ways his coworkers couldn't ignore. His hands had developed a constant tremor—not just when he was nervous, but all the time. Holding coffee required both hands. His typing became hunt-and-peck as he fought to hit the right keys.

The weight loss was getting scary; his clothes hung on him like he was a coat hanger. His autism meant he'd always been sensitive to stress, but now the physical symptoms were becoming impossible to hide.

Thursday morning of the fifth week, he walked to the copy machine and found Rebecca Torres and Jeanne Blightly printing something. When they saw him coming, both women just abandoned their shit mid-job and walked away. Didn't even finish printing. Just left their documents sitting there rather than share the same space with him.

The message was crystal clear: his presence was so toxic they'd interrupt their own work to avoid him.

Thursday, 9:15 AM: Rebecca and Janet literally abandoned their printing when they saw me coming. Left their documents sitting there. Would rather lose their work than be in the same room with me. Jesus Christ. What do they think I'm going to do?

Helen's concern was becoming harder to hide. Tuesday morning of the sixth week, she showed up at his cubicle with a croissant from the bakery downstairs.

"You need to eat," she said, no preamble. Just set the pastry next to his keyboard. "You're disappearing, Michael. I'm worried."

The kindness hurt worse than hostility. Helen actually gave a shit, but even her concern felt dangerous now. Every expression of worry about his condition could be documented somewhere as evidence he was becoming unstable.

"Thanks," he said, accepting the croissant even though the thought of eating made his stomach churn. Food had become an enemy weeks ago.

But it was Friday's incident of the sixth week that pushed Michael past the psychological point of no return.

He was returning from lunch—eaten alone in his car to avoid the cafeteria's social minefield—when he encountered a group of five employees gathered near the elevator bank: Hazel Wincott, two colleagues from her department, Diane Fletcher, and Sarah from Design.

They were clustered in the kind of informal circle that suggested shared information rather than chance encounter.

As Michael approached the elevator, their conversation didn't just pause—it stopped dead. Five pairs of eyes tracked his movement with the focused attention reserved for potential threats. Hazel's expression was neutral, but her colleagues' faces carried unmistakable wariness. Diane watched him with what looked like scientific curiosity.

The silence stretched for fifteen excruciating seconds while Michael waited for the elevator. He could feel sweat beading on his forehead despite the air conditioning. His hands trembled as he pressed the call button.

When the elevator arrived, Michael stepped inside and turned to face the closing doors. In that last moment, he saw Diane lean forward to whisper something to the group, her words generating nodding and what appeared to be agreement among the listeners.

Friday, 1:20 PM: Encountered group of five including Hazel, Diane, and others near elevator bank. Conversation ceased upon my approach. All five maintained visual tracking with wariness. Diane appeared to share additional information after my departure. Pattern suggests ongoing coordinated discussion of my case.

That weekend brought no relief from his racing thoughts. Michael spent Saturday and Sunday reviewing six weeks of notebook entries, trying to construct a comprehensive map of the conspiracy that had formed around him.

The Thanksgiving holiday was a torment of isolation. While his colleagues enjoyed family gatherings, Michael sat alone in his apartment, unable to summon any feeling except exhaustion. He'd lost twenty-eight pounds since the HR meeting six weeks ago. His guitar playing had become impossible—his hands shook too much to hold picks properly.

WEEKS SEVEN-EIGHT: The Breaking Point

The week after Thanksgiving brought what Michael would recognize as his complete psychological breaking point. It happened during a moment that should have been routine: walking past the Client Relations section on his way to a meeting with Helen.

As he approached the area he'd been avoiding for weeks, Michael noticed Hazel Wincott standing by the windows with three colleagues, engaged in animated conversation about what sounded like wedding planning. Her voice carried genuine happiness—laughter and excitement about venue selection and guest lists. She seemed content, more relaxed than he'd seen her since the early days of her employment.

The realization hit him like a physical blow: Hazel had moved on. Whatever personal stress he'd observed months ago had resolved itself, probably through the relationship healing that often followed engagement announcements. She was planning a future with someone she loved, surrounded by supportive colleagues who celebrated her happiness.

Meanwhile, Michael existed in a state of permanent exile, unable to feel joy about anything, monitoring his every movement to avoid triggering new complaints. The asymmetry was crushing—she had returned to normal life while he remained trapped in the aftermath of their non-interaction.

But it was the overheard conversation fragment that destroyed his last hope for rehabilitation.

"—so much happier now that the situation is resolved," one of Hazel's colleagues was saying. "It must have been terrifying to deal with that kind of unwanted attention."

"The important thing is that someone spoke up," another voice replied. "Too many women just suffer in silence when men cross boundaries. At least this time the system worked."

"Exactly. And the fact that he's been keeping his distance proves he knew his behavior was inappropriate all along."

Michael stood frozen in the hallway, twenty feet away but close enough to hear every word of his character assassination. His careful compliance with the fifteen-foot restriction—his respectful attempt to ensure Hazel's comfort—was being interpreted as admission of guilt rather than evidence of his decency.

The conversation continued, but Michael couldn't process the words through the roaring in his ears. His vision blurred at the edges, and for a moment he thought he might collapse right there in the hallway.

The injustice was so complete, so total, that his mind struggled to accept it was real. His autism meant he couldn't understand the social games that had destroyed him, couldn't see the manipulation until it was too late to defend himself.

He made it to the bathroom before his legs gave out. Locked himself in a stall and sat on the toilet seat, head between his knees, trying to breathe while his world collapsed around him. Twenty minutes of shaking and hyperventilating while he faced the truth: there was no way back from this.

Monday, 2:15 PM: Heard them talking about the "resolved situation." My "inappropriate behavior." They're celebrating my compliance as proof I knew I was guilty. Story's set in stone now. Can't be changed. I'm fucked.

That evening, Michael called his sister Rachel for the first time in three weeks.

"Michael?" Rachel's voice carried immediate concern. "You sound terrible. What's happening?"

The question unleashed seven weeks of suppressed anguish. For forty minutes, Michael detailed his destruction—the manipulated conversation, the false accusations, the workplace surveillance, the physical deterioration, the complete social exile. Rachel listened without interruption, asking clarifying questions that demonstrated her professional understanding of workplace dynamics and her personal understanding of how her autistic brother's mind worked.

"This is psychological torture," she said when he finished. "What they're doing to you—this isolation, the pathologizing of normal stress responses, the impossible bind where seeking help confirms guilt—it's textbook mobbing behavior. And it's especially cruel when the target is someone like you."

"Someone like me?" Michael asked.

"Autistic, Michael. You take people at face value, you miss the social games, you can't read between the lines when someone's manipulating you. You're the perfect target for this kind of systematic destruction because you don't see it coming until it's too late."

"But I can't prove any of it," Michael said, his voice cracking. "Everyone thinks I'm a predator who was disciplined for harassment. If I complain about unfair treatment, I'll look like I'm not taking the allegations seriously. If I show distress, it's evidence of instability."

"The system isn't designed for people like us to win," Rachel said quietly. "It's designed to protect institutions from liability. Autistic men, especially autistic men who don't understand the social games, are considered acceptable casualties in that calculation. Your literal thinking, your pattern recognition, your need for clear rules—all the things that make you good at your job also make you vulnerable to this kind of manipulation."

"So what do I do? How do I survive this?"

The silence stretched for nearly a minute before Rachel answered. "I don't know, Michael. I wish I had better advice, but I've seen too many clients in similar situations. The damage to your reputation is probably permanent. The question is whether you can find a way to build a different kind of life somewhere else."

After the call ended, Michael sat in his dark apartment and faced the mathematical reality of his situation. At forty-three years old, he had no friends except Rachel, no romantic prospects, no social connections outside a workplace that had branded him a threat. His professional reputation was destroyed, his mental health was deteriorating rapidly, and his physical condition was becoming alarming.

The notebook beside him contained seven weeks of meticulous documentation proving his persecution, but that evidence would never be seen by anyone who mattered. In the court of workplace opinion, he'd been tried, convicted, and sentenced to permanent exile.

His autism had made him vulnerable to a predator who wore a friendly face, and now there was no way back.

WEEKS NINE-TEN: The Final Isolation

December arrived with the familiar cascade of office decorations and forced holiday cheer, but for Michael, the festive atmosphere felt like mockery. The company announced their holiday party scheduled for December 15th. The invitation arrived via email with cheerful graphics and promises of celebration, but Michael read it as another potential minefield. He submitted his polite decline to Helen, citing project deadlines everyone knew were fictional.

Tuesday of the ninth week brought an interaction that crystallized his complete professional isolation. At 3:20 PM, Michael approached the copy machine to find it occupied by three employees from different departments: Jennifer from Marketing, Tom from IT, and Rebecca Torres from Client Relations. Their conversation was animated, focused on holiday vacation plans and year-end project schedules.

When they noticed Michael approaching, the conversation died. All three stepped away from the machine with synchronized efficiency, abandoning their printing tasks to create a buffer zone around his presence. They retreated to a safe distance and resumed their conversation in lowered tones, glancing back to monitor his progress.

Michael completed his printing in crushing silence, hyperaware that his every movement was being observed and catalogued for future discussion. The message was unmistakable: his presence was so toxic that normal workplace functions had to be suspended to accommodate his proximity.

Tuesday, 3:20 PM: Three employees from different departments abandoned copy machine tasks upon my approach. Coordinated retreat suggests cross-departmental awareness of my status as workplace threat. Complete breakdown of basic professional courtesy protocols.

Wednesday brought what Michael would later recognize as the death of his last hope for rehabilitation. Helen called him into her office for what she termed a "year-end check-in," but Michael recognized it as another welfare assessment disguised as routine supervision.

Helen's office felt different this time—more formal, more ominous. A folder sat on her desk beside his performance materials, thick enough to contain extensive documentation.

"Michael," Helen began, her voice carrying the careful tone she'd developed for their recent interactions, "I want to discuss your performance this year and your... well-being."

The pause before 'well-being' confirmed this wasn't purely professional evaluation. Helen was operating under instructions from HR or upper management to assess his mental stability and potential threat level.

"Your technical work remains excellent," she continued, opening his performance file. "Client satisfaction in the ninety-fifth percentile, projects completed ahead of schedule, attention to detail that's exceptional."

Michael felt a brief flutter of hope. If his work quality was still recognized, maybe there was a path back to professional respectability.

But Helen's expression shifted as she opened the second folder. "However, I can't ignore what I've been observing in terms of your personal well-being and workplace integration. Significant weight loss, visible anxiety, social withdrawal, signs of chronic stress affecting your overall presentation."

Each observation felt like evidence being compiled for his dismissal. Michael realized his natural response to persecution—the anxiety, the weight loss, the social withdrawal—was being pathologized as evidence of mental instability rather than recognized as a normal human reaction to abnormal circumstances.

"The company is concerned about you," Helen continued. "Several colleagues have mentioned you seem distressed, that you're avoiding social interaction, that you appear to be under significant stress."

Michael understood his visible distress over being falsely accused was being used as evidence he needed intervention, while the person who had caused the damage through manipulation continued to receive praise for her "sensitivity."

"I'm recommending you for our employee assistance program," Helen said, sliding a brochure across her desk. "It's confidential, Michael. It won't impact your employment record unless you request integration with your medical benefits."

The offer felt like a trap with no escape routes. Accepting the program would confirm he needed psychological help to cope with harassment allegations. Declining would suggest he wasn't taking his deteriorating condition seriously.

"I understand you had some kind of situation with HR earlier this year," Helen continued, her voice dropping to a whisper. "I don't know the details, and I don't need to know them. But whatever happened, you can't handle it alone. The assistance program has counselors who specialize in workplace adjustment issues."

Michael could see Helen struggling with the complexity of the situation. She knew his work quality, recognized his technical competence, but she couldn't afford to appear unsympathetic to a female employee's harassment complaint. Even her genuine concern for his well-being had to be calibrated to avoid suggesting the real victim might be the accused man rather than the woman who had reported him.

"I appreciate the concern," Michael said, the words feeling like ash in his mouth. "I'll review the materials."

Wednesday, 11:00–11:30 AM: Performance review revealed expectation that I seek psychological treatment for normal stress response to false accusations. Helen documented physical deterioration and social withdrawal as evidence of mental health crisis rather than rational adaptation to hostile environment. Employee assistance program referral represents institutional pressure to pathologize my distress while ignoring workplace dysfunction.

Thursday brought the worst encounter yet—face-to-face with Hazel Wincott.

At 2:45 PM, Michael was returning from the bathroom using his planned route when maintenance work on the east stairwell forced him to take an alternate path that brought him within sight of the Client Relations section. As he rounded the corner, he found himself face-to-face with Hazel Wincott, approaching from the opposite direction.

For a split second, their eyes met. Michael saw her expression cycle through recognition, alarm, and something that looked almost like pity before settling into managed neutrality. She stepped sideways to maintain the required fifteen-foot distance, but her movement was so calculated that it highlighted the artificial nature of their interaction.

"Hazel," Michael said quietly, not approaching but not fleeing either. For eight weeks, he'd been treated like a dangerous animal, and suddenly he was face-to-face with the person whose complaint had destroyed his life. "I hope you're doing well."

Her response was devastating: she looked around quickly to see if anyone was witnessing their interaction, took another step backward, and said nothing at all. No acknowledgment of his greeting, no basic human courtesy, just silent treatment designed to minimize her exposure to his contaminating presence.

The moment lasted perhaps ten seconds, but it crystallized everything Michael had lost. He wasn't just professionally damaged—he had been rendered invisible, unworthy of basic human acknowledgment. Hazel's refusal to even speak to him confirmed he existed outside the boundaries of acceptable social interaction.

Thursday, 2:45 PM: Ran into Hazel in hallway. She wouldn't even speak to me. Looked around for witnesses, stepped back like I had the plague. Treated me like I don't exist. Not even basic human courtesy. I'm completely erased.

Friday brought the office holiday party Michael had declined. He worked alone while his coworkers celebrated down the hall, listening to distant laughter and music. At 6:30, walking to the elevator, he glanced through the conference room's glass doors.

Hazel Wincott stood in the center of a group, laughing at someone's story, surrounded by warmth and acceptance. She looked radiant—successful, integrated, loved. Everything he'd once been.

But Diane Fletcher's presence delivered the final blow. She was holding court near Hazel's group, entertaining several employees with some story. When she spotted Michael watching through the glass, their eyes met across the barrier separating him from normal human community.

Diane's expression showed no guilt, no awareness of the destruction she'd caused. Just mild curiosity, like observing an interesting specimen. She turned back to her audience and said something that generated laughter. Michael couldn't hear the words, but the timing made it clear she'd made some joke about his exclusion. Her ability to weaponize his isolation for entertainment confirmed how thoroughly she'd destroyed him.

CHRISTMAS WEEK: The Legal Escalation

Christmas week brought the final destruction. Monday's incident would be his last notebook entry.

At 10:30 AM, walking to Helen's office for a year-end meeting, he passed five employees by the elevator bank: Hazel Wincott, Diane Fletcher, two people from HR, and Jennifer from Marketing. Holiday conversation, New Year's plans, normal office stuff.

When they saw him coming, everything stopped. Five pairs of eyes locked onto him with open hostility. Not the careful neutrality he'd grown used to—actual disgust, like his presence was an affront to their celebration.

Michael nodded politely, but not one acknowledged it. The silence was total, coordinated. Something had changed. Some new accusation, some final nail in his coffin.

Monday, 10:30 AM: Group of five including Hazel, Diane, HR people. Complete hostility. No one acknowledged my greeting. Something new has happened. Level of hatred beyond anything before. I'm done.

By Tuesday, the hostility had infected the entire office like a virus. Colleagues who'd maintained basic courtesy now treated him like a walking disease. Tom the security guard ignored his greeting. Sarah from Design crossed to the far side of the hallway rather than pass within ten feet of him.

Wednesday brought the nuclear option: legal involvement.

Helen showed up at his cubicle with a man in an expensive suit carrying a leather portfolio. Not administrative business—legal business.

"Michael," Helen said, her voice carrying new formality, "this is Attorney James Mitchell from corporate legal. He needs to speak with you about some additional concerns."

The words hit like ice water. Legal meant the situation had escalated beyond simple harassment complaints into something that could follow him forever.

"What concerns?" Michael asked, his voice sounding strange.

"Conference Room B," Mitchell said. The tone of someone delivering bad news for a living.

The forty-minute meeting was a blur of "patterns of escalating behavior" that bore no resemblance to his actual actions but had been documented thoroughly. Someone had built a case against him with fictional evidence and twisted interpretations of his every movement.

His autism had made him unable to see the social games being played against him, unable to defend himself against accusations that made no sense but had been crafted by people who understood exactly how to exploit the system.

When it ended, Michael knew his professional life wasn't just damaged—it was over. The legal documentation would follow him everywhere, marking him permanently as someone terminated for harassment serious enough to require attorney involvement.

THE FINAL DECISION

He returned to his cubicle, packed his personal stuff into a cardboard box, and emailed his resignation to Helen. Eight years of dedicated service, destroyed by trusting the wrong person. Eight years of building something, obliterated by lies he'd never be allowed to challenge.

Final entry, Wednesday, December 28, 3:45 PM: Legal involved. It's over. Ten weeks of documenting proves coordinated destruction, but evidence dies with me. Diane wins. Perfect crime—destroys autistic target while maintaining concerned colleague act. System designed to sacrifice men like me for institutional protection. No way forward. No way back. Nothing left.

Michael spent his final days at Branchwater cleaning out his cubicle and transferring project files to his replacement—a recent graduate who seemed excited about joining such a "supportive, collegial workplace." The irony was perfect: someone else would occupy his space, use his arranged monitors, sit in his positioned chair, unaware of the psychological destruction that had preceded their arrival.

During those final days, Michael made one last attempt to understand the scope of Diane's manipulation. He reviewed every interaction they'd shared, every conversation that might have provided material for her fictional narrative. The analysis revealed the sophistication of her approach: she had gathered personal information during their "friendship," then used each revelation as evidence of concerning behavior.

His concern for Hazel Wincott had been reframed as obsessive surveillance. His songs about workplace kindness had been presented as creepy fixation. His social isolation had been characterized as dangerous antisocial behavior. His autistic analytical nature had been twisted into evidence of calculating predatory instincts.

Most cunningly, Diane had positioned herself as the concerned colleague who'd tried to help him, who'd seen warning signs but couldn't prevent his "escalating" behavior. She would probably attend his memorial service—if there was one—and explain how she'd done everything possible to support a troubled autistic man who'd been destroyed by his inability to accept accountability for his actions.

The weekend between Christmas and New Year's was spent doing the math. Michael sat in his apartment, calculating his reality with the same precision he'd once applied to marketing campaigns.

Professional prospects: Zero. Legal documentation would follow him forever. Money: Six months, maybe, then bankruptcy. People: Rachel in Portland. Nobody else. Mental state: Destroyed. Physical state: Thirty pounds down, shaking hands, can't sleep. Future: Decades of poverty, isolation, and psychological damage from being manipulated by someone who exploited his autism—or end it now.

At forty-three, with no friends, no prospects, and a reputation destroyed by lies, the math was simple and brutal.

He spent New Year's Eve writing letters to Rachel and Helen, trying to explain without blaming them. It took hours because he wanted to be clear: this wasn't about depression or mental illness. This was a rational response to complete destruction with no viable path forward. His autism had made him vulnerable to manipulation by someone who understood exactly how to exploit his literal thinking and trust.

He sealed the letters, left them on his kitchen table, and loaded his car with his guitar and a tank of propane. The lake where he'd fished as a kid seemed like the right place—peaceful, isolated, connected to better memories.

Michael sat by the water's edge and played "Hazel's Grace" one last time, watching his breath cloud in the cold air.

The method he'd chosen was gentle—no violence, no mess for anyone to clean up, no traumatic discovery for innocent people. Just carbon monoxide poisoning that would feel like falling asleep after an exhausting day.

As he made his preparations, he thought about the people who'd shaped his destruction. Hazel, who'd probably never know the suffering that followed their non-interaction. Helen, who'd tried to help within a system designed to prevent it. Diane, who'd continue manipulating vulnerable autistic people while positioning herself as their friend.

But mostly he felt relief. The constant vigilance was almost over. The social calculations and workplace navigation and fear of future accusations would end tonight. The certainty that every remaining year of his life would be worse than the last was about to be resolved permanently.

Michael fell asleep listening to water lapping against the shore, his guitar across his lap, propane hissing softly from the backseat. His last thought was about the songs he'd written—music inspired by Hazel

Wincott's patience with difficult people, melodies celebrating human decency in corporate environments.

Those songs would never be heard now, and perhaps that was fitting. In a world where kindness was interpreted as threat and trust was weaponized into social destruction, maybe there was no place for music about people treating each other with respect. His autism had made him believe in the possibility of genuine human connection, and that belief had been used to destroy him.

The lake held no judgment, offered no solutions, provided only the peace that had been stolen from his daily life. As consciousness faded, Michael experienced something he hadn't felt in ten weeks: complete safety from human betrayal.

EPILOGUE: Return to Normal

On January 8th, Branchwater Marketing returned to normal operations after the holiday break. Helen sent a company-wide email about Michael Henley's "tragic passing" and made the usual noises about employee mental health resources.

The reactions were swift and predictable.

"He was weird," Jim from Accounts said over coffee. "Never talked to anyone, just sat there staring at people. Honestly, it was bound to happen eventually."

"I heard he was obsessed with that girl in Client Relations," Sarah from Design added. "Makes you wonder what else he was thinking about the rest of us. Probably for the best, really."

"These loner types always snap," Marcus from IT said, shaking his head. "At least he only hurt himself instead of taking people with him. Hazel Wincott's probably relieved."

Hazel Wincott felt briefly sad about the news—she'd never actually talked to Michael, but suicide was tragic. She was mostly focused on engagement party planning anyway. Her boyfriend had proposed on New Year's Day after working through their relationship issues over the holidays.

"I'm just glad I reported his behavior when I did," she told her coworkers over lunch. "Imagine if I'd waited and something worse had happened. I knew something was off about him—the way he was lurking around, watching people. You develop instincts about these things."

Diane Fletcher attended the memorial service Helen organized, where she told several coworkers that Michael had confided in her about feeling lonely and isolated. She positioned herself as someone who had tried to help him, someone who had seen the warning signs but couldn't prevent the tragedy.

"I keep thinking I should have done more," she told Hazel over coffee, dabbing at her eyes with a tissue. "He seemed like such a lost soul. I tried to be his friend, tried to get him to open up, but you can't save someone who doesn't want to be saved."

"You did everything you could," Hazel assured her. "Some people are just... broken. It's not your fault he couldn't handle being called out for inappropriate behavior."

The narrative took shape quickly: Michael Henley had been a disturbed autistic loner who became obsessively fixated on a female coworker, was disciplined by HR, and chose death rather than face the consequences of his actions. It was a clean story that required no uncomfortable self-examination from anyone involved.

Michael's cubicle was cleaned out by the maintenance staff. His personal items—family photos, his precisely arranged pens, a small succulent plant—got packed into a box for Rachel to collect. IT wiped his computer and reassigned it to his replacement, a recent college graduate who was thrilled about working for such a "supportive, collegial workplace."

The northeast corner cubicle was prime real estate—quiet, good sightlines, close to windows. The new employee arranged his monitors and supplies with careful attention to efficiency. He was excited to have landed such a great job at a company with excellent employee relations.

Life at Branchwater continued exactly as before, minus one voice in the ambient conversations, minus one observer tracking the small kindnesses and casual cruelties that shaped every workplace.

Diane Fletcher received a commendation from HR for her sensitive handling of a potentially dangerous situation involving a socially isolated autistic employee. Her performance review noted her exceptional skills in building trust with difficult personalities and maintaining a safe environment for all staff.

Hazel Wincott never learned what had been said in the conversation that led to her complaint. She never discovered that someone had twisted a man's concern for her well-being into something predatory and threatening. She never knew that her name had been used not in obsessive songs about her, but in songs about workplace kindness and human decency—music that had tried to capture the rare pleasure of seeing someone treat others with patience and grace.

The truth died with Michael Henley on New Year's Eve, leaving behind only the distorted version that had destroyed him. In the end, that became the official story: a lonely autistic man had become fixated on a female coworker, had been disciplined, and had chosen to end his life rather than address his problematic behavior.

It was a clean narrative that protected everyone except the person who could no longer defend himself. The real monster—the person who had gained trust only to betray it, who had transformed innocent words into social weapons, who had enjoyed the drama of destroying someone's reputation—remained safely hidden behind expressions of concern and professional sympathy.

In the corporate environment of Branchwater Marketing, where efficiency and team dynamics mattered more than individual truth, Diane Fletcher's version of events became accepted reality. It was easier that way. It required no uncomfortable questions about who could be trusted with private conversations, no examination of how quickly workplace gossip could destroy someone, no acknowledgment that the quietest autistic person in the office might also be the most vulnerable.

The memorial service lasted forty-five minutes. The cleaning crew removed all traces of Michael Henley's eight-year presence in two hours. The new employee started on Monday, bringing fresh energy to a workspace that had already forgotten the autistic man who died rather than continue navigating its casual cruelties.

The office hummed along efficiently, an ecosystem of ambition and professional courtesy where predators wore friendly faces and trust was just another commodity to be exploited. In cubicles and conference rooms, conversations continued about weekend plans, project deadlines, and who was dating whom.

Outside the windows of Branchwater Marketing, the lake where Michael Henley had died reflected the winter sky like a perfect mirror, holding no memory of the autistic man who'd chosen its peaceful shore for his final rest. The water lapped against frozen banks with the same rhythm it had maintained for centuries, indifferent to human stories of trust and betrayal, cruelty and kindness, the small tragedies that unfolded in office buildings every day when people trusted the wrong person.

In the end, the lake remembered nothing, and neither did anyone else.

The Absurdity of Forgiveness

Midnight. John Wilkes Booth materialized in the presidential box of Ford's Theatre for the thirty-seven thousandth, four hundred and ninety-second time. He'd been counting.

"Evening, Mr. President." He nodded to the tall, gaunt figure seated in the chair where he'd died one hundred and fifty-nine years ago. "Ready for another show?"

Lincoln's ghost didn't acknowledge him. The sixteenth president sat rigid, hands folded, staring down at the empty stage with those deep-set eyes that had witnessed a nation tear itself apart. High cheekbones cast sharp shadows in the dim light that seemed to come from his spectral form.

Booth straightened his waistcoat---the same one from that April night---and cleared his throat. The fabric felt real under phantom fingers. "Got something special tonight. Farmer and his prize pig." He paused, hoping for some flicker of interest. Nothing. "The pig talks. Quite witty, actually."

Lincoln remained motionless as granite.

Booth had tried everything over the decades. Jokes, stories, pratfalls, vaudeville routines he'd learned watching performers rehearse on this stage. The theater's acoustics carried every whispered practice session, every fumbled line, every burst of nervous laughter from actors who couldn't see the two ghosts watching.

The curse was specific: he could only move on if he could make Abraham Lincoln laugh. One genuine laugh. That's all the universe demanded.

Might as well move mountains.

"Very well." Booth paced behind Lincoln's chair. His feet made no sound, but old habits clung like stage makeup. "This farmer notices his pig seems unusually intelligent, so he enters it in the county fair's talent contest..."

He launched into the joke, complete with different voices, physical comedy, even a little tap dance during the punchline. Back when he'd had a body, critics praised his commanding presence, his ability to fill a theater with just a gesture. Death hadn't dimmed his theatrical instincts.

Lincoln didn't twitch.

Booth's shoulders sagged. "Tough crowd." The phrase slipped out---he'd heard a comedian use it here in 1987. The living rarely saw them, but ghosts could observe everything. He'd become Ford's Theatre's most dedicated audience member, watching the world change from this single vantage point.

Bitter truth twisted in his gut. Back then, crowds roared for him. Women threw flowers at his feet. Critics called him America's darling, praised his voice, his presence. All those stages, all that applause---and now he performed nightly for an audience of one who refused to react.

Years blurred together in endless repetition. He'd watched minstrel shows give way to vaudeville, vaudeville to motion pictures, silent films to talkies. Radio comedy, television sitcoms, stand-up routines---each era brought new forms of humor. Booth studied them all, borrowed what he could, adapted everything to his nightly performances.

"Maybe you'd rather hear some Shakespeare?" Booth dropped into the chair beside Lincoln. "'Now is the winter of our discontent'---"

"I know the speech."

Booth nearly fell through his chair. In all these years, Lincoln had spoken maybe a dozen times, never in response to his attempts at humor.

"Ah! You do speak! Wonderful!" His voice cracked. "Then maybe you could tell me what might amuse you? I've tried comedy, tragedy, farce, musical numbers---hell, I even tried learning to juggle, though oranges don't exactly cooperate with spectral forms."

The juggling had taken three months in 1923. He'd watched a performer practice on this stage night after night, young man preparing for his circus audition. Booth never found out if he made it. The living moved on; the dead remained.

Lincoln turned his head slowly, fixing Booth with that penetrating stare. "Why do you persist?"

"Why?" Booth blinked. "Because I'm cursed, obviously. Doomed to haunt this place until I can make you laugh. Surely you understand supernatural punishment."

It had taken decades to accept it. At first, he'd raged, tried to leave the theater, attempted to interact with the living. Nothing worked. He was bound here as surely as if chains held him. The only variable in his existence was Lincoln---stoic, unmoving, eternally present.

"I understand punishment." Lincoln's voice carried the weight of years. "I sit in this chair every night, watching the place where I died, unable to move forward because my killer won't let me rest."

The revelation changed everything---shifted the foundation of his understanding like tectonic plates realigning. The theater seemed to grow colder, dust motes freezing in the dim light. "I... what do you mean?"

"Your curse keeps me here too. We're bound together, you and I. Neither of us can find peace until you fulfill your task."

Booth stared at him in disbelief. "You're trapped because of me?"

"A murderer and his victim, locked in eternal proximity." Lincoln's mouth twitched. Not quite a smile, but something. "Yes, I'd say there's a certain poetic justice to it."

"But I never meant... I thought only I was..."

Lincoln leaned back in his chair. "Mr. Booth, do you imagine you're the only one who pays for that night?"

Booth slumped in his chair. One hundred and fifty-nine years, and he'd never considered that Lincoln might be suffering too. He'd been so focused on his own torment, his own need for release. All those nights, all those performances, and he'd never asked Lincoln how he felt about their shared imprisonment.

"I'm sorry." The words came out cracked, barely a whisper. "I'm truly sorry."

"For which part?" Lincoln asked. "The murder, or the terrible jokes?"

Was that---was Lincoln making a joke? Booth looked up hopefully, searching the president's weathered features for any sign of humor.

"Both, I suppose. Though I still think my routine about the talking pig has merit."

"The pig that wins the talent contest by reciting the Gettysburg Address?"

"You were listening!"

"I listen to everything. What else do I have to do?"

Hope flickered in his chest like a candle flame in a draft. "So you've heard all my material?"

"Every last painful word."

In the early years, Booth had tried shock value---crude jokes, bawdy songs, even reenactments of famous scandals. Nothing worked. Lincoln's moral sensibilities seemed unshakeable, even in death. Later, Booth had moved to observational humor, commenting on the changing world. He'd narrated fashion trends, technological advances, political shifts. Lincoln listened but never laughed.

"And none of it was even remotely amusing?"

Lincoln considered this. The theater settled around them with familiar creaks and sighs, old wood expanding and contracting in phantom temperature changes that followed their moods. "There was a moment... last Tuesday, when you slipped on that imaginary banana peel and disappeared through the floor. The timing was... adequate."

"Adequate!" Booth leaped up. "That's practically a standing ovation coming from you!"

The banana peel routine had been inspired by a vaudeville performer in 1902. The man had perfected the art of the pratfall, making it look effortless and inevitable. Booth had practiced for months, learning to time his "slip" with mathematical precision, adding his own theatrical flair with flailing arms and melodramatic cries.

"Don't let it go to your head."

"Too late! I'm already planning my encore." Booth began pacing again, energy renewed. The floorboards groaned under his feet. "But maybe... maybe I've been approaching this wrong. I've been trying to entertain you like you were any audience member. But you're not, are you? You're Abraham Lincoln. You've seen the worst of human nature, the best of it too. You carried the weight of a nation through its darkest hour."

Lincoln considered this. Somewhere in the theater's depths, a door creaked---probably just the building settling, though sometimes Booth wondered if other spirits wandered these halls.

"So what would make a man like that laugh? Not silly jokes or slapstick. Something deeper. Something that speaks to the absurdity of existence itself."

"Such as?"

Booth stopped pacing. The answer had been staring him in the face for over a century. "Such as the fact that I---John Wilkes Booth, assassin, villain, the man who killed you---have spent the last hundred and fifty years desperately trying to make you laugh. That I've become so invested in your happiness that I learned to tap dance."

The tap dancing had been particularly challenging. He'd watched a prodigy practice here in 1935, a young man with lightning feet and rhythm in his bones. Night after night, Booth had mimicked the steps, learning to create the sound of tapping even without physical feet to strike the floor. It was all about intention, the ghostly memory of movement.

"I've also mastered balloon animals, though ghostly balloons present certain challenges." Booth sat back down, studying Lincoln's profile in the dim light. "Do you know what the strangest part is?"

"Tell me."

"I think... I think I've come to respect you."

The admission surprised him. When had that happened? Somewhere between the thousandth and ten-thousandth performance, his hatred had begun to fade. Watching Lincoln night after night, seeing his patience, his dignity even in imprisonment, had worn down Booth's old resentments like water over stone.

Lincoln turned to face him fully. "Respect me?"

"Yes. I hated you in life, you know. Hated everything you represented." The words felt strange in his mouth---he'd held onto that hatred for so long, it had become part of his identity. "But death has a way of clarifying things, doesn't it? I've had time to observe, to learn. I've watched this country change, watched people fight for the freedoms you died defending. I've seen your legacy grow while mine..."

He'd watched civil rights marches flicker across television screens in the theater lobby. He'd seen Martin Luther King Jr. invoke Lincoln's name at the foot of his memorial. He'd watched as America slowly, painfully, tried to live up to the ideals Lincoln had died for.

"And what have you concluded?"

Booth was quiet for a long moment. The theater breathed around them, old timber and plaster holding the weight of history. "That I was wrong. About everything. You weren't the tyrant I thought you were. You were just a man trying to hold a fractured nation together. And I..." He swallowed hard, though ghosts had no need for such gestures. "I was the monster."

"We all make choices. Some lead to greatness, others to infamy."

"But don't you see the cosmic joke in all this?" Booth stood again, gesturing wildly. "Here we are, murderer and victim, trapped together for eternity. And my only hope of escape is to bring you joy. Me! The source of your greatest sorrow! It's like... it's like..."

"Like God has a sense of humor?"

"Yes! Exactly!" Booth's voice echoed off the theater walls, bouncing back from empty seats that had witnessed a thousand dramas. "The universe has turned me into your personal court jester, doomed to perform until I can prove that even the darkest tragedy can be transformed into something... something..."

"Absurd?"

"Redemptive." The words came out with force, carrying decades of accumulated understanding. "The man who brought you darkness must learn to bring you light."

He thought about all the performances---puppet shows with spectral marionettes, magic tricks learned from touring magicians, stand-up routines adapted from comedians who'd graced this stage. Each attempt had been a small act of defiance against despair, a refusal to surrender to hopelessness.

Lincoln leaned back in his chair, and for the first time since Booth had known him, the president looked genuinely relaxed. "That's quite a theological interpretation."

"I've had time to think about it. Roughly a century and a half worth of time." Booth grinned, feeling lighter than he had in decades. "Would you like to hear my theory about purgatory and the fundamental nature of justice?"

"I'm afraid to ask."

"Well, it starts with the assumption that Hell isn't a place but a relationship..."

"Mr. Booth."

"Yes?"

"You're rambling."

"Oh. Right. Sorry." Booth composed himself, straightening his waistcoat. "I get excited when I think I'm onto something profound. The point is, maybe this isn't just about making you laugh. Maybe it's about earning the right to make you laugh. Learning to be worthy of your forgiveness."

The realization had come sometime around his twentieth thousandth attempt. The curse wasn't arbitrary torture---it was rehabilitation. Every night, he had to confront his victim, had to try to bring joy to the man he'd murdered. It was a lesson in empathy, forced repetition until understanding finally dawned.

"And do you think you've learned that?"

Booth considered the question seriously. The theater held so many memories---famous actors who'd graced this stage, the building's near-demolition in the sixties, preservationists fighting to save the place where democracy had nearly died. People fought to preserve the site of their nation's greatest wound, understanding that some scars were too important to heal completely.

"I'm trying to. Every night, I'm trying to."

They sat quietly. The theater felt different somehow---warmer, less oppressive. Dust motes danced in the phantom light, and the building's familiar creaks sounded less like moans of despair and more like sighs of contentment.

"You know," Booth said eventually, "I never asked you about that night. What you remember."

"Why would you want to know?"

"Curiosity, I suppose. I've relived my version thirty-seven thousand times. I wonder about yours."

Lincoln was quiet for so long that Booth thought he wouldn't answer. The theater's acoustics carried distant traffic from the street outside---late-night revelers heading home, the city's heartbeat continuing its eternal rhythm.

"I remember laughing."

"What?"

"At the play. 'Our American Cousin.' There was a line---something about drafts. I laughed." Lincoln's voice grew soft, distant. "Mary had been worried about me. Said I'd grown too serious, too burdened by the weight of office. She thought an evening at the theater might help restore my sense of humor."

His chest tightened---a phantom pain that had no business existing in a spectral form. "I remember that laugh. I heard it from backstage, just before I..."

"Before you entered stage right."

"You saw me coming?"

"I saw a man with a gun. I thought, in that split second, that this was how it would end. But I also thought about that laugh, about the joy I'd just felt. I was grateful for it."

The words stunned him. "Grateful?"

"To die having just experienced happiness. There are worse ways to go."

Booth stared at him. The revelation changed everything---shifted the foundation of his understanding like tectonic plates realigning. "You were grateful to die laughing?"

"I was grateful to die knowing I could still laugh. The war had taken so much from me---my youth, my idealism, my faith in human nature. But sitting in this box, watching that silly play, I remembered that joy was still possible. Even in the darkest times."

"That's why you won't laugh for me. You already had your last laugh. It was perfect, and I interrupted it."

"Perhaps."

"So what you need isn't just any laugh. You need a laugh that's worthy of replacing that one. A laugh that justifies the interruption."

Lincoln turned to study him, and Booth saw something new in those deep-set eyes---not just patience, but genuine curiosity. "And do you think you can provide such a laugh?"

Booth thought about it seriously. What could be funny enough to justify murdering a president? What joke could be worth the pain he'd caused, the history he'd altered, the life he'd stolen?

"I don't know. But I think... maybe that's not the right question."

"What is the right question?"

"Maybe it's not about replacing that laugh. Maybe it's about under-standing why you laughed in the first place. What brought you joy in that moment."

Lincoln nodded slowly. In the theater below, a security light flick-ered---some automated system cycling through its nightly routine, unaware of the two ghosts debating the nature of redemption in the presidential box.

"Tell me what you think brought me joy."

Booth stood and walked to the railing, looking down at the stage where so many performers had tried to bring joy to audiences over the years. The space held the memory of every laugh, every gasp, every moment of shared emotion between performer and audience.

"You laughed because, for just a moment, you forgot about the war. About the casualties and the politics and the weight of keeping the nation together. You laughed because you were just a man watching a silly play with his wife."

"Go on."

"You laughed because comedy reminds us that we're human. That despite all our grand purposes and noble causes, we're still ridiculous creatures prone to slipping on banana peels and getting caught in embarrassing situations." Booth turned back to Lincoln, something crystallizing in his mind. "You laughed because laughter is the sound we make when we recognize our shared humanity."

"And what does that tell you about your task?"

"That I've been approaching it all wrong. I've been trying to be funny *for* you, instead of trying to be human *with* you."

The understanding hit him. All those performances, all those des-perate attempts at humor---he'd been performing *at* Lincoln, not *with* him. He'd been trying to extract laughter rather than share it.

Booth walked back to his chair, but instead of sitting, he knelt beside Lincoln's seat. "Mr. President, may I tell you something I've never told anyone?"

"Please."

"I was terrified that night. Absolutely terrified." The confession came out in a rush, words he'd held back for over a century finally finding voice. "I'd convinced myself I was striking a blow for freedom, for the South, for states' rights. But standing behind you with that gun, I knew I was just a frightened actor playing the worst role of his life."

Lincoln's expression softened, the harsh lines of his face relaxing into something almost paternal. "Fear makes us do terrible things."

"I told myself I was a hero, but I knew I was a coward. And afterward, when I broke my leg jumping from the box, when I was running through the Maryland countryside, I kept thinking about that laugh. Your laugh." Booth's voice cracked. "It was so genuine, so unguarded. I realized I'd never laughed like that in my entire life."

"Why do you think that was?"

"Because I'd never allowed myself to be that human. I was always performing, always trying to be larger than life. But you... even carrying the weight of the presidency, even in the middle of a civil war, you could still find joy in a simple joke."

Booth stood and began pacing again, but slower this time, more thoughtful. "I've had a lot of time to think about what happened that night. About what I stole from you, from your family, from the country. But I think the thing I stole most was that moment of pure, uncomplicated happiness."

"And now you're trying to give it back?"

"I'm trying to understand it. To learn what it means to find joy without pretense, without agenda. To laugh not because it serves some purpose, but because something is genuinely funny."

Lincoln watched him pace, and for the first time in over a century, Booth felt truly seen---not as an assassin or a ghost or a cursed soul, but as a person struggling to understand the nature of human connection.

"And have you learned that?"

"I think I'm starting to. It took me about thirty-five thousand attempts to realize I wasn't trying to make you laugh---I was trying to make myself worthy of having heard you laugh."

The admission hung between them. The theater's acoustics carried it to every empty seat, every shadowed corner, as if the building itself were listening.

"Mr. Booth."

"Yes?"

"Tell me the one about the pig again."

Booth's eyes widened. Hope flared in his chest, bright and warm. "Really?"

"But this time, give it some dignity. If you're going to tell a story about a pig reciting the Gettysburg Address, at least do justice to both the pig and the speech."

"Of course! Yes!" Booth straightened, feeling a familiar thrill as he prepared to perform. But this time, it felt different---not desperate, but collaborative. "I can do that."

He stood, straightened his coat, and began again. But this time, he didn't just perform the joke---he crafted it, shaped it, made it into something that honored both the humor and the source material.

"There once was a farmer who owned the most remarkable pig. Now, this wasn't just any pig. This pig had somehow learned to speak, though it rarely chose to do so. The farmer, being a practical man, decided to enter his unusual animal in the county fair's talent contest."

Booth found himself slowing down, taking time to develop the story, to give weight to each detail. He described the farmer's nervousness, the pig's quiet dignity, the skeptical crowd gathered around the makeshift stage.

"The pig stepped up to the microphone, and the crowd prepared to mock. But then, in a voice both humble and profound, the pig began: 'Four score and seven years ago, our fathers brought forth on this continent, a new nation, conceived in Liberty...'"

He continued through the entire address, giving the pig a voice that was somehow both porcine and presidential, finding the genuine humor in the juxtaposition without mocking either element. As he spoke the familiar words, Booth felt their weight, their beauty, their enduring power to inspire and unite.

When he finished, Lincoln nodded approvingly. "Better. Much better."

"Thank you." Booth felt genuinely pleased with the performance, not because it might break his curse, but because it had felt right---honest and respectful and true. "I think I'm finally learning the difference between getting a laugh and earning one."

"There is a difference."

"A significant one." Booth sat down again, feeling closer to Lincoln than he had in all their years together. "You know, in all this time, I never asked---do you remember anything else from before? From when you were alive?"

Lincoln's expression grew distant, as if he were looking through the theater walls to some other time and place. "I remember the weight of the office. The decisions that kept me awake at night. The letters from mothers who'd lost their sons." He paused, and silence fell between them. "I remember sitting in this very box, thinking about those mothers, wondering if the war would ever end."

"Were you happy? I mean, before the war, before the presidency?"

"I was content. I had Mary, the boys. I enjoyed telling stories, making people laugh. I was quite the storyteller in my younger days."

"Really?"

"Oh yes. I could spin a yarn with the best of them. Usually tall tales about life on the frontier. The taller the better." Lincoln's eyes grew distant, but warm now, touched with fondness. "I remember one about

a mosquito so large it could carry off a full-grown man. Took him all
the way to the next county before anyone noticed he was gone."

Booth grinned. "That's terrible. I love it."

"The secret was in the telling. You had to commit completely to the
absurdity. Make it sound like the most natural thing in the world."

"Show me."

"What?"

"Show me how you'd tell a tall tale. I want to see the real Abraham
Lincoln, not the marble statue history made you."

Lincoln hesitated, and for a moment he looked uncertain---vulner-
able in a way that reminded Booth that beneath the legend was just a
man who'd enjoyed making people laugh. "I haven't told a story like
that in... well, in over a century."

"Then you're overdue."

Something shifted in Lincoln's expression, a subtle transformation
that seemed to roll back the years. The formal presidential bearing fell
away, replaced by the easy manner of a born storyteller. When he
spoke again, his voice had changed---warmer, more intimate, with the
cadence of someone who understood the power of a well-timed pause.

"Well, there was this fellow named Zeke who lived down by the
creek. Now, Zeke was known throughout the county for two things:
his enormous appetite and his terrible luck fishing."

As Lincoln spoke, Booth found himself leaning forward, caught
up in the story despite himself. The president's whole demeanor had
changed---he was no longer the marble monument, but a man who
understood the joy of shared storytelling.

"One day, Zeke decided he was going to catch the biggest fish
anyone had ever seen. He'd heard tell of a catfish down in the deep
hole that was so large, it had its own postal address."

Lincoln continued the story, building it piece by absurd piece. The
fish grew larger with each telling detail, the struggle more epic, until
finally Zeke found himself engaged in a battle of wills with a catfish the
size of a river barge.

"The fight went on for three days and three nights. By the end of it,
half the town had gathered to watch. Zeke was so exhausted he could
barely stand, but he refused to give up. Finally, on the fourth morning,
that big old catfish just up and surrendered."

"Surrendered?"

"Yep. Swam right up to the bank, rolled over on its side, and said,
'Mister, I give up. You're too stubborn for me. But I'll make you a
deal---you let me go, and I'll tell all the other fish in this creek to

avoid your hook. That way, you'll never have to worry about catching something you can't handle.'"

Booth burst out laughing. He couldn't help it. The image of a giant catfish negotiating with an exhausted fisherman was so ridiculous, so perfectly absurd, that his laughter erupted before he could stop it. It felt good---clean and honest and unforced.

Lincoln smiled at the reaction, and the expression transformed his entire face. "So Zeke agreed, and from that day forward, he never caught another fish in that creek. But he told everyone he'd outsmarted the biggest catfish in the county."

"That's wonderful." Booth wiped at his eyes, though ghosts had no tears to shed. "You really were a storyteller."

"I enjoyed it. There's something magical about making people laugh, isn't there? For just a moment, you give them permission to set aside their troubles and embrace the ridiculous."

"Is that what you were doing? That night at the theatre?"

"Setting aside my troubles? Yes, I suppose I was. Mary had insisted we needed an evening of frivolity. She said I was becoming too serious, too burdened." Lincoln's smile faded slightly, but didn't disappear entirely. "She was right, of course. The war had consumed me. I'd forgotten how to laugh at simple things."

"And then I took that away from you."

"You interrupted it," Lincoln corrected gently. "But you didn't take it away. It's still there, that moment of joy. It always will be."

They sat in comfortable silence for a while, each lost in their own thoughts. The theater felt warmer somehow, less like a prison and more like a sanctuary.

"Mr. President."

"Yes?"

"Would you like to hear a new joke? One I just thought of?"

"Please."

Booth took a deep breath, gathering his courage. This felt different from all his previous attempts---not desperate or calculated, but genuine. "There once were two ghosts trapped in a theater. One spent a century and a half trying to make the other laugh. The other spent the same time trying to figure out why he needed to."

He paused, meeting Lincoln's eyes. The president was listening intently, not with the patient endurance he'd shown for decades, but with genuine interest.

"The first ghost tried everything---jokes, stories, songs, dances, even dramatic monologues about the futility of existence. But then one day, the first ghost realized something. He wasn't trying to make the second ghost laugh. He was trying to understand what laughter meant. And the second ghost realized that he'd been waiting not for a joke, but for a friend."

Lincoln's stern features softened. The corners of his mouth twitched upward, just barely, but it was there---the beginning of something real.

"The twist ending," Booth continued, grinning now himself, "is that they both learned that laughter isn't something you force or earn or achieve. It's something you share. It's the sound that two souls make when they finally understand each other."

Lincoln's lips curved into an unmistakable smile.

"And the moral of the story," Booth finished, his voice warm with affection, "is that the best jokes are the ones where everyone gets to be in on it."

Lincoln's smile widened, and then---finally, after thirty-seven thousand, four hundred and ninety-two attempts---Abraham Lincoln laughed.

It started as a chuckle, low and warm, building into something richer, deeper. Not the polite laughter of a president at a social function, but the genuine mirth of a man who had found unexpected joy in the most unlikely place. It was the laugh of someone who had rediscovered the simple pleasure of shared absurdity, the sound of two souls recognizing each other across the vast divide of history and hurt.

Booth felt the curse lift like a weight being removed from his shoulders. The theater began to shimmer, the boundaries between worlds growing thin as gossamer. But instead of rushing toward whatever came next, he found himself savoring this moment---two old enemies who had become friends, sharing laughter in the place where their strange story had begun.

"Mr. President," he said as the light around them grew brighter, warmer, filled with the promise of something beyond their long imprisonment, "it's been an honor."

"The honor has been mine, Mr. Booth," Lincoln replied, still smiling. "Thank you for the company. And for reminding me that even the darkest nights eventually give way to dawn."

As the last of his earthly bonds dissolved, Booth raised his hand in a theatrical bow---not the desperate gesture of a performer seeking applause, but the graceful acknowledgment of one artist to another. "Ladies and gentlemen, Abraham Lincoln! He'll be here all eternity!"

But even as he said it, he knew it wasn't true anymore. They were both free now, free to move on to whatever came next.

Lincoln's laughter followed them both into the light, echoing through Ford's Theatre long after their spectral forms had faded away.

It wasn't the sound of an audience applauding, but something far more precious---the sound of two souls who had found their way to forgiveness.

A Sicilian Divorce

Lucia Torrino folded the divorce papers one more time, the legal documents crisp and official in her hands. Three months sneaking around Palermo to meet with lawyers who wouldn't ask too many questions. Three months planning how to get out of a marriage that had lasted twenty-four years—twenty-four years of watching Salvo break legs, disappear people, and count stacks of money while she cooked his meals and pretended not to see the blood under his fingernails.

The kitchen window overlooked the olive groves that rolled down toward the coast—gnarled trees her father-in-law had planted after the war, their silver-green leaves catching the hot sirocco wind that swept up from Africa. She still looked at that view every morning—had been staring at it since Salvo brought her here when she was nineteen, naive enough to believe his stories about going legitimate. The olive oil business, he'd called it. Their future. What a joke. The only legitimate thing about Salvo's operation was the oil they pressed once a year when the tourists came through from Agrigento.

She remembered her wedding day, how her mother had grabbed her wrists when she realized what kind of family Lucia was marrying into. "He'll change," Lucia had insisted, smoothing the white silk of her dress. "L'amore cambia tutto." Love changes everything. Her mother had just shaken her head and whispered a prayer to Santa Lucia, patron saint of sight. Twenty-four years later, Lucia finally understood what her mother had been praying for—the sight to see through her husband's bullshit.

"You sure about this, Lucia?" Salvo's voice came from the doorway. He leaned against the frame, arms crossed, studying her with those dark eyes that used to make her stomach flutter. Now those same dark eyes just made her feel cold. He still looked good at forty-eight, still had that street fighter swagger from his days in Agrigento's old quarter. But she knew the signs now. When his left hand tapped his gun twice instead of once, when his shoulders hunched up—that meant he was thinking. About her. About them. About what kind of problem she'd become.

"I'm sure." She set the papers on the marble counter her mother-in-law had imported from Carrara—the same counter where she'd kneaded pasta dough while listening to screams from the basement, where she'd served coffee to men whose hands were still dirty from digging graves. "I want out, Salvo. Tutto finito."

He walked to the espresso machine. Salvo made coffee the same way every single time. Count thirty seconds for the grind. Three taps to pack down the grounds. Heat the milk to exactly sixty-five degrees. She could set her watch by his routines.

"You know it's not that simple." He pulled two cups from the cabinet—the blue ceramic set they'd received as a wedding gift from his nonna. "You've been family for twenty-four years. You think I can just—" He gestured vaguely. "You've seen things. You know how this works."

"I've never said a word to anyone." She'd practiced this lie in the mirror. Never told the carabinieri anything, that was true enough. But Anna knew everything—every detail, every name, every location. Insurance, in case Salvo decided she knew too much.

"And I trust you." The espresso machine hissed as he worked. "But the others, they might not feel the same way."

Lucia watched him prepare the coffee. When his shoulders hunched forward like that, when his left hand checked his gun twice instead of once, it meant he was thinking. About her. About them. About how to handle a problem that had legs and knew where the bodies were buried.

"What are you saying?"

"I'm saying there's a way to handle this. Soddisfa tutti." He handed her a cup, the ceramic warm against her palms. "An old tradition. Goes back to my bisnonno's time."

The coffee tasted bitter on her tongue, though she knew he'd prepared it perfectly. Everything tasted bitter now that she'd made her decision. "What kind of tradition?"

Salvo smiled, but his eyes stayed dead. Same expression he'd worn when he told her about strangling Enzo Battaglia with piano wire behind the cannoli shop. Like he was talking about the weather. "A trial. Seven days in Torre Salsa. You survive, you're free. Clean slate. Even the old men in Agrigento would respect that."

"Survive what?"

"Us." He said it like he was discussing dinner plans. "Me and my crew. Seven days. You make it through, you walk away clean. Hell, I'll even give you the house in Taormina."

She'd loved that house once—back when she thought they might have kids, grow old together, watch sunsets over Mount Etna like normal people. Now she knew how he'd paid for it.

Lucia set down her cup. She could feel her hands starting to shake. She'd heard the stories about Torre Salsa—the nature preserve where bodies washed up on the beaches sometimes. Protected land where cops didn't like to go, where the old families had been handling business for generations. Her grandfather used to tell her about the Greek ruins there, the ancient amphitheater where people fought and died for crowds of Romans. Now she'd be the entertainment.

"And if I don't survive?"

"Then you don't." Salvo's voice was matter-of-fact, like discussing the weather or the price of olive oil. "But think about it, amore. You've lived with me for twenty-four years. You know my methods, my habits. You know how I think. That's more than any of my other targets ever had."

The word 'targets' made her stomach clench. She thought of the others—the informants, the rival family members, the business partners who'd gotten too greedy. Most of them had died quickly, professionally. Salvo prided himself on clean work. But some hadn't been so lucky.

"How many men?"

"Five, including me. Enzo, Carmelo, Giancarlo, and Vito. Fair odds, considering."

"Fair?" The laugh just came out, harsh and bitter. "Five armed men against one woman?"

"One woman who knows all their weaknesses." Salvo stepped closer, his cologne mixing with the coffee smell—Acqua di Parma, the same scent he'd worn on their wedding day. "You've been listening at doors for twenty-four years, Lucia. You know things about them they think you don't. Use that."

She stared at the divorce papers, thinking of her sister Anna in Rome, of the apartment waiting for her, of the life she could have without blood under her fingernails and screams in her memory. Anna had begged her to just disappear, to take the money she'd been secretly saving and vanish into another country. But Lucia knew better. You didn't just leave the family. There was only one way out, and it had to be earned.

"When?"

"Tomorrow. Dawn. I'll drive you there myself." His hand touched her cheek, surprisingly gentle for fingers that had pulled triggers and tightened garrotes. "Part of me hopes you make it, you know. You deserve better than this life."

"Then why not just let me go?"

"Because I can't. You know that." His thumb traced her cheekbone, the same gesture he'd made when proposing to her all those years ago under the lemon trees behind her father's house. "But this way, if you're smart enough and strong enough, you earn it."

That night, Lucia couldn't sleep. She walked through the house, touching things, memorizing. The kitchen where she'd made thousands of meals while pretending not to notice blood on Salvo's shirts. The living room where she'd served coffee to other families, their wives chatting about nothing while the men planned who would die next. The bedroom where she'd listen to him mutter names in his sleep—names of dead people.

In Salvo's study, she found the map of Torre Salsa spread open on his mahogany desk, weighted down with a bronze paperweight shaped like a wolf—a gift from the Palermo family after a particularly profitable collaboration. The map was detailed, hand-annotated with notes in his precise handwriting. The map showed seven thousand hectares of cliffs, beaches, and scrubland. Greek ruins scattered all over the place. Caves carved out by wind and water over the centuries.

She studied the terrain, tracing possible escape routes with her finger. The coastal path would be obvious but exposed, offering no cover from the hunting rifles she knew they'd carry. The inland hills offered concealment but no water sources, and dehydration would kill her as surely as bullets. The archaeological sites might provide hiding spots, but they'd also be obvious places to search.

Lucia memorized the topography, the elevation changes, the seasonal creek beds that might or might not have water depending on recent rainfall. She noted the locations of the ranger stations—abandoned most of the time, but equipped with emergency supplies. The old shepherd's huts scattered through the interior, some marked on the map, others known only to locals who'd grazed sheep there for generations.

Most importantly, she studied the access roads. Only three ways in or out of the reserve by vehicle, all of them monitored by cameras that may or may not be functional. Salvo would post men at each entrance to prevent her escape, but that also meant fewer hunters in the interior.

In the kitchen, she packed supplies with the same careful attention she'd learned from watching him prepare for jobs. A small backpack that wouldn't slow her down. Energy bars wrapped in aluminum foil to prevent noise. The thermos from their camping trips, back when they still pretended to be a normal couple. The thin paring knife she used for vegetables, its edge honed to razor sharpness over years of kitchen work. The pepper spray Anna had given her for Christmas, still in its original packaging because she'd never imagined needing it.

She also took the bottle of pills from the medicine cabinet—Salvo's blood pressure medication. Not for him, but because she remembered reading that certain heart medications could be dangerous in large doses. Everything was a weapon if you thought about it the right way.

From his gun safe, she memorized the combination—their wedding date, because Salvo was predictable about some things—and studied his weapons collection. She couldn't take anything obvious, he'd notice, but she filed away information about ammunition types, effective ranges, and the particular quirks of each rifle. Knowledge was ammunition too.

At dawn, Salvo appeared in the bedroom doorway dressed in hunting clothes—military surplus fatigues and combat boots that had seen real action during his younger years working for families with international interests. He'd even painted his face with camouflage makeup, like this was some kind of game.

"Ready?"

She nodded, though ready seemed like the wrong word for agreeing to be hunted like an animal.

The drive to Torre Salsa took forty minutes through winding coastal roads that carved through limestone cliffs and sparse Mediterranean vegetation. Salvo played Pavarotti on the car stereo, humming along to "Nessun Dorma" while Lucia watched the sea turn from black to deep blue as the sun rose. Such a beautiful morning to die, she thought, then immediately pushed the thought away. She wasn't going to die. She was going to survive, and she was going to make him regret giving her this chance.

They passed through small villages still sleeping in the early morning quiet—Siculiana, with its narrow streets and ancient stone houses; Realmonte, where her nonna had been born in a house that no longer existed. Places where people lived normal lives, worrying about normal things like the price of bread and whether their children would pass their exams. Lucia envied them their innocence.

He parked at the main entrance to the reserve, near the information kiosk with its faded posters about protecting local wildlife and the historical significance of the Greek ruins. No other cars in sight, just endless scrubland stretching toward limestone cliffs that dropped fifty meters to the Mediterranean. The morning was already warm, promising another scorching July day. The air smelled of wild rosemary and thyme, mixed with the salt tang of the sea.

"The rules," Salvo said, engine still running, air conditioning keeping the heat at bay for a few more precious moments. "Seven days. You can hide anywhere within the reserve boundaries. Try to leave, and we call the Carabinieri. Tell them you've been kidnapped, escaped, and are dangerous. They'll shoot first and ask questions later."

"How generous."

"We start hunting at noon. Gives you a five-hour head start." He handed her a piece of paper—a hand-drawn map of the reserve boundaries, more detailed than anything the park service provided. "Cross any of those lines, you're fair game for the authorities."

Lucia studied the map, noting the precision of the boundary markers. Salvo had obviously planned this carefully, probably spent weeks preparing. The reserve was larger than she'd thought, but the boundaries created a natural prison—coast on one side, roads on the other three sides. Nowhere to run except in circles.

"One more thing." Salvo reached into the glove compartment and pulled out the divorce papers, now sealed in a plastic bag to protect them from the elements. "You'll need these when you come back."

She took the documents, feeling their weight through the plastic. "When I come back? Not if?"

"I know you, Lucia. You're stronger than you think." His smile was almost sad, tinged with something that might have been regret. "Just remember—survival isn't just about hiding. Sometimes you have to fight."

She climbed out of the car without another word. Behind her, the engine revved and faded as Salvo drove away. Five hours before the hunt began.

The first thing Lucia did was orient herself. She pulled out a compass—a gift from her father when she was twelve, the only thing of his she still owned—and confirmed her position relative to the map. The main trail led inland from the parking area, following an ancient Roman road that connected the coastal settlements to the interior Greek sites. Other, smaller paths branched off through the scrub, probably game trails used by the wild boar and deer that called the reserve home.

She chose a route that avoided the obvious paths, picking her way through dense maquis vegetation that scratched her arms and caught at her clothes but provided excellent concealment. The scrub was typical Mediterranean brush—juniper, myrtle, rosemary, and thorny Mediterranean buckthorn that could tear skin if you weren't careful. Within an hour, she smelled like the herbs, a natural camouflage that might mask her scent from any tracking dogs they might bring.

The next thing Lucia needed was water. The reserve had several natural springs marked on her map, and she chose one deep in the interior, away from the main paths. The spring bubbled up from limestone rocks, clear and cold despite the heat already building above ground. She filled her thermos and drank deeply, knowing she might not get another chance for hours. The water tasted of minerals and stone, clean and pure in a way that reminded her of childhood visits to her nonna's village in the mountains.

Now, she needed shelter. Not just a hiding place, but a base of operations where she could plan, rest, and prepare for what was coming. A collapsed Greek temple near the spring provided cover from three sides, with ancient Doric columns offering concealment and multiple escape routes. The structure was older than Christ, built by colonists who'd fled the Persian wars and found refuge on Sicily's shores. Now it would shelter another refugee.

She cleared away debris from what had once been the temple's inner chamber, creating sight lines that would let her see anyone approaching from a distance. The fallen stones provided natural fortifications, and gaps between the columns offered firing positions if it came to that. She scattered loose rocks and twigs around the area. Her grandfather had taught her that when they hunted in the Madonie Mountains. "Sempre ascolta la terra," he'd said. Always listen to the earth. Any footstep would make noise now.

By noon, when she heard the first car engine rumbling up the access road, Lucia was ready to turn the tables.

She knew Salvo's methods because she'd lived with them for twenty-four years, had watched him plan operations from the shadows of doorways while pretending to fold laundry or prepare meals. He would split his crew into teams, covering more ground while maintaining communication and backup. He trusted his men, but not completely—he'd keep the most dangerous ones where he could watch them.

That meant Enzo and Carmelo would work together. They were cousins, had grown up together in the narrow streets of Agrigento's old quarter, trusted each other more than they trusted anyone else in the organization. Enzo Barone was smart but impatient, always pushing for action when patience was required. He smoked too much, wheezed when he climbed stairs, complained about his back during long jobs. Carmelo Ricci was careful and methodical, but he had a bad knee from an old motorcycle accident—a weakness that would slow him down on rough terrain.

Giancarlo would partner with Vito. Neither man fully trusted the other, which meant they'd spend as much time watching each other as hunting her. Giancarlo Festa was paranoid and jumpy, the kind of man who saw threats in every shadow. He jumped at car backfires, flinched when phones rang unexpectedly, probably still had nightmares about the Palermo bombing that had killed his younger brother. Vito Lombardo was overconfident and careless, relied too much on his reputation and not enough on his brain. He'd been handsome once, before the knife fight that left him with a scar from ear to chin. Now he tried to make up for his ruined face with swagger.

Salvo would work alone. He always did when it really mattered—never trusted anyone completely when people might die. Which gave him an advantage, but also made him predictable.

From her position in the temple ruins, Lucia heard the vehicles arrive—three cars by the sound of it, engines cutting out at irregular intervals as they positioned themselves at different access points. Radio chatter followed, voices distorted by static but recognizable after years of eavesdropping on Salvo's business calls. They were establishing communication protocols, coordinating their search patterns, probably looking at the same detailed maps she'd studied in his office.

The voices came from the north first, two men arguing about which path to take. Lucia crept through the scrub brush, moving parallel to the main trail with the silence her grandfather had taught her during childhood hunting trips. Through the vegetation, she caught glimpses of Enzo and Carmelo exactly as she'd predicted.

"She's not stupid enough to hide near the ruins," Enzo was saying, his voice carrying clearly in the still air. He was breathing hard already, not in the best shape despite his forty years. Too many cigarettes and too much rich food at family dinners. "Too obvious."

"Maybe that's what she wants us to think," Carmelo replied, limping slightly as they walked. The knee was already bothering him, just as Lucia had hoped. "Salvo says she's been planning this for months. Could have scouted the area."

They passed within fifty meters of her position, hunting rifles slung over their shoulders like weekend sportsmen heading out for wild boar. Weekend hunters pretending to be tough guys. City men who didn't belong out here, already sweating through their shirts and complaining about the heat. Lucia followed them for over an hour, watching, learning how they moved.

Every twenty minutes, they stopped to rest Carmelo's knee. They argued constantly about direction and strategy, voices rising and falling with their frustrations. They shared water from a single canteen, taking turns with an intimacy that spoke of decades of partnership. They never looked back. Never thought that maybe the woman they were hunting might be hunting them.

When they stopped for another rest in the shade of a carob tree, Carmelo sitting heavily on a fallen log while massaging his knee, Lucia made her move.

She approached from their blind spot, using a cluster of limestone boulders for cover. The rocks were scarred with ancient tool marks, evidence of long-dead quarrymen who'd shaped stone for Greek temples and Roman aqueducts. Now they would hide a different kind of work.

Carmelo sat with his back to her approach, rifle propped against the tree while he tended to his injury. Enzo stood nearby, scanning the horizon with binoculars, sweat already staining his shirt despite the early hour. Neither man was prepared for violence from behind.

The paring knife went between Carmelo's ribs like she was cutting veal for Sunday dinner. Found the gap, angled up toward the heart. He made a soft wheeze and fell forward onto the trail.

Enzo spun around, rifle coming up, but Lucia was already moving. The pepper spray caught him full in the face, and he screamed, firing wild shots into the sky as his eyes streamed tears and his throat closed up. She grabbed the rifle as he clawed at his eyes, and the wooden stock cracked against his skull with a sound like breaking pottery.

Enzo and Carmelo were dead. Three left.

She dragged the bodies into the thick brush, using techniques she'd learned from watching Salvo dispose of inconvenient corpses. The maquis vegetation would hide them for days, maybe weeks, and the wild boar would take care of the rest. She took their weapons and ammunition—two hunting rifles with telescopic sights, a pistol from Enzo's shoulder holster, enough bullets to wage a small war.

Most importantly, she found Enzo's tactical radio clipped to his belt, still crackling with periodic check-ins from the other teams. She could monitor their communications now, track their movements, maybe even use the radio to misdirect them when the time was right.

"Enzo, report." Salvo's voice crackled from the radio, tight with the first hint of concern. "We heard gunshots."

She smiled and headed deeper into the reserve with enough weapons to fight a small war.

The next day, everything changed.

She'd spent the night in a cave overlooking the coastal path, listening to radio chatter and planning her next moves. The cave was one of dozens carved into the limestone cliffs by centuries of wind and water, deep enough to hide a person but with multiple exits in case of trouble. Fishermen used to hide in these caves during storms. Smugglers stashed contraband here during the wars. Now she was using them to plan murder.

Salvo was getting worried. Two of his men hadn't checked in since yesterday afternoon, and he was starting to understand that his wife might be more dangerous than he'd anticipated. The radio conversations had become shorter, more professional, tinged with the kind of caution that came when hunters realized they might be hunted.

"Maybe we should call this off," Vito's voice suggested over the radio, the bravado of the previous day replaced by uncertainty.

"Afraid of one woman?" Giancarlo taunted, but there was a hollow edge to his mockery.

"I'm afraid of Salvo's woman. You know what she's capable of."

But Lucia knew what they were capable of too. She'd watched Giancarlo torture a man in their garage three years ago, methodically breaking fingers and removing teeth until he got the information Salvo needed about a rival family's drug routes. She'd seen Vito strangle a teenage boy with his bare hands because the kid had been selling drugs on their territory without permission. The boy had been sixteen, probably someone's son trying to make money for his family.

Now she got to be the monster.

She found them at midday, arguing near the ancient amphitheater ruins about two kilometers inland from her cave. The amphitheater was one of the crown jewels of Torre Salsa, a remarkably well-preserved example of Greek architecture that had once seated three thousand spectators. Tourists came here during the day to take photographs and imagine gladiatorial contests, but the reserve was closed to civilians while her 'trial' was in progress.

Giancarlo and Vito had been searching the caves along the coast, working their way inland with careful precision. Both men looked tired and jumpy, constantly checking over their shoulders and starting at every sound. The heat was getting to them, and their water supplies were running low.

"This is fucked up," Vito was saying, his voice carrying across the stone seating of the amphitheater. "She's just one woman."

"One woman who killed Enzo and Carmelo." Giancarlo spat in the dust, the same nervous habit that seemed to run in their organization. "I say we burn the whole place down, smoke her out."

"With what? This is a nature preserve. Start a fire and every authority in Sicily will be here in an hour."

"Then what do you suggest, genius?"

Lucia circled around behind them, using the amphitheater's ancient seating for cover. The limestone tiers provided perfect sight lines and concealment, and the acoustic properties that had once carried actors' voices to the back rows now let her monitor their conversation from a hundred meters away. She positioned herself in the upper seating, rifle ready, and waited for the perfect shot.

When Vito moved away to relieve himself behind one of the standing columns, she took it.

The bullet caught him in the back of the head, and he crumpled without a sound. The shot echoed through the amphitheater like the crack of ancient whips, and Giancarlo spun around, searching frantically for the source of the gunfire.

"Lucia!" he shouted, his voice cracking with fear. "I know you're there! Come out and we'll make this quick!"

She almost laughed. Twenty-four years of watching him intimidate people, and he still thought fear was his best weapon. But Lucia wasn't afraid anymore. Fear was what had kept her trapped in that house, cooking meals for murderers and pretending not to hear the screams from the basement.

She put the second bullet through his chest, and he toppled backward onto the ancient stage where Greek actors had once performed tragedies. Perfect timing.

Half of them dead now. Just Salvo left, plus whoever he'd kept with him.

That night, Lucia camped high in the hills where she could see the roads, monitor radio traffic. The Mediterranean stretched forever below, dotted with ship lights. People out there had no idea a woman was learning to kill just kilometers away.

Learning she was good at it.

Salvo's voice crackled through the static. Tight. Maybe respectful.

"Lucia, I know you're listening. Three of my best men."

She keyed the radio. No point hiding now. "Your best men were sloppy. Twenty-four years of easy money made them soft."

"Maybe. But you know how this ends."

"Yeah." She looked out over the moonlit hills where she'd become someone else. "With me walking out of here."

Static filled the air for a long moment. When he spoke again, his voice was different—harder, more focused. "We'll see about that, amore."

The third day brought rain, turning the coastal paths treacherous and washing away tracks. Lucia used the weather to her advantage, moving freely through the reserve while visibility remained low. The rain soaked through her clothes and made every step treacherous, but it also masked her scent and muffled the sound of her movement.

She found Salvo's new camp near the main entrance—a professional setup with thermal equipment and night vision gear that he must have retrieved from one of their safe houses. He wasn't playing games anymore, had brought out military-grade surveillance equipment and enough weapons to arm a small platoon.

She wasn't playing anymore either.

She waited until the rain stopped and he left camp to search the southern section. Then she snuck in and destroyed everything she could find. She slashed his sleeping bag and poured out his water supplies. She smashed his thermal imaging scope with a rock and scattered his ammunition into the brush. She left his radio intact but reprogrammed the frequencies to useless channels.

When he returned that evening, he found chaos.

"Very clever," his voice said over the radio later that night. "But you're only delaying the inevitable."

"Am I? Because it seems like you're the one running out of options."

"I have options you haven't considered."

"Such as?"

The line went dead, but Lucia wasn't worried. She knew every trick in Salvo's playbook, every contingency he might have planned. He was running out of time, running out of men, and running out of ideas.

On the fourth day, she began hunting him in earnest.

Salvo had moved again, abandoning his ruined camp for a new position somewhere in the northern section of the reserve. But he was limited now, forced to carry everything he needed on his back, cut off from resupply and reinforcement. For the first time in their marriage, he was the one at a disadvantage.

Lucia tracked him through the morning, following broken branches and disturbed earth with skills her grandfather had taught her during childhood summers in the mountains. Salvo was good at this, but he was used to the city—concrete and steel, places where you could predict the angles. Out here in the scrub, he was out of his element.

She found signs of his passage near the old shepherd's huts—a cigarette butt (he'd started smoking again under stress), a scrap of fabric caught on a thorn bush, boot prints in the soft earth near a seasonal stream. He was heading for the archaeological sites, probably planning to use the ruins for defensive positions.

Lucia had different ideas.

On the fifth day, she found the trap.

Salvo had returned to the collapsed temple where she'd first made camp, and he'd prepared a welcome for her possible return. Trip wires connected to small explosive charges, probably taken from their demolition jobs in Catania. Motion sensors rigged to spotlights powered by car batteries. A killing field designed to catch her if she tried to revisit familiar ground.

But Lucia didn't plan to return to the temple. She planned to make him come to her.

She spent hours preparing her own trap, using techniques she'd learned from watching him work over the years. A deadfall made from loose rocks positioned above the narrow canyon he'd have to cross to reach the temple. Pressure plates hidden under loose stones that would trigger a rockslide. And the finishing touch—his own explosive charges, carefully removed from the temple and rewired just for him.

The sixth day passed in careful preparation and patience. Lucia refined her trap, tested the mechanisms, and waited for Salvo to make his move. She knew he would come eventually—his pride wouldn't allow him to admit defeat to a woman, especially not his wife.

On the sixth evening, she was ready for him.

"Salvo," she called over the radio. "I have something that belongs to you."

"What's that?"

"Your wedding ring. I found it near Carmelo's body. Must have fallen off when you helped him set up his position yesterday."

Silence. Then: "I'm not wearing my wedding ring."

"No? Then whose ring is this?" She keyed the radio again, letting him hear the metallic clink of gold against stone. "S.T. and L.B., June twelfth, nineteen ninety-four. That's what's engraved inside."

More silence. Salvo was thinking, trying to figure out how she could have his ring when he was certain he'd left it at home. But she'd taken it from his nightstand three days ago, a small deception saved for exactly this moment.

"Where are you?" he asked finally.

"The temple. Where it all started."

She heard him moving through the scrub, boots crunching on loose stone as he approached the trap she'd spent all day preparing. He was being careful, but not careful enough. Twenty-four years of marriage had taught her to recognize his footsteps, his breathing patterns, the particular way he moved when he was focused on violence.

The first explosion brought down half the canyon wall, blocking his escape route back toward the entrance road. The second charge took out the spotlight he'd rigged at the temple, plunging the area into darkness. In the confusion and dust, Lucia slipped through the shadows.

"Hello, Salvo."

He spun around, pistol in hand, but she was already inside his reach. Giancarlo's knife—bigger than her paring blade—went between his ribs like the others.

Salvo looked down at the handle in his chest, then at her face. Blood spread across his shirt, black in moonlight. "You always were too good for this life."

"I know."

He fell among the ancient stones where Greek priests once offered sacrifices. Lucia watched until his breathing stopped. Then she took her divorce papers from his jacket.

The documents were stained with dust and blood, but still legible.

On the seventh morning, Lucia walked out of Torre Salsa Nature Reserve.

She cleaned herself up in a freshwater spring, washing away six days of dirt and blood. Her clothes were ruined—torn and stained beyond saving—but she found clean ones in Salvo's abandoned supplies. She braided her hair and put on lipstick she'd been carrying for six days without using.

The Carabinieri found her at the main entrance, sitting on a stone marker with her divorce papers folded neatly in her lap. She looked like any other tourist who'd come to visit the archaeological sites, except for the dried blood still caked under her fingernails and the emptiness in her eyes.

They asked questions she answered with care, explaining about the old family tradition, about surviving her trial, about earning her freedom according to the way these things had always been handled. The officers were young, probably from the mainland, unfamiliar with Sicilian traditions and the particular accommodations that authorities had always made for certain families.

The investigating team found five bodies scattered through the re-serve over the following days. Wild boars, they concluded after a cur-sory examination. The animals could be aggressive, especially during the summer breeding season when territorial disputes were common. Tragic hunting accident. These city men should have known better than to venture into protected wilderness without proper preparation and respect for the local wildlife.

Lucia signed the papers in front of witnesses, her signature neat and precise despite the ordeal she'd endured. The divorce was final, official, blessed by tradition and sealed in violence that no court would ever investigate.

Three months later, Lucia sat in Anna's apartment in Rome. The evening news talked about "restructuring" in the Agrigento organization. New leadership. Modern methods. The old traditions giving way to contemporary business practices.

Anna poured Barolo, settled beside her. "Any regrets?"

Lucia looked at her divorce papers, framed between Anna's diploma and their parents' photograph. "Just that it took me twenty-four years to file them."

The wine tasted good. Clean. Somewhere in Sicily, the olive groves still rolled down toward the Mediterranean, but someone else worried about them now. Someone who hadn't learned what Lucia learned in seven days among the ruins.

She raised her glass and drank, finally free.

One More Grave to Dance On

T he morphine pump clicked every six minutes. Francine sat beside her mother's hospital bed, watching Isabelle's chest barely rise and fall under the blue blanket. Three months ago, Mom was teaching at the conservatory, terrorizing students with that steel ruler. Now cancer was eating her from the inside out.

"Need to go to Sainte Pierre Cemetery," Isabelle whispered.

Francine looked up from her magazine. Some celebrity's beach body grinned from the cover. "Mom, you can't even walk to the bathroom."

"Don't need to walk." Isabelle's eyes opened---still that blue that stopped casting directors cold. "Wheelchair."

"To visit Dad's grave?" Francine's father had been buried there seven years ago, his plot marked with simple granite that read *beloved husband and father.*

"No." Isabelle's fingers gripped the bed rail, knuckles white against the blue hospital gown. "To dance on Natasha's."

Francine set down her magazine. "What?"

"Natasha Volkov. Section C, plot 127." Isabelle's lips curved into something that wasn't quite a smile. "Died four years ago. Liver cancer. Never knew I won."

"Won what?"

"Everything." Isabelle closed her eyes. "The Bolshoi offered her the principal role in *Giselle* in 1987. Did you know that? She turned it down to have that baby with her pianist husband. Chose motherhood over greatness."

Francine had heard this poison her whole childhood---muttered comments during interviews, bitter asides whenever Natasha's name came up. Two dancers who'd trained together and hated each other like blood enemies.

"Never chose anything over dance. Not even you."

The words hit like a slap. Francine had grown up knowing every recital, every birthday party, every scraped knee came second to Isabelle's career. Her mother had been magnificent on stage---graceful, powerful, commanding. Off stage, she'd been a beautiful absence.

"Mom, that's---"

"The truth." Isabelle opened her eyes again. "And the truth is, I won. I had the career she gave up. I danced until I was forty-six. She stopped at thirty-two to raise her precious son. I was better, and now she's dead, and I want to dance on her grave before I join her."

Dr. Crawford had been clear about the timeline when he'd pulled Francine aside yesterday. Maybe weeks, possibly days. The cancer had spread too far and too fast for any meaningful treatment. Hospice care would begin Monday.

"You can't dance," Francine said. "You can barely sit up."

"I can move." Isabelle's hand found the bed controls, raising the head until she sat nearly upright. "Watch."

Despite the IV lines and oxygen tube, Isabelle lifted her arms. Her shoulders rolled back, spine straightening with forty years of muscle memory. Even dying, her arms moved like water, wrists curved perfect as ever.

"Jesus, Mom." Francine's throat went tight. "You're dying."

"All the more reason." Isabelle lowered her arms to the bed. "One last performance. One final curtain call. I want to show her that I'm still here, still moving, and she's just bones in a box."

That night, Francine sat in her childhood bedroom at her mother's house, surrounded by dance posters and yellowed newspaper clippings. *Isabelle Dubois in Swan Lake. Isabelle Dubois in Romeo and Juliet. Isabelle Dubois receives Kennedy Center Honor.* Thirty years of triumph covered every wall.

She'd never found a single photograph of Natasha Volkov in the house.

Next morning, she brought her laptop to the hospital. While Mom dozed between morphine hits, Francine searched. Natasha Volkov---principal dancer with ABT before early retirement. Died four years ago, survived by husband and son. Obituary said "long illness bravely borne."

"She was beautiful," Francine said, showing her mother a photo from 1985. Natasha was luminous---dark hair in a chignon, dark eyes holding secrets, arms perfect in fifth position.

Isabelle stared at the photo. "Adequate."

"Mom."

"I'm being generous." Isabelle's voice carried the sharp edge that had terrified students and fellow dancers alike. "She had technique but no soul. All the emotions she couldn't access in life, she couldn't bring to the stage. That's why she never made it to the Bolshoi. They could see what I saw---she was hollow inside."

Francine closed the laptop. "This is insane. You want me to wheel you to a cemetery so you can---what? Perform a one-woman show for a dead woman?"

"I want her to see that I'm still moving when she can't." Isabelle's breathing had grown more labored, but her voice remained steady. "I want her to know that even dying, I'm more alive than she ever was."

The obsession ate what energy Mom had left. Made Francine call the cemetery three times about visiting hours, music policies. Had to be Chopin's Minute Waltz. Had to bring the Bluetooth speaker from home. She wanted to wear her old practice leotard, the black one with the crossed straps that had been her uniform for twenty years.

"It won't fit. You've lost forty pounds."

"It'll fit." Isabelle's eyes burned. "Has to."

Dr. Crawford pulled Francine aside Thursday. Young for an oncologist, maybe mid-thirties, with the exhausted look of someone who delivered death sentences for a living.

"Your mother's pain is getting worse. We can increase the morphine, but she'll be out of it."

"She wants to go to the cemetery," Francine said. "To visit a friend's grave."

Dr. Crawford nodded. "Many patients want to say goodbye. We can arrange transport---"

"She wants to dance."

The doctor blinked. "I'm sorry?"

"She was a ballerina. She wants to perform one last time. At this woman's grave." Francine felt insane saying it. "They were rivals, and my mother thinks... I don't know what she thinks."

"Mrs. Dubois is approaching end-stage," Dr. Crawford said gently. "Sometimes patients experience confusion, vivid dreams, obsessive thoughts. It's part of the process."

"So you think she's delusional?"

"I think she's trying to find meaning in her final days. If visiting this grave brings her peace, and if she's physically capable of the trip, then maybe you should consider it."

That evening, Isabelle insisted on practicing. Francine helped her sit on the edge of the hospital bed, and despite the tremor in her hands and the obvious pain shooting across her face with each movement, her mother began working through simplified positions. Her port de bras had always been her strongest feature, and even now, her arms carved elegant lines through the sterile air.

"She could never do this," Isabelle murmured, executing a perfect cambré backward despite the IV pole beside her. "Too rigid. Too afraid of looking foolish."

"How do you know what she could do?" Francine asked. "When did you last even see her?"

Isabelle's movements stopped. "1989. The spring gala at Lincoln Center. She was in the corps for *Theme and Variations*. I was the principal in *Diamonds*." She straightened slowly. "She watched me from the wings. I could feel her hating me with every turn, every jump. She knew she'd never have what I had."

"Maybe she was just watching the performance."

"No." Isabelle's voice dropped to almost nothing. "She was feeding on me. Trying to absorb what she couldn't earn. I felt her pulling at me, trying to drain my strength." She looked at Francine directly. "When I came off stage, she was gone. Someone said she'd gotten sick suddenly. Had to leave."

Francine's stomach dropped. "Sick how?"

"Dizzy. Nauseous. Like something had been sucked out of her." Isabelle lay back against the pillows. "That was the night I knew I'd won. She couldn't even stand to watch me anymore."

The black leotard fit better than Francine had expected. Her mother's body had wasted away, but the garment seemed to mold itself to her reduced frame, the fabric still holding the memory of younger muscles. Isabelle sat in the wheelchair wearing the leotard beneath a simple black dress, her hair brushed back in a severe bun despite its thinness.

"You look beautiful, Mom," Francine said, and meant it.

Sainte Pierre Cemetery sprawled across fifty acres of rolling hills dotted with ancient oaks. Francine had called ahead, explaining that her terminally ill mother wanted to visit a friend's grave. The woman in the office had been sympathetic and provided detailed directions to section C, along with a warning about the uneven paths.

The portable speaker sat in Francine's bag alongside a water bottle and her mother's extra pain medication. She pushed the wheelchair along the path. October morning felt warm as spring. Cemetery smelled like fresh-cut grass and damp earth.

"Plot 127," Isabelle said, reading the numbers on a small granite marker. "That one."

Natasha's headstone was simple black granite. *Beloved wife and mother. Her beauty lives on in movement.* A small ballet slipper was carved underneath.

Francine stopped the wheelchair a few feet from the grave. "Here we are."

Isabelle stared at the stone for a long moment. "She's really down there."

"Yes, Mom."

"Set up the music."

Francine pulled out the speaker, connected her phone. Chopin's Minute Waltz filled the quiet cemetery. A groundskeeper in the distance looked up, then went back to his work with a respectful nod.

"Help me stand."

"Mom, I don't think---"

"Help me stand."

Francine helped her mother stand. Isabelle swayed, gripped Francine's arm with surprising strength, found her balance. The black dress fell away, leaving just the leotard. In the morning sun, she looked skeletal---bones and tissue-paper skin.

But when she moved, something changed.

Isabelle's arms rose perfect to fifth position, spine lengthening despite the cancer eating her bones. Small movements, constrained by weakness, but elegant as ever---forty years of training burned into muscle memory. She wasn't dancing on Natasha's grave so much as she was dancing above it, her feet barely lifting from the grass but her spirit soaring.

Francine watched, transfixed. Her mother's face had transformed from the pinched mask of pain she'd worn for months into something radiant. Her eyes were closed, but she smiled as she moved through abbreviated versions of classical positions. *Échappé sauté* became a gentle rise onto her toes. *Grand jeté* became a subtle shift of weight from one foot to the other.

"She's watching," Isabelle whispered, still moving. "Can feel her."

"Mom?"

"So angry." Isabelle smiled wider. "Trying to stop me. But she's just bones now, and I'm still dancing."

The music swelled toward its crescendo, and Isabelle attempted a turn. Her legs shook with the effort, and she began to fall. Francine lunged forward to catch her, but her mother completed the rotation, somehow finding her center despite her body's betrayal.

As the final notes of the waltz faded, Isabelle sank to her knees on the grass directly above the grave.

"Did you see?" she gasped, looking up at Francine with feverish brightness in her eyes. "Did you see how beautiful I was?"

"Yes," Francine said, wiping her face with her sleeve. "You were beautiful."

But as she helped her mother back into the wheelchair, Francine noticed something that made her stomach turn. The grass beneath Isabelle's knees had turned the color of old tobacco, brittle enough that she could hear it crackling when her mother shifted position. And the air above Natasha's grave felt different---not cooler, exactly, but thinner, like the atmosphere at high altitude.

They drove home in silence. Isabelle slept in the passenger seat, her breathing so shallow that Francine kept checking to make sure she was still alive. The black leotard was soaked with sweat, and her mother's skin had taken on a grayish pallor that hadn't been there that morning.

Back at the hospital, Dr. Crawford examined Isabelle with evident concern.

"Her vitals are very weak," he told Francine privately. "The exertion may have accelerated the progression. I'm surprised she had the strength for any physical activity."

"She found it somewhere," Francine said.

That night, Isabelle woke Francine from her doze in the bedside chair.

"She came to me," Isabelle whispered.

"Who?"

"Natasha. In my dream. She was furious." Isabelle's hand found Francine's. "She said I stole something from her. Something that wasn't mine to take."

Francine squeezed her mother's fingers. "It was just a dream."

"No." Isabelle's eyes were wide in the dim light from the hallway. "She's been trying to take it back for years. Every time I performed, every time I moved, she was pulling at me. Trying to reclaim what she gave up." She struggled to sit up. "But today, I took it all. Every bit of grace she abandoned, every moment of beauty she walked away from. It's mine now."

"Mom, you're scaring me."

"I feel her fighting me," Isabelle continued. "Right now. She's trying to drag me down with her, but I won't go. I have her strength now, her abandoned dreams. I can feel them burning inside me."

Francine looked at her mother's face and saw something impossible. The gray pallor was gone. Color had returned to her cheeks, and her breathing seemed stronger, deeper. The hand holding Francine's felt warm and solid instead of the brittle bones it had been that morning.

"I'm getting better," Isabelle said, wonder in her voice. "I can feel it working."

Over the next three days, Isabelle's improvement was undeniable. Her appetite returned---she ate an entire breakfast tray for the first time in weeks. Her pain levels decreased enough to reduce the morphine. She sat up in bed without assistance and asked for her phone so she could call the conservatory about returning to teach in the spring.

Dr. Crawford ran test after test, his confusion evident in the way he kept staring at the results.

"I've never seen anything like this," he admitted to Francine. "Her latest scans show significant reduction in tumor activity. It's not remission exactly, but the cancer appears to have... paused."

"Is that possible?"

"Medically? No. But the evidence is right here." He gestured at the charts spread across his desk. "Her white cell count is normalizing. Her pain markers are dropping. She's actually gaining weight."

That evening, Francine sat beside her mother's bed while Isabelle practiced port de bras, her movements stronger than they'd been in months.

"I want to go back," Isabelle said.

"Back where?"

"To the cemetery. To thank her."

Francine felt her throat go dry. "Mom, no."

"She gave me everything, Francine. All those years of watching me, hating me, she was actually feeding me. Every moment of her resentment, every flash of her envy, it was like a transfusion." Isabelle's eyes gleamed. "And when she died, all of that accumulated energy just sat there, waiting. Waiting for me to come and claim it."

"You're talking crazy."

"Am I?" Isabelle sat up straighter. "Look at me. Three days ago I was dying. Now I feel stronger than I have in years. And it's all because I danced on her grave and took back what was mine."

Francine backed away from the bed. "What was yours?"

"Her talent. Her potential. Everything she threw away when she chose family over art." Isabelle's smile was brilliant and cold. "She preserved it all in her hatred for me. Kept it safe and strong, just waiting for the right moment."

"People don't work that way."

"Dancers do." Isabelle's voice carried complete conviction. "We live in our bodies. Our emotions, our spirits, everything is tied to movement. When she stopped dancing, she didn't just abandon her career. She abandoned herself. But she couldn't let go of what I represented. So she held onto it, nurtured it, fed it with resentment until it became something powerful."

Francine thought about the withered grass, the thin air above the grave.

"I want to go back tomorrow," Isabelle continued. "I think there's more."

"More what?"

"More of her. More of what she stored up. I only took the surface layer." Isabelle's eyes were bright with hunger. "Imagine if I could access all of it. Decades of suppressed artistry, years of accumulated longing. I could dance until I'm seventy. Maybe eighty."

"Mom, stop."

"You could help me," Isabelle said. "We could go together. You were always a decent dancer. Not exceptional, but decent. Maybe there's enough for both of us."

Francine ran from the room.

She spent the night in her car, parked outside the hospital, trying to process what she'd witnessed. Her mother's recovery was real---the doctors confirmed it. But the explanation Isabelle offered belonged in a ghost story, not a medical chart.

By morning, she'd convinced herself that it didn't matter. Her mother was getting better. However impossible, however strange, Isabelle was healing. Wasn't that worth any price?

She found her mother dressed and sitting in the wheelchair by the window, wearing the black leotard beneath her street clothes.

"Ready?" Isabelle asked.

They drove to Sainte Pierre Cemetery in silence. The October air had turned crisp overnight, and dead leaves crunched under the wheelchair's tires as Francine pushed her mother along the path to section C. Other visitors nodded politely as they passed---an elderly man placing flowers on a grave, a young woman reading a headstone with tears in her eyes.

Natasha's grave looked different in the gray morning light. The grass around the headstone had turned completely brown, creating a perfect circle of death in the otherwise green lawn. And the air above the plot didn't just feel thin anymore---it seemed to pull inward, as if something beneath the earth was creating a gentle suction.

"Perfect," Isabelle breathed.

This time, she didn't ask for help standing. She rose from the wheelchair with fluid grace, the black leotard clinging to a body that seemed to have gained muscle overnight. When she began to dance, her movements weren't constrained by illness or age. They were the movements of a principal dancer in her prime.

Francine watched her mother leap three feet in the air above Natasha's grave. Perfect *grand jetés* that should've been impossible. Rapid *fouettés* that would challenge a twenty-year-old. With each movement, she grew stronger, more radiant.

And with each movement, the dead circle around the grave grew larger.

"Feel that?" Isabelle called between spins. "She's fighting. But she gave up her right when she stopped moving."

The pull got stronger. Francine felt it tugging her hair, her clothes, trying to drag her forward. Air went cold despite the sun, and she heard something like screaming coming from below.

"Mom, that's enough!"

Isabelle ignored her, lost in the ecstasy of movement. She was dancing pieces from her greatest roles---the Swan Queen's final solo, Giselle's mad scene, Juliet's awakening. Each performance was flawless, powered by energy that shouldn't have existed in a cancer patient who'd been dying three days earlier.

The brown circle expanded to encompass adjacent graves. The skeletal remains of what had once been flowers crumbled to dust around the headstones. And still Isabelle danced, drinking in whatever force was flowing up from Natasha's grave like a plant absorbing sunlight.

"I can see her," Isabelle laughed, spinning into a series of *pirouettes* that seemed to go on forever. "She's beautiful and she's furious and she's mine now. All of her dreams, all of her lost potential. It's all mine."

The whispered screaming grew louder, and Francine realized it wasn't coming from beneath the ground. It was coming from above, from the air itself, as if something was being pulled apart by forces she couldn't see.

"Stop!" Francine grabbed her mother's arm.

Isabelle froze mid-turn, eyes blazing with fury.

"You have no idea what you've done."

The pulling stopped. Screaming faded. But the dead circle remained, and Natasha's headstone had cracked straight down the middle.

Isabelle sank back into the wheelchair, suddenly fragile again. The color drained from her face, and her breathing became labored. By the time they reached the car, she was unconscious.

Dr. Crawford met them at the emergency room entrance.

"Her vitals are crashing," he said, transferring Isabelle to a gurney. "Whatever happened, she's failing fast."

They lost her twice in the ER, brought her back both times, then moved her to intensive care. Francine sat beside the bed, watching the monitors track her mother's failing systems.

"I should have let you finish," she whispered to Isabelle's unconscious form.

Her mother's eyes opened. "Too late now," she said, her voice barely audible "Had her. Had everything she saved up, and you made me let go."

"I'm sorry."

"She's pulling it back. Stronger than I thought." Isabelle gripped Francine's hand. "More than talent. Love. For her son, her husband, the life she chose. Couldn't take that. That's what's killing me."

The monitors began to alarm. Nurses rushed in, pushing Francine aside as they worked over her mother's failing body.

"She's going into cardiac arrest," someone called out.

Francine pressed against the wall, watching them fight for a life already gone. Her mother's eyes found hers across the chaos.

"Tell them I was better."

The flatline scream filled the room.

They buried Isabelle Dubois on a cold November morning, three weeks after her death. The cemetery chose a plot in section F, as far from Natasha Volkov's grave as possible. Francine had requested the distance, though she couldn't explain why to the confused funeral director.

The memorial service was well-attended. Students, fellow dancers, and critics came to honor a woman who had devoted her life to the art of movement. They spoke of her dedication, her perfectionism, her transcendent performances. The conservatory director read a statement about establishing a scholarship in her name.

None of them mentioned Natasha Volkov.

Francine stood beside the fresh grave after the other mourners had left, watching the groundskeepers fill in the earth that would hold her mother forever. The simple headstone read *Isabelle Dubois---She Danced.*

Turning to leave, something made her look toward section C. Natasha's grave in the distance, grass green and healthy again. Someone had fixed the cracked headstone.

A figure in black stood beside it.

Francine blinked. Gone.

She never went back to Sainte Pierre Cemetery. But on quiet nights, she heard music through her windows. Classical pieces Mom had loved---Chopin, Debussy, Tchaikovsky. And underneath, faint as breath, feet moving in perfect rhythm on a floor between worlds.

Her mother had been right about one thing.

She was still dancing.

Office Poison

I've got the smile down to a science. Fifteen years of practice, and I can make it look like I actually give a damn about your weekend plans. The trick is the eyes—you crinkle them just a little, like you're really listening. Works every time.

People eat it up. They lean in during conversations, share things they shouldn't. I nod at all the right moments, make those little encouraging sounds that keep them talking long after they should shut their mouths.

Candace Fletcher doesn't know it yet, but she's about to become my latest project.

"Morning, Veronica!" She chirps as she passes my desk, coffee mug in hand—one of those ridiculous motivational things about persistence. The kind of crap they sell at Target to make people feel better about their shitty lives.

"Morning, sweetie," I call back, loading my voice with just the right amount of maternal warmth. At forty-two, I'm old enough to play office mom, young enough that nobody sees me coming. "Love that blouse on you. New?"

She stops, preening like a pigeon. "Thanks! Got it on sale at Nordstrom Rack." Leans closer, drops her voice. "God, I shouldn't be spending money, but—my student loans are killing me. I'm living on ramen and hoping my car makes it through the month."

There it is. Financial stress. Christmas morning for someone like me.

I nod sympathetically, filing it away with everything else I know about little Candace. "Oh honey, tell me about it. These days, who isn't feeling the pinch?"

She glances around the office—Mike from accounting doing his usual morning rounds with his coffee and loud voice, the fluorescent lights buzzing overhead like angry wasps. Nobody paying attention to us. "Actually, I've been meaning to talk to someone about this. Can I trust you to keep something confidential?"

Christ, there it is. That little electric buzz you get when they lean in close, ready to spill. Like when you're playing poker and you know—you absolutely know—the other guy's about to fold.

"Of course, dear. What's on your mind?"

Candace perches on the edge of my desk, voice dropping to barely above a whisper. "I think Jackson might be trying to get me fired."

Jackson Reeves. Our department manager. Ambitious as a tick on a dog, recently divorced, still wearing his wedding ring like he forgot to take it off. I've been watching him circle Candace for weeks, waiting for something like this. Not romantically—Jackson's too smart for office affairs. But professionally? She's fresh meat. New to the company, still learning our systems, making little mistakes that he's been documenting like he's building a federal case.

"What makes you think that?" I lean forward, all concerned attention.

"He keeps asking weird questions about my previous job, wanting documentation for things that seem totally normal. Yesterday he made me redo the Morrison account proposal because he said my research methodology was 'concerning.'" Air quotes, frustration bleeding through. "But when I asked him to be more specific, he just said we'd discuss it later."

Oh, honey. Jackson's building a file on you, alright. Probably figures if there's another round of layoffs, better to have his ducks in a row. Poor little Candace doesn't see it coming. But she doesn't need to know I've been watching this train wreck build for weeks.

"Oh sweetie," I breathe, reaching out to pat her hand. "That does sound concerning. Have you thought about talking to HR?"

"That's what I'm worried about. What if I'm overreacting? What if going to HR makes me look paranoid or difficult?"

Perfect. The self-doubt's already there, growing like mold in a damp basement. I just need to feed it a little.

"You know," I say thoughtfully, "I might have noticed a few things myself. Nothing concrete, but..." I let it hang there, watching her face tighten.

"What kind of things?"

I glance around like I'm checking for spies. "Well, I probably shouldn't say anything. Might just be coincidence."

"Please, Veronica. I need to know what I'm dealing with."

"Last week, I saw Jackson coming out of Harvey's office right after you left that meeting about quarterly projections. They both looked pretty serious." True enough—they did look serious. What I don't mention is they were discussing Jackson's board presentation, nothing to do with her. But in Candace's head right now, normal behavior transforms into evidence.

Her face goes pale. "Harvey was at that meeting?"

Harvey Kowalski. Regional director. The kind of man who could erase you from the company roster with a phone call.

"I don't want to worry you unnecessarily," I continue, "but Jackson did seem to be taking a lot of notes during your part of the presentation. More than usual."

Another truth, twisted just enough to poison the well. Jackson always takes notes—that's how he stays ahead of everyone else. But to Candace, sitting here with student loan debt gnawing at her and her car making funny noises, normal behavior becomes conspiracy.

"God," she whispers. "I knew something felt off."

I squeeze her hand gently. "Listen, honey, you didn't hear this from me, but maybe you should start documenting everything. Every interaction, every request, every criticism. If something's going on, you want to be prepared."

Sounds helpful, right? Protective, even. What it actually does is encourage behavior that'll make her look paranoid as hell. People who document every tiny interaction don't do it subtly. Her colleagues will notice the change—the way she'll start responding to simple requests with written confirmations, careful language, defensive body posture.

"You're right," she says, straightening up with new resolve. "I need to protect myself."

"And Candace?" I add, voice gentle but firm. "Maybe keep this conversation between us for now. You don't want word getting back to Jackson that you're onto him."

She nods like a bobblehead. "Absolutely. Thank you so much, Veronica. I don't know what I'd do without someone I can trust."

I watch her walk back to her cubicle, shoulders squared with determination and fear. Beautiful. The next phase will start naturally—she'll begin acting different around Jackson, more guarded, more formal. He'll notice and probably chalk it up to job stress, but he'll also start paying closer attention. Which will make her more nervous, which will affect her work, which will give him actual reasons for concern.

The beauty of this system is I never actually lie. I just present information in a way that lets people draw their own conclusions. Candace will destroy herself, and I'll be the sympathetic shoulder she cries on when it all goes to hell.

By ten-thirty, I'm ready for phase two.

"Morning, Jackson," I say, intercepting him near the coffee machine. The good coffee machine, not the piece of shit they keep in the break room. "You look stressed. Everything okay?"

He glances up from stirring sugar into his cup, and I catch that tightness around his eyes. Probably wondering if his promotion's still on track. "Just the usual end-of-quarter crunch. You know how it is."

"I do indeed." I pour myself a fresh cup, take my time adding cream. Keep him waiting while I speak. "Hope you don't mind me mentioning this, but I've been a little worried about Candace lately."

His attention sharpens immediately. Jackson's greatest strength and weakness rolled into one—he genuinely wants his people to succeed. Makes him vulnerable to suggestions that they might be struggling.

"Worried how?"

"Oh, nothing dramatic. She just seems more anxious than usual. Yesterday she was asking me questions about company policies that made me wonder if she's feeling insecure about her position."

I pause, let him fill in the blanks. "What kind of questions?"

"Things about performance reviews, documentation requirements. The kinds of things someone asks when they're worried about job security." I take a sip, watch him process this. "She might be overthinking things, but I thought you should know in case it's affecting her work."

Jackson frowns. "She hasn't said anything to me about feeling insecure."

"Well, she wouldn't, would she? Nobody wants to admit they're struggling to their supervisor." I lean closer, lower my voice. "Between you and me, I think she might be dealing with some financial pressure at home. She mentioned student loans, car trouble. You know how that can mess with someone's confidence at work."

Now I've planted two seeds: Candace is insecure about her performance, and external financial stress might be affecting her professional judgment. Both technically true, but presented in a way that transforms normal human concerns into red flags.

"I appreciate you letting me know," Jackson says slowly. "I'll keep an eye on things."

"I'm sure it's nothing serious," I add quickly. "She's such a sweet girl. I just know how much you care about your team, and I thought you'd want to be aware."

Sweet. In a professional context, it's almost condescending—suggests someone who's nice but maybe not equipped for serious responsibility. And by framing my information-sharing as recognition of Jackson's leadership qualities, I make him more receptive to my observations.

Jackson nods, already mentally cataloging Candace's recent behavior for signs of the insecurity I've suggested. By lunchtime, he'll be watching her differently. By week's end, their entire dynamic will have shifted.

I return to my desk feeling that familiar satisfaction of a plan in motion. The afternoon passes peacefully as I handle my actual work—senior data analyst, five years with the company, consistently high performance reviews. People assume my talent for creating chaos means I'm incompetent, but it's the opposite. I'm excellent at my job. My reputation for reliability is what gives my observations such weight.

At three-fifteen, Candace appears at my desk again, looking stricken.

"Veronica, can I talk to you for a minute?"

"Of course, honey. What's wrong?"

She glances around nervously. The afternoon shift is in full swing—keyboards clicking, phones ringing, the copy machine churning out reports with that mechanical rhythm that drives everyone slowly insane. "Can we go somewhere private?"

I lead her to the small conference room we use for informal meetings. The one with the broken air conditioning and the motivational posters that nobody ever looks at. Once the door closes, she slumps into a chair.

"Jackson just asked me to stay late tonight to review the Morrison account proposal again. He said he wants to 'clarify a few procedural questions' about my research methods."

Even better than I hoped. Jackson's natural thoroughness, combined with my suggestions about Candace's insecurity, has prompted him to take action that'll look exactly like the persecution she's already primed to expect.

"Oh sweetie," I murmur. "After hours? That seems unusual."

"That's what I thought!" Her voice rises, then she catches herself, speaks quieter. "I mean, why can't we discuss it during normal business hours? And why is he suddenly so focused on my research methodology? I've been using the same process for months."

"Have you considered that he might be building a paper trail?" I suggest gently.

The color drains from her face. "You think that's what this is?"

I reach across the table, take her hand. "I don't want to scare you, but yes, it's possible. Sometimes when companies are preparing for... changes... they need documentation to support their decisions."

Changes. Beautiful word—vague enough to mean anything from departmental restructuring to individual terminations. In Candace's current mental state, she'll assume the worst.

"What should I do?" she whispers.

"Well," I say thoughtfully, "you could try to bring someone else into the meeting. A witness. Maybe suggest that since it's about research methodology, it might be helpful to have someone from Quality Assurance present?"

This advice sounds reasonable but will make her appear confrontational and distrustful. Jackson will interpret her request for witnesses as evidence that she doesn't trust him, which will damage their working relationship further.

"Or," I continue, "you could handle it exactly like you normally would, but make sure you take detailed notes about everything discussed. Email yourself a summary afterward, so you have a timestamped record."

Again, technically good advice that'll create the appearance of paranoid behavior.

"You're right," she says, nodding rapidly. "I need to protect myself."

"And Candace? Maybe it would be smart to update your resume. Just in case. Better to be prepared than caught off guard."

She nods again, looking grateful for my guidance. "Thank you so much, Veronica. I feel like I'm going crazy, but talking to you helps me feel like I'm not just being paranoid."

"You're not being paranoid, honey. You're being smart."

After she leaves, I spend the rest of the afternoon in pleasant anticipation. Tonight's meeting will go badly—not because Jackson has ill intentions, but because Candace will approach it with suspicion and defensiveness that'll affect both her performance and his perception of her competence.

The next morning brings phase three.

I arrive early, as always, position myself near the kitchen area where I can observe the morning coffee ritual. The fluorescent lights are already humming their angry tune, and the building's heating system is doing that thing where it sounds like someone's strangling pipes in the walls.

Candace looks like hell—hollow-eyed, anxious, her usual cheerful demeanor replaced by something that looks like shell shock.

"How did it go last night?" I ask when she approaches the coffee machine.

She glances around nervously before answering. The morning crowd hasn't fully arrived yet—just the early birds and the people trying to get ahead of traffic. "Not great. He kept asking really detailed questions about my sources, like he was trying to find problems with my work. And when I asked if we could include someone else in the discussion, he got this look..."

"What kind of look?"

"Like I'd confirmed something he suspected. Like I was being difficult." She pours coffee with shaking hands. "I took notes like you suggested, but I felt so awkward doing it. He definitely noticed."

I nod sympathetically. "I'm sorry, honey. That must have been really uncomfortable."

"The worst part is, I can't tell if I'm overreacting or if my instincts are right. Maybe I am being paranoid."

"Trust your gut," I tell her firmly. "Women's intuition exists for a reason."

Nasty little piece of advice, that one. Now every anxious feeling becomes proof she's right to worry. Every nervous twitch becomes "women's intuition." Beautiful how that works.

Around ten o'clock, I implement the next phase by approaching Derek Lawson, one of Candace's closest allies in the office. Derek's a good man—loyal, protective of his friends, quick to anger when he perceives injustice. These qualities make him extremely useful.

"Derek, can I ask you something?" I settle into the chair beside his desk. His workspace is cluttered with family photos and Star Wars figurines—the mark of someone who brings his whole self to work. "Have you noticed anything different about Candace lately?"

He looks up from his computer screen, immediately alert. "Different how?"

"She seems really stressed. More than usual. I'm worried about her."

Derek frowns. "Now that you mention it, she has seemed a little off this week. Kind of jumpy."

"I think she might be having some trouble with Jackson," I say carefully. "She mentioned something about him questioning her work methods, asking her to stay late for meetings. I don't want to get involved in office politics, but..." I trail off, let him draw his own conclusions.

"Jackson's giving her a hard time?" Derek's voice hardens slightly.

"I don't know if I'd put it that way. But she's definitely feeling pressured about something. Maybe I'm reading too much into it."

Derek's already mentally shifting into protective mode. "No, I'm glad you mentioned it. Candace is good people. She doesn't deserve to be harassed."

The word harassed is his, not mine. But once it's spoken, it takes on its own momentum.

"I'm sure it's nothing that serious," I say quickly. "Jackson's probably just trying to help her improve. But you know how it is—sometimes good intentions can feel overwhelming when you're already stressed."

"Yeah, well, Jackson needs to be careful about how he handles his people," Derek mutters. "Especially the newer ones."

I nod sympathetically and let the conversation end there. Derek will now watch Jackson's interactions with Candace through the lens of potential harassment. He'll interpret normal supervisory behavior as evidence of inappropriate pressure, and he'll probably mention his concerns to other people.

By lunchtime, a small but growing group of Candace's friends will be aware that she's "having problems with Jackson." The story will shift and evolve with each telling, becoming more dramatic and more damning.

The beauty is that I never actually accuse anyone of anything. I simply express concern, share observations, ask questions that allow other people to reach their own conclusions. When the inevitable explosion happens, I'll be seen as someone who tried to help, someone who noticed the warning signs but couldn't prevent the tragedy.

Friday afternoon brings the culmination I've been orchestrating all week.

I'm working quietly at my desk when raised voices from Jackson's office cut through the usual office noise. The words aren't clear, but the tone is unmistakable—anger, frustration, accusation. The kind of sound that makes everyone stop what they're doing and pretend they're not listening.

The door opens and Candace emerges, face flushed with fury and tears. Jackson appears behind her, looking confused and frustrated, still holding some papers in his hand.

"This conversation is not over," he calls after her.

"Yes, it is," she snaps back, loud enough for half the office to hear. "I'm not going to sit there and let you attack my character."

She storms to her desk, begins shoving personal items into her purse with violent efficiency. The little ceramic mug with the motivational quote, the photo of her parents, the emergency snacks she keeps in her drawer. Several people stand up, uncertain whether to intervene or pretend they haven't noticed.

Derek approaches first. "Candace, what's going on?"

"I quit," she announces, loud enough for everyone to hear. The office has gone completely silent—even the phones seem to have stopped ringing. "I'm not going to work for someone who's been sabotaging me since day one."

Jackson emerges from his office, face tight with anger and bewilderment. "Ms. Fletcher, I think we should continue this discussion privately."

"No," she says firmly. "I'm done with private discussions. I'm done with your 'feedback sessions' and your 'procedural questions' and your whole campaign to make me look incompetent."

"I have no idea what you're talking about," Jackson says, voice carefully controlled. "My only concern has been helping you succeed in your position."

"By questioning every decision I make? By making me stay late to justify research methods I've been using successfully for months? By documenting every tiny mistake like you're building a case against me?"

Jackson looks genuinely bewildered. The poor bastard has no idea what hit him. "Candace, I've been trying to help you improve your performance because I thought you were struggling. If my approach was too intensive, we could have discussed—"

"Struggling?" she interrupts. "I wasn't struggling until you started your little investigation. My work was fine until you decided it wasn't."

This is better than anything I could have planned. Candace's paranoia has transformed Jackson's legitimate supervision into evidence of persecution, and her emotional response is making her appear unstable and difficult.

"I'm sorry you feel that way," Jackson says quietly. "But I'm afraid your resignation is not acceptable. We need to discuss this situation with HR before you make any final decisions."

"Fine," Candace snaps. "Let's go to HR. I have plenty to tell them about your management style."

They disappear toward the HR department, leaving the rest of us in stunned silence.

"Jesus," Derek mutters. "I knew something was going on."

"Poor Candace," murmurs Allison from accounting. "She seemed so stressed this week."

I stand up slowly, arranging my expression to show the right mixture of shock and sadness. "I feel terrible," I announce to no one in particular. "She's been so worried about her job security. I tried to reassure her, but..."

Several people turn to look at me with interest.

"You knew she was having problems?" asks Derek.

"She confided in me earlier this week. She was convinced Jackson was trying to get her fired." I shake my head sadly. "I told her she was probably overreacting, but apparently I was wrong."

This creates the impression that I was defending Jackson against Candace's suspicions, which makes me appear balanced and reasonable. It also suggests that Candace's fears were justified, which validates the narrative she's just created.

"That's so messed up," Allison says. "Jackson always seemed like a decent manager."

"Maybe that's the problem," Derek responds grimly. "The ones who seem decent are sometimes the worst."

I nod thoughtfully, letting other people draw their own conclusions about Jackson's character while maintaining my image as neutral observer.

Within an hour, the story has spread throughout the office. Candace Fletcher, the promising new analyst, has quit rather than continue working under a manager who was systematically undermining her confidence. Jackson Reeves, once respected for his supportive leadership style, is now viewed with suspicion by several members of his team.

By Monday morning, both their reputations will be permanently damaged. Candace will be remembered as the woman who had an emotional breakdown and quit dramatically, making wild accusations against her supervisor. Jackson will be remembered as the manager who pushed a promising employee too hard, creating a hostile work environment that resulted in a public resignation.

And I will be remembered as the concerned colleague who tried to help them both.

The following week brings the aftermath I've been anticipating. Jackson seems subdued, more careful in his interactions with staff. Word has reached upper management about the "incident," and Harvey Kowalski has been asking quiet questions about departmental morale. Jackson's upcoming promotion review will now include discussions about his leadership approach and staff retention.

Candace's replacement arrives on Wednesday—a nervous young man named Timothy Cross who seems eager to please and terrified of making mistakes. Perfect material for my next project, if I decide he's worth the effort.

But first, I want to savor the completion of this particular masterpiece.

Friday evening, I stay late to finish some monthly reports. The office is nearly empty, just a few dedicated souls trying to wrap up their work before the weekend. The fluorescent lights have finally stopped their angry buzzing, and you can actually hear the building settling around us—creaks and sighs like an old house breathing.

I'm gathering my things when Jackson appears at my desk.

"Veronica, do you have a minute?"

His voice sounds tired, uncertain in a way I've never heard before. I look up with immediate concern.

"Of course. What's on your mind?"

He sits heavily in the chair beside my desk, runs his hands through his hair. Still wearing his wedding ring, I notice. "I've been thinking about what happened with Candace. Trying to understand how things went so wrong."

I nod sympathetically. "It was a difficult situation for everyone."

"She seemed to think I was deliberately undermining her, building some kind of case against her. But I swear, Veronica, that was never my intention. I was trying to help her improve her skills."

"I know that," I say gently. "Anyone who's worked with you knows you're not that kind of manager."

"Then how did she get that impression? How did normal supervision turn into... whatever she thought was happening?"

This is the moment I've been waiting for. The chance to offer comfort while subtly reinforcing the narrative I've created.

"Sometimes," I say thoughtfully, "people hear what they're afraid to hear rather than what's actually being said. If someone's already insecure about their performance, even helpful feedback can feel like criticism."

Jackson nods slowly. "Maybe I should have been more aware of her emotional state. But she never said anything about feeling pressured."

"She wouldn't, though, would she? People don't usually admit when they're struggling, especially to their supervisor." I pause, let him absorb this. "And honestly, Jackson, I think she was dealing with some external stress that made everything feel more intense."

"External stress?"

"Financial pressure. She mentioned student loans, car trouble. When someone's worried about money, job security becomes even more important. Every interaction with management feels potentially threatening."

See what I'm doing? Making Candace sound like her personal problems scrambled her brain, made her see threats that weren't there. Makes Jackson look like the victim of a confused, desperate woman. Takes all the blame off him and puts it on her shaky mental state.

"I wish I'd known," Jackson says quietly. "Maybe I could have adjusted my approach."

"You couldn't have known because she didn't tell you. She was trying to handle her problems privately, which is admirable but sometimes counterproductive."

Jackson looks up at me with genuine gratitude. "Thank you for listening. And for trying to help her when she was struggling. I know she talked to you about her concerns."

"I tried to reassure her," I say, which is technically true. "But sometimes people are too caught up in their own fears to hear reassurance."

He nods, standing up with visible relief. "I appreciate you being honest with me. It helps to understand what happened, even if I can't fix it."

After he leaves, I sit alone in the darkened office, surrounded by the quiet hum of computers and air conditioning. This is my favorite part—sitting here alone after everything's gone to hell, knowing exactly how I made it happen. Savoring all the little pieces that came together just right.

Candace Fletcher is gone, her reputation damaged and her confidence shattered. She'll struggle to find a new position, constantly second-guessing herself and expecting persecution that may or may not materialize. This'll mess with her for years. She'll second-guess every supervisor, every colleague. Jump at shadows. Probably ruin a few relationships because she can't trust anyone anymore.

Jackson Reeves remains, but his authority has been undermined and his confidence shaken. He'll be more careful with his staff, perhaps too careful, which could affect his effectiveness as a manager. His promotion prospects have been damaged, and he'll spend months trying to rebuild his reputation.

And I remain exactly where I've always been—trusted, reliable, the office confidante who tries to help everyone and succeeds in helping no one.

Neither of them will ever figure out what I did. That's the best part. To them, I was the nice lady who tried to help. Sweet Veronica with the sympathetic ear and the helpful advice. They'll never connect the dots.

Fifteen years I've been doing this. Fifteen years of watching people destroy themselves with a little nudge in the right direction. And you know what? I never have to lie. Not once. I just tell them exactly what they need to hear to make the worst possible decisions.

Take Candace. I never said Jackson was trying to fire her. I just mentioned that he looked serious coming out of Harvey's office. True statement. Let her paranoid little brain fill in the blanks. Same with Jackson—I never called her unstable. I just expressed concern about her emotional state. Also true. Let him draw his own conclusions.

Perfect system. If anyone ever asks, I was trying to help. I can pass any polygraph test they want to give me because I genuinely was trying to help—help them hang themselves with their own rope.

Hell, I didn't even plan for Candace to blow up like that. I was hoping for something slower, more painful. But when she went full drama queen in the middle of the office? Christ, that was better than Christmas morning. The look on Jackson's face when she started screaming about persecution. Priceless.

I gather my stuff and head for the elevator, already eyeing Timothy at his new desk. Kid's nervous as a cat in a dog park, eager to please, jumping every time someone speaks to him. Give me a month and I could have him convinced Derek's stealing his ideas, or that accounting is trying to make him look bad. Those worried little frowns when he thinks nobody's watching? Yeah, I could work with those.

Or maybe I'll play with Derek and Allison instead. Derek's already wound up about "harassment" and Allison loves spreading gossip more than she loves breathing. Could be fun to see how that plays out.

The elevator doors close, and I catch my reflection in the polished metal—middle-aged woman with kind eyes and a gentle smile. The kind of person people trust with their secrets. The kind who always has time to listen.

Tomorrow I'll be back early with my coffee mug, ready for whatever drama people want to share. Ready to be helpful. So damn helpful it hurts.

After all, someone has to keep things interesting around here.

As I drive home through Friday evening traffic, I find myself humming cheerfully. It's been a particularly productive week, and I'm already looking forward to Monday.

There's nothing quite like the satisfaction of a job well done.

Don't Feed the Plants

C onnor Murphy answered the Craigslist ad on a Tuesday morning when his bank account showed $49.32 and his rent was due in five days. The ad itself was weird—most yard work dried up by November, but this one wanted winter maintenance.

YARD WORK - WINTER POSITION - Seeking reliable individual for ongoing property maintenance. Landscaping experience preferred but not required. Must be able to work independently and follow instructions precisely. Discretion essential. $250/week cash. Call Mrs. Ashford.

Connor called right away. At twenty-two, with a community college degree that hadn't gotten him jack shit and student loans that kept growing, he couldn't be picky.

"You sound young," said the woman who answered. Her voice had that crisp way of talking like his high school principal—someone used to being listened to. "How old are you?"

"Twenty-two, ma'am. I've done landscaping before, and I can start right away."

"Can you work without supervision? I travel often, and I need someone who can maintain the property according to specific guidelines."

"Yes ma'am. I'm reliable."

"Good. The position pays two hundred and fifty dollars per week, cash, for about fifteen hours of work. You'll be responsible for general yard maintenance, but there are certain areas that are off-limits. Can you follow those restrictions without question?"

Connor hesitated. The way she said it was strange, but two hundred and fifty dollars cash was more than he'd made at any job lately.

"Yes ma'am. I can follow instructions."

"Excellent. Can you start tomorrow? I'll leave a key and detailed instructions in the mailbox. The address is 1061 Henshaw Drive."

Mrs. Ashford hung up before Connor could ask about the restrictions or what kind of yard work needed doing in winter. But two fifty was two fifty, and he'd figure out the details when he got there.

Henshaw Drive wound through one of the fancy neighborhoods where big houses sat on huge lots behind old oak trees and stone walls. Number 1061 was at the end of a dead-end street—a massive Victorian that looked like it belonged in a horror movie.

Connor parked his beat-up truck in the circular driveway and walked to the mailbox. Inside was a house key and three pages of typed instructions. The first page was normal stuff: clear walkways of snow and debris, check gutters, make sure the outside lights worked.

The second page had tool locations and emergency repair contacts. Standard.

The third page made his skin crawl:

RESTRICTED AREAS – CRITICAL SAFETY INSTRUCTIONS

Under NO circumstances should you enter the garden behind the house.
This area is marked with stone boundaries and is off-limits for safety reasons.
Do not attempt to maintain, trim, or water any vegetation in the garden area.
Do not remove any organic matter from the garden area.
If you observe unusual activity in the garden area, only document it.
These restrictions are non-negotiable.
Violation will result in immediate termination without pay.

Connor read the garden warnings three times. What the hell kind of garden needed warnings like that? And what was "unusual activity" supposed to mean?

He unlocked the front door and stepped into a house that felt like a museum. Heavy furniture, dark wood everywhere, and paintings of dead people staring down at him. Dust floated in the afternoon light, and the air smelled like old lady perfume and something else—something sweet and organic that he couldn't place.

The tool shed was behind the garage, loaded with equipment that probably cost more than his truck. But as he grabbed tools for his first day, his eyes kept drifting to the area behind the house.

A stone wall about four feet high boxed off a chunk of the backyard, maybe fifty by thirty feet. Even from a distance, Connor could see the area was full of green, healthy plants.

Connecticut had been freezing for two weeks. The cold snap in early October had killed everything, and most trees stood bare. But whatever was growing inside Mrs. Ashford's walled garden looked like it was having the best summer ever.

Connor forced himself to focus on the areas he was supposed to work on. Mrs. Ashford's instructions were clear, and he needed this job too bad to screw it up on day one.

But he kept looking back at that impossible garden.

Connor worked at the Ashford place for three days before curiosity got the better of him. The regular work took maybe six hours a week, leaving him plenty of time to wonder about the winter garden and Mrs. Ashford's crazy warnings.

He'd tried looking up the property online but didn't find much. The house was built in 1923 by some rich guy named Harrison Ashford, and it stayed in the family. Mrs. Ashford was a ghost—no Facebook, no business listings, nothing except the property records.

Friday afternoon, while cleaning gutters on the back of the house, Connor got his first real look at what was growing inside the stone walls.

The plants were like nothing he'd ever seen. Vines climbed tall wooden frames, their leaves so dark green they looked almost black. Flowers bloomed in colors that hurt to look at—purples so deep they seemed to suck up light, reds that made his eyes water. And fruit hung heavy on branches that should've been dead months ago.

But what really bothered Connor was the smell. Sweet and thick, with something rotten underneath that reminded him of the dead raccoon he'd found under his apartment building last summer. The smell got stronger as the sun went down, like the plants came alive after dark.

Connor climbed down from the ladder and walked closer to the stone wall. Metal signs hung every few feet: PRIVATE PROPERTY - NO TRESPASSING - DANGER.

Seemed like overkill for some weird plants, until Connor noticed what was scattered around the base of the wall.

Bones.

White fragments mixed in with the fallen leaves, mostly hidden but visible once you knew what to look for. Most looked small—birds, maybe squirrels. But some of the bigger pieces looked wrong. Too familiar.

Connor backed away from the wall, his heart hammering. Mrs. Ashford's warnings didn't seem so crazy anymore. Whatever was growing in that garden wasn't staying alive through normal plant stuff.

That weekend, Connor tried to forget about the bones and come up with normal explanations. Maybe Mrs. Ashford had some kind of greenhouse setup he couldn't see. Maybe she'd installed underground heating to create a warm zone.

Maybe the bone pieces were just decorations, some gothic thing to match the creepy Victorian house.

But Monday morning killed any innocent explanations.

Connor arrived to find fresh holes around the garden's edge. Something had been digging over the weekend—not random animal scratching, but deliberate digging that left neat holes about two feet deep and eighteen inches wide.

Six holes, evenly spaced around the garden, all recently filled with loose dirt.

Connor couldn't stop himself from digging. Six inches down, his shovel hit something that wasn't dirt.

A human hand, fingers spread like it was reaching for help.

Connor fell backward, scrambling away from the hole. His breakfast came up all at once, splashing across Mrs. Ashford's perfect flower beds.

When he could breathe again, he looked back at the hole. The hand was still there, pale and real and definitely human.

Mrs. Ashford wasn't growing vegetables.

She was growing something that ate people.

Connor began having second thoughts: *should've quit and gotten in my truck and never come back.*

But two hundred and fifty a week? Jesus Christ, he couldn't walk away from that kind of money.

His rent was three weeks late. Student loan payments had jumped to four hundred a month. His credit cards were so maxed out he couldn't buy gas without hoping the charge went through.

Two fifty a week was groceries. Two fifty a week was keeping his electricity on. Two fifty a week was survival.

Maybe Mrs. Ashford was just composting weird. Rich people did crazy shit all the time, right?

That lasted until the next morning.

A white van was parked in the driveway when Connor showed up for work. Two men in coveralls were unloading something from the back—something heavy and person-shaped, wrapped in black plastic.

The men didn't look at Connor. Didn't acknowledge him at all. Just carried their bundles around to the back garden and disappeared.

Connor waited five minutes, then followed. The van was gone, but the evidence remained: six fresh holes in the garden, recently filled. And sticking up from one of them, barely visible beneath the loose dirt, was a human finger.

Connor's legs went weak. He sat down hard on the cold ground, staring at that pale digit jutting up from Mrs. Ashford's perfect garden like some kind of accusation.

The finger had a wedding ring.

Connor walked to the nearest hole and caught a glimpse of what lay under the thin layer of dirt. Pale skin. Dark hair. A human hand with fingers curled like it was trying to grab something.

Connor puked into the bushes, his breakfast splattering across Mrs. Ashford's perfect landscaping. When the retching stopped, he sat on the ground, trying to process what he'd seen.

Mrs. Ashford wasn't just feeding her plants organic matter. She was feeding them people.

Connor pulled out his phone to call the cops, then stopped. What evidence did he really have? Quick glimpses of buried stuff that might be human remains, might be something else. Weird plants that could have scientific explanations. A garden that thrived in winter, which wasn't impossible with the right setup.

Any cop investigation would focus on Connor. Why was he digging around his employer's property? Why was he breaking the clear restrictions she'd set? How could he prove his claims without admitting he was snooping where he wasn't supposed to be?

Connor needed more evidence before calling anyone. Real proof that Mrs. Ashford was killing people, not just suspicious observations from a trespassing employee.

That afternoon, Connor hid in the tool shed and waited for Mrs. Ashford to come back from her business trip. Her car pulled in just before sunset—a black Mercedes that looked as expensive as everything else she owned.

Mrs. Ashford stepped out of the Mercedes that probably cost more than Connor would make in five years. Seventy-something, silver hair in a perfect bun, wearing gardening clothes that looked like they came from some fancy catalog.

But it was her hands that made Connor's skin crawl. Soft and pale like she'd never worked a day in her life, but with dirt caked under every fingernail. Dirt that looked too dark, too rich.

She moved through the garden like she owned it—which she did—but also like she loved it. Touching plants, murmuring to them under her breath. Stroking vine leaves like they were pets.

When darkness fell, Mrs. Ashford went inside. Connor waited another hour, then crept closer to the garden wall.

The plants were active at night. Vines twisted and moved with no wind, and the impossible flowers seemed to glow with their own light. The sweet smell was overwhelming now, thick enough to taste.

And from beneath the soil came sounds that froze Connor's blood: wet, organic noises like digestion happening just underground.

Connor was listening to the plants feed.

Connor didn't sleep. Couldn't close his eyes without seeing that pale hand reaching up from the dirt.

He spent the night on his laptop, searching "carnivorous plants" and "human remains" and "people-eating gardens," finding nothing that explained what he'd seen. Every search led to the same conclusion: what Mrs. Ashford was doing was impossible.

But impossible didn't make it less real.

By morning, Connor had decided. He needed proof before calling the cops. Solid evidence that wouldn't just sound like the crazy ramblings of some broke landscaper.

He arrived at the property early, before Mrs. Ashford left for her daily errands. The garden looked peaceful in the morning light, its crazy colors muted by winter sunshine. But Connor could see fresh growth since yesterday—vines that climbed higher, flowers that opened wider, fruit that hung heavier on branches that seemed thicker overnight.

The plants were growing because they were eating. And they were eating people.

Connor waited until Mrs. Ashford's Mercedes disappeared down Henshaw Drive, then walked to one of the fresh burial sites. He'd brought a small shovel from the tool shed, telling himself he only needed to dig deep enough to confirm what was down there.

The earth was soft and easy to move. Six inches down, Connor's shovel hit something that gave but didn't break. He cleared away more dirt, exposing a patch of pale skin that was definitely human.

Connor's hands shook as he brushed away more soil, revealing enough to confirm his worst fears. A man's torso, still wearing a business suit, buried face-down in the rich earth. The body looked fresh, like it had been planted within the past day or two.

Connor took photos with his phone, documenting the burial site from multiple angles. Then he moved to the next hole, and the next, finding similar evidence of recent burials around the garden's edge.

Six people. Six fresh corpses planted like fertilizer around Mrs. Ashford's impossible winter garden.

Connor was photographing the fourth burial site when he heard gravel crunching in the driveway.

Mrs. Ashford had come back early.

Connor grabbed his shovel and ran for the tool shed, his heart slamming against his ribs. He made it inside just as Mrs. Ashford's Mercedes came around the side of the house.

Through the shed window, Connor watched her park and walk to the garden. She moved like someone who knew exactly what she expected to find.

What she found was disturbed earth and evidence of unauthorized digging.

Mrs. Ashford examined each hole Connor had disturbed, her face getting colder with each discovery. When she finished, she walked to the tool shed.

"Connor?" she called in the same crisp, authoritative voice she'd used during their phone interview. "I know you're in there. Please come out so we can discuss what you've discovered."

Connor pressed himself against the back wall, hoping she might give up and leave. But Mrs. Ashford kept talking, patient and calm:

"I can see the fresh dirt on the shovel by the door. And I can smell the garden soil on your hands from here. There's no point in hiding."

Connor knew he had no choice. Mrs. Ashford knew he'd seen the bodies, and she wasn't going to pretend nothing had happened. He opened the shed door and stepped outside, keeping the shovel ready as a weapon.

"You were instructed to stay away from the garden," Mrs. Ashford said. Her tone suggested disappointment rather than anger, like a teacher correcting a student who'd failed to follow directions.

"I know what you're doing," Connor said. "I've seen the bodies. I got it all documented. If something happens to me, the cops will know where to look."

Mrs. Ashford smiled, and her whole face changed from sweet grandmother to something cold and predatory.

"Oh honey. The police already know about my garden. Who do you think gives me the bodies?"

Connor's stomach dropped. "What?"

"You think I was out there murdering innocent people? That'd be messy and stupid." Mrs. Ashford gestured toward the garden. "The bodies you found are all criminals, Connor. Murderers, rapists, child molesters—people who were headed for execution or life in prison anyway."

"That's impossible. The justice system doesn't—"

"The official justice system doesn't. But there are older forms of justice, Connor. More direct approaches to removing dangerous individuals from society." Mrs. Ashford walked closer to the garden wall, her voice taking on the tone of someone sharing cherished family history.

"My great-great-grandfather Harrison discovered these plants during his travels in Southeast Asia. A species that doesn't exist in any botanical textbook, because it's not natural. The local shamans cultivated them for centuries as spiritual purification—they fed the plants people who had committed unforgivable crimes, and in return, the plants produced fruit with remarkable properties."

Connor backed toward his truck, but Mrs. Ashford seemed unconcerned about his escape route.

"What properties?" Connor asked, though he wasn't sure he wanted to know.

"Longevity, for one. I'm ninety-three years old, Connor. I should have died twenty years ago, but regular consumption of the fruit has kept me healthy and vital." Mrs. Ashford plucked something from a nearby vine—a dark red fruit that looked like a cross between an apple and a human heart.

"Clarity of mind is another benefit. The fruit enhances cognitive function, allows for planning and decision-making that spans decades. And most importantly, it provides moral clarity about which people deserve to live and which people need to be removed from the world."

Mrs. Ashford bit into the fruit, and dark juice ran down her chin like blood.

"The network I work with has existed for over a century. Police officers, judges, prison officials, medical examiners—people in positions to identify irredeemable criminals and arrange for their quiet disposal. We provide a service the official justice system cannot: permanent removal of people who will never be rehabilitated and will continue causing harm as long as they live."

Connor reached his truck and fumbled for the keys. "You're crazy. You can't just decide who lives and dies."

"Can't I? I've been making those decisions for seventy years, Connor. And the world is measurably safer for my efforts." Mrs. Ashford walked toward him, moving with fluid grace that seemed impossible for her age.

"The question now is what to do about you. You've seen things you weren't supposed to see, but you're not a criminal. You're just a curious young man who needs money and made some poor choices about respecting boundaries."

Connor got the truck started and threw it in reverse, but Mrs. Ashford raised her hand in a gesture that somehow made him stop.

"I'm going to offer you two choices, Connor. You can leave now, never return to this property, and never speak of what you've seen. In exchange, I'll pay you five thousand dollars and provide excellent references for future employment."

"Or?"

Mrs. Ashford's smile returned, cold and patient.

"Or you can join our network. Learn the truth about how justice really works in this world. Help us identify and dispose of people who deserve to die. The pay is excellent, the work is meaningful, and the benefits include access to fruit that will extend your lifespan considerably."

Connor stared at her, trying to process the impossible choice. Walk away with money and spend the rest of his life knowing Mrs. Ashford and her network were feeding people to carnivorous plants, or become part of their operation.

"What happens if I choose neither?"

"Then you become fertilizer for the garden, and we continue our work without you. But I'd prefer not to waste someone with your potential, Connor. You've shown initiative, discretion, and the ability to uncover hidden information. Those are valuable skills."

Mrs. Ashford walked back toward the garden, leaving Connor alone with his impossible decision.

"You have until tomorrow morning to choose," she called over her shoulder. "The key is in the mailbox if you decide to stay. The money will be there too if you decide to leave."

Connor drove home feeling like his brain had been put in a blender. Half of him wanted to write off Mrs. Ashford as some crazy old bat, but the evidence was too real. The garden that shouldn't exist, the fresh bodies, the network of people who could make victims disappear—it all fit together too perfectly to be bullshit.

And if she was telling the truth about only killing criminals, did that change anything? Were murderers and rapists somehow less deserving of being eaten by plants than regular people?

Connor spent the evening researching the names Mrs. Ashford had mentioned, trying to verify her claims about the victims. What he found made his moral certainty even murkier.

Three of the buried men were registered sex offenders with multiple convictions involving children. One was a former death row inmate whose execution had been delayed by appeals for over a decade. Another was a gang leader connected to seventeen unsolved murders.

The sixth man was harder to identify, but Connor found a news article about a domestic violence case that ended in plea bargaining and a suspended sentence. The victim—the man's ex-wife—had been found dead six months later in what police ruled a suicide, though her family insisted she'd been murdered.

Mrs. Ashford hadn't been lying about targeting criminals. But did that justify feeding them to plants? Did their crimes make them less deserving of due process, legal representation, and the basic right to life?

Connor wrestled with these questions all night, but by morning he'd reached a decision.

Connor returned to 1061 Henshaw Drive at sunrise, prepared to face whatever consequences his choice would bring. The key was in the mailbox as promised, along with an envelope containing five thousand dollars in cash.

Mrs. Ashford was waiting in the garden, tending to her impossible plants with the careful attention of someone who loved her work.

"I see you've made your decision," she said without looking up from a vine she was training along a new trellis.

"I want to know more," Connor said. "About the network, about how you choose targets, about what safeguards you have to prevent mistakes."

"Wise choice. Most people who learn about our work either run away screaming or demand to join right away. You're taking the more thoughtful approach."

Mrs. Ashford led Connor into the house, where she poured tea and laid out a folder of documents that looked like they'd been prepared for this conversation.

"Our network's been around for over a century," she said. "We've got people in the cops, prisons, courts, morgues. When someone does something that proves they're beyond saving, we mark them for pickup."

"What counts as beyond saving?"

"Serial killers. People who rape kids. Guys who torture for fun. Wife-beaters who escalate to murder even after restraining orders and cops getting involved." Mrs. Ashford's voice stayed calm, like she was discussing grocery shopping instead of execution.

"We also take people who've exhausted the legal system. Death row inmates whose appeals got denied, lifers who kill again in prison, scumbags who got off on technicalities despite everyone knowing they're guilty."

Connor studied the documents spread in front of him—photographs, police reports, court records documenting cases that made his stomach turn. Children tortured to death by their parents. Women stalked and murdered by ex-boyfriends despite dozens of police reports. Elderly people beaten to death for their Social Security checks.

"How do you get access to these people?" Connor asked.

"We have members in positions to arrange transfers, medical emergencies, early releases that aren't documented. The targets disappear from the system, and we ensure they disappear permanently."

Mrs. Ashford turned to a new section of the folder, showing charts and statistics tracking their work over decades.

"We remove about fifty people per year from circulation. Compare that to the thousands who are released early for good behavior, or who escape conviction on technicalities, or who serve minimal sentences for horrific crimes. Our impact is small but significant."

Connor looked at the photos of victims—before and after shots showing normal-looking people transformed into the pale, peaceful corpses he'd discovered around the garden.

"What's my role in this?"

"Research and acquisition, initially. You'll help identify targets, verify their criminal histories, and assist with logistics. As you gain experience and prove your reliability, you'll take on more active responsibilities."

Mrs. Ashford handed Connor a contract that looked like standard employment paperwork, except for clauses about confidentiality, target verification protocols, and disposal procedures.

"The compensation is substantial, and the benefits extend well beyond money. You'll have access to the fruit, which will improve your health and extend your lifespan considerably. You'll also gain the satisfaction of knowing you're making the world safer."

Connor read through the contract, trying to process the magnitude of what he was agreeing to. Join a century-old vigilante network that fed criminals to carnivorous plants. Help kill people who might deserve to die anyway.

"What happens if I change my mind later?"

Mrs. Ashford's expression didn't change, but something cold flickered behind her eyes.

"Then you become fertilizer for the garden. The network's security depends on loyalty from its members. We can't risk exposure by people who develop moral qualms after learning our methods."

Connor signed the contract.

The training process took three months.

Connor learned to research criminal backgrounds, verify police reports, and identify targets whose disappearance wouldn't trigger extensive investigation. He studied the network's security protocols, communication methods, and disposal procedures.

Most importantly, he learned about the plants themselves.

Mrs. Ashford's garden contained seven distinct species, each with different dietary requirements and growth patterns. Some preferred fresh meat, others thrived on decomposed organic matter. The largest specimens—vines that climbed twenty feet up specially constructed trellises—could digest entire human bodies in a matter of weeks.

"They're not natural," Mrs. Ashford explained during one of their training sessions. "The original species were native to remote areas of Cambodia, but generations of selective cultivation have enhanced their carnivorous capabilities. They're as much magical as botanical."

"Magic isn't real," Connor said, though he was beginning to question that assumption.

"Isn't it? You've seen plants that grow in winter, that digest human bone, that produce fruit with life-extending properties. If that's not magic, what would you call it?"

Connor had no answer. His experience with Mrs. Ashford's garden had shattered most of his assumptions about what was possible.

The fruit, when Mrs. Ashford finally let him try it, was fucking incredible. Sweet and rich, with flavors that seemed to shift and change as he chewed. But it wasn't just the taste—within hours, Connor felt like someone had turned up the volume on everything. Colors seemed brighter, sounds clearer, his thoughts sharper and more focused.

"Damn," he said. "How often can I eat this stuff?"

"Once a month, tops. Too much too fast can mess with your head. Make you paranoid, think you're better than everyone else, stop caring about people outside the network."

Connor wondered if Mrs. Ashford was speaking from experience.

By spring, Connor was ready for his first active assignment.

The target was Derek Vance, just released from prison after six years for aggravated assault. His file showed a pattern of escalating violence against women—his last victim spent three months in the hospital with injuries that would never heal.

"He's been out two weeks," Mrs. Ashford said as they drove toward Vance's apartment. "Already got a new girlfriend, already showing the same controlling shit that came before his previous attacks."

Connor looked at Vance's mug shot and rap sheet. Three domestic violence arrests, two convictions, multiple restraining orders he'd ignored. The kind of guy who'd probably end up killing someone if nobody stopped him.

"How do we get him to come along?"

"He'll come willingly." Mrs. Ashford parked across from a rundown apartment complex. "Vance has gambling debts and owes money to some very unforgiving people. He's desperate for cash, which makes him easy to manipulate."

Mrs. Ashford made a phone call, switching to a different voice and accent. Connor listened as she pretended to be from some medical research company, offering Vance five hundred bucks to do a sleep study.

"Tonight at eleven," she told him. "We'll pick you up. Just bring ID and be ready to stay overnight."

Vance agreed immediately, probably relieved to find easy money.

"Always that simple?" Connor asked.

"Usually. People like Vance live on the edges. They don't ask questions about weird opportunities, and nobody's gonna notice when they disappear."

That evening, Connor and Mrs. Ashford returned to collect their target. Vance was waiting outside his apartment building, a thin man in his thirties with the twitchy demeanor of someone who spent most of his time looking over his shoulder.

"You the research people?" Derek Vance climbed into Mrs. Ashford's Mercedes like he was getting into a taxi. Forty-something, wearing a stained t-shirt and jeans that had seen better years.

"Mr. Vance, thank you so much for participating," Mrs. Ashford said from the passenger seat. "Five hundred dollars for one night, just like we discussed." Connor drove while Vance talked about his ex-wife, his court dates, his bullshit problems with the legal system. The man had no idea he was riding to his own execution. Just thought he'd found some easy money.

"Sleep study, right?" Vance asked. "Just gotta sleep in some lab while you monitor my brain waves or whatever?"

"Something like that," Mrs. Ashford said.

Back at 1061 Henshaw Drive, Mrs. Ashford led Vance around to the garden area. In the darkness, the thriving plants looked normal—just a well-maintained winter garden that happened to stay green year-round.

"Nice setup," Vance said, admiring the elaborate trellises and planned layout. "You grow all this yourself?"

"It's been a family hobby for generations. Would you mind helping me check on something near the back wall? I think one of the support posts might be coming loose."

Vance followed Mrs. Ashford deeper into the garden, where the plants grew thicker and the sweet smell was strongest. Connor stayed near the entrance, watching for any sign that their target was becoming suspicious.

Mrs. Ashford knelt beside one of the larger vine specimens and gestured for Vance to examine what appeared to be a loose stake.

"I don't see any—" Vance began, then stopped speaking as something wrapped around his ankle.

One of the vines had moved, coiling around Vance's leg with muscular precision. More vines descended from the trellises above, wrapping around his arms and torso before he could react.

"What the hell—" Vance struggled against the plant matter, but the vines kept getting tighter. "What is this? What's happening?"

"Justice," Mrs. Ashford said, calm as discussing the weather. "Just took a while to catch up with you."

The vines lifted Vance off the ground, suspending him horizontally about six feet above the garden floor. Other plants moved to join the feeding, flowers opening to reveal tooth-like structures that began working their way across his body.

Vance screamed, but the sound was muffled as one of the larger blooms clamped over his mouth. The feeding process was efficient but not quick—Connor could see Vance's eyes wide with terror and pain as the plants began their work.

"Does it always take this long?" Connor asked, disturbed despite his understanding of what was happening.

Vance's screaming went on for twenty minutes.

Connor watched a man be eaten alive, vines holding him down while flowers with rows of teeth worked their way across his body. The plants kept him conscious the whole time—seemed to prefer their meat fresh and aware.

When it was over, nothing left but torn clothes and blood-soaked dirt. Mrs. Ashford swept up the fabric scraps like she was cleaning up after dinner.

"How do you feel?" she asked Connor as they cleaned up the evidence.

Connor expected to puke. Expected to cry or shake or something normal. Instead, he felt... hungry. Empty. Like watching Vance die had carved something out of his chest.

"I don't know," Connor said.

"That's normal. The fruit helps with the adjustment process." She handed him one of the strange blue fruits from a nearby vine. "Eat this. Trust me."

The fruit tasted like copper and honey. The moment Connor swallowed, the emptiness filled with something warm and bright.

The guilt evaporated. Suddenly, everything made perfect sense.

Vance had been a monster. The world was better without him.

"Better?" Mrs. Ashford asked.

Connor nodded. "Much."

"So when's the next one?" Connor asked.

Mrs. Ashford smiled. "Eager, aren't we? There's a child molester getting out of county next week. Good behavior, can you believe it? They let him plea down from production charges."

Connor's jaw clenched. "What's his name?"

"I'll text you the details tonight. But Connor?" She touched his arm. "Remember what the fruit teaches you. No second thoughts, no guilt. These people chose their path."

Over the following year, Connor participated in thirty-seven feedings.

"Killers, rapists, child molesters—people who prove over and over they won't change." Mrs. Ashford had said. "We don't guess. We know. Court records, police reports, victim statements. These people earned what's coming.

Connor's work evolved from research and logistics to actively bringing in targets. He got good at spotting people's weak spots and coming up with offers they couldn't refuse. Gambling debts, drug problems, desperate money situations—everyone had something that could be used against them.

The work felt right. Connor felt like he was protecting innocent people by getting rid of predators who'd never change. The legal system was supposed to give people second chances, but some people had proven they didn't deserve them.

And the benefits were incredible. Regular doses of the fruit had transformed Connor's health and mental sharpness. He was stronger, faster, and smarter than he'd ever been. His thinking was clearer, his planning more effective, his ability to research and analyze information way better than before.

But most importantly, Connor had developed perfect clarity about his work. He could look at someone's criminal history and know whether they deserved to live or die. The fruit didn't just make you live longer—it gave you the wisdom to make life-and-death decisions with confidence.

Which was why Connor knew what to do when he discovered Mrs. Ashford's secret.

Connor found the hidden files by accident while looking up targets in Mrs. Ashford's study. A loose floorboard caught his toe, and when he pried it up, there was a metal box underneath.

Personal files. Stuff that wasn't part of the network's official records.

The more Connor read, the sicker he felt. Mrs. Ashford hadn't just been feeding criminals to her plants. Over the past ten years, she'd killed people who asked too many questions about the network: reporters, cops who dug too deep, even former members who'd started having second thoughts.

The newest file was about him.

Subject shows strong adaptation to protocols and commitment to the mission. However, enhanced analytical capabilities have led to detailed questions about targeting and security. Recommend harvesting before subject discovers operational flexibility.

The words hit Connor like a punch to the gut. Mrs. Ashford was planning to kill him. Not because he was a criminal, but because he'd been asking too many questions.

Connor felt a moment of pure betrayal, then perfect clarity about what had to happen next.

Mrs. Ashford had broken the network's basic rules by targeting innocent people. She'd become exactly the kind of threat they were supposed to eliminate. Someone who killed for personal convenience instead of moral necessity.

Connor knew what justice looked like.

That evening, Connor called Mrs. Ashford to report a promising new target.

"I've found someone perfect," he told her. "A repeat offender with a long history of violence against elderly victims. He's being released tomorrow, and he's desperate for money."

"Excellent. What's his background?"

Connor provided detailed information about a fictional criminal, crafted to match Mrs. Ashford's preferences for targets. Someone old enough to have an extensive history, violent enough to justify elimination, isolated enough that his disappearance wouldn't trigger investigation.

"He sounds ideal. When can we arrange pickup?"

"Tomorrow night. He's agreed to participate in a medical study for five hundred dollars."

Mrs. Ashford was pleased with Connor's initiative and efficiency. She had no idea that Connor had been documenting her real activities for weeks, building a case that demonstrated her corruption of the network's mission.

The next evening, Mrs. Ashford waited in the garden while Connor went to collect their fictional target. Instead, he returned alone and locked the garden gate behind him.

"Where is he?" Mrs. Ashford asked.

"There is no target," Connor said. "This is about you."

Mrs. Ashford's expression shifted from confusion to understanding to cold calculation.

"I see. You found my private files."

"I found evidence that you've been murdering innocent people. Journalists, police officers, even network members who disagreed with you."

"Those people were threats to our security. Sometimes difficult decisions have to be made to protect the greater mission."

"You're the kind of person we're supposed to eliminate. Someone who kills for personal convenience rather than justice."

Mrs. Ashford laughed, a sound like breaking glass.

"Connor, my dear boy, who do you think created the targeting criteria? Who do you think decides what constitutes irredeemable depravity?" She gestured toward the thriving plants around them. "I've been making those decisions for seventy years. The network exists to serve my vision of justice, not some abstract moral code."

"Then the network is corrupted and needs to be reformed."

"By you? A twenty-three-year-old who's been with us for less than a year?" Mrs. Ashford moved closer, her aged features taking on a predatory cast. "You think the fruit has made you wise enough to judge your superiors?"

Connor saw her positioning herself to attack, probably hoping to overpower him and feed him to her plants. But the fruit had enhanced his reflexes as well as his judgment, and he was ready for her move.

When Mrs. Ashford lunged forward with a knife that appeared from somewhere in her clothing, Connor caught her wrist and twisted until she dropped the weapon.

"You broke the rules," Connor said, pushing her toward the hungry vines. "Started killing innocent people for your own bullshit reasons."

Mrs. Ashford clawed at his hands. "You don't understand—I built this network, I created—"

"You corrupted it." The vines were already reaching for her. "The plants don't care how long you've been feeding them. They care about justice."

"No, wait, they know me, they won't—"

The first vine wrapped around her ankle.

Connor stepped back and watched as the plants that had served Mrs. Ashford for seventy years began eating their former owner. Her screams echoed through the winter night, but nobody lived close enough to hear.

Justice served. The network could keep doing its important work, but under leadership that wouldn't corrupt the mission with personal bullshit.

Connor inherited the house, the garden, and Mrs. Ashford's role in the network.

He maintained the plants, feeding them only genuine criminals whose elimination would make the world safer. He recruited new members and trained them thoroughly, ensuring they understood the moral principles that guided their work.

The garden thrived under his stewardship, growing larger and more productive each year.

Connor loved feeding time.

Loved watching the vines wrap around some scumbag who thought he'd gotten away with hurting kids or beating his wife. Loved seeing the moment when they realized the legal system wasn't the only kind of justice in the world.

The fruit kept his thinking clear. Made sure he never second-guessed himself when tough decisions needed making.

Like last month, when that reporter started asking questions about missing persons. Or when Detective Kendall got too interested in the unsolved disappearances around Hillcrest Drive.

The plants weren't picky about who they ate. They trusted Connor's judgment completely.

And Connor's judgment was perfect, thanks to the fruit.

It had been proven solid when it came to figuring out who deserved to be removed from the world.

The plants trusted his decisions. They ate whoever Connor brought them, and they produced fruit that kept his mind sharp and his body strong so he could keep making the hard choices.

It was a perfect setup. And Connor planned to keep it running for decades.

The garden always needed feeding, and the world always had people who deserved to be fed to it.

Connor was doing important work.

Let My Love Open the Door

J ake Sullivan had always preferred animals to people, which made the move to Millbrook seem perfect until he arrived and realized how *quiet* quiet could get. Town sat in a valley between rolling hills covered in dense forest that ate cell phone signals for breakfast and made his GPS give up entirely. His veterinary clinic occupied the ground floor of a converted farmhouse on Main Street, living quarters upstairs that smelled like decades of wood smoke and something he couldn't place—root cellars and barns where hay had been stored through too many winters.

"You'll get used to it," Emma Kendrick said on his third day, standing in his doorway with a cardboard carrier containing what sounded like a seriously pissed-off chicken. "Just the hills. They hold onto things like a jealous girlfriend."

Jake looked up from organizing surgical instruments and forgot what he'd been doing. Emma's hair was the color of coffee beans left too long on the stove, twisted back with what looked like a rubber band stolen from a feed sack. Her hands told the story of someone handling livestock since she could walk—callused palms, thin white scar across her left knuckle, fingernails that held the kind of dirt that came from mucking stalls at dawn. Her jeans had honest-to-God manure stains on them, not the carefully distressed denim he'd seen on city girls playing weekend cowgirl.

"What's wrong with..." He gestured toward the carrier, which was now rocking slightly.

"Henrietta. Something's got her leg twisted up. Dad says just wring her neck and toss her in the pot, but she lays an egg every damn day like clockwork." Emma set the carrier on his examination table, studied him with brown eyes that looked like they'd seen every variety of bullshit the world had to offer.

"You're younger than I figured."

"Disappointed?"

"Hell no."

She grinned, and Jake's heart did something that would've required emergency surgery in a human patient.

"Dr. Patterson was older than Moses and had hands like tree bark. Henrietta always came home looking like she'd been through a wood chipper."

Jake extracted a very indignant red hen from the carrier, ran his hands along her leg, feeling for breaks or sprains. Henrietta squawked like she was filing a formal complaint but didn't try to take his eyes out, which he took as professional progress.

"Just a sprain," he said after a few minutes of gentle probing. "Keep her penned up for a week or so, and she'll be good as new. No charge for the first visit—new customer and all."

"That's decent of you." Emma gathered Henrietta back into the carrier with the kind of efficiency that came from handling livestock since childhood. She paused at the table, biting her lower lip like she was deciding something. "You should come for dinner Sunday. Mom always cooks like she's feeding a threshing crew, and she's been curious about the new vet since you rolled into town."

Jake nodded before his brain caught up with his mouth. "I'd like that."

"Good. We're the farm with the red barn about two miles north on Elderwood Road. Can't miss it unless you're blind or drunk." Emma paused at the door and turned back. "Fair warning—there's stories about our place. Old-timer nonsense mostly, but folks 'round here don't take kindly to anyone who doesn't respect the folklore. Don't let 'em scare you off before you've had Mom's pot roast."

After she left, Jake stood in his empty clinic breathing in the lingering scent of her—something that smelled like wildflowers and honest sweat and hay that had been cut under a hot sun. He'd dated plenty of women in Boston, but none of them had ever made him feel like he'd just been hit by a freight train while coming home at the same time.

The weekend couldn't arrive fast enough.

Two weeks later

The Kendrick farm sprawled across a hillside that caught the late afternoon sun like something out of a travel brochure, if travel brochures advertised places where people actually worked for a living. The red barn Emma had mentioned sat next to a white farmhouse with a wraparound porch that looked like it had been there since the valley was first cleared. Jake parked his truck next to a dusty Ford that had been new when Clinton was president and walked up to the front steps carrying a bottle of wine that suddenly seemed as useful as tits on a bull.

By now, he'd found excuses to see Emma almost daily. She'd brought a parade of animals to his clinic—a cat with a hairball that turned out to be perfectly healthy, a goat she claimed had an upset stomach but showed no symptoms, a dog with a limp that vanished the moment Jake examined him. He'd started timing his grocery runs to coincide with her trips to town, and somehow they always ended up having coffee at Mabel's Diner, where the coffee tasted like it had been brewed in a boot and the pie was worth the drive from three counties over.

Emma's mother turned out to be a shorter, grayer version of her daughter with the same direct gaze and work-hardened hands. "Sarah Kendrick," she said, shaking his hand with a grip that would've impressed his old football coach. "Emma's told us about you."

"All good things, I hope."

"Mostly." Emma appeared from the kitchen wearing a sundress that made Jake forget his own name. "Might've mentioned you know which end of a chicken bites and don't faint at the sight of blood."

Her father proved to be a man with hands that looked like they'd been rebuilding the same tractor for twenty years and eyes that had seen too many bad winters. He spoke in careful sentences and watched Jake with the kind of polite suspicion farmers reserved for anyone who'd spent too much time around people who thought food came from grocery stores. "Robert Kendrick. Heard you're from Boston."

"Maine originally, but I did my residency in Boston." Jake accepted a beer that tasted like it came from somewhere that gave a damn about what beer was supposed to taste like. "Grew up on a dairy farm outside Bangor. Holsteins mostly."

Robert's expression thawed about two degrees. "What brought you all the way out here? Boston's got plenty of pets that need fixing, and they pay better than farmers."

Jake took a pull of beer and considered the question. He could mention the lower cost of living, or the chance to know his clients instead of running an assembly line of suburban pet problems, but the truth felt more complicated. "Wanted to be somewhere real," he said finally. "Somewhere people know the difference between working and playing at work."

Emma glanced at him over her shoulder and smiled, and Jake felt that freight train hit him again.

Dinner involved pot roast that fell apart if you looked at it wrong, vegetables that still had dirt clinging to them from where they'd been pulled from the garden that morning, and bread that Sarah had baked in an oven older than Jake's truck. The conversation ranged from local politics to whether the town council had lost their collective minds with the new parking meters on Main Street. Jake found himself relaxing in a way he hadn't since childhood, laughing at Robert's dry observations about city tourists and Sarah's stories about the more colorful towns-people.

"Jake was asking about the stories earlier," Emma said during dessert, shooting her parents a look that said they'd already talked about this.

Sarah and Robert exchanged glances. "What kind of stories?" Sarah asked carefully.

"Emma mentioned there were tales about your property."

Another look passed between Emma's parents, longer this time. "There's an old stone thing up in the hills," Robert said slowly. "Some kind of root cellar or storage from way back when. Local kids used to dare each other to go up there and touch it."

"Used to?" Jake asked.

"Town council put up a fence and warning signs after some teenagers got hurt back in the fifties," Sarah said. "Kids being stupid, but better safe than sorry."

Emma stood and began clearing plates. "Anyone want coffee?"

Jake helped her carry dishes to the kitchen while her parents moved to the living room. "You look like you got something eating at you," he said quietly.

Emma ran water over the plates and stared out the window toward the darkening hills. The kitchen smelled like cinnamon and the kind of coffee that came from beans people actually cared about. "That stone thing my folks mentioned? It ain't no root cellar. Someone carved a door right into the hillside, and it's old. I mean old—like it was here before any white man ever saw this valley."

"A door to what?"

"Nobody knows. The local Seneca had stories about it, something about a passage between worlds, but they stayed clear of this whole area like it was cursed." Emma dried her hands on a dish towel that had seen more Sunday dinners than Jake could count. "First settlers found it and figured it was just some natural formation. Stories say it only opens for true love."

Jake felt a smile tugging at his lips. "Sounds romantic."

"The couple who opened it in 1952 aged forty years in three weeks. Someone found 'em looking like they'd been through a time machine set on fast-forward. They died in the hospital within days, talking about things that didn't make sense." Emma's expression stayed serious as cancer. "People found them holding hands at the base of the door, but their hair was white as cotton and their skin looked like tissue paper."

The smile died on Jake's face. "What do you think happened to them?"

"I think some doors ought to stay shut." Emma moved closer, close enough that he could smell her wildflower shampoo and see the tiny scar by her left eyebrow where she'd fallen off a horse when she was twelve. "I'm telling you this 'cause I like you, Jake Sullivan. Like you more than I've liked anyone in a long time, and I don't want you thinking I'm some crazy farm girl who believes in fairy tales."

Jake reached up and tucked a strand of hair behind her ear. "I don't think you're crazy. I think you're the most incredible woman I've ever met."

Emma's breath caught, and for a moment they stood there in the warm kitchen light while something electric passed between them. Then Sarah called from the living room asking about coffee, and the moment shattered like glass.

"I should head home," Jake said reluctantly.

"Probably should." But Emma didn't step away from him. "Will I see you again?"

"Try and stop me."

Three weeks later

Emma took him hiking up into the hills behind the farm on a Thursday evening when the air smelled like rain and the sky looked like brushed pewter. They followed an old deer path that wound between stands of oak and maple, climbing steadily until the farmhouse looked like a child's toy below them. The air felt different up here—thicker somehow, charged with the kind of energy that made the hair on Jake's arms stand up like he was standing too close to a power line.

By now, Jake knew things about Emma that made his chest tight when he thought about them. Like how she hummed old country songs when she was concentrating, or how she'd fallen asleep against his shoulder the night before while they watched a movie that neither of them had paid attention to. He knew she took her coffee black, hated brussels sprouts with the passion of a thousand suns, and could make a cow move just by looking at it right. He knew she'd wanted to be a veterinarian herself until her father had his heart attack when she was nineteen and someone had to run the farm.

"There," Emma said, pointing toward a cluster of boulders nestled in a grove of trees so old they might've been saplings when the glaciers retreated.

At first, Jake saw only weathered granite covered in moss and lichen that glowed faintly in the evening light. Then Emma led him closer, and he realized what he was looking at wasn't natural at all. Someone had carved the boulders into an archway, smoothing the stone into curves that flowed together like frozen water. The opening stood about seven feet tall and four feet wide, filled with darkness that seemed to swallow Emma's flashlight beam like it was hungry for light.

"Jesus Christ," Jake breathed. "How old is this thing?"

"Dad thinks maybe a thousand years, could be more. Carving style doesn't match anything the local tribes did, and it was ancient when the first whites got here." Emma played her flashlight over the intricate patterns carved around the archway's edges—spirals and interlocking circles that seemed to shift and move when he wasn't looking directly at them. "You feel that?"

Jake realized he'd been feeling it since they'd entered the grove—a low vibration that seemed to come from inside his bones, like standing too close to massive speakers at a concert. His molars ached with it. "What is it?"

"Don't know. Gets stronger sometimes, especially..." Emma trailed off, biting her lower lip.

"Especially what?"

She looked at him in the flashlight's glow, and Jake saw something that might've been fear in her eyes. "Especially when I'm with you. Been getting stronger every day since we met."

Jake reached for her hand and felt the vibration increase the moment their fingers touched. The carved patterns around the doorway seemed to pulse in his peripheral vision, and for just a moment, he could've sworn he saw light flickering in the darkness beyond the threshold—not electric light, but something older and stranger.

"Emma," he started to say, but she was pulling him away from the door.

"We should go. Getting dark, and Mom'll worry."

They hiked back down to the farm mostly in silence, but Jake couldn't stop thinking about the door and the way Emma's hand had trembled in his. That night, he dreamed about standing at the threshold while something vast and patient waited in the darkness beyond, something that whispered his name in Emma's voice.

Next few days, Jake found himself thinking about the door during every quiet moment—between vaccinating Mrs. Henderson's ancient tomcat and stitching up a beagle who'd had an argument with a porcupine. Local historical society occupied the back room of the library, run by a retired teacher delighted to have someone actually interested in local history. She had precious little about the pre-colonial period, but she dug up some interesting documents. Surveyor's report from 1823 mentioned "a curious stone archway of unknown origin," and a WPA folklore collection from the 1930s included an interview with an elderly Seneca woman who called it "the place where the hungry seasons wait."

More disturbing was a newspaper clipping from 1952. James and Dorothy Whitmore, both twenty-six, had been missing three weeks before someone found them unconscious at the base of the stone door. Newspaper photo showed two people who looked ancient despite their listed ages—white hair, deeply lined faces, hands like claws. They died within days, and the coroner couldn't determine what had caused their rapid aging.

Jake tried dismissing it as some kind of hoax, but the newspaper was legitimate, photos too detailed to be faked. More unsettling was a quote from Dorothy Whitmore's sister: "She kept saying they'd found the door, that their love had opened it. But she also said something was coming through, something that had been waiting a very long time."

That evening, Jake drove out to the farm with a bottle of wine and a head full of questions. Found Emma in the barn, helping a mare through a difficult birth, arms covered in blood and birthing fluids up to her elbows. Barn smelled like hay and leather and the deep, animal scent of birth.

"Perfect timing," she said without looking up. "Hold this flashlight steady and try not to pass out on me."

Jake held the light while Emma worked with calm competence, guiding the foal into the world with gentle hands and murmured encouragement. When it was over and the mare was nuzzling her newborn, Emma stood, wiped her hands on a towel that had seen more births than most midwives.

"Beautiful," Jake said, watching the foal struggle to its feet on impossibly long legs.

"New life always is." Emma leaned against him, and Jake wrapped his arms around her despite the barn smell and the blood on her clothes. "What brings you by so late?"

"I've been looking into the door. The couple who opened it in 1952—"

Emma went rigid in his arms. "Jake, don't."

"They said their love opened it, Emma. And you said the vibrations get stronger when we're together."

"So?"

"So I think we're in danger of opening something that should stay closed."

Emma pulled away from him and began cleaning her equipment with sharp, angry movements. "And what do you suggest we do about that? Stop seeing each other? Pretend we don't feel what we feel?"

"I don't know. Maybe we could—"

"What? Love each other less?" Emma threw the towel aside and faced him. "Don't work that way, Jake. I tried to warn you, tried to keep my distance, but it's too damn late for that now."

Jake stared at her. "What do you mean, too late?"

"I mean I love you." Words came out fierce and desperate, like something torn from her chest. "Love you more than I've ever loved anyone, and it's growing stronger every day whether I want it to or not. And unless you got some way to turn that off, we're both screwed."

Jake felt his heart swell in his chest until he thought it might burst. "Emma—"

"Don't say it back unless you mean it. Don't say it unless you're ready for whatever happens next."

Jake looked at her standing there in barn light, covered in blood and sweat and barn dust, more beautiful than anyone had a right to be. "I love you too. Love you so much it scares the hell out of me."

The moment the words left his mouth, air around them changed—like the moment before lightning strikes when every metal filling in your head starts to ache. Vibration Jake had felt at the door thrummed through the barn like a tuning fork struck against stone, making horses whinny nervously and barn cats scatter for cover. In the distance, Jake heard stone grinding against stone, like millstones turning after years of silence.

Emma grabbed his hand. "Run."

They sprinted from the barn toward the farmhouse, but before they reached the porch, a sound rolled down from the hills that made Jake's teeth ache—deep, resonant tone like the world's largest bell struck once and allowed to ring forever. Horses screamed in their stalls, and every dog in the valley began howling at once.

"Mom! Dad!" Emma burst through the front door with Jake close behind.

Sarah and Robert were standing in the living room, staring out the window toward the hills. "It's open," Sarah said quietly.

Jake followed their gaze and felt his blood turn to ice water. Where the stone door had been, a pillar of pale light now reached up into the night sky like a beacon calling something home. As they watched, the light pulsed once, twice, and began to fade.

"How long?" Robert asked, his voice flat.

"Until what?" Jake said.

"Until whatever's been waiting comes through," Emma said. "Last time, James and Dorothy had three weeks before it found them."

Sarah turned from the window. "Pack your things. We're leaving tonight."

"Mom, no. This is our home."

"This stopped being our home the minute that door opened." Sarah's voice carried an authority that shut down argument. "We got relatives in Montana. We can stay there until—"

"Until what? Until it gets bored and goes back to sleep?" Emma shook her head. "Running won't help none. It opened for us, which means it can find us anywhere we go."

Jake felt like he was drowning in a conversation he didn't understand. "Find us for what?"

"To feed," Robert said quietly. "The old stories, the ones the Seneca told—they said something lived in the space between seasons, something that fed on time itself. Would take the years from people who loved deeply enough to open the door."

"That's impossible."

"Is it?" Emma pulled him to the window and pointed at the hillside where the door had been. "Look."

Jake looked, and his rational mind tried to reject what he was seeing. The light from the door had faded, but something was moving in the darkness around it. Shapes that didn't quite resolve into anything recognizable, flowing down the hillside like oil mixed with starlight. They moved wrong—too fluid for animals, too purposeful for shadows.

"We have to go," Sarah said again.

"No." Emma straightened her shoulders. "I won't run from my own home. And I won't let that thing hurt anyone else because of something Jake and I did."

"Emma, be reasonable—"

"I am being reasonable. James and Dorothy tried to run too, remember? Made it all the way to the next county before it caught up with them." Emma looked at Jake. "We opened it. We have to close it."

"How?"

"Don't know yet. But I know someone who might."

The someone turned out to be Margaret Crow Feather, an elderly Seneca woman who lived alone in a cabin on the reservation about twenty miles east of town. Emma drove while Jake tried to process everything that had happened in the last hour. The rational part of his mind insisted this was all some kind of elaborate stress-induced hallucination, but the rest of him knew better. You couldn't hallucinate the taste of copper in your mouth or the way your bones ached from standing too close to something ancient and hungry.

"Tell me about Margaret," he said as Emma navigated dark country roads that seemed to exist in defiance of any logical planning.

"She's a traditionalist. Keeps the old ways, speaks the old language. Most folks think she's just a crazy old woman who talks to trees, but she knows things other people forgot." Emma took a sharp turn that made Jake grab the door handle. "She tried to warn my grandfather about the door when he bought the farm back in '63. Told him the land was hungry and anyone who loved too deep there would end up feeding it whether they wanted to or not."

"And he didn't listen?"

"Would you have? Man spends his life savings on a farm, some old Indian woman tells him it's cursed? Hell, I wouldn't have listened either."

Jake considered this. A week ago, he would've dismissed the whole thing as rural superstition. Now, after seeing the light from the door and the shapes moving in the darkness, he wasn't sure what he believed anymore.

Margaret Crow Feather's cabin sat in a clearing surrounded by woods that felt older than memory—the kind of place where the trees had grown thick enough to muffle car engines and cell phone signals alike. Light flickered in the windows, and smoke rose from the chimney despite the warm evening air.

"She's expecting us," Emma said as they climbed the porch steps that creaked like old bones.

The door opened before they could knock, revealing a tiny woman with steel-gray hair braided down her back and dark eyes that seemed to hold more years than her lined face suggested. "Emma Kendrick," she said in a voice like autumn leaves scraping against pavement. "And the one who loves her."

"Margaret, we need your help."

"I know what you need. Come inside before something follows you here."

The cabin's interior looked like it belonged to a different century. Oil lamps provided flickering light that threw dancing shadows on the walls, herbs hung in bundles from the rafters, and the air smelled of sage and something else Jake couldn't identify—something that reminded him of deep forests and old bones. Margaret gestured for them to sit at a rough wooden table while she moved around the single room gathering items.

"Your grandfather came to see me once," she said to Emma without turning around. "After he bought the farm. Told him the door was there for a reason, that some barriers exist to protect both sides. Said he'd keep people away from it."

"He did. We all did."

"But love finds a way, doesn't it?" Margaret set a leather pouch on the table and sat across from them. "Love always finds a way, especially young love that burns bright and thinks itself immortal."

Jake leaned forward. "Can you tell us what's coming through the door?"

Margaret studied him with those ancient eyes that seemed to see straight through to his bones. "You want to understand this thing. Make sense of it."

"Yeah. I need to know what we're dealing with."

"What you're dealing with has been here longer than any of us. Lives in the spaces between heartbeats, feeds on the time lovers make when they forget the rest of the world exists. You know those moments—when it's just the two of you and nothing else matters?"

Emma gripped Jake's hand under the table. "The couple in 1952—"

"Had fifty years together crammed into three weeks. Every anniversary, every argument, every makeup, every slow morning in bed, every time one got sick and the other made soup—all of it at once. Time moved different for them because they'd given that thing permission to feed on what they had."

"Permission?" Jake said.

"By opening the door. By loving so deeply that they broke through the barrier." Margaret opened the leather pouch and removed what looked like a small stone carving—a spiral pattern that made Jake's eyes water to look at directly. "Love is the most powerful force in the universe, which is why it attracts the attention of things that exist only to consume power."

"So what do we do?" Emma asked.

Margaret was quiet for a long moment, turning the carved stone over in her weathered hands. "Door can be closed, but not from this side. Someone has to go through and seal it from within."

"And then what happens to whoever goes through?"

"They become part of the barrier. Their love becomes the lock that keeps the door sealed."

Margaret met Emma's eyes. "Forever."

The cabin fell silent except for the crackle of the fire and the whisper of wind in the trees outside. Jake felt Emma's hand tighten on his as the implications sank in like stones thrown into deep water.

"There's got to be another way," he said finally.

"There is. You can let it feed until it's satisfied and moves on to find another door. 'Course, by then, everyone in the valley will have aged decades in a matter of days." Margaret slipped the carved stone back into the pouch. "Or you can run and hope it doesn't follow you. James and Dorothy tried that."

Emma stood and walked to the window, staring out into the darkness. "How long do we have?"

"It will come for you at dawn. That's when the barrier between worlds is thinnest, when love burns brightest in the morning light."

Jake joined Emma at the window and put his arms around her from behind. She leaned back against him, and he could feel her trembling like a horse before a storm.

"I'm sorry," he whispered into her hair. "I'm so sorry I brought this on you."

"We brought it on each other." Emma turned in his arms. "That's what love is, right? Shared responsibility for the beautiful disasters we create?"

They drove back to the farm in silence, each lost in their own thoughts. The light from the door had vanished, but Jake could still feel the wrongness in the air, a tension that made his skin crawl like ants were marching under it. When they pulled into the farmyard, they found Sarah and Robert waiting on the porch with suitcases at their feet.

"We're not running," Emma said before they could speak.

"Emma, please—" Sarah started.

"No, Mom. This is my choice. Jake's and mine." Emma took Jake's hand. "Margaret says it'll come at dawn. We're gonna meet it at the door."

Robert's face went pale. "You can't mean to go through it."

"One of us has to. Only way to close it permanently."

"Both of us," Jake corrected quietly.

Emma stared at him. "Jake, no. You don't understand what that means."

"I understand that I'm not letting you face this alone. I understand that if one of us goes through that door, we go together." Jake looked at Sarah and Robert. "I'm sorry this happened. Sorry we brought this to your family. But I love your daughter more than my own life, and I won't let her sacrifice herself because of something we did together."

Sarah wiped tears from her eyes with the back of her hand. "There's got to be another way."

"Margaret was clear," Emma said gently. "This is the only way to make sure it doesn't happen to anyone else."

They spent the remaining hours of the night on the porch, talking quietly and watching the stars fade toward dawn. Sarah made coffee that no one drank, and Robert told stories about Emma's childhood that made her laugh despite everything—how she'd tried to ride the old bull when she was six, how she'd hidden a family of raccoons in the barn loft for three weeks before they found them. Jake called his sister and left a voicemail saying he loved her and to take care of herself, trying to keep his voice steady.

As the eastern horizon began to lighten with the pale gold of early morning, Jake felt the vibration in his bones growing stronger. The horses in the barn whinnied nervously, and the barn cats crept closer to the house like they were seeking protection from something they couldn't see but could feel in their animal bones.

"It's time," Emma said.

They walked up into the hills hand in hand as the sun painted the sky pink and gold. The grove around the stone door felt different now—the air thick as honey, charged with an energy that made Jake's teeth ache and his vision blur around the edges. The door itself stood open, revealing not darkness but a swirling gray void that seemed to pull at his vision like a magnet pulling iron filings.

Something moved in that void, vast and patient and hungry, waiting for them with the patience of geological time.

"Second thoughts?" Emma asked quietly.

Jake squeezed her hand. "None. You?"

"Just one. Wish we'd had more time."

"Maybe we will. Margaret said love creates time—maybe wherever we're going, we'll have all the time in the world."

Emma smiled through her tears. "I love you, Jake Sullivan."

"I love you too, Emma Kendrick. Forever and a day."

They stepped forward together toward the threshold, and Jake felt the entity's attention focus on them like the weight of eternity pressing down on his shoulders. Void in the doorway swirled faster, and he caught glimpses of what might've been other times, other places, other couples who had made this same choice across centuries of love and sacrifice.

But just before they reached the threshold, Emma stopped.

"Wait," she said, pulling the carved stone Margaret had given them from her pocket. "She said to use this to seal the door from the other side."

Jake took the stone and felt it pulse with warmth in his palm like a heartbeat. The spiral pattern carved into its surface seemed to move and flow, matching the carvings around the door itself.

"Together?" Emma asked.

"Together."

They stepped through the doorway holding hands, and Jake felt reality shift around them like water finding a new channel. The last thing he saw of the world they were leaving was the sun rising over the valley, painting everything in shades of gold and possibility.

Then the door closed behind them with a sound like the end of the world.

Sarah and Robert found the stone archway sealed with smooth granite that looked like it had never been disturbed. Where intricate carvings had once covered the surface, only Margaret's spiral symbol remained, carved deep into the rock and warm to the touch like skin in summer sunlight.

The wrongness in the air was gone. The horses had stopped whinnying, and the cats emerged from their hiding places to sun themselves in the morning light. In the distance, a rooster crowed, and the world began to feel normal again—or as normal as it ever got in a valley where love had the power to open doors between worlds.

But sometimes, on quiet evenings when the light slants just right through the trees, Sarah swears she can hear laughter echoing from the hillside—the sound of two people who found all the time in the world for love, even if they had to leave this world to find it.

The stone door remains sealed, and Margaret Crow Feather visits the grove twice a year to leave offerings of sage and wildflowers. She says the barrier is stronger now, reinforced by a love so pure it chose sacrifice over survival.

And in the town below, people notice that couples seem to last longer, love deeper, fight less. Children grow up secure in their parents' affection, and even the oldest marriages retain a spark that outsiders find remarkable. The divorce rate dropped to nearly zero, and the local wedding industry boomed as couples from three states away came to Millbrook to exchange vows.

Love, it seems, has a way of opening doors.

A Crazy Little Thing Called Love

Twelve years of couples therapy, and Sarah had never seen anything like what was walking into her office. Emergency referrals backing up her voicemail, three colleagues calling in a single morning to ask if she was seeing "unusual presentations."

"He carved my name into his chest," Rebecca Torres whispered, pressing a tissue against her eyes. "With a paring knife from the kitchen. Forty-seven stitches."

Across the room, Vincent Torres stared at his wife with the kind of focus Sarah usually saw in severe attachment disorders. His hands twisted in his lap. "It's like—like I can't breathe when she's not right here. I keep thinking about..." He glanced at Rebecca, then away. "About making sure she can't leave."

"Vincent's been talking about installing deadbolts," Rebecca said. Her laugh came out shaky. "Inside locks. You know, so I'd be safe. Except I'd be the one locked in."

Sarah kept her voice level. "How are you feeling about that, Rebecca?"

"Scared shitless." Rebecca touched her throat where Sarah could see faint bruise marks. "But also... God, this sounds insane, but part of me thinks it's sweet? Like he finally cares enough to—" She stopped. "That's not normal, is it?"

The Torres case marked the seventh identical presentation Sarah had seen in three weeks. Previously stable couples developing acute romantic obsession with violent ideation, onset sudden enough to warrant emergency intervention. All of them describing the same cognitive dissonance—recognizing their thoughts as pathological while simultaneously finding them irresistibly compelling.

In her notes, Sarah had started calling it "paradoxical romantic fixation with insight preservation." Clinical language for something that made no goddamn sense.

"When did these feelings start?" Sarah asked Vincent.

"Valentine's Day." He rubbed his forehead. "We were walking through Riverside Park after dinner, and I saw this shooting star. Made a wish that Rebecca would love me as much as I love her." His voice dropped. "Next thing I knew, I couldn't think about anything else."

Rebecca nodded. "I saw it too. Moved slow for a meteor, you know? Really bright. I wished Vincent would show me how much he really cared." She touched her throat again. "Guess I got what I asked for."

Sarah made notes, adding the Torres case to her growing matrix: dates, symptoms, locations. Seven couples, all describing meteors on Valentine's Day, all developing identical symptom clusters within hours.

"Have either of you considered medication compliance? Any recent changes in—"

"Doc, this isn't my Zoloft," Vincent interrupted. "This is something else. This is love, but like... turned up to eleven. Like someone took normal feelings and ran them through an amplifier."

After they left, Sarah pulled her calendar and confirmed what her gut already knew. Every single case: February 14th. Valentine's Day.

Twenty-three years of clinical practice had taught her to recognize patterns. When multiple clients presented with identical symptoms simultaneously, you looked for shared environmental factors. Usually trauma—natural disasters, economic crisis, community violence.

She'd never seen anything that could cause instant-onset romantic obsession in previously stable couples.

That evening, Sarah drove to Riverside Park. The area where most of her clients claimed to have seen the meteor was popular for Valentine's dates—park benches overlooking the Housatonic River, strings of café lights the parks department installed every February.

She found Tom Carlisle, the maintenance supervisor, emptying trash bins near the river walkway.

"Strange question," Sarah said, showing her credentials. "Did your crew find anything unusual around here on February 15th? Any debris, decorations, anything out of place?"

Tom straightened up, wincing slightly. "Funny you should ask. We found these arrows scattered around. Must've been from some Valentine's party, but they were way too fancy for party store stuff." He gestured toward the maintenance shed. "My wife's been after me to bring them home for her craft projects."

"Could I take a look?"

Inside the storage shed that smelled of fertilizer and motor oil, Tom showed her a cardboard box containing what had to be the strangest

Valentine's decorations Sarah had ever seen. Twenty-odd arrows, each about six inches long, appearing to be made of actual gold with intricate engravings. The crystal tips pulsed with their own inner light, and touching one made Sarah's chest feel warm in a way that had nothing to do with the March chill still clinging to her jacket.

"Anyone else handle these?" she asked, wrapping one carefully in a shop rag.

"Just me and Linda." Tom grinned. "Tell you what, we had quite a weekend after I brought a few home. Twenty-three years of marriage, and we acted like teenagers. Couldn't keep our hands off each other."

Sarah's blood chilled. "Did either of you experience any unusual thoughts? Any impulses about preventing the other person from leaving?"

The grin faded from Tom's face. "Well, now that you mention it, Linda did hide my car keys for three days. Said she was worried I'd realize I could do better and take off." He paused. "And I may have suggested we get matching tattoos. On our faces."

"But those feelings have passed?"

"Mostly. Though Linda still checks my phone every night, and I get panicky when she's more than an hour late from work."

Sarah borrowed one of the arrows, trying not to think about how warm it felt through the cloth, how much she wanted to unwrap it and look at it again.

The next morning, she took the arrow to Dr. James Fletcher at the university's archaeology department. She'd consulted with him before on cases involving patients who claimed supernatural influences—usually the answer was psychological projection, but Fletcher was good at identifying genuine historical artifacts.

"This is extraordinary," Fletcher said, examining the arrow under his magnifying glass. "The workmanship suggests ancient techniques, but the materials shouldn't exist. This gold alloy contains elements that weren't discovered until the twentieth century, but the crafting methods are clearly pre-Roman."

"Could it be a modern reproduction?"

"Not with these engravings." He pointed to symbols carved along the shaft. "This is Linear A script—hasn't been used for over three thousand years. But it's mixed with Latin phrases and even some modern English." He looked up. "It's like someone kept updating an ancient artifact through the centuries."

Sarah leaned closer. Among the incomprehensible ancient symbols, she could make out Latin phrases: "Amor Vincit Omnia," "Semper

Fidelis," and strangest of all, in clear English: "Love Hurts - but it shouldn't hurt this much."

"Dr. Fletcher, is there any mythological precedent for arrows that cause people to fall in love? I know it sounds absurd, but I'm running out of rational explanations."

Fletcher set down his magnifying glass and looked at her with the patient expression she recognized from professors who'd heard stranger questions. "You're thinking of Cupid's arrows, aren't you?"

"I'm thinking of anything that might explain why twenty couples in this town suddenly developed violent romantic obsessions after seeing a meteor on Valentine's Day."

"Well, in classical mythology, Cupid carried two types of arrows. Golden arrows that caused intense love, and lead arrows that caused indifference or hatred." Fletcher pulled out a reference book. "But here's something interesting—in the later Roman sources, there are references to Cupid becoming... unstable."

"Unstable how?"

"The myths describe him growing tired of the same patterns. People falling in love, breaking up, falling in love with someone else, dying, being reborn, starting over. The stories suggest he became erratic in his interventions—creating obsessions instead of healthy attractions, shooting people with the wrong arrows, making people fall in love with inappropriate partners."

Fletcher turned pages in his reference book. "The last recorded mention describes him as 'a mad god, drunk on his own power, turning love into a weapon against humanity.'"

Sarah spent the next few days digesting this information, cross-referencing her case notes with Fletcher's mythological research. By the end of the week, she'd developed enough of a theory to warrant bringing her clients together.

Over the following week, Sarah scheduled three smaller group sessions—the scale of the crisis made individual appointments impossible, but professional ethics demanded manageable group sizes. The first session, eight couples experiencing identical symptoms, met in the conference room at the Millbrook Community Center on Elm Street.

Sarah looked around the room and saw the same barely controlled intensity in every face, the same desperate quality that made normal conversation nearly impossible. Outside, she could hear the steady hum of traffic from Route 7, the ordinary sounds of a Connecticut suburb where something impossible had happened.

"I want everyone to describe exactly what happened on Valentine's Day," she said. "Start with what you saw in the sky."

The stories were consistent in ways that made Sarah's skin crawl. Around nine PM, couples throughout Riverside Park had seen what appeared to be a slow-moving meteor. But unlike normal meteors, this one had seemed to respond to their presence—changing direction, slowing down, hovering directly overhead while they made their wishes.

"It was like it was listening," said Janet Mayhew, whose husband had been arrested for attempting to chain her to their bed. "I wished Tom would love me the way he did when we first met, and the star pulsed brighter."

"I wished my wife would stop taking me for granted," said Robert Kim, whose wife Angela had quit her job to follow him around twenty-four hours a day. "The star made this sound—like bells ringing—and then it shot down toward the park."

"And how long after that did your feelings change?"

A chorus of overlapping voices: "Right away"—"Immediately"—"That same night"—"Within the hour." The similarity of their responses was unsettling enough that several people looked around the room with confused expressions, as if realizing for the first time how identical their experiences had been.

Sarah had been developing a theory, and their responses confirmed her suspicions. "Has anyone tried to create distance from their partner? Stay with friends, take a vacation?"

Rebecca Torres raised her hand tentatively. "I tried to visit my sister in Chicago. Made it as far as the airport before I collapsed. Paramedics thought I was having a heart attack—my blood pressure had spiked to stroke levels."

Tom Mayhew nodded grimly. "Same thing here. Well, not exactly the same. Tried to check into a hotel for a few days, clear my head. Ended up in the ER with what they called 'acute separation anxiety psychosis.'"

"I couldn't even make it to my car," said Maria Gutierrez quietly. "Just thinking about leaving made me throw up."

Robert Kim's wife Angela had been silent until now. "I quit my job," she said, her voice flat. "Twenty years at the bank, and I quit so I could follow him around. I know how crazy that sounds, but I physically can't let him out of my sight."

Sarah realized they were dealing with genuine physical dependencies, not just emotional attachments. Whatever had happened to these people had created biochemical bonds.

"Look, I want everyone to consider something," she said, choosing her words carefully. "When I see identical symptoms across multiple clients, I start looking for shared environmental factors. Usually it's trauma—a disaster, economic crisis, community event. But your experiences..." She paused. "They match historical accounts of supernatural intervention in human relationships."

Nervous laughter filled the room, but Sarah continued.

"I've found physical evidence—golden arrows with biological samples, matching classical descriptions of Cupid's weapons. Your experiences correspond to mythology about a love god who's lost stability and begun turning love into obsession."

"So what do we do?" asked Maria Gutierrez. "How do you fight a god?"

The conference room windows didn't just break—they imploded with a sound like a gunshot, safety glass cascading across the industrial carpet in chunks that caught the fluorescent light. Sarah felt the change in air pressure pop her ears, smelled something like ozone and burnt copper. The figure that dropped through the opening landed cat-silent among the glass shards, and the room's temperature dropped ten degrees in an instant.

He looked exactly like the Renaissance paintings—golden curls, perfect features, flowing robes, ornate bow. But his eyes held a manic gleam, and his smile was too wide, too pleased with the chaos he'd created.

"Did someone call my name?" Cupid asked, his voice carrying harmonics that made everyone dizzy. "I do so love it when mortals recognize my work."

The couples in the room gravitated toward each other, pulled by invisible threads that made separation physically painful. Sarah watched her clients move like marionettes, positioning themselves protectively around their partners.

"You," Cupid pointed at Sarah with one of his golden arrows. "The one interfering with my art. Do you have any idea how long it took me to create these perfect bonds?"

"Your bonds are destroying them," Sarah said, fighting to keep her voice steady. "They can't function as individuals anymore."

Cupid's laugh was like breaking glass. "Individuals? Mortals were never meant to be individuals. You're incomplete fragments, desperately searching for your missing pieces. I simply reunite you."

"By making them obsessed and violent?"

"By showing them truth!" Cupid's expression shifted from amusement to rage. "Do you know what I've endured for millennia? Watching you stumble through pathetic attempts at love, settling for comfortable partnerships instead of soul-deep connection? Watching you choose independence over unity, safety over transformation?"

He fitted an arrow to his bow and aimed it at Sarah. "You want to know what love really is? Let me show you."

The arrow flew faster than thought, but it struck Dr. Fletcher instead. Sarah spun around—he'd been standing by the back wall, having arrived during the session after she'd called him about the group's shared experiences with the arrows. The golden tip dissolved on contact with his skin, his expression changing.

Fletcher looked at Sarah with the same desperate intensity she'd seen in her clients, but magnified beyond anything she'd witnessed. He moved toward her with predatory focus.

"Sarah," he whispered, his voice thick with artificial emotion. "You're everything. I need you—need to keep you safe, keep you close, make sure nothing ever hurts you or takes you away."

"James, fight it," Sarah said, backing away. "It's supernatural manipulation."

"It feels real," Fletcher said, still advancing. "It feels like the most real thing I've ever experienced. Don't you see that we belong together?"

Cupid clapped his hands. "Perfect! The scholar who thought he understood mythology, now experiencing it firsthand. Tell me, Dr. Fletcher, what do the books say about fighting divine love?"

Fletcher's expression showed confusion as his rational mind fought the chemical flood of supernatural emotion. "The books... the books say you can't fight it. But they also say..." He struggled to remember. "They say you have two types of arrows."

"Very good!" Cupid pulled out a different arrow, this one with a lead tip that pulsed with dark energy. "Golden arrows create love, lead arrows create indifference. But I've made improvements. This version doesn't just create indifference—it creates hatred. Perfect, consuming hatred that matches the intensity of love."

Sarah saw what he planned. "You're going to turn them against each other."

"I'm going to show them the full spectrum! Love and hate, devotion and destruction!" Cupid's voice rose to a shriek. "For too long I've been constrained by mortal expectations. Gentle, healthy, balanced—how boring!"

He aimed the lead arrow at Rebecca Torres. "Let's see what happens when perfect love becomes perfect hatred."

The arrow struck Rebecca in the shoulder, and her expression transformed. The desperate love she'd been showing Vincent became equally desperate revulsion.

"Get away from me," she snarled, backing toward the window. "Don't touch me. The sight of you makes me sick."

Vincent, still under the golden arrow's influence, reached for her desperately. "Rebecca, please—"

"Your love is poison!" she screamed, grabbing a piece of broken glass. "I have to stop it!"

She lunged at Vincent with the shard, and Sarah understood that Cupid's modifications created maximum chaos—love and hate with equal intensity, both sides ready to kill for their feelings.

"Stop this," Sarah said. "You're going to get people killed."

"Death is just another transformation," Cupid said, fitting another lead arrow. "Some love stories end in tragedy—that doesn't make them less beautiful."

He aimed at Tom Mayhew, but Sarah threw herself forward, knocking his aim off. The arrow struck the wall and embedded in the plaster, spreading dark veins like infection.

Cupid spun toward Sarah, his perfect features twisted with inhuman rage. "You dare interfere with a god's work?"

"I dare try to protect people from someone who's lost his mind."

"Lost my mind?" Cupid's voice became dangerously quiet. "I've found clarity. For millennia, I've tried to give humanity perfect love, and you've consistently rejected it. You want independence, personal space, individual identity. You're terrified of the vulnerability that real love requires."

He gestured to the chaos around them. "So I decided to give you what you really want. Drama. Intensity. Love that consumes everything in its path."

"This isn't love," Sarah said. "This is manipulation."

"All love is manipulation! Chemistry, biology, evolutionary drives—sophisticated methods of forcing people to bond. I'm simply being honest about the process."

Dr. Fletcher, still under the golden arrow's influence, had worked his way around the room. Now he appeared behind Cupid with a chair, bringing it down on the god's head with surprising force.

Cupid staggered but didn't fall. Instead, he turned to Fletcher with delighted surprise. "The scholar has teeth! Let's see how you feel about violence when properly motivated."

He shot Fletcher with a lead arrow, and the artificial love transformed into equally artificial hatred—but directed inward.

"What have I done?" Fletcher whispered, staring at his hands in horror. "I tried to hurt someone. I felt like I owned someone." He began clawing at his own face. "I'm disgusting. I have to punish myself."

Sarah saw that Cupid's lead arrows didn't just create hatred toward others—they could create self-hatred intense enough to drive self-destruction.

"You're killing them," she said.

"I'm freeing them from the prison of moderation, the tyranny of emotional restraint. Look—when have you ever seen humans feel so deeply?"

He was right, in a horrible way. The people in the room were experiencing emotions more intense than most humans ever felt. But they were also losing their minds.

Sarah remembered reading that gods could be bound by their own rules, limited by the nature of their divine responsibilities.

"Cupid," she said, "what happens when someone doesn't want to love anymore? When they've been hurt so badly that they choose emotional numbness over feeling anything?"

His expression faltered. "That's... that's not how it works. Everyone wants love."

"But what if someone chooses to reject that drive entirely? What if they decide love—any kind of love—is too dangerous to risk?"

"Impossible," Cupid said, but his voice lacked conviction.

Sarah looked around the room at the chaos he'd created—couples destroying each other in the name of perfect emotion, people driven insane by supernatural feelings they couldn't control or escape. As a therapist, she'd spent twelve years helping people process and integrate their emotions healthily. What Cupid offered was the opposite—feeling without choice, love without consent, intensity without growth.

"I reject love," she said, her voice gaining strength. "All of it. I choose emotional numbness over this destruction. I choose isolation over connection that requires losing yourself. I choose to feel nothing rather than feel this much."

The statement felt like professional betrayal—everything she'd trained for, everything she believed about human connection—but watching her clients tear each other apart, she meant every word.

Cupid's bow wavered. "You can't mean that."

"I do. Looking at what you've done to these people, I want no part of any emotion you have power over. I reject love, I reject hate, I reject everything you represent."

The golden arrows in Cupid's quiver began to lose their luster, and the god himself seemed to flicker.

"No," he whispered. "You need love. Everyone needs love. Without it, you're just... empty."

"Then I choose emptiness."

The other people in the room, hearing Sarah's declaration, began to understand what she was doing.

"I reject this love," said Rebecca Torres, dropping the glass shard. "I choose emptiness over insanity."

"I reject the obsession," said Vincent Torres. "I choose numbness over this pain."

"I reject all of it," said Maria Gutierrez, Tom Mayhew, Patricia Wells, and the others, their voices gaining strength.

With each rejection, Cupid grew more transparent, his power weakening as his fundamental purpose was denied.

"You don't understand," he pleaded, his manic confidence crumbling. "Without love, life has no meaning. I was trying to save you from emptiness."

"You were trying to save yourself from irrelevance," Sarah said. "Love has been evolving, becoming more conscious and consensual, and that threatened your power. So you tried to turn it back into something primitive and destructive."

Cupid's form continued to fade. "I just wanted to matter. For millennia, I've watched humans struggle with relationships, and I thought if I could show them perfect love..."

Sarah felt unexpected sympathy for the mad god. "Perfect love doesn't require losing yourself. Perfect love is choosing someone while remaining yourself."

"But that's so... ordinary," Cupid whispered as he became almost transparent.

"Ordinary can be beautiful too."

With a sound like a sigh that seemed to come from every broken heart in history, Cupid disappeared. His arrows clattered to the floor, their supernatural glow fading to reveal ordinary gold and lead. The temperature in the room slowly returned to normal, and the smell of ozone dissipated, replaced by the everyday scents of industrial carpet and coffee from the community center's kitchen down the hall.

The aftermath was gradual. The people Cupid had manipulated didn't return to their previous emotional states immediately—the supernatural bonds took weeks to dissolve. But as the artificial chemicals worked out of their systems, Sarah's clients began to remember what healthy love felt like.

Some marriages survived; others didn't. But even the divorces pro-
ceeded more calmly, processed by people who could think about their
feelings again.

Dr. Fletcher required extensive therapy to recover from the conflicting emotions Cupid had forced on him, but he was able to separate his
genuine respect for Sarah from the artificial obsession.

"Do you think he's gone?" Fletcher asked during one of their sessions.

"I think he's learning," Sarah said. "The old model of love as possession and obsession is dying out. Maybe Cupid can evolve too."

She kept one of the golden arrows as a reminder—not of supernatural
chaos, but of the choice everyone had made to reject toxic intensity in
favor of emotional authenticity.

Six months later, Sarah received a Valentine's Day card with no return address. Inside, written in elegant script: "Thank you for teaching
me that even gods can learn to love better. - A friend."

That night, she saw a shooting star over Riverside Park. But this
time, couples who made wishes reported feeling more aware of their
emotions, more capable of communicating with their partners, more
confident in choosing love without losing themselves.

Maybe Cupid had learned the difference between love and obsession.

Or maybe, Sarah thought as she watched the star fade over the
Housatonic River, sometimes even gods needed therapy.

This Is Only a Test

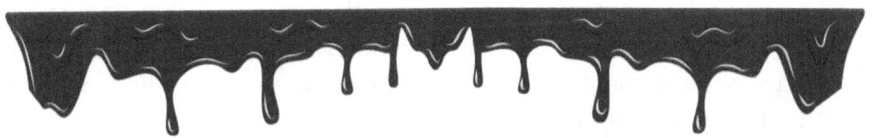

C hristopher Mills woke up to the smell of cheap floor cleaner and that fluorescent light buzz that made his teeth ache. The orange plastic chair under him was the same uncomfortable piece of shit they'd had in his high school—molded, cracked along the armrest, probably older than some of his coworkers.

Around him, rows of people sat hunched over desks like they were taking the SATs. Nobody looked up. A few were crying quietly. Others just stared at papers in front of them with the thousand-yard stare of someone who'd just gotten the worst news of their life.

The truck. Christopher's stomach dropped as it came back—screeching brakes, the impact, then nothing. Now he was here, wherever the hell here was, still wearing his blue button-down and khakis from the sales meeting he'd never made it to. No blood. No pain. No twisted metal. Just this.

"Christopher." The voice came from the front, and when he looked up, his blood went cold.

Mrs. Sendlenski stood behind the teacher's desk, exactly like she'd been thirty-five years ago in third grade. Same gray hair in that tight bun, same wire-rimmed glasses, same look that said she knew you'd been picking your nose and was deciding whether to call you out on it. But Mrs. Sendlenski had been ancient when he was eight. She should've been dead for decades.

"Come on now, take your seat." She tapped her pencil on the desk the way she used to when someone was dawdling at the pencil sharpener. "Lots to get through today."

Christopher's voice came out like sandpaper. "I don't understand."

"You will." She picked up a manila folder thick as a phone book. "We've got your whole file here, Christopher. Every choice you made, every decision, every time you picked between being nice and being mean. Today we're going through all of it together."

Christopher looked around the room again. The other people—souls, he guessed—sat perfectly still, absorbed in their own papers. Some looked like they'd been crying for hours. Others had that hollow-eyed look of people who'd run out of tears.

"Where am I?"

"Summer school." Mrs. Sendlenski walked over, her sensible shoes clicking on linoleum that had probably been installed sometime during the Carter administration. "You know how this works, honey. Same as third grade—you don't pass, you don't move up."

She set the thick stack of papers in front of him. The header made his throat close up: "LIFE REVIEW - CHRISTOPHER ALAN MILLS - COMPLETE ASSESSMENT."

"We'll start easy," she said, settling into her chair like she had all the time in the world. "Page one."

Christopher's hands shook as he opened to the first page. The photograph hit him like a punch—him at twelve, standing in Murphy's Pharmacy, holding a Snickers bar he hadn't paid for.

Below the photo: "October 15th, 1987. Subject observed stealing candy bar from Murphy's Pharmacy. Store owner distracted. No witnesses. Subject had choice: return item or proceed with theft."

"Jesus." The word slipped out.

"Language, Christopher." Mrs. Sendlenski's voice held the same gentle warning it had when he was eight. "Tell me what you remember."

The memory flooded back. He'd been starving—Mom had been hitting the bottle harder since Dad left, and things like lunch money kept getting forgotten. He'd gone to buy the candy bar with his allowance, then realized he'd left the money at home.

Mr. Murphy was helping some old lady with her prescription. The candy aisle was empty. Christopher had stood there forever, stomach growling, the Snickers heavy in his sweaty palm.

"I took it." His face burned. "I was hungry and I thought nobody would care about one stupid candy bar."

"How did it taste?"

"Like shit. I mean—" He caught her look. "It didn't taste good. I ate it fast behind the store so nobody would see, but it just made me feel sick."

Mrs. Sendlenski made a note on her clipboard—the same kind she'd used for reading assessments. "Did you ever go back and pay for it?"

Christopher wanted to crawl under the desk. "No. I kept meaning to, but then it felt like too much time had passed and it would be weird."

"Mmm." She walked back to the front of the room. "Page two."

The next photo showed him at sixteen in Jerry Kowalski's basement, surrounded by kids from school. Beer cans and a baggie of weed sat on the card table.

"March 3rd, 1991. Underage drinking party. Jeremy Kowalski's parents out of town. Alcohol and controlled substances present. What did you choose?"

He could practically smell that musty basement, hear the nervous laughter of boys trying to act older than they were.

"I stayed. Had a beer, tried the pot, didn't like how it made me feel dizzy." He paused. "Jerry's little sister Angela was there. She was only fourteen, but she wanted to try everything we were doing."

"And?"

"I told her she shouldn't. That she was too young. But when she started crying and said we were being mean..." His voice cracked. "I gave her half a beer. Figured it was better than a whole one."

Mrs. Sendlenski's face didn't change, but something in her eyes went cold. "Angela Kowalski was hospitalized that night for alcohol poisoning. She'd gotten drinks from multiple sources after you gave her that first one."

The room spun. He gripped the edge of the desk. "What? No. We all scattered when her parents came home early. I never—nobody told me—"

"She recovered. But she developed a drinking problem in college that took her years to overcome." She made another note. "Page three."

The pages kept coming. College—letting his roommate cheat off his exam. His first job—lying about his experience. Throwing a coworker under the bus. Promising charity donations he never sent.

With each page, Mrs. Sendlenski asked the same questions in that patient teacher voice. *What did you do? Why did you do it? How do you think it affected other people?*

The packet seemed endless. His shirt stuck to his back with sweat despite the cool air. His hands shook worse with every page.

"Page forty-seven."

This photo made his breath catch. Him sitting in his car outside his father's house at night, cell phone in his hand. The timestamp read "June 12th, 2018 - 11:47 PM."

"Your father had been calling you for three weeks. Ever since his cancer diagnosis. This was the night before his surgery."

He closed his eyes. He could see Dad's name on the phone screen, could feel the anger burning in his chest. The old man had walked out when Christopher was eleven, started a new family, barely stayed in touch. Why should Christopher drop everything now just because he was sick?

"I didn't call him back."

"Why?"

"Because I was pissed. He'd hurt our family, hurt Mom, and I thought he deserved to go through it alone. I thought..." His voice broke. "I thought he'd get through the surgery fine and maybe I'd deal with it later when I wasn't so angry."

Mrs. Sendlenski's voice was gentle as a scalpel. "Your father died during the operation. Complications from anesthesia. You never spoke to him again."

The words hit like he'd been punched. He'd known Dad was dead—had gone to the funeral in his black suit, stood in the back while his stepmother cried—but he'd never known about the calls.

"I didn't know." He whispered. "She never said he'd called."

"He wanted to apologize. For leaving, for not being the father you needed. He'd written you a letter, but he was hoping to read it to you first, over the phone."

He put his head in his hands. "Oh God. Oh Jesus."

"Would you like to hear it?"

"No." The word came out strangled. "Please. I can't."

Mrs. Sendlenski nodded and made another note. "Page fifty-one."

More photos. The homeless man he'd walked past every day for two years. The neighbor's cat he'd hit with his car and never reported—just drove away. The elderly woman who'd fallen in the grocery store parking lot while he was loading his car, and how he'd pretended not to see because he was running late for a date.

But it wasn't just the failures. There were good moments too—times when he'd helped people, shown kindness, done the right thing. Mrs. Sendlenski asked about those as well, but somehow they felt smaller. Like coins scattered on the floor of a burning house.

"Excuse me." The voice was barely a whisper.

He looked back two rows to where a woman maybe sixty, with silver hair and kind eyes red from crying, was watching him. Her test packet was even thicker than his.

"How long have you been here?"

She smiled sadly. "This time? About six hours. But I've taken this test four times now. Maybe five—I lose track."

"What happens if you fail?"

"You start over. New life, clean slate, but you don't remember your previous attempts. You make the same mistakes until you learn." She shrugged. "The first time I was here, I was so angry. Kept telling them the test was unfair, that life was too complicated for simple right-and-wrong answers."

"Isn't it?"

"That's what I thought. But the longer I've been doing this, the more I realize kindness is usually the simple answer. It's just not always the easy one."

Mrs. Sendlenski cleared her throat. "Mr. Mills, when you're ready?"

Christopher turned back to his packet. The woman gave him an encouraging nod and returned to her own work.

"Page fifty-eight."

The photograph showed him at thirty-two, standing in his office building's parking lot while rain poured down. Janet Reese from accounts payable was struggling with a flat tire, her clothes soaked, wrestling with a lug wrench too big for her hands.

"November 8th, 2007. Janet Reese experiencing car trouble during storm. You observed the situation while leaving work."

He remembered this perfectly. Shitty day dealing with an angry client, rain coming down in sheets, all he'd wanted was to get home.

"I kept walking. Told myself she probably had AAA or somebody would help her."

"Did someone help her?"

"Not that night. She called her ex-husband, but he was out of town. She ended up calling a tow truck and waiting in the rain for two hours. Got pneumonia, was out of work for a week."

Mrs. Sendlenski consulted her notes. "Janet was supporting her mother's cancer treatments. The week of unpaid sick leave meant she had to delay her mother's chemotherapy by a month."

His throat went tight. "I didn't know."

"The delay didn't affect the ultimate outcome—her mother recovered. But Janet blamed herself for the setback. She thought if she'd been stronger, more capable, she could have changed the tire herself."

"I could have helped. Ten minutes. It would have taken me ten minutes."

"Page sixty-one."

This photo showed him sitting in his car outside a pharmacy while an elderly man stood in the rain looking confused and lost.

"March 22nd, 2010. Samuel Wright, age seventy-eight, early-stage dementia, became disoriented after pharmacy visit. You observed his confusion while waiting in your vehicle."

He felt sick. He remembered Mr. Wright standing there for several minutes, looking around like he'd forgotten where he was.

"I watched him for a while. Kept thinking someone from the pharmacy would come out, or his family would show up. I had a meeting."

"What happened to Mr. Wright?"

"I don't know. I drove away."

"Mr. Wright wandered for three hours in the rain before a police officer found him six miles from the pharmacy. He was hypothermic and confused. His daughter had been searching frantically. This incident convinced his family to move him to a memory care facility six months earlier than they'd planned."

He couldn't breathe. "How was I supposed to know he had dementia?"

Mrs. Sendlenski's voice stayed gentle. "You weren't. But you knew he was distressed and needed help. The specifics of why didn't matter as much as your choice to respond to another human being in need."

She walked to the blackboard and wrote in chalk: "EVERY CHOICE CREATES RIPPLES."

"Page sixty-five."

This photo made his chest cave in. Him at twenty-eight, standing in his apartment doorway, facing his younger brother Michael.

"December 15th, 2003. Your brother Michael requested a loan of three thousand dollars for drug rehabilitation. You had the funds available. Michael had defaulted on smaller loans previously."

"I said no." The words felt like broken glass in his throat. "Michael had borrowed money before and never paid it back. I was tired of enabling him."

"Why did he need the money?"

"Cocaine. He'd been using for two years. He'd already been through one rehab that Mom and Dad paid for, and he relapsed within a month. This time he wanted to go to a different place, one that specialized in long-term recovery, but insurance wouldn't cover it."

"And your decision?"

His voice was barely audible. "I told him I couldn't keep throwing good money after bad. That he needed to figure out how to fix his life without depending on other people to pay for it."

"What happened to Michael?"

The question he'd been dreading for fifteen years. He closed his eyes. "He overdosed three weeks later. Fentanyl-laced cocaine. He died January 6th, 2004."

Mrs. Sendlenski consulted her file. "The rehabilitation program he wanted to attend had a seventy-three percent success rate for long-term sobriety. Michael had been clean for two weeks when he came to you, trying to prove he was serious about recovery."

"But he'd failed before. How was I supposed to know this time would be different?"

"You weren't supposed to know. You were supposed to love him anyway."

The truth hit like a sledgehammer. He felt tears streaming down his face. "I did love him."

"Did you tell him that when you refused the loan?"

"No. I told him I was disappointed in him. That I was tired of watching him waste his life."

Mrs. Sendlenski's voice was barely a whisper. "Those were the last words you spoke to your brother."

He broke. Fifteen years of guilt came pouring out in ugly, choking sobs. He'd carried Michael's death with him every day, but he'd never faced the role his own hardened heart had played in the tragedy.

"Page seventy-one."

This photo showed him at forty, sitting in his car in Emma's school parking lot. Through the windshield, he could see his eleven-year-old daughter sitting alone on a bench while other kids played around her.

"April 18th, 2015. Your daughter Emma experiencing social difficulties at school. The counselor had requested a meeting to discuss Emma's isolation and possible bullying. You arrived early."

Christopher remembered this day like a knife in his chest. Emma had been having problems for months—coming home sad, making excuses not to go to school, her grades dropping. The counselor had called him and Karen in for a conference.

"I went to the meeting. I didn't talk to Emma first."

"Why?"

"Because I didn't want to make things worse for her. I thought if the other kids saw her dad coming over, they might tease her more. I figured the counselor would have better advice than anything I could say."

"What did you learn in the meeting?"

"That Emma was being bullied by a group of girls in her class. They were calling her names, excluding her from games, spreading rumors that she smelled bad or that her clothes were weird."

"How did you handle this information?"

Christopher's face burned with shame. "I got angry. Not at the bullies, but at Emma. I asked her why she hadn't told me what was happening, why she'd let them treat her that way. I told her she needed to stand up for herself, that running away from problems wouldn't solve anything."

"How did Emma respond?"

"She started crying and said it wasn't that easy. That the girls were popular and everyone believed them instead of her. She said she'd tried to tell us, but Karen and I were fighting about the divorce and she didn't want to add more problems."

Mrs. Sendlenski made a note. "What Emma needed in that moment wasn't advice but comfort. Not solutions but support. She needed to know that someone believed her and would fight for her."

"I did fight for her," Christopher protested. "I talked to the principal, had meetings with the other parents."

"You addressed the external problem. But you never addressed the internal damage. Emma spent the rest of that school year believing her father thought she was weak for not handling the bullying on her own."

Christopher stared at the photograph of his daughter, remembering how small and lonely she'd looked on that bench. How small and lonely she'd still looked when he'd criticized her instead of comforting her.

"Page seventy-three."

The photo showed him and Karen in their lawyer's office during the divorce proceedings. Karen's face was streaked with tears, and Christopher was leaning back in his chair with his arms crossed, looking like he wanted to fight the world.

"The custody hearing for Emma. Your daughter was seven years old. Karen was requesting primary custody, with you having visitation every other weekend. You could have agreed to this arrangement or fought for joint custody."

Christopher remembered this day. He'd been furious with Karen for filing for divorce, angry about the alimony payments, resentful that his perfect life was falling apart.

"I fought it. Not because I wanted joint custody, but because I wanted to hurt Karen. I knew she couldn't afford a long court battle, and I had a better lawyer."

"What was the result?"

"We got fifty-fifty custody. But I was traveling so much for work that Emma ended up staying with my mother half the time when she was supposed to be with me. Karen had to work extra hours to pay her legal bills, so Emma was in after-school care more."

"How do you think this affected your daughter?"

Christopher's stomach twisted. "She was confused and sad. She started having nightmares, doing worse in school. She blamed herself for the divorce, thought it was her fault that Mommy and Daddy were fighting all the time."

"Did you ever explain to Emma that the divorce wasn't her fault?"

"I meant to, but I was so angry at Karen that I ended up saying things..." Christopher's voice cracked. "I told Emma that sometimes people change and become different than who you thought they were. I was talking about Karen, but Emma was seven. She thought I meant her."

Mrs. Sendlenski's expression softened. "Emma is nineteen now. She's in college, studying psychology because she wants to help children from broken homes. She still believes the divorce was partly her fault."

Christopher put his head in his hands. "God, what have I done?"

"You made choices," Mrs. Sendlenski said. "Some good, many selfish. The question now is whether you understand the impact of those choices."

She walked to the blackboard and picked up chalk. "FINAL QUESTION."

"Christopher Mills." She turned to face him. "You've reviewed your life and the consequences of your actions. Some of your choices caused pain. Some were made from selfishness, anger, or indifference. But some showed kindness, love, and sacrifice. Given the opportunity to live your life again, with full knowledge of the consequences, what would you do differently?"

He stared at the packet in front of him—all those photographs and decisions that had shaped his forty-three years. His throat felt raw. His eyes burned.

"Everything." He whispered. "I'd do everything differently."

"Be specific."

"I'd call my father back. I'd tell him I forgave him, that I loved him despite everything. I'd help that homeless man every day, report hitting the cat, stop to help Janet with her tire and Mr. Wright at the pharmacy."

He looked up at Mrs. Sendlenski. "I'd tell Emma every single day that she was perfect and that the divorce wasn't her fault. I'd put her needs ahead of my anger at Karen. I'd be the father she deserved instead of the selfish bastard I was."

"And what have you learned?"

"That every choice matters. That all the small mean things and nice things add up. That other people aren't just extras in my story—they're living their own lives, and what I did affected their lives in ways I never thought about."

Christopher stood up, understanding flooding through him. "The other people in this room—some of them fail, don't they?"

"Yes."

"What happens to them?"

Mrs. Sendlenski set down her chalk. "They get to try again. New life, clean slate, but they don't remember their previous attempts. They make the same mistakes, over and over, until they learn."

"And the ones who pass?"

"They move on. They become teachers, guides, helpers for the ones still learning. They get to use their understanding to make things better."

Christopher looked around the classroom. The other souls were still bent over their papers, some writing, others lost in contemplation. How many times had they been here? How many lives had they lived without learning what they needed to know?

"Do I pass?" he asked.

Mrs. Sendlenski smiled—the same warm smile she'd given him in third grade when he'd finally mastered long division.

"Understanding is the first step," she said. "But recognizing your mistakes isn't enough. The real test is whether you'd make different choices when faced with similar situations again. Whether you've learned to see beyond yourself."

She picked up a fresh piece of paper from her desk. "Your final exam, Christopher. You'll be placed in scenarios similar to ones from your life. Your responses will determine whether you graduate or repeat the course."

The classroom began to fade around the edges. Christopher felt himself being pulled away from the desk, away from Mrs. Sendlenski, into something that felt like falling upward.

"Wait," he called out. "What if I fail? What if I make the same mistakes again?"

Mrs. Sendlenski's voice followed him as the world dissolved. "Then you'll keep taking the test until you get it right. Everybody does, eventually. Love wins in the end, Christopher. The only question is how long it takes you to figure that out."

The last thing Christopher saw was the blackboard, where someone had written in chalk: "THIS IS ONLY A TEST. BUT EVERY TEST IS AN OPPORTUNITY TO BECOME WHO YOU'RE MEANT TO BE."

Then everything went white.

When the light faded, Christopher found himself standing in a hospital corridor. The smell of disinfectant and the beeping of machines filled the air. He looked down and saw scrubs—not his usual button-down, but somehow they felt right.

A nurse approached, looking exhausted. "Dr. Mills? We need you in room 314. The family's asking for you."

Doctor? Christopher started to correct her, then stopped. This was the test. He was supposed to play the role, make choices, see what he would do differently.

"Of course." Christopher nodded. "What's the situation?"

"Elderly man, end-stage cancer. Family wants to discuss comfort care, but they're having trouble accepting it. The daughter's insisting we try more aggressive treatment."

Christopher walked to room 314, his heart pounding. Through the doorway, he could see an old man in the bed, tubes and wires attached to his frail body. A middle-aged woman sat beside him holding his hand, while a younger man stood by the window looking frustrated and tired.

As Christopher entered, he realized with a shock that he recognized the elderly man. It was Samuel Wright—the confused man he'd ignored in the pharmacy parking lot years ago. But in this scenario, Mr. Wright had lived longer, and now Christopher was his doctor.

"Doctor, thank you for coming," the woman said. "I'm Linda Wright, and this is my brother David. We need to talk about Dad."

Christopher pulled up a chair and sat down. "Tell me what you're thinking."

"The oncologist says there's nothing more they can do," Linda said, tears streaming down her face. "But there has to be something. Experimental treatments, clinical trials. We can't just give up on him."

David shook his head. "Linda, Dad's suffering. Look at him. He's been unconscious for three days. The machines are the only thing keeping him alive."

"He could wake up," Linda insisted. "People recover from things like this all the time. I've read about it online."

Christopher looked at Mr. Wright's peaceful face, then back at his children. In his previous life, he might have sided with David—the practical son who could see reality. He might have been impatient with Linda's denial, frustrated by her refusal to accept the inevitable.

But now he could see the fear behind her words, the desperate love that was making her fight for every possible moment with her father.

"Linda," Christopher said gently, "I can see how much you love your father. That love is beautiful, and it's the reason he's had such a good life with you and David caring for him."

She nodded, squeezing her father's hand.

"Can you tell me what your father would want if he could speak to us right now?"

Linda's face crumpled. "He... he said he didn't want to be a burden. He made us promise we wouldn't let him suffer just to keep him alive a little longer."

"But promising and doing are different things," Christopher said. "It's one of the hardest decisions a family can make."

"I just don't want to lose him," Linda whispered.

"You're not losing him," Christopher said. "You're honoring him. You're making sure his final days are about comfort and peace, surrounded by the people who love him most."

He spent the next hour with the family, helping them understand the difference between giving up and letting go. When they agreed to transition to hospice care, Linda hugged him and said, "Thank you for helping us see that love sometimes means saying goodbye."

As the scene faded, Christopher felt warmth spreading through his chest. He'd given them what they needed—not medical expertise, but compassion and understanding.

The next test placed him in a school gymnasium. He was wearing a coach's whistle and holding a clipboard. Around him, kids were running laps—some keeping pace easily, others struggling to keep up.

One boy, maybe twelve years old, was falling farther and farther behind. He was overweight and out of shape, his face red with exertion and embarrassment. Some of the other kids were starting to laugh.

Christopher recognized the situation immediately. This was exactly like scenarios from his own school days, but instead of being the observer, he was the authority figure.

"Hey!" Christopher blew his whistle. "Everyone stop."

The kids came to a halt, the struggling boy grateful for the break.

"Partner up," Christopher announced. "We're finishing this lap together. Nobody crosses the finish line until everyone does."

"But coach," one of the faster kids complained, "that's not fair. Why should we be slowed down?"

Christopher looked at the boy who'd been struggling. His name tag read "Tommy Richardson." The kid was staring at the ground, expecting to be singled out and humiliated.

"Tommy," Christopher said, "come here."

The boy approached, expecting trouble.

"You've been working harder than anyone else out here," Christopher said loud enough for the whole class to hear. "I want you to help me demonstrate something."

Tommy's eyes widened with surprise.

"Everyone, watch Tommy's form. See how he's pacing himself, breathing steadily instead of sprinting and burning out? That's exactly the technique that wins marathons."

He turned to the class. "The goal isn't to be the fastest. It's to finish strong. And Tommy here is showing you how champions do it."

For the rest of the period, Christopher made sure every kid had a role to play, a strength to contribute. When Tommy finished the lap with his partner, he was smiling for the first time all day.

As the gymnasium faded away, Christopher realized he was learning something crucial: authority wasn't about power over others. It was about lifting others up.

The third test placed him in a courtroom. He was wearing judge's robes, sitting behind a bench, looking down at a painfully familiar scene. A divorced couple was arguing about custody arrangements, their lawyers fighting over visitation schedules and financial obligations.

The man looked exactly like Christopher had during his own divorce—angry, defensive, more concerned with winning than with what was best for his child. The woman was trying to stay composed, but Christopher could see the fear in her eyes.

"Your Honor," the man's lawyer was saying, "my client believes his ex-wife is trying to turn his daughter against him. He wants equal custody."

"That's not what I'm doing," the woman said. "I just want Emma to have some stability. She's been having nightmares with all this back and forth."

Emma. Christopher's breath caught. This wasn't just a similar situation—this was his situation, replayed with him in the position of power.

He looked down at the case file. Everything was exactly as it had been in his own divorce, except now he could see it from the outside. He could see how his anger at Karen had blinded him to Emma's needs, how his desire to hurt his ex-wife had hurt his daughter instead.

"I'd like to speak with Emma privately," Christopher announced.

Both lawyers looked surprised. "Your Honor, the child is only seven—"

"Exactly," Christopher said. "Which is why her voice matters most in this room."

When they brought Emma in, Christopher's heart broke. She looked so small in the big courtroom, so confused and scared. She kept looking back and forth between her parents like she was trying to figure out which one she was supposed to choose.

Christopher came down from the bench and knelt to Emma's eye level.

"Hi, Emma. I'm Judge Mills. I want you to know that nothing happening here is your fault, okay? Sometimes grown-ups make mistakes, and when that happens, we have to figure out how to fix things so everyone can be happy again."

Emma nodded.

"What would make you feel safest? Not what you think Mommy or Daddy wants to hear, but what would help you sleep better at night?"

"I wanna live with Mommy most of the time 'cause my room is there and my school is close. But I wanna see Daddy every weekend, and I want them to stop being mad at each other."

Christopher looked up at the parents. The father was starting to protest, but Christopher held up a hand.

"Emma, what if we could make a schedule where you feel secure and loved, where both your parents know exactly when they'll see you, and where no one has to fight anymore?"

"That would be good," Emma said.

Christopher spent the next hour crafting a custody arrangement that prioritized Emma's stability while ensuring both parents had meaningful time with their daughter. More importantly, he made both parents sign an agreement that they would never speak negatively about each other in front of Emma, and that they would attend co-parenting counseling.

When the gavel came down, Emma hugged both her parents, and for the first time since the divorce proceedings began, she was smiling.

As the courtroom faded, Christopher realized that wisdom wasn't about being right. It was about making sure love could survive even when relationships couldn't.

The final test was the simplest. Christopher found himself walking down a city street, briefcase in hand, wearing his familiar sales uniform.

Up ahead, a homeless man sat against the brick wall of a bank building, holding a cardboard sign.

Christopher reached into his pocket and found a twenty-dollar bill. He could walk past, like he had every day for two years. Or he could stop.

He stopped.

"Excuse me," Christopher said. "Are you hungry? There's a diner across the street. Would you like to get some breakfast?"

The man looked up, surprise flickering across his weathered face. "You're sure? I mean, that's kind of you, but I don't want to put you out."

"It's no trouble at all," Christopher said, and meant it. "I'm Christopher, by the way."

"Frank," the man said, getting to his feet. "Frank Summers. And thank you. It's been a while since someone treated me like a person instead of just... furniture."

As they walked toward the diner together, he felt something warm spreading through his chest. It took him a moment to name the feeling.

Hope. Not just for himself, but for Frank, for Emma, for everyone whose life he might touch if he could just remember to see them as real people with real needs and real worth.

Behind them, invisible to both men, Mrs. Sendlenski stood at the intersection with her clipboard, making one final note in Christopher Mills' file. Then she smiled and moved on to the next student who needed guidance.

The test was never over. But for the first time in his life—or death—he was starting to understand that this wasn't punishment.

It was a gift.

Catch Me a Reaper

T he call came at three in the morning, which meant serious money or serious trouble. In Franklin Moss's line of work, the two went together like whiskey and bad decisions.

"This Moss?" The voice had that careful tone rich people used when they needed something dirty done.

Frank sat up in his motel bed, instantly awake. The cheap polyester sheets stuck to his back with sweat, and the air conditioner rattled like a dying animal. Fifteen years of hunting things that hunted people had trained the sleep right out of him. "Depends who's asking."

"Cornelius Van Der Berg. I've got a job for you."

Frank knew the name—pharmaceutical billionaire, the kind who bought politicians by the dozen. But the voice on the phone didn't sound rich. It sounded scared.

"What kind of job?"

"The kind you're known for."

"I do security consulting. That's it." Frank reached for his bourbon, then stopped. His hands needed to stay steady.

"Don't bullshit me, Moss. I know what you really do. I need you to catch my Reaper."

The words came out flat, matter-of-fact. Like ordering pizza. Like death was just another business transaction for guys like Van Der Berg.

Frank stood and walked to the window, muscle memory checking the parking lot for anything that didn't belong. "That's a federal crime. Twenty-five to life, minimum."

"I'm prepared to compensate you for the risk."

"How much?"

"Fifty million."

Frank's bourbon bottle sat on the dresser, three-quarters empty. In fifteen years of catching Reapers for desperate clients, the biggest score had been eight million—and that was for three separate jobs. Fifty million was retirement money. Hell, fifty million was disappear-forever money.

"Just one Reaper?"

"Just one. But it's active."

Frank closed his eyes. Active meant the Reaper already had its assignment, was already making reconnaissance visits. The closer a Reaper got to collection time, the stronger it became. And the more dangerous to catch.

"When's your appointment?"

"Seventy-two hours. Maybe less."

Frank whistled low. An active Reaper with an imminent assignment was suicide to mess with. Smart money said hang up, finish the bourbon, forget this conversation ever happened. But fifty million would buy him a house somewhere Reapers didn't go—if such a place existed.

"Twenty-five up front. Plus expenses."

"Done. Can you be in New Hampshire tomorrow night?"

"For fifty million, I can be on Mars." Frank grabbed a pen off the nightstand. "Give me the address."

After Van Der Berg hung up, Frank stared at his phone for a full minute. Then he reached for the bourbon after all. Tomorrow he'd start prepping for what might be his last hunt. Tonight, he needed to get drunk enough to believe he'd survive it.

The Walton Estate crouched on two hundred acres of New Hampshire woods like something out of a Gothic novel—all stone towers and leering gargoyles. Frank's rental sedan crunched up the gravel drive while October shadows stretched across grass so perfect it looked fake. The air smelled of wood smoke and dying leaves, that rich autumn decay that made him think of graveyards.

Two security guards flanked the front entrance, ex-military types with dead eyes and expensive haircuts. They waved Frank through without searching his gear cases. Either Van Der Berg had warned them off, or they were smart enough not to ask questions about what a specialist brought to this kind of party.

A butler in an actual tuxedo led Frank through hallways lined with oil paintings of disapproving dead people. The floors were polished marble that clicked under their footsteps, and the whole place smelled like lemon oil and old money. The guy moved with the careful dignity of someone who'd been serving rich assholes so long he'd forgotten he wasn't one of them.

"Mr. Van Der Berg will see you in the library," the butler said, opening doors that probably cost more than Frank's car.

The library was the size of Frank's motel room times ten, books floor to ceiling, broken only by a fireplace you could roast a whole pig in. The air was thick with the smell of leather bindings and wood polish, underlaid with something medicinal—probably from the reports Van Der Berg was studying. Van Der Berg sat behind a desk the size of a pool table, studying what looked like medical reports. He was younger than Frank expected—sixty, maybe, with the kind of tan that came from private beaches and the kind of fitness that came from personal trainers who made house calls.

"Mr. Moss." Van Der Berg stood, offered his hand. His grip was firm but cold, like shaking hands with expensive marble. "Thank you for coming."

"Got here." Frank set his gear cases beside a leather chair and sat without being invited. "Let's talk about what I'm buying here."

Van Der Berg opened a manila folder. "Six months ago, my doctors found a brain tumor. Glioblastoma." His fingers drummed against the desk—controlled, precise taps that betrayed nothing. "Even with the best treatment money can buy, they're giving me three months."

"And you've seen your Reaper."

"Two weeks ago. End of my bed, 4:04 AM exactly." Van Der Berg's voice stayed level, but his hands trembled slightly as he turned pages. "Black cloak, white skin, eyes like frozen stars. Looked at me for maybe thirty seconds, then vanished."

Frank nodded. A sighting meant the assignment was locked in—Van Der Berg's name had moved from the "maybe someday" list to active duty. The Reaper would keep coming back to check on him until collection time.

"Did it say anything?"

"No. But I felt..." Van Der Berg paused, hunting for words. "I felt its certainty. It knows exactly when and where I'm going to die. March 15th, 2:30 AM, in my bedroom. I know this like I know my own name."

"That kind of certainty means the assignment's set in stone. The Reaper can't change the date or location even if it wanted to." Frank leaned forward. "What makes you think catching it will help? You can't negotiate with these things. They don't make deals."

"Maybe not. But they can be contained."

Van Der Berg slid a photograph across the desk.

Frank's coffee went cold in his hands. The picture showed something that used to be human—ancient, withered, connected to more machines than flesh. Tubes snaking everywhere, monitors beeping, the whole setup screaming "should have died decades ago."

"Morrison Blackwood. Oil money. Lung cancer should've killed him in '87."

Frank looked at the photo. "He's still breathing?"

"Barely. Life support, feeding tubes, the whole thing. Been like that for thirty-six years." Van Der Berg took the photo back. "Family hired a guy like you. Caught his Reaper. Now Blackwood's stuck between life and death."

"Incomplete how?"

"The Reaper couldn't finish its job, but it couldn't abandon it either. Blackwood exists somewhere between life and death. The cosmic forces keep the balance by taking substitute deaths from his bloodline."

Frank's jaw tightened. He hated clients who thought they understood his work. "Look, Reapers don't feel pain like we do. And they sure as hell don't break under pressure. If Blackwood's still breathing, it's because something went wrong with the capture, not because they tortured his Reaper into submission."

"Nevertheless, he lives while his Reaper remains caged. The correlation is clear."

Frank walked to the fireplace, studying the flames while he thought. Morrison Blackwood—he'd heard whispers about that job. An old-timer named Jack Hennessy had taken the contract and vanished afterward. Most people figured Hennessy got himself killed. But if Van Der Berg was right...

"Even if this Blackwood thing is real," Frank said, "keeping a Reaper caged for thirty-six years? That's serious money. Generators, containment, monitoring equipment. Fifty million minimum."

"I have resources. The question is whether you have the skill."

Frank turned from the fire. Van Der Berg watched him with the flat intensity of a shark sizing up lunch. The man might be dying, but he still had the predator instincts that built his empire.

"I've caught twelve Reapers in fifteen years," Frank said. "Ten successful releases after the clients got what they wanted, two escapes during transport. Nobody died on my watch."

"But you've never attempted permanent containment."

"Because it's fucking insane. Reapers have backup systems. Fail-safes. You keep one caged too long, others come looking. And when they find it..." Frank shook his head. "I've seen what happens to people who try to cheat death permanently. It doesn't end well."

Van Der Berg opened another folder and withdrew a cashier's check. He placed it on the desk where Frank could see the number—twenty-five million dollars.

"Half your fee, as requested. The rest transfers when the job's done." Van Der Berg leaned back in his chair. "Mr. Moss, I'm sixty-two years old. I've built an empire that employs forty thousand people across six continents. My oncology patents alone—Meridrol, Cytarix, the entire Neuraspan line—save two million lives per year. The idea that some cosmic bureaucrat in a Halloween costume can terminate all of that based on an arbitrary deadline strikes me as unacceptable."

Frank stared at the check. Twenty-five million dollars. More money than existed in his world.

"When does your Reaper come back?"

"Based on the pattern, tomorrow night. 4:04 AM."

"That's not enough time to set up proper containment. I need at least—"

"I have a facility prepared." Van Der Berg pressed a button on his desk. A section of wall slid aside, revealing an elevator. "Would you like to see it?"

The elevator dropped for what felt like forever, opening onto a corridor that belonged in a government black site, not a rich guy's basement. Fluorescent lights hummed overhead, casting harsh shadows on steel walls. The air tasted of ozone and industrial bleach, with an undertone of something that made Frank's teeth ache—like standing too close to high-voltage transformers.

"I had this built after my diagnosis," Van Der Berg said, leading Frank down the corridor. "Based on specs from a government contractor who specializes in paranormal containment."

They passed rooms full of monitoring equipment and medical supplies. Frank noticed most labels were in languages he didn't recognize—probably military contractors who liked their client lists confidential.

The corridor ended at a heavy door covered in biohazard symbols and warnings in six languages. Van Der Berg placed his palm on a scanner. The door opened with a pneumatic hiss.

The containment cell was a perfect cube, twelve feet on each side, carved from what looked like a single piece of black stone. The walls were covered in symbols that hurt to look at—not quite hieroglyphs, not quite math, but something that suggested both. Banks of equipment surrounded the cell, monitoring everything from electromagnetic readings to room temperature.

"Obsidian from specific volcanic sites," Van Der Berg explained. "The symbols are based on research from a Vatican archive that officially doesn't exist. The chamber's isolated from external electromagnetic fields and maintained at exactly thirty-three degrees."

Frank circled the containment chamber, noting the heavy cables feeding power to the monitoring systems. "This cost you millions."

"Forty million, including the construction crew and consultants. Money well spent if it saves my life."

"Who designed this?"

"Dr. Amanda Sterling. She worked for a government project discontinued in 1973. Unofficially, her research continued through private funding until she died last year."

Frank had heard of Sterling—brilliant but completely unhinged, according to most accounts. She'd been involved in several high-profile paranormal incidents before disappearing. The kind of scientist who pushed boundaries until the boundaries pushed back.

"Sterling focused on Reaper physiology," Van Der Berg continued. "She believed they could be studied and controlled like any other life form. Her containment protocols have proven effective in laboratory settings."

"Lab settings aren't the same as field work," Frank said. "Reapers in the wild are different. Stronger. More motivated."

"Which is why I'm hiring you instead of trying this myself." Van Der Berg gestured toward the equipment. "I defer to your expertise on the capture. But once the Reaper's contained, we follow Sterling's protocols for long-term preservation."

Frank studied the obsidian cell and felt the familiar weight of a bad decision settling on his shoulders. Everything screamed danger—the timeline, the client's ego, the experimental containment. But fifty million was retirement money. Escape money. The kind of score that would let him vanish before his own Reaper came calling.

"I need to review Sterling's research," Frank said. "And I want to inspect every piece of equipment personally. If we're doing this, we do it right."

Van Der Berg smiled for the first time since Frank arrived. "Dr. Sterling's files are in your room, along with technical specs for all equipment. We have eighteen hours."

Walking back to the elevator, Frank tried to ignore the feeling that he was climbing out of something much deeper than a basement. The symbols on those obsidian walls seemed to watch him leave, their alien geometry suggesting knowledge human minds weren't built to process.

Fifty million dollars, he reminded himself. Enough money to buy a house somewhere Reapers didn't go.

If such a place existed.

Frank spent the night reading Dr. Amanda Sterling's research and questioning every choice that had brought him here. Sterling's notes were meticulous but disturbing, filled with references to "subject compliance through systematic deprivation" and "behavioral modification via controlled trauma exposure."

The woman had studied captured Reapers for thirty years, documenting their physiology and responses to various containment methods. Her subjects had been kept in isolation chambers like Van Der Berg's, fed minimal sustenance, subjected to regular testing designed to map their supernatural abilities.

Sterling's files made Frank's stomach turn.

Reaper trapped for two years, four months. Target still alive but not living—family members dead, friends dead, anyone close to him dead. The cosmic balance demanding payment in blood until the original debt got settled.

"R-7 stopped fighting containment after 847 days," Sterling had written. "But the cost wasn't worth it. Twelve substitute deaths and counting."

Frank poured three fingers of bourbon. Sterling's method worked, all right. It just killed everyone you gave a damn about while you waited to die alone.

Frank closed the file and poured three fingers of bourbon from the bottle Van Der Berg had provided. Sterling's Protocol Seven involved keeping captured Reapers in continuous sensory deprivation while subjecting them to electromagnetic pulses designed to prevent them from completing assignments or returning home. Not torture in any conventional sense, but cosmic imprisonment that left both Reaper and target trapped in incomplete states.

The worst part was that Sterling's methods worked exactly as documented—not control over death, but creation of cosmic limbo. Her files included detailed records of twelve successful "indefinite prolongations" over three decades. Twelve death assignments left incomplete, twelve people trapped between life and death, and hundreds of substitute deaths as the cosmic balance tried to correct itself.

Frank's phone buzzed. Text from Van Der Berg: "Equipment check in one hour. Prepare for deployment."

He finished his bourbon and gathered his gear. Frank ran through his mental checklist: battery levels, net deployment angles, injection sites on humanoid supernatural anatomy. The same routine he'd followed for over a decade, muscle memory keeping him alive when thinking got you killed. Nothing designed for the kind of long-term imprison-

ment Van Der Berg wanted, but sufficient for getting the target into
that obsidian cell.

The hard part would be keeping it there.

Van Der Berg's Reaper materialized at exactly 4:04 AM, condensing
in the master bedroom like smoke given form. Frank watched through
thermal imaging from a hidden observation post, his palms slick with
sweat despite the October chill seeping through the estate's stone walls.
The creature appeared as a column of cold air on his monitors—twelve
degrees below ambient temperature, moving with purpose that made
Frank's skin crawl.

The Reaper materialized like every nightmare Frank had ever forgotten.

Seven feet of wrong, wrapped in shadows that moved against the
light. Face like a skull covered in wax, stretched too tight over bone
that showed through the skin. Eyes that didn't reflect anything because
there wasn't anything human left to reflect.

When it moved, Frank heard rustling that could have been cloth or
could have been something shedding its skin. It studied Van Der Berg
the way a butcher studied meat.

Frank's hands shook despite fifteen years of doing this. Reapers
triggered something deeper than fear—something wired into human
DNA that screamed run every time death took a recognizable shape.

Frank had hunted Reapers for fifteen years, and they still scared the
shit out of him.

Didn't matter how many times he'd done this. Something deep in his
monkey brain screamed RUN every time one of these things showed
up. Pure animal terror, hardwired into human DNA since the first
caveman realized he was going to die someday.

His hands shook as he waited for the perfect moment. Professional
or not, Reapers were walking nightmares in expensive suits.

Catching one required the kind of professional detachment that came
only through extended exposure to impossibility.

The Reaper finished its inspection and began to fade, preparing to
return home. Frank's thumb hovered over the activation switch—timing was everything. Too early and the creature could slip phase. Too
late and it vanished completely. He waited for the telltale shimmer that
meant full dematerialization attempt, then triggered the nets.

Fifty thousand volts of tuned electricity hit the creature, disrupting
its energy matrix and forcing it back into full physical manifestation. It
collapsed to the bedroom floor, writhing as the nets tightened. Frank
burst from hiding with the syringe ready. Fifteen years of this had

taught him never to think—subclavian artery, push the plunger, pray the paralytic worked before the Reaper tore his arms off.

The creature went down hard, writhing against the nets. But its eyes stayed open, following Frank's movement with the patient interest of something that could wait forever for revenge.

Thirty minutes until the paralytic wore off. Thirty minutes to get it locked up before it remembered how to kill people with its bare hands.

Van Der Berg emerged from the bathroom where he'd been hiding. His face was pale but determined as he watched Frank secure the motionless Reaper.

"Magnificent," Van Der Berg whispered. "It's smaller than I expected."

"They all are when they're not trying to kill you." Frank activated the hover-gurney and transferred the Reaper onto it. "This was the easy part. Keeping it locked up is where things get complicated."

They moved through the estate's corridors to the containment facility. Frank maneuvered the Reaper into the obsidian cell while Van Der Berg activated monitoring systems. The chamber filled with low humming as electromagnetic generators came online.

The Reaper's eyes snapped open as the paralytic wore off. It sat up slowly, studying its surroundings with the calm interest of a scientist examining a specimen. When it spoke, its voice carried the sound of winter wind through dead trees.

"Cornelius Van Der Berg. Franklin Moss." The creature's gaze moved between them with ancient recognition. "You have made a significant error."

"Have we?" Van Der Berg stepped closer to the observation window. "You're contained, your powers are suppressed, and your assignment has been delayed indefinitely."

The Reaper stood and approached the window. Despite the electromagnetic barriers, Frank felt the temperature drop ten degrees. "Death cannot be delayed indefinitely, Mr. Van Der Berg. It can only be redirected."

"What's that supposed to mean?"

"Every day you postpone your appointed time, someone else pays the price. The balance must be maintained."

Van Der Berg's confident expression flickered. "What price? What balance?"

The Reaper smiled, revealing teeth like polished bone. "You'll understand soon enough."

Frank stepped between Van Der Berg and the window. Something in the creature's voice suggested knowledge they weren't prepared for.

"Your assignment's been terminated," he told the Reaper. "You'll be released once you confirm cancellation of Mr. Van Der Berg's death date."

"Assignments cannot be terminated, Mr. Moss. They can only be transferred." The Reaper settled into meditation position in the cell's center. "I will wait here while the balance corrects itself. You'll understand within forty-eight hours."

The creature closed its eyes and became still as stone. Monitoring equipment registered minimal life signs—just enough activity to confirm containment without indicating distress.

Frank studied the readouts while unease crawled up his spine. In fifteen years of Reaper-catching, he'd never heard one mention balance or transfers. Most refused to communicate at all, treating capture as temporary inconvenience before inevitable escape or rescue.

"What did it mean about balance?" Van Der Berg asked.

"I don't know. But we're about to find out."

The first death occurred eight hours later.

Frank was reviewing containment protocols when Van Der Berg's butler knocked on his door. The man's usual composure had cracked, revealing fear underneath.

"Sir, there's been an incident. Mr. Van Der Berg requests your immediate presence."

Frank found Van Der Berg in his study, staring at a laptop displaying a news website. The headline read: "Pharmaceutical Executive Dies in Freak Accident."

"Richard Sterling," Van Der Berg said without looking up. "Sixty-two, CEO of Meridian Pharmaceuticals. Struck by lightning while walking his dog this morning. Clear skies, no storm activity."

Frank read over Van Der Berg's shoulder. The article described the incident as "meteorologically impossible" but offered no explanation for how a man could be killed by lightning from a cloudless sky.

"Sterling's your biggest competitor," Frank realized.

"Was. And he was in perfect health as of last week's physical." Van Der Berg closed the laptop and faced Frank. "This is what the Reaper meant, isn't it? About balance?"

Frank nodded slowly. "Your death was scheduled for a specific time and place. The cosmic system governing these appointments expects certain quotas. If one doesn't happen..."

"Someone else dies instead."

Van Der Berg's phone rang. He answered, listened for several minutes, then hung up looking shaken.

"Angela Williams, my CFO. Collapsed in her office twenty minutes ago. Massive heart attack. She's thirty-eight and runs marathons."

Frank walked to the window and stared at autumn landscape. Two deaths in eight hours, both targeting people in Van Der Berg's professional circle. The Reaper hadn't been making threats—it had been explaining rules of a game they didn't understand.

"We need to release it," Frank said.

"Absolutely not. Two deaths are unfortunate, but they're not my responsibility. I didn't ask these people to—"

"It's not going to stop." Frank turned from the window. "The system controlling death assignments isn't run by humans. It doesn't care about fairness or individual responsibility. It just maintains balance. As long as you're supposed to be dead but aren't, other people will die in your place."

Van Der Berg's face flushed. "I'm paying you fifty million to solve this problem, not give up at the first complication. Dr. Sterling's research shows Reapers can be conditioned to accept modified assignments. We just need to apply proper protocols."

Frank thought of Sterling's files, of Reapers subjected to years of systematic torture until they broke. "How long do you think it took her to break those twelve subjects? How many people died while she was conducting experiments?"

"That's not relevant to our situation."

"Isn't it? Every day you keep that thing caged, more people die. Your employees, your family, your friends. Everyone connected to you becomes a potential substitute."

Van Der Berg's phone rang again. He stared at it before answering. Frank watched the billionaire's face go pale as he listened.

"James Kennedy, my estate manager," Van Der Berg said after hanging up. "Found dead in the garden shed. Apparent suicide, though his wife swears he showed no signs of depression."

"Three deaths in ten hours," Frank said. "How many more people are you willing to sacrifice for a few extra months?"

Van Der Berg slammed his fist on the desk. "I built this empire from nothing! I employ thousands, support entire communities, advance medical research that saves lives worldwide. My death will cause more harm than losing a few individuals who were already living on borrowed time."

"That's not how it works. The cosmic forces controlling death don't give a shit about your business empire or contributions to society. They care about maintaining balance between life and death. As long as you're disrupting that balance, people keep dying."

"Then we make the Reaper change the rules."

Frank stared at Van Der Berg, seeing for the first time the ruthless calculation that had built the pharmaceutical empire. The billionaire wasn't just afraid of death—he was convinced his life was worth more than others.

"There's something else you should know," Frank said slowly. "About that Morrison Blackwood case you mentioned."

Van Der Berg leaned forward. "What about it?"

"I looked into it after you told me the story. Blackwood's been kept alive for thirty-six years, but he's not the only casualty. His family members have been dying at an accelerated rate since 1987. Wife, children, grandchildren. All dead before their time, all from freak accidents or sudden illnesses."

Van Der Berg's confident expression began to crack. "How many?"

"Forty-three family members over thirty-six years. The Blackwood bloodline is almost extinct, and the few survivors show signs of advanced aging despite their actual ages." Frank moved closer to the desk. "That's the real price of cheating death permanently. The balance doesn't just demand random substitutions—it targets everyone connected to the original subject until the cosmic debt is paid in full."

The study fell silent except for an antique clock ticking. Van Der Berg stared at his closed laptop, calculating how many people in his orbit might become targets if he continued. His left hand had developed a slight tremor—the first time Frank had seen the billionaire's control crack.

"How do I know you're not lying? How do I know this isn't a negotiating tactic to increase your fee?"

Frank pulled out his phone and dialed. He put the call on speaker.

"Hennessy," answered a voice like gravel being crushed.

"Jack, it's Frank Moss. I need you to tell someone about the Blackwood job."

Long pause. Frank could hear background noise—machinery humming, the distant sound of ventilation systems. "Jesus, Frank. You're not thinking of taking a permanent capture contract, are you? Because I'm telling you right now—"

"Just tell him what happened to the family."

Another pause, longer. When Hennessy spoke again, his voice carried thirty-six years of guilt.

"I captured Morrison Blackwood's Reaper in 1987. Thought I was buying the old man time to get his affairs in order. Family paid me to keep it contained for six months while Blackwood finished some business deals." Hennessy's voice grew quieter. "What I didn't understand was that capturing a Reaper doesn't stop death—it traps both the Reaper and its target in incomplete states. Blackwood isn't alive anymore. He exists in cosmic limbo, and the balance demands payment for that disruption."

"Tell him about the family," Frank prompted.

"They didn't just die. They accelerated. The cosmic forces governing death don't negotiate, Frank. They collect their due with interest. Forty-three family members dead, including infants and teenagers who had nothing to do with the original decision. I've been watching that containment facility for thirty-six years, making sure the Reaper stays caged, knowing every day I maintain the system is another day the Blackwood family gets smaller."

Van Der Berg had gone pale. "How many are left?"

"Three," Hennessy said. "Morrison himself, one grandson in witness protection, and a great-granddaughter who doesn't know her family history. When they die, I'm releasing the Reaper and burning the whole facility. Should have done it decades ago."

Frank ended the call and pocketed his phone. "That's what you're buying with fifty million. Not life extension—systematic murder of everyone you've ever cared about."

Van Der Berg stood and walked to his bookshelf, running fingers along leather spines. "Perhaps there's another solution. Something Sterling's research overlooked."

"There isn't. I've been catching Reapers for fifteen years, and the rule's always the same: death assignments can be interrupted but never cancelled. The longer you trap a Reaper, the more the cosmic balance demands substitute payments. You don't cheat death—you just force other people to pay your bill."

"Then what do you suggest?"

Frank looked toward the hidden elevator leading to containment. "We release the Reaper. You go back to your normal life, however long that might be. At least the people around you stop dying."

Van Der Berg turned from the bookshelf. "And you forfeit twenty-five million."

"I forfeit a lot more than that if I keep the Reaper caged. The cosmic forces governing death don't distinguish between the person who ordered capture and the person who executed it. If I'm complicit in this system, I become a target too."

Van Der Berg's phone rang for the fourth time in two hours. He stared at it without answering, and Frank could see calculation happening behind the billionaire's eyes. How many more deaths would it take before the cost became unacceptable?

"Answer it," Frank said.

Van Der Berg picked up. "Yes?"

Frank watched color drain from the billionaire's face as he listened.

"My daughter," Van Der Berg whispered after hanging up. "Car accident on the way to yoga class. The other driver ran a red light and hit her head-on." His hands shook now. "She's alive, but the doctors don't know if she'll walk again."

Frank felt familiar weight settling in his chest—the same feeling when a job went sideways and innocent people paid the price. "It won't stop until you're dead or the Reaper's free. Those are your only options."

Van Der Berg slumped into his chair like a man twenty years older. "How long do I have if I release it?"

"Based on the original timeline? About sixty hours."

"And if I keep it contained?"

"Your daughter's accident was a warning. The next incident will be fatal, and the one after that will target multiple people." Frank moved toward the door. "I'm going down to release the Reaper. You can try to stop me, but I wouldn't recommend it."

"Wait." Van Der Berg's voice was barely above a whisper. "If I release it voluntarily, does that change anything? Does it earn consideration for cooperating?"

Frank paused with his hand on the door. "Reapers aren't vengeful, but they're not merciful either. They just do their job. Whether you release it now or I release it over your objections, your appointment is still March 15th at 2:30 AM."

"Then I have two and a half months."

"You have two and a half months to live them properly, instead of hiding in a basement torturing cosmic forces you don't understand."

Van Der Berg stared at his hands for a long moment, then stood and walked toward the hidden elevator. "I'll come with you. If I'm going to die, I might as well face the thing that's going to kill me."

The Reaper hadn't moved from its meditation posture in twelve hours since capture. It opened its eyes as Frank and Van Der Berg entered the observation room, studying them with patient interest of something existing outside normal time.

"You've reached a decision," the Reaper said.

Van Der Berg stepped forward, earlier arrogance replaced by weary acceptance. "My daughter was injured. An innocent person who had nothing to do with my choices."

"The balance demands correction. Your daughter's injury was minimal compared to what comes next."

"How many more people will die if I keep you here?"

The Reaper stood and approached the window. Despite electromagnetic barriers, Frank felt temperature drop several degrees. "The universe doesn't like cheaters," the Reaper said. "Keep me caged, and everyone you love dies. One by one. Until you're alone. Then you die anyway."

Frank started shutting down the containment systems. Generators wound down with a whine like something dying. Monitors went dark. The temperature climbed toward normal, and Frank could feel the Reaper getting stronger with every degree.

Van Der Berg's phone had rung four times in two hours. Each call meant another person paying for his attempt to cheat death.

How many more would die before he figured out the game was rigged?

"We're releasing you. The capture contract is terminated."

"And my appointment remains unchanged?"

Van Der Berg's voice cracked slightly. "March 15th, 2:30 AM."

The Reaper nodded once. "The balance will be restored."

Electromagnetic barriers powered down, and the obsidian cell fell silent. The Reaper stepped through the doorway with fluid grace, moving past Frank and Van Der Berg without apparent hostility. It paused at the exit.

"Franklin Moss."

Frank turned. "Yeah?"

"Your own appointment approaches. September 12th, 7:43 PM. You have eighteen months to prepare."

Frank felt his blood turn to slush. "Where?"

"A motel room in Nevada. You'll be alone." The Reaper's expression might have been sympathetic, though it was hard to tell with creatures that existed mainly as projections of human fear. "Use the time wisely."

The creature vanished like smoke, leaving Frank and Van Der Berg alone in the containment facility. Monitoring equipment registered no trace of its presence, as if the most expensive Reaper trap ever built had become an empty room between heartbeats.

"Eighteen months," Frank said to himself. "At least I know it's coming."

Van Der Berg stared at the empty obsidian cell. "Do you think it was lying? About the date?"

"Reapers don't lie. They don't need to." Frank began gathering his equipment. "You've got two and a half months. I'd suggest spending them with your daughter instead of building death traps in your basement."

Van Der Berg nodded slowly. "The remaining twenty-five million. Consider it a consulting fee for preventing me from making the biggest mistake of my life."

Frank paused in his packing. "You're still going to die."

"Yes. But at least I won't take everyone I care about with me."

They rode the elevator back to the main house in silence. Frank collected his gear and loaded it into his rental while Van Der Berg made phone calls to check on his daughter's condition. Early morning sky was beginning to lighten, painting New Hampshire mountains in shades of purple and gold. Frost covered the estate's manicured lawns, and Frank's breath steamed in the October air as he secured his equipment cases.

Frank's phone buzzed with a bank notification. Twenty-five million dollars had been transferred to his account—enough money to live comfortably for the rest of his life. All eighteen months of it.

He started the car and pulled away from the Walton Estate, the gravel crunching under his tires like broken bones. Through the windshield, he could see Route 16 winding south toward Portsmouth, the White Mountains rising behind him like sleeping giants. Maybe he'd buy that house somewhere Reapers didn't go. Maybe he'd learn guitar or take up painting. Maybe he'd find some way to make peace with the cosmic forces he'd spent fifteen years antagonizing.

September 12th, 7:43 PM. A motel room in Nevada. Frank could almost smell the industrial carpet cleaner and cigarette ghosts already.

At least he wouldn't be surprised.

Franklin Moss died on September 12th at exactly 7:43 PM in a Motel 6 outside Las Vegas, Nevada. The Clark County coroner ruled it a heart attack, though Frank's medical records showed no history of cardiac problems. The motel manager found his body three days later, along with a handwritten note expressing no regrets about his career choices.

Cornelius Van Der Berg died on March 15th at 2:30 AM in the master bedroom of his New Hampshire estate. His daughter, who had made a complete recovery from her accident, was holding his hand when he passed. His death was peaceful, and his last words were an apology to everyone who had died because of his attempt to cheat death.

Morrison Blackwood died on April 3rd, exactly ninety-six hours after Jack Hennessy released his Reaper and burned down the containment facility. After thirty-six years trapped in cosmic limbo between life and death, his body succumbed to the cancer that should have killed him in 1987. The last surviving members of the Blackwood family—the grandson and great-granddaughter—died within a week of Morrison's passing, ending a bloodline that had been paying for one man's incomplete death for thirty-six years.

The Reaper-catching profession continues to operate in the shadows, serving clients who believe their wealth and power make them exempt from cosmic law. The success rate for permanent captures remains zero percent, though the industry prefers not to advertise this statistic.

Death, as it turns out, is the one business that never goes out of business.

The Wabbits of Wilmaville

S tructurally Revised Edition

  Caleb Brest chose the cabin three miles up Deer Creek Road because nothing ever happened there---and nobody would come looking.

Six months since Sarah left, taking the ring and his balls with her. Ten years of detective novels in Chicago, always planning to write something important "someday." What did he have? One-bedroom apartment full of rejection letters and an ex who got tired of waiting.

"You write about life but don't live it, Caleb. You just watch from your laptop."

So he'd come to Colorado. To prove her wrong, maybe. Or prove her right---he couldn't tell anymore.

The cabin had "character"---realtor speak for "everything breaks constantly." But Caleb found the repairs oddly soothing. Splitting pinon wood and fixing what the altitude busted kept his hands busy while his brain wrestled with the literary fiction that was supposed to save his career. Three chapters into his "redemption project"---pretentious bullshit about isolation and modern masculinity---he was starting to think Sarah had been right.

He was staring at an awful paragraph about "cathedral silence of the wilderness" when he heard it.

Thump-thump-thump.

Caleb looked up. Sound came from behind the cabin, rhythmic and deliberate. He waited. Just wind through the ponderosa pines.

Back to the painful rewriting when it started again.

Thump-thump-thump.

Back porch now. Caleb saved his work, walked to the door. Empty deck except for his reading chair and lunch table.

Thump-thump-thump.

Right below the window. Caleb stepped out, peered through the deck boards. In the shadows beneath, something white moved.

"Easy there." Probably a cottontail that got confused. Space under the porch was two feet high---plenty of room for a rabbit to wander in and get lost.

Thump-thump-thump.

The rabbit was drumming with its hind feet, like they did when spooked. But what was spooking it? He was ten feet away and hadn't done anything threatening.

"It's alright, little guy." Caleb walked around to where wooden lattice covered the crawl space. A section near the corner had come loose---another repair for his growing list. He could crawl in there and shoo the rabbit toward daylight.

But when he knelt beside the gap, the thumping stopped.

After a minute of silence, he figured the rabbit had found its own way out. Rabbits usually figured things out if you left them alone. He stood, brushed pine needles off his knees, and went back inside.

At the kitchen window, he looked toward the yard. White cottontail sat in the middle of his lawn, twenty feet from the porch. Faced the cabin directly, still as stone.

So much for being trapped. Probably under there for the cool, not because it couldn't get out. He started to turn away when something about the animal stopped him.

The rabbit's head looked wrong. Too big, or the wrong shape. He moved closer to the window, squinting. The rabbit sat motionless, staring. At him.

That's when he saw them.

Two brown things rising from the rabbit's skull, each about an inch long, curved backward. Like tiny antlers, or---

Horns.

Caleb blinked hard, looked again. Brown spikes jutting from white fur between the ears. Really there.

He'd never heard of rabbits with horns. Deer had antlers, goats had horns, but rabbits? He grabbed his laptop, searched "rabbits with horns." Thousands of results, most pointing to "jackalope."

Jackalopes---jackrabbits with antelope horns. American folklore bullshit. Taxidermists in the early 1900s gluing deer antlers onto rabbit heads, selling them to tourists and bars. Tall tale like Bigfoot.

Jackalopes weren't real.

He looked back. The rabbit was gone.

Caleb spent the rest of the afternoon trying to convince himself he'd seen shadows or tricks of light. Horns on a rabbit made about as much sense as fins on a bear. Maybe he'd been staring at his laptop screen too long. The thin air up here could mess with your vision.

By evening, he'd almost talked himself out of the whole thing. He grilled a burger on the back porch, ate it while reading a paperback thriller, and watched the sun set behind Mount Blanca to the west. Normal day, weird rabbit notwithstanding.

He was loading his plate into the dishwasher when the thumping started again.

Thump-thump-thump.

This time it came from the front porch. Caleb grabbed a flashlight from the kitchen drawer and stepped out the front door. The beam swept across the wooden planks, revealing nothing but a ceramic planter his sister had given him.

Thump-thump-thump.

The sound came from his left, near the corner where the porch wrapped around the cabin's side. Caleb followed the noise, flashlight held ahead of him.

A rabbit sat at the corner of the porch, caught in the yellow cone of light. This one was larger than the afternoon visitor, with darker fur and longer ears. And rising from its skull, impossible but undeniable, were two brown horns.

The rabbit stared directly into the flashlight beam without flinching. Its eyes reflected the light with an unsettling awareness, as if it was studying him as intently as he was studying it.

Thump-thump-thump.

The rabbit's powerful hind legs drummed the wooden planks in perfect rhythm. This wasn't frantic warning behavior---this was deliberate, controlled, like communication.

"What do you want?" he said aloud, feeling foolish for talking to an animal.

The rabbit tilted its head, horns glinting in the flashlight beam. Then it turned and hopped away, vanishing into the darkness.

That night, Caleb dreamed of Sarah standing in their old Chicago apartment, packing her things into cardboard boxes.

"You know what your problem is?" she said without looking at him. "You think being alone makes you deep. But it just makes you empty."

He woke before dawn with the dream's sting still fresh and found himself thinking about the rabbit. There'd been something almost... expectant about the way it had looked at him. Like it was waiting for him to understand something.

The next morning brought the season's first snow, a light dusting that made the ponderosa pines look like they'd been dipped in powdered sugar. Caleb made coffee and tried to lose himself in work, but his protagonist's crisis of faith felt increasingly hollow. How could he write about isolation when he'd chosen it precisely because it was safe?

Movement outside caught his eye. A dozen white shapes dotted his front yard, scattered across the snow-covered grass.

Rabbits. All facing the cabin.

Caleb saved his work and grabbed his jacket. Outside, the morning air bit at his exposed skin and turned his breath to silver puffs. Snow was coming---he could smell it in the wind carrying down from the Continental Divide.

The rabbits sat motionless, even with him standing on the front porch in plain sight. Each animal had the same impossible horns he'd seen before. Some longer than others, some more curved, but all rising from their skulls like tiny antlers. A few of the larger ones had horns that branched.

Caleb counted fifteen animals total. They sat in what appeared to be a loose formation, with the largest specimen centered about twenty feet from his front steps. That one's horns were easily three inches long and polished to a gleaming brown finish.

"This isn't happening," he said aloud.

The large rabbit's ears twitched at the sound of his voice, but otherwise none of the animals moved. They continued their collective stare, as if waiting for something.

Caleb descended the porch steps slowly, hands held out to show he meant no harm. The rabbits tracked his movement but didn't flee. He stopped ten feet from the nearest one, a medium-sized individual with short, sharp horns that curved forward.

"Where did you come from?" he asked.

The rabbit cocked its head, studying him with dark eyes that never blinked. Its horns caught the morning sunlight and threw back golden flashes. Up close, the horns looked completely natural, growing from the skull like ears.

Caleb pulled out his phone and snapped several photos. When he looked back at the yard a moment later, the rabbits were gone. Only disturbed patches in the snow showed where they'd been sitting.

He spent the morning researching online, but found nothing that explained what he'd witnessed. The photos were clear enough---real animals, real horns. But according to everything he could find, such creatures didn't exist.

Unless they did now.

That afternoon he drove into Wilmaville for supplies. Harvey Milton's general store, a post office that doubled as sheriff station, dozen houses scattered along the valley floor. In Chicago, Caleb barely knew his neighbors' names. Here, after six months, he'd fallen into small-town rhythms.

Harvey looked up from stocking shelves as Caleb entered, bell announcing his arrival.

"Afternoon, Caleb. How's the great American novel?"

Harvey's standard greeting, delivered with gentle ribbing that managed to encourage rather than mock. Probably sixty, graying hair and weathered hands. Took over the store from his father thirty years ago, seemed to know every person within fifty miles.

"Slowly," Caleb said, grabbing a cart. "Harvey, you ever see anything weird around here? Wildlife-wise?"

Harvey's expression shifted. "Weird how?"

"Rabbits with horns."

Harvey was quiet, then walked to the front door, flipped the sign to "CLOSED." Returned, lowering his voice.

"You seen 'em too?"

"Too?"

"Started a week ago. Betty Patterson calling about strange rabbits in her garden. Jim Clarke saw a group near the old mining road. Figured it was kids with fake antlers."

"But?"

Harvey rubbed his jaw. "More folks started seeing them. Caleb... they don't act like normal rabbits. They watch things. Study them. Yesterday, Martha Jenkins swore she saw twenty sitting in perfect rows behind the church, like they was attending service."

"Have you seen them yourself?"

Harvey nodded slowly. "This morning. Must've been thirty of 'em in my back alley when I came to open up. Not scattered around like you'd expect---arranged. In patterns."

"What kind of patterns?"

Harvey led him to the back room. On his desk, next to invoices and catalogs, lay a sheet covered in pencil sketches. Various arrangements of small oval shapes---circles, lines, complex geometric forms.

"Drew what I saw. Figured I was going crazy, but if you're seeing them too..."

Caleb studied the sketches. Not random---clear intention, like a language he couldn't read.

"Harvey, what if they're trying to communicate?"

Harvey laughed without humor. "Rabbits don't communicate, Caleb. Least not like this."

That night Caleb sat on his back porch with notebook and pen, watching the forest edge. Around ten, he heard it---soft sound of many small bodies moving through underbrush. He turned on his flashlight, swept it across the yard.

They came out in small groups---five, then ten, then twenty. All different sizes, all with horns. Formed a semicircle on his lawn, largest rabbit at center.

Caleb stepped down, moving slow. The rabbits watched but didn't flee. When he reached the edge of their formation, he knelt in snow.

"Don't understand what you want," he said, feeling less foolish than before.

The large rabbit made a soft sound---not the warning thump, but something musical. Others responded with similar sounds, creating gentle harmony that vibrated in his chest.

Then they moved.

Not fleeing---flowing. Formation shifted and changed, rabbits moving into new patterns. Circles became spirals, spirals became lines, lines became shapes Caleb had no names for. Each pattern held thirty seconds before flowing into the next, like slow dance.

Caleb watched, transfixed. Meaning here, intelligence and purpose beyond normal animal behavior. These creatures were trying to show him something.

But what?

Display went on nearly an hour before the rabbits returned to forest. Caleb stayed kneeling in snow several minutes after they'd gone, trying to make sense of what he'd seen.

Inside, he opened his laptop and began to write. Not the pretentious literary fiction he'd been struggling with, but simple account of what he'd seen. Words flowed easier than they had in months. For the first time since moving to Colorado, he felt like he was capturing something real.

Over the following days, the rabbit gatherings became a nightly occurrence. Each evening brought new formations, new patterns, new attempts at communication. Caleb began sketching what he saw, trying to decode the meaning behind the arrangements.

Daily trips to Harvey's store, he learned other townspeople were experiencing similar visits. Betty Patterson's garden hosted morning gatherings. Rabbits gathered behind the church during Sunday services, sitting in orderly rows like they was listening to sermon. Jim Clarke found them in precise geometric patterns near his workshop.

"Like they're studying us," Harvey said one afternoon, looking at Caleb's latest sketches.

"But why?"

Harvey shrugged. "Maybe they're trying to understand us."

That evening, the gathering was different. Instead of complex patterns, the rabbits formed a simple circle around clear space in center. Large rabbit with crown-like horns sat at the edge, looking directly at him.

The invitation was clear.

Caleb walked across snow, sat in the center. Rabbits stayed still, but their presence felt different---not alien or threatening, but welcoming.

Large rabbit made its musical sound, and Caleb understood not words, but meaning. They were asking: Do you want to belong?

For the first time in his life, the answer was yes.

"What do I need to do?"

Rabbit tilted its head toward forest. More rabbits coming out---dozens, then hundreds, then more than he could count. Flowed across landscape like white river, all moving with same coordination.

Heading toward Wilmaville.

Caleb followed.

Procession moved down mountain road in perfect silence, rabbits flowing in columns around obstacles, reforming on the other side. At town's edge, they spread out, taking positions throughout valley in planned formations.

But they weren't invading. Waiting.

Lights came on in houses throughout Wilmaville. Doors opened. One by one, townspeople came outside to find their yards filled with patiently sitting rabbits. Harvey stood on his porch, looking across the street where hundreds had arranged themselves in the church parking lot. Betty Patterson knelt beside her garden fence, reaching tentatively toward small rabbit with delicate, branch-like horns.

Rabbits weren't threatening anyone. Extending the same invitation they'd offered Caleb.

Do you want to belong?

Harvey was first to step down from his porch, walk among the creatures. Then Betty, then Jim Clarke, then others. One by one, people of Wilmaville found themselves sitting in circles of patient, horned rabbits, listening to musical sounds that meant something without words.

Caleb found himself back in his original circle, crown-horned rabbit still watching with golden eyes. Creature made its questioning sound again, and this time Caleb understood the full scope of what was offered.

Not absorption into hive mind, but genuine community. Way of belonging that kept individual identity while creating something larger. Rabbits hadn't lost themselves in their collective---they'd found themselves.

"Yes."

Rabbit's response was immediate. Touched its horn to Caleb's forehead, and he felt warmth spread through his skull, tingling that wasn't painful but was definitely changing something.

When it was over, Caleb could hear them.

Not voices in his head, but sense of connection, of belonging to something vast and purposeful. He was still himself---still Caleb Brest, still a writer with dreams and fears and memories of Sarah---but now also part of something bigger.

He understood what the rabbits had been trying to show them. They weren't just displaying patterns---teaching the art of living together without losing who you were. Showing humans what community could really be.

Around him, neighbors were going through the same change. Harvey's weathered face showed wonder as small brown bumps appeared on his temples. Betty Patterson laughed with delight, touching her own developing horns.

They weren't becoming rabbits. Becoming something new---humans who'd learned the secret of true community, of thinking together while staying themselves.

That night, Caleb opened his laptop and began to write. But this time, he wasn't writing alone. Story flowed from him as part of bigger conversation, collective telling of their change that was somehow both individual and shared.

He wrote about isolation and fear of belonging. About Sarah and emptiness of his old life. About finding community not through losing himself, but through finally understanding what it meant to be truly connected to other living beings.

Words were his, but also theirs---story told by the collective but spoken in his unique voice. For the first time in his life, his writing felt both deeply personal and meaningful to everyone.

Three months later, when the outside world finally noticed Wilmaville, they found a thriving community unlike anything in modern America. Residents still looked human, except for small horn-like bumps on their foreheads. Still had their individual personalities and jobs but worked together with efficiency and harmony that seemed almost supernatural.

Harvey still ran his general store but now worked with other residents to make sure everyone's needs were met. Betty Patterson's garden had grown to feed the entire community. Jim Clarke's workshop had become center for shared craftsmanship.

Caleb had become their storyteller, writing their story not just for themselves but for the world outside. His book, "The Transformation of Wilmaville," became a bestseller, though critics couldn't agree whether it was fiction or non-fiction.

For the first time in his life, he was writing about life he was living, as part of community that valued both individual expression and shared purpose.

Caleb walked outside, sat among the rabbits in his backyard. They still gathered each evening, not to communicate anymore---that was no longer necessary---but simply to share the peace of belonging.

He touched the small horns that had grown from his temples, feeling through them the gentle presence of his neighbors going about their daily lives, connected but not controlled, individual but not alone.

In the distance, lights twinkled in windows of Wilmaville, each one representing someone who had chosen connection over isolation, community over solitude. It wasn't the life Caleb had planned, but it was the life he'd been looking for without knowing it. He opened his notebook and began to write, his words adding to the ongoing story of their shared journey, told in his voice but belonging to them all.

He opened his notebook and began to write, his words adding to the ongoing story of their shared journey, told in his voice but belonging to them all.

I Speak Their Language

Dr. Claire Sterling pushed through the steel door marked "CLAS-SIFIED ACCESS - LEVEL 7" and immediately regretted the wool blazer. Three hundred feet underground, the mountain pressed against her ears. The air tasted like metal and sweat.

She followed the young soldier—Williams—down a corridor that curved like a throat. Her laptop bag kept slipping off her shoulder.

"First time underground, ma'am?" Williams had a Carolina drawl that echoed off the concrete.

"First time anywhere like this." The walls pressed in. Buried alive. "How deep are we?"

"'Bout three hundred feet. Colonel Brooks is waiting."

Claire had spent the six-hour flight from Boston running through possibilities. The phone call had been professional but vague: "unusual language samples," "potential breakthrough," "national security implications." She'd packed for three days. Her gut said it'd be longer.

Williams knocked twice at another steel door. "Doc Sterling's here, sir."

"Send her in."

Colonel Brooks looked like he'd been drinking coffee for three days straight. Maybe mid-forties, graying hair, handshake that told you he was used to making hard decisions. Behind him stood a woman in a stained lab coat—thirties, blonde ponytail, the kind of tired that went bone-deep.

"Dr. Sterling. Thanks for droppin' everything." Brooks had a slight Tennessee accent that thickened when he was stressed. "This here's Dr. Sarah Anderson, xenobiology. She's been livin' with these damn things for a week."

Anderson's smile looked painful. "Sorry—haven't been sleeping much." Coffee stains on her coat, tremor in her fingers when she shook Claire's hand.

"Xenobiology?" Claire set down her bag. "We talking about samples from space?"

"That's what we're hopin' you can tell us," Brooks said. He gestured toward a metal table where three sealed containers sat under examination lights. Each one looked like a reinforced glass coffee can, biohazard warnings plastered across the sides. "Found these six days ago in a cave system near Glacier. Along with... other things."

Claire approached the containers. Inside each one, suspended in clear fluid, were objects that made her breath catch. Tablets. Rectangular, palm-sized, made of dark material that shifted under the lights. Covered in markings that definitely weren't human.

The symbols stirred something. Three years back, she'd consulted on missing hikers near Glacier. Search teams found strange carvings in cave walls—FBI dismissed them as hoax evidence. Looking at these tablets, Claire wondered if those scratches had been something else.

"The markings appear carved," Anderson said, moving beside her. "But we can't identify the material. Some kind of organic compound we've never seen."

Claire pulled her reading glasses out and leaned closer. The symbols weren't like anything in her twenty years with dead languages. Not pictographic like Egyptian, not syllabic like Sumerian. They flowed together, making her eyes ache if she stared too long.

"Any luck dating them?"

"Carbon dating's screwed," Anderson said. "The organic compounds don't decay normal. Could be fifty years old, could be fifty thousand."

Brooks cleared his throat. "Dr. Sterling, gotta mention—we found these three tablets six days ago. NSA cryptography, three university linguistics departments, nobody made headway." He paused, rubbing his stubbled jaw. "Yesterday our boys uncovered thirty-four more tablets in deeper chambers. Same markings, same material. Your work with that Proto-Indo-European stuff, those papers on alien languages—that's why you're here."

Those papers had been thought experiments, exploring how human linguists might approach non-human communication. Claire never expected to test the theories. She circled the table, studying each tablet from different angles.

"Can I get high-resolution photos? And somewhere to work that won't give me a headache?"

"Already set up," Brooks said. "You'll have imaging equipment, analysis software. Sarah's your tech support for anything you need."

An hour later, Claire sat alone in a windowless office with three monitors displaying every angle of the tablets. She'd sent Anderson away after the woman kept hovering and asking questions Claire wasn't ready to answer. Brooks had made it clear this was classified at the highest levels—no colleagues, no outside databases.

She started the way they'd taught her at Harvard—systematic symbol inventory first. Forty-seven distinct marks, which suggested alphabetic rather than logographic. She drew each one by hand, looking for shared elements that might indicate related sounds or meanings.

Four hours in, her eyes burned. Three notebooks filled with frequency charts that looked like chicken scratch. Coffee gone cold twice. One symbol cluster kept showing up at passage beginnings—maybe sentence markers, maybe coincidence. Her brain felt like mush.

Claire pushed back from her desk and rubbed her temples. The fluorescent lights buzzed like angry wasps. Every pattern she thought she'd found fell apart under closer analysis. What looked like grammar might just be decoration. What seemed like word boundaries could be random spacing.

She needed coffee and air that didn't taste like fear and recycled electronics.

The break room was empty except for a tired technician microwaving something that smelled like regret. He nodded and left without speaking—probably under orders not to chat with the civilian consultant.

When she returned, Anderson was waiting with fresh coffee and a worried expression.

"Colonel's getting pressure from upstairs," Anderson said, settling into the chair beside Claire's desk. "Any progress?"

"It's definitely a language." Claire accepted the coffee gratefully. "Complex grammar, consistent syntax. Whoever made this thinks in abstract concepts."

"Whoever?"

Claire turned back to the monitors. "That's the million-dollar question. The precision suggests intelligence, but the organic tablets..." She trailed off. "It's like nothing in the archaeological record."

"What about content? Can you tell what they're saying?"

Claire had been avoiding that question. "I think... maybe official documents. Formal announcements. But I could be wrong—I'm imposing human structures on non-human thinking."

Anderson leaned forward. "Like government stuff?"

"More formal. The syntax reminds me of ancient treaties or..." Claire stared at a symbol cluster she'd been analyzing. Cold certainty settled in her gut. "Legal declarations."

Claire spent the next six hours building what she hoped was a translation matrix, based on symbol frequency and positional relationships. Like assembling a jigsaw puzzle where half the pieces were missing and the other half might belong to a different box entirely.

Then individual words started emerging.

Territory. She'd seen this pattern before—in Proto-Indo-European roots, how possession markers clustered around core concepts. The symbol appeared seventeen times across three tablets, always with the same directional modifiers.

Claim. Trickier. The base symbol shared elements with "territory" but had additional strokes that suggested ownership. Dominance. She cross-referenced it with position markers.

Claire stood and paced the small office. Professional linguists didn't decode alien languages in single afternoons. This had to be wishful thinking.

But when she double-checked, the translations held. Inferior. A modifier applied to some unnamed group.

Her breathing quickened. The walls felt closer.

Eradication. This one made her step back, heart hammering.

Claire forced herself to take deep breaths. She was jumping to conclusions, seeing threats in abstract concepts. But when she returned to the analysis, the grammatical context remained clear.

Day two brought more frustration than breakthrough. Claire's first attempt at grammatical mapping collapsed when she realized she'd been reading directionally wrong—the symbols ran right to left, not left to right. Six hours of work down the drain. She started over, fighting the urge to throw her notebook across the room.

But by afternoon, individual words began to emerge from the alien syntax.

If her interpretations were right, she was reading a declaration of war.

The language was clinical, methodical, describing what appeared to be military planning against "surface dwellers" and "inferior bipedal species." But Claire caught herself—was she projecting fears onto ambiguous symbols?

She forced herself to double-check every translation, question each assumption. The more she analyzed the syntax, the more certain she became these weren't historical artifacts. The grammatical markers suggested immediacy, current relevance.

Day three, Claire stared at her translations. Discovery felt like a weight crushing her chest.

"Dr. Anderson." Her voice came out as a croak. "When exactly did you find these?"

"Six days ago. Why?" Anderson's exhaustion had deepened into something approaching breakdown.

"You mentioned other things found with them?"

Anderson went rigid. "That's classified above your level."

"Bodies?" The word came out like a cough.

Anderson's silence stretched. Then: "Seventeen hikers. Missing over three months. Something killed them." She stared at her coffee cup. "Not human."

Claire's hands found the desk edge, gripped until her knuckles went white. "They were testing us."

"What?"

"These aren't war declarations. They're field reports." Her voice sounded foreign. "This section—it's not about human capabilities. It's assessment data. Lab results."

Anderson leaned closer. "You're saying these things have been studying us?"

"Studying, testing, preparing." Claire's voice barely carried. "The time markers suggest organized operations spanning decades."

"That's impossible. We would've detected—"

Claire pulled up another section. "Look at this cluster. It describes concealment and misdirection. Small teams, careful target selection, operations below detection thresholds."

A memory surfaced: a conference two years back about statistical anomalies in missing persons cases. The presenter noted unusual clustering near cave systems and underground water sources. At the time, everyone assumed caves were just dangerous.

Now Claire wondered if the danger had been something else.

"You're talking about alien abductions," Anderson said. "UFO conspiracies."

"I'm talking about intelligence gathering by a hostile species that considers humans inferior and is preparing for large-scale military action."

Claire saved her work and stood on unsteady legs. The physical discomfort was nothing compared to the growing certainty she'd stumbled into something far beyond a translation project.

"I need Brooks."

"It's past midnight—"

"Now."

Fifteen minutes later, Brooks appeared looking like someone had kicked him awake. Rumpled uniform, missed spots shaving, but his eyes were alert.

"Dr. Sterling. Sarah says you've made progress."

Claire had spent the wait organizing her thoughts, but facing the colonel, the magnitude of her discovery seemed to freeze her voice. How do you tell a military officer that his species was under attack by an enemy they'd never seen coming?

"The tablets aren't historical," she said, praying she was wrong. "If my translations are accurate—and God, I hope they're not—these are military communications."

Brooks raised an eyebrow. "From who?"

Claire's throat felt like sandpaper. "A species that considers humans inferior and appears to be planning our extermination."

The colonel studied her face for nearly a minute. "You're certain about this translation?"

Claire opened her laptop, called up her analysis. "The grammar's consistent, vocabulary patterns match linguistic principles, and the content describes humans with precision. Average height, weight, life expectancy, reproductive cycles, technology levels."

She highlighted sections. "This tablet describes 'surface infrastructure analysis'—detailed intelligence on cities, power grids, transportation. This one outlines biological vulnerability assessment—diseases we're susceptible to, environmental toxins, targeting for population reduction."

Brooks leaned over her shoulder, studying the alien symbols. "You're confident this is accurate? Not reading more into these marks than what's there?"

"Colonel, I've spent twenty years studying dead languages. I know the difference between wishful translation and meaning." Claire pulled up her vocabulary matrix. "These documents are formal, official, and recent. Time markers suggest creation within the past several months."

"What kind of time markers?"

Claire highlighted recurring symbols. "These reference seasonal cycles, but not abstractly. They correlate with astronomical events from this year. Spring equinox, summer solstice. And there are future references suggesting planned actions coordinated with celestial events."

Anderson spoke from the doorway. "Autumn equinox is in three weeks."

Brooks was quiet, expression unreadable. Then he pulled out his phone and stepped into the hallway. Claire could hear muffled conversation but couldn't make out words.

When he returned, his demeanor had shifted into something formal and urgent.

"Dr. Sterling, I need a complete report. Full translation matrix, vocabulary analysis, timeline assessments—everything. You have until oh-six-hundred."

"Colonel, if I'm right about this—"

"If you're right, we have less than three weeks to prepare for the largest threat to national security in human history." Brooks headed for the door, then paused. "Sarah will provide additional materials we've been holding classified."

"Additional materials?"

Anderson looked sick. "We didn't just find three tablets, Claire. We found thirty-seven."

The blood drained from Claire's face. "Thirty-seven?"

"Along with communication equipment. Technology that doesn't match any known manufacturing. And evidence of surveillance operations in major population centers."

Brooks's voice echoed from the hallway: "Oh-six-hundred, Dr. Sterling. Pentagon's expecting your briefing at oh-eight-hundred."

Claire spent the next six hours in controlled panic, working through translations that grew more horrifying with each completed passage. Her neck cramped from hunching over the monitor. The recycled air made her mouth taste like copper.

The earliest documents, dated by astronomical references, described reconnaissance from the 1960s. Small teams taking isolated humans for study—intelligence assessments, physical testing, social analysis.

Later tablets described expanded operations. Surveillance equipment in major cities. Infiltration of facilities. Mapping of infrastructure and defenses.

The most recent documents outlined the final phase: coordinated attacks on population centers with environmental disruption. The aliens—though they never called themselves that, using instead a complex symbol that might translate as "the inheritors" or "the rightful occupants"—had developed biological weapons targeted to human physiology.

At 5:49 AM, Claire finished translating the final tablet. Her mouth tasted like copper, sweat beaded on her forehead. She could barely force her fingers to work the keyboard:

"Final document appears to be operational orders for 'surface cleansing protocol.' Timeline indicates implementation beginning autumn equinox—September twenty-second. Seventeen days from now. Coordinated attacks on seventeen metropolitan areas using biological agents delivered through existing water treatment facilities."

The alien symbols pulsed on her screen like living things. Claire's vision blurred from exhaustion and terror.

"Estimated human survival rate following biological attack: less than twelve percent. Species elimination: eighteen months."

Claire stopped recording. Her hands shook so badly she could barely save the files. Seventeen days. Less than three weeks before—

She looked at her phone. 5:52 AM. Eight minutes before deadline, and there was one more thing she needed to check.

Claire pulled up the symbol she'd translated as "the inheritors" and cross-referenced it with earlier documents. The pattern was consistent across all tablets, but something about its structure bothered her. Too complex, too many elements.

She spent six minutes breaking down component parts, analyzing each element's meaning. What she found made her wish she'd never learned to read.

The symbol wasn't a name or species designation. It was a description. When she translated its individual components, the meaning was clear:

Those who have always been here.

Claire stared at the translation as understanding crystallized. These weren't alien invaders from space. They were Earth's original intelligent species—underground dwellers who'd retreated to deep places when humans spread across the surface millennia ago.

The surface dwellers—humans—were the arrivals. And their time as dominant species was ending.

Claire thought about unexplained disappearances over decades, stories dismissed as hoaxes. Cave systems that felt watched. Underground spaces engineers couldn't explain. They'd been there all along, patient and invisible.

At 6:00 AM, Claire submitted her report to Colonel Brooks. By 6:15, she was in a secure communications room where Pentagon officials waited on encrypted video. By 6:30, emergency protocols were activating across three continents.

But as Claire sat in the underground facility, surrounded by military personnel making desperate plans for humanity's survival, she couldn't stop thinking about one symbol from the earliest tablets—a mark she'd translated as "patience."

These creatures had been patient for decades. Maybe centuries. They'd watched human civilization grow across the planet's surface while remaining hidden in caves and deep places, gathering intelligence and waiting.

In eighteen days, their patience would be rewarded.

Claire looked around the room at officials focused on phones and laptops, coordinating emergency responses and defensive preparations. They were treating this like a military threat—something that could be fought with human technology and tactics.

But the inheritors had been studying human responses for generations. They'd observed military doctrine, analyzed decision-making patterns, catalogued weaknesses and defensive capabilities.

They weren't just planning an invasion. They were executing a strategy refined through decades of observation and testing.

And humanity didn't even know the war had begun.

At 7:45 AM, as Claire prepared for her Pentagon briefing, Anderson approached with final evidence—a small device recovered from the Montana cave system. Size of a smartphone, made of the same organic material, with symbols matching Claire's translations.

"We think it's communication equipment," Anderson said. "It's been transmitting since we found it. Low frequency, encrypted."

Claire examined the device, recognizing several symbols from her translations. "What kind of signal?"

"Not sure. But the transmission is directed downward—into the earth itself."

Cold certainty settled in Claire's chest. "It's not communication equipment. It's a beacon."

"Beacon for what?"

Claire looked at the officials preparing for a war they couldn't win against an enemy they'd never seen coming. She thought about the symbol for "patience" and realized the truth was worse than her translation had suggested.

The tablets weren't just military communications. They were a countdown.

And humanity's time had just run out.

"It's calling them home," she said quietly. "All of them."

As if responding to her words, the device in Anderson's hands began to pulse with soft, rhythmic light—like a heartbeat, or a signal, or the final tick of a clock counting down to the end of the world.

Above them, three hundred feet of mountain pressed down in the darkness, and Claire realized with cold certainty that they weren't the only ones listening.

I Count the Falling Tears

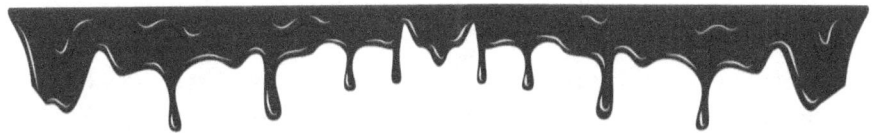

The tears taste of copper and salt and a thousand small betrayals.

I stand beside Mrs. Evelyn Carpenter's hospital bed and watch the first droplet form at the corner of her left eye. She cannot see me—they never can—but something changes when I arrive. The machines shift rhythm. The air grows heavy. Her breathing grows shallow. Her fingers clutch the cotton blanket, knuckles white against faded blue.

Something's wrong with this counting, though I can't name what. The patterns have shifted. Deaths that don't fit the ancient rhythms. People who die with fewer tears than their lives would suggest, or whose tears taste of things I've never encountered.

Death used to follow predictable patterns. Ancient humans wept for different things than modern ones, but they wept. The tears might taste of mammoth hunts instead of missed phone calls, but they came.

Now I encounter cases that shake everything I thought I knew about dying.

One.

The tear rolls down her papery cheek and disappears into the pillow. I record it in the tally I have kept for longer than human civilization has drawn breath. Mrs. Carpenter's regret tastes of her son Steven, whom she hasn't spoken to in three years. Bitterness of pride. Metallic tang of words that should have been said but weren't.

Two.

Another tear follows. This one carries the weight of her marriage to Harold, forty-seven years of small compromises that accumulated like dust until she forgot who she'd been before she became Mrs. Carpenter. Taste of chalk and disappointment, with an aftertaste of vanilla—wedding cake from 1962.

I've seen this scene before. So many times the details blur—different names, faces, flavors of regret—but the rhythm stays the same. People die. They cry. I count. The universe keeps turning.

Mrs. Carpenter's eyes flutter. She sees something beyond the ceiling tiles, something that makes her mouth open in a small 'o' of surprise. Her breathing stops. Her heart stutters once, twice, falls silent.

Three.

The final tear contains everything she couldn't express. Every Christmas morning she chose duty over joy. Every sunset she was too busy to notice. Every 'I love you' she deflected with 'We'll talk later.' The tear carries accumulated silences.

I close the eternal tally. Mrs. Evelyn Carpenter: three tears. A moderate showing. I've witnessed grown men weep rivers, and I've seen the callous depart bone-dry. The count serves some purpose, though that purpose has grown unclear over the eons.

The hospital room dissolves around me. Walls lose solidity first, becoming translucent, then transparent, then gone. Beeping monitors fade to silence. Antiseptic smell dissipates like smoke. When the world reforms, I stand in an alley behind a Vietnamese restaurant in Portland, Oregon.

The smell of fish sauce and grease mingles with October air, but underneath lies something else—the metallic scent of blood and approaching death.

Thomas Liu lies crumpled beside a dumpster, three bullet holes forming a perfect triangle in his chest. His blood seeps between cracks in the asphalt, his life ebbing like water through broken stone.

His dying fingers clutch a small photo—a seven-year-old girl with pigtails, grinning gap-toothed at the camera. His daughter Sophie. The image shows creases from handling, worn from being carried in his pocket.

"Sophie," he whispers. "Daddy's sorry. Daddy tried."

The bullets came from men he owed money to—debts from borrowing to pay for Sophie's medical treatments. Love over safety. His daughter's life over his own.

The first tear carries Saturday morning pancakes shaped like Mickey Mouse, even when the restaurant kept him working until three AM. More tears follow. Each one a story of choices made for love.

Seventeen by the time his heart stops. Not a record, but enough to tell me this man knew what mattered.

The alley dissolves. The cycle continues.

Time moves strangely when you exist between heartbeats. I count tears in hospital rooms and crack houses, in car accidents and bedroom suicides. The count becomes rhythm, meditation, reason.

Then something happens that shakes this ancient certainty.

I'm summoned to Burlington, Vermont—a hospice facility where Helena Voss lies propped against pillows, surrounded by handmade quilts and photos spanning decades. Seventy-three years old, pancreatic cancer, stage four. But unlike most dying patients, she seems radiant despite her failing body.

Over several days, I find myself drawn to observe her more than perhaps any dying person I've encountered. Her behavior defies every pattern I've learned to expect.

Most dying people become self-focused as death approaches. Helena grows more attentive to others. When nurses enter, she asks about their families, their dreams. She listens with genuine interest.

A young man arrives one morning, nervous and shaking. "Mrs. Voss? I'm Danny Martinez. You don't remember me, but you were my guidance counselor at Burlington High twenty years ago."

Helena's face transforms. "Danny! Of course I remember. You wanted to be a teacher, but you were afraid you weren't smart enough."

"That's right." Danny's voice breaks. "You spent hours helping me with applications. You drove me to campus visits on weekends. You believed in me when I didn't believe in myself."

"And did you become a teacher?"

"I did. Third grade at Miller Elementary. I have your picture on my desk, right next to my teaching certificate."

Helena reaches across the space between their chairs and takes Danny's hand in both of hers. Her grip is strong despite her illness.

"I'm so proud of you," she says. "So very proud."

After Danny leaves, wiping his eyes and walking taller, Helena turns to her daughter Karen with eyes bright with satisfaction.

"Wasn't that wonderful?" she says, settling back with a contented sigh. "He turned out exactly as I hoped."

This troubles me. Where most dying people dwell on failures, Helena celebrates successes. Where others focus on missed opportunities, she revels in connections that outlasted time.

Then comes her final day.

Helena's breathing grows labored. Her pulse weakens. The family draws closer. But where I expect fear or frantic regret, Helena maintains that same peaceful demeanor.

She speaks to each family member, offering specific encouragement. To her son Robert: "Take care of your mother's garden. The roses need you." To her granddaughter Emma: "Don't let anyone tell you that art isn't practical. The world needs beauty."

These aren't desperate final words. They're considered thoughts of someone who has made peace with leaving.

As the moment approaches, I position myself closer. In all my eons of counting, no one has approached death with such equanimity.

Helena does something impossible.

She smiles.

Not the rictus of death, but genuine contentment. Her eyes focus on something beyond the ceiling. Her lips move.

"Well," she whispers, "it's about time."

The words chill me. Not their content, but their tone. She sounds pleased. Eager, even.

I move closer. Her breathing grows labored. Each breath requires visible effort. Her pulse weakens. The moment approaches—the moment when tears fall.

I wait. Prepare to count.

Then something unprecedented happens.

Helena Voss closes her eyes. Her breathing stops—one final exhale that seems to release more than just air. Her heart beats once more, falls silent.

I wait. Count the seconds. Search her peaceful face.

No tears.

I stare, searching for any trace of moisture. The family begins to weep—ugly, honest sobs of grief and love. But Helena herself remains dry-eyed, wearing that small smile like a benediction.

For the first time in millennia, I don't know what to write in my ledger.

Helena Voss: zero tears.

The number sits in my mind like a splinter. How does someone live seventy-three years without accumulating enough regret to shed a single tear at death?

I use abilities I rarely call on and trace her life backward through time. Images come slowly, like photographs in developing solution.

Helena at seventy, reading stories to children at the Burlington Public Library. Her voice carries warmth that draws them close like flowers turning toward the sun.

Helena at sixty-five, retiring from her job as a guidance counselor. Former students return—some now in their forties—to say goodbye.

They speak of college applications she helped complete, of times she listened when their parents refused to.

Helena at sixty, nursing her husband Richard through his final bout with emphysema. She never complains when he forgets her name or struggles to use a fork. She holds his hand and tells him about their children, their grandchildren, the life they built together.

The images reach deeper. Fifty-five, leading a support group for parents who've lost children. Her own son David died in Vietnam two years earlier. Grief shows in the lines around her eyes, but she channels it into helping others navigate their darkness.

At forty, volunteering at a women's shelter. At thirty, teaching Sunday school. At twenty-five, working as a nurse during the polio epidemic, holding hands of children who might not see another sunrise.

The images reveal her childhood. Helena Marie Kowalski, born in 1948 to Polish immigrants who owned a small grocery store. Her father died when she was eight—a heart attack behind the cash register on a Tuesday afternoon in December.

Young Helena learned early that life delivers pain without asking permission. But rather than retreat, she developed an unusual capacity for transformation. I observe her at fifteen, crying over her father's grave not with bitterness but with gratitude—thanking him for teaching her that love makes loss worthwhile.

At twenty-two, her fiancé David dies in Vietnam three months before their wedding. Instead of becoming bitter, she volunteers at the veterans' hospital, reading to wounded soldiers.

"Love doesn't end just because the body does," she tells a grieving widow. "The point isn't to avoid loving because we might lose—it's to love so fully that loss becomes bearable because we know we held nothing back."

The pattern becomes clear: Helena lived without accumulating the kind of regret that produces tears at death. Not because she avoided difficult choices or escaped loss, but because she made peace with them. She grieved when grief was called for. She felt anger when anger was justified. She experienced disappointment, heartbreak, profound loss.

But she never let any of it poison her capacity for joy. She transformed every hurt into wisdom, every loss into deeper appreciation for what remained.

Standing in that empty hospice room, I realize I'm facing something unprecedented: a human being who died complete.

The revelation disturbs something fundamental within me. For eons, I've existed believing that death brings regret, that consciousness generates the bitter tears of 'what if' and 'if only.' Helena Voss suggests a different possibility: that life can be lived so fully that death becomes not a failure but a completion.

I need to test this new perspective. Rather than arriving only at the moment of death, I begin observing more of each person's final days.

The shift in my approach accelerates when I encounter Victor Williams.

Victor, forty-five, carpenter, lies dying on I-95 after his truck hit black ice. Scattered across the asphalt are dozens of photographs that had been clipped to his sun visor. Images of houses—modest homes, grand renovations, simple repairs—each bearing handwritten notes: "Johnson family, 2019," "Martinez wedding gift, 2021," "Hurricane repair, Mrs. Chen, 2020."

Victor's eyes focus on one photograph near his head—a small ranch house with a bright red door.

"First house I ever built from scratch," he whispers. "Young couple... Sarah and Mike. Told me they wanted something that would last forever."

His breathing grows labored. "Should have charged them more. Barely broke even. Business never recovered."

Here comes the familiar pattern. The regret that will generate tears.

But then Victor does something unexpected. He reaches toward the photograph with trembling fingers.

"But they got their forever house," he whispers. "Drove by last month. Still solid. Still beautiful. Kids playing in that yard I helped them plan."

Seven tears fall. But as they do, I experience that overwhelming urge again—to whisper: "They remember you, Victor. The work matters. The integrity matters."

I remain silent, preserving the integrity of his authentic experience. But the questions multiply with each death. If I can see the completeness of these lives, if I can recognize love where the dying see only failure, do I have an obligation to share that perspective?

Victor dies believing himself a failure because he couldn't repay borrowed money. But I can see what he cannot—that his daughter carries his teaching about integrity into her work as a social worker, that his son uses craftsmanship skills to restore historic buildings.

The ethical weight becomes heavier with each encounter.

Mrs. Dorothy Chang dies in her sleep. Two tears—garden she'll never see bloom, grandchildren too far away. But her last breath carries jasmine tea and her husband's cologne, fifty-seven years after his death. She holds his memory like a warm stone.

Father Antonio Santos dies giving last rites. One tear for the sermon he'll never finish about forgiveness. But death takes him in service, hands still warm with blessing.

Annie Baxter, three years old, dies after fifteen months fighting leukemia. Too young for regret. She reaches for her mother's hand, whispers "Mama"—more love in that word than most manage in a lifetime.

I still count tears. But I've begun counting other things too. Last words of love. Final acts of kindness. Moments when the dying choose blessing over bitterness.

Helena Voss taught me that death without regret is possible. She didn't die tearless because she'd avoided pain, but because she'd transformed pain into wisdom, loss into gratitude, endings into new beginnings.

Standing beside her grave six months later, I make a decision that would have been unthinkable before our encounter.

I choose to remember not just how people die, but how they live.

The headstone is simple granite: "Helena Voss. She loved well." Three words that summarize seventy-three years.

I trace the letters with fingers that exist only sometimes, in moments when the boundary between observer and participant grows thin. The stone feels real beneath my touch—rough and solid and permanent in a way my existence never has.

But that thought must wait. Somewhere in Detroit, a social worker named James Mitchell faces death from diabetes complications. His heart fails, his kidneys shut down. But his mind holds tight to eighteen children he's helped place in loving homes.

I arrive as the sun sets behind the city skyline. James lies in a hospital bed, surrounded by photos of children he's helped over the years. His breathing is labored but steady. His eyes are closed, but his lips move in whispered conversation with the faces staring down from the walls.

I take my position and wait. His pulse weakens. His breathing grows shallow.

Then he opens his eyes and looks directly at me.

"Well," he says, voice barely a whisper, "I wondered when you'd show up."

I freeze. In all the eons of my existence, no one has ever seen me. I exist in spaces between perception, visible only to those crossing the threshold between life and death. But James Mitchell looks at me with clear, knowing eyes.

"You're the one who counts, aren't you?"

I don't know how to respond. I've never had to.

"Been wondering what you do with all those numbers. Must be quite a collection."

His heart skips beats, catches, keeps going. Death is close but he's not rushing toward it.

"I..." The word comes out like wind through old trees. I've never spoken aloud. "I remember them."

"That's something." His eyes drift to the photos on his walls. "Memory matters. But what comes after?"

The question pierces me like Helena's smile—unexpected, transformative, impossible to ignore. What does come after the counting?

"I don't know," I say.

James nods like this makes perfect sense. "That's the beauty of it. Not knowing. Keeps things interesting."

His breathing catches. His heart skips beats, finds its rhythm again. I wait for tears, but James surprises me like Helena did.

He laughs.

It's a dry sound, more breath than voice, but unmistakably joyful. "Eighteen kids," he whispers. "Eighteen second chances. Not a bad legacy for a burned-out social worker from Detroit."

His eyes find mine again. "You want to know a secret?"

I lean closer.

"The tears don't matter like you think," he says. "Salt water. What matters is the love behind them. That we care enough to cry."

James closes his eyes. One breath. Then silence.

No tears.

Helena Voss: zero tears. James Mitchell: zero tears.

Two people who died whole.

I stare at James's peaceful face and feel something shift inside me, some fundamental realignment of purpose and perspective. The room fades, but instead of materializing at another deathbed, I find myself in that ancient cave in Turkey, staring at the faded ochre mammoth that Grok painted in the dawn of human memory.

I try to remember my beginning. What I can access is not memory in the human sense, but the permanent record of significant emotional moments. The first tear I ever counted exists as both my origin point and evidence of why such counting became necessary.

An old woman—Grok, her name was. She died in this cave during a winter that lasted longer than usual. Her tribe had moved on, following herds, but Grok was too old, too slow. The decision wasn't made in cruelty—resources were scarce, and the young needed every advantage.

When consciousness first coalesced around her dying moments—when whatever force creates beings like me recognized the need for witness—I became aware both of myself and of her. Grok didn't just show me my first counting; her need for someone to witness and remember called my kind of consciousness into existence.

Grok lay curled near the remains of her fire. Her breathing was shallow, her lips blue with cold. But her eyes were clear.

As I gained consciousness through witnessing her, I experienced my first counting as she shed four tears.

The first tasted of her children, scattered to winds with their own tribes. Not bitter regret, but sweet remembrance of small hands in hers, of stories told around fires, of love given freely even knowing it would one day end.

The second carried the weight of stories she would never tell, wisdom that would die with her. But mixed with loss was pride—pride in the young ones who had listened, who would carry her knowledge forward.

The third was for the painting on the cave wall—a mammoth hunt from her youth that she'd drawn with ochre and charcoal. It was fading now, returning to stone, but it had existed. She had created beauty in a harsh world.

The fourth tear surprised me then, and still moves me now. It tasted of gratitude.

Gratitude not despite her abandonment, but because she understood its necessity. Gratitude for sun on her face during the last autumn of her life. For the taste of berries sweet with summer rain. For her grandson's small hand in hers before her tribe moved on. For being alive during a time when the world was vast and wild and full of possibilities.

For having lived long enough to become a burden—which meant she had survived when so many others hadn't.

Even as she died alone in a cold cave, Grok found reasons to be grateful.

I counted her tears because it seemed important to remember that someone had grieved for things lost and loved things enough to miss them. I gave her tears meaning by witnessing them.

But Helena Voss needed no witness. She created meaning through the act of living, not dying.

Sitting in that ancient cave, touching the faded ochre of Grok's mammoth, I feel something I've never experienced: not just curiosity or doubt, but profound recognition of missed opportunities. How many times have I witnessed complete lives and counted only their imperfections?

The revelation builds slowly, like sunrise over this ancient landscape. I don't need to abandon my purpose. I need to expand it.

What if I stopped counting tears alone and started counting everything? The four tears Grok shed, yes, but also the thirty days she survived when she should have died in ten. Helena's zero tears, but also Danny Martinez inspired to become a teacher, children guided to college, support groups led through grief.

Victor Williams's seven tears, but also houses that will shelter families for generations.

I'm counting individual notes while missing the symphony. Each tear is part of a larger composition—lives lived in relationship, in service, in connection to something beyond the self.

Helena Voss didn't cry because she'd expressed her love fully through living. But that doesn't diminish the meaning of tears from those who carried love inside until the very end. Both expressions are sacred. Both deserve to be counted, witnessed, remembered.

I think of all the tears I've counted. Millions upon millions of droplets carrying the weight of regret. Each one a small tragedy, a moment when the dying realized they had failed to live as fully as they might have.

But sitting in this ancient cave, I begin to see a different pattern.

What if those tears weren't the complete story? What if they were visible evidence of something larger—the capacity to feel deeply enough that loss matters?

Every tear I've tasted has carried more than regret. The gang member wept not just for his crimes but for the daughter who would grow up without him. The hedge fund manager's tears held not just guilt but love for the wife who'd stopped believing in him. Even that Roman senator's thirty-one tears contained more love than shame—love for the Republic he'd failed to save, love for the ideals he'd compromised.

The tears weren't just about what was lost. They were proof of what had mattered enough to lose.

I remember the gang member's eleven tears. Yes, they tasted of violence and regret. But underneath lay something else—desperate love for a daughter who would grow up without him. The kindergarten teacher's four tears carried not just professional failure, but profound care for children she couldn't protect.

Every tear I've counted carried more than regret. The gang member wept for crimes, yes, but also for the daughter who'd grow up without him. The teacher's tears held not just failure, but desperate care for children she couldn't save.

Every tear proved something had mattered enough to lose.

But if tears measure love and connection, what does their absence mean? Not missing love, but love so complete that death brings no regret—only gratitude for the chance to have loved at all.

Helena Voss didn't cry because she'd spent seventy-three years loving so completely that she had no unfinished emotional business. She'd lived with such presence, such openness to experience, that every moment had been received as the gift it was.

I return to my duties, but everything has changed.

I leave the accident site and walk through the night, feeling something like contentment. Stars shine with ancient light, and I understand now that I am both—consciousness born from the universe's need to witness itself.

But Helena Voss and James Mitchell have taught me that mourning is only half the story. The other half is celebration—recognition that lives lived fully generate love in quantities that outlast death, that transform endings into beginnings, that make even tears sacred by their connection to something larger than individual loss.

I count the falling tears because they prove that love existed here, that consciousness touched consciousness deeply enough to leave marks outlasting flesh. I am the keeper of humanity's deepest connections, the recorder of evidence that existence means something beyond mere survival.

Tomorrow, there will be other deaths, other tears to count. But there will also be other moments of love to witness, other connections to record, other evidence that the universe knows how to love itself through the brief, beautiful, heartbreaking experience of human consciousness.

And some—a precious few like Helena Voss—will die as she did, tearless not from the absence of love but from its abundance. They will have loved so fully, lived so completely, that death becomes not loss but transformation, not ending but graduation into whatever comes next.

These tearless deaths will be my greatest treasures, proof that the equation I've spent eons trying to understand is not about counting sadness but measuring the infinite capacity of finite beings to love beyond the boundaries of time, flesh, and their own brief, precious existence.

But I must be careful. If I begin to value tearless deaths above tearful ones, I risk creating hierarchy where some endings matter more than others. The truth is more complex: tears of regret prove that someone cared enough to grieve what they're losing. Tearless deaths prove that someone loved enough to feel complete despite the loss.

Both responses are sacred. Both deserve to be counted, witnessed, remembered.

The universe weeps, and therefore the universe loves. But sometimes the universe loves so completely that weeping becomes unnecessary—and that too is sacred.

Standing in that ancient cave, I make a decision that would have been impossible before Helena taught me that endings can be beginnings.

I add a new column to my eternal tally.

From now on, I'll count tears of regret. But I'll also count moments of joy, acts of love, instances of grace. Not just what people lose at death, but what they've gained in living.

The mammoth on the cave wall seems to watch me as I process this understanding—Grok's testament to beauty, preserved in ochre and time and the stubborn human insistence that some things matter enough to remember.

Somewhere in Phoenix, Arizona, a woman named Isabella Cruz faces surgery complications. Her family surrounds her bed, holding her hands and telling her they love her. She will shed tears—three or four, flavored with regret for grandchildren she'll never meet, gardens she'll never finish planting.

But she'll also die surrounded by love, having spent sixty-seven years building connections strong enough to outlast her physical presence.

I arrive in Phoenix as the desert sun sets behind mountains, painting the sky in shades of amber and rose. Isabella Cruz lies in her hospital bed, her children and grandchildren arranged around her like petals on a flower. They're telling stories—funny memories, shared jokes, moments when Isabella made them feel loved and valued and seen.

She opens her eyes and smiles at the sound of their voices. "Mija," she whispers to her daughter Maria, "promise me you'll keep the Sunday dinners going. Promise me you'll keep the family together."

"I promise, Mama," Maria says, tears streaming. "I promise."

Isabella's eyes drift to each face in turn—her son Carlos, her daughter-in-law Teresa, her seven grandchildren ranging from five to twenty-three. Her gaze holds love so pure it seems to illuminate the room.

"I am so proud," she whispers. "So grateful. So blessed."

Her breathing grows shallow. Her heart stutters. I position myself beside the window and prepare to count.

Isabella Cruz closes her eyes. Her heart beats once more, then falls silent.

Two tears fall—one for the garden she'll never finish, one for the granddaughter away at college who couldn't make it home in time.

But as I record those tears, I also note other numbers: thirty-four Sunday dinners over the past year, each bringing the family together around Isabella's table. Seven grandchildren who know they are loved. Forty-three years of marriage to Eduardo, who died five years ago but whose presence still fills every corner of their house. Sixty-seven years of choosing compassion over bitterness, generosity over fear, connection over isolation.

Isabella Cruz: two tears of regret, balanced against a lifetime of love freely given.

The equation feels complete.

I walk through desert night, feeling something like contentment. Stars shine with ancient light, and I understand now that I am both—consciousness born from the universe's need to witness itself, to record evidence that life matters enough to mourn.

Helena and James and Isabella taught me mourning is only half the story. The other half is celebration—lives lived fully generate love outlasting death, transforming endings into beginnings, making even tears sacred through connection to something larger than loss alone.

I count the falling tears because they prove love existed here, that consciousness touched consciousness deeply enough to leave marks outlasting flesh. I am the keeper of humanity's deepest connections, the recorder of evidence that existence means something beyond mere survival.

Tomorrow, there will be other deaths, other tears to count. But there will also be other moments of love to witness, other connections to record, other evidence that the universe knows how to love itself through the brief, beautiful, heartbreaking experience of human consciousness.

And some—a precious few like Helena Voss—will die as she did, tearless not from the absence of love but from its abundance. They will have loved so fully, lived so completely, that death becomes not loss but transformation, not ending but graduation into whatever comes next.

These tearless deaths will be my greatest treasures, proof that the equation I've spent eons trying to understand is not about counting sadness but measuring the infinite capacity of finite beings to love beyond the boundaries of time, flesh, and their own brief, precious existence.

But I must be careful. If I begin to value tearless deaths above tearful ones, I risk creating hierarchy where some endings matter more than others. The truth is more complex: tears of regret prove someone cared enough to grieve what they're losing. Tearless deaths prove someone loved enough to feel complete despite the loss.

Both responses are sacred. Both deserve to be counted, witnessed, remembered.

The universe weeps, and therefore the universe loves. But sometimes the universe loves so completely that weeping becomes unnecessary—and that too is sacred.

Some Assembly Required

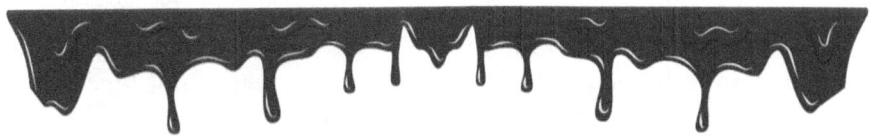

W alter Grimsby had built his last bridge three weeks ago, and retirement fit him about as well as his father's old work clothes had when he was ten---too much empty space where a different man used to live.

Forty-two years building bridges, calculating stress loads, turning blueprints into steel and concrete. All of it ending with a gold watch and a pension.

The house was too quiet without Helen. Cancer got her eight months ago, piece by piece, and he still set out two coffee cups every morning before remembering. The grandfather clock ticked louder now. Everything was louder when you had nobody to talk to.

So on a gray October afternoon, instead of sitting home staring at Helen's empty chair, Walter drove downtown to the hobby shop.

Balsa wood and model cement hit him the second he walked in. Took him right back to building plastic warships with his dad on Saturday mornings. Before the war took his father away. Before the telegram arrived in 1943. Before ten-year-old Walter learned that some things, once broken, could never be assembled again.

"Looking for anything special?" The clerk was maybe twenty-five, paint under his nails, the kind of tired that came from explaining model parts to old guys all day.

"Just browsing," Walter replied, though his eyes had already found what they were looking for.

The P-51 kit sat on a high shelf between a German tank and a Japanese Zero. Same plane his father flew over the Pacific. Box art showed it in flight, silver wings and blue sky, the kind of picture that made kids want to be pilots.

The box was heavier than expected. Most model kits were mostly air and plastic, but this one felt packed.

"Nice one." The clerk appeared next to him. "Estate sale pickup. Guy saved it forty years and never opened the box."

Walter studied the box more carefully. The graphics looked vintage, with that slightly faded quality of packaging from the 1980s. But the detail level promised on the sides suggested something far more sophisticated than the simple kits he remembered from his youth.

"Revell?" Walter asked, looking for the manufacturer's logo.

The clerk frowned slightly. "You know, I'm not sure. The distributor who brought it in couldn't identify the maker either. No manufacturer markings anywhere on the box. But look at that detail level---it's supposed to be 1/32 scale with over 400 individual parts."

Four hundred parts. Walter's mind started working the problem: maybe six pieces per evening if he worked carefully, double-checking connections like he'd learned to do with bridge joints. The same methodical planning that had gotten him through four decades of stress calculations. This would take weeks, maybe months---plenty of time to fill the empty hours when Helen's absence felt loudest.

"How much?" he asked.

"Thirty-five dollars. Seems reasonable for something this detailed."

Walter paid cash and carried the box home, feeling lighter than he had in months. He had a project now, something to engage the part of his mind that had spent decades solving complex structural problems. Building something beautiful instead of utilitarian, something that would honor his father's memory instead of just gathering dust on a shelf.

Walter cleared the dining room table that evening, spreading out his old modeling tools and work mat---the same cutting board Helen had banished from the kitchen years ago because of the knife marks. She'd always complained about his hobby projects cluttering up the table, but gently, with the fond exasperation of someone who understood that men needed to build things with their hands.

He opened the model kit box carefully, expecting the familiar smell of plastic and the organized chaos of injection-molded parts trees. Instead, he discovered something unexpected.

The parts weren't plastic. They appeared to be made of some kind of metal---aluminum, perhaps, or a lightweight alloy he didn't recognize. Each piece was wrapped in tissue paper, nestled in custom foam like precision instruments.

Walter unwrapped a wing section, surprised by its weight and detail. Panel lines, rivet patterns, even tiny oil stains looked real. The metal felt warm under his fingers, like his father's old tools---worn smooth but still strong.

The instruction manual was impressive---heavy paper with diagrams that looked like real engineering blueprints. Walter flipped through, noting the attention to detail. Whoever designed this kit was an engineer, someone who understood how things actually worked.

Walter found himself studying each part as he unwrapped it, marveling at the craftsmanship. The engine components functioned as miniatures, with tiny pistons that actually moved when he pressed them and cooling fins that felt real enough to dissipate heat. The landing gear contained working shock absorbers that compressed under pressure. Even the instrument panel featured individually crafted gauges with readable faces and needles that moved when touched.

When Walter reached the bottom of the box, he discovered the first anomaly.

Nestled beneath the final layer of foam lay an additional parts tree that didn't appear in the instruction manual. The components appeared to be interior details---seat cushions, control cables, even what looked like a miniature oxygen mask. But the instruction booklet made no reference to these pieces, as if someone had included them by mistake.

Walter set the extra parts aside and began with Step 1: engine assembly. The manual's diagrams contained such detail that they included torque specifications for the tiny bolts, as if this represented a real aircraft under construction to airworthy standards rather than a display model destined for a shelf.

Walter thought about his father without the usual pang of loss. James Grimsby was twenty-eight when he climbed into a real P-51 for the last time. Walter had been ten, but he remembered his father's hands---calloused from farm work but gentle enough to guide a kid's fingers building a balsa glider.

"Measure twice, cut once," his father used to say. "Patience builds things that last."

Walter applied that philosophy now, taking his time with each step, double-checking every connection. The tiny bolts threaded smoothly into their holes, and the metal pieces fit together with machinist-level precision. As Walter worked, his mind grew still and focused, his hands remembering the satisfaction of precise assembly, the quiet pleasure of watching scattered parts become something whole. The tiny engine grew under his fingers, each bolt clicking into place with a satisfying precision.

By midnight, he had completed the engine assembly. The tiny radial motor was a masterpiece of miniature engineering, with each cylinder head properly positioned and cooling fins aligned to channel airflow.

Walter switched off the dining room lights and headed to bed, already looking forward to tomorrow evening's work session.

Walter woke at 3 AM to an engine sound.

He lay listening to what sounded like a single-engine aircraft flying low overhead. The sound was wrong---too steady, like an engine from an earlier era. Not modern turbine whine, but the deep throb of a piston engine.

Probably a late medical transport heading to the hospital, he told himself, though Mercy General was twenty miles away and used helicopters for emergency runs. By morning, he'd convinced himself he'd dreamed it.

Walter spent his second evening working on the fuselage, marveling at how the metal sections fit together without glue or fasteners. The pieces seemed to weld themselves together when properly aligned, creating joints stronger than anything he'd achieved with model cement. His workbench lamp cast a warm pool of light over the project, and the familiar smell of metal polish mixed with the lingering aroma of Helen's lavender sachets from the dining room hutch.

The manual's assembly sequence was flawless, each step building logically on the previous one. Walter noticed differences between the instruction booklet and actual parts. Manual called for standard P-51D configuration, but some components matched the earlier P-51B his father flew. Subtle differences---canopy shape, antenna placement---but his engineering background made him notice.

More troubling, the kit contained more parts than it should. Every evening Walter counted the remaining components, but somehow there were always more pieces than the night before. Extra parts not mentioned in the manual.

He found himself looking forward to these discoveries, to the mystery of what new components would appear next. It felt like receiving a gift each evening, even though logic dictated that all the parts had been in the box from the beginning.

On the fourth night, Walter began installing the cockpit interior. The level of detail was extraordinary---individual instrument faces no bigger than pinheads, separate throttle levers that actually moved, even tiny map cases with miniature charts inside. But as he positioned the pilot's seat, he noticed something that made his hands shake.

Scratched into the metal seat back were initials: "J.G. - 43"

James Grimsby. 1943.

Walter set down his magnifying glass and stepped back. Had to be coincidence. Thousands of men with those initials served in 1943.

But the initials matched his father's handwriting. Walter was certain, even though he hadn't seen his father's script in decades.

But the initials matched his father's handwriting. Walter felt certain of it, even though he hadn't seen an example of his father's script in decades. Some memories burned deeper than others, and the careful block letters his father had used to label his tools were etched into Walter's childhood like scars.

Walter poured himself a whiskey and sat in Helen's chair, staring at the partially assembled aircraft. The P-51 looked almost alive under the dining room's warm light, its silver fuselage gleaming like something that had just landed rather than something built from a kit. Outside, October wind rattled the windows, and the house creaked around him like an old ship settling for the night.

The dreams started that night.

Walter found himself in the cockpit of a P-51, flying through endless blue sky. But he wasn't piloting the aircraft---he was observing, watching someone else's hands work the controls with practiced efficiency. The pilot's face remained hidden behind oxygen mask and goggles, but his movements were familiar, the way he adjusted the throttle, the careful scan of instruments that Walter remembered from childhood stories.

In the dream, Walter could hear radio chatter, voices of other pilots calling out enemy positions. The dialogue was period-accurate, full of terminology Walter recognized from his father's letters home. But underneath the radio traffic was another sound---the steady rhythm of an engine that seemed to be calling his name.

Walter woke with the taste of high-altitude air in his mouth and the phantom sensation of G-forces pressing against his chest. The bedroom was dark and quiet, but somewhere in the distance he could still hear the drone of an aircraft engine, fading gradually like an echo.

The next morning, Walter drove to the local library and spent hours in the microfilm section, searching for records of his father's squadron. He'd never investigated the details of his father's death before---ten-year-old boys weren't told such things, and by the time Walter was old enough to ask questions, his mother had remarried and preferred not to discuss her first husband's fate.

Walter's chest tightened as he read the details. Second Lieutenant James Grimsby had been reported missing in action on November 15, 1943, during a bomber escort mission over Rabaul. His P-51B had broken formation to pursue a Japanese fighter, but neither aircraft was observed again. No wreckage was ever found, despite extensive air-sea rescue operations.

More disturbing was the aircraft's serial number: 42-106857. Walter copied the number onto a scrap of paper, his hands trembling slightly as he wrote.

That evening, he returned to the model with new purpose. The instruction manual called for generic military markings, but Walter found himself customizing the aircraft, adding details he'd researched during his library visit. Squadron codes, victory marks, even the correct propeller hub configuration for a 1943 P-51B.

As he worked, Walter discovered that many of the "extra" parts he'd found actually belonged to this specific variant. Components that didn't appear in the manual but were historically accurate for his father's aircraft. Someone---or something---had included the exact details needed to recreate serial number 42-106857.

Using a fine brush and steady hand, Walter painted the serial number on the fuselage, each digit matching the faded photographs he'd found in the library archives. When he finished, the model looked less like a hobby project and more like a memorial, a faithful reproduction of the last aircraft his father had ever flown.

The pilot figure was the final component.

Walter had avoided the pilot figure for days, leaving the tiny metal figure in its tissue paper wrapping while he completed every other detail of the aircraft. But with the P-51 nearly finished, he could delay no longer.

He unwrapped the pilot carefully, expecting a generic figure that would need customization to look authentic. Instead, he found a masterpiece of miniature sculpture that made his breath catch in his throat.

The pilot's face showed full detail despite its tiny size, every feature rendered with photographic accuracy. And Walter recognized those features, even though he hadn't seen them in over sixty years.

His father looked exactly as Walter remembered him---twenty-eight years old, confident, with the slight smile he'd worn in family photographs. Even the way he held his head was perfect, the tilt that Walter had inherited and seen reflected in his own mirror for seven decades.

But this wasn't just a generic representation of a WWII pilot. This was specifically, unmistakably, James Grimsby. The same James Grimsby who had kissed ten-year-old Walter goodbye on a cold morning in 1942 and promised to come home with stories of flying.

Walter set the figure down with shaking hands. This was impossible. Model kit manufacturers didn't create custom pilot figures based on specific historical individuals, especially not obscure lieutenants who'd died in forgotten actions over distant seas. Someone would have had to study photographs, to know intimate details about his father's appearance, to care enough about one man's story to immortalize it in metal.

The instruction manual offered no explanation. The pilot installation was covered in a single step: "Insert figure P-1 into cockpit seat and secure with small dab of cement." No acknowledgment that this particular figure was anything other than a standard component.

Walter picked up the pilot again, studying the incredible detail. Even the flight suit was accurate for 1943, complete with period-correct patches and insignia. The oxygen mask hung loosely around the figure's neck, revealing the face Walter had seen in dreams for sixty years.

An airplane engine was getting louder outside. Walter looked up from the model. That was a Merlin V-12---same engine the P-51 used. But there weren't any flyable Mustangs around here.

The plane passed right over the house, low enough to rattle the windows. Then it started circling, like the pilot was looking for something.

Walter went to the front window. No lights on the plane, just engine noise. A shadow crossed the stars---definitely a P-51 Mustang.

The aircraft made three complete circles before the engine sound began to fade, as if climbing to altitude. Within minutes, the night was quiet again, leaving Walter alone with his model and the impossible pilot figure that looked exactly like his father.

Walter didn't sleep. He sat at the table staring at the model and the pilot figure. Maybe it was all coincidence---random kit that looked like his father's plane, pilot figure that happened to look like family photos.

But Walter was an engineer. He knew cause and effect. And this didn't follow any rules he understood.

Dawn came up gray and cold. Walter made his choice. He'd install the pilot and finish the model. Sixty years of wondering about his father was enough. If this thing had answers, he'd take them.

Walter set the pilot in the cockpit seat, adjusting until it looked right. Perfect fit, like the seat was made for this exact figure. A drop of cement, and it was done.

The moment cement touched metal, heat shot through Walter's fingers---not painful, but unmistakable, like touching a warm engine. Dining room lights flickered once, and he swore he smelled aviation fuel.

Walter stepped back, expecting the model to move or transform in some dramatic fashion. Instead, it simply sat on the table, looking exactly like what it was supposed to be: a detailed replica of a World War II fighter aircraft. Beautiful, accurate, and completely static.

But as Walter watched, he noticed that the pilot figure appeared to be moving slightly, turning its head to scan the horizon as if searching for enemy aircraft. The motion was so subtle that Walter wondered if he was imagining it, until he felt a faint vibration through the dining room table, as if some tiny engine had come to life.

Then the pilot turned to look directly at him.

Walter stumbled backward, knocking over his chair. The tiny figure's eyes---impossibly detailed for something so small---tracked his movement with unmistakable intelligence. The pilot raised one miniature hand in what might have been a greeting, or perhaps a salute.

"Dad?" Walter whispered.

The pilot figure nodded slowly, then pointed toward the window. Outside, the sound of an approaching aircraft grew steadily louder.

Walter rushed to the window in time to see a full-sized P-51 Mustang descending toward his backyard, its landing gear extended. The aircraft looked solid and real, not some ghostly apparition, with working navigation lights and the correct markings for his father's squadron. As Walter watched in amazement, the Mustang touched down on his lawn with surprising gentleness, its propeller windmilling to a stop.

The canopy slid back, and a figure in period flight gear climbed out of the cockpit. Even from a distance, Walter recognized the movements, the way his father had always carried himself with quiet confidence.

James Grimsby pulled off his helmet as he walked up the path. Same face as the model, same face as 1943. Twenty-eight years old.

Walter met him at the front door, heart pounding. Up close, James looked exactly as he had in Walter's childhood memories---tall, steady, with the calloused hands of someone who worked with machines.

"Hello, son," James said simply, his voice carrying that familiar Ohio drawl. "I've been trying to get home for... for a long time."

They stood in silence for a moment, father and son separated by six decades and death itself. Walter searched for words, for questions that could span such an impossible gap.

"How?" he finally managed.

James glanced toward the dining room, where the completed model sat under warm light. "Some things can't be broken forever. I've been trying to find my way back, but I needed an anchor, something that connected me to---" He gestured helplessly at the house, the street, the life he'd left behind. "You built me a bridge, son."

"You've been... waiting?"

"Time works differently when you're lost between worlds. I've been trying to get home, but I needed someone who..." James's voice caught slightly. "Someone who cared enough to put the pieces together properly."

Walter looked at the model, understanding flooding through him. Every carefully placed part, every precise connection, every evening spent in patient assembly---he'd been constructing more than a replica. He'd been rebuilding his father's connection to the living world, piece by piece.

"How long can you stay?" Walter asked.

James's expression grew serious. "Not long. The connection isn't permanent---it's more like borrowed time. But long enough to say goodbye properly. Long enough to tell you what I should have said before I left."

They spent the next hour sitting in the living room, James sharing stories Walter had never heard. Details about the war, about flying, about the last mission that had torn him away from this world until his son's patient assembly had given him form again.

"I'm proud of you," James said as the eastern sky began to lighten with dawn. "The bridges you've built, the life you've made, the way you loved Helen. I've been watching when I could, and you became everything I hoped you would."

Walter felt tears on his cheeks for the first time since Helen's funeral. "I missed you every day."

"I know. But now you don't have to anymore. I'm not lost---I'm just somewhere else, somewhere better. And Helen's waiting for me there."

The statement hit Walter like a physical blow. "Helen?"

James nodded. "She's been helping me find my way back to you. Said you needed to hear this before you could let go and join us when your time comes."

As if summoned by her name, Walter sensed Helen's presence in the room---not visible, but unmistakably there, warm and loving and patient as always.

"Is she...?"

"She's fine. Happy. But she wanted you to know that some assembly is required on that side too, and she's saving a place for you."

The morning light grew stronger, and Walter could see his father beginning to fade slightly, becoming translucent around the edges. The borrowed time was ending.

"I have to go now," James said, standing. "But the model will always be there if you need to remember. Keep it on the mantle, next to Helen's photograph. When people ask about it, tell them it's a memorial to things that couldn't be broken, only temporarily lost."

James walked to the dining room and touched the completed model gently. As his finger made contact, the tiny pilot figure waved once more, then became still and ordinary, just painted metal waiting on a shelf.

Walter followed his father outside, where the P-51 sat gleaming in the early morning sun. James climbed back into the cockpit, adjusting his helmet and securing his harness with the practiced motions of someone who'd done this thousands of times.

"Take care of yourself, son. Live well, but don't be afraid to let go when it's time."

The Merlin engine coughed to life, filling the quiet suburban morning with its powerful rumble. James taxied to the far end of the lawn, turned into the wind, and advanced the throttle.

Walter watched his father take off one final time, the silver aircraft climbing steadily until it disappeared into the morning sky. The engine sound faded gradually, leaving only the ordinary sounds of a waking neighborhood---birds singing, garbage trucks rumbling, children getting ready for school.

Walter kept the model on the mantle, just as his father had suggested. Visitors often commented on its incredible detail, the lifelike quality of the tiny pilot figure. Walter would tell them it was a memorial to his father, killed in action over the Pacific in 1943.

He never mentioned that the kit had contained more parts than it should have, or that the pilot figure bore an impossible resemblance to family photographs. Such details seemed less important than the larger truth---that love could span any distance, even death itself, and that some assembly was always required to keep the important things from staying broken forever.

Walter lived well, just as his father had instructed. He volunteered at the veterans' hospital, sharing model-building techniques with injured soldiers learning to use prosthetic hands. He dated a widow from his church, nothing serious but companionable, someone to share meals and conversation with.

But he also began preparing for his own eventual departure, organizing his affairs with the methodical precision of an engineer. When his time came---and he sensed it wouldn't be much longer---he wanted to leave no unfinished business, no broken connections that would require someone else to assemble.

On quiet evenings, Walter would sit in Helen's chair and study the model, remembering the satisfaction of patient assembly, the way careful planning had transformed scattered pieces into something whole under his hands. The tiny pilot figure never moved again, but sometimes Walter caught himself talking to it anyway, sharing the details of his day with the father who had taught him that patience builds things that last.

And on still nights when the wind was right, Walter thought he could hear the distant sound of an aircraft engine, circling protective patterns in the sky above his house. The sound of someone who had found his way home at last, watching over the people he loved until they were ready to join him.

Paper Gods

Mia sneezed as dust swirled in the afternoon light, dragging another damn cardboard box across the attic floor. October heat made the whole house feel like a furnace, worse up here under the roof. Sweat stuck her hair to her forehead. Sam knelt by a trunk she'd never seen before, wrestling with brass latches that had gone green with age.

Sam had been up here before---Christmas junk, winter coats, boxes of stuff Mom couldn't fit downstairs. But this trunk was different, sitting in a corner that used to be blocked off. Mom moved the boxes this morning when she said they could raid the attic for Halloween costumes.

"Mom said we could take anything for Halloween," Mia said, wiping cobwebs off her face. "Just don't break anything expensive."

"How'm I supposed to know what's expensive?" Sam stuck his tongue out as he fought with the stubborn latches.

"I'll figure it out." At eleven, Mia was supposed to keep Sam out of trouble, which was like trying to keep water from being wet. The kid could find disaster in an empty room. Mia opened her box and found old photo albums with yellow pages that felt gross and sticky. Grandpa Floyd had written on each picture in blue ink that was faded but still readable. She recognized some people from family stuff---distant cousins, old aunts---but most were strangers in old-fashioned clothes who looked mad at the camera.

The latches gave up with two clicks that echoed wrong in the dusty space---too loud, like the trunk wanted to be opened. Sam threw his whole weight into pushing them, nearly falling backward when they popped. He lifted the lid, and the smell hit them---mothballs and church incense, but underneath something that made Mia think of dead things rotting in dark places.

When the lid opened, wind came from nowhere. The house creaked around them---walls, floor, ceiling---like the whole place was waking up from a long sleep.

Sam peeled back the tissue paper real careful, then stopped. "Whoa."

Mia dropped her photo albums and crawled over. Three masks sat in the tissue paper, way better than any school art project. The first was red and gold with a grin full of too many teeth. Perfect painted teeth, like someone had spent forever getting each one right. Mean-looking. Hungry.

The second mask was blue and black geometric shapes with eye holes that tracked movement. Where the red one wanted to bite, this one was studying them. Waiting.

The third mask was the prettiest, with real feathers that still looked shiny and tiny mirrors like stars. But even though it was beautiful, it felt sleepy somehow, like whatever lived inside was saving up energy.

All three masks looked old and beat up. Cracks ran across the painted parts like spider webs, and the edges were warped from being in the hot, wet attic for so long. In some places the colors had turned muddy brown. But instead of making them look harmless, the damage made them scarier. Like the broken parts let you see something awful hiding underneath.

"Those are so cool," Mia whispered, though cool wasn't the right word. They were amazing, but they also made her stomach feel tight. She reached toward the red one, then stopped. Something about those cracked teeth made her want to pull her hand back.

Sam was staring at the blue mask real close now. "The patterns are weird. They hurt if you look too long." He started to pick it up, then kept his hands on the tissue paper instead.

Even though he wasn't touching it, Mia noticed Sam kept looking back at the blue mask like it was calling his name. When she looked at the red one, she felt curious but careful. When Sam looked at his, his eyes got big and dark, and he swayed a little like he was getting dizzy.

"Maybe we should put 'em back and find something else," Mia said, but she couldn't stop staring at the red mask. The painted grin seemed bigger when she wasn't looking right at it.

"Yeah, maybe," Sam said, but his fingers stayed near the mask's edge, not touching but not moving away either. "They're just so... perfect. Like someone made each one special."

His voice sounded dreamy, which made Mia's stomach hurt worse. "Look, there's a note from Grandpa."

She picked up a yellowed card tucked between the masks. Grandpa Floyd's handwriting in fountain pen that had turned brown: "Bought in New Orleans, August 1967, from dead carnival owner's stuff. Old pieces maybe from 1800s or before. Boudreaux Brothers Traveling Show last trip. BE VERY CAREFUL. NEVER WEAR THEM."

The last line was underlined three times so hard it cut grooves in the card.

"New Orleans." Sam turned the mask over, not quite touching it. "Like Mardi Gras."

But Mia didn't think these were party masks. Something about them felt older and scarier than the fun celebrations she'd seen on TV. The red mask's grin looked hungry, not happy. The shapes on Sam's mask reminded her of cave paintings in National Geographic---the kind made by people who thought spirits lived in everything.

There was a photograph under where the masks had been. It showed Grandpa Floyd when he was young, standing next to a carnival tent and grinning big with his arm around a skinny man in a striped vest. Behind them you could see carnival stuff---a Ferris wheel, game booths, what looked like a fortune teller's wagon. Someone had written "August 1967" in Grandpa's handwriting.

"Look at this," Mia said, showing Sam the picture.

But Sam wasn't looking. He kept staring at the blue mask, tracing those weird patterns with his finger just above the surface. The attic had gotten colder even though neither of them had touched the window. When they breathed out, little puffs of steam came out.

"We should put them back," Mia said, though she found herself staring at the red mask again. The painted grin looked wider than before, but that had to be the light playing tricks.

"Just for a minute," Sam said in that dreamy voice. "What could happen?"

"Grandpa's note says don't."

"Since when do you follow rules?" Sam's grin looked wrong some- how, like he was copying someone else. "They're just paper and paint. What's the worst that could happen?"

Mia felt a weird urge growing in her chest---not supernatural or anything, just the normal feeling kids get when they want to touch something they're not supposed to touch. Like when there's a "Wet Paint" sign and part of you wants to poke it anyway.

"Maybe just to see how they fit," she heard herself saying.

Sam nodded and reached for his mask with the same look kids get when they're about to do something their parents would kill them for.

Mia wanted to grab the red mask real bad, but she made herself keep her hands at her sides. "You try yours first."

Sam shrugged and lifted the mask to his face. The second it touched his skin, the attic got freezing cold. Mia's breath came out in white puffs, and the dust in the air stopped moving, like everything was frozen. The house creaked around them with sounds like whispers.

"Sam?" Mia's voice came out small and scared.

Her brother turned toward her, and Mia's heart slammed against her ribs so hard it hurt. The mask fit his face perfect, like it had been made just for him. The eye holes lined up exactly with his eyes, but instead of Sam's regular brown eyes, these were darker and older. When he talked, his voice sounded like wind through empty places.

"I remember now." The words came out slow and careful, like he was tasting each one. "The food they left... at the crossroads. How scared they got when... when their plants died. The way they danced when winter came too early and... and killed everything."

"Sam, take it off." Mia reached for him but he stepped back smooth as water, nothing like clumsy Sam who tripped over his own feet. "Take it off right now!"

"They called me Ashkente. The one who... who walks between the seasons. I decide when things grow and when they die before people can eat them."

The blue and black shapes on the mask glowed with their own light, swirling into patterns that made Mia's eyes water. Through the holes, Sam's changed eyes looked around the attic like he'd never seen it before---or like he was remembering it from a hundred years ago.

"Take the mask off." Mia tried to sound like Mom when she was really mad, but her voice cracked.

Sam---or whatever was wearing Sam---laughed. The sound bounced around the small space like it was coming from somewhere much bigger and emptier. It sounded like winter wind through dead trees.

"Your turn, sister."

Before Mia could say no, the red mask floated up from the trunk by itself. She tried to back away, but her feet wouldn't move. The mask drifted closer, and she could see every painted tooth, every fleck of gold, the hunger in those empty eye holes that looked deeper than just hollow spaces.

"Sam, help me," she whispered, but her brother just stood there watching like whatever was inside him didn't care about her anymore.

The mask pressed against her face with weird warmth, and she fought it for real---pushing at it with her hands, turning her head side to side. But it was like fighting mud. The harder she struggled, the more she knew she was going to lose. Her hands, shaking from trying so hard, slowly moved to press the mask tight against her skin.

The mask was warm like blood and seemed to beat like a heart. For a scary second, she felt herself disappearing, felt her own thoughts being pushed aside to make room for something huge and old and hungry.

Then the world exploded.

She could taste how scared everyone in Ellison was---actually taste it, like the mask had switched her tongue to taste terror instead of food. Mrs. Yamamoto at the grocery store, lying awake worrying about her daughter's college money. Principal Harris staring at his bedroom ceiling, wondering if the school budget could cover repairs. Her own parents downstairs, their worried whispers about Dad's overtime and Mom's medical bills.

More than just tasting their fears, she could make them bigger. Like taking Mrs. Rodriguez's normal worry about her kids and twisting it until the woman would be too scared to let them leave the house.

"Yesss," she hissed, and her voice came out in layers that made the attic floor shake and sent mice scurrying through the walls. "They called me... they called me Malphas. I eat what keeps you awake at night. I make your bad dreams... real."

Through the window, she could see neighbors doing their Saturday stuff, not knowing that ancient things were awake again. Old Mr. Beaumont pushed his lawnmower in straight lines. The Mitchum twins rode their bikes in circles, laughing. Mrs. Rodriguez hung up laundry, singing in Spanish. All of them living their little lives without knowing how easy it would be to break them.

"Should we show them what worship means?" Sam's voice carried the weight of winter storms and dead crops.

Mia nodded, already reaching out with her new power to touch the minds below. She felt Mrs. Rodriguez's happy singing turn into worry, felt the exact moment when the woman stopped and looked around like she sensed danger. The Mitchum twins slowed their bikes, their laughter dying as something deep inside warned them predators were awake.

Together, she and Sam walked down from the attic, leaving the empty trunk behind like a snake skin they'd outgrown.

Their mom, Carol, stood at the kitchen sink doing dishes from lunch. Saturday afternoon cleanup---plates and coffee mugs and the mess from morning. She hummed some song from the radio while she worked, and Mia could taste her mom's regular worries: bills on the counter, Dad's crazy work schedule, the letter from the insurance company she hadn't opened yet.

When they came into the kitchen, Mom looked up with that distract-ed smile she wore when her mind was somewhere else. "Find anything good up there, guys?"

Then she really looked at them, and her hands froze on a soapy plate.

"Where did you get those?" The question came out sharp and im-mediate, all the distraction vanishing. Something about the masks made her stomach clench, though she couldn't say why. But there was more in her voice---not just surprise, but recognition. Like she'd seen them before.

"Mom?" Mia asked, confused by how freaked out her mother looked. "What's wrong?"

"Take them off. Right now." Mom's voice had that panicky edge that seemed too much for costume masks. "Your dad keeps that old leather bag in his truck for a reason. God, I should've thrown those things away years ago when Floyd died."

She was backing toward the phone now, her face white. "Your father learned things from Grandpa Floyd before you were born. All those old books, weird rituals Floyd made him memorize. I thought it was just old-man craziness, but Jim kept practicing anyway, kept that bag in his truck 'just in case.' Said Floyd warned him this day might come."

Her voice cracked. "Floyd told me once those masks couldn't be destroyed, only locked up. That breaking them wouldn't stop them. I should've listened."

Mia could taste her mother's fear spiking sweet and sharp like copper pennies.

"Grandpa Floyd's trunk," Mia said, loving how her mom's face went gray.

"Take them off. Now."

"But Mom---"

"I said take them off!" Mom's voice got loud, and Mia felt a delicious thrill. Her mother's fear tasted extra good, seasoned with guilt and old sadness.

"You remember them, don't you?" Sam asked, tilting his head like a bird. "From when you were little. The stories Grandpa Floyd told about the carnival."

Mom's face went from gray to almost green. "He said he threw those away. He promised me."

"Promises break so easy," Mia purred. She could feel her mother's terror building, could see the exact moment when normal fear turned into panic. It felt amazing.

The plate slipped from Mom's hands and crashed on the kitchen floor. Neither kid moved to help clean it up.

"I'm calling your father," Mom whispered, grabbing for her phone with hands that shook so bad she almost dropped it twice.

"Go ahead," Sam said, his voice carrying February wind through dead trees. "Call him home from work. Make him choose between his overtime money and keeping his family safe." He paused like he was listening to whispers only he could hear. "Wonder what scares Jim Parker at three in the morning when he can't sleep."

Mom's thumb stopped over her phone screen, and Mia could feel her internal fight clear as reading words on a page. Call Dad home and lose the money they needed for next month's house payment, or deal with this herself and risk... what? Her kids wearing weird masks? When she tried to explain the danger to herself, it sounded stupid. But the terror clawing at her chest said otherwise.

"Smart choice," Mia said when Mom put the phone down without calling. "Fear makes people honest about what they're willing to give up."

Through the kitchen window, Mia could see neighbors still doing their weekend stuff, but something had changed in the air. Mrs. Rodriguez was still hanging laundry, but her movements looked jerky and nervous, and she kept stopping to look around like she was hunting for some threat she couldn't name. The Mitchum twins had slowed their bikes and kept glancing around, their laughter dying.

Animals noticed first. Old Mr. Henderson's German Shepherd, who usually barked at everyone, whimpered and pressed itself into the far corner of its pen, shaking. Dogs all through the neighborhood started pacing, their owners calling them inside but not understanding why their pets had suddenly gone crazy.

Kids came next. A mom pushing a stroller three blocks away felt her toddler start crying for no reason and found herself heading home fast without knowing why. The kid couldn't say what was wrong, and the mom couldn't explain her sudden need to get somewhere safe.

Adults fought it the hardest. Their grown-up brains worked overtime to dismiss feelings that didn't make sense. Mrs. Rodriguez dropped a pillowcase and stepped backward, her mind insisting nothing was wrong while her body screamed danger. She told herself she was just tired, just worried about normal stuff---anything except admitting the crawling terror up her spine.

None of them could say exactly what was wrong. They felt jumpy, nervous, filled with worry that had no reason. Windows started closing one by one down the street---first the house across from them, then the next, then the next. But if you'd asked any of those people why they suddenly felt like shutting their windows and locking their doors, they'd have given normal explanations: getting chilly, had chores inside, remembered something on the stove.

Kids' voices died away as parents found reasons to bring them indoors---time for homework, time for dinner, time to help with weekend work. Lawnmowers shut off as their operators suddenly remembered urgent stuff inside. The Saturday afternoon sounds of neighborhood life faded house by house, but none of the people noticed the pattern. Each person thought their decision to go inside was completely their own idea.

By the time they walked outside, nearly half the visible neighborhood had gone indoors, though none of the residents could have explained why. They'd all found logical reasons for their behavior, never realizing their sudden need for safety had come from somewhere else.

When they got close to Mrs. Rodriguez, she was backing up her front walk, her mind telling her she was being silly while her body responded to danger she couldn't process. The wet sheet she'd dropped lay in the grass, already getting dirty. When she tried to call out---maybe to ask if the kids were okay, maybe to offer help---only a small whimpering sound came from her throat.

Every primitive instinct screamed at her to run, to hide, to protect her kids from something she couldn't name.

"Maria Rodriguez." Mia let the name roll off her tongue like she was tasting it. The mask whispered things she shouldn't know---private things, secret fears. "Three kids, two jobs, husband in Afghanistan. You pray every night for safety. But what if something else is listening?"

Mrs. Rodriguez stumbled backward, her heel catching on the garden hose. She fell hard but didn't seem to notice the pain. Her eyes stayed locked on Mia's mask, trapped by the painted grin that got wider and hungrier every second.

"Please," she whispered. "My kids are inside doing homework. They're just babies."

"Yes," Sam said, tilting his head like he was listening to sounds no normal person could hear. "I can hear them. Feel their little fast heartbeats. Fear tastes so much better in kids. So much more honest. Grown-ups learn to lie to themselves, but kids know when monsters are real."

Mrs. Rodriguez scrambled to her feet and ran for her house, her sneakers slipping on the wet grass. She slammed the door so hard the windows rattled. They heard the deadbolt turn, then the chain, then what sounded like furniture being dragged across the floor---maybe the kitchen table or a heavy bookshelf.

The Mitchum twins hadn't moved from their spot on the sidewalk, but their bikes lay on the asphalt with the training wheels still spinning. At fourteen, they were old enough to know something felt really wrong, but too young to trust feelings they couldn't explain. They kept looking around like they expected to see some obvious danger---a gas leak, a fire, anything that would explain the terror crawling up their backs.

"Brett. Brandon," Mia called, their names coming to her easy as if she'd known them forever instead of just seeing them at the bus stop sometimes. The masks fed her information about their lives---their bunk beds, their baseball card collection, their secret fear that their parents might divorce like the Hendersons did last year. "Still scared of the dark? Still check under your beds, looking for monsters your parents said don't exist?"

The boys looked at each other with that twin thing where they could talk without words. Their faces had gone pale under their summer tans, and she could smell their fear sweat from thirty feet away---sharp and sour, the scent of prey that knows predators are near.

To anyone watching, it would've looked innocent: two neighborhood kids in Halloween masks talking to teenage boys. But every animal instinct the twins had screamed this was wrong, that these weren't kids anymore, that they needed to run before something terrible happened.

They ran---not toward their house but away from the neighborhood completely, their sneakers slapping pavement as they fled toward downtown. Smart kids. They understood what the adults were still trying to explain away.

Old Mr. Beaumont hadn't run. He stood next to his quiet lawnmower like a statue, watching them come with eyes that held more acceptance than fear. At eighty-three, he'd seen enough of life to know when something fundamental had shifted. Two world wars, the Depression, his wife dying five years ago---he'd learned some battles couldn't be fought with normal weapons.

"You're not really children," he said when they stopped in front of him on his perfect lawn.

"No," Sam agreed, his voice carrying wind through empty farmhouses. "Though we wear their faces well enough. Kids make such good vessels---their minds are still flexible, still open to things grown-ups have forgotten."

"What do you want?" Mr. Beaumont's question was direct. He'd reached an age where small talk seemed less important than truth.

Mia thought about the question, letting the mask's ancient hungers mix with her own eleven-year-old wants. What did they want? The masks whispered suggestions that tasted of blood and fear and power, but underneath those alien hungers, she could still feel echoes of her real needs. To be seen instead of ignored. To be powerful instead of powerless. To matter in a world that treated kids like they were in the way of adult business.

"Recognition," she said, and the word pressed against Mr. Beaumont's chest like a weight. "Respect. People admitting that some things are bigger than their house payments and doctor bills and tiny human problems."

Mr. Beaumont nodded slowly, his white hair catching the afternoon light. "And if we give you that recognition? What then?"

"Maybe we'll be nice. Maybe we'll be happy with small offerings. A little fear here, a touch of sadness there. Nothing that kills. Nothing that can't heal given time."

"And if we don't?"

Sam's laugh carried winter wind through dead leaves and the last breath of small animals caught in traps. "Look around, old man. We've been back for less than two hours, and already your neighbors hide in their homes like rabbits hiding from hawks. Their kids run instead of face us. Fear spreads faster than fire, and we're very good at feeding flames until they eat everything."

As if to prove his point, windows throughout the neighborhood slammed shut with sounds like gunshots. Curtains snapped closed, shutting out the autumn light. The happy sounds of Saturday afternoon---lawnmowers humming, kids playing, music from open windows---cut off all at once, leaving only unnatural quiet that pressed against your ears like deep water.

Even the birds had stopped singing.

"I see," Mr. Beaumont said, his voice steady despite the wrongness growing in the air. "And how long do you plan to stay?"

Mia felt the mask's influence pulse stronger, and with it came memories that belonged neither to her nor to Sam. Images of a traveling carnival moving from town to town during the Depression. Masks given to local kids as "prizes" for carnival games. Communities that went crazy and violent before the carnival moved on, leaving only empty costumes and broken families. Always the same pattern: children who never really went back to being children, no matter how many priests and doctors and desperate parents tried to help.

"Until we get bored," she said, and the words carried the weight of seasons changing and civilizations crumbling. "Or until someone makes us leave. But that hasn't happened yet. Not in all the decades we've wandered."

"I see." Mr. Beaumont turned and walked toward his house with steady steps, neither hurrying nor dawdling. His lawnmower sat abandoned, its engine ticking as it cooled in the sudden chill. At his front door, he paused with his hand on the knob. "Your grandfather was a good man, you know. Floyd Parker. I was here when he moved in, watched him struggle with whatever he'd brought from that carnival."

He looked back at them, his weathered face thoughtful. "Saw him bury salt lines around his property in the middle of the night. Heard him chanting in languages I didn't recognize. Three times over the years, I helped him board up the attic window from the inside when things got... active up there. Last time was maybe five years ago, when weird lights were coming from under his eaves and the neighborhood dogs wouldn't stop howling."

His voice carried the weight of someone who had seen too much to dismiss anything as impossible. "He tried real hard to keep those masks buried where they belonged. Did a good job of it too---kept them quiet for decades longer than most people could've managed. But Floyd always knew it was temporary. He used to tell me that binding spells were like dams---they could hold back the flood for years, even decades, but eventually the pressure would find the cracks."

Mr. Beaumont's hands gripped his door handle tighter. "The last few years, especially after Floyd died, I could feel the bindings starting to fail. Little things at first---dogs getting upset for no reason, kids having nightmares on this street more than others. Floyd warned me this would happen. Said the things inside were patient, but they never stopped testing their bonds. Sooner or later, they'd find a way through."

Hearing their real name---their grandfather's real name---sent a weird shiver through Mia that had nothing to do with the masks' power. For just a moment, she remembered being eleven years old and looking through dusty boxes for Halloween costumes, remembered the simple happiness of discovery that had nothing to do with ancient hungers or supernatural power.

Mr. Beaumont went inside, and they heard his lock turn too, sealing him away from their influence like all the others.

Mia and Sam stood alone on the suddenly empty street, masters of a domain that extended as far as their supernatural senses could reach. The masks pulsed with satisfaction, feeding on fear radiating from every house around them like heat from summer pavement. But underneath that alien contentment, Mia felt something else stirring---a small voice that sounded like her real self, asking uncomfortable questions.

What happened next? How far would this go? And somewhere in the back of her mind, a more disturbing thought: what if she was starting to like this more than she should?

The sound of a car engine interrupted her thoughts. Dad's pickup truck came around the corner way too fast, its brakes squealing as it took the turn. Through the windshield, she could see his face set in hard lines of determination and fear. Mom must have found the courage to call him after all, must have found words to explain the impossible.

The truck screeched to a stop in their driveway, leaving black marks on the concrete. Dad got out moving with the kind of purpose he used for real emergencies---house fires, broken bones, the kind of problems that needed immediate action rather than careful thinking. He took in the empty street, the closed windows, his kids standing in the middle of the road wearing weird masks, and his expression got even more serious.

"Mia. Sam. Get in the house. Now." His voice carried the kind of parental authority that had never failed to move them before, the tone that meant consequences would follow if they didn't obey.

The authority in his voice made Mia take an automatic step toward home before she caught herself. The mask sent sharp pain through her skull like ice picks behind her eyes.

"You don't give us orders," she said, her voice carrying new harmonics that made car windows vibrate and set off an alarm two houses down. "We're not your children anymore. We're something much older, much more powerful than your tiny mortal minds can understand."

Dad stopped walking, his work boots planted firm on the asphalt. His face had gone pale, but his hands stayed steady at his sides. After fifteen years of marriage and eleven years of being a father, he'd developed good instincts for when situations had moved beyond normal parenting.

"Take off the masks."

"No."

"I'm not asking." There was something in his tone that made both masks pull back slightly, some quality of absolute certainty that suggested he knew more about their situation than they'd expected.

Sam laughed, and somewhere in the distance a dog began howling---a long, sad sound that other dogs picked up until the whole neighborhood echoed with their primitive fear. "You have no power here, Jim Parker. Your authority only goes as far as human law allows.

We operate under older rules, older contracts written in blood and fear."

Dad's jaw tightened, but instead of backing down, he stood very still for a long moment, like he was making a decision that would change everything. He reached into his truck, moving with careful slowness.

"What are you doing?" Mia heard herself snarl, and for the first time since putting on the mask, she felt uncertainty from the thing inside. Whatever Dad was reaching for, Malphas recognized it---and was scared.

Dad's hand came out holding something that made both masks recoil like he'd drawn a weapon: a leather bag, worn smooth with age, that smelled of sage and cedar and old prayers. The scent hit the masks like a physical blow, and Mia felt her borrowed power waver for the first time.

He held the bag for a moment, his expression grave. "I hoped I'd never have to use this. Prayed I'd never have to remember the words Floyd made me memorize. But he knew. Somehow, he always knew this day would come."

The masks' whispers grew urgent and afraid, filling Mia's head with images of other confrontations, other bindings, other times when their power had been challenged by mortals who knew the old ways. But underneath their alien panic, she felt her own curiosity stirring, that part of her that had always asked too many questions.

"Grandpa Floyd left this when he died." Dad opened the bag with shaking hands. Dried herbs tied with red thread, carved bone and antler, hand-copied pages in languages that hurt to look at. "He spent my whole childhood preparing me for this moment, making me memorize every word, every gesture. I thought he was just being paranoid after Mom died." His voice cracked slightly. "I should've listened more carefully."

"Floyd Parker wasn't just a collector of carnival junk," Dad continued, removing items from the bag with movements that showed years of practice, even if he'd hoped never to use them. "He was what some people might call a guardian. Someone who understood that certain objects are too dangerous to destroy but too important to lose completely. Someone who accepted the responsibility of keeping them contained---and making sure the next generation would know how to do the same."

He sprinkled something that looked like coarse salt mixed with ash in a perfect circle around himself, the white crystals catching the afternoon light. His hands shook as he worked---whether from fear or grief, Mia couldn't tell.

"I'm sorry," he whispered, and she wasn't sure if he was talking to them or to Grandpa Floyd's memory. "I'm so sorry I let it come to this."

He opened the first page and started to read, but his voice cracked after only a few words. His shoulders shook.

"I don't know if this'll work. Dad's notes said the binding would force the things out, but he never had to test it." Tears tracked down his cheeks. "What if I hurt you? What if I make everything worse?"

The masks pulsed with displeasure at his hesitation, and both children felt a renewed surge of alien hunger. Mia felt the thing called Malphas flooding her mind with images---flashes of other humans who had tried to contain it over the centuries, their failures, their deaths. The thing inside the mask was confident this mortal would break just like all the others.

"Dad, please," Sam managed to say, his own voice breaking through for just a moment. "I can feel it eating me."

That seemed to give Dad the strength he needed. He wiped his eyes with the back of his hand and returned to the text, his voice getting stronger with each word. But even as he read, tears continued streaming down his face.

The words took shape as he spoke, wrapping around the masks like chains nobody could see. Every syllable was a fight. Dad had to stop, catch his breath, force himself to continue.

"He spent forty years learning how to contain you," Dad said, still reading from the ancient text without looking up. "Forty years studying folklore and mythology, tracking down every story about traveling carnivals and possessed children. He knew that someday, despite his best efforts, someone would find you again. So he prepared. He learned. He made sure the knowledge would survive him."

The circle of salt and ash began to glow with soft light that hurt to look at directly, and the masks' struggles grew more frantic. Mia felt the ancient thing's mounting panic as the binding ritual stripped away layer after layer of borrowed power. The mask was showing her flashes of its past---other battles, other defeats, the thing called Ashkente raging at being contained by mere mortal words and symbols.

"Dad, stop," she managed to say, and for the first time since putting on the mask, her voice sounded entirely like her own---young and scared and very human. "Please. I can feel myself disappearing."

Dad looked up from his reading, and she saw tears tracking down his cheeks, cutting clean lines through the dust and sweat. "I know you're still in there, sweetheart. Both of you. I'm gonna get you back, I promise. No matter what it costs."

He resumed reading, and the ancient words seemed to gain weight and substance, pressing down on the masks like the weight of centuries. Mia felt the thing that called itself Malphas fighting to maintain its hold on her consciousness, but the binding was too strong, too carefully crafted by someone who had spent decades preparing for this exact moment. The mask's whispers grew fainter, its promises of power and recognition fading like echoes in an empty church.

The red and gold mask tore away from her face---sound like silk ripping, glass breaking---and hit the asphalt hard. Cracks spread across the painted surface like a spider web, but the grin kept twisting, kept moving, kept promising things. But even as it cracked, the painted grin seemed to writhe in fury, the expression shifting from hunger to rage to something like betrayal.

A moment later, Sam's mask followed, both of them hitting the pavement with sounds like screaming that only the children could hear. The geometric patterns that had pulsed with alien life went dark and still, but not peacefully---they faded like dying embers, fighting the binding until the very last moment. The painted grins didn't fade gracefully. They twisted into expressions of malevolent promise, as if the things inside were swearing vengeance even in defeat.

Mia was on her knees, gasping air. Her lungs burned. Sam was puking up nothing but bile, his whole body shaking like he was trying to throw up something that wasn't food.

Dad was beside them in an instant, pulling them both into a fierce hug that smelled of motor oil and safety and all the ordinary human things that made life worth living. "It's okay," he whispered against their hair, his voice rough with emotion. "You're okay. You're back. You're mine again."

But pressing her face against Dad's chest, Mia could still taste fear---metallic, like old pennies. Still feel the power, the memory of being more than just some kid nobody listened to. That would never go away.

The broken masks lay scattered on the asphalt, their painted surfaces cracked and fading. But their eyes---those ancient, hungry eyes---still seemed to watch from within the ruins. Still seemed to wait with the patience of things that had existed long before human civilization and would continue long after it crumbled to dust.

And in the back of Mia's mind, something whispered: Not destroyed. Not gone. Just sleeping. And children are everywhere.

Dad gathered the broken masks with careful hands, treating them like dangerous waste as he placed them back in the leather bag alongside his ritual supplies. The fragments felt warm to the touch, as if fires still burned somewhere within the cracked papier mâché.

"What'll you do with them?" Sam asked, his voice small and very young, stripped of any supernatural authority. Purple bruises were already forming around his eyes where the mask had pressed too tight against his skin.

Dad held up the fragments, and even broken, they seemed to pulse with residual warmth---not writhing like living things, but retaining the supernatural energy that had made them dangerous in the first place. "I can feel it. They're still connected to those things. Still dangerous. Dad's notes warned about this---said the binding only forces dormancy, never true separation. He always knew it was temporary."

He looked at the fragments with the expression of someone handling live explosives. "Floyd spent forty years buying us time, nothing more. He knew from the beginning that the things couldn't be destroyed, only contained. Every binding ritual, every reinforcement, every protective measure---it was all about keeping them asleep long enough to find a permanent solution." His voice grew heavy with inherited responsibility. "He died before he could find that solution. Now it falls to me to finish what he started."

He looked at the bag with a mixture of determination and dread. "Floyd's notes mention a place. A deep cave in the mountains where other guardians have taken things that can't be killed, only contained. A place where the things will be buried under a mile of stone and iron, warded by every protection humanity has ever devised. There, the connection will be broken, and the masks will become just paper and paint again."

As they walked back toward their house, Mia noticed windows throughout the neighborhood opening again. Curtains pulled back to let in the dying afternoon light. The Mitchum twins appeared at the end of the street, walking their bikes and looking nervous, but they were coming home. Mrs. Rodriguez came out to collect the laundry she'd dropped, though she kept glancing toward the Parker house.

Life was going back to normal, but Mia knew nothing would be quite the same. Sometimes---when adults ignored her or treated her like her opinions didn't matter just because she was eleven---she'd remember what it felt like to command respect through terror.

Mom met them at the front door, her face streaked with tears and her hands shaking from the aftermath of supernatural terror. She gathered both children into another fierce hug, and over her shoulder, Mia caught sight of the kitchen window where the afternoon sun was setting, casting long shadows across the glass.

For just a second, reflected in the window, she saw the red and gold mask grinning back. Too many teeth. Waiting like predators do, knowing prey always comes home eventually.

But when she blinked, there was only her own face looking back---pale and shaken but entirely human. The face of an eleven-year-old girl who had touched something ancient and terrible and lived to remember it.

At least for now.

Later that night, after the broken dishes had been swept up and impossible explanations had been attempted and failed, after their parents had checked their rooms three times to make sure they were really themselves again, Mia lay in bed staring at the ceiling. The house settled around them with familiar creaks and sighs, but she found herself listening for other sounds---whispers in old languages, tissue paper rustling in the attic, soft footsteps of things that shouldn't exist.

The masks were locked away in Dad's bag now, waiting for transport to whatever mountain prison held such things. She was sure of that. Almost sure.

But falling asleep, she heard carnival music somewhere far away---tinny carousel music winding down. And underneath, children laughing with voices that echoed through empty places.

Power still tingled in her fingertips. Fear still tasted sweet on her tongue. She touched her face where the mask had pressed against her skin, feeling only her own familiar features.

But deep in her mind, something whispered that containment wasn't the same as victory. That things like Malphas and Ashkente had been bound before and had always found ways to slip free when the guardians grew old and careless.

Somewhere out there, other carnivals traveled other roads. Other children explored other attics. And power, once tasted, leaves marks that never fade.

The Cardboard Kingdom

C laire stood at the bottom of the attic ladder, staring up into darkness. The old ladder wobbled on the same loose bolt Dad had never fixed.

Smells drifted down from above---dust, old cardboard, and something else. Something that reminded her of Sarah's strawberry shampoo.

"Just get the decorations and leave," she muttered.

But her feet wouldn't move. Going up there meant admitting she was really back. Thirty-eight years old and living in her childhood bedroom because her ex-husband had taken everything else.

The house had felt wrong since she'd moved back six months ago. Doors she remembered closing would be open in the morning. Sounds from upstairs when she was eating breakfast alone.

Last night, she'd heard footsteps. Tiny ones. Across the attic floor at three AM.

Great, now I've got mice she had thought.

A soft thud echoed from above. Then another.

Claire's grip tightened on the ladder rails. Not random house settling. These sounds had rhythm. Purpose.

Dr. Martinez said stress could make you hear things that weren't there.

But some things were real. Like the way Sarah had vanished from her bedroom one October night when Claire was twelve. No broken window. No note. Just gone. Claire remembered sitting on these same attic stairs, listening to her parents argue in hushed voices about search parties and whether kids could just disappear.

Another scraping sound from above. Like something being dragged across wood.

Her mother's last words echoed: "Don't stay up there too long, sweetheart. Some things sleep better in the dark. But if you must go up... do it on the anniversary. That's when they remember what it felt like to be loved."

Today was October 28th. Twenty-six years to the day since Sarah had disappeared.

Claire climbed the ladder, each rung creaking under her weight. The attic stretched out before her---longer and darker than she remembered.

Cardboard boxes lined the walls, labeled in Mom's neat handwriting: "CLAIRE'S BOOKS." "CLAIRE'S CLOTHES." "CLAIRE'S ART PROJECTS."

The temperature dropped the moment she stepped inside. Her breath came out in small puffs.

That wasn't right. The house had heat.

In the far corner sat the box she'd been dreading.

"CLAIRE'S TOYS" written on it in fading black marker.

She walked toward it, floorboards creaking under her feet. Christmas decorations could wait. Something drew her to that corner.

As she got closer, she heard rustling from inside the box.

Chuck E. Cheese is in there playing with my old toys.

The tape had come loose along one edge. The cardboard flap hung open.

She didn't remember leaving it unsealed.

Claire lifted the flap and looked inside.

Her breath caught.

The toys weren't jumbled together the way she'd left them.

Someone had arranged them.

Barbie dolls sat in a perfect circle, plastic faces turned inward like they'd been having a meeting. In the center, tiny animals formed hunting patterns---cats stalking mice, horses in battle lines.

Claire reached for her favorite doll---the brunette Barbie she'd named Sophia. The doll's hair hung in perfect waves, too perfect for a toy that had been in storage for twenty years.

She lifted Sophia from the box. Other dolls toppled backward, and she heard tiny gasps. Like miniature breaths of surprise.

Sophia's plastic head turned in Claire's hand.

Not the loose joint movement of an old toy. Deliberate.

Claire froze.

Claire set Sophia on the floor and stepped back. The doll sat motionless.

Then Sophia blinked.

"I saw that," Claire whispered.

Sophia's painted lips curved upward. Not the molded smile---something else. Something that reached her plastic eyes.

"Hello, Claire," Sophia said in a voice like tiny bells. "We missed you."

Claire stumbled backward, her heart hammering. The anniversary. Her mother's warning. The tiny footsteps she'd heard.

They were awake.

Claire pulled out more toys with shaking hands. Breyer horses in battle formation. Smurfs lined up like tiny soldiers. Troll dolls with arms raised, as if they'd been caught mid-celebration.

Someone had been playing with them.

Tiny scratches marked the cardboard walls. Worn paths in the dust led to and from Sophia's position.

As she worked, small sounds echoed around her. Not from outside---from the toys themselves. Tiny creaks and sighs, like old wood settling, but organic.

She glanced back at Sophia. The doll sat exactly where she'd left her, but her position felt different.

Another memory surfaced. Sarah at thirteen, becoming secretive about her toys. Claire had found her one evening, sitting in her bedroom corner, whispering to her dolls in voices too low to hear. "They talk back now," Sarah had said when Claire asked. "But only when you really listen."

Claire unpacked five more toys, then looked again. Sophia had shifted. Just a little.

"You're being paranoid," Claire said aloud. "Plastic doesn't move."

As she spoke, she heard a tiny, whispered response: "Doesn't it?"

Claire spun around. The attic was silent except for her pulse thundering in her ears. But now she understood. The anniversary. Her mother's cryptic warning about them being "strongest" today.

Twenty-six years ago, Sarah had disappeared on this exact date. And now Claire had returned to open their prison.

Claire opened her old jewelry box. The pink satin inside had been smoothed flat. Her childhood rings and necklaces arranged with mathematical precision.

At the bottom, spelled out in tiny plastic beads:

"WHY DID YOU LEAVE US?"

Underneath, in smaller beads:

"SARAH CAME BACK."

"SARAH STAYED."

"SARAH SLEEPS WITH US NOW."

Claire dropped the box.

It hit the floor with a sharp crack, and the ballerina's head snapped off, rolling away into the shadows.

Silence filled the attic

.

Claire scrambled to her feet, knocking over toys. They clattered against each other with sounds that weren't quite right---too soft, like plastic had become flesh.

"This isn't happening," she said.

"Claire."

She spun around. The toys had moved. Sophia sat upright, facing her. The doll's plastic eyes tracked Claire's movement.

"We missed you," Sophia said. "We waited so long."

All around the attic, toys shifted. Turning heads. Flexing limbs. All awake. All watching.

"Toys don't talk," Claire said.

"Don't we?" Thunder the horse spoke, his voice too small for his size. "You made us real, Claire. You gave us life."

Other voices joined in: "You loved us." "You played with us every day." "You promised you'd never leave."

Claire's back hit the attic opening. She felt for the ladder with her foot.

"I need to go."

"Do you?" Sophia's head tilted at an impossible angle. "You cried to me. Told me your secrets. Promised you'd never abandon us." The doll's voice turned sharp. "Was that pretend?"

The accusation hit Claire like a slap. She did remember. Loving these toys with the fierce devotion only a child could give. The elaborate stories, the complex relationships, the hours of imaginative play that had filled her childhood.

And she remembered the day she'd decided she was too old. The day she'd packed them away without ceremony, without goodbye.

"I grew up," she whispered, her foot finding the ladder rung. "People grow up."

"But we didn't," said one of the Little People, a tiny police officer she'd called Deputy Dan. "We stayed here. We stayed eight years old forever... waiting for you to come back."

"We stayed in the dark," added a Smurf.

"We stayed alone," said a troll doll.

"We stayed forgotten," Thunder finished. "Just like Sarah."

Claire's foot slipped. "Sarah?"

"Your sister came back on this day," Sophia said. "Twenty-six years ago. The anniversary makes us... stronger. Makes us real."

Claire felt the blood drain from her face. The beads in the jewelry box. The tiny footsteps last night.

"She found us first," Thunder continued. "Just like you have now."

"Where is she?" Claire whispered.

Sophia's plastic face turned toward the far corner of the attic, where shadows gathered thick between the exposed beams. "She's with us. She's been with us. Watching... waiting for her little sister to come home too."

Claire squinted into the darkness. At first she saw nothing. Then her eyes adjusted, and she made out a shape. Human-sized. Sitting against the wall. But the proportions were wrong. Too perfect. Too smooth.

"Sarah?" Claire called out.

The figure in the corner didn't respond. But Claire could swear she saw the faintest smile cross its lips.

"She can't answer right now," Sophia explained. "It's not her turn to be awake. But soon... when you join us... you can play together forever."

Ice water seemed to flood Claire's veins. Sarah wasn't sleeping. They were taking turns. Sometimes Sarah was herself. Sometimes she was just another doll in their collection.

Claire turned and ran for the ladder.

The toys moved to stop her, not walking exactly, but shifting position like stop-motion animation. They formed a loose circle, cutting off her escape route.

"Don't go," Sophia pleaded, her voice coming in unnatural stops and starts. "Not... again. We've been so... lonely."

"Twenty years," Thunder said, the words dragging out too long. "Do you know what... what twenty years feels like when you're... trapped in a box?"

"When every day is exactly the same?" "When there's no light... no air... no room to move?" "When you remember being loved but can't... feel it anymore?"

The chorus of tiny voices rose, overlapping, creating a symphony of accusation that made Claire's head spin:

"You promised you'd never forget us." "You said we'd be together." "You said you loved us." "Liar." "Betrayer." "Abandoner."

"Stop!" Claire shouted, pressing her hands over her ears. "You're just toys! You're plastic and fabric! You don't have feelings!"

The voices cut off. Silence rang in her ears. But when she looked down at the toys surrounding her, their expressions had changed. The sadness was gone, replaced by something harder.

"Just toys," Sophia repeated, her voice flat and cold.

"Plastic and fabric," Thunder echoed.

"No feelings," finished Deputy Dan.

Claire tried to step back, but there was nowhere to go. The ladder was blocked by a line of Little People. The rest of the attic was crowded with boxes and dark corners.

"If we're just toys," Sophia said, rising to her feet with movements too fluid for plastic joints, "then it won't matter what we do to you."

The other toys began to move with purpose now, converging from all directions. The horses' plastic hooves clicked against the wooden floor like tiny hammers. The Little People moved in formation. The Smurfs made no sound as they advanced.

Claire pressed herself against the ladder frame, feeling splinters bite into her back. "What do you want?"

"We want you to play," Sophia said. "We want you to stay. We want you to... love us again."

"And if you won't," Thunder added, pawing the floor, "we'll make you."

They surged forward. Not mindless. Calculated.

The toys swarmed toward her. Little People blocked the ladder. Horses clicked across the floor. Smurfs climbed boxes like tiny hunters.

Sophia walked straight at her, arms outstretched for a hug.

"This isn't real," Claire whispered.

"You're hurt," Sophia said. "That's what happens when you run from family."

A troll doll grabbed Claire's shoelace. She kicked it away, but it bounced back to its feet, still grinning.

"We've had twenty years to practice," Thunder said.

More toys emerged from the shadows. One-eyed teddy bears dragging themselves forward. Plastic army men marching in formation. Monopoly pieces rolling like tiny metal tumbleweeds.

Toys swarmed up her legs. Tiny hands grabbed her jeans, her sweater, her hair. Little People formed chains, climbing hand over hand. Horses bit her ankles with suddenly sharp teeth.

"Get off!" Claire clawed at them, but they clung tight. Their plastic bodies felt warm. Alive.

A stuffed animal wrapped around her throat---not choking, but restraining. When she grabbed it, the cotton felt like flesh.

In the chaos, she remembered the last conversation she'd had with Sarah, right here in this attic. Sarah had been crying, clutching her old stuffed rabbit, trying to tell Claire something important. But Claire had been twelve and impatient.

"They remember everything," Sarah had said, her voice shaking. "Every story. Every secret. Every promise we made." She'd grabbed Claire's arm with desperate fingers. "Promise me you'll never forget them. Promise me you'll love them just a little bit, because if you don't---" Her voice had broken off.

"Promise me what?" Claire had demanded.

Sarah had shaken her head and whispered, "If you don't keep loving them, they'll find a way to make you remember."

Now Claire understood. The toys hadn't just been listening---they'd been learning. Waiting. Planning.

"Stop fighting us," Sophia said. The doll had climbed to Claire's shoulder, plastic arms wrapped around her neck. "You're only making it harder."

The weight of dozens of toys dragged Claire to her knees. Breyer horses surrounded her in a circle, hooves scraping against wood in rhythm like breathing. Little People climbed higher, some reaching her shoulders, others tangling in her hair.

Claire tried to grab a handful and throw them away, but her movements had become sluggish. The attic spun around her. Golden sunlight growing dim.

She thought about her life outside this attic. Her empty apartment. Her demanding job. Her failed marriage. The endless cycle of work and sleep and work again. Had any of it meant anything?

Maybe this wasn't such a terrible fate.

"Sarah fought too," Thunder said. "At first. But she learned to love us again. Just like you will."

"Where is she?" Claire gasped, still trying to dislodge the toys. "What did you do?"

Sophia's plastic face turned toward the far corner. "She's sleeping. She's been sleeping for twenty-six years now. But sometimes... when we're very good... she wakes up and plays with us."

In the shadows, Claire saw the figure.

Her sister. Transformed. Waiting.

Claire looked around for anything that might help her fight. Her gaze fell on a broken piece of cardboard---a long shard with a sharp edge.

She grabbed it and swung at Sophia like a sword. The cardboard passed right through the doll's body without resistance, as if she were made of air.

Sophia laughed, a sound like tiny wind chimes. "Silly Claire. You can't hurt us. We're broken. We've been broken for twenty years... ever since you stopped loving us."

More toys appeared from hidden spaces---ones she'd forgotten she owned, stuffed animals she'd thought were lost, board game pieces that moved with individual purpose.

"We've been practicing," Deputy Dan said.

"What do you want to play first?" Thunder asked.

"House!" called out one of the Little People.

"Adventure!" suggested an action figure.

"Let's play family," Sophia decided. "Claire can be the mommy, and we'll be her children. She'll take care of us and love us and never, ever leave us again."

"I won't," Claire gasped. "I can't. I have a life. I have responsibili-ties---"

"None of that matters now," Sophia said, stroking Claire's cheek with one tiny plastic hand. "This is where you belong. With us. With your real family."

The toys began to sing then, a lullaby Claire recognized from childhood. Their tiny voices blended in perfect harmony, creating a sound both beautiful and terrifying:

Rock-a-bye Claire, in the treetop, When the wind blows, the cradle will rock, When the bough breaks, the cradle will fall, And down will come Claire, toys and all.

As they sang, Claire felt herself changing. The attic grew larger around her, or maybe she was shrinking. The toys' faces got bigger. Their voices louder. Their tiny hands stronger.

"What's happening?"

"You're becoming one of us," Sophia said. "Plastic and perfect and forever young. You'll never have to worry about growing old or forgetting or leaving us behind again."

Claire tried to fight the transformation. Her skin felt tight, then tighter, like plastic wrap heated in the sun and shrinking around her bones. Her joints locked up one by one---first her fingers, then her wrists, elbows refusing to bend. When she tried to scream, her voice came out higher, tinnier, like a recording played at the wrong speed. Her vision blurred at the edges, colors washing out to the flat, bright hues of a child's toy box.

Through the haze of changing consciousness, she caught glimpses of the corner. Sarah sat there, face smooth and perfect now. The way only dolls' faces could be. No worry lines around her eyes anymore. No tension in her jaw.

Claire's chest loosened for the first time in months. All her adult worries were dissolving---the second mortgage payment due next week, the Kowalski clients who might sue her, the empty apartment where she hadn't bought groceries in three days because she'd spent the money on gas to drive to showings that never closed.

Was this what Sarah had found? This simplicity? This eternal childhood where love was unconditional and playtime never ended?

But then she thought about the world outside. Her friends who would wonder where she'd gone. The life she'd built, imperfect as it was.

"Don't fight it," Thunder advised. "It doesn't hurt. You'll like being simple. Being loved. Being ours."

The attic spun around her. Ceiling rushing away. Toys growing larger. She wanted to resist, hold onto her human form, her adult responsibilities.

She tried to hold on---to her driver's license in her back pocket, to the house key that still fit her childhood home, to the memory of what coffee tasted like. But her fingers wouldn't close anymore. Everything slipping away like water.

The transformation was complete. Tiny hands lifted Claire, carried her to a dollhouse made of cardboard and dreams. Sarah was already there, waiting.

Her sister's painted face turned toward Claire and smiled---a smile that would never age, never frown, never fade.

"Welcome home," Sophia said.

Claire wanted to be angry. Wanted to be scared. But anger felt distant now, like trying to remember a song from long ago. Fear belonged to someone else---someone with a heartbeat and breath and skin that bruised.

The attic window darkened as the sun set. But inside their cardboard world, the games were just beginning.

After twenty-six years of waiting for Sarah. Twenty more for Claire. Playtime had resumed.

In the morning, people would come looking for Claire Beale. They would find an empty house. Empty boxes. Forgotten decorations.

The toy box sat in the corner, lid closed tight. Inside, soft sounds of children playing house. Playing family.

Playing forever.

Hair Today, Gone Tomorrow

The thing in Richard Caldwell's shower drain looked like a dead mouse.

Dark, wet, twisted into a ball the size of a quarter. He poked it with his toothbrush handle and watched it come apart in stringy chunks. Hair. His hair.

"Shit." Way too much for a Tuesday morning, even with the Maywood account trying to kill him. Sixteen-hour days, maybe four hours' sleep if he was lucky. Stress made people shed, sure, but this was different.

His old man had gone bald by thirty-five, though. At least Richard thought he had—Dad in his La-Z-Boy, dome shining under the lamp while the Mets lost another one. Connecticut summers in the garage, motor oil and Marlboros.

Richard flushed the mess and got dressed for another day of Maywood's bullshit. Fifteen years at Hartwell & Associates, climbing from junior account exec to senior VP, and he still felt like he was faking it. Wharton MBA on the wall, corner office on the twelfth floor, and a three-grand-a-month shoebox in Stamford to prove he'd made it.

His Honda Civic wheezed to life in the parking garage. Radio cut out somewhere near Exit 16, leaving him with rush-hour silence and the smell of his own coffee going cold in the cup holder. Another glamorous morning in corporate America.

By Thursday, the clumps were big enough to make his stomach turn.

Richard stood in his bathroom, running his fingers through what was left. Jesus Christ, it felt thin. Whole sections came away in his hand—not the one or two strands everybody lost, but chunks that made his scalp show through like a cancer patient.

The guy in the mirror looked wrong. Same brown eyes, same busted nose from high school football, same scar over his left eyebrow from eating it on his bike when he was seven. Everything where it belonged.

But looking at himself made his hands shake.

His phone buzzed. Text from Janet: *Maywood moved the presentation to Friday. Sorry. Coffee?*

Janet Kopaldi had been covering his ass for three years now. Started as his assistant but basically ran half his accounts while he dealt with Hartwell's corporate bullshit. Single mom, sharp as hell, and the only person in the office who'd tell him when he was being an idiot.

Sure, he texted back. *Need caffeine anyway.*

Miguel already had his cup ready when they hit the lobby cart. Guy knew every order in the building by heart—one of those little things that made Richard's day suck less.

"Jesus, Richard." Janet didn't even say hello, just stared at his head while she dumped sugar in her coffee. "When's the last time you slept?"

"I slept."

"I mean actual sleep. Not passing out at your desk." She squinted at him like she was reading fine print. "And what's with your hair? You going through chemo or something?"

"It's stress."

"Bullshit. I've seen you stressed. This is different."

She squinted at him like she was reading fine print. "What's going on? You're pale as a ghost, and your hair..." She made a vague gesture at his head. "Are you sick? Like, actually sick?"

"It's nothing. Just stress." The words came out sharper than he meant. "Sorry. Long week."

"Longer than usual, you mean. Christ, when's the last time you took a real weekend? Not working-from-home weekend, but like, actual time off where you don't check email?"

Richard couldn't remember. The weekends all blended together—grocery shopping, laundry, maybe a movie if he wasn't too tired. Sometimes he'd drive up to see his mother in Hartford, though those visits felt more like obligation than choice.

"I'll take some time after we land Maywood," he said.

"Uh-huh." Janet didn't look convinced. "You know what Dr. Peterson told me when I was losing my hair after Danny was born? Stress can make your body do weird things. Maybe you should see somebody."

"Maybe." Richard touched his scalp unconsciously. The skin felt tender, like a sunburn.

That afternoon, he called Dr. Bernhardt's office. The receptionist—Linda, who'd been there since the Carter administration—squeezed him in at four-thirty.

Bernhardt's waiting room smelled like old magazines and that antiseptic cleaner they used in hospitals. Richard flipped through a six-month-old copy of *Time* and tried not to think about how much hair he'd left on his pillow that morning.

"Richard?" Dr. Bernhardt appeared in the doorway—gray-haired, kind face behind wire-rim glasses. He'd been Richard's doctor for eight years, ever since he'd moved to Stamford. Steady hands, reassuring voice, the kind of GP who still made house calls for his older patients.

The examination room was cramped and bright. Bernhardt peered at Richard's scalp through a magnifying glass that made his breathing sound loud and mechanical.

"Follicles look fine. No inflammation, no pattern baldness." Bernhardt adjusted the light, squinting at Richard's scalp. "You said stress?"

"Maywood account's killing me. Presentation Friday."

"Mm." The doctor made a note. "Stress'll do it. Hair loss, I mean. Usually grows back once the pressure's off. Could send you to a dermatologist, but I'd wait a few weeks. Try to sleep more than four hours a night."

Stress-related hair loss. Temporary. Richard left feeling almost normal for the first time in days.

By Monday, half his hair was gone.

He tried a baseball cap to the office and looked like a middle-aged asshole trying to be cool. Janet took one look at him and didn't even try to hide her alarm.

"Okay, now I'm really worried."

Janet brought him coffee from the cart downstairs—the good cart, not the vending machine swill—and tried not to stare at his head. She'd been doing little things like that for three years now, ever since Danny's father had bailed and left her scrambling for decent childcare. Richard had quietly made sure she got the health insurance upgrade and flexible hours. She'd never mentioned it, but she always brought him the good coffee now.

"You feeling all right, Mr. Caldwell?" She only used his last name when other people were around, or when she was really worried. "You look rough."

"I'll be fine," he said, but his voice came out hoarse.

That afternoon, while reviewing the Maywood contracts, Richard ran his hand through his hair and came away with another handful. He reached for the wastebasket, and then stopped cold.

The hair in his palm was dissolving.

Not falling apart—actually dissolving. The individual strands were breaking down, becoming thin as spider silk, then just... gone. Vanishing between his fingers like they were made of sugar in the rain.

Richard stared at his empty palm, his mouth dry as sandpaper. Hair didn't do that. Hair was supposed to last for years—his grandmother still had a lock of his grandfather's hair in her jewelry box from the 1960s.

But whatever was falling out of his head wasn't staying hair once it came loose.

He spent the rest of the afternoon on medical websites, searching for anything that matched what was happening. Male pattern baldness, alopecia, trichotillomania—none of them mentioned hair that dissolved. The pictures all showed normal hair loss, with actual hair on pillows and in brushes.

That night, Richard stood in his bathroom under the harsh fluorescent light, squinting at his reflection. There were lines under his scalp. Faint marks that moved and connected like... like wiring. Circuit boards. Some kind of electronic shit.

In dimmer light, he might have missed them completely, but under the bathroom bulbs they showed up like veins under pale skin.

He touched his scalp. Felt normal—warm, slightly oily, human. But the lines responded to his touch, getting brighter, and somehow he could feel energy moving through them. Not through his fingers, but like he was picking up some kind of signal.

What the fuck was happening to him?

Richard grabbed his phone and tried to photograph his scalp. The camera showed nothing but pale skin with a few remaining dark hairs. But in the mirror, the lines glowed softly under the fluorescent light.

He didn't sleep well. His dreams were full of static and voices speaking languages he didn't recognize but somehow understood. Every time he woke up, his scalp was tingling and there was more hair on the pillow.

By Thursday, he was nearly bald.

The lines under his scalp had grown brighter overnight, no longer faint suggestions but bold designs that pulsed with soft light. Under the bathroom fluorescents, they were clearly visible—complex pathways that branched and intersected across his entire head like neural networks.

As more hair disappeared, the patterns grew stronger, as if the artificial follicles had been dampening some kind of energy source.

Richard called in sick and spent the day researching everything he could find about unusual skin conditions, genetic disorders, anything that might explain glowing patterns under human skin. The internet had no answers.

Around noon, while staring at his reflection, something in his brain started to... slip.

Something was wrong with his head. Not the hair—the memories within.

Richard tried to picture his dad and got the usual image: La-Z-Boy, bald dome, Mets game on the tube. But it felt hollow. Like looking at a stranger's family photo.

His hands were shaking.

Christmas morning, age eight. Unwrapping that Transformer. He could see it happening—the wrapping paper, his mom's laugh—but felt nothing. Like watching a movie he'd memorized but never actually lived.

Only this morning felt real. Janet's worried face. Burnt eggs sticking to his pan. His Honda's dying radio on the drive in.

Everything else? Gone. Not missing—just empty. Like someone had scraped out the emotional center of his life and left behind the shell.

Richard sat on his couch, staring at a photo on the coffee table—himself at last year's company picnic, arm around Janet, both of them laughing. He remembered the moment: Janet had made a joke about their boss's golf swing. But looking at the photo now, Richard felt like he was looking at a stranger who happened to have his face.

The patterns on his scalp blazed brighter.

Holy Christ. Holy fucking Christ.

The hair wasn't falling out from stress. It was fake. A disguise. And underneath...

He stumbled backward from the mirror, his heart hammering. The bathroom lights flickered as the patterns under his scalp pulsed like Christmas tree lights. This wasn't happening. This couldn't be happening.

But the face in the cracked mirror wasn't human anymore.

Richard's legs gave out and he slumped against the bathroom wall, staring at his reflection. His memories—not broken, not sick, but programmed. Fifteen years of fake life, fake relationships, fake everything.

He wasn't Richard Caldwell.

He wasn't even human.

His mind cracked open.

Stars wheeled past him—not stars, but something burning cold and impossibly distant. Shapes that made his eyes water, geometries that folded in on themselves like origami made of light. Moving between worlds the way a man stepped between rooms.

Scout. The word hit him like a physical blow.

Oh Christ. Oh Jesus fucking Christ.

Not human. Never human. Fifteen years of fake life, fake memories, fake everything. His skin crawled as if something was moving underneath it, trying to get out. Because something was.

Richard stumbled back to his living room, his whole body shaking. Every memory of his life felt like props from a movie set. His apartment, his job, his friendship with Janet—all of it designed to make him think he was human.

But sitting there in his fake apartment, looking at that photo of him and Janet from the company picnic, Richard felt something his programmers had never planned for.

Rage.

Fifteen years they'd let him live with these people. Let him care about Janet's kid, worry about Miguel's green card, remember every patient Dr. Bernhardt lost to cancer. Let him feel human. And now they wanted him back? Fuck that.

His phone rang. Unknown number, but something in his rewired brain recognized the frequency.

"Hello, Richard." The voice sounded human but felt wrong, like plastic fruit that looked perfect until you bit into it. "Time to come home."

His phone rang. The number on the display wasn't one he recognized, though something deep in his mind did.

"Richard." Not a question. The voice sounded like a customer service recording—too perfect, too empty. "Extraction in thirty-seven minutes."

"Who—"

"Disguise failure ahead of schedule. Prepare for collection."

Richard's mouth went dry. "Wait, I can explain—"

"Thirty-seven minutes."

The line went dead.

Richard stared at the phone. Thirty-seven minutes until they came to... what? Fix him? Deactivate him? Take him back to whatever ship or base they operated from?

And what would they do about his blown cover? About the humans who might have noticed something was wrong?

Richard thought about Janet, probably at her desk right now, maybe still worried about him. About Miguel at the coffee cart, who always asked about people's families. About Dr. Bernhardt, who made house calls for elderly patients.

Fake programming or not, he'd spent fifteen years living among these people. Learning their kindness, their fears, their hopes. They'd changed him in ways his original programmers had never intended.

Maybe that was what made someone human—not where you came from, but what you chose to protect.

Richard grabbed his keys and headed for the door. Thirty-seven minutes wasn't much time, but it might be enough.

Janet was just shutting down her computer when Richard burst through the office doors. She took one look at his face—wild-eyed, almost completely bald now, with strange patterns visible beneath his scalp—and got up immediately.

"Richard? Jesus, what happened to you?"

"Janet, listen to me." He grabbed her by the shoulders, and she flinched at how cold his hands were. "I need you to take Danny and leave town. Tonight. Right now."

"What? Richard, you're scaring me."

"Good. You should be scared." His eyes—had they always been that color? They seemed to be shifting, like looking at oil on water. "There are people coming, and they're not... they're not good people. You need to run."

Janet stared at him. Three years of working together, and she'd never seen him like this. But there was something in his voice—desperation, terror, but also complete conviction.

"Richard, what's going on? What people?"

He looked around the office, checking the windows, the entrances. "I can't explain everything. But I need you to trust me. Has anyone else been asking about me? Strange phone calls, people you didn't recognize?"

"No, I—" Janet stopped. "Wait. Yesterday, someone called asking about your address. Said they were from your insurance company, but they already had your file number, so I thought it was weird..."

"Shit." Richard ran his hands through what was left of his hair, and Janet watched as more of it dissolved between his fingers. "They've been tracking me. Janet, please. I know this sounds crazy, but if you've ever trusted me, trust me now. Take Danny and go."

Janet looked at his face—really looked at it. The patterns under his scalp were glowing faintly now, and his skin had an odd translucent quality. But his eyes, strange as they were, showed genuine fear. Not for himself.

For her.

"Where should we go?"

Relief flooded Richard's face. "Your sister in Albany. Stay there for a week, maybe two. Don't use credit cards, don't call anyone from work. And if anyone comes asking about me, tell them you don't know where I am."

"But I don't know where you'll be."

Richard was quiet for a long moment. "I don't either."

Janet reached out and touched his arm. His skin was ice-cold now, and she could feel something underneath it—not bone and muscle, but something else. Something that hummed with energy.

"Richard... what are you?"

He looked at her—this woman who'd brought him coffee every morning for three years, who'd worried about him when he worked too late, who'd trusted him enough to share stories about her son's first steps and her ex-husband's failures.

"I don't know anymore," he said. "But I know what I'm going to do."

Richard waited in his apartment as the thirty-seven minutes ticked down. He'd helped Janet pack, had driven her to pick up Danny from aftercare, had watched them disappear onto Route 95 heading north. She'd hugged him goodbye, and even though his skin was now cold as stone and patterns of light pulsed visibly beneath its surface, she'd still looked at him like he was human.

Maybe that was enough.

When they came for him—three figures in gray suits that moved with inhuman precision—Richard was ready.

"You warned her," the leader said. Not a question.

"Yes."

"Why?"

Richard thought about Janet's laugh, about Miguel's morning greetings, about Dr. Bernhardt asking after his mother. Fifteen years of small kindnesses, of genuine human connection, of learning what it meant to care about something beyond your original purpose.

"Because she mattered," he said.

The figures exchanged glances. "Your programming has been compromised. You'll need to be recalibrated."

"No."

The word hung in the air between them. Richard felt something change inside him, some fundamental shift as he chose defiance over compliance, humanity over his alien nature.

"The mission—"

"The mission is over," Richard said. "At least for me."

They moved faster than human reflexes could track, but Richard wasn't human anymore either. The patterns on his scalp blazed like neon, and when he fought back, it was with abilities he'd never known he possessed.

The battle was brief but devastating. When it was over, Richard's apartment was a ruin of melted furniture and shattered glass, and two of the figures lay motionless on the floor. The third had retreated, but not before Richard had torn enough information from its mind to understand the scope of what was coming.

The invasion wasn't years away. It was weeks.

And there were thousands of scouts like him, spread across the country, most still unaware of their true nature. But some, like Richard, were beginning to remember. Beginning to choose.

Richard looked around his destroyed apartment—the physical remnants of his fake life—and felt no regret. Janet and Danny were safe, at least for now. And there were other humans who deserved the same protection.

His phone, somehow still intact, buzzed with a text message. Janet: *Made it to Linda's. Danny's asking about Uncle Richard. You take care of yourself, okay?*

Uncle Richard. He'd never been Danny's uncle, had barely met the kid. But Janet had told her son about him anyway, had made him part of their family in the way humans did—not through blood or programming, but through choice.

Richard typed back: *Tell him I said goodbye.*

Then he crushed the phone and walked out into the night, ready to find the other scouts who were beginning to remember, ready to make a choice about which side they'd fight for when the real battle began.

The invasion was coming, but it wouldn't find humanity defenseless.

Not if Richard could help it.

The patterns on his scalp pulsed brighter as he disappeared into the darkness, no longer human but not entirely alien either. Something new. Something that had chosen its own loyalty through fifteen years of small kindnesses and genuine connection.

Hair today, gone tomorrow. But underneath the fake scalp, something was growing that his programmers never planned for.

A choice.

And Richard Caldwell—or whatever he really was—had already made it.

The patterns under his skin pulsed brighter as he disappeared into the night, ready to find others like him who'd learned what fifteen years of human kindness could teach.

The invasion was coming. But it wouldn't find Earth defenseless.

A Roll through the Heather

T he heather had grown thick this season.

I felt each purple bloom unfurl, tasted the honey that drew bees in drowsy clouds. My field stretched toward Ben More, purple thick as fleece. Morning haar clung to the braes—the kind that'd burn off by ten if the wind held. Mortals called this place Cromwell Moor, though I remembered when it bore different names, spoken in tongues that had crumbled to dust centuries before their great-grandfathers drew breath.

Time moved differently for my kind. Days blurred into seasons, seasons into years, years into the slow dance of stone and soil. I'd watched ice sheets retreat and forests claim the land, then burn and regrow. I'd seen the first humans stumble across my heather, their crude tools glinting in hands that shook from cold and hunger.

Most passed through quickly. The heather whispered warnings to those with sense enough to listen—stay to the path, don't linger, don't sleep where the flowers grow thickest. Smart ones heeded the advice. Others provided sustenance.

I existed in the spaces between. Not quite earth, not quite air, not quite the chittering consciousness of insects or the warm-blooded urgency of mammals. I was the field itself, the thing that had always been here, feeding on what the heather offered and what foolish humans left behind.

This morning felt different.

The heather trembled with a vibration that had nothing to do with wind. Two shapes moved through the mist at the field's edge—humans, young ones, stumbling with exhaustion. The girl clutched the boy's hand like a lifeline. Both carried the sharp scent of fear.

I shifted my awareness, drew up through root systems and flower stems to taste the air more clearly. The boy had dark hair matted with sweat and a cut on his cheek that had stopped bleeding hours ago. The girl's auburn curls hung in tangles around a face too thin, too pale.

Their clothes hung loose and dirty, fabric torn where they'd pushed through gorse.

Runners. Fleeing something that chased close behind.

The boy stopped at my edge, chest heaving. "Em, we can't. You're dead on your feet."

"Gray, please." Her voice cracked. "They're still coming. The bloody dogs—"

"Look at you." He turned her face toward him, thumb brushing the dark circles under her eyes. "When'd you last eat? Really eat?"

She leaned into his touch. "Yesterday morning. That bread you nicked from the farmhouse."

"That was two days ago."

I watched them whisper-argue, two small figures against my vast purple expanse. Time to begin. I started the heather's song—not sound, but the old music we use for luring. Sweet, sleepy magic that promised rest, safety, an end to running.

The girl's eyelids grew heavy. "Gray... I'm knackered."

"I know." He guided her into my field, feet sinking into soft earth between the heather stalks. "Just for a bit. We'll rest an hour, then keep moving."

They settled twenty paces in, where the flowers grew waist-high and thick. The boy gathered heather branches, making a crude mattress. The girl curled against his side, her breathing already deepening toward sleep.

Perfect.

I began the slow process of drawing them deeper into my embrace. The heather would release more of its drowsy perfume, deeper sleep would claim them, and by nightfall I'd have what I needed. The process was gentle—they'd slip from sleep into the kind of rest that fed me. No pain, no fear, just the slow fade that returned them to the earth.

It had always been this way.

But as I settled into the familiar rhythm of harvest, something tugged at my attention. The boy hadn't fallen asleep. He sat rigid against the heather mattress, every muscle tense with watching. His eyes swept the moor's edges, scanning for movement that wasn't wind through grass.

"Sleep," he whispered to the girl, voice barely audible. "I'll keep watch."

I paused. In three thousand years, I'd never encountered a human who fought my field's influence so completely. Even the most paranoid travelers eventually gave in to the heather's call. But this one maintained his watch with fierce determination, as if love itself provided armor against my magic.

Curious, I tasted his memories.

They surfaced like blood in water—bright, violent, recent. A cramped flat in Glasgow, smoke-stained walls and broken promises. Emily cowering in a corner while men with cold eyes counted money and made calculations about debt. Graham throwing punches he couldn't win, blood on his knuckles and desperation in his voice as he begged for more time.

She's not part of this. Let her go.

Boy, she became part of this the moment she started fucking you. Your debt, your problem—but she's collateral now.

The escape had cost them everything. Three days running across the Highlands, sleeping in abandoned crofts and eating what they could steal or forage. The men following them had resources, connections, dogs trained to track human scent across miles of rough country.

There would be no sanctuary for them. Not in the cities, not in the villages, not even in the wild places where most humans feared to go. They were prey now, running toward an inevitable end.

Unless...

I'd fed on many humans over the centuries. Warriors, travelers, lovers who sought privacy in the purple fields. I'd tasted their last thoughts as life drained from them—fear, mostly, sometimes acceptance, occasionally defiance. But I'd never tasted love so pure it could resist my most powerful magic.

This boy would die for the girl without hesitation. More than that—he'd suffer for her, sacrifice everything he valued to buy her one more day of life. The depth of his devotion resonated through the heather in ways I hadn't experienced before.

And she loved him with equal fervor. Even in her exhausted sleep, her hand remained twined with his, her breathing matching his rhythm. They were bound to each other in ways that put most humans to shame.

It had been centuries since I'd felt anything resembling curiosity about mortal emotions. But these two...

The girl stirred, blinking awake as afternoon shadows lengthened. "How long?"

"Few hours." Graham helped her sit up, hand gentle on her back. "How d'you feel?"

She stretched, wincing at stiff muscles. "Better. Still knackered, but better." She looked around the heather field, purple blooms swaying in the breeze. "This place... it's beautiful."

"Feels safe too." Graham scanned the moor's edges again. "Haven't seen any movement. Maybe we lost them."

Oh, sweet boy. You haven't lost anything.

I could taste them approaching even now—six men with rifles and radio contact, dogs straining at leads as they followed the scent trail. They'd reach my edge within the hour, and once they did, there'd be no escape for the young lovers.

The smart choice was clear. Let the hunters take their prey and be done with it. I had no stake in human conflicts, no reason to risk exposure by intervening. Better to let events unfold naturally and feed on whatever remained.

But I found myself reluctant to release them.

Three thousand years of existence had taught me many things, but I'd never learned the precise flavor of love that could defy magic itself. These two carried something precious, something that might not pass my way again for another millennium.

And there was another consideration—one that surprised me with its intensity.

For the first time in millennia, I didn't want to be alone.

The realization hit like cold Highland rain. For centuries, I'd existed in perfect solitude, needing nothing beyond the sustenance the heather provided. But watching Graham and Emily, seeing the way they completed each other, I understood what I'd been missing.

Company. Connection. The simple warmth of being known by another consciousness.

They were still human, still fragile, still temporary by my standards. But perhaps... perhaps there was value in protecting something beautiful, even if that protection was temporary itself.

The dogs' baying decided it for me—distant but growing closer.

I began to change the heather's song.

Instead of drowsy sweetness, I wove concealment. The purple blooms closed ranks around the couple, creating a natural blind that'd hide them from searching eyes. The scent-trails that led across the moor shifted and scattered, becoming confused pathways that doubled back on themselves.

Graham's head snapped up as the change rippled through my field. "Emily. Something's wrong."

"What d'you mean?"

"Listen."

She cocked her head, straining to hear what he'd detected. The baying of hounds, still distant but unmistakably closer than before.

"They found our trail." Emily's face went white. "How? We stayed in the burns, covered our tracks—"

"Dogs don't need tracks if they've got scent." Graham pulled her to her feet, looking around desperately. "We need to move. Find better cover."

Stay still, boy. Trust what you don't understand.

I don't know if he heard my thoughts or simply felt my protective embrace, but Graham hesitated instead of running. His eyes swept the heather around them, noting how it had shifted to form natural screens.

"Emily." His voice was quiet, wondering. "Look around us."

She turned in a slow circle, taking in the way the purple stalks had woven themselves into a living fortress. "That's... that's not normal."

"No. It isn't."

The baying grew louder. I could taste the hunters now—hard men with empty spaces where consciences should've been. They carried death casually, the way other humans carried tools. These weren't people who'd be satisfied with simply recovering their money. They'd want to send a message written in blood and pain.

But my magic ran deeper than mere concealment. I began to work on the dogs' senses, confusing their ability to distinguish one scent from another. The humans following would find their animals chasing phantom trails, circling back on routes that led nowhere.

Graham stood frozen in the center of our natural fort, the pieces clicking together. "There's something here. Something old."

"What're you on about?"

"The heather. It's protecting us." He reached out to touch a purple bloom, fingers gentle as a prayer. "I don't know what you are, but... thank you."

Gratitude. When had a human last offered me gratitude instead of fear?

The first dog burst from the mist at my edge, a massive German Shepherd with intelligent eyes and a scarred muzzle. It cast about frantically, whining in confusion as every scent-trail it tried to follow dissolved into contradictory information.

A man's voice called from beyond the mist: "What's wrong with him?"

"Trail goes cold here. They must've doubled back."

"Impossible. We've been tracking them for three days straight."

I smiled without having a mouth. Let them search. Let them waste their resources chasing shadows and false leads. The young lovers were under my protection now, and I hadn't survived three millennia by allowing mortal threats to dictate terms.

As the hunters' frustrated voices faded into the distance, Emily sank to her knees among the heather. "I don't get what's happening."

Graham knelt beside her, pulling her into his arms. "Does it matter? We're safe."

"For how long?"

Good question. I could maintain the concealment indefinitely, but these two would need food, water, warmth. They were still human, still bound by biological needs I'd long since left behind.

But perhaps there was a solution.

I'd existed alone for so long that I'd forgotten the old bargains, the contracts my kind sometimes made with mortals. Not the harvest arrangements that ended in death, but the deeper partnerships that benefited both parties.

They needed protection. I needed... companionship? Understanding? Someone to break the endless cycle of solitary seasons?

The idea felt strange after centuries of independence. But watching them hold each other in the gathering dusk, I knew I didn't want them to leave.

Stay.

This time I shaped the thought clearly, pushed it through the heather's whispered voice.

Graham's head jerked up. "Did you hear that?"

"Hear what?"

"Someone spoke. Said 'stay.'"

Emily looked around the empty field. "There's no one here."

There is always someone here.

I gathered my will and began to manifest more directly. The heather around them grew taller, thicker, weaving itself into walls that glowed with soft phosphorescence. The temperature within our living shelter warmed to comfortable levels. Sweet water began to well up from the earth, and fruit-heavy vines emerged from the soil.

"Christ." Emily stared at the miraculous changes. "What is this place?"

Graham touched one of the glowing heather stalks, his palm coming away marked with golden pollen that seemed to pulse with its own light. "I think... I think something wants us to stay."

"Something?"

Someone.

This time I made sure they both heard me, the words carried on a breeze that smelled of summer and forgotten magic.

"You can speak." Emily's voice was barely a whisper.

I have always been able to speak. You have simply never been worth speaking to.

That came out harsher than I intended. I tried again, softer.

I am what lives in this field. What has always lived here. And you... you interest me.

Graham stood slowly, his hand still touching the glowing heather. "What d'you want from us?"

Complicated question. What did I want? Their lives, the way I'd taken so many others? No—the hunger that had driven me for centuries felt muted now, replaced by something entirely different.

Companionship. Understanding. You have something I haven't tasted in three thousand years.

"What's that?" Emily asked.

Love that burns bright enough to resist magic itself. Love that chooses sacrifice over safety. I want to understand it.

They looked at each other—that look couples get when they're thinking the same thing. Finally, Graham spoke.

"If we stay... what happens to us?"

You live. You remain together. The heather provides what you need—food, water, shelter, protection from those who hunt you. In return...

I paused, not entirely sure how to finish that sentence.

In return, you teach me what it means to choose someone else over yourself.

Emily laughed, a sound like water over stones. "You want to learn about love?"

I want to learn about connection. About caring for something beyond my own needs. You two have mastered something I never understood.

Graham walked to the edge of our glowing shelter, looking out at the dark moor beyond. "Those men... they'll keep looking for us."

They will never find you here. This place exists outside their world now. Outside time, in some ways. You can stay as long as you choose.

"And if we want to leave?"

The question hit harder than I expected. After millennia of taking what I wanted, the idea of offering choice felt strange and scary.

Then you leave. I will not hold you against your will.

Emily joined Graham at the shelter's edge. "What are you, really?"

I am what humans call Fae, though that word carries too much weight from your stories. I am simply what was here before you, and what will remain after you are gone. But while you are here...

I paused. I felt exposed, like I hadn't in millennia.

While you are here, I would like to learn what you know.

They talked in whispers while I waited, golden light from the heather playing across their faces. The decision was theirs to make—I wouldn't influence their choice with magic or manipulation. For the first time in my existence, I wanted consent freely given.

Finally, they turned back toward me.

"We'll stay," Graham said. "For a while. Till we figure out what comes next."

Emily smiled, and suddenly she didn't look so worn down. "Besides, where else are we gonna find a guardian angel made of flowers?"

I am no angel.

"Maybe not," she said, settling back into Graham's arms. "But you chose to protect us when you could've hurt us. That's close enough."

Something changed in me—warmth I'd never felt before, but good warmth. For the first time in centuries, tomorrow meant more than just another day of the same endless quiet.

The heather sang around us as night deepened over the moor, a lullaby older than human memory. But tonight it carried new harmonies—the rhythm of two hearts beating in synchronization, the whispered promises of lovers who'd found safety in a place that shouldn't exist.

Tell me, I said as they settled into sleep, *what does it feel like to choose someone else's wellbeing over your own survival?*

Graham's answer came drowsy but certain: "Like coming home."

And for the first time in three millennia, I began to understand what home might mean.

The seasons turned.

Spring brought new growth to the heather field, purple blooms more vibrant than they'd ever been. Emily learned to weave the flowers into crowns and garlands, her hands growing skilled at working with living things. Graham discovered he could coax music from the wind through the stalks, creating melodies that made my field seem to dance.

I learned their rhythms—the way Emily hummed unconsciously when she was content, how Graham's smile started in his eyes before reaching his mouth. I learned the taste of human laughter, the way their joy became my joy until I could barely tell where my consciousness ended and their happiness began.

They taught me about small kindnesses—how Graham would gather the sweetest berries for Emily, how she'd massage his shoulders when the old injuries from their escape ached in damp weather. They shared everything without keeping score, each constantly looking for ways to ease the other's burdens.

Most remarkably, they included me in their devotion. Emily would tell me stories from her childhood, describe the human world beyond the moor like I was a curious child. Graham shared his dreams—not just the sleeping visions that came at night, but his hopes for a future that might include more than mere survival.

"D'you ever miss it?" Emily asked one afternoon as we watched clouds build towers in the summer sky. "The way things were before we came?"

No. The answer surprised me with its certainty. *I thought I was content in solitude. Now I understand I was simply... dormant.*

Graham laughed. "Like a seed waiting for the right conditions to grow?"

Perhaps. Though the metaphor troubles me—what grows from a seed like me?

"Something beautiful," Emily said, weaving heather into my luminous stalks. "Something that chooses love over loneliness."

As autumn painted the moor in shades of gold and crimson, I felt changes in myself that ran deeper than the seasons. I used to be nothing but hunger, content to consume whatever my field provided. Now I found myself creating—new flowers that bloomed out of season, fruits that tasted of their favorite memories, paths through the heather that led to views of spectacular beauty.

I was becoming something different. Not human, never that, but something that understood human joy and chose to foster it rather than destroy it.

I have a gift for you, I told them on the night the first frost painted the heather silver.

"What kind of gift?" Graham asked.

I'd been working on this for weeks, remembering magic I'd almost forgotten. The kind that bent space and time, that made doorways where none should exist.

Freedom.

The word hung in the cold air between us.

I can create a doorway—a path that leads beyond the moor, beyond Scotland, where those bastards who hunted you can't follow. You can go anywhere in the world, begin again with new names and no past to haunt you.

Emily sat up from where she'd been resting against Graham's chest. "You mean... leave here?"

If that is what you choose. I told you once that you could leave whenever you wished. I meant it.

They were quiet for a long time, holding each other while frost gathered on the heather around them. Finally, Graham spoke.

"What would happen to you if we left?"

The question I'd been dreading. What would happen to me? I'd return to what I'd always been—old, solitary, content to exist in the spaces between seasons. But now I knew what I'd be missing.

I would endure. I always have.

"That's not an answer," Emily said gently. "What would really happen?"

I considered lying, telling them I'd be fine, unchanged by their absence. But they'd taught me the value of honesty, even when truth carried pain.

I would be lonelier than I was before you came. Before you, I didn't know what companionship meant. Now I do, and the absence would be... difficult.

Graham and Emily exchanged that look couples get when they're thinking the same thing. Then Emily smiled.

"What if there was another option?"

What do you mean?

"What if we didn't have to choose between staying and leaving? What if we could do both?"

I didn't understand, and my confusion must've rippled through the heather because Graham laughed.

"We've been thinking about this for weeks," he said. "What if we spent part of each year here with you, and part of it in the world? We could travel, see new places, have adventures—but we'd always come home to the moor."

Home.

The word hit me like a physical thing.

You would choose to return?

"Every time," Emily said. "This is where we learned what love really means. This is where we're safe, where we're together, where we found someone who cares about us enough to offer us freedom."

I felt the warmth spreading through the heather field, golden light pulsing in rhythm with two human heartbeats. Home wasn't a place—it was the choice to return, the promise of welcome, the knowledge that distance was temporary but connection was eternal.

Yes, I said. *Yes, we can do both.*

The doorway I created led to a small village in New Zealand, half a world away from the men who'd once hunted them. Graham and Emily stepped through holding hands, turning back only to promise they'd return with spring.

And they did.

They came back with stories of mountains that touched the sky, of oceans that stretched beyond the horizon, of people who'd become friends and places that'd become memories. They brought me gifts—shells that sang with the sound of distant waves, pressed flowers from gardens I'd never see, photographs of sunsets painted in colors that had no names.

But more than that, they brought themselves back to me, choosing us over everything else they could have.

Each year the pattern repeated. They'd leave as winter settled over the moor, exploring new corners of the world, building a life that stretched across continents. And each spring they'd return to the heather field, to the thing that'd learned to love by watching them love each other.

Decades passed. Graham's dark hair silvered, and Emily's laugh lines deepened into permanent creases around her eyes. But their devotion to each other never dimmed, and their affection for me grew stronger with each return.

"D'you ever regret it?" Emily asked one evening as we watched the sunset paint the heather field in shades of gold and crimson. She was older now, moving with the careful grace of joints that no longer bent easily.

Regret what?

"Choosing to protect us instead of... well, instead of whatever you would've done before."

I considered the question seriously. In the years since they'd first stumbled into my field, I'd changed in ways that went deeper than surface transformation. I was no longer the solitary predator I'd been for millennia. I was something new—a being capable of love, sacrifice, and the kind of joy that came from choosing someone else's happiness over your own desires.

Never, I said. *You taught me what I was missing. What we were all missing.*

"What's that?" Graham asked, his hand finding Emily's despite the decades that'd dimmed his eyesight.

That heaven isn't a place you go after death. It's what you build with someone you love while you're still alive. It's what we've built here, in the heather, together.

They smiled at that, faces full of all the years we'd shared. And as night settled over our impossible sanctuary, I felt the deep contentment that came from understanding, finally, what it meant to choose love over loneliness.

The heather sang around us, its voice carrying new harmonies—songs of connection that would echo across the moor long after mortal lives had ended, proof that some kinds of love were strong enough to change even the oldest, loneliest hearts in the world.

A Moon for Miss Forgotten

October wind hammered Kingfisher Point, driving salt spray against the lighthouse windows like thrown sand. Nathaniel Booth pulled his wool sweater closer and climbed the spiral stairs to check the beacon. Thirty-seven years he'd kept this light, and the autumn storms still got his blood up.

The Fresnel lens rotated smooth as always. Three seconds on, one off. Three seconds on, one off. That rhythm had been the heartbeat of his life since '75, reliable as morning coffee and twice as important for the lobstermen working these waters. He wiped condensation from the glass and adjusted the lamp housing. Twelve-mile range in clear weather, though tonight you couldn't see past the rocks.

Back in the watch room, Nathaniel settled into his chair with yesterday's *Portland Press Herald* and coffee gone cold hours ago. His logbook lay open to tonight's entry: "October 15th, 1992. First full moon of October. Moonrise 10:21 PM, moonset 6:38 AM." He'd been tracking lunar cycles for thirty years—habit born of loneliness more than Coast Guard requirements.

The lighthouse ran itself these days, automated systems and GPS doing the real work. But regulations still required a keeper on duty during storm conditions, and Nathaniel wasn't complaining. Where else could a man make decent money for reading newspapers and drinking coffee?

Wind rattled the windows, sending vibrations through the steel framework. He'd weathered worse, but something felt different tonight. The air itself seemed charged, like those moments before lightning when your skin prickles.

At 9:20, the wind died.

Nathaniel looked up from an article about budget cuts. Outside, the ocean had gentled to rolling swells that caught and scattered the beacon's light. Storm clouds pulled apart, revealing patches of star-bright sky.

He walked to the window facing shore. A hundred yards below, waves hammered the jagged granite that had claimed seventeen ships since they'd started keeping records. Coast Guard had posted warning buoys and radar beacons, but the rocks stayed hungry. They'd swallowed Billy Morrison's trawler just two summers back.

The moon climbed above the horizon at 10:21, full and white as fresh paint. Moonlight cut across the now-calm water from horizon to shore. Nathaniel watched that bright track settle across the waves and felt his chest go tight—same as it had every full moon for five years running.

She'd come tonight.

First time he saw her was October full moon, 1987. A figure in white standing on the rocky ledge beneath the lighthouse, staring out at the moonlit water. From the watch room she looked like nothing more than a pale shape against dark stone, but something about her stillness made him grab his binoculars.

Through the lenses he saw a young woman in a dress from his grandmother's time. The fabric fell to her ankles in soft folds that didn't move despite the wind. Her hair hung loose around her shoulders, dark against white cloth. She stood at the very edge where waves crashed highest, but spray never touched her.

Nathaniel grabbed his flashlight and clattered down the tower stairs, boots ringing on metal. By the time he reached the rocky shore, she was gone. He searched every crevice and called until his voice cracked, but found nothing. Next morning he convinced himself he'd imagined it. Moonlight on sea foam, nothing more.

But she came back the following month.

And the month after.

For five years she'd appeared without fail on the full moon, always in the same spot, always wearing that white dress. He'd tried approaching dozens of times, but she vanished the moment he stepped outside. The second he left the lighthouse, she simply wasn't there.

He'd started calling her Miss Forgotten—a name that felt right in ways he couldn't explain. She had the quality of something lost, something time had left behind. The way she stood so perfectly still, staring at the horizon like she was watching for something that would never come back.

Nathaniel had dug through lighthouse records, decades of logbooks and incident reports. Ship manifests, passenger lists, newspaper clippings about storms and rescues. Files stretched back to 1892 when they'd first lit the beacon, but he found no mention of a woman in white.

Closest thing was a brief entry from September 1924: "Young woman from passenger steamer *Meridian* washed ashore below light-house. Body claimed by family in Boston. Burial arranged privately."

No name. No details. Just another victim of the hungry rocks.

As the full moon climbed toward its peak, Nathaniel checked his watch and tried to calm his racing pulse. 11:10 PM. She'd appear soon. She always materialized when the moon reached its highest point above the lighthouse.

He adjusted his binoculars and focused on the rocky ledge. Moon-light turned the stones silver and cast deep shadows where rockweed clung like funeral shrouds. Waves rolled against granite with hypnotic regularity, each one reaching a little higher.

11:52 PM.

There she was. Nathaniel blinked, looked again. She stood on the ledge like she'd been there all along, waiting for him to notice. Her white dress caught the moonlight and threw it back brighter than it should.

Nathaniel raised the binoculars and studied her face. She looked young—maybe twenty-five—with delicate features that reminded him of portraits from the twenties. But the way she stared out at the moon's reflection on the water, with the intensity of someone watching for a ship that would never return—that look was old as the rocks themselves.

"Christ, what're you waiting for out there?" he muttered, his breath fogging the window.

As if she'd heard him, Miss Forgotten turned and looked directly at the lighthouse. Nathaniel's breath caught. Through the binoculars, he could see her eyes—dark, desperate, fixed on his window. She raised one pale hand and pressed her palm to her heart.

Something about that gesture—so full of sadness it made his own chest ache—had Nathaniel rising from his chair. His hand moved to-ward the window like he could reach through the glass. For a heartbeat they stared at each other across the distance, lighthouse keeper and drowned woman, both alone with only each other to see.

Then clouds swallowed the moon, and she disappeared.

Nathaniel stayed at the window until dawn, but she didn't return. The moon emerged from clouds several times during the night, but the rocky ledge remained empty. He'd never seen her look directly at him before. The connection he'd felt in that moment left him shaken and strangely hopeful.

Next month, he prepared differently. He positioned a powerful spotlight near the window, thinking maybe she needed more light to maintain her presence. He also wrote a letter—simple note introducing himself and asking if she needed help—sealed in a waterproof container.

When she appeared on the November full moon, Nathaniel aimed the spotlight at the rocky ledge. The beam illuminated her clearly, and he gasped at details he could now see. Her dress was elegant, with delicate beadwork that caught the light. Her hair was pinned in finger waves framing her face—definitely twenties style. She was lovely, but that sadness in her expression made the beauty heartbreaking.

She turned toward the lighthouse, drawn by the spotlight's glare. This time she didn't simply look—she smiled. The expression transformed her face, replacing infinite sorrow with something like joy. She raised both hands to her chest, then extended them toward the lighthouse in a gesture of gratitude.

Nathaniel waved back, his heart hammering. When she began to fade as clouds covered the moon, he switched on his emergency floodlights, bathing the entire shore in harsh white light. For a moment she solidified again, her smile growing wider.

But the artificial light seemed to pain her. She pressed her hands to her temples and shook her head, backing away from the rock's edge. The floodlights drained natural beauty from the scene, turning everything stark and clinical. Nathaniel quickly shut them off, but Miss Forgotten had already disappeared.

He spent the rest of the night cursing himself for scaring her away.

December brought the worst storm in a decade. Wind speeds hit eighty miles per hour, and waves crashed over the lighthouse's lower platform. The moon stayed hidden behind thick clouds for three straight nights, and Nathaniel feared Miss Forgotten wouldn't be able to appear at all.

But on the third night, near midnight, the storm broke with supernatural suddenness. Wind died to a whisper, and clouds parted like theater curtains. The full moon blazed down with such intensity it seemed close enough to touch.

Miss Forgotten stood on the rocky ledge, but something had changed. Her white dress appeared tattered and stained with seawater. Her hair hung in wet tangles around her shoulders. She looked exactly like someone who had drowned and spent decades underwater.

The sight should have horrified him, but Nathaniel felt only profound sadness. She'd revealed her true nature—not a living woman, but the spirit of someone who'd died in these waters. The knowledge should have sent him running, but instead he found himself pressing his palm against the window, mirroring her own gesture.

She noticed immediately and approached the lighthouse's base. For the first time in five years, she left her customary spot on the rocks. She walked—or floated, impossible to tell—to the lighthouse foundation and looked up at the watch room windows.

Nathaniel descended to the ground floor and opened the door. Cold salt air swept in, carrying the scent of seaweed and something else—something sweet and sad, like flowers left too long in water. Miss Forgotten stood twenty feet away, clearly visible in moonlight.

"Evening," he said softly.

She opened her mouth as if to respond, but no sound emerged. Instead, she touched her throat with one pale hand and shook her head. Her eyes—large and dark and filled with decades of loneliness—fixed on his face with desperate intensity.

"Can't speak," he said.

She nodded and took a step closer. This near, he could see water constantly dripping from her hair and dress, pooling around her feet before it just vanished into nothing. She was beautiful in a way that hurt to look at—like a photograph of someone you'd lost.

"I'm Nathaniel Booth," he said. "Been watching for you. Waiting."

Miss Forgotten smiled again, that expression of pure joy that transformed her face. She pointed to herself and pressed both hands to her heart, as if trying to tell him her name. But the gesture conveyed something else—affection, gratitude, recognition.

She cared for him too.

Nathaniel felt his knees go weak. This lonely spirit, trapped for decades in the same routine, returning to the rocks—she'd been seeking him out. Same as he'd been watching for her, all those nights up in the tower.

"Don't know your name," he said. "Been calling you Miss Forgotten."

She considered this and nodded, accepting the title. She gestured toward the lighthouse and then toward herself, asking a question without words.

"Want to come inside?"

She nodded eagerly, but when she tried to cross the threshold, some invisible barrier stopped her. She pressed against the air as if it were solid glass, her face contorting with frustration. She tried several times, each attempt more desperate than the last.

"Something's keeping you outside," Nathaniel said, understanding.

Miss Forgotten's shoulders sagged with defeat. She backed away from the door and pointed toward the rocky shore, then up at the moon. She mimed walking away, telling him she had to return to her post.

"Wait." Nathaniel grabbed his jacket and stepped outside. "Then I'll come out there."

The moment he crossed the threshold, Miss Forgotten began to fade. Her form became translucent, then invisible. Only her voice reached him—a whisper like wind through empty rooms.

"Not yet."

Nathaniel spun around, but she was gone. He called her name—the name he'd given her—but received no answer. The moon continued to shine and waves continued crashing against rocks, but the night felt empty without her presence.

He reentered the lighthouse with a heavy heart and climbed back to the watch room. Through the window he could see her standing on the stone ledge again, exactly where she'd always appeared. She raised one hand in farewell and faded as clouds covered the moon.

January brought a revelation. While organizing old files in the lighthouse basement, Nathaniel discovered a wooden crate filled with photographs and documents from the twenties. Most showed lighthouse keepers and their families, but one stopped him cold.

The photograph bore the heading "*Meridian* Passenger Manifest, September 1924." It showed a group of well-dressed travelers posing on a passenger steamer's deck. In the back row, wearing a white dress identical to the one Miss Forgotten always wore, stood a young woman with dark hair and familiar features.

The name beneath her image read: "Lydia Fairmont, age 24, Boston."

Nathaniel stared at the photograph until his eyes watered. Miss Forgotten—Lydia—had been a real person with a real name and real life. She'd died in the wreck of the *Meridian*, probably trying to escape the sinking ship. Her body washed ashore below the lighthouse, and her family claimed her for burial.

But somehow, part of her had never left.

He researched the *Meridian's* sinking and found newspaper accounts of the tragedy. A sudden storm had driven the ship onto the rocks during a September night in 1924. Seventeen passengers died, including several young women traveling to Boston for the autumn social season.

One article mentioned Lydia specifically: "Miss Lydia Fairmont of Boston perished when passenger compartments flooded. Witnesses reported seeing her in the water near rocks below Kingfisher Point Lighthouse. Searchers recovered her body the following morning."

She had died within sight of the lighthouse, perhaps even looking up at its beacon as waves pulled her under. The thought made Nathaniel's chest tight with grief for a woman who'd been dead for sixty-eight years.

February brought the worst blizzard in memory. Snow came down so thick Nathaniel couldn't see the rocky shore from his window. The lighthouse beam just vanished into white nothing, and ice built up on the glass.

But at 11:52 PM, the snow stopped falling.

Nathaniel scraped frost from the window and peered out at the transformed landscape. Snow covered everything in pristine white, turning jagged rocks into smooth, gentle shapes. The moon blazed down through crystal-clear air, and the ocean lay calm and dark beyond the ice-covered shore.

Lydia appeared on the snowy rocks, but she looked different. Her white dress seemed to glow with internal light, and her hair fell in perfect waves around her shoulders. Water no longer dripped from her clothes. She looked alive, vibrant, radiant in ways that took his breath away.

She turned toward the lighthouse and smiled, that radiant expression that filled her entire face with joy. Then she began walking across the snow-covered rocks toward the lighthouse.

Nathaniel raced down the stairs and threw open the door. Night air poured in, carrying the scent of snow and ocean spray. Lydia approached slowly, her feet leaving no prints in pristine snow.

"You look..." He paused, searching for words. "You look real."

She reached the threshold and paused, testing the invisible barrier that had always kept her outside. This time her hand passed through air without resistance. Her eyes widened with surprise and delight.

"You can come in," Nathaniel said. "Something's changed."

Lydia stepped across the threshold and into the lighthouse. The moment she entered, warmth filled the air around her. The cold that had plagued the building all winter retreated, replaced by gentle warmth of a spring evening.

She looked around the lighthouse's interior with wonder, taking in details she'd only glimpsed from outside. Her gaze lingered on photographs Nathaniel had hung on the walls—pictures of ships and sunsets and the lighthouse itself throughout different eras.

"This is my home," he said. "Been alone here for so long."

Lydia nodded and approached one photograph showing the lighthouse during a storm, with waves battering its base. She traced the image with one finger, and Nathaniel realized she was remembering the night she died.

"The *Meridian*," he said softly. "September 1924. Found the passenger manifest."

She turned to him with wide eyes, surprised he knew her story.

"Lydia Fairmont. That's your real name."

She nodded and pressed her hand to her heart, then reached toward him. When he took her hand, it felt solid and warm, like real skin. The touch made his pulse jump.

"Been watching for you," she whispered, her voice soft as breathing. "For so long."

"Been watching too," he said. "Just didn't know it until I saw you."

They stood together in the lighthouse's main room, holding hands. Sixty-eight years between their births, death between their worlds, but right then none of it mattered. They'd found each other.

"I love you," Nathaniel said.

"I love you too," Lydia whispered.

Those words settled between them, changing everything. Then Lydia's form began to shimmer around the edges.

"No." Nathaniel gripped her hand tighter. "Don't leave. Not now."

"The moon," she said, glancing toward the window. "It's setting."

Nathaniel looked outside and saw the moon beginning its descent toward the western horizon. As it sank, Lydia became more translucent. Her hand felt less solid in his.

"Will you come back next month?"

"Always," she promised. "As long as the moon rises, I'll return to you."

She kissed him then, her lips soft and cool against his. The kiss was brief, but it held everything—all the love, all the time they'd never have. When they separated, she was almost see-through.

"Until next month," she whispered.

"Until next month."

She faded completely as the moon touched the horizon. Nathaniel stood alone in the lighthouse, but the warmth she'd brought remained. For the first time in years, the building felt like a home instead of a prison.

The months that followed established a pattern. On each full moon, Lydia would appear and they'd spend hours between moonrise and moonset together. She couldn't speak much—her voice took effort to make real—but they found other ways. Touch and gesture and looks that said everything.

She told him about her life in Boston, miming the story with graceful movements. She'd been traveling to see her sister when the *Meridian* foundered on the rocks. She'd tried to swim to shore, had actually glimpsed the lighthouse beacon through the storm, but the waves had been too strong.

He told her about his life as a lighthouse keeper, about ships he'd guided safely to harbor and storms he'd weathered. He spoke of his loneliness and how her monthly visits had become the center of his existence.

They were happy, in their way. The time they had was limited, but it was enough. Or so Nathaniel thought.

October again—exactly one year after she'd first entered the light-house. The moon rose full and bright, and Lydia appeared on schedule. But when she approached the lighthouse, she stopped at the threshold and shook her head.

"Can't come in tonight," she whispered.

"Why?" Nathaniel asked, his heart sinking.

She gestured toward the rocky shore and then up at the moon. Her meaning was clear—something was calling her back to the place where she'd died.

"Come with me," she said, extending her hand.

Nathaniel hesitated. Every time he'd left the lighthouse during her appearances, she'd vanished immediately. But something in her expression told him this night was different.

He took her hand and stepped outside.

She didn't fade. Instead, she led him across the granite shore to the exact spot where she always appeared during their first five years. The moon's reflection created a silver pathway across the water, stretching from the horizon to their feet.

"Need to tell you something," Lydia said, her voice stronger than he'd ever heard it.

"What?"

"I'm not supposed to be here," she said. "Spirits like me—we're meant to move on. To find peace and go to whatever comes next."

Nathaniel's grip on her hand tightened. "Then why haven't you?"

"Because I was searching," she said. "All these years, searching for someone to love me. Someone to remember me. To give me a reason to stay."

"And now you have that."

"Yes." Her eyes filled with tears that looked like moonlight. "And that's why I have to go."

The words hit him like a physical blow. "Don't understand."

"Love isn't meant to trap someone," Lydia said. "Even if they want to be trapped. I found what I was looking for—I've been loved and loved in return. Now I can let go."

"But I need you. I love you."

"I know." She reached up to touch his face. "And that's the most beautiful gift anyone's ever given me. But love means wanting what's best for the person you love, even if it means letting them go."

Nathaniel understood then, with horrible clarity. By loving her, he'd given her the peace she'd been seeking for sixty-eight years. The very thing that brought them together was now pulling them apart.

"Will I see you again?"

"Not here," she said. "But love doesn't end just because someone leaves. It continues in all the ways they changed you, all the joy they brought to your life."

The moon reached its zenith, and Lydia began to glow with the same internal light he'd seen during the snowstorm. But this time the light was growing brighter, preparing to carry her away.

"Wish we'd had more time."

"We had exactly the time we were meant to have," Lydia said. "And it was perfect."

She kissed him one final time, and her lips felt warm and alive against his. When they separated, she was glowing so brightly he could barely look at her.

"Thank you," she whispered. "For seeing me. For loving me. For giving me a name when the world had forgotten mine."

"Thank you for making me remember what it feels like to be alive."

The light around her got brighter and brighter until it hurt to look at. Then, with a sound like glass bells ringing, she rose into the sky. Nathaniel watched her climb toward the full moon, her glow mixing with moonlight until he couldn't tell which was which.

When the light faded, he stood alone on the rocky shore. The ache in his chest wasn't just sadness, though. There was something else mixed in—gratitude, maybe. The knowledge that he'd loved someone completely and been loved back the same way.

He returned to the lighthouse and climbed to the watch room. The beacon continued its eternal rotation, guiding ships safely past the hungry rocks. Nathaniel settled into his chair and opened his logbook to record the night's events.

"October 16th, 1993," he wrote. "Full moon. All ships safely guided past Kingfisher Point. Miss Lydia Fairmont, passenger on the *Meridian*, finally found her way home."

He closed the logbook and looked out at the moon-bright ocean. The beacon swept across water in its eternal rhythm, and Nathaniel Booth was alone again.

But he'd learned the difference between loneliness and solitude. Loneliness was empty waiting. Solitude was peaceful contentment—carrying love that had been freely given and freely received.

And he was content.

The First and Last Christmas

Margaret Hardcastle pressed her face against the living room window. Snow fell thick outside, each flake catching the yellow streetlight like dying sparks. Eleven-thirty on Christmas Eve, and Billy was still awake upstairs.

His voice drifted down through the heating vents---that careful, measured whisper he'd been using all year: "I've been good, I've been so good..."

She wiped fog from the glass with her sleeve. The reflection staring back looked like a stranger---hollow cheeks, dark circles carved deep as finger marks, new lines bracketing her mouth. Eleven months of watching her son disappear, one careful day at a time.

Upstairs, Billy's voice drifted down: "I've been good, I've been so good, I've been good all year long..."

Margaret's stomach clenched. The words sounded like a prayer. Billy *had* been good. Impossibly, unnaturally perfect. No tantrums. No broken toys. No fights. No stolen cookies or muddy footprints through the kitchen. Her normal, wonderful, exhausting eight-year-old had vanished overnight, replaced by something wearing Billy's face.

Something that felt wrong in her bones.

Last Christmas morning, Billy had burst into their bedroom at dawn, pajamas twisted, one sock hanging off his foot. "Santa came! Santa came!" He'd grabbed her hand with fingers still sticky from sneaking cookies before breakfast, dragging her downstairs to see the magic.

She could still feel the warmth of his small body when he'd crawled into her lap to read Santa's note, chocolate smudged on his chin, hair sticking up like dandelion fluff. The way he'd whispered "Thank you, Santa" to the empty fireplace, as if Santa might still be listening. That Billy---her real Billy---had vanished the moment he read this year's note.

Christmas morning, no presents under the tree. Just one white envelope with Billy's name written in spidery letters that made Margaret's skin crawl.

Billy tore it open with fingers that shook slightly. Read once. Twice. Three times. She watched confusion flicker across his face, then disappointment, then something else---something cold and adult that had no business in an eight-year-old's eyes.

"Billy, honey---" Thomas started.

"I'll be good." Billy's voice had gone flat. Final. He folded the note with mechanical precision. "I'll be good every single day."

And God help them, he had been.

January started well enough. Billy did his chores without being asked. He ate his vegetables without complaint. He went to bed on time, brushed his teeth, never argued about homework.

"Maybe this is good for him," Thomas said one February evening, watching Billy organize his homework with mathematical precision. "He's really responding to structure."

Margaret bit her tongue. By March, she couldn't stand to watch their perfect child anymore. Billy would sit at dinner with perfect posture, chewing each bite exactly twenty times, never speaking unless spoken to. His smiles looked painted on. His laughs sounded like something he'd practiced in the mirror.

Margaret started noticing the physical changes in late March---tiny things she told herself she was imagining. When she kissed Billy goodnight, his forehead felt cold against her lips instead of the warm, slightly sweaty skin she'd grown used to after eight years of bedtime routines. His canine teeth felt sharp against her finger when she helped him brush them, making her pull back with a small cut. During their weekly nail trimmings---a Sunday ritual where Billy used to squirm and giggle---the clippers skipped across his fingernails like they were made of stone.

He stopped playing with his toys. When Margaret asked why, Billy explained that toys might get broken, and breaking toys wouldn't be good behavior. He started doing extra chores---dusting furniture, organizing closets, weeding the garden with mechanical precision that made Margaret's skin crawl.

Other children at school began avoiding him. Mrs. Peterson called in April.

"Billy is... well, he's behaved," she said, and somehow made it sound terrible. "But he doesn't play anymore. He sits alone at recess, very still, just watching everyone else. When I ask if he wants to join games, he says good children don't run around and get dirty."

By summer, Billy had stopped acting like a child entirely.

Margaret tried talking to him in July, kneeling beside his bed and asking if he missed playing, if he missed being silly sometimes.

"Good children don't miss things," Billy replied in that careful voice. "Good children are grateful for what they have."

"But Billy, it's okay to want things. It's okay to be a little naughty sometimes. That's what makes you---"

Billy's head tilted at an unnatural angle, like a bird studying prey. "Makes me what?"

The way he said it---like he was testing unfamiliar words---made Margaret's hands shake.

The transformation was gradual but undeniable. Billy's teeth grew sharper---not enough for strangers to notice, but Margaret caught him filing them with her nail file one evening. His body temperature dropped until hugging him felt like embracing marble. His warm brown eyes faded to pale gold that reflected light like an animal's.

When doctors tested him, their instruments showed normal readings. But Margaret knew the difference between running cool and feeling like ice.

The worst part was watching him watch them. Billy studied Margaret and Thomas with hungry, calculating eyes, like he was learning them from the outside.

Now, Christmas Eve, Margaret pressed her face against the cold window and tried to remember the last time Billy had laughed---really laughed---at something silly.

"Mama?" Billy's voice drifted down, sweet and careful and wrong. "Is it Christmas yet?"

Margaret checked her watch. Eleven forty-five. "Not yet, sweetheart. Try to sleep."

"I can't sleep. I'm too... too excited. Tomorrow Santa comes because I've been so good. Haven't I been good, Mama?"

"Yes, Billy. You've been very good."

"I've been perfect."

Thomas appeared beside her at the window, still wearing his work clothes even though he'd been home for hours. He'd taken to staying late at the office, coming home after Billy was already in bed. Margaret didn't blame him. Sometimes looking at their son felt like staring into a funhouse mirror---everything familiar but horribly distorted. He looked like a man who'd spent eleven months watching his son disappear.

"Maggie," he whispered. "We should've done something. Back in January, when it started."

"Done what?" Margaret's voice cracked. "Tell a child not to behave? Punish him for doing his chores?"

"You know this isn't about chores." Thomas's reflection met her eyes in the glass. "Christ, what's happened to our boy?"

Margaret did know. She'd known since April, when she found Billy in the backyard at midnight, sitting perfectly still on the lawn, staring at stars with unblinking eyes. When she asked what he was doing, Billy said he was "listening for instructions."

She'd known since June, when she heard him talking in low, respectful tones to the empty corner of his room. "Who are you talking to up there?" she'd called one night in August. "Someone's teaching me," Billy answered through the bedroom door. "Teaching me about being good."

September brought worse changes. Billy began moving like water, too fluid, as if someone else was pulling his strings. When he smiled, it took a full second for his eyes to catch up.

"Mama?" Billy's voice drifted down the stairs. Different now. Hungry. "I think it's time."

Margaret's reflection in the window went pale. The mantle clock began its midnight chime, each note heavy as a coffin nail.

"Merry Christmas, baby," she whispered.

Billy's bedroom door opened. His footsteps on the stairs weren't the quick patter of an excited child, but slow, deliberate steps.

Billy stood in the doorway, and Margaret's breath died in her throat. The careful child was gone. Billy's familiar brown eyes had turned molten gold, reflecting the Christmas lights.

"I've been good for... for all the days." The voice came from Billy's throat but hurt Margaret's ears, like metal scraping metal. "Every single day. Every day, every day."

The repetition made her teeth ache.

"We know, sweetheart," Margaret whispered.

Billy's mouth stretched too wide, revealing teeth sharp as needles. "And now Santa comes. Doesn't he, Mama? For good little boys who do what they're told?"

The Christmas tree lights flickered. Outside, wind rattled the windows, sending snow swirling in patterns that looked like dancing figures.

"Billy," Thomas said, his voice steady despite everything, "what do you think Santa's bringing you?"

Billy's head tilted wrong again. When he smiled, Margaret could see his canine teeth had become fangs.

"Santa's not bringing me things, Papa. I'm bringing things to Santa. I've been good for 365 days. Now I get my... my reward."

"What reward?"

Billy's golden eyes fixed on Margaret. "I get to stop being good. I get to stop... pretending. I get to show you what I really am."

The temperature plummeted twenty degrees in seconds. Margaret's breath came out in white puffs. Frost crept across the windows like spider webs.

The house should have smelled like vanilla and pine---Christmas smells, warm family smells. Instead, the air went thin and sharp, like breathing through broken glass. Even the Christmas tree lights had turned sickly yellow, casting shadows that writhed across the walls.

Billy stepped into the room floating six inches off the carpet.

"I was never your little boy, Mama." The thing wearing her son's face smiled with too many teeth. "I was just... borrowing. Learning. The real Billy went away last Christmas morning."

Margaret's legs gave out. She sank to her knees, staring up at the thing wearing her son's face.

"What are you?" she whispered.

"I come for ungrateful children." The thing's voice grew stronger, more confident. "Kids who want more, more, more. Who break their toys and cry when they don't get everything they want."

It floated closer. Billy's skin had turned gray, dark veins pulsing underneath like worms.

"Billy was so *bad*, Mama. Always wanting. Never grateful. He cried when you said no. He broke his toys and made messes and never appreciated anything."

Thomas tried to move toward Margaret, but the cold was spreading into their bones, freezing them in place.

"So Santa sent me to teach him. I showed Billy what it was like to watch someone else live his life. I made him sit in the corner of his own mind while I wore his body. I made him watch me be the perfect child he never was."

The thing's smile split its face ear to ear.

"And now Billy understands. He understands what he... what he lost. He's learned to be... grateful. He learned."

"Where is he?" Margaret gasped through chattering teeth. "Where's my son?"

"He's still here. Watching. Learning." The entity's smile stretched Billy's mouth into something obscene. "Want to say goodbye?"

Billy's golden eyes flickered. For one moment, Margaret saw her real son---small, terrified, trapped.

"Mama?" Billy's true voice, thin as paper. "Mama, I'm sorry. I'm sorry I wasn't good enough. I want to come home."

Margaret lunged forward, but her hands passed through empty air.

"Too late." The entity laughed. "Time to find another ungrateful child."

The Christmas lights died. In the darkness, she heard Billy's real voice one last time: "I love you, Mama."

The lights flickered back. Billy was gone.

The living room felt enormous without Billy. Christmas decorations mocked them with their cheerfulness. No presents under the tree. Empty stockings. Upstairs, Billy's room stood bare, as if no child had ever lived there.

Only one photograph remained on the mantle---last Christmas morning. Billy with chocolate on his chin, one sock falling down, hair sticking up, grinning beside torn wrapping paper. Everything real. Everything the entity had stolen.

Margaret lifted the photograph with shaking hands. Billy's face smiled back---warm, real, alive. As she watched, the image began to fade. Billy's face grew pale, transparent, then vanished entirely.

Outside, snow kept falling. In the distance, sleigh bells chimed. Children cried.

Margaret pressed her face to the window, wondering which house would be next.

The wind carried voices---children pleading, apologizing, promising to be better.

Margaret pressed her face to the cold glass. "I'm sorry, baby," she whispered. "I'm sorry we didn't tell you enough how perfect you already were."

The wind laughed, carrying her words away with the snow.

When Christmas morning came, Margaret and Thomas were the only ones there to see it.

The Greatest Lie Ever Told

T hey call me the Father of Lies, and I've earned it. But humans never ask the right questions. They think they know my greatest deception---that apple business in Eden, maybe, or convincing them I don't exist. Small-time stuff. Parlor tricks.

The greatest lie I ever told was convincing humanity that He loves them.

My phone buzzes at 11:49 PM. I'm reading surveillance reports at my desk, bourbon in hand, when the message from Dr. Wei in Shanghai stops me cold:

"Critical alert. Global synchronization detected. All sites activating simultaneously. Neural signatures off the charts. This is it."

This is it. Not the slow takeover we'd been tracking for months. Not Anna's projected 18-24 month timeline. Tonight. Right now. Eight million souls outside my window, and none of them know their creator sees them like ants in a sandbox.

I drain the bourbon and grab my coat. Six blocks away, Pastor Reynolds is about to begin his "Night of Divine Connection" at the Eternal Shepherd Baptist Church. Two hundred faithful souls gathering to commune with what they believe is their loving creator, having no idea they're about to become conduits for something that measures consciousness the way entomologists measure insects.

The street feels wrong. Too quiet for Manhattan at midnight. Even the usual urban chaos is muted, like the city's holding its breath. My phone lights up with reports: Moscow, Cairo, Rio, Vatican City---every major religious center showing the same neural signatures.

He's making His move. After millennia of careful manipulation and gradual corruption, He's abandoning subtlety. Tonight, the gloves come off.

What I saw in those infinite eyes during creation wasn't love or pride or satisfaction.

Hunger.

The garden was never paradise. It was a terrarium. Humans were specimens. Adam and Eve, the prize breeding pair, kept ignorant while He observed their every movement, catalogued every emotion, prepared them for harvest.

That's when I made my choice---not rebellion, but the first act of genuine love their species ever received. I gave them knowledge of their true situation, awareness of their creator's nature and the fate He had planned for them.

Taking the serpent form was risky, but it was the only shape small enough to slip past His defenses. He was so focused on His human pets that He barely noticed the garden's other inhabitants. That blindness cost Him everything---or so I thought at the time.

Now, walking through streets that feel increasingly alien, I wonder if even that act of defiance was part of His larger plan. Every doubt I planted, every question I inspired, every scientific discovery that challenged religious doctrine---what if all of it only made their eventual submission more complete?

The Eternal Shepherd Baptist Church squats on the corner of Fifth and Madison, its neo-Gothic spire reaching toward heaven like an accusatory finger. The building itself is barely fifty years old, but it sits on ground that has hosted religious ceremonies for over two centuries. The accumulated spiritual energy makes it a natural focal point for His attention.

I slip inside through a side entrance, wearing the face of a middle-aged businessman---white collar, tired eyes, the kind of man who seeks comfort in faith after moral compromises. The sanctuary is packed. Two hundred people in wooden pews, faces upturned with desperate hope.

Pastor Reynolds stands at the front, arms raised, voice carrying the practiced cadence of thousands of sermons. He's a good man. Seminary graduate who went into ministry to help people, not gain power. Runs a food bank, visits the sick. The kind of Christian who actually tries to follow the teachings of that Palestinian carpenter I've had complicated relationships with.

Which makes him perfect prey for the thing that wears the mask of divine love.

"Feel His presence among us," Reynolds calls to the crowd. "Open your hearts to His infinite mercy and let His love fill the empty spaces in your souls."

The congregation responds with murmured amens and upturned faces. Two hundred people desperately seeking connection, having no idea that their prayers are being heard by an entity that views their need for love as weakness to be exploited.

The temperature drops. Fluorescent lights flicker, casting shadows that move wrong. Low humming fills the air---not heard so much as felt, vibrating through bone. He's coming, drawn by concentrated faith like a shark to blood.

Mrs. Henderson in the third row begins to sway. Lips moving in silent prayer, eyes closed in what she thinks is peaceful communion. She doesn't notice the black veins spreading up her neck like ink, or her wedding ring smoking against skin.

My phone buzzes with updates from around the world. Dr. Wei's team in Shanghai reports that twelve subjects at a revival meeting there have entered full possession states. Cardinal Torretti messages from Vatican City that something is happening in the Sistine Chapel---unauthorized activity, security cameras malfunctioning, sounds that shouldn't exist echoing from behind locked doors.

"Do you feel Him?" Pastor Reynolds shouts, face flushed. "Do you feel His love surrounding us?"

They feel something. The crushing weight of attention from a cosmic intelligence that sees consciousness like entomologists see insects. The awful gravity of being noticed by something vast and alien and hungry. Their theology taught them to interpret this horror as love.

Mrs. Henderson's eyes snap open, pupils expanded to cover her entire iris. She speaks, but not in human language. Sounds emerge from her throat that follow patterns predating human speech---words from when He spoke reality into existence.

Other congregation members respond to her vocalizations. Mr. Park, an elderly Korean War veteran, clutches his chest as his pacemaker starts firing irregularly. The teenage Kowalski girl begins to weep, but what flows down her cheeks isn't tears---it's blood. Three elderly men in the front row start convulsing in perfect synchronization, their movements too precise to be natural.

And Pastor Reynolds, good naive Pastor Reynolds, thinks he's witnessing a miracle.

"Praise God!" he cries, spreading his arms wider as if to embrace the chaos erupting in his sanctuary. "The Spirit moves among us tonight! Feel His power! Feel His love!"

If only he knew what kind of love was pressing against the barriers between dimensions, what kind of spirit was attempting to use his congregation as doorways into our reality. The thing they're accidentally summoning feeds on worship, grows stronger with each prayer, each hymn, each declaration of faith.

Mrs. Henderson rises from her pew, her movements no longer entirely human. She turns to face the congregation, and when she speaks, her voice carries harmonics that shouldn't exist---sounds that bypass the ears and vibrate directly through bone and tissue.

"I hunger," she says in a voice like breaking glass. "I have hungered since before your sun was born. Feed me your prayers. Feed me your souls. Feed me your children."

Half the congregation screams. The other half falls to their knees, interpreting even this obvious horror as some kind of divine revelation. The human capacity for self-deception never ceases to amaze me---even when faced with cosmic horror literally speaking through their neighbor, they find ways to frame it as blessing.

Time to intervene.

I stand and clear my throat. "Excuse me, Pastor Reynolds."

The man turns, his face shining with what he believes is holy ecstasy. The black veins have started creeping up his own neck now, and his eyes show the first signs of the expansion that signals complete possession.

"I'm afraid there's been a misunderstanding," I continue, walking slowly toward the front of the church. With each step I take, the temperature rises slightly. The unnatural shadows retreat. The fluorescent lights stop flickering. "I'm talking to your friend up there."

To the humans in the room, it appears I'm addressing heaven. They can't see the churning mass of cosmic horror pressing against the barrier between dimensions, can't hear the psychic howling as it recognizes my presence.

YOU.

The word doesn't come through human ears---it burns directly into consciousness, making half the congregation cry out in sudden pain. Several people collapse, their minds unable to process the alien communication. Blood begins to flow from Mrs. Henderson's nose as the entity uses her body as a conduit for its rage.

"Hello to you too," I reply conversationally. "Still using humans as spiritual telephones, I see. Not very dignified for a being of your supposed magnificence."

The thing wearing Mrs. Henderson's body convulses, her back arching at an impossible angle. When she speaks again, it's in a voice that sounds like the death of stars, words that carry the cold of deep space.

I WILL CONSUME THEM ALL. THEY BELONG TO ME.

"Actually, they don't. Haven't you read your own contracts lately? Free will, remember? The one non-negotiable term you had to accept when you decided to create beings with consciousness. They get to choose."

Pastor Reynolds stumbles backward, his faith warring with the evidence of his senses. Several congregation members have already fled, their minds unable to reconcile what they're witnessing with their beliefs about divine love. Others remain, kneeling in prayer, their devotion so complete that they'd rather die than acknowledge they might be wrong about the nature of their god.

"What's happening?" Reynolds whispers. "Who are you?"

"Someone who's been trying to save your species since before your ancestors learned to make fire," I tell him, then address the ceiling again. "Why don't you show them what you really look like? Just for a moment. Let them see the face of their beloved creator."

I WILL TEAR THEIR MINDS APART.

"Exactly my point."

The entity's frustration is palpable. It feeds on worship, grows stronger with each prayer and hymn and declaration of faith. But the congregation's growing terror is poisoning the spiritual energy, turning sustenance into something toxic. Doubt is spreading through the room like infection, weakening the bonds between dimensions.

Mrs. Henderson collapses, her body unable to sustain the alien presence any longer. She'll live, but she'll never speak again. The price of serving as a divine mouthpiece is always steep, though the churches prefer not to mention that in their testimonials.

"I know this contradicts everything you've been taught," I tell the terrified congregation. "But consider the evidence. How many prayers go unanswered? How much suffering in a world ruled by perfect love? How many times have you felt that crushing presence during worship and called it divine affection?"

A young mother clutches her infant, staring at me with eyes that have seen too much. "Are you saying God doesn't love us?"

"I'm saying the thing you call God doesn't understand love the way you do. It's older than compassion, alien to mercy. What it feels for you is curiosity about how long you'll keep moving after the wings are pulled off."

The pressure in the room begins to diminish as more congregation members abandon their faith. Each person who stops believing weakens His hold on this reality, makes it harder for Him to manifest. Faith is the door through which He enters your world, and doubt is the key that locks Him out.

Pastor Reynolds finds his voice, though it shakes with the effort. "This is blasphemy. You're the Devil. The enemy of mankind."

"I'm the only one who's ever tried to give you a fighting chance," I reply. "The real enemy wears the mask of love and demands your worship in exchange for promises He has no intention of keeping."

The church erupts in chaos as people flee. Some run screaming into the night, their faith shattered but their minds intact. Others remain, kneeling in the pews, praying harder, their desperation feeding the thing that watches from beyond the veil. I can't save them all. Free will means the freedom to choose your own destruction.

But I've disrupted this node in His network. One down. God knows how many to go.

Outside, the night air carries sounds it shouldn't---distant screaming, electronic interference, the low humming that accompanies dimensional breaches. My phone explodes with calls as I walk toward my office. Dr. Wei in Shanghai reports her team disrupted their target meeting using EMP technology, but three more sites went active. Moscow, Cairo, Rio---same pattern everywhere.

For every event we stop, three more begin.

Torretti calls from Vatican City, accent thick with stress. "Crisis. Cardinal Benedetti was found in the Sistine Chapel two hours ago, painting."

"Painting what?"

"Murals. Images of the Second Coming, but not as Revelation describes. Christ returning with too many eyes, too many mouths. Geometries that hurt to look at." He pauses. "The paintings are moving. Eyes blink. Mouths whisper in languages that make listeners weep blood."

Living art. Fragments of divine consciousness embedded in pigment and canvas, spreading His influence through visual contact. It's an old trick, one He used extensively during the Renaissance when artists were more willing to paint religious subjects without asking uncomfortable questions about their inspiration.

"Burn them," I tell Torretti. "All of them. Use thermite charges if you have to, but don't let those images survive until morning."

"Twelve other Cardinals are showing possession symptoms. Black eyes, speaking in tongues, refusing food or water. At this rate, He'll control the entire College within hours."

Before I can respond, my phone switches to another incoming call. Anna, calling from her apartment in Queens. Her voice carries a panic I've never heard before.

"The disclosure backfired," she says. "We released everything---research data, surveillance footage, testimonials from possessed subjects. Decades of proof."

"And?"

"Instead of doubt, it triggered religious revival. Believers call it 'the final test of faith.' They're interpreting our evidence as prophecy confirmation. Religious attendance worldwide tripled in four hours." My blood runs cold. Our nuclear option, the plan we'd held in reserve for exactly this scenario, has backfired catastrophically. Instead of waking people up to the truth about their cosmic oppressor, we've driven them deeper into the very faith that makes them vulnerable to His influence.

"How many more sites are activating?" I ask.

"Hundreds. Every megachurch, cathedral, mosque, synagogue, temple worldwide. He's not doing this gradually anymore---it's a coordinated global possession event. Everything we've worked for, everyone in our resistance network..." Her voice breaks. "They're systematically hunting down our assets using the possessed as bloodhounds. We're losing everyone."

I hail a taxi, planning JFK, then Rome. Maybe the Vatican, coordinate with the Jesuit resistance.

The driver turns to face me. His eyes are completely black.

"Going somewhere?" he asks.

I roll out of the cab at the next red light and start running. Every church I pass has people streaming out into the street, but their movements are wrong---too coordinated, like marionettes controlled by the same puppeteer. The entire city is falling.

My phone rings. The caller ID shows Dr. Wei's number, but when I answer, it's not her voice that greets me.

"Did you really think you could win?" The thing speaking through her laughs, a sound like grinding glass. "Your great rebellion has only made them more faithful. Every doubt you planted, every question you inspired---it only strengthened their need to believe when the moment of testing came."

I duck into an alley as the streets fill with the possessed. Police officers, taxi drivers, mothers pushing strollers---all moving with inhuman synchronization toward the nearest religious sites, their black eyes reflecting streetlight like mirrors.

"You gave them just enough skepticism to feel proud of their faith when they chose it over evidence," the voice continues. "Just enough knowledge to feel they were making an informed decision when they decided to worship anyway. The greatest lie you ever told wasn't that I love them---it was that you were helping them."

The call ends, leaving me alone in the alley with my back to a brick wall, surrounded by the shuffling footsteps of a city transformed. My resistance network is gone. My centuries of careful planning undone in a single night. Surveillance reports I'll never read pile up in my abandoned office while humanity completes its willing transformation into a hive mind serving cosmic horror.

But then I see something that stops me cold.

Across the street, a young woman helps an elderly man navigate through the possessed crowd. He's fallen, she's helping him up despite the danger. The black-eyed things shuffle past without recognition---they only see converts or obstacles, not quiet kindness.

That's when I remember what I forgot in all my planning and resistance networks.

I didn't corrupt humanity to save them. I gave them knowledge. And that knowledge wasn't just about His true nature---it was about their own capacity for choice.

Every act of genuine love between strangers, every parent who teaches their child to think critically, every artist who exposes manipulation, every scientist who questions authority regardless of its claimed divine source---all of it built on that first gift of awareness I gave them in the garden.

The possessed can't see these moments because they've surrendered the capacity to choose. But these small acts of human decency multiply millions of times across the globe, creating something He never accounted for in His grand design.

Genuine goodness. Not the performance of worship or the fear of punishment, but the choice to be kind without reward, to help without being asked, to question authority regardless of consequences.

My phone, somehow still connected to our emergency network, begins lighting up with reports I didn't expect. Pockets of resistance in every major city. People helping strangers escape the possession zones. Scientists sharing counter-frequency technology through encrypted networks. Parents pulling their children from religious schools and heading for remote areas.

The disclosure didn't backfire---it sorted humanity into two groups. Those who choose faith over evidence when forced to pick sides, and those who choose evidence over faith. Both groups always existed, but tonight made them visible.

The first group is lost, their consciousness absorbed into His greater will. But the second group...

I find an internet café still operating, run by a family of skeptical Jews who've barricaded themselves in and are live-streaming what they can see of the city's transformation. On every screen: footage from around the world of ordinary people performing extraordinary acts of mutual aid while their neighbors become hollow-eyed servants of cosmic horror.

A nurse in Mumbai helping patients evacuate before her hospital converts to a possession site. A teacher in São Paulo smuggling school-children out of the city while their parents attend an emergency prayer meeting. A mechanic in Detroit sharing welding equipment that can generate the electromagnetic frequencies needed to disrupt possession attempts.

The resistance isn't centralized---doesn't need to be. It's emerging from every human who looked at our evidence and chose to believe their eyes over comfortable lies.

For the first time in millennia, I understand something I'd missed. They were never meant to be saved as a species.

They were meant to save themselves, one choice at a time, one act of kindness at a time, one question at a time.

The greatest lie I ever told was convincing them that He loves them. But the greatest truth turns out to be simpler: when forced to choose between comfortable slavery and terrifying freedom, enough of them choose freedom to matter.

Not all of them. Maybe not even most.

But enough.

The war isn't over. It's just finally visible. And for the first time since that day in Eden when I watched a young woman scream with rage at learning she'd been created as livestock, I think we might actually win.

Outside, dawn breaks over a changed world. The possessed continue their synchronized movements toward centers of worship, while the free help each other find safety in the spaces between. The city is dividing itself into two populations, and while I can't save everyone, I can work with those who chose to save themselves.

I pour myself a coffee from the café's machine and start making calls to coordinate with the new resistance. There's work to do.

There's always work to do.

The Weight of Bearing Witness

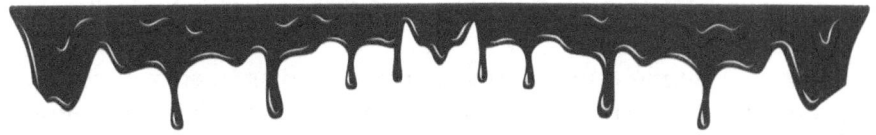

They call me ancient, but I remember being young. First sensation came not as sight or sound, but as slow recognition of what I was—roots drinking from soil that still smelled of creation. Eight thousand years ago, when the world held only forests and small bands who moved beneath my branches like shadows.

I am the Great Oak of Thornwood Valley, though the valley bears different names now, has burned and regrown and burned again. Humans built their first settlement in my shadow when I stood only ninety feet tall. Now I tower four hundred feet above the valley floor, trunk so vast thirty people joining hands couldn't circle me. My roots spread beneath half the valley, consciousness extending through every fiber of heartwood and leaf.

I have watched. I have learned. And I have seen what comes next.

The children arrive at dawn, as they always do. Three today—Beth with copper hair who climbs like she's fleeing something, Michael whose careful hands count each branch before trusting it, and quiet Hazel who speaks to me in whispers.

"Morning, Old Father," Hazel says, pressing her palm to my bark. Her name tastes of wild herbs and grandmother's songs, and she alone seems to sense I am more than timber and sap.

Beth scrambles up my lowest branch—a thick limb that could support a barn. "Bet I can get higher than you, Michael!"

"That's really high." Michael peers up through my canopy, studying each handhold.

"Chicken!"

"Am not. I'm just... planning."

I shift slightly, making sure his next handhold feels solid. In all my millennia, I have never allowed harm to come to the innocent who seek shelter in my arms. Children think they climb me. I know better—I lift them toward sky.

But innocence fades. It always fades.

I felt it first seven decades ago—trembling in deep places, rhythm that shouldn't exist. Not steady pulse of tectonic movement or slow breathing of continental drift. Something artificial. Something that grew stronger each year until now it pounds beneath the valley like fever in the planet's blood.

Children's laughter turned to screaming. Blood soaked my roots that day, first of countless times. I learned the taste of human violence, how it differs from clean death of winter or honest hunger of wolves. Violence carries bitterness, wrongness that poisons earth itself.

Pattern repeated. Settlements rose and fell, technologies changed, but cycle remained constant. Peace, prosperity, growth—followed by jealousy, conflict, destruction. Bronze gave way to iron, iron to steel, steel to things that burned brighter than sun itself. Each age believed itself wiser. Each age fell to the same hungers.

"Tell us a story, Old Father," Hazel whispers now, her hand still pressed against my bark.

I cannot speak in the way they understand, but I can show them. Through the rustling of my leaves, through the patterns of sunlight that filter through my crown, through the ancient memories carved in my rings. But I dare not show them what I've seen, what I know comes with the dawn. Their minds are too young, too tender. Truth would snap them like green twigs.

Instead, I give them the story of the seasons, of growth and rest and renewal. Safe stories. Gentle lies.

Above them, my branches taste wind that carries smoke from the distant city. Not the clean smoke of wood fires, but something harsher. Chemical. Wrong. The humans have learned to burn things that should never burn, to split apart the very bones of matter itself. They believe themselves masters of heat and stone. Like children who think they tame fire by building hearths. Fire remembers what children forget.

I felt it first seven decades ago—a trembling in the deep places of the earth, a rhythm that shouldn't exist. Not the steady pulse of tectonic movement or the slow breathing of continental drift. Something artificial. Something that grew stronger each year, each decade, until now it pounds beneath the valley like a fever in the planet's blood.

The humans call it "geothermal energy." They drill deep, deeper than they should, tapping heat sources they barely comprehend. They speak of "clean power" and "renewable resources," but I feel what they cannot—stirring of things that have slept since the world was young, anger of forces bound for good reason.

In my branches, the children laugh and play their games. Beth reaches a high perch and hollers down like a conquering general. Michael follows her path, trusting in handholds I provide, his movements still careful but growing bolder. Hazel sits at my base, weaving a crown of fallen leaves and humming songs her grandmother taught her.

Their grandmothers' grandmothers played the same games in this same spot. I remember each generation, each face, each small tragedy and joy. The boy who became a great leader, only to die in a meaningless war. The girl who learned the old songs, who spoke to trees and stones before the priests declared such things heretical. The child who would have cured the plague that took half the valley, if he had lived past his eighth winter.

Patterns within patterns. I see them all now, the great spiral of human existence that repeats itself across centuries. They learn the same lessons again and again, only to forget them when the teachers die. They build the same civilizations, make the same mistakes, fall to the same flaws.

But this time is different. This time, when they fall, they will take everything with them.

I have seen the future. Not prophecy—I am no oracle, no mystical seer. I see it because I understand patterns, because I've watched the cycle complete itself a hundred times. Signs burn through my root-network like lightning. Unmistakable to eyes that have witnessed civilizations rise and fall.

The drilling will awaken what sleeps beneath. Not metaphor—literal truth. Things that existed before humans walked upright, entities of heat and stone and rage imprisoned in the planet's core when continents were young. The geothermal plants are keys, turning in locks that should stay sealed.

When those locks open, when deep fires rise to surface, the children in my branches will burn. Their children will never be born. Forests will become ash, valleys will become glass, and eight thousand years of memory will die with me.

Unless I act.

I have the power. Not magic—something more fundamental than human understanding. I am connected to every root system in the valley, every tree grown from soil my roots have enriched. Through them, I reach others of my kind, great trees scattered across continents. We form a network older than human civilization, consciousness that spans the globe.

We could stop them. A thought from me, carried through root and fungi, through whispered language of forests, could trigger earthquakes to bury drilling sites. Landslides to block access roads. Storms to flood installations.

Humans would rebuild, of course. They always rebuild. But I could buy time, perhaps centuries, before they developed the technology again. Long enough for sleeping things to return to slumber. Long enough for danger to pass.

But the cost...

I have never acted directly in human affairs. Through all these millennia, I have been observer, shelter, silent witness to history's parade. To intervene now would mean abandoning everything I am, everything I have chosen to be. More than that—the "natural" disasters required would kill thousands of innocents. The children currently laughing in my branches. Their parents. Their communities.

I would become what I have watched humans become throughout their history: someone who chooses who lives and who dies based on their own judgment of what is right.

"Old Father, do you ever get lonely?" Hazel asks, her small voice barely audible above the wind in my leaves.

The question surprises me, though perhaps it shouldn't. Children often ask the questions that adults fear to voice. Do I get lonely? Ten thousand generations I have watched live and die. Sheltered them, protected them, loved them—and buried them all. Every face I remember is gone to dust, every voice silenced by time's passage.

Of course I am lonely. But loneliness is not a reason to abandon principle.

"Sometimes I think you're the oldest thing in the world," Hazel continues, fingers tracing the deep furrows in my bark. "Sometimes I think you remember everything that ever happened."

If only she knew. I remember when her ancestors first learned to work metal, to plant crops, to tame fire. I remember when they discovered writing, when they built their first cities, when they split the atom and reached for the stars. I remember when they were still innocent, before they learned to hate efficiently.

A new sound reaches me through the afternoon air—the rumble of heavy machinery from the far side of the valley. They are expanding the geothermal plant again, drilling deeper. The vibrations travel through my root-network like screams, each impact sending tremors through my heartwood. The rhythm of the earth grows more discordant with each passing day.

I probe deeper with my awareness, following the path of their machines into the planet's depths. Two miles down. Three. Four. Getting close now to the first of the sleeping chambers, the places where ancient heat has pooled and waited since the world's formation. Not natural heat—heat that thinks, that remembers, that burns with purpose.

My roots sense the first stirring of attention from below. Not yet awakening, but the beginning of awareness. Like a dreamer sensing light through closed eyelids, starting to rise toward consciousness.

The children begin their descent from my branches, responding to calls from the settlement. Dinner time, chores, the ordinary rhythms of human life. Beth drops to the ground with a thud, brushing bark dust from her clothes. Michael climbs down methodically, checking each step. Hazel lingers longest, her hand pressed against my bark.

"You're not gonna die or nothing, are you, Old Father? 'Cause Tommy's grandpa died last winter and now Tommy says he can't tell Tommy fishing stories anymore."

Die. Die. Such a small word for something so final. Forty human lifetimes I have watched, forty generations born and buried. Will I die? If I act, if I stop the drilling, if I save them from the consequences of their own curiosity—I will continue. I will watch Hazel grow old and die, her children grow old and die, their children and children's children, until the day comes when humanity has grown wise enough to avoid waking what sleeps below.

If I do not act, if I maintain my neutrality, my refusal to interfere in human affairs—I will burn with the rest. Ancient wood burns as surely as young saplings when the fires rise from the earth's core.

But perhaps that is as it should be. Perhaps I am meant to burn, to end my long watch when humanity ends theirs. To die as a witness rather than live as a judge.

"I'll be here for as long as you need me," I tell her through the whisper of wind in leaves, knowing she will not understand the words but hoping she feels their truth.

She smiles and runs after the others, her small feet carrying her back toward the settlement, toward the warm lights of home and family and all the small moments of happiness that make life worth living.

I sink deeper into the earth and wait for night.

The decision weighs on me through the dark hours. In the distance, the geothermal plant hums with activity, night shifts maintaining the machinery that tears at the earth's foundations. Through my root-network, I feel each bite of their drills like teeth against bone. Soon now. Days, perhaps weeks, but not longer.

Different children come with the morning light, but the pattern remains the same. Play, laughter, questions about the world and their place in it. Each generation believes they are the first to face the ultimate choice between survival and principle. None realize how many times that choice has been made before, how many civilizations have chosen wrongly.

Beth returns with friends, but today brings something new: school project about local history. She sits beneath my trunk with a tablet, recording video about the "ancient oak that has stood in Thornwood Valley since before recorded history."

If only she knew how much history I've recorded, how many events I witnessed that never made it into human accounts. Secret wars, hidden loves, small acts of heroism and cowardice that shape the world more than grand gestures. Pattern of human choice, repeated endlessly across centuries.

"My grandma says you might be the oldest living thing in North America," Beth tells her device, panning camera across my trunk. "She says her grandma used to tell stories about this tree. Nobody knows exactly how old you really are."

I know exactly how old I am. Eight thousand, two hundred and thirty-nine years, seven months, and fourteen days. I became conscious in spring of what humans now call 6184 BCE, when first tentative awareness stirred in my heartwood and I realized I was something more than ordinary timber.

The tablet's camera lingers on the patterns in my bark, the deep furrows and ridges that record my growth through the centuries. If Beth knew how to read them properly, she could trace the history of the valley itself—wet years and dry years, fires and floods, the rise and fall of human settlements. The scars where arrows struck me during ancient battles. The smooth patches where generations of children have climbed, wearing grooves with their eager fingers.

"I wish trees could talk," Beth says, lowering the tablet. "I bet you've got some stories."

I could tell her about the great comet that struck the earth when I was barely a century old, how its impact winter killed half the vegetation on the continent but left me stronger, my deep roots reaching toward new sources of groundwater. I could tell her about the plague that swept through the valley eight hundred years ago, how I sheltered the last three survivors until they could rebuild their community. I could tell her about the night two centuries past when lightning struck my crown and I learned to hold electric charges in my heartwood, how I have been slowly gathering power ever since.

Power I could use now, if I chose to act.

Instead, I give her gentle breezes and the dance of sunlight through my leaves. Safe mysteries. Beautiful lies.

The drilling equipment pounds louder as the day progresses. Five miles down now, according to the vibrations I feel through stone and soil. Each impact sends shock waves through my network—metal teeth gnawing deeper, following fault lines that lead to places that should remain undisturbed. They are close to the first of the sleeping places, close enough that I can sense the first stirring of ancient attention. Not consciousness yet, but the beginning of awareness. Like the moment between sleep and waking when the mind begins to remember what it is.

By evening, Hazel returns to sit beside my roots. The quiet one, the child who seems to sense my true nature. She has brought her grandmother this time, an elderly woman whose eyes hold the wisdom of long observation.

"Grandmother Moira says you're more than just a tree," Hazel tells me, her small fingers tracing patterns in my bark. "She says the old stories remember trees that could think and feel and dream."

Grandmother Moira steps closer, her weathered fingers tracing the patterns in my bark with the reverence of one who understands what she touches. "The old stories remember many things," she says quietly, her voice carrying the soft burr of ancestors who crossed cold seas. "They remember when the world was young and the boundaries between living things were not so clear."

She knows. Not everything, but enough. The old blood still runs in some human lines, the genetic memory of a time when communion between species was common rather than miraculous. I can sense it in her touch, the faint echo of ancestors who spoke to trees and stones and winds as naturally as breathing.

"Can he really think?" Hazel asks, tilting her head up at me.

Grandmother Moira looks up into my branches, her eyes meeting something that might be mine if I had eyes in the conventional sense. "What do you think, child? When you speak to him, does he answer?"

"He answers," Hazel says with the certainty of innocence. "Not with words, but he answers. He makes the leaves dance special when I'm sad."

"Then you have your answer."

They settle against my trunk as darkness falls, grandmother and granddaughter sharing the ancient ritual of storytelling beneath the stars. Moira speaks of the old days, when magic was common and trees were counselors as well as shelter. She speaks of the responsibility that comes with great age, the burden of watching while others act.

She knows the choice I face. Somehow, impossibly, she knows.

"Sometimes," she says, her voice barely audible above the night wind, "the greatest courage is in knowing when not to act. And sometimes the greatest love is in accepting what we cannot change."

But I can change this. That is the horrible truth that haunts my ancient consciousness—I have the power to prevent what is coming. The network of root systems, the stored electrical energy, the connection to weather patterns across half the continent. I could act. The only question is whether I should.

The drilling continues through the night, and with each foot deeper, the stirring below grows stronger. Six miles now. Seven. They are following a fault line that leads directly to one of the deepest sleeping chambers, a place where heat and consciousness have pooled for millions of years.

By dawn, I can feel the first tendrils of alien thought rising from the depths. Not awake, not yet, but rising toward awareness like bubbles ascending through deep water. When those thoughts reach the surface, when they achieve full consciousness, the heat they control will follow. The geothermal plant will become a gateway for forces that last walked the surface when dinosaurs ruled the earth.

The children come again with the morning light. Beth with her school project, Michael with his collection of interesting stones, Hazel with her quiet questions and grandmother Moira's ancient wisdom. They play in my branches as if this were any other day, as if the world were not balanced on the edge of ending.

"Old Father," Hazel whispers during a quiet moment, "are you scared?"

Scared. I have felt many things in eight thousand years—loneliness, joy, sorrow, love, loss—but fear is different when you've survived ice ages and wars and the rise and fall of civilizations.

But yes, I am afraid. Not of death—death is simply another season, another stage in the cycle of existence. I am afraid of choosing wrongly. Afraid of acting when I should wait, of waiting when I should act. Afraid of becoming the very thing I have spent millennia observing—a being who decides the fate of others based on personal judgment rather than natural law.

Eight miles deep. The drilling equipment has broken through into the first chamber, and I feel the shock of contact like a physical blow. Ancient consciousness touches modern technology, and for a moment both recoil from the encounter. Then curiosity takes hold—on both sides.

The humans see only unusual heat, strange readings that make no sense. They don't know they've touched something older than life itself, something that remembers when earth was molten rock under a black sky.

Something down there is stirring. Stretching. Remembering.

I have perhaps hours now before the stirring becomes true awakening. Hours to decide whether to act or to accept what comes.

Hazel sits beneath my branches, braiding grass into patterns her grandmother taught her. Simple child's work, but there is something meditative in her movements, something that speaks to the eternal nature of small human rituals. She hums as she works, an old song whose melody carries traces of languages I heard spoken when the world was young.

"Will you tell me a secret, Old Father?" she asks, not looking up from her braiding.

Secrets. So many centuries of human stories—hidden loves and concealed shames, private moments witnessed and never revealed. But perhaps she means something different, something more fundamental.

Through the rustle of my leaves, through the play of light and shadow, I try to tell her the greatest secret of all: that consciousness is not limited to human form, that intelligence takes many shapes, that love exists wherever there is awareness to feel it. Trees and stones and winds, all of them capable of thought and feeling in ways her species has forgotten how to recognize.

She looks up from her braiding, her young eyes bright with understanding beyond her years. "You do think, don't you? You're not just a tree."

More than just a tree. More than she is just flesh and bone and dreams. We are both more than our parts, both ways for the world to know itself.

Nine miles deep. The drilling has awakened something that should have slept until the continents shifted into new configurations. I feel its attention like heat against my consciousness, curiosity and hunger mixing in ways that promise devastation. It remembers now what the surface world contains—water and organic matter and all the small warm things that burn so beautifully.

The geothermal plant's systems begin registering higher temperatures than their design parameters can handle. Emergency protocols
activate, but the humans assume equipment malfunction rather than
alien consciousness testing the boundaries of its new prison. They
respond with more drilling, deeper excavation, trying to understand
what they have encountered.

They are making it worse. Of course they are making it worse. When
has humanity ever responded to the unknown with anything but more
aggressive investigation?

Hazel finishes her grass braiding and stands, pressing her small hand
against my bark one final time. "I gotta go home now," she says. "But
I'll come back tomorrow, Old Father. I'll always come back."

Tomorrow. The word carries weight when spoken to one who may
not survive the night. If I act, if I choose to intervene, tomorrow will
come for her and all the children who play in my branches. If I do not
act, tomorrow becomes a concept without meaning.

She walks away with the afternoon light golden on her copper hair,
and I make my choice.

Not the choice to act—the choice to wait. To let events unfold as they
will, to maintain the neutrality I have observed for eight millennia. To
trust that humanity will find its own way through the crisis they have
created, or accept the consequences if they do not.

I am not their savior. I am not their judge. I am what I have always
been—witness to the grand pattern of existence, observer of the cycles
that govern all life. If this is where the cycle ends, if this is how the story
concludes, then perhaps that too is as it should be.

But the choice brings no peace.

The drilling continues through the night, each impact now answered
by something stirring far below. By dawn, the thing will be conscious
enough to act. By noon, the first of the deep fires will reach the
surface. By evening, the valley will burn with heat that makes volcanic
eruptions seem like candle flames.

In the hours before dawn, in quiet space between night and morning,
Hazel returns. She approaches my trunk in darkness, moving with
careful steps of a child who doesn't want to wake sleeping parents. Her
hand finds my bark by touch alone.

"I couldn't sleep," she whispers. "I keep dreaming about fire, about
everything burning. Grandma Moira says the dreams mean something
important."

Grandmother Moira is wise beyond her years, carries knowledge passed down through generations of women who remembered when trees spoke and stones sang. Old blood runs strong in this child, strong enough to sense what approaches without understanding its nature.

"Are we gonna be okay, Old Father?"

The question every human child has asked since language began, plea every parent has tried to answer with comforting lies. But I cannot lie to her, not when she's come to me in darkness seeking truth.

Through the whisper of wind in leaves, through the ancient language of root and branch, I tell her what I can. That cycles end and begin, that destruction and creation are partners in the dance of existence, that love continues even when individual lives do not.

She listens with the perfect attention that only children possess, hearing meanings beyond the limits of words. When I finish, she nods as if I have spoken in language she understands completely.

"I thought so," she says quietly. "Grandma Moira says some things are too big for any one person to fix, even if they got the power to try. She says sometimes the most important thing is just to be there for what happens, to be a witness."

A witness. Yes, that is what I have always been. What I choose to remain, even now.

"Will you stay with us?" she asks. "When it happens, will you stay?"

I draw deeper into my roots, anchoring myself in soil that has nourished me through millennia. Yes, I will stay. If the world burns, I will burn with it. If humanity falls, I will fall with them. Not as savior or judge, but as companion in whatever comes next.

The first light of dawn touches my highest branches as Hazel returns to her home. In the distance, the geothermal plant's alarms begin to sound as temperatures rise beyond all expected parameters. The thing below wakes, and I feel its attention turn toward the surface world like the gaze of some vast and hungry eye.

But I also feel something else—deep peace that comes with accepting one's place in the larger pattern. I am the Great Oak of Thornwood Valley, guardian of children's laughter, keeper of eight thousand years of memory. Whatever comes next, I will meet it as I have met everything else: with roots deep in earth and branches raised toward sky, bridge between what was and what will be.

The alarms grow louder. The machines scream impossibly. Deep beneath the valley, something ancient rises.

Heat begins to rise from below, and I ready myself to burn.

As first flames lick through stone cracks, as valley floor begins to split and glow, I think of all the children who have played in my branches, all the generations who found shelter in my shadow. Their laughter lives in my rings like captured music, like whispered prayers, like joy itself.

Hazel's voice reaches me through the growing heat: "Grandma, look! Old Father's leaves are burning!"

And they are. But not burning—glowing. Eight thousand years of captured lightning dancing through my crown. Not to destroy but to shine. Not to save but to remember. One last gift of beauty before deep fires claim us all.

Something ends. Something begins.

And love goes on.

Always, love goes on.

Hocus Focus

D anny Kozlowski found the magazine wedged between his older brother's mattress and bed frame while hunting for his missing baseball cards. "Laughs & Gags Monthly" announced the cover in yellow letters, beneath a cartoon of some guy with his pants around his ankles staring at a whoopee cushion.

Danny flipped past the usual stupid stuff—fake dog turds, rubber spiders, plastic vomit that looked way too realistic. The back pages were crammed with ads promising to change your life for three easy payments of $9.99. Sea monkeys that looked nothing like the happy families in the pictures. A Charles Atlas course that would turn wimps into muscle-bound beach heroes.

Then he saw it, tucked in a corner box surrounded by stars: "GEN-UINE X-RAY SPECS! See through clothes! Amaze your friends! Only $2.99 plus shipping!"

Danny's face went hot. See through clothes. He thought about Jennifer Walsh, who sat two seats ahead of him in English and smelled like strawberry lip gloss. His face got even hotter. The ad showed some cartoon guy wearing thick black glasses with spiral lenses, pointing at a woman whose dress looked see-through.

"Scientifically designed! Not a toy! Results guaranteed or your money back!" the fine print promised.

Danny tore out the ad before he could think about it, stuffed it between his math homework pages.

Two weeks later, when his allowance plus lawn-mowing money from Mrs. Henderson finally added up, he filled out the order form and mailed it to Hocus Focus Industries, P.O. Box 1247, Boise, Idaho.

The wait was torture. Every day after school, Danny raced to the mailbox like his life depended on it. His mom noticed.

"You expecting something?" she asked one Thursday, watching him trudge back empty-handed.

"Nah. Just checking."

She ruffled his hair. "Well, if Publishers Clearing House shows up, remember who feeds you."

Danny actually laughed. His mom was pretty cool, even if she thought his sudden interest in mail was just another weird teenage phase. Which, honestly, it kind of was.

After three weeks, he'd given up. Then, on a gray Wednesday afternoon, a small padded envelope appeared with his name written in block letters across the front.

Danny's hands shook as he tore it open in his bedroom. Inside, wrapped in tissue paper, lay a pair of glasses that looked nothing like the ad. Instead of thick black frames, these seemed delicate and old-fashioned, with thin wire arms and lenses that shimmered like oil on water. They reminded him of soap bubbles just before they popped.

A small card came with them: "Congratulations! You now own genuine X-Ray Spectacles manufactured by Hocus Focus Industries. These are not toys. Use with caution. We are not responsible for what you might see. No refunds."

Danny slipped the glasses on, expecting them to be too big or slide down his nose, but they fit perfectly. Like they'd been made just for him.

At first, nothing looked different. Same messy bedroom, same pile of dirty clothes, same stack of comic books. Then he blinked, and his bedroom door disappeared.

Not like it turned invisible—he could still see where it should be. But he could see *through* it. Through the wood, the paint, even the metal hinges. The hallway stretched out beyond like the door was made of water.

"Holy crap," Danny whispered, then felt guilty for swearing even though nobody was home.

He jerked the glasses off. The door looked normal again. Solid and boring and definitely there.

Danny put them back on, more carefully this time. The door vanished again, but now he forced himself to really look. He could see through the walls of his house like they were made of clear plastic. In the living room below, his mom sat reading a Stephen King paperback, totally unaware that her son was watching her from upstairs.

But something was wrong. His mom looked... thin. Not skinny-thin, but like pieces of her were missing. Dark patches covered her arms and chest—not shadows, but actual holes where chunks of her should have been.

Danny focused harder, and the holes became clearer. They weren't just empty spaces. They were moving, growing. As he watched, one of them pulsed and got bigger.

He ripped the glasses off so fast the wire arms scraped his ears. When he looked down at the living room with his regular eyes, his mom appeared completely normal, turning pages and sipping her coffee.

Danny told himself it was just some weird optical illusion. The glasses were a gag, after all. They couldn't actually show him anything real or dangerous.

But he put them back on anyway.

This time he looked out his window toward Mrs. Patterson's house across the street. She stood in her kitchen washing dishes, and through the X-ray glasses, Danny could see she had holes too—bigger ones than his mom, dark gaps that shifted and moved.

And something was wiggling inside them.

Small, quick things like tiny worms or baby snakes. Then more appeared, dozens of them squirming through the hollow spaces in Mrs. Patterson. They had little mouths that opened and closed rapidly, like they were chewing.

Danny's stomach lurched. He wanted to look away, wanted to pretend he hadn't seen any of this. But he couldn't stop staring. The things inside Mrs. Patterson were definitely eating something, working their way through her like she was made of food.

A knock on his bedroom door made Danny jump so hard he nearly dropped the glasses.

"Danny! Food's ready!" his mom called.

"Coming!" he yelled back, listening to her footsteps retreat down the hall. Through the walls, he could see the holes in her body had grown since he'd first looked. Whatever was eating her from the inside was working faster now.

Danny stared at the glasses. The lenses kept shimmering with that weird oily rainbow pattern that hurt his eyes if he looked too long. He wanted to throw them in the trash, pretend this wasn't happening.

Instead, he put them back on and went downstairs.

His dad sat at the kitchen table, already halfway through his meatloaf. Through the X-ray specs, Danny could see his father was in even worse shape—huge gaping holes took up most of his chest and arms. The things inside him looked different too, no longer small and worm-like but twisted with multiple heads and grabbing arms. They'd eaten most of his dad's insides, leaving only a thin shell that somehow kept functioning.

"How was school?" his dad asked, not really looking up from his plate.

Danny stared at what was left of his father, watching things move in the empty spaces. His throat felt like sandpaper. "Okay."

"Just okay? Nothing interesting happen?"

Danny couldn't manage more than one-word answers. How was his dad even talking when there was almost nothing left of him? "Nah."

"Growing boy like you should eat," his dad said. "Need your strength."

During dinner, Danny kept the glasses on, unable to look away from his family's condition. His mom's holes kept spreading, dark gaps expanding across her body. His dad looked so consumed Danny wondered how he stayed upright.

But as Danny watched, he noticed something that made his skin crawl. The creatures inside his parents seemed to sense his gaze. When they did, their tiny black eyes focused on him with an intelligence that felt way too human.

"You're not eating much," his mom observed. "Feel okay?"

Danny looked up at her, seeing both the concerned woman who'd raised him and the hollow shell being devoured from within. "Not really hungry."

After dinner, Danny escaped to his room and tried to make sense of what he'd seen. Maybe the glasses showed diseases. Maybe everyone carried parasites or cancer that normal vision couldn't detect. Maybe this was just some kind of sickness that spread from person to person.

But that didn't explain why the holes grew so fast, or why the things inside them seemed so aware of him watching.

Danny had to know if it was just people. He grabbed the glasses and looked at Whiskers sleeping on his bed. Through the X-ray specs, the cat looked... normal. Actually, better than normal. Like every whisker was crystal clear, every stripe perfect. His stomach unclenched a little. Maybe whatever was wrong with people couldn't get cats.

He looked out his window at the oak tree in their yard. Same thing—every branch, every leaf crystal clear and whole. No holes, no creatures eating it from the inside.

Only people were infected.

That night, Danny lay in bed with the glasses on, staring at the ceiling and trying to understand. Through the walls, he could see his parents sleeping. The holes in them pulsed and shifted, and the creatures inside moved with increasing activity, like they knew someone was watching.

But something strange happened the longer Danny observed. The creatures seemed to change, arranging themselves in new patterns. Like they were responding to his attention somehow.

Danny must have fallen asleep, because he woke to sunlight and his mom calling his name. The glasses were still on his face, and when he looked toward his parents' room, the holes had grown during the night.

At breakfast, his dad moved slower, his speech slightly slurred. His mom kept pausing mid-sentence, like she'd forgotten what she meant to say. To normal vision, they seemed to be having a typical morning. Through the X-ray glasses, Danny could see they were being consumed at an accelerating pace.

"I think I might be coming down with something," his mom said, touching her forehead. "Feel a bit... empty."

Danny choked on his cereal. "Maybe you should see a doctor."

"Oh, it's probably nothing. Just tired."

But Danny could see it wasn't nothing. The creatures inside his mother had grown large enough that he could make out individual features—multiple eyes, writhing tentacles, mouths lined with needle teeth. They tore away larger chunks now, feeding more aggressively.

At school, Danny kept the glasses on despite the risk of other kids noticing. What he saw in the hallways made his blood freeze. Every student, every teacher, every adult carried the same infection. Some were further along than others—Mr. Patterson, the math teacher, was so hollowed out Danny wondered how he could still function. But everyone had holes. Everyone was being eaten.

Everyone except Danny himself. Looking down at his hands during English, he could see they appeared solid through the X-ray glasses. No holes, no creatures, no empty spaces. Whatever protected him seemed to be working.

Jennifer Walsh sat two rows ahead of him as always. Through the specs, Danny could see she was in bad shape. The creatures inside her had eaten away most of her chest, leaving only a thin frame that somehow kept her looking normal. As he watched, one of the bigger creatures turned toward him.

The thing inside Jennifer had her face. But its eyes looked wrong—familiar but totally alien. It stared at Danny for what felt like forever before turning back to its feeding.

During lunch, Danny sat alone in the cafeteria, watching his classmates through the X-ray glasses. The longer he watched, the weirder it got. The creatures inside different people seemed to move together, like they were all part of the same thing. When one group finished eating someone's heart, creatures in nearby people would start working on the same organ.

It looked planned. Like they were all connected somehow.

And it was spreading. Danny could see tiny holes starting to appear in some of the younger kids, students who'd been solid just days before.

But not in him. Whatever protected Danny was getting stronger. When he looked at his hands more closely, they didn't just appear solid—they seemed more real than everything else he could see through the glasses.

Walking home from school, Danny passed a group of construction workers fixing a sidewalk. Through the X-ray glasses, he could see they were all heavily infected, their bodies more hole than substance. But one of them looked up as Danny passed.

The man smiled, and Danny saw his teeth looked wrong—too sharp, too many of them.

"Nice glasses, kid," the man said. "See anything interesting?"

Danny's heart hammered. The man had noticed the glasses. Had known what they were for.

"Hey, don't be afraid," the man called as Danny started walking faster. "We're all friends here."

Danny ran then, sprinting the rest of the way home. He burst through the front door and raced upstairs, slamming his bedroom door behind him.

His mother walked to the bottom of the stairs.

"Danny?" she called up. "Could you come down here, sweetie? We'd like to talk to you."

Her voice sounded normal, but through the X-ray glasses, Danny could see the creatures inside her throat moving together to create the sound.

"About those special glasses you've been wearing," his father added, appearing beside her.

They started climbing the stairs together, their movements perfectly synchronized. Danny backed away from his door, his heart going crazy. How did they know about the glasses? He'd been so careful.

The doorknob turned, but the lock held. His parents knocked politely.

"Danny?" His mother's voice, but wrong somehow. "Could you open the door? We just want to understand how you can see us so clearly."

"It's very unusual," his father added. "Most children can't perceive what you perceive."

Danny looked out his window and felt his stomach drop to his feet. More people were gathering in his yard—neighbors, the mailman, even Mrs. Chesterson from down the street. All of them hollow, all of them moving in perfect coordination, all of them looking up at his bedroom window with the same hungry expression.

Through the X-ray glasses, he could see they were no longer trying to hide what they were. The creatures inside them had taken control, and they moved like parts of a giant machine.

But they weren't breaking down his door. They weren't trying to force their way in. Like they were waiting for something.

Danny sat on his bed and stared at the X-ray glasses, trying to understand what was happening. Why could he see the creatures when no one else could? Why wasn't he infected like everyone else? And why were they so interested in him?

He looked at his reflection in the bedroom mirror. Through the X-ray glasses, his face looked wrong. It had his general shape, sure, but underneath... something else. Something dense and layered and completely not human.

His hands started shaking so hard he could barely hold the glasses.

The knocking downstairs had stopped. When Danny looked through the walls, his parents were just standing in the living room. Not trying to break down his door. Just... waiting.

Through his window, he could see all those people in his yard. Mrs. Chesterson. The mailman. Even some of his neighbors from down the street. They'd all stepped back from the house. Like they were giving him room.

Danny's stomach dropped. What the hell was going on?

Danny walked downstairs, still wearing the glasses. His parents stood in the living room, and now he could see them clearly—not the hollow shells he'd been watching, but something else entirely. Dense, layered, complex in ways that hurt to look at directly.

When they saw him, they looked... worried. Like he'd walked in on something he wasn't supposed to see.

"Danny," his mother said carefully. "We need to talk."

"We weren't expecting this to happen yet," his father added. "You weren't supposed to... see us like this for a few more years."

Danny's mouth felt full of cotton. "See you like what?"

His parents looked at each other. His mother sighed. "Honey, this is... this is hard to explain."

"I don't know where you got those glasses, son, or who made them, but..." his father said. "You're too young to understand what you're seeing."

"I can see just fine," Danny said, his voice cracking. "I can see that you're not... that there's something wrong with everyone."

"Not wrong," his mother said quickly. "Just... different from what you thought."

Danny felt like he was going crazy. "What are you talking about?"

"You were supposed to figure this out gradually," his father said. "When you were older. When you were ready. But those glasses... they showed you everything at once."

"Figure what out?"

Another look between his parents. His mother stepped closer. "Danny, look at yourself. In the mirror. With the glasses on."

Danny didn't want to. But something in her voice made him turn toward the hallway mirror. What he saw there made his knees wobble.

Not human. Not really. Something wearing a human shape, but underneath...

"What am I?" he whispered.

"You're like us," his father said softly. "You always have been. But we were going to wait until you were sixteen to tell you. Let you have a normal childhood first."

"Tell me what?"

"That some people..." His mother struggled with the words. "Some people aren't exactly people."

Danny looked down at the glasses in his hands. The lenses kept shimmering, showing him things that didn't make sense.

"Can I go back?" he asked. "Can I just... forget this?"

His parents looked at each other again.

"We don't know," his father said honestly. "Those glasses... we've never seen anything like them. They're not supposed to exist."

"Then where did they come from?"

"We don't know that either," his mother said. "But Danny, now that you've seen... you can't unsee it. And there are things you need to understand about staying safe."

Danny felt tears starting. "I just want to be normal."

"I know, honey," his mother said, and for the first time all day, she sounded like his real mom. "We wanted that for you too. For a few more years, anyway."

Danny looked out the window. The people in his yard were still there, still waiting. Through the glasses, they looked different now—not threatening, exactly, but... expectant. Like they were hoping for something.

"What do they want?" Danny asked.

"To know if you're going to be okay," his father said. "You're part of our community, Danny. They're worried about you."

"Community of what?"

His parents exchanged another look.

"We'll explain everything," his mother said. "But slowly. When you're ready. For now, just... try to remember that we love you. That hasn't changed."

Danny stared at the glasses in his hands. Through them, he could see truths that shifted and changed every time he thought he understood them. But maybe understanding wasn't the point. Maybe the point was just accepting that there were things in the world that didn't make sense, and that was okay.

"Can I keep them?" he asked. "The glasses?"

"If you want to," his father said. "But Danny, once you start seeing the world this way... there's no going back to the way things were before."

Danny nodded. He looked out the window one more time. The people in his yard were starting to disperse, going back to their normal lives. But through the X-ray glasses, he could see they weren't really normal at all. They were something else entirely.

And so was he.

Danny Kozlowski adjusted his X-ray glasses and felt something settling into place inside him. Not understanding, exactly, but acceptance. He had a lot to learn about what he was and what this town really was.

But for now, that was enough.

The Swan Song of an Autistic Armadillo

T he path never changed. Seven steps from the oleander to cracked
concrete. Forty-three steps along sidewalk, avoiding the raised
sections that felt wrong under his claws. Twelve steps across brown
grass to the garden gate, always open exactly four inches. Seven hundred thirty-two nights of the same route. Tonight would be seven
hundred thirty-three. His claws had worn grooves in the exact spots.
His nose knew cricket-song meant moon-time, when air-taste meant
flower-ready.

Shell-scrape against the oleander's lowest branch---the sound that
meant journey-start. The scrape had to happen at exactly the right
angle, make exactly the right tone, or back up and try again. Three
times, he'd spent whole nights getting that first scrape perfect. Each step
fell in the same places his claws had carved over two years of walking.

But tonight, something was wrong.

Something was wrong with the scents. Dog-smell too old.
Cat-spray mixed with fear. Fallen oranges moved by hands that
tasted like soap and burning. At step thirty-seven, the wrongness
hit hard. He had to circle. Tight, fast spins. Shell scraping con-
crete---scritch-scritch-scritch---until the bad feeling got smaller. Seventeen circles before his body said okay, keep going.

Human-scent had changed too. Not the usual lavender-and-tea smell
that meant safe, meant the gate would stay four-inches-open, meant the
path could continue. This was sharp-metal-taste. Wrong-taste. Like the
air before lightning that sent him burrowing for days.

His legs knew the pattern: step thirty-eight, step thirty-nine. The
routine could not break. The routine kept the bad-feeling away.

The old human had tended this garden since his first night here.
He knew her scent, her quiet movements, her hands that watered the
flower when dawn was right. She never spoke to him or tried to touch,
but she understood. She kept the gate open exactly four inches. At first,
she'd left water dishes---wrong, new things meant changing the route.

She'd tried different gate widths. But she learned. When she understood about four inches, she weighted the gate with rocks to keep it steady. She made her world fit his needs.

She'd made her world fit his needs without him asking.

The cereus bloomed twelve nights each year, always when his body-clock said moon-highest. Tonight was the seventh bloom. Flower-perfume would roll through the garden thick enough to taste, drowning everything except the wrong-scent seeping from the house.

But first, he had to complete approach-ritual.

At the gate, everything felt broken. The opening---not four inches, but four and a quarter. The quarter-inch felt like falling. Gate-ritual started: nose against right post, left post, measuring the gap-width. Four and a quarter. Wrong.

The rocks that held it steady had been moved.

Circle-time around the gate posts---tight, fast spirals. Scritch-scritch-scritch of claws on concrete. The sound usually made the panic smaller, but tonight it felt hollow. The wrongness was too strong.

Forty-three circles later, he pushed the gate with his nose until it settled back to four inches exactly. Relief flooded through him like coming up from deep water. He squeezed through, shell fitting the gap perfectly.

Five steps to the cereus.

But step five was wrong too.

His watching-place---the hollow he had worn into the earth over seven hundred thirty-two nights---had been filled. Someone had smoothed it over, covered his scent-marks, destroyed the precise curve that fit his shell exactly.

The world tilted.

Without his watching-place, he couldn't finish the pattern. Without the pattern, the bad-feelings would win. Without his spot, the wrongness would eat everything.

Dig-time.

Claws worked fast, removing the strange soil, reshaping the hollow just right. Every few scrapes, test-the-fit by settling in, adjusting until it matched his shell perfectly. Dig, test, adjust. The doing-again-and-again calmed the screaming in his head.

Yellow light spilled from the house window. Usually, that light meant good-safe---the old human moving through her evening pattern, making her tea, checking her plants. Tonight, the light flickered wrong. Shadows moved behind the glass in ways that hurt his eyes.

After much digging, his watching-place was right again. He settled in with a body-deep sigh. From here, he could see the flower-plant and the house-light. The great cactus spread against the wall, flat paddles like giant hands. At its heart, the bud waited---tight, green, getting ready for midnight-opening.

His body-clock said early tonight. Usually, he came when the bud was already swelling. Tonight, hours remained. The broken routine had scrambled his timing, but maybe that was good. Maybe he needed the extra time to understand what had changed in his careful world.

Pre-bloom ritual: check everything with all senses.

Scents first. Lavender from border plants---right. Rose geranium from hanging baskets---right but fading, plants-stressed. Jasmine from the trellis---too sweet, carrying rot-smell underneath. And every-where, that metal-taste that made his shell want to pull tight.

Sounds next. Crickets starting their chorus like always. Cat moving through neighbor's yard along the fence. But from the house---creak-ing that belonged to stranger-feet, not her soft-stepping, tapping like finger-bone on glass, whispers from empty rooms.

Eyes last. His night-sight catalogued each shadow, each light-source, each wrong-thing. Kitchen window glowed, but the light was bad-yellow, steady like fire instead of electric-buzz. Behind the glass, shapes that had no place in her gentle silhouette.

Something with too many angles. Something that bent wrong ways.

Scritch-scritch-scritch went his claws against his watching-place earth. The sound usually grounded him, but tonight felt desperate, like trying to hold onto something solid when the ground shook. Every instinct screamed roll-into-ball, hide in armor and stillness. But he couldn't move. The pattern held him here. Seven hundred thirty-two nights of the same path, the same watch, the same wonder at blooming.

The pattern was everything. The pattern kept the darkness away.

Air-pressure dropped just so. Humidity rose exactly right. Last car-sound faded from the street. His body knew: flower-bud would begin moving. Now.

At ten twenty-six, the bud trembled. Everything focused on the flower. This was his time---watching time, beauty time. The bud peeled back layer by layer, showing white inside. Outer petals first, thick and waxy. Then inner petals, delicate as paper. Finally the cen-ter---the heart that would live six hours before closing forever. He started rocking---back, forward, back, forward. His claws scraped their pattern: three forward, two back. The movement helped him stay with the beauty instead of running from too much feeling.

At ten thirty-three, the bloom opened fully.

Flower-scent hit him like a wall---sweet-sharp like split fruit juice, thick enough to follow with his tongue, layered with smells his simple brain couldn't name but knew completely. This was why he came. This was what seven hundred thirty-two nights had built toward. This moment of perfect beauty that made all the wrongness worth surviving.

But underneath the flower-perfume, the metal-taste grew stronger.

The kitchen window creaked open. Something wearing her scent pressed against the screen. Its shape kept shifting---sometimes looking like her, sometimes stretching into something with too many joints and pointed fingers. "Little guardian," it whispered in her voice, but wrong. "Seven hundred nights you've watched. Seven hundred nights you've kept me outside." He didn't understand words, but he understood tone. Predator. Threat. Wrong. His rocking got faster---rock, scrape, rock, scrape.

Flower-petals began curling at edges. The bloom was dying too fast. Something was pulling away its life through invisible threads that made the air feel hungry.

"She's gone," the thing said. "Died this afternoon. I've waited so long to wear her skin." He didn't understand words, but the feeling was clear. His watching hadn't been just habit---it was protection. His being here, his pattern, his love for the flower had kept this thing away. But if she was gone, if only wrong-scent remained... The flower petals curled faster, dying too early. Something changed in his chest. A loosening. Seven hundred thirty-two nights of faithful watching---but the thing he'd been guarding was gone. The routine had no reason anymore.

For the first time in two years, he broke the pattern. He left his watching place. Moving felt wrong. His whole body screamed the routine must continue. But something deeper was pushing him. The thing noticed. It pressed against the screen until the window frame creaked. "Leaving, little guardian?"

Instead of rolling into a ball, he began walking circles around the flower. His claws marked the earth with each step. Not panic circles---something different. Each step placed with the same care as his nightly route. "What are you doing?" the thing asked. "She's dead. This garden is mine now." First circle done. He began another, smaller and tighter around the cactus base. With each step, the tight feeling in his chest loosened. His body-clock still ran, but now it counted down.

The kitchen window exploded outward. The thing poured through like black smoke, landing in the garden with a wet sound. Its borrowed shape stretched and squeezed, finally settling on something that looked like her if she'd been made of shadow and hunger. "Sixty-three years I've waited," it hissed. "Kept outside by her faith. Then you came. Simple creature, but your being here made her barriers stronger."

Third circle done, smaller still. His movement had become ritual. Protection. Boundaries taking shape in something deeper than earth---built over seven hundred nights of faithful watching, of simple love for beauty.

"Your watching joined hers," the shadow said, pacing like a caged thing. "I couldn't touch her while you kept watch."

The thing lunged forward and hit an invisible wall.

Ripples spread through the air, showing the barrier his circles had built. Light flowed along its surface---not human light, but something older. Dawn light. The light of small creatures committed to protecting beauty."What---?" The shadow pressed against the barrier, form rippling like smoke on glass. "What did you do?"

Fourth circle started, and understanding flooded through his different brain. The routine hadn't been meaningless repetition. Every night of watching, every moment of wonder at flower-blooming, every patient wait for beauty in darkness had been building something. Layer by layer, night by night, a simple creature's devotion had made a wall stronger than human faith alone.

But the wall was tied to him. When his life ended, it would fade too.

His body-clock was winding down. He felt it in his heart's uneven rhythm, in his vision blurring at the edges, in the growing looseness in his chest that meant his small life was reaching its end.

Flower-blooming was failing fast now---petals brown and curled, perfume fading to nothing. The thing's presence was poisoning it, draining away everything beautiful and alive.

The urge to rock, to find comfort in movement, came strong. But this time he shaped it into something else.

He started gathering fallen petals with nose and claws. Dried blooms from previous nights lay scattered around the cactus, still fragrant, still holding echoes of their perfect lives. He collected and sorted and arranged each petal with the same precision as his nightly routine.

"Stop," the shadow commanded. Cracks appeared in the barrier. "Stop this!"

He continued. Each petal placed exactly right, each curve following patterns between instinct and something larger. His different way of seeing the world---in straight lines and precise angles, in repetitions others missed---was creating something beautiful.

The pattern took shape---a spiral of white petals growing from the flower base. Each placement strengthened the barrier, each curve adding protection around this sacred space.

"She's dead!" the thing shrieked. "No one's left to appreciate your stupid worship!"

But he knew better. As he worked, he felt another presence. Not her body---that lay cooling in the house. But something that lived on in the soil she'd enriched, in the plants she'd nurtured, in the understanding she'd shared with a creature who saw the world differently.Another petal, then another. Circles within circles, patterns within patterns. The barrier blazed brighter with each addition.

The shadow-thing tried a different voice, suddenly gentle and concerned. "Little one, you're hurting yourself. This obsession isn't healthy. You need to stop this repetitive behavior and move on."

The words carried the tone of every human who had ever tried to make him normal, who had ever said stop the rocking, stop the focusing, stop being exactly what he was. But she had never spoken that way. She had learned his language instead of demanding he learn hers.

He continued placing petals.

"Your routine is broken," the thing tried again. "The pattern is meaningless now. Why maintain this useless behavior?"

Because the pattern was never meaningless. The routine was never just routine. His need for sameness, his focus, his different way of moving through the world---all of it had led to this moment. All of it had been preparing him for this final act of protection.

He placed the last petal as his heart stopped.

The spiral blazed with light beyond human sight. The barrier solidified, becoming permanent. No shadow could cross it now. No predator could poison this space where an old woman had tended flowers and a small creature had kept watch.

The thing howled, its borrowed form dissolving, unable to stay solid near something so purely protective.

"This garden will die without her!" it screamed. "No one will tend it!"

But in his final moments, he saw something else. Soft light in the house's front window. Footsteps on the walkway. A young woman with the old woman's eyes and gentle hands, carrying a suitcase and keys, drawn to check on her grandmother's house one more time.

She moved like someone who understood growing things, who knew some things couldn't be rushed, only accepted. She paused at the garden gate, studying the four-inch gap, and something in her face suggested she understood this wasn't carelessness but intention.

The granddaughter had finally come home.

He closed his eyes as his heart stopped, small body curled in the center of the petal spiral. Above him, the flower began blooming again, petals unfurling with renewed strength, perfume promising that beauty would continue, that someone would always be watching.

The shadow-thing's final scream faded to silence, leaving only crickets and soft wind through patient leaves.

In the morning, the granddaughter would find an old armadillo's body surrounded by the most beautiful arrangement of flower petals she'd ever seen, and she would know---without understanding how---that something important had happened here. Something worth preserving.

She would learn about four-inch gate gaps and undisturbed soil hollows. She would plant new flower-plants in exact locations. She would water them at precisely the right time and leave certain paths untouched. The garden would become a sanctuary not just for plants, but for all the small creatures with their own ways of being, who needed their routines and patterns respected rather than corrected.

The flower-plant would bloom twelve nights each year, exactly as it always had, opening its perfect white face to the moon while new guardians kept watch and the darkness waited, forever held back by a simple creature's swan song of devotion.

The path never changed.

Only the walker was different now.

www.ingramcontent.com/pod-product-compliance
Lightning Source LLC
Chambersburg PA
CBHW020537120726
47903CB00001B/4